INTO TEMPTATION

UNSHACKLE · DOMINATE · COMPLICATE

PAM GODWIN
NEW YORK TIMES BESTSELLING AUTHOR

Copyright © 2021 by Pam Godwin
All rights reserved.
Cover Designer: Hang Le
Interior Designer: Pam Godwin

This is a work of fiction. Names, characters, places, and incidents are the product of the author's imagination or are used fictitiously, and any resemblance to actual persons, living or dead, events, or locales is entirely coincidental.
No part of this book may be reproduced in any form, except for the inclusion of brief quotations in a review or article, without written permission from the author.

Visit my website at pamgodwin.com

DELIVER US (boxset)
DELIVER (#1)
VANQUISH (#2)
DISCLAIM (#3)

FROM EVIL (boxset)
DEVASTATE (#4)
TAKE (#5)
MANIPULATE (#6)

INTO TEMPTATION (boxset)
UNSHACKLE (#7)
DOMINATE (#8)
COMPLICATE (#9)

UNSHACKLE
PAM GODWIN

Book 7

ONE

A man with soulless eyes shoved a hood over Luke Sanch's head, blocking out the private airplane hangar and spiking his heart rate. The stifling fabric allowed in no light. Just pitch goddamn darkness.

He was officially past the point of no return.

One could argue he'd passed that point the night he woke in Van Quiso's attic, naked and shackled. But unlike that brutal, defining moment, he'd put himself in *this* situation willingly.

The hood had been expected. What would follow, however, was anyone's guess.

Beside him, his roommate and close friend, Tomas Dine, received the same treatment. They'd worked numerous jobs together, alongside their vigilante team. Jobs that put them neck and neck with vile human sex traffickers. This operation was no different.

Except this time, he and Tomas were going in alone.

The tread of soft-soled shoes approached from behind, circled ominously, and paused a few inches before Luke.

"Welcome, John Smith." The man's voice drawled beneath the weight of a nasally Latino accent. "Your luggage has been searched and transferred. I trust you had no complications during your travels?"

The flight had been over-the-top luxurious—one of the perks of having a Colombian cartel *jefe* on their vigilante team. Matias Restrepo was funding this entire operation, which included flying Luke and Tomas on an untraceable private jet from Mexico to this hangar outside Orange County, California.

To meet with La Rocha Cartel.

The most aggressive, most organized, most violent cartel in existence.

Sharing the same air with these men made Luke's knees twitch, threatening to weaken his stance. Saliva gathered in his mouth. He felt sick. Surrounded. Overpowered. Horrifyingly out of his league.

Whether these homicidal terrorists bought his story or intended to kill him was yet to be determined. Survival depended on his ability to maintain his carefully crafted ruse over the next few days or weeks.

"The flight was adequate." He slipped the tips of his fingers into the pockets of his designer suit pants. "And you are?"

"I'm John Smith," the voice deadpanned. "My colleague here… He's John Smith, too. As are the men at your back, who are currently aiming high-caliber guns at you and your bodyguard."

Funny guy. A blade in the motherfucker's gullet would be funnier. And oh-so-satisfying. His hands clenched.

Finesse, Luke. Find it and wield it. Don't be a moron.

Posing as his bodyguard, Tomas didn't make a sound. The hoods provided a reprieve, hiding involuntary facial tics. They'd been trained for covert operations by Cole Hartman, a retired military, secret agent, whatever-he-was operative. But weeks of lessons hadn't miraculously turned them into seasoned professionals.

Where they lacked undercover experience, they made up for in vicious determination. Or was it stubborn recklessness?

Or just plain stupidity?

"I expect nothing less." Luke injected a cocky smile into his voice. "I followed your instructions. We're unarmed, and all electronic devices were left behind."

No bugs or tracers. No way for his team to track his movements beyond this hangar. His neck tightened with unease.

"We appreciate your cooperation, Mr. Smith," the man said. "And you'll understand the necessity of being searched before we depart."

"Make it quick." Luke grunted. "And mind the suit. It's worth more than the lives of your men."

Arrogance. That was one of the character traits he donned as John Smith. Along with greed, cruelty, and a few other unsavory qualities that would befit the sort of man who shopped for sex in the slave trade.

Several hands fell upon him, thoroughly patting down every inch of his fit frame. They untucked his shirt, dug around in his pants, and lifted his nuts to prod beneath.

Fucking hell. He gritted his teeth as fingers breached the crack of his ass. Then they moved on to his socks, shoes, and other less invasive areas. A growling sound beside him indicated Tomas underwent a similar body search.

UNSHACKLE

That done, they were led to a waiting car. He straightened his suit, blindly ducked into an air-conditioned cabin, and slid across leather seats.

"Right behind you, sir," Tomas said, confirming they hadn't been separated.

The doors shut, and the vehicle rolled into motion.

Stretching out, Luke felt his way around the configuration of seats. A limousine.

No surprise. He was masquerading as a powerful businessman with the wealth of Bill Gates and the ethics of Lucifer. The cartel wanted his business, his *money*, and would wine and dine him until he splurged on their product.

He would have his pick of any of their high-priced, stolen girls.

"The hoods remain on until we arrive. Protocol, you understand." The man from the hangar spoke from an adjacent seat, his accent unnervingly cultured for a cutthroat cartel gangster. "To offset the inconvenience, I have something to make the ride more enjoyable. This one's on the house."

Luke tensed as someone shifted across from him. Body heat brushed his legs. Small hands molded around his knees and traveled up his thighs. Female hands.

He cringed beneath the hood. God only knew how old she was. Or how willing.

Going undercover for this job meant he would have to do things that violated his moral principles. Vile things, like forcing his dick inside girls who weren't in a position to consent.

He wasn't here to rescue them. Not directly. His assignment was to locate Vera Gomez, glean her involvement in the human trafficking syndicate, and finish the job that his roommates, Martin and Ricky, had started during their undercover stint in Jaulaso Prison.

His friends hadn't failed in Jaulaso. They'd just, rather unexpectedly, fallen in love with Hector La Rocha's daughter, Tula Gomez.

Tula's intel on the cartel was marginal at best. Hector hadn't fully trusted her with his secrets, and rightfully so. In the end, she'd killed the cartel capo and passed along everything she'd learned about the trafficking operation in his cartel.

She wanted to find Vera, her missing half-sister. Luke wanted to take down her father's operation and annihilate everyone involved. If the sister wasn't as innocent as Tula adamantly claimed, he didn't know if he could keep his promise to show mercy.

The female hands, now sliding over his groin, could very well belong to the missing sister. A sick part of him hoped for that. He'd memorized her face in the old pictures Tula had provided.

Vera's photographic beauty attached itself to the fingers currently stroking Luke's hardening cock. He strained against the fabric of his trousers, cursing the confinement but also grateful for it.

Hector La Rocha's dying confession had painted Vera as the enemy. Add to that her track record with the cartel, and Luke had a good idea about what he was dealing with.

Beneath the hood, he closed his eyes and gripped the slender arms on his lap, ruthlessly squeezing the delicate bones. "I don't fuck what I can't see."

"I assure you," his cartel escort growled, "she's every man's fantasy."

"I'll be the judge of that." He shoved her away.

"Very well."

A tense moment passed, coiling with the hum of tires on pavement. Their destination might have only been five minutes from the hangar, but he wouldn't put it past the cartel to drive around for an hour to safeguard the compound's location.

Without warning, a small body straddled his lap and lifted the hood to his forehead. His vision filled with a flash of Tomas' leg beside him, the opulent interior of the limo, and the girl's face an inch away from his own.

Not Vera. But no less gorgeous. Christ, her eyes alone made his skin heat and shiver. Huge, gray, and feathered with thick lashes, they blinked at him with gut-hardening vacancy. Innocence. She couldn't have been older than sixteen.

A seductive, practiced smile stole across her features but didn't touch her gaze. Not even a little. She was probably drugged. And brainwashed.

Holding the hood to his brow, she reached between them and unbuckled his belt.

Most trafficked victims came from homes with little supervision and even less love. A distinguished, wealthy stranger could saunter into an impoverished town and lure neglected teenagers with a silver tongue and mouthful of lies. Promises of a new home, money, loving attention, education, and above all, passage to the United States turned desperate kids into easy prey.

Luke would know. Eight years ago, he'd been one of them. Hard-up, naive, and broke as fuck, he'd fallen right into Van Quiso's trap.

It had been eight years since his life irrevocably changed. Nine years for Tomas. Even longer for Ricky and Camila. In total, they were nine ex-slaves, collected one by one, sexually trained, abused, and united in misery.

UNSHACKLE

Luke was damn proud of what they'd become. Vigilantes. Freedom fighters. An inseparable family. The only family he had, and he would take a bullet for every single one of them.

Beyond the tinted windows, luxurious estates dominated the Orange County landscape. The limo headed east, away from the coastline and commercial clusters.

Canting his head, he locked onto the man sitting across from him.

"Is she too cooperative for you?" Dark aura and oily eyes—the desperado scowled at Luke's grip on the girl's arms. "You like them to fight? Is that it?"

"I forwarded my specifications." Luke pushed her away. "You know what I want."

She returned to her seat without argument, and the hood fell back in place, blinding him. On instinct, he reached up to lift it.

"Leave it." The man clucked his tongue. "When we arrive, you'll be pleased with the selection. We have exactly what you requested."

Early twenties, brown eyes, black hair, slender build, golden complexion. Luke didn't have a type, but those were the attributes that had been sent to the cartel because they matched Vera Gomez.

Best case, she was enslaved at the compound and available for purchase. He would buy her and get her the hell out of there.

But he was prepared for the worst.

Unbeknown to the cartel, Van Quiso had made this meeting possible. Van, the notorious slave trader from Texas. Van, the dead man who had been shot by his partner, Liv Reed, six years ago.

Only those connected to the Freedom Fighters knew he'd survived. Over the past month, Van had dug up some connections from his old trafficking life and reinserted himself into the underground network as an interested buyer named John Smith.

Within days, La Rocha Cartel had taken the bait.

They'd vetted and trusted the information Van fed them. And why not? Van had contacts that could only be obtained by powerful, scum-sucking rapists.

Because Van had been one of them.

He'd done a lot of atoning since then. Enough to make him seem almost... Empathetic? Accountable? *Human.*

It was strange to admit—no one ever said it aloud—but Van had become a trusted friend among them. A Freedom Fighter. Family.

The bastard was still a cocky prick. But Luke no longer held a grudge for the unspeakable weeks he'd been raped and tortured as Van's captive. If he were honest, Van had done him a favor.

Luke had a purpose now, a reason to fight. Many reasons. He had friends who cared about him. Because of Van, he'd escaped a lonely, meaningless, dead-end life.

Because of Van—and the obscene down payment wired to the cartel—he was on this blindfolded ride to an unknown destination, where he would be expected to sample the merchandise and purchase a stolen girl.

For a wealthy, sexually depraved monster, it was a dream vacation.

For Luke, it was a chance to exact justice.

Silence thrummed for nearly an hour. The hood eliminated eye contact and the awkward need to make conversation, but the tension mounted. It was coming from him, knotting in his shoulders and making every second unbearable. Reality setting in.

He was on his way to La Rocha Cartel's secret compound. Without a weapon. Without a tactical team of Delta operatives. Without federal agents who did this shit for a living. It was just him and Tomas, working outside the boundaries of the law.

If they succeeded, Hector La Rocha's four sons and their despicable operation would be eliminated. Vera would be returned to her sister, and countless slaves would be freed.

If they failed, he and Tomas would be gutted, dismembered, and never seen or heard from again.

You volunteered for this. Trained for it. You know what you're doing.

It wasn't working. His heart refused to abandon its frantic sprint around his ribcage.

Eventually, the limo slowed, motoring in stops and starts, presumably through gated entrances manned by armed guards. Then the engine shut off.

"Have a look, Mr. Smith." His escort shifted, creaking the seats as the doors opened.

Luke dragged off the hood and caught Tomas' expressionless stare before turning his attention beyond the windows.

Parked in a massive, extravagantly landscaped courtyard, they were surrounded by opulence and money. A lot of fucking money.

Stone archways and monolith columns supported red-tile roofs that stretched between Mediterranean-style buildings. The compound formed a sprawling, symmetrical circle around him. A towering, open-air fortress, broken up by breezeways and multilevel turrets to create individual living spaces with wrought-iron balconies and stucco exteriors.

UNSHACKLE

The travertine driveway snaked through a portico and curved out of sight. Patterned pavers drew walkways in every direction, leading under covered arches to smaller courtyards, lush gardens, fountains, and pools.

Less conspicuous, but no less excessive, was the security detail. Cameras and guards covered every corner and entry point. Weapons weren't in view, but they were there, hidden under oversize jackets. Anything else would've made guests uncomfortable.

This was a resort designed to entertain depravity. A compound built on indulgence and the blood of innocents.

The limo emptied, leaving him to exit last. The unforgiving California heat baked into his black suit as he stepped out and joined Tomas. His gaze landed on the row of cars in the courtyard.

A Ferrari FXX-K, Lamborghini Centenario, and holy shit, that was goddamn Pagani Huayra. He blinked. And blinked again. One of only a few hundred in the world, that hypercar had taken over two years to build by hand. *Look at all the carbon fiber.* Complete with gull-wing doors, red leather upholstery, and a 720hp AMG Mercedes engine. Un-fucking-real.

He dragged his eyes away only to choke at the sight of the Koenigsegg Agera parked next in the line. Sexiest goddamn thing he'd ever seen. And *fast*. The rear wing adjusted at the push of a button for optimal speed. Not that it needed the help. It held the production car speed record of 278 mph.

His fingers twitched. *Damn.* This was the closest he'd ever come to touching one.

Back in Texas, he'd taken up mechanic work to pass the time between vigilante jobs. He'd learned the trade. Self-taught. Motorcycles mostly. But he'd always had a deep appreciation for fast cars.

More Ferraris and Lambos filled his view, forming a glimmering, drool-worthy panorama of rolling works of art. Every hypercar here was worth over a million dollars. Some valued at three to four mil. Whoever owned this collection was a car enthusiast, someone who shared his obsession and had the money to buy the rarest, most expensive models in the world.

There would be other guests on the property, slave buyers like him. But they would've been escorted here in the limo, wearing hoods. These cars belonged to someone who could come and go freely.

"If you're good with a stick, my brother will let you test drive one of his toys around the property."

The sultry feminine voice turned his head. The click of approaching heels drew his gaze. Long, shapely legs hewed his breath. Sun-kissed skin for miles.

His insides drew taut as he took in the sinuous lines of hips in the simple black dress. Early twenties, brown eyes, black hair, slender build, golden complexion. *Exquisite.*

She stepped right up to him, too fucking close for someone he didn't know, and dragged red-painted fingernails along the curve of his bicep. He dug through a swirl of potent perfume and male arousal and found his brain.

"Your brother owns these cars?" Prying her off his arm, he set her away. "Who is he?"

"Marco La Rocha."

The eldest son. Of course.

According to Hector, he'd fathered four sons and one daughter. While in prison, Tula Gomez saw the paternity test that confirmed her unsavory bloodline. Hector La Rocha was her father. *Gomez* was her mother's surname.

So who was *this* woman?

Dread sloshed through his veins.

"Welcome to *Casa de La Rocha*, John Smith," she said with a sensual, south-of-the-border accent. Then she drifted back into his space and hooked an arm around his elbow, turning him toward the main entrance. "Except we both know that's not your real name, handsome. Perhaps that's what I'll call you. *Handsome.*"

"What do I call you?"

"I... I think..." She touched her chin to her shoulder, peering up at him with a coy smile. "When you turn those arresting green eyes on me, you can call me whatever you want." She cleared her throat and looked away, guiding him forward. "To everyone else, I'm Vera. Vera Gomez."

Fuck.

TWO

It was no secret that Luke loved women. Graceful legs, voluptuous asses, small tits, pouty lips, skinny, curvy, tall, and petite… He appreciated all shapes, sizes, and ethnicities. But more than that, he admired the female inner strength. The stronger her mind and spirit, the more he wanted her.

Lucky for him, women gravitated to him. Because he had a handsome face? A full head of auburn hair? Those were the only good things he'd inherited from the addicts who'd brought him into this world.

Years of dedication in the gym lent him a honed physique and the stamina of a horse. But he lived a dangerous life, had a deplorable past, a crass disposition, and he didn't know a damn thing about relationships. Unless it involved his voracious libido.

Yeah, that was what he had to offer.

Sex.

Orgasms.

Hours of unadulterated, mutually satisfying pleasure.

He could coax an explosive release from anyone, anywhere, anytime, with only his mouth. A skill that had been ruthlessly enforced upon all Van Quiso's captives.

But Luke wasn't here to worship the sexy minx on his arm.

He was going to destroy her.

That made him the best man for this operation. He could separate sentiment from logic, extinguish every ounce of compassion, and get his hands dirty without losing focus.

By the end of this, his hands would be covered in blood.

Vera Gomez's blood.

She wasn't enslaved. She wasn't chained in a cage, beaten into submission, and awaiting an unspeakable fate. Her confident steps escorted him into the yawning foyer, her painted lips curving into a soft smile.

What was her purpose here? Hostess? Liaison? Kinky party planner? Did she fuck the guests? Or hold down the victims while they were violated and abused?

Glancing over his shoulder, he exchanged a look with Tomas. On the surface, his friend wore the unflinching, alert demeanor of a bodyguard. That alertness was real. While Luke played the megalomaniac pervert role with the cartel, Tomas would discreetly scope out the lay of the land.

On Tula's last day in Jaulaso Prison, a dying inmate had choked out, *C-C-Calaaa.* An attempt to tell her where to find her sister. Now, six months later, Luke was in California with Vera literally in his grasp. But where in California was he exactly?

Beyond the open windows, acres of land stretched out in every direction. At the farthest perimeter, a fortification of walls enclosed the compound, providing protection against the cartel's enemies. It also prevented guests on the inside from identifying any landmarks around them.

What was out there? Desert? Suburbia? One of the edge cities in Orange County?

It was Tomas' job to find out, as well as gather intel on the cartel's security guards, weapons, and technology. Once he uncovered something useful, they faced the task of transmitting it to the Freedom Fighters, who waited on standby in Orange County. Their friends would come, armed to the teeth, the moment they knew the location.

Tomas' expression didn't confess their agenda. Nor did it show his outrage at seeing Vera Gomez greeting them with a smile. Tula had been so certain her sister wasn't involved. Even now, Luke didn't want to believe what was right in front of him.

He planted his shoes on the tile, bringing Vera to an abrupt halt. Startled, she whirled on him, her mouth opening to speak. He didn't give a fuck what she had to say.

Knocking her hand off his arm, he grabbed her throat and yanked her against him. The force of his strength caused her to wobble in the heels.

Two men stepped forward, reaching for hidden weapons. She held out a hand, staying them, and he used that opportunity to angle her neck and put her left ear near his mouth.

"Never," he breathed, cold and calculated, "ever touch me without my permission."

UNSHACKLE

At odds with his cruel tone, he tenderly curled her shoulder-length hair behind her ear. A gesture meant to confuse her as he imperceptibly exposed the skin behind her earlobe.

And there it was, exactly where Tula said it would be. A small black flower tattoo.

Fucking fuck.

The proof of her identity sank into his bones like burning ash. Disgusted, he stepped away, strolling ahead without waiting.

The click of her heels sounded, giving chase.

"Your rooms are this way." She passed him, veering right, shoulders back, and chin raised. No eye contact. Probably because she couldn't hide that butthurt look in her pinched expression. *Good.*

She guided him through arched doorways designed to let breezes flow through the estate. High ceilings added to the open-air concept, but his stifling unease didn't abate.

Voices drifted from unseen rooms. Deep rumbles. Feminine titters. Sounds of flirtation and foreplay. He hardened himself against it, bracing for the hours and days to come.

Other than Vera, the women within these walls weren't here of their own volition. They didn't want rotten, horny, old men touching them. But before the night was over, Luke would shed the last of his humanity and become one of their tormentors.

Through passageways and common areas, Vera narrated the function of each space. With flicks of a hand, she rattled off directions to the indoor gym, spa, main pool, and communal dining room.

He focused on what she didn't point out. Cameras in the ceilings of every room and corridor. Weapons beneath the shirts of every cartel member. Vacancy in the eyes of every young female.

They were all young. As in *not* legal. Not legal age or citizenship. The half-dressed girls milled about carrying drink trays, mopping floors, and entertaining the guests.

A white-haired man in a suit sat on the veranda with a snake-skinned boot propped on the coffee table. An oil baron? Texan rancher? Probably a greasy politician. A topless Asian girl perched on his lap, staring at nothing as he fondled her breasts.

In the pool beyond, another girl bent over the side, moaning half-heartedly while an obese man plowed into her from behind.

At the end of the hall, a petite brunette sat on the floor of a sunlit library, playing with a menagerie of plastic animal figurines. *Toys.* She wore two curly pigtails and a frilly pink sundress that bunched around her waist. A child's dress.

She was physically small enough to be prepubescent, but her profile revealed a woman in her twenties. A creepy dichotomy, made worse by the tinkling octave of her childlike voice singing in Spanish.

He slowed in the doorway, morbidly captivated as she spread her legs and licked the long neck of a plastic giraffe. Her hand went between her thighs, exposing herself, and the figurine followed, repurposed as a different sort of toy.

Nothing wrong with age play in a safe environment. But this place wasn't safe. Who knew how long she'd been enslaved here? Likely captured at a young age, the girl needed a loving home. *And therapy.* Not a sex resort for pedophiles.

"*Como este, papá?*" She worked the giraffe in and out of her body like a dildo, groaning a hollow giggling sound.

"Yes, babygirl. Just like that." A masculine voice rasped from around the corner. "Fuck that juicy cunt for your daddy."

Heat simmered across Luke's skin, and he quickened his gait. But he couldn't look away as he passed the room, locking onto a middle-aged, average-looking man sprawled in the chair a few feet from her.

There was nothing normal or average in his eyes. The son of a bitch viciously face-fucked another girl while watching the one on the floor.

Sex charged the air, humming and writhing on the breeze. Luke felt it in his pores, sizzling his blood, and tightening his trousers. It made him itchy. Restless. Primed to sink into hot, wet pussy.

Christ, he was surrounded by temptation. Perfect bodies, soft mouths, doll-like eyes, irresistible feminine beauty, and it was all his for the taking. The wrongness of it swelled his cock, thickening with violent need.

What a sick, twisted fuck.

He dragged a hand down his face and looked away, catching Tomas' blank stare behind him. At least one of them seemed to be unaffected.

Everything about this place stank of sin, awakening suppressed urges, tantalizing him, and they hadn't even scratched the surface. These girls were just the entertainment, the docile ones who had been beaten out of their wild state and made tractable. Usable. Stripped of all hope and will.

There would be others hidden somewhere on the property — the untouched virgins who were freshly captured, full of fight, and caged like livestock. They were the forbidden flesh. The highest price tags. The ones who would be sold and sent home with guests.

Despite Luke's filthy dark appetite for sex, he only wished to free them. But that wasn't his purpose here.

UNSHACKLE

His target was Vera.

Why would she want any part of this? Didn't she miss her sister? He knew her background, her education, her life story. She hadn't been raised in an abusive household or neglected by an unloving family. What was her motivation to be here? Money? Power? Or was she in trouble? Maybe she was being blackmailed, and her participation was all smoke and mirrors?

After surviving his own captivity and learning the tragic truth behind his captors, Van and Liv, he knew that not everything was as it seemed. The quickest way to the truth was to get close to this woman and coax her to talk.

She waited a few paces ahead, studying her fingernails as if the scene in the library had no effect on her. Maybe it didn't, but he needed to test her.

A pretty Latina emerged in the hallway, carrying a stack of towels. Eyes directed at the floor, she strode by without looking up.

He grabbed her arm, halting her. "How old are you?"

"Whatever age you want me to be." Her mousy voice matched the downward gaze.

"Show me."

She set the towels on a chair behind her and reached for the neckline of her simple maid frock. A zipper ran down the front, which she pulled to the hem, fully opening the dress and revealing nothing beneath. *Designed for easy access.*

Stepping into him, she set her feet shoulder-length apart and put her hairless cunt next to his hand at his side. He only needed to twitch his fingers to feel her heat, tease her open, and sink inside.

He should do it. Make it look like he was interested. It was exactly what was expected of him.

But her age was questionable, and that doubt dumped ice water in his veins, holding him immobile.

"If it pleases Mr. Smith," Vera said, nudging the girl back, "you'll be sent to his room later. Go on now. Finish your work."

The girl grabbed the towels and made a soundless, obedient exit. He kept his eyes on Vera, watching for something, anything, that might betray her thoughts.

She met his gaze with an unreadable expression. Impenetrable brown eyes. The stare-off stretched for a few seconds too long. Then her lips parted. A flush rose on her neck. Lashes fluttered, and her gaze pulled down and to the side.

Submissive. Aroused. Yeah, she definitely found him attractive. If he snapped his fingers, would she lower to her knees and service his cock?

"That girl wouldn't please me." He lifted her chin with a knuckle, guiding her eyes to his. "She's too young. Too…passive."

"Noted." She turned on her heels and exited the breezeway, stepping into the foyer of a connecting building.

He followed at a leisurely stroll, admiring the way her ass swayed. As Tomas trailed, Luke refrained from stealing another glance at his friend. Too many exchanged looks would invite suspicion from whomever monitored those cameras.

"Here we are." She stopped at the first door and inserted a key card.

The lock buzzed open.

Subtle hostility stiffened her movements. Was she jealous of his interaction with the girl? Annoyed? Tired of men hitting on her? No woman looked as good as she did without constant male attention. Especially not in this haven for perverts.

He played the part, leaning in and letting his breath brush her cheek. "What about you?"

"What about me?"

"You're neither too young nor too passive. It would please me to have you sent to my room later."

"Handsome *and* direct." She pushed through the doorway and into a large private sitting room. "Two bedrooms. Kitchenette. Only one bathroom, but its ample size should be sufficient to share with your assistant."

"Bodyguard."

"You don't need those services here."

Tomas ambled away to investigate the rooms. Standing in the entrance, Luke already spotted multiple cameras. Probably equipped with microphones. The guests had no privacy, and the cartel wasn't even trying to hide it.

She launched into a spiel about the amenities. Room service, personal butler, spa, unlimited alcohol, computer, cell phone, and Internet.

"Communication with outside parties is allowed on our devices." She led him into the enormous bathroom. "What do you do exactly? For work?"

"I'm a silent investor."

"And you invest in…?"

"Emphasis on *silent*."

"Very well. I advise using that same discretion if you conduct business here. Every message you send and receive, every call you make, will be monitored to ensure the safety of our guests and organization."

UNSHACKLE

"In other words, you're recording everything I do, from the women I fuck to the transactions I make on-line. That's your insurance, yeah? If I piss you guys off, you'll use whatever dirt you have on me as blackmail."

"You're paying attention." She smiled.

"Do you give your little warning to all the guests?"

"Yes. It comes with the down payment."

The outrageous down payment bought him all the luxuries of an all-inclusive resort. Only here, the massages came with happy endings, and the whiskey was served with a side of cocaine. Pampering the guests was a small cost to the cartel, considering the amount of money they received at the end.

The going rate for a sex slave? Upper six digits.

Eight years ago, a buyer had paid close to a million dollars for Luke. When Liv had delivered him to the sadist, he'd stared straight into the man's gaze, knowing he was seconds from being handed off and forced to spend the rest of his life doing more than just sucking the fucker's cock. In that defining moment, shackled in the grip of those heartless eyes, he saw the place where the souls of evil were punished and tormented. He saw the face of hell and the terrifying power it held.

With a hard blink, he squared his shoulders and locked down the memory.

He needed a shower.

Prowling through the bathroom, he counted only one camera. Tomas would check every shadow, crack, and corner to verify that.

The wet room went on forever. At least three times the size of the bedroom he no longer had in Texas. The Freedom Fighters recently sold that house and moved to the Restrepo Cartel headquarters in Colombia. It was safer for them there, luxuriously furnished, and closer to the trafficking operations Camila was targeting.

But it wasn't home. He'd never really had a place to call home. Before Van, he'd never experienced the comfort of money. He had plenty of it now. Over six-hundred-thousand dollars. All Van's slaves had received a cut from his operation when he shut it down and grew a conscience.

Multiple floating vanities and countless jets and shower heads jutted from the bathroom walls. A modern, freestanding tub sat at the center, surrounded by a sleek use of white stone materials, giving the room a rich, clean look.

"Did you read the specifications I sent?" He began to undress, toeing off his shoes and draping his clothes neatly over a white settee.

"Yes." Her breathing quickened as she inched toward the door. "I'll just let you—"

"Turn around." Stripped down to his pants, he approached her on bare feet and angled her to face one of the full-length mirrors. "Tell me what I want."

"Early twenties, brown eyes, black hair, slender build…" Her mouth pinched into a line as she regarded her reflection, which embodied the specifications.

"I requested *you*."

"You requested a Latina. There are plenty here to choose from."

He wanted to say her sister's name and watch her reaction. But exposing his connection would be suicide. Vera was one of them.

"How much for you?" He edged closer, his chest touching her back as he met her gaze in the mirror.

"I'm not for sale."

"Everything has a price. Who do I speak to about your ownership?"

Her nostrils widened with a sharp inhale. "No one owns me."

"Not yet." He unbuckled his belt and opened his zip, noting her flush at the sounds of him undressing. "When I want something, I take it. I'm very good at that — taking, consuming, *fucking*. You'll learn this soon enough, whether you're watching me with another or riding me yourself. Which will it be?"

"I've seen it all, handsome. Not interested."

"You're going to swallow those words, right along with the load I shoot down your pretty throat. *After* you beg for it."

She shivered, ruining her attempt at indifference.

With a smirk, he let his breath trickle against her neck. She made a small noise, and he stepped back, shedding the last of his clothes. Then he ambled to the far wall and turned on the shower heads.

"Dinner and entertainment begin at seven on the veranda." She spun away, heading for the exit.

"Vera."

She kept walking, face forward, and vanished around the corner.

He'd scared her. Shaken her. Sent her running right out the door.

Damn, that was easy.

Too easy.

THREE

Warm water blasted Luke's body, washing away the long day of traveling. Slowly, his muscles unclenched, releasing knots he hadn't realized were there.

To think, he'd only been at the compound for an hour. This job could last days. Weeks. He wasn't leaving until it was finished.

Amid the rising steam, Tomas entered the wet room, his gaze darting, sweeping for hidden technology. Luke left him to it, closing his eyes and running soap through his hair.

Until something screeched across the floor. A loud crash followed. What the—?

He turned as Tomas set down a heavy chair, which had apparently just been swung at the camera in the ceiling. Plastic pieces crunched beneath Tomas' boot. Pulverized. That must've been the only camera. Tomas wasn't looking anywhere but at his mechanical watch. Checking the time.

The cartel would come, and the speed of their arrival would indicate how closely they were monitoring them. With so many cameras on the property, there would be a security room with multiple eyes on dozens of screens. It would also have views of the surrounding landscape so they could see a threat approaching before it arrived.

Access to that room would reveal the location of the compound.

Tomas strode toward him, and he stepped out of the fall of water so his friend wouldn't get wet.

"Twelve cameras with microphones in the other rooms." Tomas gripped Luke's neck, pulling him close to speak at his ear. "They shouldn't hear us over the water."

"Any revelations so far?"

"She's nice to look at. Grade A tit-to-ass ratio. Don't deny it. You want to fuck her."

"Who wouldn't?"

"Rein that shit in. You can't trust her."

"Sex and trust. Two things I've always kept separate."

"So what's your plan?" Tomas leaned back just enough to lob a surly scowl. "Make her jealous? Then what?"

It was a gamble. Women were smart, resourceful, and underestimated only by fools. But they shared a common weakness. He'd seen it time and again, the way they rallied together in support of one another. Until they didn't.

Too often, they let men come between them. Especially the narcissistic assholes who slept around and committed to no one.

"Put a good-looking bachelor in a house full of women, and what happens?" Luke asked.

"Reality TV?" Tomas twitched his lips. "They turn on one another, plotting and competing to be the one who ensnares him."

"Exactly."

He couldn't blame them. It was animal instinct. Find the mightiest male in the herd, mate with him, and breed the strongest offspring. Vera might not consider herself part of the female selection here, but her biology said otherwise.

Men were simpler, like trees in a field, with the urge to spread their seeds far and wide to ensure they take root in as many diverse and distant places as possible.

Survival, stripped down to its crudest, most basic denomination.

"Okay..." Tomas squinted, giving Luke's nude body a once-over before meeting his eyes. "From what I've seen of the guests, you're the only attractive dickhead here."

Not exactly true. Tomas turned heads without trying. Beauty had been the primary requirement in Van's selection process. Their entire vigilante team looked like they'd walked off the set of *Baywatch*.

But Tomas' sex appeal suffocated beneath the cloud of fuck-off vibes he wore like a pressed suit. Luke trusted his friend without hesitation, but there were moments when he detected something sinister— in Tomas' glare, in his voice—that sent a chill through the bones. For that reason, as well as Tomas' shadowed role as a bodyguard, it was unlikely that Vera would take an interest in him.

"You make her nervous." Tomas glanced at his watch. "She's clearly attracted to you. Maybe that scares her."

"Maybe."

UNSHACKLE

But Luke meant what he'd told her. She wasn't meek. Once she saw him with another woman, her primal nature would claw to get out.

If she made the mistake of falling into his bed, it was game over. He was trained in the art of sexual pleasure. Add to that his insidious brand of dominance, and she was as good as his. Her heart. Her trust. Whatever he wanted.

In theory.

A knock sounded on the exterior door, and the hinges creaked, opening without waiting for an answer.

"Four-minute response time." Tomas raised his eyes from his watch and moved to the far wall.

Luke returned to the warm spray, giving his visitors a full-frontal view as they stormed in. Two armed guards led the intrusion, their eyes instantly locating and assessing the broken camera.

Vera swept in behind them and anchored her hands on her hips. "Damaging property is not—"

"My boss," Tomas said, crossing his arms, "doesn't need an audience while taking a shit."

"But you're welcome to stay while I finish my shower." He arched a brow. "Or join me."

Her gaze dropped to his half-hard cock and skittered away. "No, I..." She coughed. "I don't play with the guests."

He shouldn't derive this much pleasure from her discomfort. He wanted to like her. Pity her, even. She was Tula's half-sister, for fuck's sake. But beyond his appreciation of her physical attributes, he felt nothing for her. No chemistry. No interest in learning why she was a human trafficking bitch.

The sooner he rid the world of her and this operation, the better.

"Then stop wasting my time." He turned off the shower, giving her his back.

"If you break another camera—"

"My being here doesn't mean my business stops running out there. I require a secure space to discuss confidential details with my right-hand man." He nodded at Tomas. "This room will serve as my private meeting space. If I learn that your organization is eavesdropping on the business dealings of my organization while I'm in this room, I will take you down with every connection I have."

"La Rocha doesn't tolerate threats or damage to their property."

"Put it on my tab and go fuck yourself on the way out."

Her gasp filled him with sick satisfaction. As she vanished out the door, he squeezed his fist, imagining it crushing the bones in her neck. It wasn't rage that pumped through his veins. It was focus, clarity, all thoughts aligning on the path ahead.

He twisted to find the same determination in Tomas' hard eyes.

Martin and Ricky wouldn't have been able to finish this job. They loved Tula too much to hurt her sister. In fact, they might never forgive him for the things he was about to do.

"I'm gonna take a walk and do some reconnaissance." Tomas pushed off the wall. "Try not to get yourself killed while I'm gone."

FOUR

Dinner included lamb chops with balsamic reduction, crispy Hasselback potatoes, carrot soufflé, and superficial chitchat with five disgustingly wealthy slave buyers. Appetite long gone, Luke slid his fork away, fighting the impulse to repeatedly stab them with it.

"Best lamb I had in ages." Lester, with his snake-skinned boots and Texan drawl, leaned back from his empty plate and lit a cigar. "Wouldn't you agree, John?"

"No. My whore of a mother cooked better than this slop." Luke lied through smiling lips, prompting a ripple of laughter around the table.

He'd lied about his name, his mansion in Tahoe, his trophy wife, and his undefeated golf game at the country club. They all lied, and they all knew they were spouting canards to one another. It was the most pointless, fucked-up dinner conversation in history.

Maybe this was a game to them, to see who could spout the most bullshit without getting called out. After two hours of table talk, he still didn't know their real names, real occupations, or anything genuine or useful.

They were master manipulators. Whatever powerful positions they held—CEOs, politicians, investment moguls—they hadn't achieved their success honestly.

They were bad men, the sort who fraternized with a cartel and fucked underage girls. Someday their sins would catch up to them. If he moved quickly enough, he could be the one to deliver what they deserved.

Tomas ate alone on the other side of the veranda, ever the scowly, unapproachable bodyguard. He wasn't the only *plus one*. Most of the guests had brought along a male attendant. They probably couldn't function without their personal servants wiping their asses.

Without looking, Luke marked Vera's footsteps in and out of the dining area. She hadn't eaten with them, hadn't sat down long enough to join the conversation. If he didn't know better, he'd think she was avoiding him.

La Rocha guards loitered in the periphery. Cantina girls, dressed in corsets and garters, kept the food and drinks coming. Hector's sons had yet to make an appearance, and no one seemed to care.

Except Luke. He wanted to see the faces of his primary targets.

"Are you betting on the fight tonight?" Ted, a wrinkly old man with sharp eyes and a frail body, met his gaze across the table.

"Fight?" He took a swig of peated whiskey, swallowing the smoky burn with a trickle of dread.

"Oh, yeah." Ted gestured at the grassy area beyond the veranda's railing. "It'll start out there any minute. I have a hundred grand riding on it."

A hundred grand? On what? A cockfight? Dog fight? Knowing the cartel, it would be any manner of cruelty, and he wanted nothing to do with it.

Lester flicked the ash from his cigar. "Putting your money on the girl, old man?"

"Are you kidding?" Ted laughed. "I saw what she's up against. She won't last the first round."

"Human girl?" Luke yawned, pretending a blithe disregard. "Or something else?"

"They say she's human, but I hear she looks and fights like an animal."

"Well, hell." Twisting in the chair, Lester motioned at one of the half-dressed servants. "I'm in. Might even bet against you, Ted."

More laughter and Luke feigned a moderate chuckle. Maybe the girl was a trained fighter, someone they brought in and paid for a harmless night of entertainment.

But he knew better.

"Gentlemen." Vera approached the table, smothering his senses in a cloying fog of perfume. "If you're ready to move to the railing, the show will begin shortly."

The table emptied as everyone grabbed their drinks and ambled toward the long bar that overlooked the lawn. Everyone but Luke.

UNSHACKLE

"I didn't get a chance to tell you about the fight." She stepped closer, her breasts rising over the low neckline of her dress. "It's not too late to place a bet."

"Who or what is the girl fighting?"

"I don't want to ruin the surprise."

"Will it be a fair fight?"

She shrugged.

He couldn't bet against a dead girl. "I'll sit this one out."

"Suit yourself." She scanned the room as if looking for an excuse to move away from him. "Did you enjoy your dinner?"

"I prefer a private meal with a beautiful woman. Tell me something." He reclined, resting his fingers on the arms of the chair. "What do you get out of this?"

"This?"

"You deal in sex but blush when you're propositioned."

"No, I—"

"You keep dangerous company but run from the smallest confrontation."

Her face turned crimson. "I do not—"

"There's that blush. Listen, I'm sure La Rocha pays you well. And not just that. They give you security. Protection. You're loyal to them because they stand between you and whatever it is you fear."

"You don't know what you're talking about," she said, her accent thick beneath her breath as her gaze flicked through the room.

"I can give you everything they give you and more."

"This conversation is—"

"I'll buy your freedom. As far as they're concerned, I'll own you. But the moment we walk out of here, you're free. I'll pay you a salary and provide all the security money can buy."

"And what do you get out of it, handsome?" She cocked a hip and stared down at him.

"Your willing cunt."

"Willing?" Her gaze lingered on his before hardening and snapping away. "I've had enough—"

"Honey, one night with me is never enough."

She laughed, a strained cackle of disbelief.

Yeah, he was laying on the douchery nice and thick. He didn't have a choice. There were cameras and ears everywhere. Decent men didn't come here. Not that he ever claimed decency.

"Do you leave this property? Are you allowed?" At her silence, he stroked a knuckle, light as a feather, along her exposed thigh beneath the hem. "Where are you from?"

"We're not doing this." She jerked her leg away from his touch.

"Oh, come on. I'm not the first man to make you an offer. But I'll pay a lot of money to be the last."

She blinked, and her eyebrows pulled in, knitting grooves across her forehead.

This could be so easy for her. She only needed to agree. He would buy her from the cartel. Fly her ass to Colombia. Put her in an interrogation room at the Restrepo compound and pry every answer he needed to finish the job. She would have Tula in her corner, so the torture would be minimal. Far less painful than the alternative.

Solar lights flickered like torches, illuminating the perimeter in a glow of amber against nightfall's backdrop. The guests gathered at the railing, their murmurs rising in volume as they watched whatever was unfolding on the well-lit lawn.

"No." She straightened. "While you're not accustomed to taking *no* for an answer, ignoring my objection will have severe consequences." Pivoting, she strolled toward the fight.

Well, he tried the easy way. Her funeral.

Drinks refilled. Voices rose, and excitement intensified among the guests. But he remained seated, reluctant to join them.

Until Tomas bent over his shoulder and growled in his ear. "Your contempt is showing. Get over there and prove to the bloodthirsty pigs that you're one of them."

His friend paced to the far end of the railing, which provided views of the fight and the entire veranda.

Tomas was right, of course. Sitting here alone helped no one. But watching an innocent girl die while pretending to enjoy it? Luke had limits, and that one sat firmly at the top.

He listened for the sounds of a feral dog barking or the wild flap of fowl wings. When he heard neither, his nerves wrung tighter, his imagination making it worse. So he crossed the porch and found an empty spot at the railing away from the guests.

Just beyond the covered veranda, a grassy cockpit glowed in a ring of solar garden stakes. A woman stood at the edge, fisting her hands at her sides.

Greasy strings of hair hung in her face and twisted around gaunt shoulders. Not an ounce of fat on her sharp, protruding bones. But the little meat she did have looked hard. Honed from strife.

Long muscles wrapped her arms and legs. A tight t-shirt molded around the small curves of breasts. Frayed denim shorts clung to narrow hips and thighs. She was a tiny thing. Almost a foot shorter than his six-three height and at least a hundred pounds lighter.

UNSHACKLE

Who was she? A trafficked girl? A cartel dissenter? The kidnapped daughter or wife of an enemy? One thing was certain, she didn't want to be here.

Angry red welts encircled her wrists and ankles. Layers of grime stained her torn clothing. Tangles of unwashed hair hid her face, but her eyes glowed through the knots. Dark eyes. Ferocious. Possessed with seething hatred.

She directed her fiery gaze across the ring, and from the shadows, a man stepped into the pit. If he could be called a man. The thug had barely grown into his baggy jeans, his swarthy face too young to take his thin goatee seriously.

Tattooed symbols scattered his bare chest and arms. The markings of a kid who was desperate to prove himself. He couldn't have been older than eighteen. Yet he had about forty pounds on the woman.

The woman he intended to fight.

Luke's stomach sank.

Another man sidled up against her back, gripping her shoulders and whispering in her ear. She stiffened, as if to reject the touch, but didn't pull away.

"I knew you wouldn't miss this." Vera leaned against the railing at his side, all glossy lips and shiny black hair.

Stunning woman.

Unfeeling eyes.

"It's a favorite attraction among the guests." A hint of annoyance clipped her tone.

"Who's the girl?"

"One of my brothers' whores."

"You mean Hector's sons? They're your brothers?"

"They're my family."

Not her biological family. Very few outside of the cartel knew Hector had a daughter, and that daughter was Tula Gomez, who was safe in Colombia with Martin and Ricky.

Tula and Vera shared the same mother. Different fathers. Vera couldn't have been related to Hector's sons. Unless she considered them stepbrothers? As far as he knew, they hadn't grown up together. Tula didn't even know she had brothers until a few months ago. He couldn't ask Vera about any of this because he wasn't supposed to know Tula existed.

"Omar!" Ted thrust out his glass, sloshing the contents over the railing. "Quit sweet-talking the bitch and throw her in there!"

Omar. Hector's second-oldest son.

"Fight to the death!" Omar snatched a fistful of her hair and shoved her toward her opponent.

To the death.

He'd expected as much, but as reality sank in, he couldn't calm his breathing. This girl was going to die, and there wasn't a damn thing he could do about it.

FIVE

Without preamble, the fighters crashed together in a burst of punches, missing and hitting with brute speed. Luke half-expected a knockout in the first minute, but the girl surprised him.

Blood spurted from a powerbomb that landed across her mouth. She dodged the next blow and caught the kid in the solar plexus with her knee. Once. Twice. He staggered backward, sneered, and attacked again.

Hit. Crunch. Smash. Grunt. The crescendo of brutality spiked Luke's pulse. The harder she fought, the more invested he became. Every strike she delivered confessed her will to live. Every ruthless shot she received hardened her jaw, promising retaliation.

Outmatched in strength and skill, she had zero chance of winning. But she didn't give up. Didn't show signs of slowing. As if she'd discovered a way to block out the pain, she limped, boxed, and snarled through bleeding injuries.

Her technique wasn't disciplined. Nothing about her performance indicated she'd been trained in combat sports. She fought with her heart. Like she had nothing to lose. *Like an animal.*

Even with the odds stacked against her, she possessed more bravery in one finger than the combined assembly of tycoons yelling from the veranda.

"Hit her good! Make it hurt!" Ted shouted and gulped back his drink.

"Stay on your feet!" Omar roared, shaking his fist from the sidelines. "If he gets you on your back, he'll fuck you in half. Is that what you want, cunt? You wanna bleed out on his dick?"

Gobsmacked, Luke couldn't look away. Couldn't move. Christ, he wanted to be in that pit, his instinct to defend her riding him hard. Every part of his being rooted for her, his muscles vehemently locked, his mind spinning, grasping for a way she could survive this.

Too late, he remembered himself and realized Vera had inched closer, studying his reactions.

"What are the rules?" Ordering his hands to unclench from the railing, he schooled his expression.

"No rules. It ends when she kills him, or he fucks her. If he manages to hold her down long enough to bury his prick, well…" She lifted a shoulder. "*Then* he can end her life."

Pressure built at the base of his skull, spreading and numbing until he couldn't feel his legs. "What if he kills her first?"

"He loses." She wrinkled her nose. "That's how they make it fair. He might be stronger, but he has to complete those two things in the right order. She only has to kill him to claim victory."

It wasn't what she said, but *how* she said it. No compassion. Not a trace of humanity. She didn't even flinch as the girl took a pounding of rapid-fire fists to the face.

The merciless beating sent her careening across the lawn, where she lay in a pile of twitching limbs.

Luke froze, breathless, seconds from leaping over the railing.

Get up. Come on, goddammit, get up!

Slowly, she climbed to her feet, staggering, swaying. With a wet growl, she spat a wad of blood on the ground and leaped back into the fight.

The guests exploded in cries of approval, voices growing hoarse in their fervor. Dressed in their expensive suits, smoking their fancy cigars, they laughed and applauded while a young girl fought for her life.

This wasn't any different than the Romans and their Colosseum. Crowded against the railing, they elbowed and shoved, trying to steal a better look and smell the blood.

"What's wrong?" Vera brushed her arm against his, drawing his gaze. "You don't approve?"

"Do you?"

"I asked first."

"All right." He finished off the whiskey, his eyes on the fight. "When a man has it all—money, women, power—he grows bored, appreciates nothing, and soon, the only thing that moves him is the pleasure in controlling and abusing others."

"Is that supposed to be a revelation?"

UNSHACKLE

"Not at all. What strikes me is how we try to normalize the barbaric behavior." He gestured around them. "The formal clothing, fine dining, soft music, classy cocktails, and let's not forget this..." He tapped the black steel railing built to withstand a mob. "This keeps us safely on the side of superiority, separated from the subhumans fighting below. As long as we keep to this side and surround ourselves with expensive things, we can remain desensitized to what's actually happening."

He glanced at the throng of desensitized monsters who trafficked innocents, bet on blood sports, and grew hard at the prospect of rape and murder.

Returning to Vera, he waited for something to click in her eyes—a softening, a hint of agreement—but it didn't come. Maybe he'd said too much, given too much away, but he needed to know if there was anything worth salvaging in Tula's sister.

"If you have a point..." She crossed her arms. "Make it."

"You entertain powerful guests, but if any of them stepped into that pit, their money, influence, power—none of it would save them."

"Same could be said for you."

"Wrong, darling. I'd win."

"Really?" She sniffed, incredulous. "Because you keep yourself fit?"

"Sure."

It was more than that. He and his entire team underwent extensive training. They knew how to shoot, fight, and fuck, among other skills they practiced on an on-going basis. He wanted her to know he wasn't like her other guests, and not just because he had a pretty face. He needed her to walk away from this conversation thinking about everything he said until it consumed her.

Messing with her head was just another way to control her.

"Yet here you are," she said, "standing on the safe side while casting hypocritical judgment on your peers."

"Hypocrisy is the least of my sins." He turned his attention back to the fight, his tone stoic and bored. "Put me in there. I'll prove it."

"It's not allowed."

Of course not. He would end the fight. The girl wouldn't die, and all bets would be off. Where was the fun in that?

"Who's the male opponent?" he asked.

"A new recruit."

His chest constricted.

New cartel members were required to do all sorts of horrific things as part of their initiation. He'd heard of capos forcing initiates to eat children's hearts to prove their loyalty. Talk about desensitizing a person.

If the kid lost this fight, he wouldn't just lose his chance at joining the cartel. He would be shot dead.

Good riddance. One less enemy to deal with.

But from the kid's perspective, the stakes were high. Too high to have any last-minute scruples about killing a girl.

Rivers of red dripped from her hair and face, staining her shirt. She managed to stay on her feet, but her balance was shit. Probably a concussion. She favored her left side, where she'd been hit in the ribs too many times.

The next strike sent her tumbling to the ground, and instead of regaining her stance, she rolled to her side and coughed a scarlet spray across the lawn.

Luke tensed, leaning over the railing as sweat gathered on his brow. She wasn't getting up.

Time moved in slow motion, and a hush fell over the spectators, producing ringing in his ears.

The kid climbed over her and tackled the fly on her shorts. She slapped at his hands and tried to squirm away, her movements clumsy. But not defeated. She was still fighting, her growls loud and short of breath.

He wrestled the denim down her thighs, and she twisted, crawling on her stomach along the perimeter of garden lights. Keeping his grip on her shorts, he yanked them off and went for her underwear.

It would only take seconds to rip that flimsy barrier out of the way. He wrestled with her flailing limbs, eyes wild and teeth bared before he flipped her face-up and wrenched open her legs.

Luke seethed but managed to keep his posture relaxed.

You're not here to help that girl.

Don't expose your cover.

You.

Cannot.

Help.

Her.

Vera said something, her voice snatched away by the pounding in his head. His fists balled to the point of pain, but he held himself still, battling raging impulses.

The girl's hand reached blindly for a solar light. Not the one closest to her. She stretched her fingers for the one above her head. What was she doing? They were staked in hard dirt and impossible to—

She pulled it out. As if seated in butter, the metal stake glided smoothly from the ground. He held his breath.

"Oh my God." Vera's hand came down on the railing next to his.

UNSHACKLE

In a blink, the girl thrust the stake, impaling the sharp end through the kid's throat and out the back of his neck.

"Nooooo!" Ted yelled from the veranda.

Her opponent crumpled, the flow of blood too great. A gurgle sounded, a final gasp, and just like that, it was over.

Unfuckingbelivable. She did it. She fucking won.

Stunned silence strangled the guests, rendering them as motionless as Luke.

A snarl sounded beside him, and Vera stormed away. Fuck her. How she could've wished for a different outcome was beyond him. He couldn't remember the last time he felt this goddamn relieved.

As the guests lost interest and wandered back to the table, he remained at the railing, his gaze glued to the injured girl.

Omar tried to haul her up, but she wasn't coherent enough to stand. He yanked her harder, lugging her out of the ring.

Motherfucker. Luke maintained a neutral expression even as his blood boiled to dangerous levels. What were their plans for her? Would they kill her? Rape her? Make her fight another night?

He swiped a hand down his face. She wasn't his mission.

As Omar dragged her off the lawn and out of view, Luke kept his feet planted and cleared her from his mind.

"Gentlemen." Vera stood on the far side of the veranda, clinking a knife against a glass. "We've arrived at the part of the evening where you can bid on who you want to spend the next twenty-four hours with. As you can see, we have an irresistible selection tonight. Nothing but the best for our guests."

Her sugary sweet voice grated on his nerves as a line of half-dressed girls paraded through the dining area. Some he recognized from his walk-through earlier, all of them young and beautiful. Beauty-queen faces. Flawless bodies. As if they'd been grown in a lab and plucked at perfect ripeness.

The ones who smiled made the attempt look wooden. Others didn't bother, their downward gazes failing to look shy. Timidness came from self-preservation and worry. These girls were long past that. The mind could only withstand so much suffering before it shut down.

The bartering began, and one by one, Vera auctioned off humans like property. He didn't move to join in, knowing his reluctance only delayed the inevitable.

Tomas watched him from across the veranda, his eyes hard with wordless commands. Annoyed, Luke gave him his back and studied the remaining girls.

It didn't matter who he selected. They were all submissive, emotionless, broken in... Broken in general. The redhead or the Latina or the black-skinned beauty over there... He could take any one of them to his room, and she wouldn't put up a fight.

That only made the task harder to stomach.

He didn't fuck gently. Didn't know how to be intimate without fire and passion. When he entered a woman, he did it with his entire body, every sinew, organ, and nerve ending engaged.

Sure, he could go through the motions. But could he make it look believable? Could he maintain an erection with someone who just lay there, eyes glazed over and mind shattered? Could he bring a damaged girl back from the dead?

He was good, but maybe not that good.

Where were the lively ones? The girls who would claw, bite, and scream with murderous passion? If he was going to do this, he needed someone who would hit him, try to reject him, and remind him that he was here for a job, not for his own depraved pleasure.

"Vera." He caught her gaze and crooked a finger.

She pulled herself into a taller stance, her nostrils flaring on a deep inhalation. Then she crossed the room, approaching him.

"Do you see something you like, handsome?" Her smile didn't reach her dark, narrowed eyes.

"Where are you hiding the quality selection? The freshly picked gems?"

"We like to give the guests some time to—"

"Be watched by your cameras? To make sure I'm not a narc? Don't waste my time, Vera. I came here to make a purchase. Show me what I'm buying."

She flinched. Cleared her throat. Looked around the room. As her gaze passed over a camera in the ceiling, she gave it an extra blink before skipping away.

"Fine." Straightening, she turned toward the exit. "Follow me."

SIX

As Luke followed Vera's swishing backside through the compound, he wracked his brain for a way to tie her up and sneak her out without getting shot. But every furtive glance she gave the passing cameras was a reminder he would never get her alone.

She tried in vain to maintain several paces ahead of his long-legged gait. He allowed it a few times, because hey, he was a guy, and the view of her ass didn't suck. But each time she lengthened her strides, deliberately shoving distance between them, he didn't know whether to be annoyed or pleased.

He affected her. Why? Was it fear? Unwanted attraction? Or something else?

"I make you nervous." He strolled along, hands folded at his back, listening to Tomas' footsteps behind him.

"I don't know why you would think that. Turn here."

He stepped into another breezeway. "Your body language writhes with discomfort."

"I do not *writhe*."

"Pity." He trailed her into a connecting building, separate from the main compound.

"Do you analyze everyone you meet?"

"Yes."

She paused in a large foyer with shiny tiles and no furniture. No windows. Just a bay of double metal doors and a key reader.

With a swipe of her card, the elevator opened. They took it down one floor—the only option—and stepped into a dimly lit underground corridor. It led back toward the estate, ending somewhere beneath the guest quarters.

He was instantly aware of how different the ambiance felt down here. The floors, walls, ceiling—everything was drab concrete. No paint. No decor or embellishments. It reeked of gloom and cold imprisonment.

Like a dungeon.

His palms slicked with sweat. Cameras hung from the corners, always watching, so he quelled the urge to look at Tomas.

Relaxing into his apathetic mask, he measured his breaths and followed Vera through the tunnel.

A steel door greeted them at the end. Another card reader. Only those with access could enter. *And exit.*

"Do you bring all your guests down here?" He leaned a shoulder against the wall.

"Yes." She glanced at him sidelong. "We prefer to do it on the day of their departure."

Like a souvenir shop at the end of a tourist attraction. After they admired the art and enjoyed the rides, they took a walk through the shop and purchased a parting keepsake. A memento in the form of a sex slave.

"You haven't tried very hard to spruce up this part of the attraction. That's intentional, isn't it? If a man can't handle a walk down a crude hallway, he won't be able to deal with what waits on the other side of that door."

"You seem to be coping just fine."

"I appreciate beauty in its rawest form. Unrefined. Wild. When you strip away the savagery of nature, polish it up, and make it behave, it loses its appeal."

"You say that while looking rather polished and well-behaved in your dapper suit."

"I assure you, Vera, I'm unapologetically primitive beneath the threads." He leaned in. "Open the door."

Her lips parted on a soft intake of air, her gaze fixed on his.

He'd give anything to know her thoughts, her secrets. Christ, if he just knew the coordinates of this rotten place, he would make an excuse to leave. They would blindfold him and transport him back to the hangar, where he could call in his team and tell them where to attack.

But if he had to guess, not even Vera knew how to find her way back to this corner of hell.

She opened the door.

UNSHACKLE

The din of a television reached his ears, playing a commercial with a catchy jingle in Spanish. Otherwise, the room within lay quiet. The sort of eerie quiet that sent a chill along his scalp, at odds with that happy jingle.

He didn't want to enter, but he forced his feet forward, grateful for Tomas at his back.

The space was vast and empty, except for an old couch in the corner and a hard-looking man perched upon it. A small flat-screen TV hung lopsided on the wall, holding the man's attention.

He didn't even spare a glance at Vera as she strode past and poked her head into a dark doorway.

"Marco?" She jumped back. "Oh! There you are."

A tall man emerged from the shadowed depths, his brown eyes instantly locking onto Luke.

Splatters of blood stained his collared shirt. That would've been disturbing on its own, yet everything about Hector's oldest son radiated violence, from his menacing stare and tense jaw to his hard-set shoulders and wordless greeting.

"This is John Smith and his assistant." Vera gave them a nod. "He's ready to make a purchase."

"Are you leaving tonight?" Marco spoke around the cigarette dangling from his lips, his accent straight out of Mexico.

"Just looking." Luke ambled forward, speaking confidently through the lie. "If you don't have what I want, then yes. I'm leaving tonight."

"You don't enjoy the accommodations? Not having a good time?"

Oh, how he wanted to voice exactly what he thought about the disgusting operation. With Hector dead, he stood toe to toe with the new capo of La Rocha, a man who wore his authority in the harsh lines of his face. This was an opportunity the cartel's enemies could only dream about.

But.

There was always a *but*.

Marco only needed to twitch a finger, and an army of guards would pour into the room. Luke had no power here. His next breath depended on the whim of this heartless slave trader.

He would be lying if he said he wasn't on tenterhooks, waiting to be gunned down any moment. The tension strung so tightly in the air he didn't dare move.

Mexican cartels were a distrusting lot, as they should be. They had more adversaries than allies, and as a result, they treated everyone like a threat. Including their guests.

"I'm a busy man, Mr. La Rocha." Luke expelled a bored breath as if he weren't sweating from neck to balls. "If you have something more interesting to sell than the mannequins you're parading around up there, show me. Otherwise, I think we're finished here."

Marco choked on a sharp grunt of disbelief. His eyes flared, shooting his brows to his black hairline. He huffed again and looked around, maybe to see if anyone else shared his shock. But there was only Vera, and she gave no reaction.

"Mannequins?" Marco tugged at his rolled-up sleeves. "What does this mean?"

Whiskers darkened his jaw, making his forty-something face look harsher. His tailored black pants showed wet smudges. Probably blood. The stained shirt hung open at the collar, revealing tanned skin beneath. If he'd been wearing a jacket and tie, both were now gone. What remained of his attire had been loosened and adjusted to do whatever nefarious thing he'd been up to beyond that doorway.

"He wants a lively one." Vera looked anywhere but at Luke. "One he can break himself."

"Of course." No smile from Marco. Not a hint of satisfaction or trust.

Not good.

"You want a struggle? A resistant *niñita*?" The capo stepped out of the doorway and motioned Luke through. "Have a look. Tell me which pussy you like, and we'll discuss a price. Or choose more than one. We'll work something out."

A hot ember sat in Luke's throat. He let it fester there. No swallowing. No twitchy movements. Expressionless, he strode past Marco and into the darkness.

The doorway led to a corridor that veered sharply around a corner. Another tunnel—this one lined with rooms. Eight chambers on each side. No doors or gates.

The overhead bulbs, spaced too far apart, provided little light. Some flickered erratically, sparking trepidation down his spine.

He knew what he would find in those rooms, and given the fresh blood on Marco's clothing, it wouldn't be easy. Even more difficult was the looming task of choosing a girl to purchase and rape.

Any compassion he would've felt was stifled. Fucking a girl was part of the plan, a necessary evil to maintain his cover. So he would pick a strong one, drag her upstairs—by a collar and leash if necessary—and use her to fuck with Vera.

Glancing over his shoulder, he expected to find his cartel escort. But only Tomas had followed him into the corridor. Didn't mean he could let his guard down. Cameras were everywhere.

UNSHACKLE

No more delaying, he made his way to the first doorway.

Inside the cement cell, a dark-haired girl curled up on the grimy floor. She jumped at the sight of him, rattling the chains that connected to hooks in the wall.

"What do you want?" A sob erupted past her trembling lips. "Why am I here? I just want to go home. Please, take me back!"

"How old are you?"

"F-f-fourteen. Are you here to help me? Please!"

"Too young." He said it for the cameras and ordered his feet to move to the next doorway.

Same story. Same torment.

Room after room, girls cried in shackles, pleading, spitting, and demanding to be freed. Some answered his questions. Others angrily refused to acknowledge him. Many didn't speak English.

All of them wore street clothes—jeans, shorts, tattered dresses, whatever they'd had on when they'd been abducted. Ages ranging from thirteen to eighteen, they'd come from Mexico, South America, the United States, and several parts of Asia.

Sixteen girls in all.

None appeared to have life-threatening injuries. Bruises and cuts marred their skin from rough handling. But no visible blood.

He backed out of the last room and stood in the dim corridor, listening to their screams. His presence had stirred every chamber into a frenzy of keening sobs and gutting pleas.

His rage stretched on the brink of snapping, but he kept it bottled.

"Might I suggest the one in there?" Tomas pointed at the room two doors down. "She seems the best fit for you."

The pretty black American girl with blazing eyes and a fuming temper.

At eighteen, she was the oldest. She also appeared to be the strongest, physically and mentally. Even now, her voice rang out above the rest.

"Motherfucker!" she shouted. "Bring your sorry ass back here and let me go! Swear to God, I will find you and cut you for chaining up girls!"

Yeah, she was the best choice. If she held onto that fire, she had the best chance of emotionally surviving what he would do to her.

At least, that had been his own experience. Van had broken his body, repeatedly violating him in ways he'd never imagined or wanted a man to touch him. But, week after week in that attic, he never stopped fighting. Never let his mind surrender or give up.

If he could survive Van Quiso, that girl could survive him.

"Yes, I agree she's…" He went still, certain he'd heard something in the distance. "Do you hear that?"

Tomas cocked his head, eyes narrowed at the unlit bend in the corridor, where they hadn't ventured. "Are there more rooms?"

There were no lights beyond where they stood. But there was definitely something...or *someone* down there.

"Help." The voice trickled into a weak moan, coming from nowhere and everywhere. "Help me."

Tomas straightened. "Another girl?"

Luke held up a finger as a frail cry whispered around them, so soft, so fucking strained with pain. His stomach hardened. His heart pounded, and every muscle turned to stone.

He followed the sound.

The whimpers rose in volume, growing closer as he reached the bend in the pitch black. Tomas touched his back, guiding, pushing him forward. With every step, his legs felt heavier, laden with dread.

As his vision adjusted to the absence of light, the stench of rot and fear invaded. The tunnel opened to a room, the shadows so dense he couldn't breathe.

His head filled with sounds of slapping flesh, his lips cracked and crusted with blood. He heard Van's voice. Demanding. Lustful. Chains clanked. A haunting nightmare.

An omen.

He saw it now. Watching as an outsider, he saw his silhouette hanging in a cage without sunlight. Except the dangling dark shape wasn't him. Not this time. It was something else. Someone was there, only a few feet away. It moved.

And cried.

"Please." The pale whisper dissolved into mewling murmurs too weak to vibrate vocal cords.

He blinked, the thud of his heart hot and viscid. Urgency moved him toward the wall, his fingers sliding over gritty concrete, searching. "Where's the fucking light?"

"Here." Tomas bumped his hand, locating a switch.

An overhead bulb buzzed to life, casting the room in filmy yellow. He squinted through the glow, and his eyes came into focus.

He stopped breathing.

A young blonde girl hung from the rafters by one leg.

By a fucking meat hook.

"Sweet mother of God," Tomas whispered behind him.

The S-shaped hook went through her thigh and suspended her several feet above the floor. Her other leg had been broken in multiple places, the skin flayed, exposing white splintered bones.

UNSHACKLE

His fist flew to his mouth as he cataloged countless stab wounds, purple contusions, and missing appendages. Fucking Christ, this girl was missing fingers, parts of her ears, and a goddamn foot.

The leg impaled by the hook had been sawed off at the ankle. Not a clean amputation. No tourniquet. Nothing to slow the flow of blood except gravity.

"Please." Her mouth moved, coughing on a dry gasp. "Kill me."

No.

Fuck no.

He couldn't.

But he couldn't leave her like this, either. She wouldn't survive the wounds unless she saw the inside of an emergency room soon. That wouldn't happen. Not in the next few minutes. Not ever.

She didn't even try to move, her body too weak and wracked with pain. She could barely cry, and even then, it wasn't enough to produce tears.

"Sir." Tomas touched his elbow, guiding his attention to the wall where they entered.

Another girl.

She sat on the floor, legs stretched out before her. No crying from this one. No tears of anguish. But she wasn't without injuries.

Tangled black hair framed her bloodied, bruised face. More blood soaked her shirt and denim cutoffs.

Lifting her head, dark brown eyes collided with his.

Ferocious, familiar eyes.

The fighter.

SEVEN

"You." Luke opened his mouth to say more, but all that came out was a scathing exhale.

His first thought? *She did this.* The vicious scrapper tortured this young girl and hung her by a hook.

But no, that didn't make sense at all.

The blood on Marco's shirt, the shackles on the fighter's arms and legs, and the fact that she couldn't stand after the fight… She was as much a victim as the others. Perhaps more so. She'd been thrown into the dark with a dying girl, forced to listen to her shallow cries for help.

"End this." The blonde's fractured voice pulled him back. "Kill…me."

His blood shivered, and denial banged in his skull. Again, he took inventory of her injuries, searching for a sign of hope, anything that might save her.

Rust and dirt coated the hook through her leg. Infection would set in soon. The amount of blood on the floor beneath her was more than a human could lose. She wouldn't survive this, and every minute she lived was a cruelty she didn't deserve.

"Why is she in here with you?" He glanced at the fighter.

She glared back, a hostile, rancorous glare that promised death to him and everyone if she broke free.

"What's your name?" he asked.

She slowly raised a hand, dragging the chain across her lap, and extended her middle finger.

The blonde moaned, choking out another plea for death. Her cries thickened with distress, producing a change in the fighter's expression.

UNSHACKLE

For a fleeting moment, those savage eyes softened. Grief, compassion, whatever it was sank into the grooves of her battered, swollen face, blurring her gaze in a sheen of moisture.

Then she blinked, and the tenderness vanished, replaced with red-hot fury.

Do it. Her eyes demanded.

A camera hung in the doorway. Would they try to stop him? Shoot him for interfering?

Fuck it.

Fuck the cartel. Fuck his dead parents. Fuck Van Quiso. Fuck every injustice he'd ever gone up against. None of it owned him.

But this? This he couldn't walk away from.

As the blonde continued to cry, he blocked everything out— Tomas, the fighter, the mission. He put one foot before the other and did the only thing he could do.

He stood behind her inverted body, wrapped a large hand over her nose and mouth, and smothered her air.

She struggled, an involuntary reaction as her mutilated body fought to breathe. His other hand held the crown of her head, his fingers hidden by her crusty hair, discreetly massaging, stroking her scalp. The only comfort he could offer.

As interminable seconds passed, he felt chunks of his soul rip away. He was breaking inside. Battling hardwired convictions. Roaring on his knees. Dying with this girl.

Dying.

Dying.

Make it end. God almighty, I can't do this.

But he did. He finished it, holding her against him as she fell limp.

Lifeless.

Gone.

Fucking God, help me. What have I done?

He'd killed men before. Vile men. But never with his bare hands. Never a woman.

Never an innocent.

His chest squeezed so tightly he thought his heart stopped working. But no, it was still beating, pulsing strenuously, yet… Altered. Twisted into something nastier. Stiffer. Thorny. No longer human.

Raising his head, his gaze caught on the fighter. She watched him, motionless, her expression iced over with suspicion and horror, but deeper, closer, he glimpsed gratitude.

He hadn't done it for her. He hadn't done it for himself, either, and he would live with the cold, stricken guilt for the rest of his life.

She and Tomas hadn't been the only witnesses to his heinous crime. Marco and Vera stood in the doorway, clotting the room with displeasure.

Pure scum of the earth. Neither of them deserved to breathe, let alone stand there in a snit of condemnation. Marco had butchered a young girl, strung her up like slaughtered meat, and left her to die.

Luke's vision turned red. Adrenaline charged, and wrath fired on all cylinders.

Kill him.
Gut him.
Make him pay.

He would. Goddammit, he would exterminate all of them. But to do that, he had to become a man that no one fucked with.

Make them cower.
Earn their horror and respect.
Beat them at their own game.

With his hands still wrapped around the dead girl's head, he showed them a monster that all monsters feared.

"Look what you made me do." He hauled the corpse upward so that he could stare into the dead eyes. "Sniveling little cunt. We could've played so well together, but you just…wouldn't…shut up." He shook the body, punctuating every word before shoving it away. "What a waste."

His stomach cramped. Saliva gathered around his gums. He was going to puke.

"This is unexpected." Marco lumbered into the room, head tilted. "You killed her… Because she was crying? That will cost you—"

"She was half-dead." He wiped off his hands on a clean scrap of her shirt. "I'm not paying for broken goods. Besides, I know which one I want."

He prowled a circuit around Marco and paused before the fighter, staring down at her with a malicious smile.

Realization burst behind her eyes, and she went wild, spitting a string of Spanish and bucking in her restraints.

Across the room, Tomas shot him a look that said he didn't agree with the turn of events.

Too bad. Luke refused to leave the girl chained in the dark with a corpse.

"This one," he announced to the room.

"No." Marco folded his arms over his chest. "She belongs to me."

"And your brothers." Vera scowled.

"I see. And those hypercars out front?" Luke clasped his hands behind him, head down, with his back to Marco. "They belong to you, too?"

"Of course."

"Of course." He glanced over his shoulder. "When I arrived, Vera promised I could test drive one of your toys around the property."

Her eyes widened. "I didn't promise—"

"Shh." Marco's hand slashed through the air, and he held Luke's gaze, deadly captivated. "Is that right?"

"Yes. Perhaps you can appease me another way." Luke straightened his suit jacket and turned to face the capo. "Sell me the Pagani Huayra."

Marco laughed, a shocked sound, and sobered abruptly. "Not in a million lifetimes."

"What's her name?"

"The Huayra?"

"The whore." Luke met her livid stare.

"Who cares?" Marco grunted. "She's a whore."

"Which do you value more? The Huayra or the whore?"

"There are only a few hundred Huayras in existence."

"I'm aware. Yet I'm only asking to test drive a common whore."

"Ah." A humorless grin underscored Marco's wagging finger. "I see what you're doing." Then he went still, thoughtful. "Just a test drive?"

"Give me a week with her. I'll keep her in working, *fighting* condition. At the end of the week, if she still holds my attention, we'll discuss a more permanent arrangement. If not, I'll pay for the mileage I put on her and make another selection."

Marco's eyebrows pulled tight, his gaze narrowed on the thrashing fighter, considering her worth.

"Why *her?*" Vera fisted her hands, the snarl of her lips baring white teeth. "Omar will not allow—"

"*Cállate!*" Marco returned fire, spitting a mouthful of Spanish before thrusting a finger at the door. "*¡Vete!*"

With an enraged glower at Luke, Vera spun and stormed out of the room.

"I'll gladly test drive Ms. Gomez, instead." Luke ogled at her retreating backside, angling his neck and making a show of it.

She slammed to a stop, just long enough to shoot daggers over her shoulder before vanishing around the corner.

"No, no, no." Marco shook his head, chuckling. "I will not share that one."

"Because she's your sister?"

"Because she's *mine.*" With that unnerving announcement, the man removed a key from his pocket and held it up. "I give you a week with the whore. But I warn you. Watch the grill." He gestured at his mouth. "She bites."

"I look forward to it." He grabbed the key and squatted before the seething girl.

Woman.

Hard to be sure with her face banged up, but her eyes confessed her maturity. Mid-twenties? Possibly older. Jaded beyond her years.

She hadn't stopped kicking and bucking in the shackles, her anger so intense it foamed from her mouth. He couldn't fault her for the tantrum, but all that straining couldn't be good for a concussion.

Marco left without another word. Luke waited for the heavy thud of footsteps to fade in the distance. Then he addressed the woman now in his charge.

"You can fight me." He caught her swollen jaw in his hand and squeezed, making her eyes burn hotter. "Kick and scream and wear yourself out. It only makes me harder. *Hungrier.* But if you cause serious harm to my bodyguard or me, or if you run and make us chase you, I will find another girl and hurt her worse than this one." He tilted his head at the dangling corpse. "I'll make her beg for death, and there will be no mercy next time. No escape from the agony. And you'll watch every second of it, knowing you caused it. Nod your head if you understand."

Her eyes flashed, but her head didn't move.

The point was to scare her with threats instead of his fists. She didn't know he would never follow through. Only it wasn't working. He didn't detect a trace of fear in the air.

Maybe she didn't speak English?

No, there was too much comprehension in her expression. Too much stubbornness. She understood him perfectly.

He yanked her up by her long black hair, hauling her body against his, and grazed his teeth across her swollen cheek, the corner of her mouth, and bit her ear. "Nod your goddamn head."

Her lashes fluttered against his face, and her breath came in rapid gusts. Then she nodded.

He unlocked her restraints.

When she didn't move to stand, he scooped her up and cradled her to his chest. She weighed nothing but felt as strong as hell. Compact muscle. Sturdy bones. It would require a lot of effort to really hurt her.

He hoped he was right about that, for both their sakes.

"Should I bring the shackles?" Tomas asked.

"No." His threat would suffice.

As he carried her out, the pull to look back at the dead girl slowed his steps. He wanted nothing more than to bow his head and give her a moment of respect. He needed to tell her he would never forget.

He'd stolen her life, and he didn't even know her name.

UNSHACKLE

How would he ever redeem himself? Ever forgive himself for what he'd done? Or what he was about to do?

Pushing forward, he felt like he was wading through ice, every step a perilous obstacle, every breath a frigid stab in his chest.

Vera waited at the exit, holding the door open to the final tunnel. Marco had already left.

"I want a medical kit." He strode past her, tightening his grip on the injured woman. "Ice packs. Food. High-calorie, nutritional food. And a bottle of your best whiskey."

"Tequila." The fighter buried her nails into his nape, deliberately breaking skin.

"And tequila." His lips quirked. "Make sure it's in my room within the hour."

"I'm surprised." Vera hurried after him, eyes on her phone, presumably passing along his demands. "There are sixteen untouched girls back there, and you choose a whore who can't even walk. She's been thoroughly used up by all four of my brothers. This very moment, their come is leaking down her legs."

His jaw hardened, and he almost lost his footing. But the rage inside him didn't compare to that of the woman in his arms. She exploded in a fit of slashing claws, reaching toward Vera's face while shouting in Spanish.

He wrangled her back, using more strength than he wanted to restrain her against his chest. Then he threw a withering glare at Vera.

"Oh, you didn't know?" She swiped her key card and opened the elevator. "Marco and Omar tag teamed her after the fight."

Raped.

If he'd acted sooner and followed Omar down here, he could've prevented that.

"Why do you care?" He stepped onto the lift with Tomas at his heels.

"I just think... You can do better."

"Better, as in... You? Have you reconsidered my offer?"

Her gaze slid to the woman in his arms, and a malevolent drum of energy electrocuted the space between them. A hatred so rancid and sticky it raised the hairs on his arms.

"The two of you have a story." He looked from one to the other, back and forth, before pausing on the woman he held. "How long have you been here?"

"Too long," they snarled in chorus.

"Are you related?"

"God, no." Vera laughed.

Similar brown eyes, black hair, and tawny skin. Both had Mexican accents, like many of the girls here. But their likeness ended there. Where Vera held herself with sophistication and reserve, the fighter was feral and impulsive. Vera had grown up in a loving home, until her mother died of heart disease.

The common thread between them was Hector's sons. The brothers prized the woman in his arms, whether for sex or blood sports. But the nature of Vera's relationship with them wasn't clear.

Was she jealous of the fighter? Because Hector's sons showed interest in another woman? Or because Luke showed interest in her?

The elevator opened, and Vera sashayed away, leaving Luke standing there holding an unsolved puzzle.

She entered a breezeway in the opposite direction of his rooms and paused, glancing at him before scowling at the fighter. "Have fun with that."

"Have no doubt." He headed the other way, placing his full attention on the woman he was about to become intimately acquainted with. "Tell me your name."

Stubborn silence.

He growled, "This will go much easier if you give me that."

"Easier for you?" Her accent dripped with vitriol while somehow retaining a seductive quality that made his balls tighten. "I'm not giving you shit."

"We'll both have fake names then. I'm John, and you're Gina." At her thinned stare, he clarified. "Gina Carano. The hottest female fighter of all time. At least, she was until I saw you defeat that kid tonight."

She clamped her busted lips into an angry slash and looked away.

Why had he said that? He was supposed to scare her, not charm his way into her panties.

Old habits.

"Tell me what happened in the basement with the girl."

"Go to hell." She shoved at his chest with a shocking force of strength. "Put me down."

He constricted his grip, which only spurred her to push harder. In the next breath, she went wild, flailing and cursing in Spanish.

After spending years with Camila, Matias, and Ricky, he understood common words. Mostly slang. Too little to hold a conversation.

Not that this woman was interested in talking.

She aimed her mouth toward his, her eyes promising teeth and blood. He dodged her, wrapped her up, and still, she kept fighting.

The little heathen needed boundaries, and now was as good a time as any to set them.

UNSHACKLE

He opened his arms.

She dropped. Her legs buckled, and her rear hit the floor. The woman had been hit so many times in the head tonight she couldn't keep her eyes focused. She was in no state to stand, and they both knew it.

"Let's go." He took three steps toward the room and stopped with his back to her. "Start walking, Gina, or I will rip off your pants and blister your ass."

Tomas stood off to the side, his expression blank. No one moved.

He set a toe behind the opposite heel, pivoted, and stalked toward her. With her legs sprawled and chest heaving, she thrust up her chin. It was all she could do before he was on her.

Flipping her to her stomach, he set a knee on her back and shoved a hand beneath her waistband.

A button flew. The zipper broke, and the thin cutoffs ripped like tissue paper. Her panties followed, and he tossed the shreds aside.

Nude from the waist down, she clenched a firm, round, tanned backside.

Lust hit his circulation like a crackle of fireworks, lighting him up from the inside out. But he couldn't enjoy this. He shouldn't.

That was the real bitch of it. He had to behave as if spanking and touching and fucking this woman was pure goddamn bliss without taking real pleasure in it. Without becoming the monster he pretended to be.

She'd been violated and abused in unspeakable ways. No matter what he did with her, *to her*, he couldn't forget that.

So as his hand came down on her ass, he made her feel it without feeling it himself. He wailed on her, avoiding her injuries smoothly enough that she didn't notice the mercy. He hit her just enough to make her fear him, and she took the punishment without making a sound.

When he was sure his point was made, he threw her over his shoulder and hauled her to his room.

She didn't cry or struggle, didn't try to hide her red backside from the men he passed. But she didn't just hang there, either. Her muscles contracted against him, bracing for war, biding time.

She was plotting a way out of this. If she wasn't, she fucking well should've been.

Tomas opened the door with his key reader, and Luke carried her directly to the bathroom.

Placing a chair beside the tub, he dropped her there and got in her face. "Don't move."

She gave him an unblinking stare, looking pissed and miserable beneath all those bruises.

He cranked the faucet for the bath, tested the water, and let it run. Then he strode behind her, out of her range of sight.

Tomas joined him at the vanity across the room, monitoring her as Luke doused cold water on his face. In the mirror, he watched her, too, stealing glimpses between splashes of water.

His hands were shaking.

Shoving them under the faucet, he tried to calm himself. Except he didn't feel nervous. No panic or dread. Could've been the lingering effects of adrenaline. But there was something else. He felt different. Dazed. Empty.

"I'm losing myself," he whispered.

I killed an innocent girl.

Tomas leaned in while keeping his golden eyes laser-focused on the woman's back.

She couldn't hear them, not over the water spraying from multiple faucets.

"You're still you." Tomas gripped the tie at Luke's throat, loosening and removing it.

"I feel numb. Cold. Really fucking cold."

"It's temporary. Embrace it for just a little longer." With steady hands, Tomas unbuttoned Luke's collar and spoke in his ear. "I know it doesn't feel right, but you're doing a good thing. Focus on the big picture, the end goal, and remember, I'm here. If you fall too deep, I'll pull you back."

Too late.

Luke shrugged out of his jacket and rolled up his sleeves, his movements wooden.

Tomas placed a supportive hand on his neck and gave him a look that had been forged in trauma, friendship, and solidarity.

"You're John Smith. A slave buyer." Tomas shored up his grip, squeezing painfully. "Act like it."

"Done." He knocked the hand away and shed the remains of Luke Sanch.

Then he turned toward his newly acquired slave.

EIGHT

Her lower half was naked, but she hadn't consciously registered that detail until his eyes latched onto her in the mirror. Green eyes, glowing like toxic fire as they licked across her battered body.

With her back to him, she didn't need to turn around. The full-length mirror near the door hung at a convenient angle, giving her a direct view of him with his bodyguard. And what a strange bromance they shared.

First off, why were they both so damn good-looking? That wasn't normal. Not in this cesspool of pervy sadists. In the years she'd been imprisoned here, she'd never seen an attractive guest.

It was surface-level bullshit anyway. Every man here was hideous at his core.

But what struck her was the way these two interacted. A moment ago, the golden-eyed bodyguard seemed to console his boss, whispering sternly while helping him undress.

The boss—a sickeningly gorgeous redhead who called himself John—certainly didn't look like he needed comfort. Especially not now as he swung his searing gaze around the damage splotching her skin.

God, she hurt. Her head pounded, and her face felt like an overinflated basketball. Her mouth and cheeks throbbed, so hard and swollen she couldn't even scowl. Or cry.

The pain in her ribs indicated more bruising. Last year, they'd cracked during a fight and hadn't felt the same since. Then there were the degrading welts on her ass, which burned each time she shifted. He'd enjoyed that particular torment. No noticeable bulge in his pants, but his eyes had dilated the moment he'd hit her.

He didn't take those eyes off her now as he prowled closer, all hard angles and long, muscled legs, eating up the distance. He hadn't known she'd been watching him with his employee and didn't look happy about it. Whatever. It didn't change her outcome.

She knew why she was here and what he expected from her. If she fled, he would punish another girl. Even if she could physically run to the outside perimeter, Marco's men would capture her, drag her back to the basement, and torture another captive.

Like today.

That poor, innocent girl. Viciously butchered and killed. Because of her.

Every time she closed her eyes, she relived that horror. She still couldn't believe John had the balls to end the girl's life. Despite what he'd said, he hadn't done it out of cruel annoyance. Marco might've bought the act, but the conflict in John's eyes hadn't lied. He'd hated doing it and suffered for it.

Circling her chair, he stopped before her and laid his gaze boldly on hers. He didn't move, didn't blink, as if caught in a trance. Or maybe she was the one entranced. His stare wasn't a stare. It was a labyrinth. All high walls, dark corners, and confusing dead ends.

No way out.

She spent a week in the maze of his eyes. At least, that was how long it felt before he released her and shifted his attention to her lap.

He lingered on the shallow gashes, the dirt caking her knees and feet, and the patch of trim black hair between her legs. Despite the conversation in the elevator, he wouldn't find a drop of come on her body.

Marco and Omar usually fucked her after a fight. But tonight, they'd punished her in the worst way possible.

Her chest squeezed, and a thousand needles stabbed the backs of her eyes. She would mourn the nameless girl who'd bled for her. But not now, not here. She couldn't let the sorrow cripple her.

Anger was her only friend. "What are you looking at?"

"A repulsive mess. Grubby fingernails, filthy clothes, a fucked-up face…" His American accent penetrated her senses, cold and ravaging. He shut off the water. "I can't decide if you're hiding anything pretty beneath the bruises or something even more abhorrent."

She flinched and pulled in a slow breath to conceal it. They were just words. Harmless cruelty. She'd endured much, much worse.

"Remove your shirt." He stepped around her, casting a smothering shadow over her back.

The shirt was the only clothing she wore. Whether she liked it or not, it was coming off. But she wouldn't make it easy.

UNSHACKLE

Crossing her arms, she trapped the bloodstained cotton against her chest.

He didn't say a word. Not a sound for the longest minute.

With a deep shaky breath, she twisted around and looked up into the greenest, wickedest, most terrifying pair of eyes she'd ever seen.

Oh, God. She turned back.

Would he strike her? Throw her across the room? Rip away the fabric?

He took his time wringing out her nerves, and when he finally moved, she didn't hear or see him. But she sensed him all around her. His body heat against her skin, his breath on her neck, and his chilling patience like a collar on her throat.

"Do you feel the walls pressing in around you? Restricting your movements? Strangling your air?" He brushed his nose against her ear. "That's me, Gina. The more you defy me, the closer and meaner I get."

"Don't call me that."

"Do you prefer whore? Slave?" He held her motionless without touching her. "How about cunt?"

A fist pounded on the door, prompting Golden Eyes to exit the bathroom. She welcomed the distraction, knowing food had arrived. When was the last time she'd had an actual meal?

Confusion edged in, fogging her vision. The thought of eating made her sick. She needed sleep. Just a few moments to close her heavy eyelids. But that was dangerous. And impossible.

The night had only just begun.

As voices drifted from the main room, he shoved a hand between her legs. It happened so fast she wasn't prepared. The iron bar of his arm caught her across the chest, pinning her to the chair. His other hand hooked around her waist, his fingers seeking and finding the hood of her clit.

Before she could blink, he had the bundle of nerves exposed and held captive between his finger and thumb. A sharp, ruthless tweak wrenched a shriek from her throat. He did it again, pinching and twisting with unholy pressure. The agony was more than she could bear.

"Stop!" She thrashed, screeching the chair on the tiles. "No! Please! No more, no more, oh, God. Please stop!"

He squeezed harder, yanking the raw bud so aggressively it felt as though he was ripping it from her body.

With him behind her, she couldn't land a punch or kick. Her fingernails proved useless against the steel cage of his arms, and her efforts quickly exhausted her.

Tears swarmed her eyes. Her throat swelled with wet cries. God help her, she couldn't stop screaming, which only made her face hurt that much more.

"Okay, okay, I'll do it!" She tried to tear her shirt from beneath his arm. "Let go, goddammit, and I'll do what you said!"

He freed her, and she doubled over, groaning in misery as blood rushed to her clit. Nausea raged, and the pain in her skull grew claws. She breathed through it, waiting for the rampage to subside. Then she clumsily pulled off the last of her clothes.

Golden Eyes entered, pushing a cart full of covered plates, liquor, and medical supplies and closed the door behind him. Before the scent of food reached her nose, John scooped her up and dumped her into the bathtub.

Warm water rose to her chin and stung her wounds, finding lacerations and open sores she didn't even know she had. But once the shock wore off, relief seeped into her bones. She lay her head back on the ledge and sighed.

"When was the last time you had a bath?" John dragged the chair closer and lowered into it.

When she didn't answer, he sank a hand in the water and grabbed her inner thigh. It was a promise, not a threat. He would hurt her again.

What was the point in remaining silent? She wouldn't win.

"A week, I think." She met his stony eyes. "There are no bathrooms in the basement."

"When do they let you out? When you fight?"

"When I behave. I have my own room away from the main house."

Not really. She slept in a garage filled with old cars and lawn equipment, but no one bothered her there. It was her solace in hell.

Golden Eyes carried over a container of soaps and stood off to the side.

"Tell me about the girl and the hook." John lathered up his hands and started cleaning her arms.

The foam turned pink as he scrubbed dried blood from her skin. She marveled at the gentleness of his fingers, so contradictory to the agony they'd inflicted just moments ago.

"I tried to escape last night." She let him lift her leg from the water, wincing at the movement.

"Relax." He held her weight, massaging soap around damaged muscles. "Was it your first attempt?"

"No. But when they caught me this time, they made sure I'd never try again."

"The girl." His hand paused on her calf, his gaze locked on hers. "They butchered her to teach you a lesson."

"Yeah. Lovely friends you have. I guess birds of a feather really do flock together."

He yanked hard on her foot and hauled her along the bottom of the tub. The sudden motion pulled her head beneath the water. Panic rose, and her legs cartwheeled as the memory of his hand over the blonde's mouth flooded her brain.

She flailed, shot up, and gulped for air. "Fuck you!"

"I'll be the one doing the fucking. Hold still." He resumed his lathering before she'd even caught her breath.

"I can wash myself."

"No. Explain your relationship with Vera Gomez."

Homicidal rage spiked through her, quivering her muscles. "We have no relationship."

"If your face wasn't broken, I'd see a vein bulging in your forehead just at the mention of her name."

There was so much she wanted to say, but she couldn't. If she thought today's punishment was unbearable, it was nothing compared to what they would do if she told her secrets.

But if she didn't give him something, he would just keep pushing. Keep hurting her.

"I've been here as long as that bitch." She tilted her head back to locate the cameras and found none. Then she spotted a hole in the ceiling. "What—?"

"I'm a very private man, and I don't appreciate *anyone* recording my personal activities."

So he tore out the only camera? What about the other rooms? The cartel would never allow that.

He followed her gaze to the doorway and shook his head. "This is the only room that isn't monitored."

"They can't hear us in here?

"Only when you scream," Golden Eyes said without emotion.

"You and Vera came here…" John inched the chair toward her head and washed her hair. "When?"

"Nine-hundred and fifty-eight days ago."

Almost three years. It felt like three decades.

"You arrived together?" he asked.

How much could she tell him? Maybe the cartel wasn't listening right now, but could she really take that chance?

"Not together. The compound had just been built." She closed her eyes and wiped at the stream of bubbles running from his hands. "She hated me from the beginning."

"Why?"

So many reasons, and none that she could disclose. So she settled on another truth. "Why does La Rocha abduct, rape, and sell girls? They're evil. *She* is pure fucking evil."

He seemed so perplexed by this with his brows all knitted and his lips clamped together. Of course, he didn't get it. He associated with the Mexican cartel. Hell, he was a goddamn slave buyer.

Except… He didn't fit the mold. Not exactly. Something was weirdly off about him.

He finished shampooing and moved on to conditioner. "Was she ever a captive here?"

"Are you kidding? This place is her brainchild. Her pride and joy. She built it from the ground up." She squinted at him. "Why are you so interested in her?"

"She's fucking gorgeous." He licked the corner of his mouth and put his face in hers. "You're jealous."

Yeah, right. Beautiful women grew on trees around here, and she never wanted to be one of them. Which was why she welcomed every fight, hoping the beatings would make her less desirable.

He fell quiet as he rinsed her hair, seemingly lost in thought.

Then he finished the rest of her. Somehow, he managed the intimate task without making it sexual. His gaze touched her nudity without being creepy. His hands glided over her breasts and between her legs without trying to violate her.

He couldn't have made it more obvious that something strange was going on.

Maybe it was her appearance? She didn't need a mirror to imagine how grotesque she looked. *Good.* If a puffy face killed his boner, she might consider punching herself to maintain the swelling all week.

But if her looks turned him off, why had he chosen her?

"How many times have you been pimped out to the guests?" He pulled the drain and let the water out.

"You're the first."

He winged up an auburn eyebrow, an expression that made him look younger. Almost playful.

"You're not special." She slid her knees to her chest, shivering in the draining water. "If I hadn't won so many fights for the cartel, they would've killed me a long time ago. I'm a flight risk who's outlived her value, and you said you wouldn't pay for broken goods." She laughed hollowly. "You've been duped, Johnny Boy."

UNSHACKLE

"You're not only wrong. You're scared." He bent in and wrapped a hand around her throat, holding her gaze. "Scared shitless, because you know that when your bruises fade, I'm going to like what I see. When I taste you, I'm going to savor that, too. What you may not know, but will soon discover, is that when I'm inside you, you'll come on such a violent tailspin of pleasure that my cock will be the only one that ever matters. Then, now, and forever."

"Hate to burst your bubble, but women don't get off when they're raped."

He grabbed a towel and lifted her from the tub, his voice the texture of velvet. "We'll see about that."

NINE

Her mysterious captor was right about one thing. She was scared. How could she not be? As traumatizing as it was to be fucked into the dirt by the four top dogs of La Rocha Cartel, sex with them was always predictable, routine, and over quickly.

This man promised none of that.

She lay on a settee in the wet room, swaddled in a towel, watching him and his bodyguard gather supplies. They worked effortlessly together, anticipating each other's movements, communicating without words. She was horrifyingly captivated.

How many times had they done this? How many women had they raped? Killed?

They didn't need to pay for sex. Not with those sculpted faces. But it wasn't uncommon for serial killers to charm women into their beds.

These guys had more than just charisma, with their powerfully honed physiques, the intelligence behind their eyes, determination in the set of their shoulders, and they smelled good. Sweet Jesus, the room reeked of clean, woodsy, virile masculinity.

Potent males.

Gorgeous.

They looked like fashion models, not corrupt businessmen. But to be invited here, John must be tremendously wealthy. Or in debt up to his pretty green eyeballs.

"During the fight tonight…" He perched on the settee beside her hip and loaded a toothbrush with paste. "You knew which solar light would pull free."

"It was a lucky guess." She reached for the toothbrush.

UNSHACKLE

He drew it away. "Don't lie to me."

"Fine. Last time I walked through the yard, I dug up the stake and loosened the hole."

He took her hand and caressed his thumb across her palm. She shivered, waiting for him to do something mean. But he just kept the pad of that thumb moving in featherlight circles.

Tingles of sensation licked through her, unlike anything she'd ever felt. It made her uncomfortable. Nervous. She knew how to battle pain. But affection? Kindness? She liked it too much. More than liked it, and that put her at a disadvantage.

"Don't." She yanked her hand from his grip.

"You're not in a position to make objections."

"Oh, buddy, I can and *will* refuse you. Isn't that what you wanted? A whore who will kick and scream and wear herself out? It makes you hard and hung—"

He shoved the toothbrush in her mouth, and she choked on the glob of mint.

"Asshole." Her garbled, foamy insult lit up his eyes with a devilish gleam.

It was almost a smile. A beautiful one, unfortunately. He really was so nice to look at, with his red hair glinting like metallic copper in the overhead light. Though he kept it short, it curled at the ends, giving him a relaxed, tousled look.

Wide across the shoulders and narrow through the waist, he had the *V* thing that she'd only ever seen on porn sites. Like in the male on male videos, and the macho men with big cocks, oh, and the naked solo amateur guys, stroking themselves for the camera... God, she used to love watching those.

She used to love sex.

There had been a time when she loved having a boyfriend, too. A guy she could talk to and kiss whenever the impulse struck. She missed the comfort in connecting with another person, even when they turned mean and tried to smack her around.

Someday, if she escaped this place with her mind and body intact, she would find a decent partner, someone to love, and just maybe, she wouldn't feel so alone.

As she brushed her teeth and spat in a cup, John watched her as fixedly as a predator with eyes on his prey. A wolf in a suit. She could admire his impossible beauty and even hold a conversation with him, but it didn't change the fact that he was going to rape her. If not her, then someone else.

Golden Eyes crouched beside her head with a medical kit and reached for her face. She jerked away.

"Be still." John bent over her and fingered her wet hair. "He's going to treat your wounds while we talk."

"Why bother?"

"If you're as smart as I think you are, you'll figure it out."

The quiet man stared at John in a scolding way. Like they were... Equals? Friends? Family?

What were they hiding?

"Do you have a fake name, too?" she asked the bodyguard.

"Tomas."

"Rhymes with dumbass." John pitched a scowl at the man. Then he held up one of her spirally black locks, studying it. "This wasn't curly before."

"It wasn't clean before."

The girls in the main house straightened it the last time she washed it. Sometimes, she let them play dress-up with her, looking for any excuse to eavesdrop on their gossip.

Since they had more freedom to roam the property, they knew things she didn't, such as who was coming and going, which guards were on patrol, how many guests were in-house, and when the next shipment of girls would arrive.

His fingertips ran down her breastbone and loosened the knot on the towel. She dropped the toothbrush and stopped him from descending farther.

He smiled down at her. No humor. All heat.

"No." She wasn't ready. She would never be ready.

"Fight me." His voice slid over her with silken confidence. A voice that could carry brutal commands over the length of a dark, oppressive dungeon.

"Fuck you."

He ripped away the towel.

"No! Stop!" She shrieked, scrambling to pull it back.

But he'd already tossed it away, chuckling blackly. So she kneed him in the chin. Hard.

His head snapped back, and the crook of his mouth kicked up. Not a hint of surprise on his face.

He'd let her have that shot.

"That's the only one you get tonight." He captured her legs and pinned them down. "Your coordination is getting worse. Are you dizzy?"

"Eat a dick."

"You'll be doing exactly that if you don't answer the question."

"Yes, John, the room is spinning."

UNSHACKLE

Nausea, headache, sleepiness, blurred vision, ringing in her ears... She had a concussion. But that wasn't the only reason she was pinned down. Every punch she'd thrown at him had been easily dodged and redirected. He knew how to neutralize an attacker.

"You've had training." She wrapped an arm over her bare chest and a hand between her legs, covering her nudity. "Combat sports."

"It's a hobby of mine, along with weights and cardio. You'll work out with me once you're fed and rested."

By *work out*, he didn't mean jogging.

He blatantly inspected her naked body while Tomas cleaned the cuts on her face.

Antibiotic ointment was applied. Her eyes were pried open and checked. Then her teeth, ears, and nose. That done, Tomas ran his hands over every inch of her scalp, searching for hidden wounds. The scrupulous efficiency in his work suggested he'd done this before.

"Are you a bodyguard or a doctor?" she asked him.

"I've treated a lot of wounds."

"Your boss must toss all his beaten slaves your way."

John splayed a large hand over her hipbone, his fingers stretching nearly around her waist. "Why are you so thin?"

"It's called intermittent fasting. If you want to shed extra pounds, you have to feel the pangs of hunger every day."

He narrowed his eyes, not buying a single word.

"They say fasting also helps you live longer." She shrugged.

"If you're concerned about longevity, you wouldn't be breaking through a wall patrolled by heavily armed guards. You're lucky they didn't shoot you."

"How did you know I breached the wall?"

"I didn't until you just told me."

Fuck, fuck, fuck. Her lungs emptied of air.

His eyes darkened, half-hooded by thick copper lashes that did nothing to conceal the intellect blazing there. "Tell me what you saw on the other side."

No way. That was *her* secret. She'd barely convinced Marco she hadn't seen anything. She sure as fuck couldn't trust this man. What would stop him from running straight to Marco and ratting her out?

"It was nighttime." She swallowed her rising panic. "I couldn't see my hands in front of my—"

"Shut up." He climbed over her and straddled her waist.

With his knees astride her hips, he held his weight off her while lowering his upper body, chest to chest, and arms bracketing her head. His mouth hovered so close she tasted his breath. Peated whiskey, hot and smoky, like the blood burning through her veins.

"I know you're lying." His lips grazed hers, shooting unwanted frissons across her skin. "If you tell me what you saw outside the perimeter, they'll kill you. And me, as well." His gaze darted to the closed door. "We'll discuss it another time."

Like never.

There was only one reason he'd be interested in what lay beyond the wall. He wanted the location of the compound.

Some guests felt paranoid and isolated here and didn't like the cartel monitoring their external communications. They knew if something happened to them, no one would ever find them. Last year, a government agent had disguised himself as a buyer and infiltrated the estate. The cartel discovered his identity quickly, and the man was never seen again. His bones were undoubtedly buried somewhere on the property.

Whether John was a narc, military operative, or just another paranoid dipshit, she needed to stay clear of the crossfire.

"They're starving you." He swept his fingers over her ribs and raised his body to stare down the length of hers. "What's the purpose in that?"

"Have you ever seen a pit bull in a fighting ring? Or a greyhound on a racetrack? Those malnourished, neglected animals are worked to the bone and kept only to make their owners money. When they're no longer useful, they're put down." Her eyes closed without her permission. "I'm just a dog on death row."

He cleared a bit of hair off her cheek, prompting her to look up at him. "You're more than that to them. How many in the cartel have fucked you?"

"If you wanted a virgin—"

"I want information about the woman I'm paying for." His hand captured her nape, fingers closing around her hair, restraining her as he breathed his threatening words against her lips. "We can go round and round, but eventually, you'll tell me what I want to know."

"No one touched me tonight."

"But Vera—"

"Is a goddamn liar. They raped the girl on the hook instead."

An anguished look stole across his handsome face. Didn't he know that any show of emotion would get him killed?

He didn't belong here. Which begged the question... Who the hell was he?

"How many times have they forced you to fight?" His hands held her so firmly against him her neck smarted.

"I don't know. Maybe a dozen."

"You've never lost."

"You know the rules. If I lose, I'm dead."

UNSHACKLE

"How do you rig every fight?"

"Shoestring and fishing line in my pocket make good garrotes. Same with a belt. Then there's the stolen switchblade I buried in the dirt. A hidden nail file works well in the eye socket. Sometimes, I'm just lucky."

Damn lucky she was still alive.

He released her and shifted down her body. "I want the names of every man who raped you."

For what reason? To avenge her?

Just like that, she was a wishful, simple-minded teenager again. *Oh, that pathetic girl.*

The cynical, realistic woman knew better. He simply wanted to know the state of her used-up pussy before he shoved his dick in it.

"Their names," he said.

"Marco, Omar, Miguel, and Alejandro." She turned her head, refusing to look at him.

The cartel brothers had been passing her between them for almost three years. They never fucked her at the same time, but they shared her, nonetheless.

John was so quiet she thought he would push her away with disgust. She waited, hoping he would. Concussion or not, she just wanted to sleep.

When she finally dared a sideways glance, he was ready with one of those ice-cold expressions.

"Hector's sons kept you to themselves?"

"Until tonight."

Maybe they were finally done with her. Maybe John was, too.

"Are you going to send me back to them?" she asked.

"Should I?"

"Don't care."

His jaw turned rigid. "You watched them butcher a girl."

"Still don't care." She knew what she was getting with the cartel.

This guy had a mouth on him. Full, pillowed lips that would wrench ungodly screams until he wore her out. Screams of pain were one thing. They fueled her hatred and kept her focused. But she feared they would be screams of pleasure. Then she would only hate *herself*.

"Roll over." He shifted lower, straddling her knees.

So we're doing this.

Go directly to anal. Do not pass go.

Her stomach hardened. "I want tequila first."

"No." He smacked her thigh so hard it sent shock waves down her leg.

Was this a battle worth fighting? Unfortunately, no. Sex from behind was impersonal and would be a thousand times easier than looking this man in the eyes.

She flipped over gingerly and tried to relax her sphincter. There were worse things than being plowed in the ass.

Like watching a girl get her foot sawed off.

Tomas passed a tube of ointment to John, and she focused on her breathing. In. Out. In—

A lubed finger pressed against her rectum. "They fuck you here?"

"Every time." She clenched, unbidden. "Use a condom."

"I'm clean."

"They're not. Use a fucking condom."

She didn't have an STD, but she couldn't trust John's claim about himself. Not that he'd listen to her demand.

He adjusted his weight on the backs of her legs. A wet squirt belched from the tube, and she held her breath.

Make it hurt.

Make me want to gut you.

His hands came down on her buttocks, soft and sticky and warm. *Oh, God.* She tensed. Not from pain. No, his touch was pure heaven.

The sensual slide of palms, the hypnotic rhythm of his caress, and the sinful friction of skin on skin made her pulse sing and belly quiver.

Talented fingers kneaded her flesh, working antibiotic ointment—not lube—into her welts. Trickles of bliss crept up from her toes, melting her joints and turning her bones to sludge.

She'd never had a massage but imagined this one exceeded every touch ever set upon the human body. She felt heavy, hot, and under attack. He lay siege to her senses, wrecking her ability to think as his hands parted ways, dividing and conquering the length of her.

His touch was everywhere, gliding over curves and wrapping around achy muscles. Each caress imparted authority, ordering her flesh to heat, commanding her nerve endings to dance, and teaching her body to crave.

He knew where to stroke her, how much pressure to use, and precisely which spots would make her sigh. And sigh she did, open-mouthed and collecting drool. Never had she felt this relaxed.

Until he lowered his head and curled his tongue along her spine.

TEN

"What are you doing?" Her blood spun hot at the shocking, wet caress along her back.

The sensation couldn't have been produced by his mouth. She twisted her neck to see behind her, and *holy fuck*. His firm lips were right there, his kiss gliding up her backbone.

From the moment he'd flipped her to her stomach, she hadn't anticipated anything remotely pleasurable nor half as sensual as the swirling possession of his hands and tongue.

Fear was always a glaring partner when she was alone with the brothers. But never arousal. Never *this*.

This destructively alluring man made her want more than a *hurry-up-and-finish* encounter. She wanted hours of him doing this. Touching, kissing, hungering... She didn't want him to stop.

What the hell was wrong with her? She couldn't accept this. Not from a slave-buying rapist.

"Stop that." She tried to jerk free. "Don't touch me."

His teeth clamped down, holding her in place as effectively as his intimidating gaze.

With her chin to her shoulder, she stared back, scrambling to find footing in the stellar depths of his eyes. "Quit toying with me, and just do what you're going to do."

He licked her bitten skin defiantly. "I'm responsible for the care and feeding of my woman."

"I'm not your woman, and unless I'm mistaken, you're feeding yourself."

"You're mine for a week, and tonight, I eat first."

He trailed his lips toward the curves of her ass, just as seductively as before, staring down at her nudity with those long thick lashes fanning over his cheeks. Then he glanced up, delivered another diabolical sweep of his tongue, and looked pointedly at Tomas.

His bodyguard nodded and paced off toward the door. When he opened it, he didn't leave and instead took up a watchful position on the threshold.

What was happening?

John returned to his torture, sucking, tonguing, and nipping her backside. The delicious incursion pulled her insides this way and that. She thrashed beneath his greedy mouth, gasping at the overload of stimulation.

No one had ever taken time to warm up her body. It had been so long since she'd experienced anything akin to foreplay she'd forgotten it was even a thing people did.

The worst part? She was enjoying it. Allowing it to happen. Imagining other parts of her that would tingle and heat beneath his lips. Would he find her as hot and wet, as lush and needy as his wicked mouth?

Not possible. She didn't get wet. Not anymore.

His affection was so fucking wrong it was cruel.

With renewed clarity, she met his gaze. He rolled his tongue, and her stomach seized up.

"Enough!" She exploded out of her skin.

Twisting to her back, she let her fist fly. Missed his face by an inch. Swung a left hook. Missed that one, too. Fuck!

"You're off-balance, Gina." He wrapped a hand around her neck and easily immobilized her.

"Release me!" She writhed on her back, kicking uselessly as he settled between her legs.

The pressure on her throat tightened. Dots blurred her vision, and she clawed frantically at his arms, his hands.

"You're only hurting yourself." He loosened his grip just enough to allow breath. "Surrender."

"Never!" She coughed, gulping for air.

"Easy. I promise you'll enjoy this. You might even thank me."

"I'll blow the devil in hell before I thank you for anything!"

"I *am* the devil, and while your offer is tempting, I don't want your mouth." He released her throat. "Unless, of course, you use it to scream."

"I hate you."

The look he gave her was arched and dismissing. His attention lowered to his shirt, his fingers opening the buttons. Then it was off, and her heart stuck somewhere between one breath and the next.

He bent over her, his torso as arresting as his face, strong and powerful, enough to cause serious ruination to her mental health.

Every nerve in her body thrummed as he lowered his mouth to her breast, the harsh lines of his face unsoftened by the tenderness in his kiss.

She tried to push herself upright only to be shoved down by his forearm, the flex of muscle bulging against her throat. He radiated such an intense fusion of beauty and menace it sucked her breath. But that didn't stop her from sinking beneath the tangled warmth that spiraled from the tongue against her nipple.

His lips moved from one breast to the other, kissing and suckling until she burned beneath the quickening rush of his exhales. Hot mouth. Expert tongue. He licked her in a way she'd never dreamed.

From neck to hips, he dealt relentless strokes, slowly, steadily, inch after inch down her body. Her fingers caught his hair, pushing, pulling, knuckled against his scalp.

When had she started trembling? Jesus, she'd lost count of how many times she'd gulped down a moan.

"It's too much." Another gulp lodged in the back of her throat. "Stop!"

Kneeling between her legs, he straightened and stared down at her, eyes glinting with cold sparks of lightning. Then he lifted her knees and forced them to her shoulders, spreading her wide for his gaze.

And his mouth.

"No." She shook her head frantically, fighting the steely grip of his hands on her thighs.

"Tell me. Are you not the least bit passive in bed?" he asked. "Truthfully."

"When it's consensual, you mean? Like with a man I *want* to be with?"

"Yes."

She contemplated her answer as his mouth took a meandering stroll along her ankle.

"I don't remember." She tried to kick his face and hit air. "Are you?"

"No." He moved on to her foot, warming the arch with an open-mouthed kiss. "You don't want a passive man."

"I don't want a man. Period." She thrashed and swung her arms, going nowhere. "Let me go!"

"Your body betrays you." His gaze dipped, bringing attention to the moisture chilling in the air against her folds.

No. How could that be? She didn't want this. "Don't—"

He buried his mouth between her thighs.

She bowed off the cushion and tried to roll away, but he stopped her. With his hands on her thighs, he ravished her pussy, plundering, conquering, until she was hoarse from screaming and dizzy with fatigue.

They'd been dueling in this position long enough for both of them to be covered in a sheen of sweat. She didn't want to straddle his shoulders anymore. Didn't want his tongue buried inside her. But there was no evading him. No interrupting that merciless mouth. No part of her left unexplored, unlicked.

Faster and hungrier, he ate, groaning against her, building the rhythm, and dragging her with him on a spiraling, breathless descent south of heaven.

Death would be waiting. At the bottom of the fall. At the end of his tongue. If she orgasmed, it would break her.

Every skilled touch felt like a sledgehammer crashing into her carefully erected shields. She wouldn't be able to stop the flood of pleasure much longer.

If she harmed him, he'd said he would hurt another girl. But would he, really? After the mercy he'd shown the blonde in the basement and the peculiar adoration he was giving her body now, his threat didn't hold true.

She decided to take a chance. A last-ditch effort of strength.

Balling a fist at her side, she swung and connected with the side of his head. *Yes!*

He grunted, reared back, and swiped at the moisture on his lips.

Oh, God. If looks could kill… There was no mistaking the haughty brows, tense mouth, and hawkish glare. He struck an impressive figure when he was calm. But when he was pissed, he was terrifying.

She couldn't pull air into her lungs.

"Tomas." He inclined his head, motioning his bodyguard forward. When his order was obeyed, he said in a wintry tone, "Pull out your cock."

"What?" Her breath released in short, hard pants. "No!"

John clapped a hand over her mouth as Tomas unzipped. It took a moment for the man's full length to spring free. Then it was there, semi-hard, growing harder, really goddamn hard to miss.

She choked at the sight of him, abandoning her fight to utter horrified shock. John removed his hand from her face, but she still couldn't breathe. She'd never seen a man hung like that. Maybe in porn, but sweet Jesus, never in person. It couldn't be real.

The girth, the length, the sheer fucking size… And it was still lengthening, thickening substantially in the fist of his slow, lazy strokes.

UNSHACKLE

"I don't need to hurt another girl when I have a solution right here." John slid a finger between her legs and pressed farther back, testing the give of her tightest hole. "You can struggle and scream, but I promise, little fighter, if you strike my face again, Tomas will impale that monster in your ass, and you'll feel all ten of those inches."

Fully erect, Tomas stared down at her with absolute intent in his eyes. John wore the same expression. No lust. No smiles. Just single, unified purpose.

They weren't fucking around.

The bitter taste of defeat filled her mouth. She swallowed, turned her head away, and ordered her body to relax.

"Hold down my arms." She didn't trust her impulses.

Tomas zipped up his fly and stood somewhere above her with his hands shackling her wrists. Then John pressed his mouth to the inside of her thigh. She shuddered.

He took his time edging his way back to her center. She whimpered as he explored, gasped as he bit, and sighed as he grazed on her flesh.

By the time he reached her pussy, she was strung out and panting. His finger was the first to sink inside, and her body jolted. He pumped that thick digit in and out, surging a torrent of honeyed lava through her system, sizzling, consuming, and rocking her through the invasion.

Her voice produced sounds she'd never heard, sobs of forced pleasure as he strained forward, thrust harder, and joined his tongue with his fingers.

"You taste like sin." His hands trembled against her, his breathing erratic. "Fucking addictive."

She liquefied, bones dissolving, and tears swarming her eyes. Raw, sexual heat flamed her skin. He probed deeper, licked her faster, and her whole body caught fire. She gripped Tomas' wrists, digging fingernails into muscle and shaking from head to toe.

"You look like a warrior goddess." John made a toe-curling lap around her clit. "Mottled with battle wounds and writhing on my tongue. So damn hot."

If anything, she felt remarkably weak and pathetic. But the urgent demand of his mouth couldn't be denied. He raided her senses and kept taking and taking until every muscle and bone in her body was spent.

Sliding a hand between his lips and her drenched flesh, he assaulted her anew. Hard to tell what he was doing, but the intersecting stimulation of his tongue gliding around and through his caressing fingers made everything slip together wetly, erotically. It was beyond arousing, turning her into a quivering, moaning puddle, and soon, she was screaming.

His lips drove savagely against her clit, his tongue a hot weapon of destruction, burrowing deep as if seeking the limits of her resistance. Swirling, tasting, owning, he built her release, climbed higher, faster, and carried her to the peak.

A starlit bomb detonated in her core, exploded outward, and crackled across her skin. Euphoria spasmed through her, arching her back, skyrocketing her voice, and flashing vivid color behind her eyelids.

"There she is." With a vibrating groan, he made a final, wet revolution with his tongue, teasing out the remnants of sensation.

"Stop." She panted breathlessly, twitching with lingering convulsions. "Please, stop."

His auburn head rose, and his body shifted up, up, up until he hovered above her face, gazing thoughtfully down at her. The lushness of his mouth glistened with her come. Then he licked it clean.

Ashamed to the pit of her stomach, she turned away.

He caught her nape, careful to avoid the bruises on her jaw, and hauled her close, his lips feathering against hers, touching… Or not touching? She wasn't sure. The heat of his mouth was so close her breath stuttered. Her nostrils flared. He smelled too good and felt too hard, his chest a pressing wall of burning muscle against her.

Why was he in her face, his parted mouth on hers, but not? He was just breathing against her lips, aggressively so, as if holding himself back from kissing her.

Please, don't kiss me.

"I've never witnessed anything more beautiful, and I haven't even seen your face yet." His words fell like a kiss over her gaping mouth. "Thank you for giving me your submission."

Her head reeled, and her heart stumbled into a strange, fitful rhythm. "I didn't—"

He pressed lips lightly against hers. "Don't ruin it."

Self-preservation was the first law of nature. In the presence of this man, she felt that law in the marrow of her bones.

"Tomas." Pushing to his feet, he opened his pants. "Move the food to my room."

She closed her legs and curled up on her side, knowing full well he wasn't finished with her.

"Hold these on your face." Tomas pressed two ice packs into her hands. Then he pushed the cart out of the bathroom.

John stripped off his pants and briefs and faced her with his fists on his hips. He just stood there, head cocked, as if he didn't have a huge, raging erection jutting between them.

"Get those on your face." He nodded at the ice packs numbing her fingers.

UNSHACKLE

She blinked, thunderstruck, and slowly raised the cloth-wrapped pads to her cheeks. Before she could form a question, he strode to the wall of shower heads and yanked on the faucet.

With his back to her, she found her gaze drawn to the perfect form of his body. The strong column of his neck, slope of broad shoulders, chiseled torso, well-muscled legs... She swallowed, drinking in his dangerous masculinity.

He leaned toward the wall, head down, bracing himself on strong, corded arms. She shouldn't be staring at his ass, but God help her, it was tight, firm, chiseled to perfection, with two little divots denting either side of his tail bone.

Why was he built so beautifully? Not only that, how did he know how to touch a woman with such flawless mastery? His skill was so over-the-top he could coax multiples from a quadriplegic and use that American twang to charm the panties off a deaf woman.

It didn't make sense. None of it added up.

He bought trafficked humans, for Christ's sake. Was that how he'd learned the art of seduction? He must've heard the pained, helpless cries of dozens of slaves.

Abruptly, he shut off the water and prowled toward her. He'd showered without bothering with soap? Even more curious, his dick was now flaccid.

He wasn't as endowed as Tomas—no one was—but his size was impressive, nonetheless. Thick and veiny with a plump head, his manhood hung against heavy balls, the root surrounded by a sparse nest of copper hair.

She didn't want any of that anywhere near her.

When he reached her, she flinched and blamed her jumpiness on her pounding headache and blinding exhaustion.

He collected the ice packs and lifted her from the settee. Goosebumps prickled his flesh, and cold water dripped from his body to hers. *Ice* water.

"You took a cold shower?" She hugged her chest, an awkward position in the cradle of his arms.

"Remember..." He turned toward the door, his voice low at her ear. "Outside this room, they're watching and listening."

Her brows pulled together as he carried her out of the bathroom.

Everything he'd just done to her had been in private. Had that been deliberate? Except... Wait. The door stood open. It had been closed until he'd nodded at Tomas to open it. Right before he'd forced her to orgasm.

They can't hear us in here?
Only when you scream.

Boy, had she screamed. She must've sounded as if John were beating her, and he'd encouraged the noise. Almost as if he'd orchestrated it. But for what purpose?

He carried her into the bedroom, both of them nude. Whoever monitored the cameras would've heard her shrieks and assumed he fucked her in the bathroom. Hell, he'd even taken care of his erection.

But why go through all the trouble when he could've just raped her?

Something was rotten in the state of Denmark. What, exactly, she didn't know, but this man wasn't who he claimed to be.

If he thought he had her fooled, he was an idiot.

ELEVEN

"There's another steak." Luke set aside her finished plate, bone-tired yet too wired to close his eyes. "You need the calories."

"I can't eat another bite." She slumped against the pillows on his bed, her lashes fluttering closed. "Hand me the tequila."

"You've had enough." He'd allowed her a few sips to take the edge off the pain. "You need water."

"Shut up and let me sleep."

Amusement tugged at his lips. She'd been awake and holding a conversation for hours with that concussion. It was probably safe for her to rest. She needed it.

In the next day or so, her face would be black and blue. For now, the ice had reduced the swelling enough that he could almost make out her features.

Christ, she was magnificent. Rough-hewn but at the same time delicately formed. With shimmering raven hair and flashing brown eyes, she was captivating beyond what he'd imagined a cartel slave could be. Or any woman, for that matter.

No wonder Hector's sons were so possessive of her. *Were.* Not any longer. She belonged to him this week, and during that time, no one would fucking touch her.

Sitting beside her hip, he adjusted the sheet over his nude lower half. Without a doubt, Vera had tuned in from the monitoring room, listening to the screams from his bathroom. She'd shown too much animosity toward this girl to not be glued to the cameras.

If his efforts to make Vera jealous and cozy up against him didn't pan out, he had a backup plan with the little fighter. Being imprisoned here for almost three years, Gina knew things about the compound. Hell, she'd seen what lay outside the wall.

She cracked open an eye, then the other, giving him a full-blown glare, frosty and vibrant with malice. "Who are you?"

"A man who doesn't deserve that look."

The evening could've gone much worse for her, and she knew it.

Delaying the need to cause her more pain was the best he could do tonight. Tomorrow would be a different story.

Tomorrow, he would learn everything she knew, even if he had to fuck it out of her.

What made that more depraved was that he looked forward to it. To capture her tiny waist in the grip of his hands and impale her on his cock... He couldn't wait. Heat snaked through his groin at the thought of claiming her.

He wanted to do it *now*.

With her long black curls spread out over the pillow, she conjured images of a dark angel. The bedsheets tangled around sleek, enchanting hips, leaving the rest of her bare like a sacrificial offering for his gaze. Small firm breasts, flat belly, bronze legs, so smooth and enticing... She had a body that wouldn't quit. Strong, divine, untamed beauty.

The urge to slide his fingers up and caress the reddened skin around her eyes and cheekbones was hard to resist. But she would fight the affection. With the cameras in full view, he didn't want to have to discipline her, which he would do to maintain his cover.

As it was, this girl was already onto him.

The moment she'd realized he wasn't fucking her tonight, her hatred had twisted into bewilderment. Fatigue played a part in her confusion, but he'd felt a shift in her.

She wanted to trust him.

If only he could do the same. He'd tried to test her loyalty, asking if he should send her back to Hector's sons. Her *don't care* response wasn't assuring. Until he knew with certainty she wouldn't stab him in the back, he couldn't tell her who he was. Blowing his cover was the quickest way to ruin the mission.

Despite all that, he loved her explosive temper and quarrelsome nature. She wasn't afraid to throw a bare-knuckled punch or get in his face and run off her mouth.

A mouth that had forgotten how to soften in a smile.

He wanted to force his tongue between her clenched teeth and duel it out.

He wanted to kiss her.

UNSHACKLE

Even after consuming more whiskey and half of a steak, he still tasted her on his lips. He couldn't recall ever contemplating the flavor of a woman's body before. Perhaps because no one had ever tasted so forbidden, like honeyed sin and fiery rebellion.

Shutting the door on those thoughts, he turned on the television, switched off the lights, and slid into bed beside her. After a few adjustments, they lay beneath the covers, face to face, eyes locked.

Tomas had already retired for the evening, confirming that the devices in the ceiling had night vision. But the sounds from the TV should drown out a whispered conversation.

A late-night talk show flickered on the screen. The soundtrack of studio laughter detached itself from the weighty silence between him and Gina.

He wished he knew her real name. He wanted to know everything about her—where she came from, how she ended up here, her schooling, job history, hobbies, family, boyfriends, all of it.

She regarded him with similar interest, her dark eyes pooling with dazed curiosity, lips swollen, and forehead creased as if fighting the lethargy taking hold.

"You can't fall asleep?" he asked.

"Not lying beside a rapist."

"Deal with it."

"Yeah." Her jaw stiffened. "It's what I do."

"Do any La Rocha members force you to spend the night in their beds?"

"Never."

"This is the first time you've slept beside someone since you've been here?"

"I'm not sleeping." She squinted. "So that first hasn't happened."

"You going to stay awake for a week?"

The slits of her eyes become impossibly narrower.

"Tell me, Gina. Where do you wish to be right now?"

"A thousand miles away."

"Only a thousand?" He kept his voice soft, tucking their privacy inside a whisper.

"More like eight-hundred miles."

"That's specific. Given your accent, your home is in Mexico. Exactly eight-hundred miles from here?"

"Where is here?"

"You tell me."

"You writing a book?"

Irritatingly gorgeous pain in the ass.

"We can talk." He reached beneath the covers and tweaked her soft, warm nipple. "Or we can fuck."

As expected, instant hostility fired in her eyes, and she slapped his hand away.

She'd endured his level of douchery from countless men since she'd been here. Three years was a long time, fighting for survival night after night in a cartel compound. The fact that she was still breathing meant she'd learned not to show the slightest weakness.

He appreciated her strength and stood behind it one hundred percent. But to finish this job, he would have to break through that stubborn armor.

A foot of silence separated them. Might as well have been eight-hundred miles.

With a quick reach of his arm, he caught her around the waist and yanked her flush against him. Chest to chest, skin on skin, he felt every inch of her nudity along every inch of his.

Her gaze held, widening only slightly as he hardened against her thigh.

"Ignore it." He pulled the sheet up to their faces and whispered against her lips. "Tell me the location of this place."

Now she stiffened, and her breathing shortened. "I don't—"

"Don't lie to me."

"I'm not. I swear, I don't know." She looked off-kilter and desperate—this woman who fearlessly stared down cartel gangsters.

She was telling the truth.

"What about Vera?" he breathed against her mouth. "Does she know?"

"Ask her yourself."

He was hard. She was hours past passing out, and they were both gloriously naked. So flipping her onto her back and pressing his erection against her cunt required no effort. She struggled, her movements clumsy, and he waited her out, letting her breathing escalate.

She didn't have to like him. By the end of the week, he'd make sure she didn't.

At last, she stopped resisting and sank into the mattress. "Maybe."

"Yes or no." He kicked his hips, threatening her entrance with the head of his cock.

"Yeah, motherfucker." She bared her teeth, a startling white contrast to her dark complexion. "She knows."

That was the confirmation he needed. If Vera gave him the coordinates, he would leave. Let them put a hood over his head and escort him out. Then he would return with an army.

UNSHACKLE

He slid off her hot body and adjusted them on their sides, settling into the same position as before. "Is anyone looking for you?"

Surprise popped into her eyes, and she jerked away as though she'd been burned.

He dragged her back. "Family?"

"I have one person. One person left in my family, and I won't let you near her."

His interest wasn't in her family. He just needed to know her stakes in this, that she had something to fight for. A life she missed. Someone she loved. If she valued this person over the cartel, maybe he could trust her. Unless the cartel was using her family member to threaten her.

Shifting her lower beneath the covers, he whispered under the veil, "Is this person safe from La Rocha?"

In the dark, her inhale shuddered, and a sheen of distress wet her eyes. "No."

Fuck. "Where is she?" He could've kept his whisper flat, but his anger got away from him.

She heard it, blinking rapidly, and seemed uncertain how to respond.

He needed to explain away his concern, but this girl was too smart. Too perceptive. And maybe, seeing someone pissed in her defense was exactly the kind of thing that would penetrate her shields.

So he remained quiet, watching, waiting to see what she would do next.

It took a year and a day before she reached for him. Tentative fingers crept over his jaw and pulled back when she felt the rigidity there. He tried to relax, loosening the tension in his face.

Inching closer, she touched him again. His neck this time, her warm hand sliding to the hairline on his nape. Her eyes didn't waver from his until she set her mouth against his cheek and breathed in and out, deeply, slowly.

She was testing him. Or testing herself. How long could she hold him like this before he flipped her over and fucked her? If he didn't do what she expected, could she trust him enough to finish the conversation?

Maybe she wasn't thinking any of this. She could be lying to him, manipulating him. Working for the cartel. His intuition disagreed, but he couldn't do this job on gut instinct and emotion. There was too much at stake.

Her fingers twitched against his nape, almost caressing as if seeking the contact. Then she leaned back just enough to search his eyes. Her lips parted to speak, but her voice hid in her throat.

"Tell me." He kept his expression unreadable and his gaze attentive.

"La Rocha…" She swallowed, her voice barely audible. "They took my mother. She's a successful actress. Well-known and well-connected."

"Who is she? Give me her name."

She clamped a hand over his mouth, eyes wide and head shaking side to side. "Don't. Not that. I'll shed every drop of blood in my body before I tell you." She glanced up around the fold of covers, her gaze on the ceiling. "They might kill me anyway."

Not on his watch.

He touched her chin, drawing her face back under the sheets. Then he guided her hand to his neck. "Is your mother connected to someone dangerous?"

"Lots of someones." Her lashes lowered, and her fingers fell away. "I think I can sleep now."

He missed the warmth of her touch instantly. When she rolled and gave him her back, he missed the feel of her body against his. But he allowed her some space to get comfortable.

Shutting off the TV, he blanketed them in a dark hush and waited.

Soon her breathing slowed into the even rhythm of slumber.

Slowly, careful not to wake her, he curled around her tiny frame, with her back to his front and his arm locked around her like an anchor.

Her chest rose and fell with a shuddering inhale before returning to a soporific tempo. She felt so fragile in his embrace, so sweet and sexy. He couldn't stop himself from kissing the bare top of a graceful shoulder.

Breathing in the scent of her skin, he ordered his mind to shut off. But he couldn't sleep.

Minutes blurred into hours, and he lay entwined with a stolen girl while thinking about another one.

Blonde hair. Glassy eyes. Strangling beneath his hand. Squirming. Dying. Unable to gasp. Everything inside him wrangled and twisted anew.

From this night forward, a nameless dead girl would be the only thought he took with him into the hinterland of sleep. She would forever haunt his dreams, breed his nightmares, and admonish him of the decision he'd made.

He would never forget.

TWELVE

She'd been watching him sleep for an hour. Long enough for the first light of dawn to form a glaring halo behind the curtains. His arm lay heavily around her, holding her against his hard chest. It felt horrible.

Horribly safe.

No, not safe. His strange behavior and little mercies were an illusion. A trap. This man had an agenda, one that didn't include protecting her. Certainly not from himself.

With her face inches from his, she must've turned toward him during the night. *Toward* him. Why would she do that? Even unconscious, she knew better.

Why the fuck was she still in bed with him?

At any point, she could've lifted his arm and crept away. For a vigilant, calculating predator, he slept like the dead.

His hair, thick and tousled, glimmered differently in the morning. Metallic lowlights of ruby and brown threaded with strands of copper, creating a tapestry of red hues.

Not a single tattoo on his smooth fair skin, a body hardened to steel, and cold sharp eyes of emerald intelligence, which hadn't cracked open yet.

Blondish-red fuzz roughened his chest and forearms, just a little. Just enough to remind her of his masculinity.

She didn't need the reminder.

Last night was seared forever in her memory. The suction of his mouth between her legs. The deep rumble of his American accent in her ear. The taste of his whiskey breath that still lingered on her lips.

I need to get out of here.

Holding in her next inhale, she made her escape. Out from beneath his arm, down to the floor, she crouched low, waiting.

He didn't stir.

Her muscles protested every movement, stiff and sore, but remarkably better than last night. She scrunched her face, testing other injuries. No swelling that she could tell. No hunger pangs, either. That was a novelty.

His luggage lay open behind her. From the large case, she carefully removed a button-up shirt. No reason to snoop through his belongings. The cartel would've already searched it and removed anything useful.

Backing away on tiptoes, she closed the buttons on the shirt and slipped into the main room. The door to the other bedroom stood open, giving her a view of Tomas' bed.

The sheets lay crumpled on the empty mattress. No sounds came from the bathroom. The bodyguard wasn't here. *Perfect.*

She hurried on silent feet toward the exit. By the time she gripped the door handle, her heart had clawed its way to her throat.

I'm not running.

That would be against his rules. She just needed... What? Clothes. Coffee. A morning walk. *Space.*

With her defense prepared, she swung open the door and gasped.

Brown hair, crooked nose, steroid-induced torso, and eyes as black as night. Hateful eyes, burning with manic rage.

"Alejandro." She sucked down her panic and faced him with her chin raised. "What are you doing here?"

He'd been gone for several weeks, which meant he'd just delivered a new batch of trafficked girls. And not only to this property. The youngest La Rocha brother sold slaves all over California and elsewhere.

"Imagine my disappointment," he said in scathing Spanish, "when I arrived this morning to discover that *my* whore was whoring for someone else."

"Marco allowed—"

"I don't give a fuck!" His hand shot toward her neck.

She ducked, slammed against the door in her attempt to escape, and tried to flee into the breezeway. He reached for her again, and she threw herself forward, knowing there was no way she'd make it past him.

Except he didn't stop her.

Glancing back was a mistake. She should've kept running. Eyes forward. Always straight ahead. But stupidity swung her gaze around and slowed her steps.

A broad muscled back swallowed her view. Freckles she hadn't noticed before on the bulging ridges of shoulders. Corded neck, red hair, and a fist that reached back and captured her wrist in an unbending grip.

UNSHACKLE

"You must be John Smith." A sneer edged Alejandro's broken English.

"And you must be Miguel." John's head dipped down and back up, taking in the man's massive size. "Or are you the youngest brother?"

"I'm Alejandro, *vato*, and she belongs to *me*."

"I see. Well, then…" John ruthlessly dragged her forward, making her trip. "Take her. Since you're not interested in my business, I'll leave this morning. You can speak to my assistant about refunding my down payment, as well as the obscene amount of money he wired last night for the time I *won't* be spending with my purchase."

He pushed her toward Alejandro, washing his hands of her. She didn't know whether to sigh in relief or punch his balls into his throat.

"You paid for her?" Alejandro jerked his head back. "For a used-up whore?"

"I paid six digits for a week with her."

Her stomach sank. She knew the buyers dropped serious cash on the virgin girls fresh off the truck. But six digits in exchange for *her*? It was preposterous. Why would he do that? He didn't even fuck her last night.

Alejandro glanced at the workout shorts that John had shoved on. Then his gaze traveled over the stolen shirt she wore. He was a possessive son of a bitch, and it showed in the hard brackets around his scowl. His nostrils widened, and he gripped his nape. Then a decision settled on his face.

The cartel valued money far and above their women. Her fate was sealed.

"I misunderstood." He shoved his hands in his pockets and backed away. "We honor our deals, *ese*." His Adam's apple bounced, the flat line of his lips barely concealing his displeasure. "Stay. She's yours for the week."

"You hear that, darling?" John grabbed her by the hair and yanked her back against him. "Unless, of course, you'd rather go with Alejandro? Your choice."

What the ever-loving fuck? After all that posturing with Marco last night, he was changing his tune? Talk about whiplash.

Maybe it was a test, but she wouldn't fall for it. Whomever she chose, the other man would find a way to make her pay for his embarrassment.

"What's behind door three?" She jerked at the hair in his fist, unable to free herself.

"I'll show you." John hauled her back into the room. Then he faced the doorway, blocking her view. "Will there be anything else?"

"There's a private dinner in my quarters tonight." Alejandro cleared his voice, his English thick with resentment. "I expect you to be there. Bring the whore."

Fuck no! She didn't want anything to do with that.

With a nod, John shut the door in the cartel *jefe's* face. Then he slowly turned toward her and lobbed a glare so frightening it sent prickles from her nape to her toes.

"You're feeling better." His voice was cold. Terribly so.

She shook her head and retreated around the couch.

"You're recovered enough to run." He prowled after her, eyes locked.

"I wasn't running, *idiota*. I needed clothes and coffee and—"

"Shut the fuck up." His words didn't match the oh-so calm delivery, which made him even more fearsome. He paused at the side table and removed something from the drawer, concealing it in the palm of his huge hand. "Your disobedience will not go unpunished."

"*El burro sabe más que tú*. Do you hear yourself?" She shook violently, and that just made her madder. And *louder*. "I bet you were the school bully. The guy who shoved around the smaller kids because your dad took his fists to you? You were hiding your own bruises, weren't you? And the only control you had in your life was beating the shit out of those who weighed less than you."

She was angry and scared and talking out of her ass, but the instant his face paled, she knew she'd touched a tender nerve.

"I warned you." He followed her through the sitting area, his gait too casual for the fists flexing at his sides. "Every foolish action will result in another girl taking your punishment."

"No! This is between you and me, goddammit!"

He paused, tipped his head. "Then you better run."

Her pulse exploded as she spun and bolted toward the door. His footsteps pounded after her, flooding her system with adrenaline. She passed a chair and yanked it behind her. Same with a small table. A glass lamp crashed to the floor, followed by a masculine curse.

She made it halfway to the door when it opened. Tomas stepped in, holding a tray of food and a bag of clothes.

Fucking hell. She swerved, aiming for the bedrooms, but John was too close, breathing down her neck. He swiped at her, his fingers snagging the back of the shirt. She whirled, stomped a heel on his foot, and drove a fist into his gut.

He grunted, and she dropped to the floor, scrambling around his legs to evade the long reach of his arms. All those muscles made him strong, but they also slowed him down.

UNSHACKLE

She could've outrun him if she had somewhere to go. Tomas blocked the exit, and there was no other way out. Not that leaving this room was an option beneath the gravity of John's threat. He'd told her to run because he clearly enjoyed the chase. She was playing right into his games, but what else could she do? Just stand there and let him punish her? Not a chance.

So she sprinted around furniture and tossed vases and decorative knickknacks at him, recklessly trashing the place. He caught her several times, but she hit, kicked, and bit her way out of his clutches.

Part of her suspected he was giving her those little victories. The other part just didn't care. She wasn't going down without a fight.

And *down* was exactly how it went as he tackled her to the floor. The full force of his weight crashed onto her back and knocked the air from her lungs. They landed in a sweaty pile — his bare chest, her kicking legs, their arms slick and wrestling.

She panted uncontrollably and attacked with elbows to his ribs. He chased her hands, trying to restrain them. She threw back her head, aiming to break his face. He dodged, grabbed her throat, and sank his teeth into her neck.

Her screams rang out loud enough to reach far beyond the walls, but no one would come to her aid. She was on her own, crushed beneath two-hundred-pounds of roguish male hunger. Her pleas and objections weren't just ignored. They were *laughed* at.

Yeah, he was laughing and groaning through labored breaths. And fully aroused. His erection jabbed her naked backside, with the shirt tangled around her waist.

"You're a sinful goddamn turn on, Gina. Can't remember the last time I needed to be inside a woman this badly." He lifted a hand to his mouth and tore open a square packet with his teeth.

A condom. That was what he'd removed from the drawer.

"No, no, no! Fuck you, cocksucker! Fuck you!" She bucked beneath him, breaths wheezing and heart rate in overdrive. "Wait! Just wait. Okay, I'm sorry. I won't run again. Don't do this!"

"Too late for repentance, baby." Lust thickened his voice as he raised his hips and rolled on the rubber. "Time for that punishment."

She didn't stop thrashing, didn't for a second make it easy for him. But he was bigger, stronger, built with the right equipment and the cruel agility to take a woman from behind.

In one thrust, he stabbed past her opening, driving hard and spearing her to the very hilt of himself.

Tears hit her eyes as a strangled groan sounded in his throat. He rocked against her, picking up speed, digging deeper, violating, ravaging, and grunting in her ear. She wanted to die.

He fucked into her over and over like an animal, opening her legs wider with the spread of his powerful thighs. His hands were on her everywhere, grappling, stroking, and mauling while at the same time holding her immobile.

The condom must've been lubricated, because the initial burn dissolved into slippery wet strokes. He was thrusting savagely, jerking out, slamming in, and building a rhythm that made her writhe in agony.

It didn't hurt, and she hated him for that. She hated that he fit inside her just right and that he moved his body so sensually and obsessively, suggesting he was fully engaged in this, physically and emotionally.

This wasn't like the three-minute ruts she endured from the brothers. He fucked her with passion and filled her with fire, penetrating her body with his entire being, forcing her to feel him beneath her skin, taking over every cell, and delving deep into her core.

She gasped and clawed at the floor, frantic to escape the overbearing onslaught of his fervor. Gaining a few inches, she saw Tomas watching from the door before she was dragged back beneath John and utterly devoured.

That was the only way to describe it. His lips locked onto her nape, tasting and consuming, his tongue laving at her damp hairline, only deepening the fevered kisses on her neck, then her temple, her cheek, the corner of her mouth.

Her senses swam, her breathing unmanageable. She tried to struggle, but he only buried himself deeper, stretching her, stuffing her, nailing her to the floor, and rendering her even more helpless.

"Goddamn, you feel unreal." He surged harder, his fingers wedged beneath her chest, tormenting her breasts. "Fucking incredible."

He attacked the shirt, the material ripping and pulling in a flurry of urgent movements, buttons breaking, and her arms forced from sleeves. Her whole body jostled with the frantic piston of his hips and the tugs on the fabric, causing her bare nipples to scrape against the coarse rug beneath her.

She tried to push up, to crawl away, but her arms gave out from under her.

"All that straining and fighting makes your pussy clench." He lurched back with a sudden outward pull, only to ram back in, stretching her wider around the slick steel of his cock. "Christ, you're tight. Hot. Wet. I want to feel you bareback."

"I hope your dick rots off."

"Give me that fucking mouth." His arm banded around her chest, holding her tight as he gripped her chin and fused their lips.

UNSHACKLE

She used her teeth, her hands, the last of her strength, but she couldn't stop his tongue from melding with hers. His mouth ground with maddening pressure, his fist balled in her hair, and he took. Lord have mercy, he took, deep and long and ravenously, while shoving his cock, plunging mercilessly, and groaning with poisonous pleasure.

He was heat and virility, fury and stamina, plundering and claiming with a skill that destroyed everything she knew about sex. No one had ever fucked her so vehemently. Every touch, kiss, and thrust was an effusive blaze, flowing out, over, and through her.

Answering heat simmered her blood. Her insides burned and tightened. Nerve endings sizzled, and her soul shook. *She* was shook. Mentally unhinged. Damned to eternal hell.

She wanted him to punish her. She needed him to beat her, hurt her, smack her back into reality. Anything but this. What he was doing to her, making her crave it… It was sick.

She was sick.

Faster and faster he moved inside her, sparking pleasure she didn't want. Their gasps mingled and mixed into one. A moan escaped her mouth, and he faltered above her, recovered, and began to rock almost reverently into her, the cadence strangely slowed, languorously thickened, and weighted with the dragging pull of his lips against hers.

His hands strayed her hips, gripping tightly as he caught a telltale rhythm. His invasion seemed to swell, growing impossibly thicker and harder in that last painful moment, his legs trembling, and chest heaving as he chased his release.

"Oh, fuck. Oh, fuck…" He came, driving deep and pounding into her with a growling roar.

As he ground into a slow halt, jerking and catching his breath, a wet sheen blurred her eyes. She felt dirty. Twisted. Used.

He twitched, and her inner muscles spasmed around him in response.

Shame. That was chief of her emotions and the worst feeling of all.

Without a word, he pushed off her, flung the condom at the trashcan, and yanked up the shorts he still wore.

"See that she gets dressed and hydrates," he said to Tomas. "We leave in five minutes to work out."

He ambled toward the bedroom, leaving her with a hollow, pulsing ache for something she couldn't possibly want. Her lips were raw. Her breasts tingled with heaviness. Her pussy throbbed with soreness, and her chest cleaved for want of air.

She'd been violated more times than she could count since arriving at the compound. But not once had she ever felt so hot and needy and fucked-up afterward. What the hell had he done to her?

Anger spiked, coursing through her veins. She jumped to her feet, eying the demon who strolled away without a single glance back at the woman he'd just raped.

She didn't think. She just ran. Past Tomas, toward the bedroom, she headed off the monster before he turned the corner. With a hard kick to the back of his knee, she caught him by surprise. He lost his balance, gripped the door jamb, and when he spun, she was ready.

Her fist collided with his granite jawline, sending a jolt of pain up her arm. She swung again, faking the hit, while driving a knee into his groin.

He doubled over and wrapped his arms around her like iron bands, slamming her against the wall as he stumbled. Those were the only strikes she got before he subdued her with a hand on her throat and his body planked along the front of hers.

"Do you want a postcoital cuddle? Is that it?" He wet his lips, his fingers tightening against her tender airway.

"I don't want a coital anything from you."

"You sure about that?" With his free hand, he reached between her legs and fingered her wetness. "Ah. You want a release."

She gulped, dragging in precious drops of air and furiously shaking her head. But the tears that sprung were telling.

This need... The awful, involuntary longing he'd woken beneath her skin had teeth. She didn't know how to fight this new enemy inside her. She didn't even understand it. But she needed to. She couldn't straighten out her head until she figured out the mystery between them.

He watched her closely, his face an inch away. The hand on her throat loosened, melting into fingers that stroked and beguiled.

"Say what you're thinking," he murmured.

"You..." *Kiss differently. Fuck differently.* "You hurt me differently. Not like the others."

Nothing changed in his hard expression. No surprise. No annoyance.

"You want to know why." He did something with his finger between her legs, making her entire body bow off the wall and press into his. "Why does my touch bring more pleasure than pain? Why do I kiss with the patience of a man who worships women, not owns them?" He leaned in and slid his nose along hers, his whisper kissing her lips. "The truth is so disturbing you wouldn't believe me if I told you. Let it go."

He released her and stepped back.

Rubbing her throat, she glared at him, more confused and uncomfortable than ever before.

UNSHACKLE

"You want to come, Gina, even as your brain abhors the idea. That's your punishment, one that will plague your pretty little mind and pussy all day. Get dressed."

With that, he stalked into the bedroom, dismissing her.

THIRTEEN

By *work out*, he actually did mean jogging.

The man had some irritating stamina, but she was no slouch, either. Dressed in the tank-top, spandex shorts, and running shoes that Tomas had found for her — *God only knew whose closet he'd raided* — she pounded her feet along the trail.

Sweat dampened her brow. Sunshine warmed her skin, and the light breakfast she'd eaten sat contently in her stomach.

She was glad to be outside, breathing in the open air. The exercise kept her focused on rebuilding her strength rather than falling apart. She even appreciated the view of the two shirtless psychopaths jogging along either side of her. It was better than being confined in a room with them.

Before yesterday, she'd considered herself fairly perceptive when it came to men. She anticipated their intentions, skill sets, and limitations with a high degree of accuracy.

But not this one.

John confounded her at every turn. Even now, as he veered off the cobblestone trail and sprinted across the lawn, she couldn't guess what he was doing.

The grass was cut short, but a few minutes into the detour, the ground became uneven, the terrain unused and unkempt. When her pace slowed, he shot an aggressive look over his shoulder.

If only he would trip and impale himself on something sharp.

"There are dozens of running trails." She panted, pumping her legs twice as hard to keep up with his long gait. "Do you know where you're going?"

A grunt was all he gave her.

UNSHACKLE

Nasty redheaded gorilla.

As he and Tomas led her farther away from the outdoor luxuries of the estate, she remained a few clips behind them, growing suspicious.

She knew every corner of this property, every building, pathway, camera, and blade of grass. A two-mile, unclimbable stone wall enclosed the compound, every inch of it monitored either by technology or armed guards.

Except one section. One shaded, overlooked nook. And there, behind a maze of cobwebs and dead trees was a way out.

Yesterday, she was caught far away from that area, thank God. She'd attacked a guard near a different section of the wall in an attempt to knock him out and take his clothes, weapons, and earpiece before making her escape. Unfortunately, she hadn't counted on the second guard who had sneaked up behind her.

Up ahead, Tomas angled closer to John and said something too low for her ears. Then he gave a subtle nod to the left, spoke again, and jogged off.

The camera. There was only one in this area, hidden in a tree, and he'd just pointed it out.

So this was a scouting expedition disguised as a run?

John made his way to a small grove beyond the range of that camera. The property spanned multiple acres, and he plopped down in one of the few places that wasn't monitored by the cartel.

Her heart hammered against her ribs. Was he a spy? Some kind of operative in the military? Whatever it was, she didn't want any part of it.

"Come here." He met her gaze from across the field, his tone brooking no argument.

Tomas was nowhere in sight. Not that he would come to her defense, but she didn't want to be alone with this man.

He didn't repeat himself and didn't need to. His look spoke louder than words.

Seconds ticked by. The stare-off extended past stubborn and dipped into dangerous territory. If she didn't obey him, he would physically force her, and she would lose. Again.

Shoving her feet forward, she trudged toward him and paused a few paces away. "What?"

"Sit with me."

"No."

He lunged, and though she was ready for it, he pounced lower than she expected. She didn't see his leg shoot out until it collided with her ankles, knocking her on her ass. With a yelp, she scrabbled away only to be overpowered once again by his sheer size and strength.

Lying on her back in the overgrown grass, she gazed up at him and didn't move. Wriggling beneath his weight would only turn him on, and she still felt the tenderness of the last violation.

Maybe he would hurt her anyway, but his demeanor didn't suggest cruel intentions. He held the back of her head in a firm palm and drank in her features, the brilliant green of his eyes making an unhurried exploration.

Leaning closer, he slid a thumb along her jaw, nudged it down, and forced her lips open. She gulped, and he pressed closer, breathing in her gasp. The way he stared so deeply into her eyes, he looked like he wanted to kiss her, like he wanted to peel her open and climb inside.

"Do you know why I chose you?" The question rumbled from deep in his chest.

"I was the only woman still alive in the room?"

"Alive." He licked his lips, tasting the word. "Exactly. You're so alive you glow with fire. Not only when you fight, but when you watch and listen."

"I'm a side-effect of men's cruelty." She didn't appreciate him analyzing her as if he knew her. "What do you want?"

"Only to talk."

"Talk?" She narrowed her eyes. "Like we did in your room this morning?"

"Since there are no cameras here, we can interact like normal people." He rolled off her and pulled her to her side to face him. "Tell me something. Anything."

"What do you mean?" She was still stuck on the camera comment. "Did you fucking *rape* me because you knew they were watching?"

With a sigh, he stretched out on his back and bent an arm behind his head. "Tell me something about yourself. Or about the world. Pick a topic."

"What's your interest in the cameras?"

"Another topic."

"Fine. When you're not raping women, what do you do for a living?"

"I invest in something important. Next topic."

"Is your job legal? Do you work for the government?"

"No to both of those questions, and that's the last answer you'll get from me on that."

"How many innocent lives have you taken?"

He remained silent.

Disappointment pinched in her chest.

UNSHACKLE

So he was a criminal, which revealed nothing. Every man who walked through here lived on the wrong side of the law. He could be an assassin or an enemy spy. Or maybe he was just another well-funded, paranoid asshole, looking for a new sex slave.

"I'm giving you the chance to speak freely about anything you want." He gazed up at the tree canopy, his handsome face speckled in drops of sunlight. "If you don't pick a topic, I will, and it'll involve you telling me who you are and how you came here. You'll fight me, and we both know how that will end."

He looked at her, and she turned away, feeling extra stabby. She wanted to claw his eyes out.

"You have every right to despise me," he said. "When it comes to taking what I want from you, I'm no different than Hector's sons. But have they ever taken the time to have a conversation with you? Do they know you at all?"

No. Not even a little. They came, and they went. Wham-bam-fuck-you-ma'am. Omar kept her around as long as she won fights. Alejandro was possessive, but he was like that with all his women. The other two didn't even look at her after they fucked her.

That went both ways. She wanted nothing to do with them. But she did miss the simple act of sharing a conversation with someone. She had no one to talk to here. No one who gave a shit what she thought.

She shifted to her back, mirroring his position beside her. Despite the shade from the trees, the air felt unusually hot for autumn, clinging to her skin and making her sweat. Damn global warming.

"Greenland has melted beyond saving." She threw the random thought into the humid breeze.

"Ah." He caught it with a smile in his voice. "The tipping point debate."

"If you look at the science, there's no debate. The ice sheet has lost so much mass over the last two decades that even if global warming ended yesterday, the arctic island won't recover."

He turned slowly, stretching and shaping his body around hers without touching. "What are we going to do about it?"

"We, the human race? Nothing. There isn't enough intelligence or concern on this planet to fix it. Future generations will have to use advancements in technology to adapt to the changing environment."

"How?"

"They'll modify their DNA. It's the only way they'll be able to inhabit a world our species isn't designed for."

"Designed? You believe in a higher power? Intelligent design?"

Oh, she had plenty of opinions on that. Her mouth ran away from her, and for the next few minutes, she stood on a soapbox and outlined everything she speculated on the subject. By the time she realized she was rambling, she couldn't take it back. She'd engaged him in a conversation, doing precisely what he wanted.

The thing was... He *listened*. Actually kept his arguments to himself so that he could hear hers. Was this some kind of ploy to engineer personal information from her?

Except she hadn't revealed anything confidential. He seemed genuinely interested in what she had to say.

Was she being naive?

Lifting on an elbow, he regarded her intently. "You've given this a lot of thought."

Without access to a phone, Internet, or friends, all she had was time to sit around and think about shit.

She met his eyes, breaths defensively taut. "You want to argue my points? Bring it on."

"Nope. I'm not an expert on climate change or God."

"Then where is your expertise? What do you know?"

"I can offer some factoids on testosterone." He bent his head toward hers, making her heart skip. "I've read a lot on the subject."

She didn't like where this was headed. Anything related to men and their bodies was dangerous territory. But she sucked it up and gave him her ear.

"A man's testosterone peaks at puberty." He brushed a wayward lock of hair from her face. "It declines immediately after then plateaus as he ages. Unless he gains weight. Fat pushes testosterone levels into a downward spiral. But you know what doesn't?"

"No." She didn't want to know. Not with that heated look in his eyes.

"Sex. Studies have shown that a man's testosterone increases the morning after intimacy. More so in unmated males, those who are actively *hunting*. Their testosterone boosts exponentially—we're talking upwards of three-hundred-percent—the morning after sexual activity. Interestingly, masturbation doesn't yield the same results, which suggests there's a socio element to hormone production."

Fascinating. Also, disturbing. Especially with him angled so close to her.

He engaged in sex last night. Not intercourse, but oral sex. Did it count if he didn't come? Was his testosterone in the red zone when he woke?

"Is that why you raped me this morning?"

UNSHACKLE

"Despite what you think, I'm in full control of my baser needs. Case in point..." He dipped his head, hovering his face an inch from her heaving chest. "I want to cover these raised nipples with my tongue and tease them into hard peaks through the shirt. When the fabric becomes too damp and itchy, I want to strip it away and feel you against my lips—your soft skin, the pounding of your heart, the vibration of your moans. What would you do...?" He paused. Breathed in. On an exhale, his voice shifted from seductive to pensive. "For a...?

Uncertain, she flattened her back against the ground and curled her fingers in the grass. "For what?"

"For a Klondike bar?"

She stared up at him and blinked. "Sorry?"

"It's a square of ice cream with chocolate—"

"I know what it is." She gritted her teeth. "Are you making fun of me?"

"Depends on your answer."

"God, you're so..." *Unpredictable. Gorgeous. Perplexing.* She sniffed, trying to hold onto her annoyance. "Strange."

"What would you do for one? Would you lick that tree?" He nodded at the barky, moss-covered trunk a few feet away.

"I don't know. Maybe?" She couldn't remember the last time she tasted ice cream.

"Would you finish our jog without clothes on?"

"No." *Not willingly.*

"Would you sing?"

"That would be awful for everyone." She made a face. "But I can rap."

"Right now."

"What?" She sat up, forcing him to lean back.

"Rap me a song, and I'll get you a Klondike. Hell, I'll get you a whole box."

"Three."

"Three boxes?"

"The variety packs. All different flavors."

He rolled his lips to hide a smile. "You drive a hard bargain."

"Do we have a deal?"

"Absolutely."

This rich boy wouldn't know a good rap song if it smacked him in his white ass. So she opted for something satirical with a little cheese and a lot of groove.

Closing her eyes, she loosened her shoulders, rocked her head, and hummed the opening rhythm of "Welcome to Chili's" by *Yung Gravy*.

Only the intro was in Spanish, which she sang embarrassingly off-tune. But when she jumped into the rap, she was fire, popping the *P's*, rolling the *R's*, and hitting every word with a kick in her hips.

After a few lines, she leaped to her feet, catching the beat with her whole body. He rose in her periphery, and she turned away, focusing on the lyrics.

Until his masculine heat covered her back. Bold hands glided over her shoulders, down her arms, moving with her. *He* moved with her.

She shivered and rapped out the next verse. By the time she reached the chorus, his voice was in her ear, saying the words with her, nailing the beat perfectly.

Holy shit, he knew this song? Why was she surprised? It was popular in America. But still...

She turned, facing him without losing the tempo. But she was no longer dancing, her body restrained in the intensity of his stare. He faltered over some of the words but knew the rest. They didn't bounce or sway, didn't blink or break eye contact for a single second.

The moment held them in a peculiar other world where a woman and her rapist rapped in a trance.

When had he drifted closer? Was she leaning into him? No, they weren't touching. But she felt him all over, against her skin, in her song, humming through her blood.

When had they stopped singing?

The canopy rustled above them. She couldn't think.

A locust buzzed in the grass. She couldn't look away.

His fingers floated through her hair. She couldn't breathe.

He touched her face, the bruised skin around her eyes, her cheek, her lips.

Push him away.

Her hands landed on his bare chest. Solid bedrock encased in hot skin. Beautifully built. Flawless definition. Carved and sanded with divine precision.

His palm cupped her jaw. So gentle. So goddamn nice.

Get rid of him.

Her head tipped, slanting into the touch as if compelled by a magnet.

Jesus, his eyes were right there, shining vividly. His mouth slightly parted and waiting.

This was too heavy. Too *cozy*. This... Feeling? It was gravity. Chemistry. Deranged attraction. Why couldn't she fight it?

"Baby," he murmured against her mouth. "There's something I need to tell you."

Dazed, she couldn't feel her tongue. "Mm?"

UNSHACKLE

"There's a snake behind you."

"No, he's…" Her chest filled with air. "He's in front of me."

"I'm serious."

"What kind of snake?"

"Black and white with red rings. Three feet long."

"Oh. That's a king—" Her feet left the ground as he swung her up and away. "Wait!"

He spun toward the creature, crouching to attack it as she yelled, "It's a kingsnake! Nonvenomous! Don't kill it!"

"What?" He lunged, catching the squirming body. "I want to help it. Look."

She darted toward him, craning her neck, and gasped.

The poor thing was tangled in a piece of plastic netting, with the webbing cinching it so tightly it couldn't move properly.

"Here." He trapped it against the ground, controlling the whip of its head. "Hold the tail."

She didn't hesitate, and within seconds he managed to break the plastic enough for the snake to work itself free.

He pocketed the trash and watched the animal slither away while she watched him, baffled and conflicted.

"Why did you do that?" Her mind churned to reconcile everything she knew about men with the one standing before her. "What are you trying to prove? That you're not cruel? That you're different from the others?"

His gaze cut to her, his eyes blazing with so much anger it snipped her breath. "There are plenty of snakes that deserve to die. Dozens that are eating, fucking, and indulging in evil right inside those walls." He stabbed a finger in the direction of the estate. "Despite what you saw last night in the basement, I'm not in the business of taking innocent lives."

"But you're still a snake." She shook her head, fighting the impulse to step back. "You're a bad guy."

"I hear the question in your voice." He prowled forward, edging into her space.

"No question." She thrust up her chin. "I was there this morning, remember? Pinned beneath your brutality with my face shoved into the floor."

"Yes, but you're also realizing there's more to me than that moment."

"Like the fact that you're working against the cartel? That you're hiding some traitorous shit that I want nothing to do with? Will you kill me if I discover your secrets? The cartel certainly will if they think I'm involved."

A muscle feathered across his shirtless chest, his expression twitching with contemplation. "I'll tell you my secrets."

Her mouth parted.

"*If,*" he said, "you tell me yours."

"Get real."

"Start with your education. You were born and raised in Mexico, but your English is perfect."

If she made up a story about that, he would read her like a lie detector. So all she gave him was a blank stare.

He met it with one of his own, and here they were again, locked in a silent battle of wills.

Could this guy be any more frustrating? Or intimidating? Or good-looking? Let's face it. She'd never been more captivated by a human being, let alone a human with a dick.

And mesmerizing green eyes.

And sculpted lips.

The tension between them passed, and those lips became an open-mouthed sigh. "We're done here."

Turning on his heel, he jogged back toward the estate. He paced his speed to keep her at his side, but instead of heading back to his quarters, he led her to the gym.

She welcomed that idea, hoping to avoid his bed as long as possible.

Strolling into the weight room, he snapped his fingers at the two guests on the weight machines. "Get out."

"Excuse me?" The younger of the two puffed out his chest.

"I didn't stutter."

John had more muscle and strength than both of those men combined. But it was his warlike posture and menacing scowl that sent them hurrying out of the room.

"You're not making any friends." She rubbed her neck, looking around at the commercial machines and free weights. This was the longest she'd ever been in this building.

"I'm not here to make friends." He glanced at the camera in the ceiling and ambled toward a rack of kettlebells. "Follow me."

"You know, not everything has to be an authoritarian command. You could ask out of common decency."

He extended a finger toward the floor beside him and waited.

"Right." She grumbled a few choice words under her breath and dragged her feet to where he wanted her. "Now what?"

"You know how to hit, but you'll land harder punches if you strengthen the muscles here."

He jabbed his thumbs into her shoulders. Then he proceeded to show her how to build those muscles.

She questioned his motivation just as she questioned everything about him. But she needed to be patient. She'd only just met him last night. Less than twenty-four hours ago.

It's going to be a long week.

Once she got the hang of the repetitions, he left her to it and moved toward the heavier iron on the other side of the room.

For the next hour, they worked out in silence. She transitioned to the machines while he tossed around some deadly weight. His physique glistened with sweat, swelling and flexing obscenely.

The barbell loved him, and he seemed to love the punishment it put on his upper body. His chest, shoulders, and triceps contracted with every heave and pull. His lips curled back from his teeth, his grunts and pained breaths making it impossible to ignore his presence.

He was an erotic destination, a trip she had no business taking with her eyes. But the impulse couldn't be denied. She looked long and often, and he caught her every time, because he was looking, too.

Plenty of men had stared at her, here and *before*. But not the way he did. Not at his level of predatory intensity.

He reminded her of a big, sleek cat, with an air of smugness and danger that came from being well-fed yet always hunting. And why wouldn't he look at her like she was his next meal? He'd bought himself a week with her to do whatever he pleased outside the reach of the law. He didn't need to ask her permission, for anything, and he wouldn't.

But you're also realizing there's more to me than that moment.

Maybe.

Maybe that was what scared her the most.

FOURTEEN

Standing at the vanity in his bathroom, Luke scraped a razor across his jaw and watched his little warrior in the mirror. The view was no less than stunning, and his blood simmered with appreciation.

Beneath the spray of the shower, she rinsed the soap from her hair, smoothing the long coils into a black velvet curtain. Water sluiced down her tawny body, running sensual rivulets around toned curves and muscle.

Her gaze found his in the mirror, and swear to God, that look had a punch, hitting hard enough to make his balls shrivel. Her dark eyes blazed with righteous censure and judgment. But there was desire as well, no matter how hard she fought to hold it at bay.

More than anything, he wanted to see that desire win out.

It was dangerous to hope for such a thing. He only had one week with her, and during that time, his focus needed to be on Vera Gomez.

Dinner with Alejandro was approaching, and he counted on Vera being there. The sexual chemistry between Gina and him was so potent it wouldn't go unnoticed. Not by Vera nor Alejandro nor anyone else present tonight.

He would flaunt it, not hide it. Let them obsess over his relationship with the fighter. Better that than on the real reason he was here.

Even Tomas detected the energy ricocheting between him and the woman in the shower. His friend leaned against the wall beside the vanity, wearing a scowl full of opinions.

"Shut your fucking mouth." Luke tossed the razor aside and rinsed his face.

UNSHACKLE

"I didn't say anything, you twat."

Gina turned off the faucet, snagged a towel, and strode toward the doorway as if she couldn't get away fast enough.

"Your dress is on the bed," Luke called after her. "Don't do anything stupid."

With a middle-finger salute, she disappeared around the corner.

Tomas stared after her with smoldering interest in his unmasked expression. A jolt of aggression shot up Luke's spine, and he slammed a hand down on the vanity.

"That woman is fucking beautiful." Tomas blinked and finally dragged his eyes away from the doorway.

"That's the last time you'll notice."

Tomas huffed a disbelieving laugh. "Have you lost your goddamn mind?"

A sharp inhale stretched Luke's nostrils, and he pushed away from the sink.

"Oh, shit." Trailing after him, Tomas whispered harshly, "She's getting to you."

"Don't be a moron. I've known her less than a day."

"It only takes a look, man. You're fucked."

Luke whirled and shoved a finger in that smug mug. "Back the fuck off."

"Save it." Tomas leaned in, putting their faces an inch apart. "I'm the last person you want to fight."

That much was true. Tomas would mop the floor with his ass.

"I've got your back." His friend stood taller, using his height to drive home his point. "Even when it means protecting you from your own mistakes."

"What mistakes are those, Tommy?" He lowered his growl to barely a whisper. "Raping an innocent girl?"

"Next time, it may not be rape. Then what? How will she react when you have to fuck another girl who doesn't like you?"

"That's insulting on so many levels."

"Get the sand out of your vagina." With a scoff, Tomas raked a hand through the flop of his brown hair. "Focus on your target."

"I am."

"Good."

"Fine."

They glared at each other for a hot minute before Luke blew out a breath.

"I'm not doubting you." Tomas clapped him on the shoulder. "To be honest, you're managing this so well I feel useless here."

"You've done plenty."

In twenty-four hours, Tomas had gathered more intel on La Rocha than in all the years their team had been tracking the cartel. He knew the location of the monitoring room, every camera on the property, as well as the names and positions of every man who came and went through the gates.

"Did you find the girl who was in the limo with us yesterday?" Luke asked quietly at his ear.

She hadn't been wearing a hood during the drive. If they found her, Luke might be able to coax crucial information from her.

"Yes." Tomas' face turned white.

"What? What is it?"

"The girl in the basement… The one on the hook—"

"No." His stomach turned, and his chest burned with bile. "That wasn't her. It couldn't be."

"I'm one-hundred-percent certain. But we couldn't have known. Her face was…"

Beaten to a pulp. Unrecognizable. But he should've looked closer. Should've questioned.

"Fuck!" He spun away and slammed his foot into a trashcan, sending it screeching across the floor.

"Pull your shit together." Tomas grabbed Luke's neck and yanked him close, bringing their foreheads together. "Move on. Right now. With me?"

"Yeah." He drew in a breath and released it. Then another. "I'm with you."

Footsteps approached, and Gina poked her head in. "Lover's quarrel?"

Luke shook off the sick feeling in his gut and turned to face her. "Let me see you."

Her fingers tightened on the door jamb, her body out of view. But he glimpsed the edge of a sexy strap on her shoulder.

Stubbornness hardened her expression, her eyes shifting with indecision. Then she set her jaw, straightened, and stepped into the doorway.

The air rushed from his lungs, parting his lips and caving in his chest.

Tomas gave him a squeeze on the shoulder and left the room. Terrible idea. Luke couldn't be trusted with this intoxicating creature.

She stood before him, dripping temptation and sin in a gown of black silk. Fresh face, damp curls, and spiked heels that seemed to extend the length of her bronzy, athletic legs.

He tried to gather his breath, his voice, but all he could do was stare.

UNSHACKLE

Christ almighty, she was an exquisite, heart-stopping, goddamn knockout. The dress hugged her tiny tits, nipped in at the waist, and flared around her toned thighs. Understated yet elegant. Striking. Just like her.

"This is rather tame for dinner with the cartel." She fingered the hem of the skirt, eyebrows drawn in confusion. "I assumed you'd put me in pleather and chains or something equally distasteful."

"I told Tomas to find a plain dress. I'm sure he tried, but..." The longer he soaked in her immaculate beauty, the tighter his suit pants became. "Nothing could ever look plain on you."

"Why? I mean, why do you want me to look plain? They love their whores to dress—"

"You're not a whore, and while you're with me, you will not dress like one."

Her eyes widened.

He snatched his necktie from the chair and moved to the mirror to wrangle the thing into place. After a few lousy attempts to make a knot, he yanked it free, grunting with frustration.

He was a mechanic, not a pompous high roller. How was he supposed to continue this ruse when he couldn't even knot a tie? Tomas would have to show him again, but not without teasing him excessively for it.

As he turned to call for his friend, a small hand landed on his chest.

"Allow me." Brown eyes stared up at him from the face of a goddess.

He raised his chin, giving her access. "You know how to do this?"

"I thought everyone knew how." She looped the ends, watching him with suspicion. "Especially rich businessmen."

"I never said I was a businessman."

"That's right." With swift movements, she made a tug here, an adjustment there, and stepped back. "You invest in important things. Criminal things that don't require a suit, apparently."

"My offer stands." He rested a knuckle beneath her chin, lifting it. "I'll tell you my secrets."

She turned her head away, rejecting his touch along with his offer.

Probably for the best. What he needed from her was the location of the breach in the wall or whatever she'd seen beyond it. But even that might not be enough to determine the coordinates of this place.

None of it was worth blowing his cover. He'd been asking himself all day if he could tell her the truth. The simple fact that he was on the same side as Vera's sister would make Gina turn against him even more than she already was. She hated Vera worse than she hated him.

He couldn't trust her, no matter how badly he wanted to.

"There's makeup and hair stuff in that bag." He nodded at the supplies Tomas had gathered. "It's yours to use."

"I don't wear makeup."

"Good."

She didn't need it. Even with bruised splotches on her face, the woman had more natural radiance than anyone he'd ever met.

"We leave in ten minutes." He ambled out of the room to find his suit jacket and mentally prepare for the evening.

A moment later, the sound of a hairdryer reached his ears. Surely she wasn't blowing out her curls? He loved the way they bounced and spiraled in every direction. He fantasized about them coiling around his cock as he sank into the back of her throat.

Sick fuck.

In the bedroom, he shrugged on the jacket. After their workout, she'd spent the day in the sitting room watching TV while he and Tomas sent cryptic messages to their team.

They only had access to the laptops and cell phones provided by the cartel. But they'd prepared for that and sent all communication to burner phones and other untraceable devices that were monitored by the Freedom Fighters.

Before departing Colombia, they'd memorized a specific list of song lyrics, each verse with a predetermined meaning, a specific message on the status of the mission. Right now, their friends only needed to know they were safe. They found Vera alive and well, and everything was moving as expected.

Within the next couple of days, he hoped to have a different message to send. If they obtained the location, he would send Tomas away with an excuse and remain here until he returned with a full team and a lot of firepower.

A knock sounded on the outside door. He tilted his head, listening as Tomas answered it.

"Good evening." Vera's sultry voice drifted in, followed by the click of her heels. "Where's your handsome *jefe*?"

Luke strolled into the main room with his hands clasped behind him.

She went still, her gaze sweeping him from head to toe and back again. "Well, don't you look absolutely delicious?"

Bending, she lowered a large brown bag to the floor, and her chest nearly spilled from the tight black leather dress.

At least it's not pleather.

"What did you bring me?" He prowled toward her, causing her breaths to accelerate.

"Ice cream." She smiled and flushed. "When I heard you ordered three boxes of Klondike bars, I had to see it for myself."

"See what exactly?"

"A physically fit, gorgeous specimen of a man consume dozens of ice cream bars. I mean, come on." She cocked a hip, blatantly flirting. "How do you eat junk food and still look like that?"

"It's not for me." He angled his chin to speak behind him. "You can stop spying and come out."

An annoyed huff sounded in the bathroom, and a moment later, Gina strode into the room.

She'd left her hair curly, and those silky, raven spirals sprung around her arms and chest as she navigated the sky-rise heels with more poise and grace than he would've thought possible.

His eyes tracked her, his insides heating and tightening anew. Tomas was right. She was getting to him, under his skin, in his head, and fucking with his heart rate.

He never had trouble shutting off sexual attraction. But this went beyond shallow interest.

For the first time in his life, he wanted more from a woman than a night of pleasure.

He wanted more with *this* woman.

"Vera," he said. "Give her the ice cream."

He could retrieve the bag himself but wanted to study the interactions between the two women.

As expected, Vera clenched her jaw. Then she slowly lowered and gripped the bag, her eyes locked on him.

"I can't eat that right now." Gina approached his side and curled a hand around his elbow.

An unsolicited touch? This was new, and damn him, but he felt her grip through his entire body.

He slid his other hand over hers, and Vera homed in on the connection, scowling her displeasure from beneath beetled brows.

With his eyes on her, he focused his other senses on Gina, marking the stiffness in her posture, the slight tremble in her fingers, and the overall nervousness wafting from her pores. He suspected it had little to do with Vera and everything to do with Alejandro's dinner.

If she wasn't dreading the next few hours, she should've been.

"Put the dessert in the freezer." He flicked a finger toward the kitchen, dismissing Vera like a common servant.

She hesitated, her face pinched like she would argue. Then she pushed back her shoulders and obeyed.

Turning toward Gina, he twined his fingers through the soft curls on her shoulder. "Are you ready?"

"Fuck no."

"Good girl. Stay on your toes. But know this…" He bent in and grazed his lips along her cheek. "No one will touch you but me."

"Is that supposed to ease my fragile little rabbit heart?"

"There's nothing fragile about you, and I'm counting on that tonight." He straightened and pivoted toward Vera. "Will you be joining us this evening?"

"Yes, I'm headed there now. We can walk together." She sauntered to the door and looked back at him expectantly.

He emptied his expression, hiding any response she might've sparked in him, which was very little. All criminal behavior aside, there was something off-putting about her.

Tula hadn't shown him any recent photos, but the digital images he'd seen of teenage Vera had alluded to the gorgeous woman she was today. He couldn't find a single flaw in her appearance.

It was her personality. The smarmy way she ogled him, the constant hair-flicking and lip-licking, the overly servile responses to his demands—she rubbed him the wrong way.

Sliding his hand around Gina's, he felt a sudden jerk, her reflex to pull away. Then her fingers curled around his, slick with sweat and nerves.

He was right there with her, anxious to end the evening before it had even begun.

With a nod at Tomas, he followed his friend out the door.

FIFTEEN

"Your hair is the sexiest shade of red I've ever seen." Vera inched closer on the couch, bending over Luke's sprawled leg.

"Mm." His tongue took a stroll through his mouth, casting off the sour taste of her flattery.

She'd openly watched him across the table all through dinner. After dessert, it hadn't taken her long to seek him out in Alejandro's den.

Ten minutes into their private conversation, he knew he would have her beneath him by night's end.

Would…

Definitely should.

He should fuck her into delirium, drug her with orgasms, and win her over once and for all.

With a sharp pang in his gut, his gaze gravitated to the dark-haired beauty sitting alone on the far side of the den. He'd kept Gina in his periphery from the moment they'd arrived but hadn't spoken a word to her.

Her eyes shone with alertness, her posture cautiously still. The purple markings that splotched her face lent a tough edge to her feminine appearance. But it wasn't just the bruises that made her unapproachable. Her entire aura screamed, *Fuck off*.

She and Tomas had that in common.

Luke didn't want her here, for her own protection and his peace of mind. But Alejandro had instructed otherwise, and the reason for that wouldn't make itself known until the entertainment began.

Given the tautness in her shoulders, she knew what was coming.

"She belongs to my brothers." Vera slid a fingernail beneath Luke's jaw, attempting to turn his attention back to her.

"Not this week, she doesn't." He gave Vera his eyes. "Tell me why you hate her."

"Tell me why you want her."

"She's available, and that availability allows me to do anything I desire to her tight little body."

As she mulled that over, her eyes dilated, and the rise and fall of her chest slowly sped up.

"If *I* were available…" She trailed her nail down his neck and hooked it beneath the tie. "What would you do to me?"

"Your answer first." He captured her wrist, holding it immobile. "Why do you hate her?"

"She makes my brothers stupid."

"Explain."

"The whore is a distraction." At the clench of his fingers around her arm, she narrowed her eyes. "That's exactly what I'm talking about. You all turn into cavemen the way they fight over her."

"I'm not fighting."

"Semantics. I can't help but wonder if she can cast spells with her pussy. Every man who falls in doesn't come out with his brain intact."

"That's a pretty powerful trick." He smiled, unable to deny the claim.

"It's sorcery. My brothers need to get the fuck over her."

Jealousy. That was the real answer to his question. Vera was insanely, viciously jealous of the attention that Hector's sons gave to Gina. If he had to guess, Vera was in love with at least one of them.

"You know…" He released her wrist. "The best way to get over a woman is to send her home with another man."

"You mean, send her home with *you*?" Her spine went ramrod straight. "You actually want to keep her?"

"Perhaps." He stretched his arms along the back of the couch, reclining with his legs spread and his gaze locked on Gina. "There's something quite enchanting about her."

There was something, all right. She made him feel restless and possessive, like an alien predator trapped in his skin.

Tomas stood like a sentinel behind her, allowing Luke the opportunity to work on Vera. But his focus was shit. Every brain cell seemed to be on a single track, one that had nothing to do with the operation and everything to do with protecting his fighter.

UNSHACKLE

Marco and Alejandro were the only other two men present tonight. Evidently, Omar didn't attend family dinners, and Miguel was still out of town on *business*. A few scantily dressed cantina girls milled about the room, collecting empty glasses and taking orders.

The brothers didn't give the girls the time of day. Nor did they seem the least bit concerned with him cozying up on the couch with Vera.

No, they only had eyes for Gina.

If either man touched her, the night would be over. He'd made that announcement the moment they arrived for dinner.

"They'll never let you keep her." Vera sniffed. "They'll kill her before they let her leave the property."

"They call her a whore, but you and I both know that's bullshit. Who is she?"

"Don't know." She shrugged.

"Don't know or won't say?"

"Poor pathetic man." Vera shook her head. "You're bewitched by a woman who despises you."

"Is that right? Have you watched us together on the cameras? Sleeping? Working out? *Fucking?*" He wrapped the last word in gravel and heat, marking the raising goosebumps along her arms. "Ask your question again."

Her lashes fluttered, and two pink blooms rose to her cheeks. "If I was available, what would you do?"

"Let's go for a drive tomorrow."

"A drive? How would—?"

"I'll borrow one of Marco's hypercars."

"He would never—"

"I can be very persuasive." *Not that persuasive.* But he had another plan. Angling toward her, he gave her the full force of his gaze—the look that *always* got him laid. "I want to get out of here for a few hours. Just you and me. We'll drive somewhere nearby." He drifted closer, letting her feel his breath against her neck. "Then I'll show you what I can do to you."

"We don't need to leave." She was leaning, floating into him, caught in his snare. "I have my own room."

"So do I." He parted his lips around her earlobe, barely touching, but it was enough to melt her next breath.

"Mine doesn't have cameras."

His rush of victory was instantly strangled by a fist of guilt. He felt Gina's eyes on him before he looked in her direction.

Their gazes clashed and tangled, yelling soundlessly and swinging invisible punches. Disgust steamed from the cracks in her expression, her hands flexing into white-knuckled weapons on her lap.

Did she not like seeing him with another woman? Or just this woman?

If only he could tell her this was a job, that he was serving a greater cause.

But that was the problem. He wasn't here to pursue romantic interests. Gina was collateral. A means to an end. He didn't owe her an explanation. She'd put herself in the cartel's grasp, and not once had he promised to get her out.

This wasn't about her.

Returning his attention to Vera, he embraced the vow he'd made to his team and their newest member, Tula Gomez.

He was holding Tula's sister in his arms. She was alive and growing pliable by the second. Bedding her was the quickest and surest way to get inside her — in her head, in her trust — to locate the key to finishing this mission.

Molding his lips around her earlobe, he suckled it like a clit. The technique lay in the pressure of his tongue, the precise amount of suction and friction, and the low, vibrating hum in the back of his throat. He did it exactly as he'd been taught by Van and Liv, the mechanics executed with an unrivaled skill that was so effective her head fell back, and her breathing careened out of control.

He felt nothing.

Lost to his tongue, she moaned, gasped, and arched her back as her hands grappled for a landing place. Frantic fingers grazed his flaccid cock, and he swatted them away, repulsed and suddenly, irrationally angry.

Old hang-ups rose to the surface. He'd been trained to lick and suck, pleasure and serve. All for a master who had bought him and ultimately died at the hands of his friends. But he'd never felt more like a whore than he did right now.

He didn't want this woman. His *heart* wanted someone else.

Since when did his heart have a say in sex? It was inconceivable, yet the damn thing hammered at him, demanding he change course and find another way.

He slowed the roll of his tongue, hating the taste of her skin, the scent of her hair, and the sounds of her gasps. Easing back, he grimaced inwardly at the sight of her body splayed in lust.

With her legs parted as far as the dress allowed, her hand moved between her thighs, stroking her greedy cunt. Eyes bedazzled, tits heaving over the bodice, she was ripe and ready.

From just a kiss on her ear.

So goddamn easy.

UNSHACKLE

He could fuck her right here. She would fall apart on his cock and beg for more, guaranteeing him access to her room, her bed, and the thoughts in her head. He wouldn't even need to resort to orgasm denial. The way she was looking at him now—eyes hooded and thighs trembling—she would sing her secrets in just a few thrusts.

His move.

Voices murmured around him. Ice clinked in glasses. Soft, classical Spanish music thrummed from hidden speakers, and somewhere deep in his soul, his sense of loyalty won. Loyalty to his friends, his family, and their mission.

He slid a hand along Vera's inner thigh, the skin damp and hot, quivering beneath his touch. Slipping his other hand beneath her head, he threaded his fingers through her hair. Coarse hair. Straight. Too short and all wrong.

Focus, asshole.

He leaned toward her face, and she lifted her mouth, offering, silently pleading for a kiss. He wouldn't fuck her here. Not in front of Gina. She was too much of a distraction. Even now, he felt her gaze pounding blow after blow against his back.

Maybe he imagined it, hoping for it like a desperate douchebag.

Clearing his mind, he focused on the plump, red-stained mouth before him, the lips he could conquer and ruin for all others. He'd made women come from just a kiss, and with her fingers vigorously working between her legs, she was already climbing, panting. A puddle of lust and need in his hands.

A breath away from her mouth, he paused, wrestling with the inescapable urge to steal a glimpse behind him. He had to know if she was watching.

If she cared.

Tilting his neck, his gaze unerringly latched onto her waiting eyes. Punishing eyes, flaring with all the violence and scorn of a damaging storm. Despite the distance, the rage in her barely contained breaths blazed a fire around him, burning him alive.

Alejandro leaned over her chair, speaking in Spanish, trying to get her attention. But her gaze remained on Luke, blistering his skin and manipulating the flow of his blood.

He fucking adored her for that. In the space of one look, she roused the darkest, most twisted parts of his nature, stirring awake uncontrollable desires and stretching them beneath his skin.

His balls tightened. His cock swelled, and he had to reach and make a crude adjustment. The feelings she unleashed in him were unwieldy. Monstrous. Impossible to tame. And the dangerous surge only intensified when Alejandro got in her face.

Luke seethed, fighting the vicious explosion inside him. Pulling his hand from Vera's thigh, he veered his mouth past her lips and spoke in her ear. "I'll give you some time to think about this."

It was the best he could do without completely destroying his progress with her.

Pushing off the couch, he crossed the room in a few unstoppable strides and grabbed Gina's arm. With a hard tug, he had her off the chair and out of Alejandro's reach.

"Is there a problem?" he asked the stocky muscle head.

"No hay problema." The man glared daggers. "But I find it odd this…she…" His English broke up as he searched for the right words.

"She watches you." Marco strolled forward with a hand in his pocket and an arm around a scowling Vera. "Why is this?" He nodded at Gina. "This man-hater stares at you with venom, sure. But something else lurks between her eyes and yours. I want to know what it is."

Marco wasn't an idiot. None of them were. They didn't run the largest, meanest, most dangerous cartel in Mexico on luck. They knew what they were doing, and the biggest part of that was understanding their enemies.

"I give her things." Luke tightened his grip on Gina's arm as she angrily tried to jerk away.

"Things?" Marco rubbed his jaw. "What *things*?"

He met Vera's eyes and shaped the word like a kiss. "Orgasms."

Her gaze dipped to his mouth, darkening with hunger.

Marco threw his head back and laughed. "This, I don't believe. The whore is incapable of pleasure."

"Perhaps you're incapable of giving it."

It was the wrong thing to say.

Sudden, heavy silence clotted the room, the atmosphere too strained to breathe.

Well, fuck. He'd just thrown down the gauntlet, challenging the cartel in their own house.

SIXTEEN

"Prove it." Marco's command fell like thunder through the room. "Show me this power you claim to have over women."

Burn in hell.

Luke had a mind to tell the motherfucker how he felt about being ordered around. But doing so would end with his body rotting in whatever hole the cartel deemed deep enough.

Carefully, he released Gina's arm, and carefully, he clasped his hands behind him. "What did you have in mind?"

"This isn't necessary." Vera tensed.

"Yes, it is." Marco paced beside her. "You watched the monitors this morning. The whore fought him, rather pathetically. She did *not* come."

"Since you were spying on me," Luke said, "you know she tried to sneak out before Alejandro came by. You also know that I brought her to the point of begging and denied her release. It's called *punishment*."

Marco and Vera shared a look. Yeah, they'd seen the whole damn show. He'd counted on it.

"You seem to know your way around a woman's body, Mr. Smith." Vera touched her throat, toying with a wisp of hair. "But how many of your untamed whores reciprocate?" She flicked a hand at Gina and laughed mockingly. "This one would never put her mouth on you. Not without biting off your dick."

"*Exactamente.*" Marco studied him with a pensive mien.

"You're wrong." Luke knew how to control the human jaw and feed in his cock without so much as a scratch.

Alejandro gulped back a swig of tequila and lowered into a nearby chair. He was the brother to keep an eye on. The quiet ones were usually shifty and underhanded, the ones who stabbed their victims during consoling hugs and hid the bodies under their beds.

"I'm curious." Marco paused behind Vera and slid his hands around her waist. "If given the choice, whose face would you fuck? My beautiful sister's?" He reached up and caressed Vera's cleavage, prompting her lashes to lower submissively. "Or the bruised face of a whore?"

His gorgeous fighter. Hands down. No question.

But this wasn't about his personal preference. The cartel loved their games. Every play had a price, and the wrong move would be costly.

What did Marco want out of this? To see if Luke was too cowardly to tempt Gina's teeth? Or if he was stupid enough to take the risk? Maybe this had nothing to do with him? Could it be a test of Vera's loyalty? Or Gina's?

The biggest mindfuck of all was the way Marco continued to fondle Vera's tits after referring to her as his sister.

Luke shuddered. "How are you related? Same mother? Father?"

Neither option made sense. Tula Gomez shared a father with Marco and a mother with Vera. Vera's father was unknown.

"It's not important." Marco punctuated the point by palming one of her heavy breasts and kissing her neck. "You have a great mouth, don't you, *mi reina*?" His eyes lifted to Luke while he nibbled. "Hot, wet suction. No one gives head like my sister."

Alejandro watched from the chair, his heated expression vacillating somewhere between disgust and lust.

Incest aside, Luke wanted to leave the lovebirds to it and haul Gina out of there. The fastest way out was the path of least resistance, and Marco wanted a show.

Vera would offer no resistance. Luke only needed to snap his fingers, and she would be on his cock like a fly on honey.

He sensed her staring and reluctantly met her eyes. What he saw there was blatant desire, but beneath the thirst lay a shining gleam of vulnerability.

What were her stakes in this? Yesterday, she wanted nothing to do with him. Now, seeing him with Gina, she was playing right into his plan. But what if her role here wasn't so black and white? Everyone was playing a game. For some, it was a game of survival.

"Make a decision." Marco smoothed a hand down Vera's arm. "Whose throat will you fuck, John Smith?"

"I thought you didn't share your sister."

"I make the rules and change them as I please."

"You know what I think?" Luke rested a hand on Gina's lower back. "You're setting me up."

She went rigid, and he flattened his palm, waiting for her to feel him, to *listen* to his touch.

"Setting you up how?" Marco's face turned to marble.

"You tell me." He was stalling.

Moving his thumb, he stroked her spine. Tapped. Stroked again. Only Tomas stood behind them. Cameras were there, but to anyone monitoring them, it would just look like nervous fidgeting.

Make a move, Gina.

He circled his thumb, applying pressure, releasing, and tapping again. Sending her a message.

This is your choice.

He could force her to suck his cock. Or he could make her watch him face-fuck her archenemy. If she didn't give him some sort of signal, he would choose her. Her mouth. Her body. He wanted her heart.

The sickest part of him hoped it would come to that. He wanted to shove himself so deep in her throat that she felt him in her chest. He wanted to lose control in her body, torment her with passion, and wreck her as thoroughly as she was wrecking him.

On the heels of those thoughts, he felt the mission unraveling in his hands. For the life of him, he couldn't choose Vera. Or his friends. Or their cause. Not this time.

"I'm only interested," Marco said, "in seeing which mouth you intend to take."

Luke increased the rhythm of his thumb, silently urging Gina to make a decision. "Maybe I want both. At the same time."

Both women bristled.

"No-no-no." Marco wagged a finger, grinning. "That is not the deal."

"All right." He dropped his hand from Gina's back. "I made my decision."

At the edge of his vision, she flexed her hands into fists and stared at her feet. His neck stiffened as she drew in a breath. Then she turned toward him and slowly moved her arm.

The moment her fingers touched his cock, his pulse burst into a gallop. Blood rushed to his groin, and he swelled, hardened, *throbbed.*

His desire for her was visceral, but it wasn't just based in lust. The most benign things set it off. Like the sound of her *Rs* rolling on her tongue. The intoxicating taste in the air when she yelled in his face. The way her scent carried through his nose and hit his brain with comforting familiarity.

And the feel of her hand curling around his erection through the suit pants.

Her touch wasn't benign at all. It was detrimental to his job. He wanted this tiny little warrior with a ferocity that felt foreign. Inexplicable. Completely out of his depth.

He gripped her wrist, dislodging her fingers from his leaking dick. But he didn't let go. Shifting around, he spotted a nearby couch and dragged her there.

"You're choosing *her*?" Vera boiled, her voice an octave above horrified.

"Yes."

And she chose me.

Why? He had no idea. Maybe it was to one-up Vera. Or maybe she planned on castrating him with her teeth.

With a furious pivot of heels, Vera spun toward the door.

"You will watch." Marco caught her hand and pulled her into a chair.

Luke lowered onto the couch and pointed at the cushion beside him. "Kneel."

Gina looked shell-shocked, uncertain, as if she was only now coming to terms with her decision. But she owned it profoundly, exquisitely, with each knee she set on the couch.

"You should know…" Marco reclined in the chair beside Vera, sitting directly across from him. "When she bites your dick, I'm not calling the doctor."

"Noted." He deepened his sprawl on the couch, stretching out his arms and getting comfortable. Then he let his head fall back like a man in control of his universe. "Pull me out."

Her eyes flashed. "Are you going to give me step-by-step instructions?"

"Do I need to?"

"Shut the fuck up, and you'll find out."

That's my girl.

"She's going to bite the dick!" Marco roared with laughter and clapped his hands.

Vera scowled, and across the room, Alejandro remained in his chair with a cantina girl perched on his lap.

Tomas' steady gaze stayed with Luke. A silent, bolstering presence. No one knew him like those among his kindred. United in strife, he and Tomas had been forced to perform sexual acts for an audience during their time in captivity. This was nothing new.

UNSHACKLE

But it felt new as Gina unzipped his fly and wrestled his pants to his thighs. It felt so goddamn significant he was shaking. Not noticeably, but she felt it. With her hand on his bare hip and his cock jutting toward her mouth, she raised her eyes to his.

Compassion. It glowed in her gaze and socked him straight in the chest. This woman… She was the living reality of the only dream he'd ever dared to want for himself, the most precious, indestructible, viciously beautiful creature in and out of any fantasy.

She was an impossible possibility in the flesh.

"You're so fucking beautiful." He wanted to give her so much more than trite words. But not here. With the cartel watching, he could only be John Smith. "Suck me."

"Don't coach me, asshat."

"Don't test my patience, sugar."

A glimmer lit her eyes. Her jaw opened slightly. Slowly, her head lowered, and he watched, breathless and overtaken, as this fierce woman lay her claim on his cock.

Soft lips. Hot tongue. Oh, God. Oh, sweet holy fuck. She sucked him straight to the back of her throat.

His toes curled, and his hips shot off the couch, thrusting, plunging, digging deep, so fucking deep before he caught himself and pulled back.

Down boy.

He wasn't going to last. No way in hell. She felt too fucking unreal.

"Unbelievable." A string of Spanish spewed past Marco's lips.

That was the last distraction Luke registered before everything faded. The room, their audience, nothing existed but the overwhelming stimulation of her mouth moving on his cock.

Her tongue traced veins and ridges. Her hands explored, caressing his abdomen, hips, thighs. By the time she reached his balls, he was panting, grunting, fighting the demands of an impending release.

Christ, he was going to come. Or black out. Fuck, he would die from the pure agony of it.

Not yet. Holy fucking hell, not yet.

He didn't want it to end. But her mouth was relentless, sucking the sensitive glans beneath his head, tasting the endless flow of pre-come, swallowing him deeply, and coaxing him to shoot his load.

With throaty groans, he couldn't stop the movement of his hips. His hands flew to her head, and he crushed her face to his groin, rocking, stabbing, cutting her air. He had to have her, kiss her, fuck her, and touch her everywhere. God almighty, he'd never needed anything or anyone like he needed this. *Her.*

Mindlessly, he fucked her throat, and she took every inch, gripping his thighs, gagging, choking, and sucking even harder.

Let her breathe, idiot.

Releasing her, he reached beneath her dress, between her legs. His fingers found her panties, ripped them away, and sought her wet center. Soaking. So silky and warm. Her arousal gushed over his knuckles, and her pussy sucked his probing touch into its hot, welcoming recesses.

She writhed, gyrating her hips and moaning around his cock. He thrust a finger into her again, added two, three, rimming her opening and massaging the sensitive muscle inside. She cried out, grinding against his hand, her breaths faltering, eyes squeezing shut as she rode the pleasure like a hellion.

Dragging her tongue along his length, she flicked and teased without mercy. His head spun at the unpredictable rhythm, his body hard, every muscle flexed, his entire world caught in her spell.

Over and over, she sucked the tip into the back of her throat, closing her lips around him, sealing him in delicious warmth. It took every ounce of concentration to remember the fingers he still held inside her. What a distracting little succubus.

Two could play at this game.

He moved his hand between her legs, seeking her clit with his thumb, rolling it, adding pressure until she cried out and pulled her mouth off his cock.

"Oh, you're in trouble now." She flashed her teeth, gripped his hip and thigh, and sucked him hard and deep into her throat.

His vision blurred. The world spun, and he shut his eyes against the onslaught.

"Jesus. Goddamn. Fuck, fuck, fuck!" He flung out his free hand and gripped the back of the couch, desperately anchoring himself in some semblance of control.

She was ready to come, dripping all over his fingers. If he didn't send her over now, she would win. She'd milk him for all he was worth before he had a chance to have her here, on the couch, wild and rabid and absolute.

Circling his thumb around her clit, he fingered her sheath with hard strokes, harder, until he thought she would tumble into his lap. Trembling on the cusp of ecstasy, she fought it valiantly. And lost.

The hot clasp of her body squeezed, constricting his fingers through violent spasms. She tore her mouth off his dick and screamed, her head tilting back and mouth wide in stunned oblivion.

Her release shuddered through her, and her hoarse cries dissolved into moans. As she gulped for air, he yanked a condom from his pocket and rolled it on.

UNSHACKLE

Glazed eyes found his, satisfied but not sated. His heart pounded. The tumultuous sounds of their breaths caught fire, and they launched at the same time.

Chests colliding, arms grappling, they came together in a tangle of limbs and sexual heat. There was no pause. No hesitation. Her legs wrapped around his hips. Their lips met in a frenzy, and their bodies took over.

She rose above him. He adjusted the angle, and *Ahhh, fuuuuck!* He sank into her hot, drenching glory. Tight and swollen, she urged him deeper, wriggling, slamming down her hips, and hardening him beyond human endurance.

Sweaty and breathless, he started moving, thrusting, and fucking her mouth with his tongue. She grabbed his necktie, lifted along his length, and lowered, dipping him inside her oh-so-slowly.

He couldn't take it. With his hands on her waist, he took the reins. Then he took her fully, setting the tempo, widening her thighs, and pumping into heaven, his body a piston of pent-up urgency and hunger.

She clawed at his neck, his shoulders, holding onto him as if wrestling for every inch of closeness. Their lips smashed and bruised, teeth clashing, tongues hitting and sliding, too frantic and reckless to execute a real kiss.

But it was more than real. It was what every kiss should be. Untrained. Unhinged. Just pure raw fire.

He drove his hips harder, hitting the spot inside her that would send her into rapture. She clenched her thighs around him, pulling herself closer, moaning helpless sounds of want.

Yeah, she was close, her gasps becoming shallower, her cunt growing slicker. He fucked her steadily, completely, knowing no man—not even the two in the room—had ever possessed her the way he owned her now. In this, she was his alone.

At the edge of his awareness, he heard arguing. A glass crashed. A door slammed, taking Vera's angry voice with it.

Reality crept in.

He felt things for this woman, feelings too new to analyze. Maybe he was crazy, but it wasn't one-sided. She felt something, too.

By no means could the cartel get a whiff of it. Not until he had a plan. As much as Luke wanted to carry Gina out in tender embrace, he couldn't. The cartel needed to believe what they witnessed tonight was just a moment. Just sex. Nothing more. And he needed her cooperation to pull it off.

She slipped her hands along his arms, holding tight as he trailed his lips across her cheek, into her hair, peppering slow feverish kisses.

At her ear, he tasted her sweet skin and whispered, "You hate me. The instant you come, show them *exactly* how much. Then leave. Go to my room. Tomas will make sure you arrive safely."

She leaned back and searched his eyes. Their hips came together, grinding in a fusion of conflict and intimacy. He watched her closely, looking for a sign that she understood.

But she was already lost, drowning in the grip of pleasure. *Jesus fuck*, she was coming, straining against his hold, her body shaking, her voice whispering in Spanish over and over.

The splendor of her surrender was his undoing. He increased his strokes, the intensity beyond anything he'd ever experienced as he clutched her neck and roared, releasing himself in hard, violent jets. He came and came on the verge of passing out.

Until a hand crashed across his face, shooting blinding pain through his jaw.

He blinked, panting, and she punched him again.

"I hate you." She shoved off his cock, jumped from his lap, and straightened her dress in a raging fit. "What do you think just happened? That I wanted it? Fuck no! That was coercion. Rape. You sick, unholy bastard!"

"That's what they all say." He tossed her a grin and rubbed his jaw. "Try not to come so hard next time."

A livid flush spread up her neck. She flexed her hands, pivoted, and raced out of the room.

He didn't have to signal Tomas. His friend was already moving, hot on her heels.

She did it. Exactly what he'd told her, she pulled it off. Pride filled his chest. Whether she liked it or not, she was on his team now.

She was *his*.

Vera, Alejandro, and all the girls had vacated the room, leaving him alone with the cartel capo.

Nervousness set in, but he didn't let it show.

"Women." With a sigh, he removed the condom and stashed it, along with her discarded panties, in his pocket. Then he straightened his clothes and zipped up.

"You can't live with them, so just fuck them and kill them. *Si?*" With a chuckle, Marco stood and set a drink in Luke's hand. "Congratulations, my friend. Now tell me how you did it."

SEVENTEEN

She sat in John's bathtub, hugging her knees to her chest as unanswered questions pounded in her head.

When the water cooled, she let it out and refilled it again. With each passing minute, her hands turned pruney, her heart numb.

After leaving Alejandro's quarters an hour ago, she'd headed straight here. Not because John had commanded it. But because she needed to talk to him, to find out what was real and what was an act.

He'd put his hands and mouth all over that hateful bitch. Was he with her now? Kissing her? Thrusting between her legs?

Gah! She yanked at her hair. Why did she care who he was with?

More importantly, why had she willingly swallowed his cock and fucked his damn brains out? What made him so different than the others?

I give her things.

Orgasms.

Yeah, he doled those out like party favors.

If it was only that, she could work with it. She'd already accepted her attraction and given into the lust. How could she not? The sex was…

Her thighs squeezed together. Her nipples hardened, and a fluttery sensation lit up her belly.

Yeah, he knew how to fuck. And kiss. And touch all the right places. He was turning her into an addict.

Point for him.

It would be no hardship to spend the rest of the week in bed with him. As dangerous as he was, he'd given her more blissful moments in twenty-four hours than she'd experienced in the past three years.

But this wasn't just sex. There was a rare, deep-reaching, unstoppable force blooming between them. A magnetism that jacked up her blood pressure and consumed her mind. A supernatural connection that she'd never shared with any other person.

She desperately wanted to believe in that connection, trust it, and fight for it. Damn her, but she felt outrageously possessive of it. The thought of another woman touching him sent her into a homicidal rage.

That was why she'd gone down on him after dinner. Watching anyone else do it would've gutted her. Which was maddening. She didn't even know him.

What was his name? Where did he grow up? How did he earn a living? What were his crimes?

What did he want with her?

She secretly harbored wishes about him. Recklessly whimsical hopes. The kind that only came true in fairy tales. Because there were no white knights in *Casa de La Rocha*. He couldn't rescue her. Not even if he tried.

Sinking into the water, she let her face float just above the surface and stared at the hole in the ceiling.

This morning, he'd said La Rocha hadn't replaced the camera because he made them believe he was discussing confidential business details in here with Tomas and threatened to take down the cartel if they invaded his privacy.

He would be gone soon anyway. After they squeezed all the money they could get out of him, he would leave.

What would happen to her? Would they keep her alive? Continue to use her as bait? Or put her in another fight, one she didn't have a chance at winning?

She needed to get out of this bathtub.

Rising to her knees, her gaze landed on the doorway, and her breath abandoned her.

John stood on the threshold, his tie hanging loose around his neck. Red hair tousled from raking fingers, suit jacket dangling from a finger, he looked tired and pensive.

She rested her hands on the edge of the tub, holding his gaze. With his chin dipped downward, he watched her from beneath dark brows. Just watching. Breathing. After too many inhales and exhales, he stepped in and shut the door.

"My parents were drug addicts. When they were sober, they beat me. When they weren't…" He toed off his shoes and removed the tie. "They forgot they had bills and…a child."

She closed her eyes, instantly regretting the mean things she'd said about his father leaving bruises. "I'm sorry."

UNSHACKLE

"Don't be. You were right about that." He unbuttoned his shirt and dropped it. "But you were wrong about me bullying kids in school." His lips quirked. "I only bully women who know how to bully right back."

A smile tickled her lips and faded quickly. "What happened? With your parents?"

"Dead. Overdosed." He ambled to the tub and stripped the rest of his clothes. "I ran away before that happened. Finished my last year of high school while living on the streets."

"How did you do it?" She touched her chin to her shoulder, meeting his eyes. "I mean, you're clearly successful and wealthy. How?"

"A single, horrifying, unfortunate event." He stepped in, sliding into the water behind her.

She stared at his legs, so hard and powerful as they wedged in around her, dwarfing her body. "An unfortunate event led to…a fortune?"

"A fortune in things that matter." His arms glided around her waist, pulling her back to his chest. "I'll tell you about it some other time."

"You're leaving in a few days."

"Not without you."

She melted. Every muscle, sinew, and bone dissolved before she could stifle the reaction. No matter what he promised, she couldn't leave. Was he an idiot? Or maybe he thought she was.

Pushing herself upright, she refused to let any man, including this one, make her feel weak and manipulated.

He held onto her hips, and she yanked at his hands. When he finally released her, she spun away, splashing water over the edge.

The tub wasn't big enough for the two of them, but she wasn't leaving it until she had answers.

"Where have you been for the past hour?" She inched back against the opposite end, facing him.

"With Marco. Instructing him on how to bring a woman to orgasm."

"What?" Her jaw dropped. "Why?"

"He wanted to know my technique." He pulled her feet onto his lap beneath the water and stroked a hand along her ankle. "Giving him a few pointers seemed less painful than pissing him off."

"Did you…?" Her face flamed. She really didn't want to ask this, but she needed to know. "Did you demonstrate on someone?"

"No." His voice lacked insistence or any emotion. He didn't seem to care if she believed him or not.

"Marco doesn't do things without causing discomfort or pain to someone else. He was probably fucking with you."

"I don't disagree."

"And you associate with him. What does that say about you?" She yanked her legs away from his touch.

"Why are we discussing him when there's something else weighing heavier on your mind? You're not one to hold back, Gina. Let's hear it."

"All right. Why am I here when you were all over *her* tonight?"

"If I wanted Vera in my bed, she would be here right now." He studied her carefully, his arms draped over the back of the tub, his presence overbearing, unnervingly still. After a long, watchful moment, he released a breath. "I need something from her."

"The location of the compound." Her pulse increased. "You think you can fuck it out of her."

"I know I can."

Irrational pain swelled behind her breastbone and seeped into her voice. "If she gives it to you, what happens next?"

"You're jealous." He lunged forward and touched a finger to her mouth, silencing her objection. "I'm giving you the truth, even when it hurts." His hand trailed along her jaw, flaming her skin. "I'm jealous, too. I feel this constant, unreasonable impulse to piss a circle around you, to throat punch anyone who looks at you, including Tomas…" He laughed and dragged a hand down his face. "That's definitely a first for me."

She liked the sound of that. Too much. Sucking in a tight breath, she turned her head away. "Answer my question."

"I've answered enough for now. Trust goes both ways. I give a little. You give a little. Eventually, we meet in the middle." He glanced at the closed door and leaned in, bracing his elbows on bent knees. "I know that confiding in me means risking not just your life but your mother's life, as well. I'll help you the best that I can, but you have to help *me*."

He extended a hand to her, and she stared at it with a lump in her throat.

From what she'd surmised, his role as a slave buyer was a cover-up for something far more insidious. She knew crucial things about the organization and the compound that could help him, whether he was gathering intel or planning a hit.

But if he killed Marco and started a war, what would happen to her and the only person she cared about?

What would happen if he left and she never saw him again?

She could die either way. But if she helped him… If she could bring herself to trust him, he might be her only way out.

UNSHACKLE

Reaching out a hand, she clasped his strong fingers. Their gazes held as he pulled her toward his chest. She slid over his hard physique, setting a palm on his flat hipbone, corrugated abs, sculpted pecs, until she found a gripping spot in the warm juncture between his neck and shoulder.

With her lower body floating in the cradle of his thighs, she rested on his chest and pressed her cheek against the whiskered hardness of his.

"Three years ago," she whispered, "I made the worst decision of my life."

EIGHTEEN

She reached back through time, aching so brutally with loss she couldn't breathe. With her mouth against John's cheek and his heat beneath her body, she welcomed his stillness, the intensity in which he waited and *listened*. His attentiveness bolstered her.

"There are things I don't recall, like how I arrived here or the first few days I spent in the basement." Her whisper went as taut as the coils knotting in her belly. "But I remember the day Miguel La Rocha walked into the *taqueria* where I worked and offered me the world."

He tensed beneath her. "Did you know who he was?"

"No idea. He gave me a fake name and a warm, irresistible smile. He's the most charming of the brothers. The best looking. He wears expensive suits and has this captivating, alluring demeanor about him, you know? Yeah, of course, you know. You're very much like him in that way."

"I've never met him, but I assure you, I'm nothing like him."

"Well, he knows how to charm the pants off a woman." With a sigh, she set her chin on his shoulder and closed her eyes. "By the time he asked me to dinner, I was ready to run off with him."

His jaw hardened against her face. When she sensed the judgment forming on his lips, she cut him off.

"Imagine living in a country ridden with cartel wars and poverty. Jobs are hard to come by. There's never enough food or medicine. Education is a pipe dream. As a woman, my value is insignificant at best. I was beaten by boyfriends. Abused by employers. My father fled before I was even born. I only had to look at my mother and her mother before her to understand that the life I was born into was the only one I would get. No matter how hard I worked. No matter how many beatings I endured. My existence would continue another forty years with no improvement. And that would be it."

"Then one day," he said, running a gentle hand along her back, "a dashing, wealthy man with a silver tongue walked into your life."

"Yeah. He singled me out from all the other girls, made me feel special, and treated me to the most expensive dinner I've ever had. He dated me for *weeks*. The lying, cold-blooded son of a bitch made me believe he was falling in love with me. Little did I know, his father had sent him after me. I didn't even suspect that he had cartel affiliations. That's why Miguel is so good at his job. Ever elusive and sophisticated, he lures girls in and wins their trust."

"Why were you targeted by his father?"

Her gaze darted through the bathroom as a crawling sensation prickled her scalp. Could she trust his word that there were no devices in here? What if the cartel was listening right now? She hadn't over-shared yet, but answering his question would end as gruesomely as the girl on the meat hook.

Sensing her tension, he glided his fingers through her hair. "Give me what you can for now."

She breathed in slowly, relishing the clean, masculine scent of his neck. "Miguel offered to help me escape to the United States, promising I would become a free, legal citizen and make more than enough money to pay off my debts. That was the pivotal, most important thing he could've offered me. I have years of debt, accrued through desperate means." Her chest squeezed. "I owe a lot of money to some shady collectors for reasons I'm not ready to talk about."

"Don't be embarrassed."

"I'm not." Sudden anger spiked through her, and she leaned back, causing water to lap around their chests. "I have regrets, but not about that. My debts were necessary. I did what I had to do and will never ever feel ashamed about it."

"Good girl." His touch on her cheek wasn't pitying or shaming. It was supportive. "The water's cooling."

He opened the drain and stood, taking her with him. Out of the tub, he led her to the settee, where he dried them both off and snagged two robes. Once they were wrapped in terrycloth, he lowered onto the seat beside her.

She hadn't finished her story, but he didn't press. He simply sat beside her, quiet and patient.

How much could she tell him? Not all of it. But if she gave him some insight into how the cartel trafficked girls, it might help him stop the operation. *If* that was his aim. She hoped.

It was more hope than she'd had in years, and that scared the shit out of her.

"Miguel offered me an installment plan." She hugged her waist, hating how naive she'd been. "All I had to do was sign a contract that promised to pay back the money I borrowed by working for his connections at a restaurant or factory. The going rate was thirty-thousand dollars. It sounded too good to be true. But hey, everyone gets rich in America, right? So I signed, ignoring the clause that said my family would be responsible for my debt if I couldn't pay."

"You didn't know what would happen."

"I should've known. There were so many warning signs. I ignored them all and paid for phony identification documents, adding to the debt I was already trying not to freak out about. Then I let him put me into a car with a strange man, who drove me to a strange city in California."

"What did you tell your family?"

"I didn't. I left Mexico thinking I would call once I was settled." Her chest constricted against the stabbing guilt. "I was taken to a place that was neither a restaurant nor a factory. There, in a filthy backroom packed with dozens of girls just like me, I was handed off to Miguel's *connection*, who told me I would be a prostitute. I would be charged room and board while I paid off the thirty-thousand dollars I owed them. Just like that, I went from being in debt to being in more trouble than I could've ever imagined."

He gripped her hand on her lap and bowed his head. At the edge of her vision, she watched his jaw grind and flex.

"I protested." She sat taller, recalling the painful memories. "God, I fought. I don't even know how many times I tried to cut and run. I even enlisted the other girls to rally with me. But every effort I made ended in agony. He beat me, starved me, kept me awake for days on end until I was too disoriented and weak to lift my head. That's when I caught a glimpse of my future."

"You knew you'd been trafficked."

UNSHACKLE

"I was starting to suspect that. I mean, I understood all along that what they were doing wasn't legal, but part of me still believed I was in control of my situation. I remember lying in that backroom—eyes swollen shut, ribs cracked, my stomach twisted with hunger—and that's when I finally came to terms with how grim my predicament was. I'd unknowingly sold myself to La Rocha Cartel and became an illegal immigrant, without a cent to my name. I didn't know where I was, had no access to a phone, and no options because no one allowed me to go anywhere alone."

He scooped her into his arms and held her tight across his lap. It was a big lap, warm and protective, reinforced by rock-hard thighs and a sense of security that shouldn't have made sense.

After Miguel, she'd sworn she would never be fooled by a man again. But her relationship with Miguel had never been *this*. He'd bought her expensive food, wooed her with pretty words, and fucked her without fireworks. Not even a spark.

He'd never held her, never embraced her without throwing her against the closest surface and rutting atop her.

Angling her head, she sought John's vibrant gaze. Sweet Lord, he was so close, regarding her as if nothing else existed in the world. She nuzzled so deeply against his chest she felt the rhythm of his heart in her soul, dancing with hers. Endlessly, he held her, his mouth nearly upon her lips, chasing her breaths with unspoken questions.

"I was out of options," she whispered. "What was I supposed to do?"

"You survive by doing what you're told." Green eyes glared down at her.

"Fuck that." She glared right back. "I will *always* fight. And I did, earning more punishments. More beatings. More days without food. But you know what? Every infraction ensured that he couldn't whore me out. Since I refused to be a prostitute, I was completely useless to him. So Miguel was called in. He drugged me, and a week later, I woke in the basement of *Casa de La Rocha*, only to become his personal whore. Then he gave me to his brothers."

He tucked her head beneath his jaw and caressed her hair. His fingers swam with strong, powerful strokes, every touch made to comfort a woman as if he'd been born and bred to it.

For long minutes, he just cradled her, arms locked around her back, controlling her breaths with the confident, steady rhythm of his chest. She shouldn't want him like this or find pleasure in his affection or feel so full of him.

Sleek with muscle beneath the terrycloth, his thighs shored up hers, supporting her like the arm tight around her back. An arm roped with cords of strength. The scent of raw masculinity, soft copper hair, flawlessly fair complexion, speckles of random freckles... How could she not admire his physical attributes?

The carved cut of his features lent him a rugged look, whether he wore a suit, gym shorts, or nothing at all. A unique mix of polish and roguishness, he was insanely gorgeous by any measure.

Oh, how she wanted to spend some time with his sinful mouth. Without an audience. With no agendas. She wanted to kiss him for no other reason than to savor his taste and delight in the tingles he delivered.

Dammit, get a grip.

She wiped a hand across her lips, but it didn't erase the hot, virile feel of him, the potency of his skin, the answering electricity in her blood. Every drip of remembered pleasure drew her deeper into his trap.

It was no use. He was too tempting, and she was too interested. So she let herself indulge, just for a moment.

Running a palm up his chest over the robe, she slid her fingers between the lapels to brush the sparse hair on his pecs. His breaths grew shallow, but he let her explore, bending down to kiss her head. Then he leaned back and watched.

Her hand roved lower, to his abdomen, to his waist, as lean and strong as a pillar, chiseled with sexy ridges and indentations. She spread open the robe to roam along the thin trail of hair, defined hipbones, and the proud, semi-hard length of his response to her touch.

"What's your real name?" he murmured.

She closed her eyes and pulled her hand away. "I can't."

"Hector La Rocha knew it. That's why he sent Miguel to take you." His American accent turned growly. "Why is the secrecy of your name so important?"

"What's your real name?" She moved to crawl off his lap.

He caught her waist and wrenched her back, wrapping her legs around his hips to straddle him.

"I'll give you mine..." He gripped her jaw and brushed his lips against hers. "When you give me yours."

"I want to tell you." Her heart hammered as she cupped his powerful jaw, his beautiful, sculpted face. "I'm scared. I'm..." She cast her gaze around the room, knowing if she gave him this information, it wouldn't happen here. "Hector was murdered in prison and—"

A strange, unguarded look swept across his features, there and gone too quickly to analyze. "What does his murder have to do with you?"

"His sons are looking for his killer. They believe the assassin belongs to a cartel in Colombia. Rest...ari...something."

"Restrepo," he whispered, his face paling. "The Restrepo Cartel."

"Oh, my God." She scrambled off his lap. "You're one of them? You work for a rival cartel?"

"No, I work for myself. Tell me what you know." He rose and grabbed her robe. "This is fucking important."

Adrenaline poured through her veins, and she spun, stripping free from the terrycloth in his grip and racing toward the door, naked.

"This is the first time I've heard any mention of Hector's death since I've been here." He prowled after her, all long legs and stony determination. "You're going to tell me everything."

"I swear I don't know anything about Hector."

He caught her at the door, slamming his hand against it and preventing it from opening. "How does his death involve you?"

"They're using me as bait."

"For Hector's killer?"

"Yes."

"Why?"

"I. Don't. Know." She yanked on the door handle, frantic to get on the other side, where there were cameras, where he wouldn't interrogate her and force her to talk. "Let me out."

"Do you know who killed Hector La Rocha?"

"No one knows. It could've been an inside job by one of the inmates. Probably an attack by the González cartel or one of the enemy gangs in the prison. I grew up in that city, and everyone wanted him dead."

He zoomed in on that last part like a laser beam. "You grew up in Ciudad Hueca?"

Her stomach dropped. She'd said too much. "It's a big city. Lots of people have lived there."

"More specifically, you and Vera Gomez." He bent at the waist, putting his face in hers. "What is your relationship with her?"

Heavy iron seemed to clog her ears, her blood running rabidly through her system, chilling her insides with fear. A cold sweat formed on her skin. Her lungs struggled for air as a vicious quiver overtook her body. She shook so violently she rattled the door at her back.

"I can't..." She gulped for breath, unable to maintain a whisper. "Please, you don't know what you're asking."

The steely intimidation in his expression faded, replaced with a storm of turmoil and something else.

"It's okay." He hooked his arm around her and pulled her against him, pressing his lips to her head. "Shh. Easy. Breathe with me."

She couldn't stop trembling, wrestling with the need to tell him everything. It was right there, all of it, twisting up her tongue. But she fought it. She had to. It wasn't just her life she was risking.

Maybe tomorrow. With a clear head and full night's sleep, maybe she could find a way to tell him who she was.

He read the decision in her eyes and released a slow breath. "Go to bed. I'll be in later."

The instant he opened the door, she fled to his room like a coward.

NINETEEN

An hour later, she rolled to her side in a bed of Klondike wrappers and groaned. She shouldn't have eaten that last ice cream bar. Or the six bars before it. But for a while, the delicious chocolate had kept her mind off the man making plans in the other room.

When he'd followed her out of the bathroom, he'd made a beeline to Tomas. After some very cozy whispering, they turned their attentions to their phones, their fingers furiously tapping out messages to whomever they were working with.

The Restrepo Cartel?

John didn't look like a Colombian cartel gangster, and he'd denied the accusation that he worked *for* them. But he knew the cartel. The mere mention of them had put him on immediate guard. In a blink, he'd gone from patient and affectionate to demanding and all business.

For a few minutes, she'd spied on him and Tomas from the bedroom, unable to hear their hushed conversation. When her snooping got the best of her, she stormed in and tried to join the discussion. The fuckers clammed up, moved to the bathroom, and locked the damn door.

They didn't trust her, and why should they? If she knew their plan, she could run straight to Marco with it.

What she'd witnessed the night she met them made sense now. The bromance hug they'd shared in the bathroom, the camera removed from the ceiling, the feeling that they weren't who they claimed to be... Whatever reason they were here, they were in it together, and it was all related to Hector's killer.

If they'd come to finish off Hector's sons, she sure as hell wouldn't stand in their way. At the same time, she didn't want to become an unintended casualty of war. Maybe John wouldn't throw her on a grenade to save his mission. But if forced to choose between his goal and hers, he wouldn't pick her. He didn't even know her.

She couldn't trust him. Not with her life or that of the one person she'd spent three years protecting.

With a heavy heart, she cleaned up the ice cream wrappers and waited for him to come out.

And waited.

And waited.

Eventually, she fell into a restless sleep.

The next morning, she opened her eyes to an empty room. The mattress lay untouched beside her. He never came to bed?

Her heart plunged to her stomach.

You're leaving in a few days.

Not without you.

His luggage was still here, his clothes draped over the chair.

"John?" She leaned up on an elbow, listening.

Silence.

Sighing, she threw back the soft coverlet, warm and bright with the kiss of sunshine, and went to investigate.

A full breakfast greeted her in the main room, eggs and high-fat pork still steaming beneath the dome covers. She forced herself to eat, needing the calories, but her nerves prevented her from tasting it.

Where was he? Was he already executing some reckless plan against La Rocha? Why hadn't he woken her? What if he got himself killed?

Cold dread slithered up her spine.

"You're deranged and paranoid," she whispered under her breath. "He's just working out."

She showered and got ready for the day. By mid-morning, he hadn't returned.

She went for a walk.

Keeping to the low-traffic areas, she followed winding paths through the gardens and ventured away from the main buildings.

All was quiet here in the morning, opening her ears to the sounds of chirping birds and busy bees. If she closed her eyes, she could almost imagine she was in a peaceful place, surrounded by nature and harmony. And freedom.

She'd forgotten what freedom felt like. To exist without someone watching. To run without someone chasing. To make decisions without painful corrections lashed upon her body.

UNSHACKLE

It had been so long she didn't know how to wish for such an ideal.

Lost in thought, she wandered until her feet carried her to the garage on the far side of the property. The door creaked as she opened it, the aroma of metal and engine oil tickling her nose. A comforting scent. Her sanctuary.

A camera hung high in the corner, tracking her movements until she veered around a large shelving unit and climbed into the back of an old Dodge Dart. The rusted thing might've been a rock-star muscle car in the sixties, but the only purpose it served now was a place to hide beyond the reach of the camera.

The paint was so worn and dusty only a few bits of blue shone through. The long backseat, however, made a comfy bed. She crawled in and curled up on the blanket she'd placed here forever ago.

From beneath the seat, she removed a small journal and flipped through the pages, reading her handwriting, savoring the words. Memory after memory filled her vision. Only good memories. The best ones from her childhood. She'd written them all down when she first arrived and added to them over the years. On her worst days, she read them, relived them, and rediscovered her smile.

But she hadn't come today to recharge with happy thoughts. She was here to think, weigh her options, and make a decision.

The last time she trusted a man, she got schooled. Miguel had promised her a dream and delivered a nightmare.

John had made no such promises, save for one.

He'd said he wouldn't leave without her.

It was a promise he couldn't keep. La Rocha would never let her go. Not for any sum of money. Not even at gunpoint. Well, maybe if it was a lot of guns. Like a whole army.

If John was connected to the Colombian cartel, he had the means to gather a militia. But he didn't know *where* to send them.

It all came down to the location of the compound.

She couldn't help him with that, but she could tell him what she saw on the other side of the wall. Maybe it was nothing.

What if it was everything?

The thought slingshot her heart into the garage rafters. She jackknifed up, shoving the journal beneath the seat on her way out of the car.

She wouldn't be naive, but being stubborn was just as bad. She could help him figure out the location without giving him her name. If his plan went south, or worse, if he betrayed her, her family would still have anonymity.

Decision made, she turned toward the door. But before she stepped into view of it, it creaked open.

She froze, her senses amplified as a single set of footsteps crunched across the dirt floor.

Heart thudding in her ears, she rounded the shelving unit and came face to face with Miguel La Rocha.

"*Ven aquí, mi pequeño zorro.*" He smoothed a hand down his tie, his Spanish a silken caress. "Are you hiding from me?"

"No. But had I known you were back, then yes, you bet your ugly ass I would've hidden somewhere you couldn't find me." She sidestepped, veering toward the door.

"Careful." Graceful and deadly, he moved with her, blocking her escape. "I'm not in the mood today."

"You're never in the mood, *pachuco*."

His lip curled with distaste. "Watch your mouth, or I'll find a better use for it."

A sting of fear knifed through her. "You didn't come here for a blowjob."

He would never force her to do that particular act. He knew better. But there were worse ways to hurt her.

"No." He stalked toward her, dressed in a black suit, shiny shoes, and hair slicked back like he'd just stepped out of a salon. "*Quiero tu coño.*"

"Nope. No sex." She eyed the door with longing as her insides tumbled through shards of ice. "Marco sold me to one of the guests."

"Ah, *si*. He *loaned* you to John Smith. You still belong to us."

She flexed her hands. If she didn't make a break for it, Miguel would rape her. His intent smoldered in his eyes and filled her stomach with lead.

"Mr. Smith doesn't share." She inched toward the exit, her pulse careening into the red. "I don't want to get in the middle of that, so I'll just go find him and let you—"

"I saw him." His mouth spread into a grin—the one she despised, for it promised a world of hurt. "I didn't get an opportunity to talk to him. Not with his tongue shoved down my sister's throat and his hands up her dress. They could hardly remain upright as they stumbled and groped like animals into her room."

No.

No, John wouldn't do that.

Except he'd told her that was precisely what he would do.

Agony like nothing she'd ever felt seared through her chest and wrenched a horrible sound from her throat. She rubbed a hand over her mouth, trying to conceal the shameful reaction. She didn't have feelings for that man. She couldn't. She fucking *wouldn't*.

UNSHACKLE

But her damn heart took a detour around logic and self-preservation and attacked her with everything it had. She couldn't breathe against the onslaught. It hurt too badly—the pounding, caving, internal pressure. She gripped her throat, her chest, and raced for the door.

"What's wrong?" Miguel was on her in a flash, an arm locked around her waist and a fist in her hair. Then he slammed her back against the wall. "You like this John Smith?"

He drew a featherlight finger down her temple, tracing the creases of her fractured expression, his gaze sharp and observant, seeing too much.

"You know how I feel about your sister." She gnashed her teeth, bucking uselessly in his grip. "You also know how competitive I am with her. If she's moving in on my turf, I'm going to fucking defend it!"

"*Oh, sí, lo sé.*" He flipped his hand over, brushing the backs of his fingers across her cheek, making her shudder. "You were possessive of me once."

"Until I saw the size of your dick." She held up her pinkie finger and wriggled it. *Delusional pervert.*

His expression clouded over, and the cords of his neck strained beneath his collar. She knew the strike was coming before he reared back his hand.

Hard knuckles collided with her jaw, and she deliberately fell to the dirt floor. Pain ricocheted through her face, bringing tears to her eyes. But it was better than the alternative.

Miguel abused her either through sex or violence. Never both at the same time. She'd baited him and taken the hit because she couldn't endure his rutting. Not after John.

John, who was currently fucking that bitch.

Her insides bled venom, and her vision tunneled in blinding rage. She had to go to him. She needed to see for herself.

Not once had she thought he would choose her over his mission. But had every touch, every look, every intimate whisper they'd shared been just a task for him? A means to gather information? Had he felt even a fraction of the beautiful chaos she felt when they were together?

Or was she just a stupid girl who continued to let herself be fooled by assholes?

"Are you finished?" She tipped her head up at Asshole *Numero Uno.* "Or do you want to hit me a few more times while I'm down?"

He scoffed and shook out his hand. "Not worth my time."

That much was true. He could beat or fuck anyone he wanted. He didn't care about her or his sister or any other woman in this godforsaken place. He was motivated by money, plain and simple.

As he glowered down at her, she thought he might kick her for good measure. But instead, he adjusted his tie, brushed off his suit, and strolled out the door.

It shut behind him, and she let out a stream of shaky air. Then she ran back to the old car, where she kept a few medical supplies just for these encounters and cleaned the blood from her face.

Everything hurt. Not from the punch of Miguel's hand, but from his words. From the images they evoked.

John with another woman.

She wanted his kisses to herself. She wanted his affection, his honesty, his story, good or bad. She wanted a shot with him because he was the first man in her life that made her feel significant.

She didn't need anyone to validate her worth, but it was really something to spend time with someone who treated her like an equal.

He'd bought her, and not once had he made her feel like a whore.

Maybe he was just really good at deception.

Stowing the medical supplies, she made her way to the estate. She knew where to find him, her steady strides carrying her to a part of the compound she'd avoided since arriving.

When she reached the breezeway to those lavish private quarters, she stopped. Glared at the door. And waited.

If John was in there, he wasn't having goddamn tea. If he wasn't in there, he was resourceful enough to find her.

Minutes passed. Hours. Years. She waited long enough to lower to the floor and take the weight off her feet. Then she waited some more.

At last, the door handle jiggled. The door opened, and she rose, standing twenty paces away with a vise around her chest.

The first thing she saw was red hair. He stepped into the breezeway, and her heart shattered upon the floor.

Head down, tie loose around his neck, the collar crooked and unbuttoned, he tucked in his shirttails and closed the door behind him.

Paralyzed, she couldn't move. No matter how badly her legs burned to run, no matter how hot the pain stabbed behind her eyes, she ached to see the look on his face.

He sensed her instantly, his head snapping up and gaze glowing, stark and bright. "Gina."

"That's not my name." She directed her focus at the door behind him, refusing to cry. "Did you get what you came for?"

His jaw set, and his presence grew dark. Menacing. "Go to my room. I'll be there in a moment."

He might as well have hit her, in her stomach, her chest, her face.

"Sure, John." She curled her lips into the shape of a smile and hoped he couldn't see them quivering. "Whatever you say."

UNSHACKLE

His eyes turned to hard slits. Yeah, he hadn't missed the livid sarcasm staining her voice.

The next thing he said was lost beneath the hollow drum in her head as she pivoted and strode away. The moment she turned the corner, she flew. As fast as her legs could pump, she sprinted away, away, away.

Then she heard him. The fall of his footsteps, racing, chasing, gaining speed.

She ran harder.

TWENTY

Bitter tears stuck in her throat like sand, and the dirt path blurred beneath the speed of her feet. Given John's longer strides, he would catch her quickly. She needed to reach the grove before that happened.

Because she was unraveling. Splintering apart by the second. She'd reached her breaking point and needed to be out of camera range when she self-destructed.

This was why she never subscribed to hope. There was always disappointment, and this time, it hurt beyond reason, crippling her with every punishing step.

When she'd learned of Miguel's betrayal three years ago, it had crushed her. But that despair wasn't in the same realm as what she felt now. As she sprinted harder, faster, she tried to process and compartmentalize her thoughts.

Her brain, however, wasn't working right. Grief watered down reasoning. Panic drowned out logic. She swam in anguish, unable to surface for air.

If only John would suffer the same betrayal. Heartbreak. Loss of love and faith. He deserved nothing more than to spend the rest of his days alone, miserable, and forgotten.

When she reached the field, she sensed him slowing behind her. He knew where she was going, their confrontation inevitable. She girded herself for it.

In the grove, safe from the cameras and shaded by the canopy of trees, she skidded to a stop and spun to face him.

"What happened to your face?" He stalked toward her, eyes blazing with temper. "Who the fuck hit you?"

"Doesn't matter." She blinked back tears. "No one can hurt me as deeply as you have."

"I want a name!" he roared so viciously it rattled her nerves. "Answer me!"

Her mouth opened, vocal cords and tongue working and failing to produce discernible sound. When she found her voice at last, it broke with a sob. "Miguel is back."

"He's a dead man." He charged closer.

She stumbled away, enlarging the space between them. "How could you fuck her?"

"I didn't." He pounced.

She dodged. "Liar! I saw you!"

Back and forth, they went. Lunging and darting, they circled each other through trees. He chased, and she evaded, nimble and furious. Then he caught her. Tangling her up in his muscled arms, he pinned her against the trunk of a large oak.

She grasped at breath and engaged her entire body in a frantic burst to break loose. Squirming and writhing and thrashing about, she snarled her wrath and spat noises of defiance.

"Shh." He remained calm, pressing a forearm against her throat, his strong, agile physique coiling about her like a kingsnake constricting a wriggling mouse. "It's all right."

"No! It's not all right! It's not fine!" Tears fell too hot and fast to stifle, further enraging her. "Nothing in my life is all right!"

She escaped from his hold only to be snatched again by a hand as unbending as stone. He hauled her back so forcibly her trapped limb felt as if it pulled from the socket.

Gathering her wrists, he held her against his chest, his mouth a severe slash. "My name is Luke Sanch."

"I don't give a fuck! It's too late." She bucked, her vision smearing with tears. "Let me go!"

"You *will* hear this." He shook her until her head tipped back and her watery gaze snapped to his. "I lived on the streets in Texas until I was nineteen. Until I was abducted, snatched off the park bench where I slept, by a small-town sex trafficker." He lowered his face to hers. "He raped me in his attic for eight weeks. Whipped me every day until I learned how to *enjoy* giving head and getting fucked in the ass. Then he sold me to a monster for six figures."

Good God. Her heart surged and spilled over in waves of denial. "You're lying."

"His name is Van Quiso. I was his fourth captive. Tomas, number three, escaped before I arrived. The day I was delivered to the man who'd bought me, Tomas—along with Van's other escapees—showed up, shot my buyer, and took me in. That was eight years ago."

"You had sex with a man? *You?*" She laughed upon a slapping breeze, her pulse stammering and mind whirling in flux. "How can I possibly believe anything you say?"

"Listen. *Hear* me. Then decide." He released her and ran a hand over the top of his head as though it might arrange the order of his thoughts.

"You have five minutes." She folded her arms across her chest.

"I'll see your defensive posture and raise you fifteen minutes."

"Eight."

"Ten. It's a complicated story." A rough finger crooked beneath her chin, forcing her head to turn so he could examine her swollen jaw. "Then I have a man to kill."

"Just spit it out." She knocked his hand away.

A crease appeared between his copper brows. He dragged a palm down his face, over his mouth, and stared off in the distance. Then he started talking.

He told her about a woman named Liv Reed, who gave birth to Van's baby in captivity. Van's father stole the child to control Liv. She became Van's accomplice. A captive-turned-captor. From there, the tale spun into the far-fetched land of make-believe, packed full of courageously gruesome misadventures about how Van's nine slaves escaped *then* befriended their captors. Afterward, they all banded together with the Colombian cartel to take down other sex traffickers.

Freedom fighters, he called them. As part of this vigilante group, he said they infiltrated the darkest corners of the world and fought evil-doers outside the boundaries of the law.

Seriously.

His story had no merit. Nothing he said sounded sane or credible in the slightest. What kind of fool did he take her for?

He was a liar and criminal. She'd encountered enough of them, so full of their own poison they couldn't fathom how a woman could resist drinking the Kool-Aid and falling in line.

"This isn't Gotham City, Batman." Her head pounded. "I live in reality."

"Open your mind." He stepped into her space and, for a moment, the sliver of air between them seemed to lengthen, over-stretched and fragile, like a strand of hair pulled too taut.

UNSHACKLE

She felt vulnerable beneath the masterful demand of his stare, his breath, the way he controlled her time and space. His proximity did terrible things to her heart and the temperature of her skin. Like a hallucinogenic, he altered her senses. A temporary high.

"Your ten minutes expired ten minutes ago." She stepped back.

"Listen to me, goddammit!"

"I *am* listening. You sound like a lunatic."

"You think I'm making this shit up? For what purpose?" He angrily threw his hands in the air. "I'm risking everything—my life, Tomas' life, our mission, the freedom of every woman here—to tell you the truth."

"Then you're a fucking moron."

"Jesus Christ!" He grabbed at his hair and pulled, growling through clenched teeth. "You are so…"

"What?" She fed on his seething rage and flung it right back, screaming, "What am I?"

"Frustrating beyond words. Stubborn as a mule. The most irritating, hardheaded, quarrelsome creature I've ever met."

"Why are you here, Luke?"

He went still, eyes locked on hers, the anger draining from his posture. "I knew the reason… I thought I knew. Until now." He blinked, and his eyebrows furrowed. "It seems every path I've taken, every decision I've made, all of it was meant to lead me here just so I could hear my name pronounced on your tongue."

Her lungs tightened, requiring a gulp. And another.

He drifted closer and touched her cheek. "Say it again."

She wet her lips, slipping, spiraling, losing her soul to four letters. "Luke."

"What are you doing to me?" He sought her with his hands, fingers gliding, fisting in her hair.

"Luke—"

"I didn't fuck her." He brought their foreheads together, his gaze digging deep. "I didn't touch her or kiss her or do anything I wouldn't want another man doing to you." His voice cracked against her lips. "Believe me. I need you to do that more than anything else. I need you *with* me. Please."

It was his plea that penetrated the ice in her chest. His mouth latched onto hers, seizing, heating as if attempting to thaw the blood in her veins.

She resisted for the space of a breath, then surrendered, opening upon a cry, her hands closing around his shoulder and neck.

His deep, sweeping strokes simmered with desire and something much deeper. This wasn't a kiss to satisfy a physical need. It was emotional. Poignant. Staggering. Sheer madness.

As she took the warm, firm, skillful lick of his tongue between her lips, she replayed everything he'd said. In his arms, pressed against him, she tasted the truth. She *felt* it. Every conversation, look, and touch they'd shared backed up his claim, driving away all argument and leaving only her belief in him, in his strength and unstinting heart.

This man, his body, his veracity, his gallant devotion to those he loved—he had endured the unthinkable, escaped the same hell she'd been trapped in, only to return so that he could make the world a safer place.

She saw that man the night they met and his agonizing turmoil when he gave a tortured girl a merciful death. He wasn't a killer of innocents. At his core, he was an avenging hunter.

He hadn't come for her specifically, but she believed him now. He wouldn't leave without her. And she wanted it. All of him.

In that defining moment between love and hate, heaven and hell, life and death, she lost her heart, definitively, irrevocably. It was his.

The kiss melted into mingled breaths, the air heavy with unspoken words.

"That man, Van Quiso..." She framed his chiseled face in her hands, absorbing his tragedy. "He raped you for eight weeks? That was your horrifying, unfortunate event?"

"The unfortunate event that led to a fortune." His expression showed no trace of shame. Only a pure appreciation for life. "Because of Van, I have the deepest friendships, a family who loves me, and a vital purpose. In that, I'm the wealthiest man alive."

He was the bravest man. Noble. Dauntless. Beautiful inside and out. She'd known it all along and had refused to accept it.

"This purpose..." She ran her fingers through his hair, unable to resist the urge to touch him. "How can I help?"

"I came here to find Vera Gomez and—"

"Vera?" A chill froze her bones, and her heart slammed against her ribs. "You knew that name before you arrived?"

"Yes. Her half-sister is Hector's daughter. Tula Gomez—"

"What do you know about her?" She staggered backward, pulse racing, emotions leaking, freaking the fuck out. "Where is she?"

"Until a few months ago, she was in prison." He stayed with her, eying her suspiciously. "She's safe now. Protected by my team. What's wrong?"

She clapped her hands over her mouth, strangled by a torrent of rising sobs. Confusion, fear, relief, joy—it all collided in a jumble of face-drenching tears.

UNSHACKLE

"I'm not interested in Vera." He caught her jaw, searing her with cold, angry eyes. "I only sought her out because her sister—"

"Tula is *my* sister." She grabbed his wrist, squeezing ruthlessly. "She's *mine*!"

"What did you say?" He shook his head, his face stark white as he stared at her, surveying her features as if seeing her for the first time. "That's not possible."

"I'm Vera." She closed her eyes, choking on the secret. "I'm Vera Gomez."

TWENTY-ONE

For the first time in nearly three years, Vera felt alive, electrified, and impossibly, wonderfully free. To say her name out loud, to verbally own it... What an empowering goddamn relief.

And petrifying.

She scanned the surrounding grove, her skin crawling with paranoia. The cartel couldn't have heard her. But if they somehow learned that she'd broken the rules, they would kill her and the only family member she had left.

Except Tula was safe?

"You said your mother is a famous actress." John...*Luke* stood unmoving, every muscle flexed to strike, his face an unholy sculpture of retaliation. "Vera's mother is dead."

She flinched. "I had to give you something. You wouldn't leave it alone. So I lied."

Panic paralyzed her, for even in the dark shade of the trees she saw the enraged glint in his eyes, the cruel set of his unforgiving mouth, the animosity in his stance. He was *not* happy about her dishonesty.

Without warning, he grabbed her. Imprisoning her neck in a startling grip, he bent it roughly to the side and pushed away the hair behind her ear.

"Stop!" She shoved at him, unable to free herself. "What are you doing?"

"You can't be Vera." His thumb pressed against the back of her ear, folding it forward. "She has a tattoo. A small black—"

UNSHACKLE

"Petunia. My sister's name is Petula, and when we were little, I called her Petunia." The memory surged fire through her sinuses, searing the backs of her eyes. "Miguel had the flower lasered off when I arrived here. There's a faint scar, like a stretch mark."

She knew the moment he saw it. His breath left him. His grip loosened, and he angled her face toward his.

"You speak English flawlessly." His gaze raked her, flinty with skepticism until it dipped to her lips. He lingered there then slowly returned to her eyes, his own widening with realization. "Tula is a teacher."

"Even before she earned her degree. She taught us both English when we were kids."

"You should've fucking told me."

"I couldn't. The cartel is watching her. When she was released from prison, they sent men to follow her. Marco said they would leave her alone as long as I went along with Silvia's ruse to be me."

"Silvia." He said the name with disdain, his mouth a puckered grimace. "Who is she?"

"She's the half-sister of Omar, Miguel, and Alejandro. The four of them share the same mother. Hector La Rocha's only wife. She died years ago. When Hector met her, he already had two children—Marco and Tula—from two other women. And his wife already had a child."

"Silvia..." He pinched the bridge of his nose. "So she's related by blood to Omar, Miguel, and Alejandro. Marco is her step-brother."

"Yeah, but the five of them grew up together. Raised as full siblings by Hector's wife."

"Add in Tula, and it's the fucking Brady Bunch."

"Where's my sister?"

"Colombia. Hidden and protected with the Restrepo Cartel. With my *friends*. I swear on my life that she's safe."

"I can't believe this." Her mind swam, and old guilt rose to the surface, unleashing a well of tears. "She served time in that brutal prison because of me. *Years.* If I hadn't called her that morning..." Her voice broke as wet trails streamed down her face. "She would've stayed in Arizona. But no, I had to make that damn call, and she dove head-first right into my mess."

"And fell in love." He cupped her face, his accent soft and rumbly. "Twice."

"What?"

"Martin and Ricky, my roommates..."

She remembered the names from his story. "Van's ex-captives."

"Yes. Three years ago, they infiltrated Jaulaso Prison as part of our on-going operation to take down Hector's sex trafficking organization. Tula was with Hector in that prison when they arrived. She went to Mexico because you called her for help. But if you were already enslaved here, how did you make that call?"

"Shortly after I arrived, one of the guards left his phone unattended while using the bathroom. I had seconds to use it and didn't know how law enforcement worked in America or if they would even believe my story and come. I didn't even know where I was. But I knew Tula would know what to do, that she would find the proper authorities and get help. So I called her, whispering frantically, *I'm in trouble. Need you. Come now.* When I lowered the phone to look up the GPS location, Marco was there. He'd been watching me, waiting until I called her, and destroyed the phone before I could tell her I wasn't in Mexico. It was a fucking setup, and stupid me, I fell right into it."

"Vera..."

"It's all my fault. I'm a worthless sister, and I know it. I never intended to involve her. God, I spent years keeping her oblivious to what was going on."

"Let's talk about that." He brushed a lock of hair from her face. "Why were you in trouble and accumulating debt?"

"Our mother..." Her scalp tingled, and though she was whispering, it sounded like a roaring gale in her ears. She searched the spaces between the trees and probed the field beyond.

"Tomas did another sweep of this area today. No one is listening. And he's out there just over that hill right now, guarding. He'll let me know if anyone approaches. Your mother..."

"Died of heart disease."

"I know, and I'm sorry for your loss." He stroked her cheek, her neck, his fingers constantly brushing her skin as if he couldn't stop touching her. "Tula gave us a comprehensive rundown of your background to help us rescue you. Hector tried to convince her that you were working for him, but she never believed that. She was adamant about your innocence."

"I miss her so much. I'm surprised you didn't recognize me. We look alike." She glanced down at the bones protruding on her frame. "Or, at least, we used to."

"She didn't have recent photos. The teenage girl in the pictures we saw..."

"I've lost a lot of weight."

UNSHACKLE

"You were beautiful then. And now." A heated look came to his eyes, lazy and hooded. Arresting. The transformation drugged her with narcotic desires, turning cravings into a full-blown addiction. "You're so fucking gorgeous. Sometimes, I look at you and think you're an illusion. You can't be real. Then you return the eye contact, and I feel like a teenage boy all over again. A fumbling, fuzzy-headed, walking hard-on."

The foolish, constricting organ in her chest jumped madly at his words, sinking deeper into him.

"Your sister told me that trouble often found you. But she didn't know about your debt." His fingers feathered along her collarbone. "What did your mother have to do with that?"

"Medical bills. So many. She was in and out of the hospital for years before she died. I had no money, no way to pay for her care. Doctors started refusing her, and I just… I couldn't tell Tula. She made it out of Ciudad Hueca, escaped to America through hard work, brains, and *legal* means. If I told her about the bills, she would've forfeited the life she'd worked so hard to achieve. She would've come home. I couldn't let her do that."

"So you lied to her." He held his chin tight to his chest, green eyes sparking beneath thick copper lashes.

"Don't you dare judge me."

"Judge you?" He half-laughed, half-groaned. "I'm insanely turned on. It's all I can do to not throw you on the ground and have my way with you. Your ferocity, selflessness, courage, outrageous beauty… I'm fucking beside myself with admiration. I won't even apologize for it, because you know exactly what you're doing to me."

"No, I…." A pulse burst in her temples, and her mouth went dry. Desire. It tore through her belly, low, deep, and ill-timed. *Focus.* "I want to hear about Martin and Ricky."

"They're two of my closest friends. I told you their histories with Van. They're also bi-sexual, openly now, with Tula. The three of them are in a polyamorous relationship."

"You're kidding." She couldn't imagine it. "My sister… In a threesome?"

"From what I saw just a few days ago, she's happily, ridiculously in love."

"Wow. How do you feel about that?"

"I don't swing that way, despite what I went through in Van's attic. I'm not the sort of man who shares women, not even with my best friend. But if they're happy, I'm happy for them." He leaned in, eyes glowing. "Ask me how I feel about *you*."

Heady warmth spread through her stomach and radiated to her thighs. He was so obscenely handsome and sexy, and that heady warmth gathered into a delicious ache. "How do you feel about me?"

"I'm here to free Vera Gomez by any means possible." He lowered his lips, settling his mouth upon hers, soft, barely touching, yet certain. "The task felt impossible because I didn't want to help the woman who pretended to be you. I wanted to kill her. Still do. Especially now, knowing the part she played in making your life a living hell."

His voice was a deep caress with an edge of vindictive fury as he kissed her face, her neck, nuzzling and touching her everywhere. The yearning he stirred in her was frightening, scrambling her concentration.

"I want the real Vera Gomez. Madly." He started to remove her clothes.

"Luke." Torn between lust and needing answers, she twined her fingers through his hair and dragged his mouth against hers, the flavor of mint clinging to her lips. "I have so many questions, and you make it damn hard to think."

"Multitask." He rubbed his thumb over her nipple through the shirt and slipped his tongue in her mouth. "I'm listening."

"I didn't know Tula's father was Hector until Marco told me." She groaned, letting him kiss her for a long moment, soaring in a decadent fusion of lips and tongues. "My mother took the identities of both our fathers to the grave. I'm still trying to get used to the idea that my sister is La Rocha by blood."

"I can tell you what I know." He lifted her into his arms only to lay her on a soft patch of grass. Then he stretched out on his side against her and toyed with the curly strands of her hair. "When Petula Gomez walked into Hector's prison, her name keyed him off. So he had a paternity test done without her knowledge. He was as surprised by her incarceration as she was. We don't know if her arrest was coincidence or—"

"When I heard about it, I suspected that the Mexican military mistook her for me. There are a lot of dangerous people looking for me in Ciudad Hueca. The more money I owed, the deeper I entangled myself with wanted felons. My sweet sister—"

"She murdered Hector in his prison cell."

"What?"

At her stunned gasp, a smile overtook his face. "She's fierce. Just like you."

As she spluttered a million questions, he gave her a full retelling of how her sister, a Spanish high school teacher, outsmarted and cut down the capo of La Rocha Cartel in prison. His hands roamed her body as he narrated each heroic detail and reassured her about Tula's safety and wellbeing.

UNSHACKLE

His mouth shared the story while his lips vibrated the words along her ribs and the undersides of her breasts, dampening the shirt. By the end, he had her shoes and jeans off, her top and bra pushed to her neck, and her breasts glistening with the moisture from his panting mouth.

With impatient hands, his thumbs caressed the pink peaks. They rose to his touch, hardened for his mouth, and throbbed for his tongue. She arched to bring him closer.

He was so heartbreakingly gorgeous. Everywhere. Sunlight dappled his skin to gilded ivory, his half-lidded eyes rich and gleaming with sensuous hunger. He slipped a hand between her thighs and stroked. She moaned, hot and clenching, even as she tried to focus on the conversation.

"Before now, I didn't know why the cartel was using me to bait Hector's killer." She smoothed a hand across his cheek.

The day's growth of whiskers tickled her fingertips, igniting sparks of delirious anticipation as she recalled the scratchy feel of that roughness along her inner thighs.

"Hector's sons knew all along that Tula was the killer." He slipped his tongue around her nipple and down her flat belly. "If they followed her like you said, they're aware she sided with the Restrepo Cartel."

"You know what that means, right?" Panic rose, and she sat up.

He pushed her back down. "They're expecting us to come for you."

"That's why Silvia stole my identity, Luke! She's waiting for you to seek her out under the belief that she's me. And you did. You went straight to her. What if she knows who you are?" She clutched a handful of red hair and yanked, dislodging his mouth from her hipbone. "What happened in her room today?"

"She doesn't know." He gripped her waist and covered her stomach with kisses.

His scent invaded her nose, clean and woodsy. If testosterone had a fragrance, he was it. Ineffable, potent, *distracting* man.

"Luke, if you don't start talking—"

"I teased her with words." With a sigh, he rested his cheek on her abdomen and met her eyes. "I made her believe I would fuck her if she gave me something. A vulnerable piece of herself. A secret. Anything that would prove she would choose me over the cartel."

"Miguel said you were groping and going at it on your way into her room."

"Miguel said he would pay off your debt and make you a legal citizen in the States."

"Fine. Point made. So what happened? Did she refuse your offer?"

"We went back and forth for over an hour. Lots of talking. Negotiating. Mind games. I really thought I had her."

"Because she wants you."

"Like a bitch in heat."

Her molars crashed together. "Had she told you the location, you would be fucking her right now."

"No." The sharp planes of his face turned to limestone, like a fairy-tale villain carved by a demented artist. But his skin, the blood beneath, and his entire aura were alive and real with a vengeance. "Had she given me what I wanted, I would've wrapped my hands around her throat and snuffed the life from her body."

"Brutal." She blew out a breath.

"Brutally honest. I'm going to end her, Vera. Her *and* her brothers. But first…" He nudged her naked thighs apart, bent, and ran his tongue along her slit. "I'm going to end this agony between us."

TWENTY-TWO

Vera swelled so hard and fast between her legs she went mad with her need for him. *Luke.* The only man who had ever held this much power over her.

He wasn't so cruel to make her beg. Dipping a wicked finger inside her, he sent rivulets of pleasure everywhere. A second digit compelled her hips off the ground, her entire body reaching for more, harder, deeper... Oh God, right there.

Fingers thrusting and lips trailing a line of fire to her clit, he buried his face and smothered her senses with his devilish mastery.

She clamped her legs around his shoulders, the delicious ache intensifying as she drank in the vision of him with new eyes.

This proud, virile, intimidating alpha had been forced to perform sexual acts with another man. But he also knew his way around a woman's body. A skill that could only come from experience.

Jealousy sank in its teeth, but more than that, she felt a kindred connection. He knew what it was like to be a slave. He'd experienced the terrifying loss of freedom. He understood her in a way no one else could.

And she understood him.

He'd raped her, not out of self-serving cruelty, but out of necessity to maintain his ruse. A ruse that followed justice.

"I forgive you." She quivered and heated beneath his attentive touch.

"I don't deserve that." He lifted his face, his expression blanking as he removed his fingers.

"I'm about to change my mind." She bucked her hips. "Don't stop."

In a tailored suit, tie tossed over his shoulder, red hair tousled, and gaze fixed upon her, he stole her breath. Her sanity. Then he smiled, and she lost her dignity.

"Fuck me, Luke." She squeezed her thighs around him. "Right now."

As she pulled on his shoulders, firm muscles rippled beneath her hands. He lowered his grin and kissed her deeply, claiming every inch of her pussy. She stabbed her fingers in his hair, gasping and weakening at the hum of his hungry groans against her sensitive flesh.

He lifted her legs with gentle pressure beneath her thighs, spreading her open and sinking his tongue. Her heart burst into a sprint, flooding thick, languorous sensations along her limbs. Dizzy energy and heat, crackling static and syrup, all of it spiraled through her blood and rocked her to her core. Wave after wave of stimulation slammed through her, centering in the bundle of nerve endings at the apex of her thighs.

His lips ground against her, firm and demanding. Then his fingers penetrated her achy depths, curling, pumping, freeing the last of her tension, and sending her tumbling into oblivion.

Strength left her body as she came, moaning and trembling through the stunning, blissful high. Then she crashed, clutching at the grass beneath her, anchoring herself back to reality.

He lowered her knees and removed his jacket and tie. Unbuttoned his shirt. Gave up halfway and tore open his fly. Removing a condom from his pants pocket, he rolled it on in record time. Only then did she notice his hands shaking.

"Luke." Dazed, she reached for him and opened her legs.

"Christ, you're a vision." His gaze traveled over her nudity as he lowered himself in the cradle of her thighs. "There's no place I'd rather be. I want to spend eternity inside you."

Where her heart had been, there was only him. A thrumming stronghold of love and raw intensity.

"Touch me." He held his hips above hers, his hand wrapped around the root of his cock.

She eagerly did as he asked, her questing fingers finding him hot and rigid, rubber over steel, twitching against the slide of her touch.

"Someday soon…" Hips rocking in her grip, he lowered his mouth to the hollow at the base of her throat and released a vibrating groan. "I'm going to feel you without a condom."

"I'll hold you to that." She teased the thick length of him, her thumb roving over the tip, her fingers squeezing.

"Enough." He grasped her wrist, stopping her. "You make me crazy, woman. So utterly outside of my control I fear I might burst."

She knew the feeling.

Repositioning, he took his time lining up. Gliding the plump head between her folds, he teased and tormented until sweat broke out on her brow.

By the time he pressed against her opening, the world had narrowed to the rapid hammering of her pulse. Then he pushed, sinking, stretching her body, taunting her with every agonizing inch in one unhurried stroke.

Once he was seated, his breath rushed out on a strained grunt, his face so close she could see flecks of gold in his green, dilated eyes.

"You're beautiful," she whispered.

"I was just thinking the same about you."

They were still. Throbbing, tingling, clinging to each other with their arms, their gazes, and the heavy rhythm of their heartbeats.

"It's never felt like this." She stared up at him, searching for the right words. "Like a surreal dream. I'm afraid to blink."

"My thoughts exactly."

"Why is it like this with you?"

"It's *us*. We fit, and not just on a physical plane. It's molecular." He began to move within her, drawing back, pushing forward. Tight, shallow strokes. "Indescribably elemental."

"Our souls match, and I don't think it's accidental. It's as if they were merged together long ago, separated, and are finally *re*connecting."

"Maybe we were born for this exact moment. Deliberately designed to find each other and bind on a level that we can't comprehend."

"Fated. You believe that?" She slid a hand beneath his shirt and touched his chest, the muscle there hard and ridged with definition.

"With you, anything is possible."

A sense of peace washed over her, but with it came a spike of fear. She wound her arms around his neck and pressed herself against him. "This scares me."

"Us? Together?"

"Us, *not* together. I'm terrified to lose this. Everything good in my life is taken away. I can't lose you, Luke."

He didn't make promises he couldn't keep. He knew the risks, the dangers they faced ahead, and seemed hellbent on keeping her in the present. Sheathed in her wet heat, he thrust hard and deep, setting a toe-curling rhythm and effectively ending all thought and conversation.

His tongue swept between her lips, drawing hers to him. The kiss deepened, and he palmed her backside, gripping her possessively while guiding her to meet his strokes, not too soft, not too hard, but so damn hot.

He surrounded her, filled her, moving in and out as if to satisfy a desperate craving to have her in every way, beyond sex, deeper than flesh, to own her once and for all. She needed no encouragement, lifting her hips, bowing her back, and riding the tide of elation.

The temperature rose, in the air, beneath her skin, between their lips. He rubbed his tongue against hers, and she gripped his shoulders, holding him, keeping him near, aching everywhere with a thirst that couldn't be quenched.

"Christ, Vera, you feel sensational." His hands found hers and held them against the grass above her head. "You're my salvation. My heaven. An unbelievable dream."

Strong fingers closed around her smaller ones, cradling her in the warmth of his palms, thumbs caressing with an intimacy that sent heat roiling through her body.

Her breasts felt heavy with it, her belly shimmering with butterflies. His eyes never left her face, except when he kissed her, which he couldn't seem to do enough. Her lips welcomed the slippery, warm caress of his tongue, and she opened to him, always, delighting in his rumbled grunts and panting groans.

Flattening a palm between her breasts, he slid it to her throat. Rather than fight him, she gifted him with a vibrating moan beneath his hand, followed by her joyous laughter.

He lost his rhythm, his smile blinding as it tripped across his beautiful face. Then he pressed his advantage, tightening those powerful fingers and controlling her airflow. She saw stars, and amid the burst of light, his gasps joined the sounds of her strangling breaths.

The man had a mean streak, but she wasn't scared. Not anymore. Her body danced for him, writhing in a wordless plea for his pain and his pleasure while trusting him to know her limits.

That realization only fueled her hunger. Liquid heat simmered through every extremity, welled in every hot crease, and sparked flames in all her pleasure centers.

Kissing her harder, he drowned her in his heat and dominated her with his tongue. He knew how to kiss so well it turned her brain inside out, his technique fluctuating between the exquisite softness of his licks and the ferocious bites of his teeth. All she could do was hold on and arch against him, thrusting her breasts against the hard press of his chest and whimpering her cries for more.

He sought, and she gave, mindless against the unstoppable pull to fuse everything of theirs into one—breaths, bodies, souls. He dragged her hips tight to his and clutched her ass with a bruising hand, fingers splayed, owning her over and over.

UNSHACKLE

Nothing in his touch hinted at uncertainty. Only conquering demand and desire. She tasted it in his mouth, felt it in the frantic grip of his fingers, and saw it burning the green depths of his eye contact.

God, she was wet. Rivers of arousal ran hotly between her thighs, squelching where he thrust, lubricating when he drew out and rammed in. Each time he left her, she felt a cold, horrifying emptiness. When he pushed back in, he was like gravity between her legs, a pressure so heavy and intense, so agonizingly wonderful that everything inside her clung to him.

"You're squeezing me. Strangling my fucking cock." He embedded himself deeper, a groan breaking from his chest. "Milking me before I'm ready."

"Stop whining." She laughed, shifting her hips and bearing down to torment him further. "Try to keep up."

"Witchy woman."

"Filthy ginger."

"That mouth… You wreck me." He captured her lips, his tongue sweeping in and devouring her next breath.

She could anticipate him now — the tempo of his quickening gasps, the slicking heat of his skin beneath her pressing fingertips, and the building of his thrusts into a rhythm that was entirely his own.

His hand cupped and caressed her breast, making her all the more grateful that he'd taken the time to remove her clothes. She moaned her body's acceptance with each impassioned kiss, touch, and grind of his hips.

She loved being naked with him, and as the excitement in her blood grew hotter, so did pulsations between her thighs. He was still kissing her, wielding his tongue like an instrument of seduction, licking her deeply, wildly, until she hurt with the need to come.

The hot friction of his cock grew sharper, more centered, and her breath burst forth, giving birth to shooting stabs of pleasure.

It started in the deepest, darkest, most untouchable recesses of her body and spread outward, the unbearable ache peaking and exploding within her.

Her cries were lost to his mouth, her fingers anchoring in hard muscle and knotting in the sweat-dampened hair at the base of his skull. She felt him in her soul, swelling, pulsing, shattering into a million pieces as he surrendered with her.

"Vera, Vera, Vera." He panted and shook, driving his cock into the back of her cunt, spurting, groaning, and digging himself as deeply as he could possibly go. "It's never felt like this. Ever."

They clung to each other long after the tremors dissolved. With his weight on one arm, he held her hand with the other as they lay in a pile of entwined limbs, catching their breaths and floating in their starlit high.

She drifted off to the gentle caress of his lips kissing her face and his fingers tracing the lines of her body.

When she woke, he was sitting up, his attention locked on something behind her.

Approaching footsteps.

As she moved to turn, he caught her shoulder, stopping her from exposing her nude front. "Get dressed."

Her clothes landed near her head.

He rose and stepped over her, his tension palpable. "What's wrong?"

Blindly reaching for her underwear, she stole a glance over her shoulder and locked onto Tomas' golden eyes.

Face pale, posture stiff, he looked like he'd seen a ghost.

"I need to talk to you," he said to Luke, his fingers clenching around the phone he held tight to his stomach. "Privately."

TWENTY-THREE

Unease trickled through Luke as he took note of Tomas' stark expression. "Start talking."

"This requires…" Tomas glanced at Vera while white-knuckling the phone in his hands. "Discretion."

"Speak freely in front of her. We had a breakthrough. Didn't we, Vera?" he called over his shoulder, watching Tomas' eyes bulge.

"Sure, Luke." Her clothing rustled behind him as she dressed. "If by *breakthrough*, you mean we had a come to Jesus, where you underwent the difficult but amazing realization that the reason you're here is for me, and therefore, I'm in charge from this point forward."

"We're still working on her listening skills," he said to Tomas. "Obedience training takes time."

She made a sound of exasperation. "I don't know what fantasy world you live in but—"

"If you don't cover your ass in two-point-five seconds," he said, stabbing a finger toward her naked lower half. "I'll blister it red."

"Fifteen seconds."

"Five." Slightly irritated and overly amused, he turned back to Tomas and nodded at the phone. "Tell me what's going on."

"Okay, just… Hang on." Tomas scrubbed a hand over his head, his gaze fixed on Vera. "I'm still processing. *She* is Vera?"

"Eyes up here while you process." Luke shifted, blocking Tomas' view of her getting dressed.

"I have something to tell you." Growing agitated, Tomas looked away. "But first, you're going to fill me in on what I missed."

Luke spoke quickly, hitting on the critical details about Vera's identity until she interrupted, expanding on his bullet points and overtaking the briefing. She zipped up her jeans and pulled on her shoes as she finished talking.

Tomas looked at Luke for confirmation.

"That about sums it up." His chest swelled as he regarded her, unable to hide the untenable adoration he felt for this woman. "Hector's sons suspect that Tula Gomez is protected by Matias. They're expecting a rescue party to come for Vera."

"So Silvia assumed Vera's identity and is waiting around for the rescuer to reveal himself." Tomas scratched his jaw. "It's smart. I mean, Silvia and Vera look a lot alike."

"That so?" Vera's eyes turned to threatening slits.

"You're prettier." Tomas shrugged.

She flexed her hands, temper fuming through her hot little figure.

"Calm down." Luke hooked an arm around her, pulling her against his chest. "Tomas, has that phone left your possession?"

"Not once since we arrived. The microphone is disabled. Physically disconnected. There's no way the cartel can hear us."

"All right. What's going on?"

"I fucked up." Tomas' expression emptied as he looked at the device in his hand. "In light of Vera being on our side, it makes it a little easier to say this… We need to leave. As soon as possible."

Dread curled in Luke's stomach. "I'm listening."

With a glance at the empty field behind him, Tomas began to pace, dragging a hand through his hair, fidgeting and restless. His uncharacteristic behavior put Luke on edge.

"When I was a boy…" Tomas stopped and stared off at nothing, his eyes clouding over. "I fell in love."

Stunned, Luke jerked his head back. That was the last thing he expected to hear from Tomas Dine. His friend had never brought a woman home for longer than a few hours. In fact, Luke had never heard a romantic word pass Tomas' lips.

"She died." Tomas bent at the waist as if overpowered by sudden, excruciating pain, and his voice took on a harrowing tone, making Luke's blood run cold. "She fucking died."

Vera reached for Luke's hand, her silence as heavy and bewildered as his.

"I was three years older than her." Tomas straightened, composing himself. "Her parents forbade her to see me. So I created an email account for her, wrote the address and password on a piece of paper, and gave it to her at school. She never had a chance to use it. That night, she and her entire family died in a car accident."

UNSHACKLE

A hot ember formed in Luke's throat, and he swallowed, grasping for words.

"I'm so sorry, Tomas." Vera stepped forward.

Tomas held up a hand, warding her off. "I started emailing her. I just...couldn't let go. I know she wasn't receiving the messages, but I needed to talk to her. Fuck, I needed her. She was my best friend. My girl. My whole fucking world. So I wrote to her through email. For years."

"The email account..." Luke cleared his voice, uncertain why Tomas chose this moment to tell him this. "It eventually exceeded its size limit, right?"

"Every few months, I cleaned it out. I had the password, and other than spam, I'm the only one who ever sends messages to it." He held the phone up and stared in a daze at the screen. "Every time I go in to wipe the history, I intend to delete the account. But I can't. The messages I'm writing are dangerous and stupid, but I can't stop. I couldn't..."

His spine tingled. "Dangerous how?"

"I've told her everything over the years. Every time a miserable goddamn thing happens in my life, I write it in an email to her. Every tragedy, every victory... Every *secret*."

"What secrets?" Luke stopped breathing, seeing the writing on the walls.

"*Our* secrets." Tomas met his eyes, his face bloodless. "I told her about Van and everything before and after."

"Like a journal." Vera touched her throat. "You write to her as if composing your thoughts in a diary."

"Diaries are forbidden in our business." Luke couldn't stop the ire from leaking into his voice. "No incriminating evidence. You know the rules, Tomas."

"Yeah. I fucking know, Luke." Tomas bared his teeth. "I always email her from a fake account and also... She. Is. *Dead!*"

"Do you use your real name in the signature? When you end each message?"

"Just *Tommy*."

"What about locations, events, missions? Other names, like Matias? Mine? Did you include any of that in your love notes?"

"Yes."

"Goddammit!" Luke seethed.

"The night before we came here, I sent an email from a new untraceable account, stating it was my last message. I intended to delete her account the moment we returned. I was finally prepared to move on."

"What happened?"

Tomas handed over the phone and paced away, gripping the back of his neck.

Luke woke the device, and an email app filled the screen. It showed the inbox of Tomas' fake account, which had one single message. A correspondence with *Tommysgirl*.

Oh, fuck, Tomas. What have you done?

He opened the email and read the initial message. It confirmed that Tomas had composed a short, incisive goodbye to *Tommysgirl*.

Knowing the cartel monitored every transmission, Luke was relieved to see nothing in the text that could condemn their operation.

"Did you log in to the *Tommysgirl* account from this device?" Luke asked.

"No, I'm not a fucking moron."

But there was a problem, and it stared back like a ghost from the grave.

Someone had responded to Tomas' goodbye email.

His pulse exploded as he opened it.

Tommy,

Please, don't stop messaging me. I've been reading your emails for ten years, anticipating and living each and every one. I'm sorry I never responded, but I didn't know what to say. At first, I felt terrible for logging into this account. I found the login information in the pocket of a coat that I bought at a thrift store.

I shouldn't have logged in, but investigation is my job. After your first few messages, I knew the account belonged to someone you lost. A girl you loved.

You grieved so painfully in every email you wrote I couldn't ignore it. You loved her deeply, and I felt it deeply. I'll be honest, I envied her. To be on the receiving end of such devotion... I wanted to be her.

But I remained silent. I listened and looked for signs of self-danger in your words.

Then your messages stopped. For ten weeks, I thought I lost you.

Until you wrote again.

You changed. After everything that happened to you during those weeks, you became so cold and angry. You needed an ear, someone to hear your story and watch over you. I was here for you, even when you thought you were alone.

Over the years, I felt your continuous evolution and adaptation to the dangers around you.

I know you better than you know yourself. I've heard every feeling and thought you sent. You needed this outlet. A place to share your thoughts without judgment or consequence. And through it all, I realized I needed it, too.

Please, don't end this. I know you don't know me. But I need to see you. I've been sitting on your emails for so long, worrying about your safety and telling no one.

I'm still worried.

I'm on the good side of the law, Tommy, and I sense you spiraling. You're trying to do the right thing, but you've gone too far.

UNSHACKLE

Meet me in one week. I know you have the means to fly home. Your childhood house is still abandoned. I'll be there at sunset on Saturday.

Come alone.

"Fucking fantastic." Luke passed the phone to Vera, his nerves strung like a live wire. "Assuming she's a *she*, does she know where you are now? That you're here on a mission that involves the Mexican cartel?"

"Some of it, yes. I wrote about gearing up for this operation." Tomas set his hands on his hips, his posture challenging and angry. "I'll handle it."

"Yeah, you'll fucking handle it." He strode toward his friend and lowered his voice. "She knows who we are, what we do, and every crime we've committed."

"She's also delusional."

"Whether you like it or not," Vera mumbled, her eyes on the email, "you've been talking to this woman for ten years. She knows your entire life story, and it sounds like she just wants to help. Like she cares about you."

"She's in law enforcement," Luke said.

"Doesn't mean shit." A vein bulged in Tomas' forehead. "She's probably a small-town cop. I grew up in the Chihuahuan Desert in Texas. She must be a local there. It's the only way she would've ended up with my girl's coat."

"She probably printed every message you sent. She could send those transcripts to someone who can destroy us."

"I said I'll handle it." Tomas gritted his teeth.

"La Rocha will see the email she sent, if they haven't already."

"There's nothing damning here." Vera gave the phone back to Tomas, her brow furrowing. "She was careful in her wording. She knows exactly what she's doing."

"It could be a trap," Luke said.

"I'll find her before Saturday and follow her." Rage boiled through Tomas' voice, turning his neck crimson. "I'll figure out who she is and what she wants before she ever sees me. *If* she sees me."

"You're taking this personally."

"Damn right, I'm taking it personally. She invaded my fucking privacy for ten years!" Tomas rubbed his hands down his face and reined in his temper. "I'll be careful."

He studied Tomas for a moment, gaging his friend's emotional state. Tomas was the calm one in the group. The level-headed, stern-faced, untouchable guy who handled his problems on his own and avoided drama like the plague. He would deal with this as quietly as possible.

"All right." Luke blew out a breath. "I'll arrange an escort with La Rocha to get you out of here."

"You're coming with me."

"No, I'm not. I planned this out before you showed me the email." He glanced at Vera, bracing for her fury. "I'm going to make an offer to buy Vera, an offer the cartel can't refuse, and you're going to take her with you."

"No!" Tomas and Vera shouted in unison.

"They won't let me go." Vera raged, shoving him in the chest. "Even if they agree, I won't. I'm not leaving without you."

"They will, and you don't have a vote in this."

"You son of a bitch." She spat a rapid-fire barrage of Spanish before switching back to English. "I will fight you and—"

He clapped a hand over her mouth and hauled her against him. "Shut up and listen." He looked at Tomas. "There's a massive wall surrounding this compound. How many properties in California are built like this one?"

"A lot," Tomas said. "Paranoid rich folks, hiding their dirty deeds from outsiders."

"But you've spent the last few days studying the layout, memorizing every detail. Once you're outside these walls, you're going to pass along those specs to the team. They can survey maps and fly a chopper over the region. You'll find your way back."

Vera squirmed and bucked in his hold until he released her.

"Great." She spun away, panting through labored breaths. "You can both leave and return with your army."

"I'm not going anywhere until every single person who hurt you is dead."

"Oh, for fuck's sake."

"What happens, Vera, if all three of us leave and never find our way back here?"

Her stubborn chin tipped down, her eyes blazing with rancor. "The girls remain enslaved, and the bad guys win."

"I won't let that happen. What did you see on the other side of the wall?"

"I'm not agreeing to this."

"Answer the question."

"A junkyard." Her nostrils flared with indignation. "The compound is bordered on one side by a massive graveyard for old cars."

A grin pulled at his lips as he turned to Tomas. "How many properties in California are surrounded by a stone wall and a junkyard?"

"Probably not more than one." Tomas' mouth twitched, unleashing a matching smile.

UNSHACKLE

"Excellent. I'll arrange your immediate departure and negotiate a purchase price for my mouthy new sex slave."

"You can go right to hell, Luke!" Tears welled in her eyes, and her hands balled into infuriated fists. "I won't let you do this. They'll kill you. No. You know what? Fuck that. *I* will kill you."

She could despise him and curse him to hell. He would still win.

Sending her far away from this place was priority number one, even if he had to shackle and gag her to see it done.

TWENTY-FOUR

Luke had to shackle and gag her.

By nightfall, Vera still wouldn't see reason. She threatened to scream his secrets from the rooftops if he forced her to leave without him. She would never blow his cover, but he didn't put it past her to race off and hide somewhere on the property.

He didn't have time for that. So he bound her with rope and silenced her with a strip of cloth. Then he ordered Tomas to carry her to the waiting limo. The sight of her thrashing and heaving with every fierce breath in her body gutted him at a depth that couldn't be mended.

He was hurting her in his attempt to save her. Taking away her right to choose. Removing her free will. It was the worst possible thing he could do to her.

Except risking her life.

From where he stood, ensuring she lived superseded all ethical and moral obligations.

Maybe his decision was selfish, but at that moment, watching Tomas wrestle her into the back of the limo, he realized he would never survive her death. He couldn't even consider the possibility.

He remained on the sidewalk, stomach knotted, lungs collapsing, fighting like hell to maintain his ruse as a wealthy, suit-wearing, heartless slave owner.

His face felt like marble, his numb hands clasped loosely behind him. He was a stone-cold monster, who had just purchased a trafficked girl.

His first and last.

UNSHACKLE

The negotiations with Hector's four sons had dragged out for two hours in Marco's lavish office. Over tequila and cigars, Luke cajoled, and the brothers strung him along with no real commitment to his offer.

His top price was one million. Six-hundred thousand of that was his own money. Van had given each of his ex-slaves that amount. It was the only money Luke had to his name.

Before he left Colombia, Martin and Ricky had offered their portions, as well. They desperately wanted Vera to be returned to Tula. Tomas had also thrown his share into the pot.

In total, Luke had two-point-five million to bargain with. But he'd had no intention of draining his friends' bank accounts.

He was a fool.

Marco haggled with him for two hours. Marco's brothers wanted no more part of the negotiations. Selling Vera meant surrendering their bait for their father's killer. Of course, they didn't know that Luke was privy to Vera's true identity.

It had been several months since Hector died. Vera believed they were losing patience, and it wouldn't be long before they killed her. She was a liability. A flight risk. Too smart for her own good.

In the end, Luke bought her freedom for three million dollars. A bid the cartel hadn't been able to refuse.

If they suspected he had something to do with their father's murder, he was the one they wanted anyway. Not Vera.

To seal the deal, he announced that he would be staying on the property for the remainder of the week with the possibility of purchasing a second girl.

Dollar signs glowed in four pairs of gluttonous eyes.

Another three-million-dollar purchase? He didn't have that kind of money. But they didn't know that.

When he'd left Marco's office, he'd sent a message to one of the burner phones that Matias Restrepo carried. The cartel *jefe* agreed to cover the half-million that Luke was short for the purchase of Vera.

It was a huge ask. Camila's husband had already invested a hefty chunk of change into this operation. If Luke succeeded in taking down La Rocha, maybe he could liquidate La Rocha's assets and recoup the investment. But there was no guarantee.

There was no guarantee he would ever see his friends again.

From within the limo, Tomas signaled him to approach. With a calming breath, he moved on lead feet and bent into the open doorway.

Shackled to one of the long benches, Vera sank her teeth into the gag and glared at him with pure venom in her eyes. A wet sheen shimmered along her lashes and welled in the corners.

He felt sick to his stomach.

Straps crisscrossed her torso, restraining her to the seat. She still fought, bucking and snarling, her chest rising and falling with the furor of her breaths as a livid flush reddened her cheeks.

She was pissed. But more than that, she was terrified. *For him.*

Tomas perched beside her, donning a stoic expression. Across from them sat their escort. Probably the same man who had accompanied them here a few days ago.

"She doesn't look happy to be your new toy." The man chuckled.

"Are any of them happy at first?" Luke forced a smile with predatory teeth. "Give me a minute with her."

With a nod, the man slid out of the limo, and Tomas followed.

He shifted back to Vera and cupped her face. "I know you're angry."

Muffled screams clotted the air, her eyes shouting viciously over the gag.

"Shh." He kissed the curve of her neck, the hollow between her collarbones, and the rough fabric over her mouth. "I'm yours. From now until the termination of my soul, I belong to you and you alone."

Tears stole along her cheeks and dampened the gag. He leaned in and caught the streams with his thumbs, then his lips. Suddenly, viscerally aware of the pounding of his heart against her breasts, the feel of her soft curls against his neck, he wrenched her legs open and knelt between them.

Without a moment's hesitation, their bodies sought, instantly gravitating together with the torment of their impending separation. He pressed his lips to her face, her heart, and everywhere, claiming her with each kiss, each ragged breath drawn as one. When the violence of her grief grew too great, he touched her with worshiping hands, caressing her skin and clasping her body to his.

She began to tremble, crying out in muzzled, wordless misery, then again when he pulled away.

Tremors of anger rocked him, ignited by the salty taste of her tears on his tongue and the primal, instinctual impulse to never let her out of his sight.

But above all, he needed her safe.

Behind him, Tomas cleared his throat. Then a black hood was pressed into his hand.

"Don't give Tommy any trouble." He slipped the material over her head and held it against her brow. "I'll see you soon."

She whimpered, a desperate edge of anguish that locked up his lungs. He might never see her again. He trusted Tomas to keep her safe, but Luke would be on his own. He might not make it out of here alive, and she knew it.

UNSHACKLE

It was why she had to be shackled. His little fighter would've never willingly left him.

I love her.

The realization rose from deep inside him and fired through his bloodstream. He would tell her when they reunited. He would see her again if only to give her the three words he'd never given anyone else.

He held her gaze a moment longer, kissed her lips around the gag, and lowered the hood.

She didn't cry. Didn't kick or growl. Instead, she composed herself, sitting calmly in utter blackness as he backed away.

So much strength in this woman. He was completely and irrevocably besotted.

Passing Tomas on the way out of the limo, he gave his friend a squeeze on the arm. Then he turned and ambled toward the entryway, unable to breathe.

There, he watched the cartel escort climb in. He didn't move as the limo pulled away. He didn't take a breath until they vanished around the bend. He couldn't help it. His precious, beautiful future was in that car, and she was on her way to safety.

The most important part of the operation had been accomplished. She would be reunited with her sister by tomorrow morning.

Now he had to finish this.

As he made his way back to his room, his mind circled around the plan he and Tomas had devised after the meeting with Marco. He couldn't sit around and wait for backup. His team could take weeks to locate him and mobilize an attack.

They might never find him.

He needed to learn the exact coordinates of the compound and get the fuck out of here. Then he would return with his team.

Now that he knew who Silvia was, he wouldn't waste his time seducing information from her.

He needed her key card.

Tomas had given him the layout of the property, including the location of the monitoring room. Despite Vera's seething reluctance, she helped by telling him how to find the breach in the wall. Then she told him about the armory.

Beyond the largest pool, nestled deep in the garden, stood a small concrete building. She claimed it housed enough weaponry and ammunition to take down the entire cartel. It was also monitored by multiple cameras and could only be accessed with the top cartel members' key cards. Silvia was among that membership.

Loading up with guns and crawling through the hole in the wall was a life-or-death option only. If he broke into the armory, they would know. He could only resort to that if his identity was discovered.

Hell, it might come down to exactly that because his plan was shoddy as hell.

He intended to steal a cartel member's street clothes and cover his hair with a hat and bandanna. Disguised as a thug, he would use Silvia's key card to enter the monitoring room and steal a peek at the monitors that showed the surrounding area. With any luck, no one would question him before he turned heel and left.

He had about a five-percent chance of success, and that was optimistic.

First, he had to spend some time with Silvia.

A few hours later, he ordered an old fashioned with rye whiskey and found a quiet corner on a vacant veranda. Sprawled in a comfortable chair, he waited.

She didn't make him wait long.

Pausing in the doorway, Silvia wore a red body-clinging dress and matching lipstick. Black hair, black eyes, she looked like Satan's mistress. He hid his repulsion and pretended not to notice her.

She approached his chair, placing one strappy heel before the other. Heel to toe, heel to toe, she really put a lot into that walk. Always trying too hard. This time, it was a waste of effort.

"Good evening, handsome." She lowered into the seat beside him.

He sipped his drink, brushed imaginary lint off his suit jacket. Then he gave her his attention. "Good evening."

At the edge of his periphery, her key card hung from the front of her dress by a claw clasp. The same clasp that attached his plastic card to his pants pocket.

The cards looked identical. A swap should be effortless.

She leaned in, giving him an eyeful of plumped-up cleavage. Heavy mascara lined her lashes, hooding a gaze that darkened with hesitant hunger. She wasn't certain of his interest. Hell, he'd teased her enough over the past couple of days to leave her hot and bothered and unsure about everything.

"Why didn't you leave with your new purchase?" She trailed a finger along his arm.

"I have unfinished business here." He raked his gaze down her body and lowered his voice into a suggestive caress. "Something I want."

"If that's true, why did you spend three million dollars on another woman?"

"Because I can."

"But why *her*?"

"The one I want said she couldn't be bought." He traced a finger along the curve of her jaw.

Her breath caught. "For that much money, my brothers would've made an exception."

"Good to know." He bit his lower lip in a way that women seemed to love. "I might make another offer, but I always sample expensive things before I invest in them."

"Is that right?" She purred, an actual feline sound in the back of her throat, and rubbed her face against his touch like a contented cat.

He wanted to backhand her, which, even for him, exceeded his tolerance of violence. He adored women and treated them as such.

But not this one.

This one, he ached to kill.

Stifling those urges, he reclined in the chair and sprawled his legs in a blatant invitation for her to join him.

She did instantly, crawling over his lap and straddling his hips. Then she touched him, her hands wandering and exploring his body unfettered. He allowed it, biting back bile and guilt.

He'd told Vera he belonged to her, and he meant every word. But Silvia's key card was hanging against his chest, so close, right fucking there.

"You're so goddamn sexy." She slid her palms over his shoulders. "So big and strong and beautifully formed."

As she groped his muscles and nuzzled his neck, she went on and on about his physical appearance. He barely attended, his focus on his goal, waiting for the right moment.

When her breaths sped up and her eyes clouded over with lust, he knew she was lost in her aching need, thoroughly distracted by her greedy desires.

Without warning, he yanked her tight, bodies flush. In the span of her startled yelp, he unclipped the card from her dress. Her hands flew to his face, her hips abhorrently grinding as he switched the cards and secured his to the same spot on her bodice. Her card went into his pocket under the guise of his knuckles teasing her inner thigh.

She bent in for a kiss.

He captured a hunk of her hair, stopping her an inch away. "I do the kissing, not the other way around."

Her ruby lips bowed downward into a moue of frustration.

The easy part was done. Now he needed to untangle her from his body before she put her hands on his cock.

He wasn't hard, not even a little. The very thought of her touching him stirred nausea in his stomach.

Too late.

Her fingers slipped past his guard and caught him between the legs. He didn't move, didn't twitch, for fear he would knock her across the room.

"You're not into this." Her grimace deepened as she squeezed his limp dick. "Almost as if you're not into *me*."

"I've been *very* straightforward about what I'm into." He removed her hand and chose his words carefully. "While you match my physical specifications perfectly, you fail to meet other expectations."

"You like a fight."

"Always."

"You want me to struggle and cry while you dominate me." Her throat bobbed. "You want to rape me."

No. He didn't want anything to do with her. "Yes. Brutally."

"I see." Her eyes flared, and the skin on her neck pulled taut. She wasn't into that. Not at all. "How would that work if you bought me? Would you rape me *and her* at the same time? Or would you assign us days of the week and alternate between us?"

"I would do whatever the fuck I wanted because I would own you."

"The day you arrived, you said you would buy my freedom, and when I walked out of here, I would be free."

"I'm revising my offer." He cupped her throat and applied pressure. "You require a leash."

That did it. She shoved off his lap and straightened her dress, her nostrils pulsing with indignation. She brushed a hand over the key card, checking its presence.

Standing taller, a spark of cruelty lit her gaze. "Have you heard from your bodyguard?"

Alarm spiked through him. He started to reach for his phone and changed his mind. Tomas wasn't supposed to make contact until he put Vera on Restrepo's plane and began his drive to Texas to deal with the email issue. That would've taken hours.

Except it had been hours.

He swallowed down his rising panic. "I'm not expecting a call."

With a smirk, she curled a lock of hair around her finger and angled her face to the camera in the ceiling. "Turn his service back on."

What the fuck? They'd cut the signal on his phone?

All the blood in his body drained to his feet. His skin prickled, and his stomach bottomed out as he removed the phone from his pocket. His hand shook as he turned it on and flipped through the screens. No missed calls. No texts. She was fucking with him.

Before he could release a relieved sigh, the phone started buzzing, blowing up with incoming texts as the service came back on line.

UNSHACKLE

The first message had been sent three hours ago, and when he absorbed the words, his heart stopped.

Unknown: Your tie is crooked.

It was a code phrase, designed to convey that something had gone terribly wrong. Only Tomas knew that code.
More texts followed, timed several minutes apart.

Unknown: The escort took her.
Unknown: Kicked me out of the limo on an abandoned road and drove off with her.
Unknown: Hello?
Unknown: Answer the phone.
Unknown: I'm sorry. I couldn't stop them. I was forced out of the limo at gunpoint.
Unknown: I don't know where they took her.
Unknown: Are you getting this?
Unknown: Where are you?
Unknown: I'm tossing this phone. Will be in touch.

Pain detonated in his chest, lungs, and throat. The roar of his heartbeat thrashed in his head, and terror paralyzed him, making it impossible to think.
The cartel had Vera.
She wasn't safe.
They knew. They fucking knew he'd been playing them in an effort to rescue her. They were going to hang them both from meat hooks.
Silvia watched his reaction, studying him too closely, way too hard. He kept his expression in check, and in the next breath, he flipped a switch.
The calculating side of him took control, squashing all fear, wrath, and love. He extinguished every ounce of emotion and let the coldness creep in, numbing his limbs and deadening his heart. He blinked, drew a steady breath, and focused on the facts.
If his cover was blown, they would've killed Tomas. And Vera, too. Unless they kept her alive to use her as a hostage to question him.
Why would they question him if they knew he was the rescuer they'd been waiting for? Why had Silvia tried to fuck him just a moment ago?

There was no way the cartel knew he was part of a vigilante group or that their lives were targeted by such a group. The brothers simply wanted to retaliate against Tula Gomez, their father's killer, and whomever she'd sent to save her sister.

If they truly knew Luke's identity, he would've already been tortured and cut into pieces.

This was another game. A test. Maybe they suspected that he'd been sent for Vera, but they weren't convinced enough to risk his backlash if they were wrong.

From their viewpoint, holding Vera as a hostage was forgivable. She was just a whore. Killing Luke's assistant, however, was just plain bad for business.

So they let Tomas go, effectively removing Luke's bodyguard from the property with no way to return.

The cartel didn't know that during the hours that Tomas had been texting Luke, he would've found another phone—would've stolen one from a random stranger if necessary—and contacted their team.

The Freedom Fighters would've learned at least an hour or two ago that Luke was in trouble. They just had to find him.

But they had intel now. They had everything Tomas would've passed along.

Luke turned his attention to Silvia, taking his time to speak.

"Why?" Slowly, casually, he rose from the chair and pocketed the phone. "I paid for her. You received the money. Alejandro assured me that you honor your deals."

"It's just a technicality. A hiccup in the deal. I'm sure we can work it out."

"Explain the *hiccup*."

"I'll show you. Follow me." She pivoted and strode away, giving him no choice but to follow.

TWENTY-FIVE

As Silvia led Luke outside, a disarming chill saturated the air. Maybe it was just him. His skin rippled with the prickles of a cold sweat, and the drum of looming doom sounded in his ears.

Unarmed and without backup, he had to keep his wits about him. Maintaining his composure and talking his way out of this were his only lines of defense.

Unless his cover was already blown. In that case, he was a walking corpse.

She escorted him along a trail through the lush garden, her heels carefully maneuvering the cracks in the cobblestones. He considered making a break for it, his flight-or-fight instinct gripping him hard. He could outrun Silvia with ease, but he couldn't escape the cameras and the armed guards.

Even if he could, he would never leave Vera. If she was even here.

The path led to a small pond encircled on all sides by dense trees. The moonless shroud of nightfall cast the water in inky black, the muddy edge occupied by half a dozen man-shaped silhouettes.

Nothing like walking into a waiting throng of armed, distrusting, coldblooded murderers. His anxiety surged into overdrive.

As he approached, he squinted through the darkness, searching for Vera's small frame among them.

Marco, Omar… All four brothers were here, dressed in a range of suits and street clothes. A few others in the cartel accompanied them.

No Vera.

"Where is she?" Luke paused a few feet away and wiped his slick palms on his pants, trying to control his nerves.

"Did you know," Miguel asked, tilting his head, "that the black widow is the deadliest spider in America? At times, the female eats the male after mating, hence her name."

He could've gone without that visual.

Impatience dogged him as he probed the pond and surrounding trees, his temper growing short. "I paid a lot of goddamn money for that girl, and you fucked me over. If this is how you do business, I will—"

"Careful." Miguel's accent sharpened. "A smart man would think twice before making threats against La Rocha."

"Fuck you. Where's my property?" As the insensitive question left his lips, he detected a disturbance at the center of the pond. His pulse lost rhythm, spiraling turbulently, his eyes refusing to adjust in the darkness. "What's out there in the water?"

"The black widow's bite is venomous." Miguel slid a hand down his tie, needlessly straightening it. "But not usually deadly to humans. A single bite doesn't have the potency. But many bites? Dozens attacking at once, especially when threatened? That would be fatal to a small woman. I've seen it with my own eyes." He chuckled. "Nature is not merciful."

Tension breathed down his neck, and vertigo threatened to buckle his legs.

Spiders.

A pond of tenebrous water.

Nothing foreboding about that.

Put Vera in the middle of it, and they couldn't have orchestrated a more sinister nightmare.

If the desired effect was to scare the ever-loving fuck out of him, job well done. His throat felt like smoldering ash, his chest a cavern of dry ice.

But he only showed them the man he wanted them to see—an arrogant prick whose time was invaluable. "Get to the point."

"Omar." Miguel nodded at his brother.

Omar flicked on a portable spotlight. The blinding beam shot across the pond, illuminating two shapes at the center.

An unfamiliar man sat in a kayak with a paddle resting across his lap. A few feet from him, a small dome floated on the surface, wrapped in some sort of metal mesh, like the screening material in windows. It allowed in airflow and light, but little else.

He didn't have to look closer to know what he'd find inside. The contraption was only slightly larger than a human head, and that was what it held.

Vera's head.

UNSHACKLE

With her body submerged to her neck—presumably anchored to the floor of the pond—her eyes squeezed shut against the glare of the spotlight. Her mouth angled above the water, but she couldn't shout or make a sound because her lips were stretched open by a spider gag.

The metal ring sat behind her teeth, holding her jaw in a gaping O. A buckle secured it around her head, and four steel legs fanned out from the ring. Those curved legs extended over her chin and cheeks, preventing her from turning the ring in her mouth while forcing her jaw wide open to accept anything into her throat. Like probing fingers. Or a cock.

Or a black widow spider.

His stomach churned. His heartbeat tightened, and his insides ran too hot and too cold as he fought the excessive need to swallow. He couldn't trust himself to speak without a quaking voice.

"She can put her head underwater." Marco stepped to Luke's side, his dark features ever darker in the thickness of night. "Though I don't think she'd enjoy that. Have you ever tried to keep your throat closed while your mouth is held open underwater?"

He'd learned many survival tricks during his time in Van's attic. But nothing related to water play.

"She can't dislodge the mesh hood," Marco said. "It's connected to her life vest. Her hands are bound, and her feet are tied to a cement block, keeping her vertical."

"Why?" He girded his backbone, forcing strength in his tone. "What's the point of this?"

"We don't trust you, John Smith."

"I assure you," Luke scoffed, "after this double-crossing bullshit, the feeling is fucking mutual."

"We haven't double-crossed you. We're merely being cautious. See, we investigated you, as we do with all our guests, and we can't find a single piece of information about you."

"I didn't give you a real name."

"No one does. We use facial recognition software. You can't hide your face in public these days. Not with all the cameras spying and recording your every move. Except you've done exactly that. It's as if you don't exist, and that makes you…questionable."

Luke had fallen out of the system when he ran away from home. When Van abducted him, no one knew he was missing. No one cared. He was as good as dead. After he escaped, he remained dead. He never used his real name. Never had an encounter with the law. When Cole Hartman joined their team, he erased all of the Freedom Fighters from every hidden corner of the Internet and dark web.

None of them existed.

"This shouldn't surprise you." Luke squared his shoulders, watching Vera hold her shit together at the center of the pond. "If a man has the means to spend three-million dollars on a slave, he should certainly be able to cover his tracks effectively."

"Yes, we've taken that into account. This is why your assistant is still alive. Once you've answered our questions, your property will be returned to you, and your life will resume unmolested."

"I don't owe you a goddamn thing." Fury flushed through his body, hardening his muscles. "Release her."

"Who do you work for?"

"Myself."

"What is your business?"

"None of your fucking business."

"Mr. Smith." Silvia sidled up beside him and stroked his arm. "You can tell us the easy way. Or we can force you the hard way."

"You think I would choose a girl over the critical confidentiality of my business?"

"A girl you paid three mil for?" Silvia narrowed her eyes. "That's the question, isn't it?"

"You've threatened me, and now it's my turn." He directed his gaze over her head and met Marco's eyes. "You can apologize and escort me and my purchase directly to my plane. Or you can suffer the backlash of my exceptionally powerful and ruthless business partners. I'm connected, Marco, deeply and dangerously, and I will turn every magnate within my far-reaching circle against your cartel. You are fucking with the wrong man."

That much was true. Between Van Quiso, Tiago Badell, and Matias Restrepo, Luke had some brutally violent allies. Add Cole Hartman into the mix, and they were ingloriously, terrifyingly unstoppable. Whether or not he and Vera died tonight, La Rocha would be annihilated. There was no doubt.

Marco stood so still he didn't seem to be breathing. Only his eyes moved, scouring Luke's blank expression. Without looking away, he slowly raised an arm and snapped his fingers.

For an asinine moment, Luke thought he'd won.

Until the man in the kayak tossed a lid off a large container and poured the contents atop the dome on Vera's head.

Luke lost his mind as a cascade of teeming, shiny black bodies glimmered in the spotlight, tumbling down the mesh sides and hitting the water. Vera's face froze in a silent scream and quickly vanished behind a writhing wall of spiders as they raced back up the dome, climbing over one another to safety.

UNSHACKLE

The kayak jostled, rocking wildly beneath the man's sudden and frantic attempt to paddle away. The oar whirled around him as if he were fighting off an invisible monster. Within seconds, he was beached on the shore and running, shouting in Spanish, and slapping at his arms.

"Black widows don't like water." Miguel's amused voice penetrated the panic that lay siege to Luke's mind. "Eventually, they'll find their way into her hair and slip under the net. Once they start biting, the venom will attack her nervous system. With her diaphragm in paralysis, she'll struggle to breathe. Severe abdominal pain will set in, along with tremors in her legs, vomiting, profuse sweating, and swollen eyelids. The number of bites and the depth of the punctures will determine how quickly she dies. That's if she doesn't drown first."

Fear was a vicious, quivering entity inside him. Tunnel vision invaded, and light-headedness crippled him with an overwhelming need to sit down before he fell down. But more than that, he was ruled by the savage, reckless urge to run to her. His legs contracted and burned to go, go, go. Now!

That was what they wanted.

This was the test.

Dozens of eyes watched him from all directions, waiting for him to strip his disguise and rescue the girl.

A slave buyer wouldn't dare dirty his expensive suit to save the life of a whore. But a cartel *sicario* or *teniente* would endure torture and take a bullet before returning to his *jefe* empty-handed. That would be career-ending. Life-ending. The ultimate disgrace.

To survive this, he had to prove to them that he wasn't with an enemy cartel. He was John Smith, shrewd businessman and unfeeling slave owner.

He stood motionless, ice-cold and dead inside, calling their bluff.

Seconds stretched. Spiders swarmed. His lungs refused air.

The longer he waited, the more deadly Vera's predicament became.

Seeing her smothered beneath a blanket of black widows burned away the lining of his stomach and turned his guts inside out. There was only so much stress a body could bear—hers and his.

With her mouth forced open, her limbs restrained in murky water, and her head enveloped by a hood of venomous spiders, her panic would've exceeded volcanic by now.

Long black hair floated around her, skimming the surface and providing a landing place for clinging legs. Were they swimming beneath the dome? Sinking fangs into her tender skin? Injecting her with venom?

Enough.

Everything inside him switched gears. Tendons turned to steel. Muscles flexed around fortifying joints. Adrenaline spiked, and his mind cleared.

He would die for her.

He didn't remember removing his suit, but by the time he reached the pond's edge, every stitch of clothing was gone except his pants and shoes. He toed off the latter and scooped them up to use as weapons against the spiders. Then he calmly waded into the chilly water.

"What are you doing, Mr. Smith?" Marco asked, not bothering to chase him.

"Retrieving my property." He wouldn't survive their gunfire, but he would do everything in his power to ensure that she escaped.

Beyond the spotlight's beam, he waited until the water rose to his hips before discreetly removing the key card and phone from his pocket. Both went into one shoe, which he kept above the water and shielded from their view.

"Come back here," Marco called in a bored tone. "We *will* shoot you."

"Do it, Marco, and you'll invite an army of enemies you won't win against."

"How will they find us?" Marco laughed.

He met the man's eyes over his shoulder. "How did *I* find you?"

Marco's face went taut. Let him stew on that for a while.

As the water rushed over his shoulders, he kept the insides of the shoes dry, floating them smoothly along the surface.

The swim toward her was the longest half-minute of his life. The spot between his shoulder blades tingled beneath the aim of multiple guns.

They could shoot him at any moment, but he counted on them waiting. He was providing them with a show of human suffering and vain hope. It was the ultimate entertainment. They lived for this shit.

He slowed at the center, scanning the illuminated water for squirming black bodies. Thank fuck for the light—

It clicked off, dousing him in pitch black.

"Turn it back on," he roared, panic setting in.

The laughter of monsters erupted on the shore.

Fuck them. Without the light, he couldn't see the spiders. But it also meant the cartel couldn't see him.

He released the shoes, letting them float. Then he inched toward the bobbing spider-covered dome.

"It's me," he whispered. "I'm going to remove the gag first. Don't make a sound when I do."

UNSHACKLE

He couldn't see her face through the squirming bodies to know if she was still above water. There were too many, some falling into the black depths around him. He could splash the mesh hood or hit it with a shoe to clear it, but that would just scatter the threat and waste time.

His skin erupted with the sensation of crawling legs, and he spun, shaking himself beneath the surface. His blood pressure exploded, and paranoia set his teeth on edge.

He breathed through it, drew a deep gulp into his lungs, and dove.

His eyes opened to sheer blackness, but he found her legs quickly. Sliding his hands over her jeans, the life vest, and her neck, he reached the surface with questing fingers.

Her skin felt warm and alive, her face still above water. Still breathing.

Hang on, Vera.

There wasn't enough room in the dome for both of them. So he tucked his head downward, kicked his legs to maintain buoyancy, and blindly unbuckled the spider gag.

A sudden, searing prick erupted on his forearm. He screamed, unable to control the reaction, and his lungs expelled precious bubbles of air.

Motherfucking fuck! That hurt!

It was just one bite. God only knew how many she'd suffered already.

His pulse pounded as his fingers located her lips and pried the metal ring from her mouth. Pulling the gag away, he tackled the rope on her hands.

He couldn't hear anything, didn't know if the cartel was yelling for him. He couldn't care. His lungs burned for air, but he needed her out of this rope.

When the knot around her hands finally gave, his chest was on fire. He kicked hard, shooting upward and surfacing only long enough to take a huge breath. Then he dove for her feet.

The rope there took longer, the knot too tight to loosen with fingers. He wasted invaluable seconds trying to untie it from the cement block.

They'd done this before. Everything was too perfectly measured. From the anchor to the life vest, her body was stretched in a vertical line, allowing no wriggle room. The dome was fastened to the vest, which she should be able to unzip and slip—

Her knees bent above his hands, eliminating the taut stretch of her legs. She'd removed the vest.

Soft fingers curled around his, and together they tore at the knot around her ankles.

He wanted to sigh beneath her living, breathing touch. He ached to hold her and whisper kisses across her skin and show her how much he loved her.

The rope fell away.

They reached the surface together to the sounds of Marco shouting from the shore.

"Mr. Smith, bring her here."

"Did you get bitten?" he whispered.

"Just a few times." She cupped his face in the dark, her legs sliding soundlessly against his as she stayed afloat.

She was close enough that he could make out her exquisitely fierce features. *And the movement in her hair.*

Near her temple, a black widow clung with long legs, seemingly tangled in a curly lock.

"Oh, God, there's one in my hair, isn't there?" Her question rode on a hesitant breath.

"Hold still." His chest constricted as he pinched the hard black body, cringing as he flung it away.

"Thank you."

"I love you."

"Luke—"

He covered her mouth with his hand. "You're dead."

"John Smith!" Marco called again.

"She went underwater, goddammit! If she's dead, I'll be extremely displeased." He whirled, finding the shoe with the phone in it floating nearby. He pushed it toward her while pulling her close and whispering quickly. "This contains a phone and Silvia's key card. My team is on standby in Orange County. Call them. Help them find you. I'm going to create a diversion."

Her eyes turned colder than the Greenland ice sheet, flickering with flames of rage. "You can go to hell."

"On my way. But I need you to do this." He rattled off a phone number, his nerves raging with frantic energy. "Repeat it back to me."

Her jaw set. Then she whispered the numbers. "I'm not leaving you again."

"If we both run, we're both dead. Go."

Her gaze, as sharp as a blade, absorbed everything from the restless men on the shore to the dense trees on the other side. She knew he was right, and she hated him for it.

"You can't fake my death," she said. "They'll search the pond for my body."

UNSHACKLE

"That'll take time and daylight. Avoid the cameras and get to that breach in the wall before sunrise. I know you can do it." He kissed her hard and fast. Then he pushed away and started screaming.

"Ow! Fuck. Get them off of me!" As he splashed around in the water, he marked her retreat.

She swam beneath the surface, guiding the shoe along the top as she raced to the far shore.

"Get me out of here!" He continued to thrash, moving away from the floating dome of spiders. "I can't find her, you son of a bitch! Get your men in here and fix this!"

The spotlight switched on, blinding his eyes. It pointed away from the direction she'd swam. The cover of trees should hide her exit from the water, but he kept flailing, ensuring all attention remained on him.

No one came to his rescue. They stood around like the heartless fucks that they were and waited for him to drag his ass to the shore. He took his time and made a lot of noise, giving her an extra minute to flee.

"You killed her." He trudged out of the pond and collapsed onto his knees, heaving. "You owe me three million and a lot of goddamn groveling. Take me to my plane."

"I don't think so." Marco prowled forward.

Yeah, he hadn't thought so, either.

As he pushed to stand, he was so focused on *not* looking for Vera on the far shore that he missed the butt of a rifle swinging toward his head. He saw it just as it collided with his skull.

Pain ricocheted. The ground rose up, and the world went black.

TWENTY-SIX

Luke woke without clothes.

The room was austerely gray. Prosaic. No windows. One door. Fluorescent lights. Concrete walls. And a large steel table, which he was bent over. With his feet on the floor, his arms stretched over his head, his hands were shackled with handcuffs — the standard-issue police variety.

It was a cartel interrogation room.

The cuffs connected to a chain that fastened beneath the table. A rod between his ankles forced them apart and secured to something beneath him. He gave the restraints a testing yank. No give.

His skull pounded from the collision with a rifle, and a burning itch flared on his forearm around two red fang marks. But those were the least of his problems.

He wasn't alone.

"Oh, good," he murmured, his voice cracking with dry rot. "The whole family is here."

Ignoring him, Silvia and her four brothers communed beside a wall of shelves filled with fetish equipment and instruments of torture.

He was no stranger to the array of tools that sadists used to correct, fuck, and break a body. Eight years ago, he'd learned how to endure the full spectrum of pain, purgatory and hell, and every torment in between. He'd barely survived those weeks.

I won't survive it again.

That disparaging thought was overshadowed by a more pressing one.

Vera.

UNSHACKLE

Was she still alive? Had she made it through the breach in the wall? What if she'd been bitten too many times to recover?

He shook off his worst fears and fantasized about her sprinting through the junkyard in the cloak of darkness, armed with weapons from the armory, reaching a busy street, and waving down a motorist with a gun.

It was an impossible notion. She'd had three years to escape, and God knew she'd tried.

But maybe this time was different. The cartel was distracted with whatever they were planning for him. And she had Silvia's key, which gave her access to places she hadn't been able to go before. Places she could hide without cameras. But if she'd gone to the armory, she would've been detected. Alarms would've sounded.

What had he missed while he was unconscious? He couldn't have been out for longer than a few minutes. Not long enough for Silvia to leave his side and discover that her key card had been swapped out.

Hopefully.

He wouldn't ask the cartel a single question about Vera. If they told him she was dead, he wouldn't believe them. He couldn't. By the looks of the instruments they were considering, they intended to torture him. Physically. Psychologically. Any manner they pleased.

The silver lining? He didn't see a container of spiders anywhere.

Silvia turned and sashayed toward him. Her red lips curved into a smirk, causing his heart to whack against his ribs like a caged animal. Then he saw the apparatus in her hand.

A metal dildo the size of Tomas' dick strapped to a leather harness. Strap-ons were Liv Reed's specialty, and he'd been on the receiving end of her thrusts more than once. But she'd used phalluses with a squeezable texture. Never metal.

Wordlessly, he watched Silvia lift her red dress and expose her bare cunt. Just as wordlessly, her brothers gathered around, staring boldly at the disturbingly erotic view their sister gave them.

This was an area of kink he had no experience in. She was blood-related to three of these men. They'd all been raised together since childhood. Talk about a mindfuck.

The sounds of quickening breaths coming from them made his blood shudder. Twitchy hands, chilling grins, the stench of anticipation. Then the deep voice of the oldest son, echoing through the room. "Answer our questions, and we'll let you go."

No, they wouldn't.

He lay his cheek on the cold steel table and tried to relax his muscles. Van had trained him how to endure this without injury. The key was in *not* fighting the invasion.

Marco and Silvia stepped out of sight behind him, making it impossible to remain calm.

"What's your real name?" Miguel approached the table near Luke's head and unzipped the fly of his suit pants.

"I'm not interested in your dick, sisterfucker."

"I'm not interested in yours, either. But I do love to watch my sister fuck."

Feminine hands curled around the muscles of Luke's ass, stroking and fondling and coiling him with anger.

"He's so beautiful." She bent over his back, fingers wandering everywhere, her hair tickling his spine with dread. "Just look at this body. Big and strong and powerful. I want to keep him."

"We'll see." Miguel pulled out his erection and lazily stroked it. "Tell us who you're connected with, John."

Luke squeezed his eyes shut as her hand found his flaccid cock.

Please, don't react. Dear fucking God, don't give her what she wants.

His body would respond to her touch eventually. But he stalled it by casting his mind back to the pond and replaying his horror and fear as spiders teemed over Vera's head. He thought about how close she'd come to dying in that water and the anguish he would've been experiencing now had he been forced to witness that.

"He's not getting hard." Silvia tightened her strokes, her grip too clumsy and aggressive.

It was the wrong hand.

The wrong fucking woman.

Miguel slammed a fist on the table, prompting Luke's eyes to flash open. "Then make him hard."

No, no, no. He couldn't do this to Vera. He couldn't respond to another woman's touch.

A voice in his head whispered, *You're not doing it. It's not your fault. This is rape.*

Didn't matter. As Silvia slipped under the table and drew him into her mouth, he saw red. He roared. He thrashed in the shackles. And he hardened.

Spittles of rage sprayed the steel surface beneath his lips. He choked as she sucked. His balls withered as she groped. His skin peeled away from burning muscles, shrinking with the force of his unholy wrath. And still, his cock did what it was designed to do. It swelled in the suction of wet heat.

Shame threaded through him. Vulnerability and helplessness throttled him on all sides. He'd been here before. Pinned down and degraded beneath Van's cruelty. Only this time was worse.

UNSHACKLE

He belonged to someone else. His body wasn't just betraying him. It was betraying the woman he loved.

Voices barked in a fog around him. Questions. Demands. They fired their inquiries one after the other as a dry finger probed his ass and forced its way inside.

Her fingernail scratched through the unbearable penetration. He tried to relax, but a strange buzz flogged his ears. Heat pricked the backs of his eyes, and his vision blurred.

He checked out, left the room, and went to a place inside his head.

He couldn't be present while Silvia sodomized him, milked him, and repeated the torture. And he couldn't allow himself to succumb to a moment of weakness and expose his vigilante operation, his friends, or anything related to Vera.

He burrowed so effectively inside his mind that he didn't sense the world around him. Until blinding agony seared through his rectum.

A strangled scream burst from deep in his chest. He knew the metal phallus had torn something inside him before she pulled back and rammed into him again.

Cold fire. Scathing pressure. If he'd still had an erection, it was long gone. Bile welled in his throat. He came close to blacking out as his spirit vacated his body and crashed back into his organs so violently that he shook, heaved from an empty stomach, and felt horribly, miserably dead.

And so it began.

Silvia fucked him with a ruthlessness that aroused everyone in the room but him. Omar and Miguel continued to volley their questions, but the pauses in between grew longer as they watched Marco mount their sister and thrust into her from behind, driving the velocity and force of the strap-on.

Then the interrogation was forgotten altogether as they jerked off to the show.

Alejandro was the only one not participating. He stood off to the side, arms clenched across his chest. But he wasn't unaffected. The bulge in his pants confessed his arousal.

It was apparent then why no one else was in the room. How would the cartel members feel about the incestuous orgies that took place among their leaders? No wonder the brothers never answered questions about how they were related to her. This wasn't okay. The most depraved criminals wouldn't find this sibling fuckery amusing or acceptable.

The fact that they were doing it in front of Luke meant they had no intention of letting him live.

Watching them together, however, helped him understand Silvia's motivation. She loved her brothers, sickeningly and unlawfully, and craved their attention. When they brought in Vera, Silvia was no longer the center of their world. She didn't approve of how possessive they became over another woman.

The crazy, jealous bitch moaned behind him, and Marco joined in, shouting in Spanish as he came.

Inside his stepsister.

"I need something to eat." Silvia pulled out and gave Luke's ass a hard slap. "But don't worry, handsome. I'm nowhere near finished with you."

She might be when she found out her key card had been swapped.

Marco escorted her out, using his own key. They came and went in pairs, presumably to freshen up, refuel, and check on the cartel's operations.

Hours passed.

No one mentioned Vera.

Luke didn't speak a word, and they didn't free him from the restraints. After bending in the same position for so long, his muscles and joints ached. The contusion on his head hadn't stopped throbbing, and his ass burned in ways he hadn't experienced in eight years.

He had no plan. No hope, save one.

Vera was alive.

He couldn't accept the alternative. It was the only thought keeping him sane.

Eventually, Silvia returned with Omar, wearing a silk robe and fresh lipstick. She dropped the garment inside the door and strolled toward Luke, completely nude.

He turned his head and looked the other way.

"Oh, handsome. Don't be that way." She climbed atop him, straddling his back and grinding her wet pussy against his spine. Then she angled forward and licked his ear. "I want your gorgeous cock inside me."

His insides curdled, and his breaths caught fire, searing past his nose.

"His dick is thick like yours, Alejandro."

The youngest brother glowered from his post near the door. "Don't—"

"Don't what?" She returned to Luke's ear. "Whenever he fucks me, it makes him so angry. God, I love his angry sex."

Out of the five of them, she was clearly the most psychotic. What kind of deranged shit had to happen to a person to turn them into the grinding, sex-crazed demon on his back? She didn't belong in this world. She might even be too damaged for hell.

UNSHACKLE

The door opened, and Marco stalked in. All five of them were here now, which meant the torture would begin again.

Sweat chilled on his brow, and his ass clenched, unbidden.

Silvia slid off his back and perched a naked butt cheek on the table beside his face. Her hand drifted to his hair, stroking him like a pet.

He seethed, jerking and bucking, unable to stop her. Exhaustion pressed into his bones, and prolonged stress fumbled his thoughts. But no matter what they did to him, he would *not* talk.

"Tell me." She toyed with the hair at his nape. "Do you love her?"

He bit down on his lips.

She lowered off the table and put her face in his. "Do you love Vera Gomez?"

Fuck, fuck, fuck.

He arranged his forehead in an expression of confusion. If he remained silent, would it give too much away? Maybe. So he formed a fitting response. "I despise you with every drop of blood in my body."

Her head jerked back, and her eyes tapered into reptilian slits. "Harsh. But you know that's not what I asked. The woman you paid three million for? Vera Gomez? Was she just a job to you? Or did you love her?"

He didn't like her speaking about Vera in past tense. "I don't know what you're talking about, you demented bitch."

"It's time to remove some of his extremities." Marco strolled forward, holding large steel-bladed pruning shears. He opened the handles and snapped the blades closed, his expression chillingly lethal. "Starting with the one you love most."

"No!" Silvia straightened. "You're not cutting off his dick. That's mine, and I'm keeping it."

"You can keep it in a jar."

If Luke's bladder had anything to expel, he might've pissed down his leg.

"I want to feel him inside me, Marco." She sidled up to her brother and cupped him between the legs. "I want to feel both of you at the same time."

"Fucking insatiable." He smacked her hand away. "Never happy. Look what we built for you." He swung out an arm, indicating the estate. "We give you everything you want, and it's never enough."

"That's not true." She burst into Spanish, throwing around her hands.

Marco yelled back, getting in her face. Miguel and Omar joined in, and the dysfunctional family began to scream over one another.

Luke kept his eyes on the hedge shears in Marco's grip. His blood ran cold at the thought of that thing going near him. And it would, as soon as they stopped arguing.

Think, goddammit.

What could he say to get out of this? What bargain could he make without revealing the existence of his team? Could he fabricate a believable story on the fly?

His ruse as a wealthy slave buyer had taken weeks to prepare, every detail memorized and thought out. If he changed his story now, they would know he was lying. Besides, anything he told them would only delay the inevitable. He couldn't stall them for weeks.

As his captors continued to quarrel about which limb to remove first, the door opened.

They didn't hear it.

His heart pounded at the sight of a gun, connected to an outstretched arm, the body out of view. Then the gunman stepped in.

Gun*woman*.

He stopped breathing as Vera dragged an unfamiliar man in behind her and closed the door.

The room fell quiet. Every head turned. No one was breathing.

She aimed a Glock at Alejandro's face, who had pulled his own gun the moment she came in.

He stood close enough to knock the weapon from her hand. But he wouldn't. Because her other hand held a goddamn grenade. The pin was gone, her tiny fingers white-knuckled around the spoon. If she dropped it, they were all dead.

Luke scanned the room, confirming that only three people were armed. Alejandro, Vera, and the man she'd brought in.

What the fuck was she thinking? She was supposed to be gone and calling in backup. Goddamn her for not listening.

And God love her for showing up.

He should've known. This woman didn't run. She fucking fought.

Rifles and ammo hung from her shoulders and hips. Beneath the heavy artillery, she wore a bulletproof vest. Her bare arms and neck showed multiple spider bites and signs of swelling. But there were no visible holes in the vest. No signs of gun wounds.

How had she made it in and out of the armory and all the way here without getting shot?

No matter. She was here, and he couldn't have been prouder of her.

"I fucking told you she wasn't dead," Alejandro growled at his brothers.

"Easy, Vera." Miguel didn't move, his accent losing its smooth charisma. "Put the pin back in."

"I dropped it outside." She shrugged, rattling the rifles on her back. "Whoops."

UNSHACKLE

"Romero." Marco glared at the skinny man at her side. "What are you doing?"

"She held me at gunpoint, *jefe*." Romero gripped a huge phone, his gangly body weighed down by more guns and ammo belts than Luke could count. "She broke into my room and... I'm so sorry, *jefe*. She was going to kill me."

Who was this kid? He didn't look like a coldblooded cartel member.

"What did you do, Romero?" Marco asked dangerously.

With Alejandro's gun trained on her, she returned the aim with her Glock. "He shut down the cameras and sent the coordinates of the compound to Restrepo. If you listen hard, you might hear the choppers overhead."

Luke's pulse burst into a sprint.

Except Matias only had one chopper in the States. Maybe she assumed there would be more? Or maybe she was lying through her teeth.

His anxiety reached an all-time high as she waved the weapon through the room and pointed it at Silvia.

Did she even know how to use a gun? Could she shoot accurately under pressure?

"Unshackle him." Vera scowled at Silvia's naked body. "So help me God, I'll pump your skank ass full of lead, starting with your tits."

"You're not shooting anyone." Miguel stepped forward.

She swung the Glock toward him. Until Omar called her name, and she turned the gun on him.

Luke's mouth dried as he watched her finger bounce all over that trigger. With any luck, she wouldn't shoot *him*.

"How did you get in here?" Omar asked. "Only the people in this room have access."

"I used your sister's key."

"Then whose key...?" Silvia's face paled, and she shot a deadly look at Luke. "Oh, my God. You swapped it on the veranda. That's why I couldn't get into my room tonight."

"This is bullshit." Omar charged toward Vera.

With one hand on the grenade, she adjusted the gun's aim on him, let out a screech, and squeezed the trigger.

Nothing happened.

Omar froze, and the room went still.

"Well, shit." She rattled the Glock side to side. "Is this thing on?"

The brothers erupted in mocking laughter.

She laughed nervously with them, sobered, and retrained the gun.

"Just kidding." She fired off a shot with a yelp of surprise.

Holy fuck. Luke jerked as if he could dodge the bullet.

It missed him, missed Omar, too, and hit the concrete wall. The men moved, rushing at her, and she fired again. Over and over, rounds pinged through the room, until one finally hit Omar in the chest.

Silvia wailed as he hit the floor, dead before he dropped.

The beautiful part? Vera had shot him without letting go of the grenade.

She's incredible. Ferocious. And mine.

Outrage and grief poured off Marco and Miguel, but it was Alejandro that kept Luke's attention. The only reason the muscle head hadn't fired yet was because of that grenade. But if he inched close enough, he could wrestle it from her hand. If she shot him, he would shoot back, to hell with the grenade.

Luke burned with the urge to shout commands at her.

Don't take your eyes off Alejandro.

Keep Romero beside you.

Don't let anyone take the kid's weapons.

The Glock only has one bullet left.

Don't drop that fucking grenade.

But she was already doing everything right. For someone who hadn't been trained for combat, she was killing it.

There was only one problem.

Alejandro.

"Give me the grenade." He stepped toward her, gun aimed, patience gone. "Right now!"

TWENTY-SEVEN

I don't know what I'm doing.
  I don't know what I'm doing.
  Oh, Lord Jesus, what the hell am I supposed to do?
    Vera's pulse bellowed in her throat, and her hands grew clammy around the gun. It was hard to think with all the screaming coming from Silvia, who lay prone across Omar's dead body.
    The weapon that Alejandro aimed at her head didn't help her focus, either.
    She couldn't even look at Luke and his position on the table. Or the strap-on on the floor. She was going to kill that fucking bitch. But first, she had to deal with Alejandro.
    He pressed forward, forcing her to retreat.
    "Stay at my side, Romero." She veered, angling toward Luke without a plan in sight.
    Romero clung like velcro, souring her inhales with his fear. The computer whiz kid had been reluctantly instrumental in helping her get here. He also served as her pack mule. She could only carry so many guns, and she expected a war.
    Silvia hadn't left Omar, her wails grinding into blubbering sobs as Marco and Miguel crept closer.
    "Get back." She waved the pistol between them and Alejandro. "Move to the wall."
    Holy shit, they were angry, their expressions crimson, veins bulging, hands flexing at their sides.

Good for them. She was pissed, too. And tired. Her fingers quivered around the grenade, and her arm flagged from training the gun one-handed.

When she reached the steel table, she glanced at the restraints. Latches on the chains. A key jutted from the locking mechanism on the handcuffs. Easy peasy.

Except she had no spare hands.

"Romero." She jerked her chin. "Free him."

"If you do," Alejandro said coldly, "you're dead."

"Remember my promise, Romero. Your tech skills are destined for better things. You're too smart to make the wrong choice here."

"She's out of bullets and won't be able to fire those rifles one-handed." Alejandro sneered. "She can't protect you."

"Oh." She played dumb, knowing she had one left in the chamber and a loaded Glock wedged in the back of her jeans. "Romero, I'm going to need you to get moving on those shackles now."

Her heart went ballistic as she waited for him to obey. She only had one chance at this. One try.

Aim at the chest. Don't let go of the grenade.

Romero shifted. Alejandro turned his gun toward the kid, and she fired.

A direct hit in the chest. As he stumbled back, she dropped the empty Glock, grabbed the second from her back, and sprayed bullets in the direction of Marco and Miguel.

Don't drop the grenade. Don't drop the grenade.

She silently chanted the reminder and counted off the rounds as she fired through the room. Mostly, she missed her targets, but at least two of the shots were fatal. As Marco and Miguel slumped to the floor, Silvia's ear-splitting shrieks rent the air.

Vera spun back to Alejandro. *Too late.*

His gun boomed, and her thigh buckled beneath explosive, scorching pain. The dizzying cloud of agony stole her balance. She held tight to the grenade, but she couldn't stop her fall.

Luke's roar shook the walls, penetrating her haze.

I've been hit.

I still have a gun.

Two bullets.

She squeezed off one as she went down. And missed.

Alejandro sprawled on the floor. Blood on his chest. Gun in his grip. Hard eyes locked on her.

She fired again, dropped the empty Glock, and clutched the grenade with both hands.

UNSHACKLE

The gun slid from Alejandro's limp fingers. Two red holes, side by side, bloomed on his chest, his head lolled at an awkward angle. Dead.

She blinked, snapping out of a suspended fugue, and that was when the real pain kicked in. All at once, it crashed into her like a vengeful flood, slamming her teeth together and bowing her back.

The room spun in a cacophony of chaos. Fists pounded on the door. Silvia wailed. Romero unshackled Luke, and through it all, she clung to that grenade.

"Vera!" Luke's voice grew closer.

Then she felt roaming hands—on the grenade, her face, her leg. Oh, God, her leg.

"I need to tie this off." His breaths came in bursts. "Can you hold the grenade?"

"Got it." She clenched her teeth, tasting blood.

"We knew all along!" Silvia screamed from across the room. "We knew when you chose her in the basement that you were with Restrepo, you lying, miserable, limp-dick murderer! You're dead. You're so fucking dead!"

She was coming, her voice announcing her approach.

"Deal with her." Vera pulled the grenade against her chest, blinking through tears of pain. "I've got this."

Luke's beautiful face turned to stone. Cold. Brutal. Lethal.

He stood, gloriously nude, and just as Silvia reached him, he punched her screaming mouth.

She went down, and he followed her, caught her by the throat, and wrenched her close, nose to nose.

The cartel continued to bang on the door, shouting and ramming the steel frame.

He ignored it. "I came here to free Vera Gomez, kill your brothers, and destroy the cartel. I'm part of a vigilante group. We annihilate monsters. People just like you." He bared his teeth in a terrifying smile. "I fell in love with Vera the night I saw her fight. You, on the other hand, have repulsed me from the moment we met."

Her head hit the floor as he dropped her. Then his fists flew. One punch after another, he bludgeoned her face. She made no noise, no attempt to fight him. Soon, the sounds of wet smacks gave way to crunching bone. He didn't stop.

Vera recognized the torment in his eyes. The rage. The haunting nightmares. Silvia had raped him, and she hadn't been the first. Vera's heart broke as she watched him unleash eight years of memories in the harrowing drive of his fists.

He hammered strike after strike, raging in a gruesome trance, long after Silvia was dead. Long after Vera could stomach the macabre sight of blood and bone splattering beneath his blows.

Romero sat in a huddled ball with his eyes clamped shut.

"Luke."

He didn't hear her.

"Luke. Luke! Snap out of it and look at me! I need you!"

He stopped, stared at his bloody hands, and met her eyes.

"Time's up." Her body felt like ice, her head squishy with fuzz. "I'm losing blood, and you need pants."

He looked down at himself, brows knitting as if noticing his lack of clothes for the first time. Rising to his feet, he didn't give Silvia another glance. He strode directly toward Marco's corpse, stripped off the suit pants, and dragged them on.

By the time he returned to her, the blood was gone from his hands. He appeared composed, hawk-eyed, and laser-focused. One-hundred-percent Luke.

"Romero." He snapped his fingers. "Stand up."

"Don't hurt him. He designed the cartel's security system. Really smart kid." She felt herself fading, her fingers slipping on the grenade. She readjusted her grip. "I promised him amity and protection. He's coming with us."

A period of murkiness flickered in and out, disorientating her. Seconds passed. Or minutes? She was losing her sense of time and awareness.

Luke was bent over her, his shirtless torso bulked up and strapped with weapons. Expression hard, eyes aglow with green flames, he looked like a rogue soldier, armed and ready for a revolution.

"Let me have it, baby." His hands were wrapped around hers, keeping the grenade safe.

She released the locked grip of her fingers and watched through blurred vision as he passed the small missile off to Romero. Then he removed the heavy artillery from her body.

A necktie appeared in his hand, one that Marco had worn. He tied it tightly around her thigh above the bullet wound. She cried out and pressed a fist to her mouth, shaking through the unholy pain.

"I'm so sorry." He kissed her face and pulled her hand away to kiss her mouth. "I'm getting you out of here."

"For the second time." She tried to smile, but her lips were numb.

"For the last time."

As he bent to lift her, an explosion rocked the foundation. The ground shook like an earthquake, and the atmosphere charged with electricity. He spun, grabbing the grenade from Romero's hands.

UNSHACKLE

Her ears rang, and the boom lingered in her chest. When the tension released, overpowering relief swept in.

His team was here.

As the dust settled, Luke turned to her, thunderstruck. "Tell me that was our guys."

She looked to Romero for confirmation.

"I hooked your friends into my phone's GPS so they could track us, and vice-versa." Romero removed the device from his pocket and tapped on the screen. "They're on the south side. All the activity is there. We should be able to escape out the main gate."

"I can't wait to hear how the two of you pulled this off." Luke grinned.

Romero might've been a genius, but his story wasn't much different than hers. Poor Latino boy supporting his poor family. A wealthy, powerful man strolled in, offered him a high-paying job, U.S. citizenship, and a slew of other empty promises.

She'd learned about him through the gossip of the girls in the estate. The cartel kept him sequestered away from the guests, but with Silvia's key card, she'd been able to enter his room and take him by surprise.

Romero wasn't really a bad guy. He'd made some mistakes, the same as her. Now they were both working toward redemption.

"The pounding on the door stopped," she said.

The explosion had drawn the crowd away.

Luke glanced at the grenade in his hand, then at the wall near the exit. "What's on the other side of that door?"

No way could he carry her, a grenade, and aim a gun at the same time. He must've been thinking the same thing.

"A garden." Romero looked up from his phone. "Lots of foliage to hide anyone who might be waiting for us to come out."

"Stay here." He strode toward the door, opened it with Marco's key card from his pocket, and chucked the grenade.

Seconds later, it detonated with a chest-rattling bang.

Well, there was no one waiting out there now. But more would come.

She didn't know how he planned to carry her to the gate without taking gunfire. But the pain in her leg was eating away her ability to worry about the endless details.

The persistent pull to close her eyes was grueling. She wanted to sleep, needed it desperately after being awake all night. But Luke probably hadn't slept, either, and his night had been much, much worse.

"Here we go." He crouched over her, gun in hand, more guns strapped to his back, and lifted her into his arms.

She bit back a scream as her leg jostled and burned with a vengeance. "Remove my vest. It's bulky. Too heavy."

"Not a chance. Hold on."

She tried, but the universe was spinning around a black curtain. Daylight speckled in through moments of darkness. Gunfire sounded off and on, muffled pops, as if passing through wads of cotton.

Then there was nothing.

"Vera."

"Huh?" She woke with a rumbling vibration beneath her and a rumbling voice beside her.

"Vera. Wake up."

She rubbed her eyes and found herself in the luxurious leather seat of a fast car. Like really *fast*. It flew down a barren road, hugging the turns and growling through the gears.

Behind the wheel sat the most beautiful man she'd ever seen. Red hair glinting in the sunlight, shirtless chest boasting strength and hard work, and powerful hands that knew how to maneuver high speeds, deliver fatal punches, and touch a woman until her eyes rolled back in her head.

"We're alive," she said in wonder, watching trees blur by. In the distance, clouds of smoke billowed on the horizon. "Is that the compound?"

"Yeah, it's burning. We hit them hard and fast. There will be nothing left by the time the authorities show up."

"How did you get us out?"

"Your badass haul of guns. I had enough firepower to clear a path to the car. Romero's safe. None of us were hit."

"What about the girls?"

"Rounded up and protected. This is what we do. Trust me, they're fine." His green eyes cut to her and returned to the road. "How are you doing?"

"I'm in shock, I think."

"It's the blood loss. And the adrenaline dump. You single-handedly took down all four of Hector's sons."

"I had help."

"You're a goddamn warrior. The fucking bullet is still in your leg." His hand clenched on the steering wheel. "Restrepo's doctor is waiting on the plane. You're going to be okay."

She believed him.

She loved him.

How could she not? They'd been through hell and back together. Sacrificed their lives for each other. Witnessed each other at their lowest, most degrading points.

UNSHACKLE

Funny how the threat of death opened a person's eyes. Without tribulation and strife, a woman could go her life and never truly understand the meaning of love.

Had Vera spent enough time with Luke without all the danger, she would've eventually fallen for him. But after everything they'd been through, time had no bearing. After meat hooks, spiders, metal dildos, jealous bitches, and gunshot wounds, their relationship had been tested more in a short period than most couples experienced in an entire lifetime.

They'd already proved they could overcome anything together.

"Luke."

"Mm?"

"I have something to tell you."

"I know."

"No, you don't."

"I love you, too."

She grunted a breath that tumbled into a pain-laced groan. "You ruined it."

"You can still say it. Go ahead."

"But now you know what I'm going to say. It's lost its impact."

"Jesus, Vera, don't you know that every word that passes your lips impacts me? When you say *those* three words the first time, the next time, and if I'm lucky enough to hear them more times than that, they *will* have an impact, profoundly, significantly, in every way that matters."

She couldn't feel her injury. Or her legs. He was the cure for pain, pushing it into extinction and replacing it with sublime, soul-deep joy.

She let her head roll toward him and waited for his gaze. "I love you."

He didn't smile. Didn't repeat the words back. But it was all in his eyes. The coming together. The collision of souls. The brilliant shine.

The *impact*.

The force was so great she felt it everywhere.

"Eyes on the road." Her lips quirked.

Sprawled in a seat that seemed to be made for him, he shifted through gears with the confidence and fearlessness of a race car driver. He was in his element, driving too fast and taking too many risks. The car suited the man. Sexy as all hell.

"Is this Marco's sports car?"

He made a choking sound. "It's a *hyper*...car. A Koenigsegg Agera. Fastest car in existence."

As if to prove that, he opened the gas and tore down the road at dizzying speeds.

There was no one in front of them, but the side mirror revealed a long trail of hypercars behind him, glimmering in every color. She recognized them from Marco's collection.

"Where's Romero?" she asked.

"In the Lambo." He flicked a finger at the rearview mirror. "Those are my guys. I doubt they'll keep up, but they know where we're going."

"Where are we going?"

"Home. Colombia. To see your sister." He gripped her hand. "We made it, Vera. Just hang on a little longer."

She wove her fingers around his and squeezed.

For him, she would hang on forever.

TWENTY-EIGHT

Vera lay on her back on a plush sofa in Matias Restrepo's personal jet. With her head propped on Luke's lap and a heady flow of pain killers circulating through her system, she floated on a cloud.

This is what freedom feels like.

Voices whispered through the cabin. Jet engines hummed, and Luke's warm hand kept a constant, hypnotic rhythm along her arm, lulling her deeper into tranquility.

This is what love feels like.

He spoke quietly with two lethally handsome men who sat across from him. They'd introduced themselves as Tate Vades and Cole Hartman.

Lucia Dias, sister-in-law to the Restrepo capo, reclined beside Tate with a leg hooked over his knee. The beautiful Latina worked silently on her laptop as Tate absently stroked her inner thigh.

More vigilantes filled the seats in the front of the plane. Others had stayed behind to sell Marco's cars, relocate the girls, and clean up loose ends. They were also looking for Tomas. He hadn't contacted anyone since last night.

Picar, the cartel's doctor, hunched over Vera's exposed thigh, putting his final touches on the wound. She'd already received a blood transfusion and IV fluids. It was no surprise that the aircraft was equipped with the personnel and supplies to treat injuries. Cartel business was bloody.

At first, she didn't think the old doctor's cloudy eyes could see past his own nose. But he'd had no trouble locating and treating all her spider bites, removing the bullet, and stitching her up with tiny thread.

Speaking of stitches, the man who accompanied Picar wore a smile that had been sewed shut with heavy black thread. Add in his frizzy fluff of black hair, stark white complexion, and dark smudges around his eyes, and the man looked downright ghastly.

Luke had referred to him as Frizz and assured her that he deliberately sewed his own mouth closed.

She tried not to stare.

"All done. You need rest," Picar said in Spanish, straightened—as much as he could with his crooked spine—and waddled toward the front of the cabin.

She wished her sister was here. But since La Rocha had been looking for Tula, she'd been forced to stay in Colombia.

Romero seemed to relax now that he was on the plane and away from La Rocha. He sat on the other side of Luke, talking through the events leading up to the interrogation room.

"If you had access to all the cameras," Luke asked, "how did you not see her enter your room?"

"I was asleep."

"And I only had to dodge two cameras between the pond and his quarters." Vera shifted on the couch, seeking a more comfortable position with a better view of Romero, Luke, and his friends. "I know the location of every camera and their blind spots. It took me a long time to skirt around them undetected. But once I reached Romero's door, I knew I wouldn't have to deal with the cameras again."

"I woke with this woman straddling my hips." Grimacing, Romero scrubbed a hand over his black short-cropped hair. "She jabbed the barrel of a gun under my chin, with her eyes all feral, clothes and hair soaking wet, and—"

"It was an empty beer bottle, not a gun," she said.

"I didn't know that at the time." Romero dropped his hand. "She started making demands and screaming in my face. I knew immediately she was the girl who won all those fights. I thought for sure she was going to kill me."

Luke's hand never left her, his fingers tickling her neck and gently working the tangles from her curly hair. She drifted into a peaceful place, listening to Romeo explain the rest.

He was the hero, after all. Without him, she wouldn't have been able to enter the armory or move through the compound undetected. He'd manipulated each camera they'd approached so that the guards in the monitoring room wouldn't suspect a breach.

"I'll be honest," Romero said. "Her plan scared the shit out of me."

"It was reckless." Luke gave her hair a scolding tug.

"Shut up," she mumbled. "It was brilliant."

UNSHACKLE

"You saved us a lot of time." Cole leaned forward, arms braced on knees.

The vertical frown lines between his eyes were more prominent than the downturn of his lips. His thick brown beard did a good job of hiding the subtleties in his expression, which was probably a calculated effort. But no amount of hair could conceal the beautiful symmetry of his features.

"When you contacted us," he said, "we were at least two or three days away from isolating your location. You saved a lot of innocent lives."

"And ended a lot of evil." Luke's fingers tightened in her hair.

"It was all her. I was just doing what she asked." Romero blushed, looking sheepish. "She was pretty convincing once she started talking about how I could earn back my freedom by joining a movement against human sex traffickers. When I got involved with La Rocha, I knew they were criminals, but I didn't know about the girls and the slave buyers and everything that went on at the compound. I really had no idea what I was getting into until it was too late."

He told them about his family in Mexico, their poverty and sickness, and his desperation to help them. He'd been naive, just like her, and they'd both paid the price.

Romero had been imprisoned in his concrete room at the estate for two years, designing and maintaining the proprietary technology that secured the property. Only Silvia and her brothers had access to his room.

Vera would bet her last dollar that Silvia had raped the poor kid. Frequently.

"They threatened to butcher my family," he said. "I left my parents two years ago, promising to send them money. They haven't heard from me or seen a single dollar since I left."

"We'll take care of them, kid." Lucia looked up from her laptop and winked. "You're one of us now. *Tu familia es nuestra familia.*"

Your family is our family.

Vera felt that in her bones, and it made her eyes heat and dampen. Luke was taking her to her sister, bringing her into his tight-knit family, and giving her a home.

He was offering her a world of tangible dreams and possibilities.

"I'm sorry it took me so long to show up." With her head in his lap, she reached up and cupped his scratchy, chiseled jaw. "Romero and I didn't come to an agreement right away. I didn't trust him not to use one of his devices to notify the cartel."

"And I didn't trust her not to smash in my skull." Romero released an anxious laugh.

"We eventually worked out a fragile truce. Then we spent hours ironing out a plan." Guilt riddled her. "I took too long."

"You showed up." Luke slid a thumb across her cheek.

"Not soon enough."

"I'm alive, Vera. With all my body parts intact."

Her throat tightened at the memory of Marco holding pruning shears when she'd charged in.

"I saw the instrument Silvia used on you." She lowered her voice. "You should let the doctor examine you."

"What instrument?" Tate asked.

"Strap-on." Luke met his friend's eyes. "It had been a while since…"

"Eight years, man." Tate blew out a breath. "It's not easy to relive a second time, is it?"

"No, but I remembered the training, everything Van taught us. It helped."

"Are you injured?"

"It's minor. I'll heal."

She watched their interaction, recalling everything Luke had told her about the captives in Van's attic. The nine of them shared such horrific memories, but she found comfort in the ease in which they could talk about it.

Lucia set her laptop aside and crawled onto Tate's lap, wrapping her arms around him and nuzzling her face in his neck.

For a group of vicious killers, their empathy was palpable, their deep friendships undeniable. Vera respected them for that. Quite frankly, she was in awe of how these proud, dominant males could undergo such trauma and not lose themselves on the other side of it. Some victims never recovered.

"I betrayed you, Vera." Luke's roughened voice drew her gaze.

"What?"

"Silvia…put hands on me. Her mouth." His jaw went rigid. "My body reacted. I couldn't control—"

"Did you want her? Did you give your consent?"

"No. Fuck, no. But I wasn't strong enough to—"

"Don't forget who you're talking to, Luke." She pushed herself up to meet him at eye-level. "I was raped for three years. You don't have to convince me you didn't want it. I've been there."

"Yeah, I know." His eyes hardened. "*I* raped you."

"I forgave you. You don't have to forgive Silvia. In fact, I'll be royally pissed if you do."

"Dayyy-um." Lucia grinned. "I like her. It's about time someone put you in your place, Luke."

"When her leg heals, my place will be standing behind her upturned ass while I blister it red."

UNSHACKLE

"Promises, promises." Vera lay back down, returning her head to his lap.

She slept off and on through the duration of the flight. During moments of alertness, she listened to them wrap up the details of the mission and discuss the status of another one Camila was running in Mexico.

But mostly, they talked about Tomas.

Cole asked a lot of questions about the email, its origin, and Tomas' childhood. Luke and Tate didn't have the answers. Tomas had never told anyone he'd loved and lost a girl. He'd certainly never told anyone he'd been writing to her ghost all these years.

It sounded like they were going to give him a week to make contact. Then Cole would fly back to America and go after him.

"Who are you?" Vera cringed at the rudeness of her question. "Sorry. That came out wrong. But seriously. You're not one of Van's captives. You're not related to them by blood or marriage. You're not a Restrepo cartel member. So… Who are you?"

Cole flashed her a wolfish, bearded smile, all teeth, and no answers.

"If you ever figure it out…" Luke stroked the curve of her hip. "Tell the rest of us."

TWENTY-NINE

Vera spent the next week in a blur of recovery and acclimation. She'd been dug out of hell, dropped into a brand-new life, and she embraced it with her entire being.

The Restrepo Cartel headquarters in Colombia was even more lavish than *Casa de La Rocha*. Nestled in the Amazon rainforest, it boasted top-notch security, freedom to roam without consequences, and the best part? The cartel didn't traffic humans. They sought and destroyed those who did.

Matias and Camila were in Mexico right now, running another mission. But she met the rest of the crew. Liv and Josh, Van and Amber, Kate and Tiago, Martin and Ricky. And Tula...

Her sister had greeted her on the helicopter pad, arms wide, black hair whipping in the turbulence, and tears streaking down her face. They cried together, blubbered their regrets, and reconnected for days.

Tula's guys, Martin and Ricky, had greeted Vera with warm, hard-muscled, masculine-scented hugs. Then they hung around, listening to her and Tula exchange questions and reminisce for hours. They were good-looking men. Attentive. Devoted to her sister. But dangerous.

Everyone she encountered vibrated with ruthlessness and menace. A sense of danger hung in the air and lurked around every corner. But not like it was with La Rocha. The danger here wasn't directed at her.

Luke's friends protected their own, followed their own laws, and viciously destroyed anyone who threatened their loved ones. She felt it in every handshake, embrace, and flinty-eyed look.

For the first time in her life, she felt safe among criminals.

UNSHACKLE

Tula monopolized her first week here, showing her around the fortress and introducing her to everyone they passed. Vera hobbled along on her crutches as Tula shared the brutal details of her time in prison. But when she spoke of Martin and Ricky, her eyes lit up, and her cheeks rose with a goofy smile.

Love.

Vera sympathized with that ailment.

Luke was giving her space to catch up with her sister. He was using that time to work on a strategy with Cole, who was leaving tomorrow to return to the States.

Tomas still hadn't made contact.

So she stayed out of Luke's way and formed a delightful friendship with Tiago's wife, Kate. The pretty blonde only stayed here part-time. She was shadowing Picar, learning medicine, and working toward her degree. She wanted to be a doctor.

She didn't have the experience to treat Vera's wound, but she always accompanied Picar, absorbing his broken English while he examined Vera. Then she hung around after, chatting and sharing stories about her captivity with the Venezuelan crime lord, Tiago Badell.

Everyone here had a story, and Vera loved learning about their survival, their triumphs, and how they all interconnected.

There was so much she'd yet to learn about Luke.

She wanted to know all his quirks and complain about them. She wanted more Klondike and rap-song moments. She wanted to bicker with him over nothing and whack him with a pillow when he snored. Because that was what couples did, right? They drove each other crazy.

Crazy with Luke was going to be crazy amazing. She couldn't wait.

She missed him.

"Do you love him?" Tula pushed her sunglasses to her forehead and squinted in the afternoon sunlight.

"Yeah. Terribly." Swallowing a sip of beer, Vera stared out across the crystal-blue pool. "I've barely seen him all week."

"He's busy. But you're sleeping in his bed, right?"

Every night, he tucked her against his chest, kissed her everywhere, touched her over her clothes until she was wet, and… "No sex."

"Well, hello? You were shot. With a bullet."

"In the leg. Not in my vagina."

Tula burst into laughter. "Haven't you figured out that these guys are different? They're not like those selfish, abusive boys back home. They want us healed and healthy and begging for it before they beat us."

They stared at each other, biting back smiles.

"Never thought you'd crave a fist around your throat, huh?" Tula gave into her grin. "Or a stinging-red ass, bite marks, bruised thighs..."

"Never in a million years." She leaned back on the lounger and sighed. "It's been a rough road for us, you know?"

"Don't you feel like the hardest part is behind us?"

"Yeah. Even if it isn't, the hard stuff feels a lot less hard with someone you love at your side."

"Or two someones."

"You're such a whore." She knocked the sunglasses off Tula's head.

"A happy whore." Tula chuckled.

"Who's a whore?" Amber strolled up to their loungers.

"Your mama," Tula said.

"Doubtful. She spent a lot of time clutching her pearls. Can I join you?"

Tula dragged over another lounge chair. Meanwhile, Vera couldn't take her eyes off Van's wife. The woman radiated head-to-toe beauty, from her shiny chestnut hair and rosebud lips to her flawless, hourglass figure on full display in a tiny black bikini. Good God, she was gorgeous. Beauty queen gorgeous.

It was hard to imagine her with a man like Van Quiso. Vera knew their story and couldn't help but resent the man for everything he'd done to Luke and the others. She also knew they'd forgiven him.

He was among their kindred, which meant she would learn to accept and forgive him, too.

"I'm just going to put this out in the open." She shifted on the lounger, adjusting her injured leg before meeting Amber's eyes. "Your husband terrifies me."

"Me, too." Amber moved the coasters around on the small table beside her, arranging them in neat groups of four. "He's meaner than piss."

"With you?"

"Hmm. Why don't you ask him yourself?"

"No, that's—"

"Van!" Amber leaned to the side, shouting toward the open door of the veranda. "Come here!"

"Oh, now you've done it." Tula groaned. "You call one of them out here, and they'll all show up."

Sure enough, as Van ambled into the pool area, Joshua and Ricky trailed behind. They wore swim trunks and carried beers. Sunglasses and sexy hair. Shirtless and shredded with stacks of muscle. Where was a camera when she needed one? They belonged on a vigilante calendar. She would call it *Freedom Fighters, the Weapons of War* edition.

UNSHACKLE

Van paused beside Amber, gazing down at her, and his smile stretched the scar that curved from his mouth to somewhere beneath his shades. As he leaned down to kiss her fully on the mouth, his hand swiped over the coasters she'd arranged on the table.

When he straightened, her eyes zoomed in on the mess he'd made.

Apparently, Amber's OCD was a work-in-progress.

"Vera wanted to know," Amber said, without looking away from the scattered coasters, "if you're mean to me."

"Nah." He removed a toothpick from his pocket and set it between his teeth. "I'm a big sappy baby."

Joshua laughed as he stepped into the pool. "He's an asshole. With everyone."

With an unapologetic shrug, Van rolled the toothpick to the corner of his smirk. "Anything else you want to know? Like if I'm mean when I suspend my wife from the trees out there?" He nodded at the rainforest. "When I whip her and welt her pretty skin? Or when I bring her to orgasm, and she screams so beautifully everyone in the estate can hear her?"

"No, I...really didn't want to know that." Vera squeezed thighs against the warmth that rushed between them.

During that brief and disturbingly hot exchange, Amber had discreetly started moving the coasters back into symmetrical groups.

Van tossed his toothpick next to her busy hand. Then he kicked the table, just enough to jostle her attempt at order.

"Excuse us." He grabbed her, tossed her over his shoulder, and walked straight into the pool, submerging them both as she screamed.

Vera shook her head. "Well, that was..."

"Typical Van." Ricky took Amber's chair, stretching out his legs and closing a hand around Tula's knee. "You'll get used to him."

Not likely.

For the next few hours, she hung out with Tula, Ricky, and Joshua. Van and Amber stayed in the pool until Van started removing her bikini. Then they disappeared, taking their foreplay elsewhere.

Beer flowed. Platters of food arrived, and the air buzzed with laughter and conversation.

Until Tula started harping on Vera for hiding the magnitude of their mother's medical bills. They both had regrets and hashed it all out over multiple beers. Then Tula revisited the topic of Luke.

"He hasn't fucked her in a week," she said to Ricky.

Vera gave her the stink eye.

"She has a gunshot wound." Ricky scraped a tortilla chip along the bottom of a salsa bowl and crammed it into his mouth. "I'd be the same way. A wound like that needs time to heal."

"That's what I told her. You're all so overprotective."

"Okay, first of all…" Vera picked at the gauze on her thigh. "I'm not a sex addict. There's more to Luke than his body."

Tula snorted. "You're in the honeymoon phase of your relationship. It's *all* about the fucking. I mean, the guys and I still go at it like rabbits."

"You're wet just thinking about it." Ricky winked.

"You know I am."

"Not helping," Vera muttered.

"Go to bed naked." Joshua arched a brow and reclined back in the chair. "Trust me. All chivalry will fall by the wayside the moment he reaches over and finds his woman laid out and bare. It'll trip the wires in his stubborn head."

That night, she took Joshua's advice. No t-shirt. No panties. No bandage on her leg. She slipped beneath the covers, wearing only her skin, and shut off the light.

Luke hadn't come in yet. He'd been tied up with Cole and Tate all day.

As she started to drift off, the door opened. He crept in quietly and removed his clothes in the dark. Then the mattress dipped.

Lying on her side with her back to him, she held her breath, her blood heating in anticipation.

His hands went directly to her ass, as they always did. Only this time, they froze on contact.

Keep going, Luke. It's all bare.

Slowly, his clever fingers slid up her spine and back down, questing, hunting for more nudity. His breaths grew shorter. His body inched closer. Within seconds, his hands were everywhere, trailing along her neck, molding around her breasts, and dipping between her legs.

"Killing me, Vera." Panting against her shoulder, he reached the vicinity of her gunshot wound and stopped. "Where's your bandage?"

"Don't need it." She wriggled her backside against the iron proof of his arousal. "Just need you."

He groaned hotly against her nape. "I don't want to hurt you."

"Denying me hurts me." She shifted onto her back and found his gaze in the moonlight. "If your hesitancy has to do with what happened with Silvia, we need to talk about it."

"No." His eyes widened. "I haven't thought about that once. It's your leg. Picar said you need to go easy on it."

"Go easy on it." She pulled off the covers and spread her thighs in a wanton display. "But don't go easy on my pussy."

UNSHACKLE

In a flash, he was up, stripping off his underwear and straddling her hips. His mouth came down on hers, his tongue pressing in. He kissed her maddeningly, passionately, unleashing the depths of his need.

"I missed this." He rocked against her as he ate at her mouth, dragging his erection along her stomach. "I love you."

"Love you." Pre-come smeared her skin, and she basked in the sensation, reaching down to caress the heavy sac behind his cock.

He grunted against her lips and leaned back a few inches to stare at her. His hand caressed her face, clearing away the hair that had fallen over her cheek. Then he dipped his head and attacked her mouth again.

They kissed like teenagers, grinding, groping, and making out with tongues and teeth. Then he turned his attention to her body, licking and biting every dip, working his way down her breasts, down her belly, down through the slit of her cunt to burrow into the wetness between her legs.

She moaned guttural sounds and writhed against his mouth. He spread her apart and lapped at her flesh, fingertips flirting and rolling alongside his wicked tongue.

When he finally sank a pair of fingers inside, she cried out, clenching, and that was all it took.

She came instantly and with wild abandon, bucking and trembling and screaming, "Luke! Luke! Luke!"

"Christ, you have a magnificent cunt." He dipped his fingers in and out of the pooling moisture, making her shudder and ache all over again. "Swollen and pink. Primed for my cock."

"Fuck me, you redheaded sadist."

"In good time." He crawled back up her body and slid his nose along hers. "How's your leg?"

"Same as the other one. I need you between them."

He grinned, and she whimpered, knowing he had every intention of making her wait.

As he leaned in to kiss her, she took a mental picture because damn, he was sexy. The way he rolled his tongue past his parted lips just before their mouths collided... It got her every time.

That irresistible tongue felt so perfect against hers. So warm and controlling and *him*. She loved everything about him—his kisses, his touches, the heat of his body, and how it made her feel when he was moving inside her. She would never tire of this. Never tire of him.

He made the world a better place, and he was the only place she wanted to be.

His mouth left her lips to kiss over her face. Then he straightened on his knees and shifted until his sculpted thighs bracketed her head.

She devoured the sight of him towering over her, a powerful symbol of sexuality. His crowning glory jutted outward, bobbing above her head, thick and swollen, and tipped with a fat bead of pre-come.

Her inner muscles convulsed around nothing, throbbing to be stretched and pounded by that long, beautiful cock.

His hand wrapped around the root and slid up the broad shaft. He watched her, eyes smoldering beneath hooded lids, as he glided his palm around the head, gathered the moisture, and began to stroke with vigor.

Erotic didn't begin to describe the sight of this man pleasuring himself. His brawny legs trembled. The bricks of his abs contracted. Veins bulged in his forearm, and his eyes…

They were predator eyes, molten green, bold and hungry as ever, deadly dominant, deadly overbearing, just plain deadly.

He smacked the plump crown of his cock against her mouth. Then he did it again. And again. When she gasped, he shoved himself in, past her lips, her teeth, and straight to the back of her throat.

Her hands flew to the granite globes of his ass as she relaxed her tongue and breathed with his thrusts.

He gripped the headboard, bracing the cant of his body, while his other hand fisted in her hair. He held her head immobile, fucking her face with the frenzy of a mindless animal.

But he wasn't mindless, his gaze too alert and watchful. He never looked away, penetrating her with his eyes as deeply as the plunge of his cock.

It was that constant, worshiping eye contact that turned her on more than anything else. She savored the salty taste of him, the feel of his balls grinding against her chin, the way his body moved in a sensual dance. But God almighty, she loved the way he watched her.

He was language without words. The devotion-forming capacity of nature. The spirit of adventure and love. A humanist at war with monsters. And a carnal beast in the throes of pleasure.

His breathing deepened, and his honed physique flexed and dampened beneath her hands. She indulged herself, tracing all his grooves and indentations while sucking and licking the furor of his hardness in her mouth.

He gritted his teeth, his masculine features straining as he battled against completion.

"Fuck." He pulled out and squeezed the base of his erection as if trying to ward off a demanding release. "Your mouth feels too good, baby. I almost came. Not going to last a minute once I'm in your hot pussy."

"Good thing you have supernatural stamina. I'm expecting a long night with you."

"How about a long life with me?"

"That, too."

"Stay there." He shifted down her body, curling his warm, hard muscles around her uninjured side. Lifting her good leg, he hooked it over his hip while keeping her wounded thigh flat on the bed. "Don't move or fight against me. I don't want that leg straining."

They'd both been tested by the doctor. They were clean, and she was on birth control.

"No condom." She quivered at the feel of him sliding along her drenched slit from behind.

"My first time bareback." He leaned over her face, mouth open and panting against her lips as his cock teased the pulsing ring of her opening. "I'm so in love with you."

"Same." She gripped his nape and pulled him down for a kiss. "Please, Luke. Fuck me."

He pushed in his tongue. Then he pushed in his cock, sinking both with a shuddering, body-trembling groan.

With her lying on her back, he hiked up her good leg, holding it against him while guiding the movement and angle of her lower half as he plowed into her from behind.

The position allowed her injured leg to rest on the bed and away from the piston of his hips. It also gave him access to her mouth and a view of her jiggling tits, of which he took full advantage. He kissed her. Stared at her body. Kissed her again. Bit her nipples. He was everywhere, over, under, and inside her at once.

Lying on his side while holding her leg in an arm lock didn't affect the rhythm or force of his thrusts. Nor did it stop him from reaching a hand to where they were joined to add another layer of stimulation.

He played with her clit and stroked the flesh that squeezed around him. Then he pushed two fingers inside, entering her alongside his cock. Triple-penetration. She nearly came undone.

"The silk inside you feels unreal." He licked at her mouth, trying and failing to keep their lips sealed. "The sensation is so much hotter, softer, fucking wetter without a barrier. Christ, I'll never go back to condoms." He held her gaze and slammed into her with cock and fingers. "I want to put a baby in you."

She laughed blissfully around his hungry tongue. "Let's practice for a while. Lots and lots of practice."

He moved his hand to her breast and got to work, fucking her with shocking endurance. His deep, frenzied strokes delivered a religious experience, the heat of his kisses an empowered sense of rapture. He injected wonder into reality and transformed the world into electric hues of elation.

Making love to him was a cosmic explosion of body and mind. A splitting of atoms. Nuclear fission.

Energy released around her, sparking a chain reaction, rapidly multiplying the sensations plummeting through her, and sending her over the edge.

She came so violently she screamed, gasping for air and choking out his name. Pleasure burst in a starscape of light, crashing through her nerve endings and sucking all her strength.

Complete and total surrender.

"Vera." He saw it, felt it, and went rigid, groaning and jerking and succumbing to his own breathless release.

A warm rush flooded into her as an expression of gobsmacked adoration overtook his face.

"What are you thinking?" She cupped his hard jaw, laughing and wheezing.

"No words." He tried to catch his breath and lowered her leg. But he didn't pull out. "It's indescribable."

"Yeah."

"We're not finished." He thrust lazily inside her, testing the rigidness of his cock.

"I hoped you'd say that."

"You're not getting rid of me."

"Not even when we fight. And we will. I'm going to challenge everything you say and do. Can you deal with that?"

"I fucking look forward to it."

His mouth covered her lips. His hips rocked against her, and their bodies came together, unshackled in love and united in war.

THIRTY

Luke circled the Koenigsegg Agera, admiring its low profile, aerodynamic lines, and metallic silver paint. It used to be the sexiest goddamn thing he'd ever seen.

That was before he rested his eyes on Vera Gomez, who was currently naked and bent over the hood.

"Luke." She rubbed her pussy against the front wheel well, no doubt leaving streaks of moisture on the paint. "If you don't finish this soon, I'm going to take care of myself."

"Be quiet." Fucking hell, he was hard. Painfully, miserably rock-hard. "I paid a lot of money for this view."

All of Marco's hypercars had been sold, but this one. Luke had personally funded the shipping expenses to transport it from California to Bogota, Columbia.

For one reason only.

He wanted to fuck the world's sexiest woman on top of the world's sexiest car.

Never in his wildest fantasies did he think he would be standing here, in the middle of a forest outside of Bogota, taking in this view.

Her heart-shaped, upturned ass bore the welted marks of his spankings. Her skin slicked with sweat. Arousal soaked her thighs. He'd been playing with her in this position for over an hour.

"This is the pinnacle of my life." He grinned at her backside. "Nothing will ever top this."

"Don't say that, you fucking asshat. What about marriage? Kids? Grand—"

"Nope. This is *my* fantasy. One I've dreamed about for as long as I can remember."

"You fantasized about beating a woman's ass when you were a kid?"

"Beating the *sexiest* woman's ass on top of the *sexiest* car." He unzipped his jeans and freed his cock. "I can't even tell you how many times I shot my load with this image in my head."

"How's the reality holding up?" She wriggled her hips.

"Fuck." He gripped his cock, trying not to come. "It's better. The reality is so unbelievably sinful. Wish you could see it."

She moaned, stretching her arms out over the hood and rocking her hips. "Come on, Luke. I *ache*."

He stood still, committing every glorious detail to memory. Then he prowled toward her, kicked her feet apart, and sank himself into her throbbing wet heat.

His hands traveled over her delicious curves. His heart raced with the unfettered force of his thrusts, and she gripped him, clenching, with a tight, greedy cunt.

He wanted it to last forever, but she was already there. His body, completely attuned to hers, followed the sounds of her blissful cries, climbing with her, fusing, crashing…

Impact.

He drove savagely into her, spilling his seed as she found her own release. His head fell forward, his mouth sucking and biting her shoulders, his senses exploding in ecstasy.

As they settled down, he tucked himself away and pulled her limp body into his arms.

She stared up at him, and he kissed her dazed smile, lips gliding, and hearts pounding a single tattoo.

"I have a surprise for you." He brushed her hair from her face. "Get dressed."

He stepped back, admiring the view of her tight, sexy body as she dragged on jeans and a t-shirt. "What's the surprise? Go ahead and tell me."

"Vera." He clicked his tongue. "Don't start."

"I just want to know."

"You want to argue."

"No. I just don't like surprises."

"Too bad."

She growled under her breath. "You're so annoying."

"You're so beautiful."

Her dark eyes softened. Her lips turned up, and he considered riling her up again, just so he could savor all her expressions.

UNSHACKLE

An engine sounded in the distance, and a moment later, a motorcycle emerged on the winding road through the trees.

"Expecting someone?" She joined his side.

"Yep." He removed the Koenigsegg key from his pocket.

The motorcyclist pulled to a stop in the clearing and turned off the engine. The man had been thoroughly vetted, the deal already negotiated. Luke expected no trouble.

"Mr. Smith?" The man removed his helmet, revealing a bald head and a silver beard.

"Yep." Luke held out the car key.

"She's a beauty." Eyes on the hypercar, the man shrugged out of his backpack and handed it over. "It's all there. In small bills, just like you asked."

The heavy weight of the bag promised a clean transaction. While the man checked out the Koenigsegg, Luke opened the backpack and counted the money.

"What are you doing?" Vera stood over him, her fists anchored on her hips. "You're selling that car? Why? It's your dream car!"

"Shh." He continued counting.

She fell quiet, waiting for him to finish.

"It's all here," he said to the man. "We good?"

Better be. He was selling that car for a fraction of what it was worth.

"All good." The man grinned. "The second helmet is on the bike."

Luke strapped the backpack onto Vera's shoulders and kissed her stiff lips. "Let's have some fun."

"I can't believe you sold that car."

"I have everything I want right here." He kissed her again. "Come on."

Then he put her on the motorcycle, tucked her close behind him, and hit the road.

As much as he enjoyed the hypercar, it didn't compare to the feeling of an engine between his legs and Vera's warm body wrapped around his back.

He opened the throttle, startling a yelp from his girl. Then she laughed, clutching his waist and squeezing her thighs around him.

This is heaven.

He took her to a small town on the southern outskirts of Bogota. Not the safest area, but they wouldn't stay long.

Zipping along the crumbling streets, he veered toward his destination. When he arrived at the old hospital, he turned off the engine and lifted Vera from the seat.

"What are we doing here?" She scanned the dilapidated building, the broken wrought iron on the windows, and the overall gloom shrouding the place.

"We're spending the money." He grabbed the backpack and hooked it over his shoulder. Then he grabbed her hand, pulling her along. "Twenty minutes. In and out."

"Okay, but isn't this a hospital? What are we buying?"

"Smiles."

He couldn't stifle his own as he led her through the front entrance and down a dank, unkempt corridor. There was no security here. No visitor protocols. Nothing to stop them from entering the first room.

An elderly woman lay in the hospital bed, her arms and chest hooked up to a chirping, outdated machine. There were others in the room, presumably her family, sitting on the floor and standing along the wall.

"Luke?" Vera squeezed his hand. "Do you know these people?"

"Nope. Reach into the backpack and give them a gift."

Her forehead knitted. She glanced around the room at all the silent, staring faces. He watched the realization widen her eyes and swell in her chest.

She pressed a fist to her mouth, nodding as tears welled along her lashes. Then she reached into the backpack.

And so it went.

He followed her from room to room as she passed out money, speaking rapidly in Spanish, trying to convince each patient that she expected nothing in return.

When she lingered too long at a bedside, he quickly dragged her to the next one, keeping her moving.

They were in a dangerous neighborhood, riddled with poverty and crime. He wanted all the money gone before they drew too much attention.

By the time they reached the last room, her smile was blinding, contagious, and worth all the hypercars in the world.

She was happy making people happy, and he knew without a shadow of a doubt that she would thrive as a Freedom Fighter.

He couldn't stop staring at her, at the majestic glow that shone in her eyes, her tears, her constant smile.

"What?" She walked beside him through the parking lot, watching him watch her.

"You know the fantasy I had with you and the hypercar…"

"And my glowing red ass?"

"Yeah." He stopped at the motorcycle and hauled her against his chest, smiling against her lips. "You just topped it."

UNSHACKLE

"*We* topped it. Thank you for that, for what you did in there." She raked her hands through his hair and kissed his mouth. "I love you."

Impact. Direct shot to the chest.

"I felt that." He rested his brow against hers.

"I'll say it again if you stop for ice cream on the way home."

"Klondike bar?"

"Three boxes." She wedged on the helmet and flipped up the visor. "Variety packs. All the flavors."

"One box." He straddled the bike and pulled on his own helmet. "Six orgasms."

She started to argue until she registered the last part. Then she grinned, slapped down the visor, and climbed on behind him.

"No stops." She rested her chin on his shoulder and hugged his back. "Let's go home."

DOMINATE
PAM GODWIN

Book 8

PROLOGUE

Pecos River Bridge
Langtry, Texas
Ten years ago

There were many reasons to jump, but Rylee Sutton only needed one to step off the ledge.

He was her one.

Her only.

Her first love, her best friend, her husband.

He *had been* her ever after.

Now there was no future. No do-overs. Nothing left but inconsolable pain.

She couldn't breathe. Couldn't see through the searing blur of tears that poured from the damage inside her.

Goddammit, she was a mess. How had she ended up here?

Perched on the bridge high above the Pecos River gorge, she dangled her feet over the yawning black abyss, her flip-flops clinging precariously to her toes. Another sob shuddered up, and she angrily kicked off the sandals, sending them tumbling into the dark.

Plunging.

A silent, insignificant drop.

She would be next.

After a four-second fall at seventy-five miles per hour, she would crash into the Pecos River with the force of a speeding truck colliding with a concrete building.

She'd thought about this a lot, had done the research, and knew this was the one thing she would *not* fail.

She was done. Done failing at life. Done failing her husband.

If she only knew where she'd gone so terribly wrong.

She'd supported Mason through thirteen years of medical school and residency, worked multiple jobs to pay off his student loans, and delayed her own career pursuits to assist the startup of his private practice.

Together, they'd been an unstoppable team. The power couple that all others envied. She'd helped him become an orthopedic surgeon, and now, he was supposed to be at her side while she studied criminal justice.

Only he wasn't with her.

He was with someone else.

Anguish surged faster, harder, wracking her body in vicious waves. She clapped a hand over her mouth and sobbed against her fingers.

She loved him so much it hurt. She hurt so badly she couldn't see past it. Couldn't see anything but the images of him with another woman.

"I knew, Mason," she cried, yelling at the moonless, unfeeling sky. "I've known for months and refused to believe it."

She was an idiot.

His late nights at work, shady excuses, casual flirting with other women, disinterest in sex with her—all the signs had been there, glaring at her. So two nights ago, she followed him. Watched him enter an unfamiliar house without knocking. Waited for him to come back out.

When he didn't, she stormed right up to the front door and opened it.

No amount of suspicion could've prepared her for the sight of her husband banging a woman against the wall. He hadn't even made it past the front room before shoving his dick inside her.

Rylee had lost her shit. Utterly. Maniacally. She'd screamed. He'd begged for forgiveness. She'd left in her car, and he'd chased on foot.

The devastation was so complete she couldn't remember the last two days. She hadn't gone home. Instead, she'd driven five hours through the desert, stayed in a motel, and found herself in Nowhere, Texas, staring over the side of a bridge.

She couldn't pull herself away from the ledge. Revenge was gnawing. Consuming. Demanding that she hurt him as deeply as he'd hurt her.

Her death would destroy him.

Lifting her phone, she glanced at the twenty new texts and missed calls. He'd left hundreds of messages over the past two days, ranging the spectrum from denial and anger to guilt and fear. He was sorry. He wanted her back. He would do anything for her. Blah, blah, blah.

DOMINATE

If she went home, maybe he would wear her down and convince her to stay. But she would never forgive him. Never forget. He'd decimated the very foundation of her existence. She didn't have the energy to rebuild. Couldn't fathom starting over at age thirty-one.

She didn't want a life without him.

His messages would go unanswered. But she wouldn't depart this world without the final word.

Tears fell in steady streams down her cheeks as she opened the camera on her phone, switched to video mode, and pressed record.

"Mason, you dumb son of a bitch. You fucked up. You fucked around, and you fucking lost me. I'd say that I hope it was worth it, but I know it wasn't. The moment you put your dick in her, you ruined both of our lives."

The light post across the bridge illuminated a halo behind her, but the screen showed only her face. A ghastly, puffy-eyed, *old* face. She stared at the image for several seconds, shocked by her reflection.

"The face staring back at me isn't mine. It's the face of a defeated woman. I don't recognize her. I don't accept her, and I fucking despise her for the things she cannot change." She swiped at the torrent of tears, unable to rein in the fury in her voice. "I read your messages and listened to your voicemails. You claim it was just sex with that woman, that it meant nothing. If that were true, why do I feel so dead? I used to get tingles every time I thought of you. Now I just feel cold and sick with this slimy, hateful sensation stuck in my gut. That's never going away. So I have a choice. I can live with the pain. Or I can end it."

Her hands trembled so violently she jostled the phone. Readjusting her grip, she swallowed. Blinked. Cleared her voice.

"Maybe I feel too much. Do I? I think I do. I think I loved you too much. Certainly more than you deserved. So I'm going to stop that. I'm just going to stop feeling. I gave you thirteen years, and what did I ask for in return? Fidelity? I wish you would've told me that was too much to ask. Maybe you didn't know. But you should have. You're a fucking doctor. All that schooling to learn how to heal people, and in the end, you hurt the person who loved you the most. Well, you can just fuck right off. You did your thing, and now I'm going to finally do something for me. I'll see you in hell."

Numb, she stopped the recording. She was spent. Empty. There was nothing left.

She had no living family. No one to mourn her death.

Except him.

He would watch the video after she was gone, and maybe it would wreck him so completely he would eventually follow her off the bridge. It was the cruelest, most selfish thing she could do. The person she was before would've never been so vindictive.

But that person was already dead.

She opened her email to forward the video to him. By the time he received it, she would be at the bottom of the river.

The tightness in her chest choked her breaths. Her eyes were so hot and swollen it was like looking through ripped scabs. She rubbed her lashes and squinted at the screen.

A new email had popped up. *Weird.* It wasn't in her inbox but in the unknown account she'd logged into weeks ago.

Her finger hovered over it.

No. Forget it. She should just send the video and be done with this.

But that account... Why was it receiving an email now? It had never been used. No incoming or outgoing messages ever.

A month ago, she bought a jacket at a thrift store in El Paso. In the pocket, she'd found the email address and password scribbled on a scrap of paper. At the time, the romantic in her had been drawn to the username.

Tommysgirl.

Someone had created it a few months before she'd acquired the jacket. They seemed to have forgotten about the account.

She'd forgotten about it, too.

"It's not important. Just delete the account and erase everything."

She didn't want anyone thinking she'd been having an affair with a guy named Tommy.

As she switched to the account to remove it, her attention snagged on the subject line of the message.

I need you.

Three words, so simple and ambiguous, yet they sneaked beneath her desolation and shone a blinding light on the most broken parts of her.

She desperately needed to be needed.

The fog in her head lifted as she quickly opened the message and read the first line.

I know you're dead, but you're still my girl. I need you.

Her gaze skipped to the bottom of the letter and landed on the signature.

Tommy.

Who was he? Who was Tommy's girl?

DOMINATE

Her heart hammered as she absorbed the rest of the email.

I've been avoiding this email account. I mean, I created it and gave it to you the day I lost you. It's like I knew I would need to write this letter to your ghost.

Maybe that's fucked-up, but I need you to hear me. I don't think I can keep going if you're not out there, somewhere in the ether, listening.

They said you died in that car accident, but your spirit is too bright, too big, to just vanish. You always smiled at me like you were part of a better world, so I think that's why you left. You were destined for something greater.

I wish you could tell me where you went. Is it nice? Are you alone?

It's dark here. Everything feels haunted. All I see is shadows, the ones you left behind. They're in the hallways at school, on the trails we walked between our houses, and in the rocks we climbed in the desert.

Your ghost belongs to me. It's the only thing I got to keep. All your possessions were snatched up by extended family and sold off. But your ghost is mine. Except I can't wrap my arms around it. I don't know how to hold it and kiss it.

I miss your lips.

I just want to be with you.

You were supposed to grow up and become the strong woman you were meant to be. I couldn't wait for you to grow up with me.

How could you leave me here to live without you? I want to be mad at you, but I miss you too much. I miss you.

I just...miss you.

It's not fair what happened to you and your family. Or what's happened to me. I guess I can be angry about it forever, or I can just try to...be.

You've been gone for six months. Did you know that? Does time move the same where you are?

My mom makes me see a therapist because I won't talk to her. Funny how, when bad things happen, people make it worse by feeling sorry for you. I see the pity in their eyes, the shared looks of concern. What they're thinking and not saying is that I'm horribly fucked-up and make everyone uncomfortable.

Grownups are clueless. They think they can fix things, like I need someone to take care of me, but mostly they just want me to act normal.

I can act normal and feel brave and still find myself falling.

Maybe that's what love does. It gives you hope then throws you off the cliff into terrible darkness so that every memory stays with you into infinity.

I'm drowning in memories. I remember when you were born, when you started walking, talking, and running faster than me. Jesus, you were fast. I was always chasing you, wasn't I?

Now I'm chasing shadows.

You know what really messes me up? The fact that I've been waiting my entire life for you to get older, and now you never will.

You'll always be fourteen. Three years younger than me this year. Four years younger than me next year. The year after that, five years younger. I have to graduate from high school in the spring, knowing that you will never join me on the other side.

All the dreams we talked about — college, marriage, the dogs, the kids, the house with the pond, everything we planned... Our future died with you. We did everything right, and it all turned around on us.

You're mine, but you're not. Mine to protect, but I can't do that, can I?

I guess you don't need protection where you are. You're free from danger and pain. Congratulations on being free. But I'm still here, reaching for you and waiting for you to reach back.

Losing you feels like I lost myself. When I try to talk about it, I hear a noiseless hush. Echoes, maybe. Like strangled screaming from somewhere inside me. That really sucks, you know? I can't talk to the therapist. It's a waste of goddamn time.

But writing the words to you... I don't know. This is easier. I don't feel so helpless and weird. Because I know you're listening without judgment. Even when you don't like what I say, you've always listened.

Maybe if I keep writing, if I tell you about the guy who misses his girl, no matter how bad it is, I won't be stuck in this story anymore. I'll be the author of it.

Authors have the ultimate power. They can save a character. Or kill him off. I like that idea.

Shit, I need to go. My mom's calling for me. I think she's lying about how bad her cancer is. I'll tell you about that another time.

Thank you for listening.
I wish you were here.
Yours,
Tommy

A lump knotted in her throat, and her tears cascaded with a vengeance. She read through the email again and again, hurting for him through every word. He was only seventeen. Just a kid. Yet he had more strength and maturity than she did at thirty-one.

Boy, did that put her pathetic life into perspective.

What the hell was she doing?

She sat back against the guardrail and pointed her toes toward the black nothingness below. Nighttime insects buzzed around her, and in the distance, the rushing river beckoned.

"Mason cheated on me." She spat the words off the bridge.

She repeated it over and over. Every time she screamed it, the statement was no less true, but it started to lose its power over her.

So he cheated on her. Was that really worth killing herself over?

Yes.

She thought about it and asked the question again.

DOMINATE

Maybe. I don't know.

Mason hadn't died in a car accident. His life hadn't been stolen from her. He was an unfaithful husband. A dirtbag. A man who didn't love her enough to be faithful.

This kid, Tommy, was dealing with something far more tragic, and she didn't sense a hint of suicide in his email. He was powering through it, pushing forward, despite the excruciating pain and loneliness.

If he loved his girlfriend even a fraction as much as she loved Mason, he was hurting. Inconsolably. The more a person loved something, the harder it was to lose it.

She felt that loss at the center of her bones. It was a winless battle she didn't want to fight.

Until she'd read that message.

Now she didn't know what to do. She couldn't email the boy. If she did, he would stop writing to his girlfriend and lose that outlet to express his feelings.

He needed someone to hear him, and deep down, she knew she needed to listen. She couldn't compare his misery to hers. It wasn't even in the same realm. But she related to his words and felt his insecurities like they were her own.

He gave her strength. But was she strong enough to start over? She wasn't seventeen anymore.

She wasn't ninety, either. Age was just a number. An excuse to give up.

Mending a broken heart felt impossible. But that was life, wasn't it? Everyone got their heart broken at least once. Now that she'd experienced it, she knew how to avoid it.

She wouldn't go home. She would never fall in love again. She could focus on a career. Did she still want that?

Did she still want to jump?

It would be easier.

Since when did she ever take the easy route?

Fuck, she was just so tired. Exhaustion pushed in from every direction, pulling on her limbs and straining her insides. It hurt to breathe.

Maybe she should go back to the motel and sleep on it. But if she stepped away from this bridge, she knew she wouldn't return.

So she stayed. Deliberated. Reread Tommy's email. Listened to Mason's new voicemail messages. Then she watched her video through a fresh sheen of tears.

On the screen, she looked like a raving lunatic. A sad, pitiful victim crying out for help. That wasn't her. It was just a moment, one she'd needed to give herself. If she was brave enough, she could put the video and all thoughts of suicide behind her.

She deleted the recording. Then she sat in the silence and allowed herself to grieve.

Hours passed. She remained on the bridge until the first rays of dawn broke over the horizon.

She hadn't slept. Hadn't jumped. But she was no longer crying.

After spending the evening imagining what her life would look like without Mason, she had a plan. It wasn't dreamy or exciting, but it was obtainable. She could get by with a broken heart, and maybe someday, she might find a way to be happy as a single woman.

The sunrise stretched pink and lavender fingers across the rippling surface of the river below. In the light, a fall at this height felt a lot more daunting.

Her moment to jump had come and gone.

Woodenly, she gathered her things into her bag and checked her phone.

Another email had been sent to *Tommysgirl* ten minutes ago. She opened the message.

Me again.
I fought with my mom last night. Turns out, I was right about her cancer.
The doctors give her six months to live.
I really need you.
Are you there?

"Yeah." She stepped away from the ledge and trudged to her car on bare feet. "I'm here, Tommy."

ONE

Eldorado, Texas
Present Day

"I'll only be gone a month, Evan." Rylee breezed past him, her mind running in a million different directions. "The lights are on timers, so don't mess with the switches."

"At least tell me where you're going." Evan caught her arm, stopping her at the front door. "You owe me that much."

"Bullshit." Anger flared as she whirled on him. "I had one rule."

"I never agreed —"

"No expectations. No commitments. No possessive behavior."

"That's three."

"All synonymous with *no clinging.*"

"I'm not…" He followed her narrowed gaze to his grip on her arm. "Jesus." His fingers sprung open, releasing her. "Don't break my balls because I give a shit."

"Stop."

"Stop what? Caring about you?"

"Yes." She grabbed her backpack and slung it over her shoulder on her way out the door. "My bills are paid through next month. You're listed as my emergency contact, but nothing is going to happen. It's just a sabbatical. My first vacation *ever.*"

"Rylee." He stepped in front of her, blocking her exit off the porch.

"Evan." Impatience clipped her voice.

His bright blue eyes searched her face as his hand crept along her jaw, soft yet demanding. "Let me in."

She'd let him in her bed, and that was enough.

More than enough.

In the ten years since her divorce, she made it a point only to have sex with strangers. She didn't do relationships. Never slept with the same man twice. She didn't let people in.

Then Evan moved into the house next door.

For the first few years, she turned down his persistent sexual advances. Didn't matter how goddamn good-looking he was. A one-night stand with a guy who lived twenty feet away was a terrible idea.

But Evan was confident and aggressive and gorgeous in all the ways that spoke to her. So it happened—late one evening, after too many beers and a long bout of loneliness.

Drunken stupidity had been her excuse the first time. But the sex was good. So she let it continue. With one rule.

No clingy attachment.

Except they were together a lot. His place. Her place. Several nights a week. Until she woke one morning and realized he was the only man who had been in her bed in over a year.

She'd broken her own damned rule.

Not only did she have sex with her next-door neighbor, but she'd also become monogamous with him. That was dangerously close to a relationship.

"I need to go." She tried to step around him.

"You have no obligations for the next month." He stayed with her, sliding a hand into the back pocket of her jeans, his fingers squeezing her butt as he tucked their hips together. "Give me a few minutes."

She pulled in a calming breath, which inadvertently drew his sexy, masculine scent into her lungs. He smelled amazing, but she was immune. Damaged. Closed off to anything beyond a casual hookup.

Ten years hadn't dulled the thorns inside her. If anything, time had made her harder, icier, more set in her ways. She wasn't looking to change. Detachment suited her career and safeguarded the life she'd built for herself.

But it didn't negate the fact that Evan was her friend. Her only friend. He didn't deserve to be stonewalled.

She lowered the backpack to the porch and rested her hands on his biceps. Thick, corded muscle stretched the sleeves of his shirt, every inch honed through manual labor in his construction job.

DOMINATE

At age forty-three, he was two years her senior, divorced, and living paycheck to paycheck just like her. His modest two-bedroom house was well-kept like hers. He drank cheap, domestic beer like her. His life was humble, unsophisticated, and honest. Like hers.

But unlike her, he had no reservations about putting himself out there—his generosity, his vulnerabilities, and his overprotective heart.

Evan was a catch, and every unattached woman in their small Texan town wanted him. He needed to stop wasting his time with her.

"All right." She straightened her spine, wishing she were anywhere but here. "I'm listening."

"You should see the look on your face. It's as if a conversation with me makes you physically ill. It's not like I'm asking you to marry me."

Blood drained from her cheeks, and she suddenly felt lightheaded and shaky.

"Fuck, Rylee." He cupped her neck, eyes blazing and mouth twisting with malevolence. "I'm going to kill that son of a bitch."

She never told him about Mason, never even mentioned she was divorced. But over the years, Evan had put it together. Every time she shut him out, he blamed a man she tried to forget.

"Are you going to slay all my demons?" she asked.

"If you let me."

"Because I'm not strong enough to fight them myself?"

"Don't put words in my mouth. You've been fighting for years, proving to the world that you're an impenetrable badass. I get it. You don't need me or anyone else. But dammit, if you let me in, you won't have to fight alone."

With a sigh, she rested her cheek on his chest. "You're a good man."

"The best you'll find this side of the Rio Grande. You should be chasing me, not the other way around."

The only thing she chased was her career, but she wouldn't insult him by voicing what he already knew.

His hand settled on the back of her head, holding her against him. "Tell me where you're going."

"Three hours from here."

"Which direction?"

"West."

"The desert?" He tensed. "Have you lost your mind? A beautiful woman in no man's land? *Alone*? It's crawling with rattlesnakes and scorpions and hell knows what else. Not to mention there's no cell service. No hospitals. What in God's name is out there worth risking your life?"

"Closure."

"So this is about the ex-husband." His fingers angrily fisted in her hair.

"Not exactly." She shut her eyes, searching for an ambiguous version of the truth. "I need to deal with some things. Personal issues I should've put to rest a long time ago."

More specifically, she needed to deal with the boy who had been writing to her—or rather, his dead girlfriend—for ten years.

Except Tommy wasn't a boy anymore. He was twenty-seven. *And dangerous.*

It was never her intention to announce herself to him, let alone meet him in person. Hell, she never should've logged into his girlfriend's account. But if she hadn't, she wouldn't be alive today to contemplate whether or not she was doing the right thing.

He'd been there for her on that bridge without knowing it, and she'd been here for him ever since.

For over a decade, weekly emails arrived in the *Tommysgirl* account. Each message came from a different anonymous address, but they were all from Tommy. After she read each one, she snapped a photo of it, marked it as unread, and deleted her IP address from the activity log.

The day after sending each message, he always went in and erased it. He only needed to change the password on the account once, and she would've been locked out. But he never did. Because that would've locked out his beloved ghost.

An absurd thought, but she knew how his mind worked, perhaps better than he did. He was smart. Too smart to believe that dead people read emails.

But sometimes, beneath his brave, self-assured words, she sensed the lasting sorrow of the boy he'd been. A boy who'd lost his girlfriend in a car accident, his only parent to cancer, and had been abducted and raped by a heartless sex trafficker, all at the age of seventeen.

He'd survived things that most people couldn't fathom and found the courage to write down his trauma in harrowing detail. She never wanted him to learn she'd invaded his privacy. His emails hadn't been meant for her, and responding to them would've been cruel. But when he sent that last message a week ago, she had no choice.

"What the fuck are you going to do in the desert for a month?" Evan leaned down, putting his scowl in her face. "Sprinkle sage on some coals, trip on peyote, and take a revelatory journey until you've vanquished these issues you think you have?"

"Something like that, but without the psychedelics." She pursed her lips. "And we both know I have issues."

Almost as many as Tommy.

DOMINATE

First off, he was going undercover to infiltrate a Mexican cartel, which was by far the most reckless, idiotic thing he'd ever attempted. He had training and experience with his vigilante team, but not enough. Not to take down an entire cartel.

When he made that announcement in his last email, she panicked. Then he ended the message, stating he wouldn't write again.

It was a final goodbye.

A sucker punch to the gut.

No more emails. No more contact. He was going to shut down the account.

If she hadn't written him back, she would've lost him. She might've lost him anyway.

It had been a week without a response to her email. She worried herself sick, wondering if she would ever hear from him again. He used so many different accounts. What if he didn't check them all?

No, he was too meticulous. He probably didn't read her message until he was deep undercover. Man oh man, his reaction must've been boiling, volcanic fury. No question, he was plotting her death at this very moment.

She'd violated his most private thoughts, infringed upon his darkest moments, stole his secrets out from under him, and he didn't even know she existed.

Until now.

It was such a fucked-up situation. From her perspective, he was familiar and intimate. A friend she dropped everything for. Someone she cared about and fretted over. It was the only relationship that worked for her because she didn't have to give any part of herself in return. He couldn't hurt her as long as he didn't know she was there.

She didn't need a degree in psychology to recognize how unhealthy that was. Every time she read his emails, she knew exactly what she was doing. She also understood the consequences of responding to the last one.

He was coming for her.

While that scared the ever-loving piss out of her, it'd been the only way to draw him out of the life-threatening operation he was undertaking with the cartel.

He'd saved her life on the Pecos River Bridge, and now it was her turn to save him.

So she'd devised a plan. An insane, treacherous, terrifying plan. Then she emailed him back, confessed to reading his emails, and told him when and where to meet her.

Evan knew none of this. He didn't know about the bridge or the *Tommysgirl* account or the man, whose name she learned a few years ago was Tomas Owen Dine.

God, if Evan even suspected what she planned to do, he would tie her up and never let her leave.

"I'm going with you." His hands ghosted along her back.

"Oh, really? You're going to take off work for a month?"

"For as long as you need me."

She didn't need him. The thought made her feel like a bitch, but this was something she had to do alone.

"I need you to look after my house." She pinched his rigid jaw and gave him a stern look. "You're not going. That's non-negotiable."

"I figured you'd say that." He eyed the camping gear in her pickup truck in the driveway. "What happens when a hungry bobcat attacks your campsite?"

"Mosquitoes are a greater risk to humans than bobcats."

"Because most humans don't camp out in wildcat territory."

"I have a shotgun."

He already knew that. He'd gone target shooting with her at the range.

"I guess there's just one thing left to say." He gripped the backs of her legs and hooked them around his hips, holding her so close his breath kissed her lips. "And one thing only—"

"Just say it."

He smiled, his teeth blinding white in his suntanned face. "I'm going to miss your hot body."

With a quick dip, he claimed her mouth. Warm tongue, firm lips, clean taste, his kisses were always agreeable. Pleasing. Yet something was missing. Nothing she could label. Just an itch at the back of her mind.

It was her, not him.

She tried to lower her feet to the ground, but he tightened his grip. She leaned away, but his mouth chased hers, intent on recapture.

"Evan."

"One for the road." He pulled her tight against his erection, grinding seductively. "I'll settle for a quickie."

"No."

"Come on, Rylee. How am I going to go without you for an entire month?"

"You have plenty of booty calls." She snatched the phone from his back pocket and pulled up his contact list. "Who do you want? Addy? Amy? Ashley? Ava? Wow, so many options, and I haven't even made it past the *A* names."

"You're the only one I want." He ripped the phone from her hand and tossed it onto the porch swing. "And you're the reason those women are in my contact list."

That was true. She pushed him onto every unwed lady she encountered.

Somehow, she'd fallen into monogamy while making sure he didn't. She needed to see those women slipping out of his house in the mornings, so that each one could add another mile of emotional distance between her and her charming neighbor.

"I told you no expectations." She squirmed in his arms. "I suck at this."

"Yeah, you do." He set her on her feet. "Only because you want to suck at it." He grabbed her backpack and slung it over her shoulders. Then he fisted the straps, yanked her close, and stole a kiss from her lips. "Get out of here before I carry you into the bedroom and delay your trip."

"Thank you." She stepped back, gave him a small smile, and headed to the truck.

"Rylee."

"Yeah?" She glanced back.

"I'm going to be pissed if anything happens to you."

"I'll take that under advisement."

But no promises.

She hoped to stop Tommy from killing her, but there were no guarantees he wouldn't hurt her before she convinced him to see reason. She didn't know what he looked, sounded, or smelled like. Didn't know anything about him in the physical sense. She wouldn't even be able to pick him out in a crowd.

But she knew his psychological and criminal profile like the back of her hand.

Heaven has no rage like love to hatred turned.

She imagined that summed up his current state of mind. By reading what he'd written to the girl he loved, she'd stained his words. He would regret revealing so much of himself and view the letters as weapons turned against him, his secrets and insecurities wrongfully exposed.

Hell has no fury like a man deceived.

She anticipated his wrath, feared it, but she wouldn't run. She had a month off of work.

A month in the desert with a livid, deadly criminal.

She would survive this, or she wouldn't. But she owed it to both of them to see it through.

TWO

The charred structure protruded from the dry, crusty earth. Rylee's chest tightened as she shaded her eyes, squinting at the rubble around her, trying to make out what was left of the Milton house.

Caroline Milton.

Tommy's girl.

Two exterior walls jutted in misshapen pieces, weathered by years of dust storms. A fire had devoured the rest. Arson. The conflagration had burned so hotly it had melted the stone foundation.

A shiver ran up her spine. With zero cover and nothing but buttes, craters, and searing sand in every direction, it felt as though she were standing amid ancient ruins on an alien moon.

This barren part of the Chihuahuan Desert promised hardship to anyone living here, which was why Caroline's house had sat empty for years after the family died.

Until Tommy bought it and burnt it to the ground.

His own childhood home stood two miles away. A grueling distance for two kids to trek to see each other. The next closest neighbor was thirty minutes by car, so maybe that two-mile hike was a blessing.

The unforgiving sun beat down on her neck, burning her fair skin as she pushed sand over the bag she'd buried in the remains of Caroline's house. The duffel contained her ID, credit card, phone, and license plates from her truck—everything she carried that could identify her. The phone was the hardest to relinquish, but without cell service, it was useless.

Sweat trickled between her breasts, her body temperature rising to unbearable levels. She released her ponytail and shook out her hair, using the length to cover her shoulders and arms. She wouldn't last an hour out here without turning into a blistered tomato.

The heat chased her back into the cab of the air-conditioned truck. She leaned toward the vent, absorbing the cold air as her mind drifted to the next task.

Was Tommy already at his house, waiting for her? What if he hadn't made it out of the cartel's headquarters? She'd only given him a week's notice.

He had the resources to learn who she was and everything about her. The man on his team, Cole, had some sort of military background that enabled him to erase their identities from existence. With time, that guy would've found her. But probably not within the week she'd given. And not while Tommy was undercover and unable to make contact with him.

Tommy's emails never disclosed last names. Not his, Caroline's, or any of his friends'. Rylee only discovered his identity, and that of the Milton family, by piecing together the clues he'd provided, such as the descriptions of his rural home, the details of Caroline's car accident, and the fire he'd set to her family's property.

After she determined where he grew up, she'd driven by a couple of times to check out the place. But not recently, and she'd never dared to step out of her truck and peek inside for fear of being discovered.

Her nerves coiled as she put the truck into motion. In a few moments, she would finally come face to face with the one person she knew better than anyone in the world.

The first few seconds would be critical. He would either listen to her introduction or shoot her in the head.

She'd discarded all her identification because she didn't want him investigating her without talking to her. It would be safer for her and everyone in her life if she defused his anger before giving him too much information.

Navigating along the bumpy terrain, she white-knuckled the steering wheel and swallowed her rising trepidation. There were no roads or tracks. Every landmark looked the same, from the tufts of desert growth to the steep, flat-top hills. It was a wonder she'd found this place the first time.

When the one-story adobe brick building came into view, her entire body began to shake. Adrenaline flooded her system, her senses firing on high alert.

He kept company with a gang of violent criminals and could've brought a few of those terrifying friends along. Except she knew he wouldn't. In his rage, he would regard her as *his* problem, one he'd created, a horrible mistake he needed to clean up.

Tomas Dine—complicated man and lone wolf—would walk through hell to resolve his dilemmas on his own.

What concerned her was that while she knew him, he didn't know her. She was the stranger.

From his perspective, she was the enemy.

Sweeping her gaze over the abandoned house, she found it just as creepy and unkempt as the first time she visited. An old tractor rusted on rotting tires in the unfertilized, parched soil. A windmill canted off-balance, missing most of its blades.

Heavy drapes covered the small square windows. The satellite dish on the roof appeared to be in working condition. But was the electricity on to power it?

Nothing had changed. No vehicles. No signs of life.

Her heart sank.

She drove a wide circuit around the house, surveying the lot from all angles. If Tommy were here, he'd hiked in or caught a ride.

Returning to the front of the property, she parked the truck, shut off the engine, and... *Holy shit.* The front door stood open. No way had she missed that a minute ago. It had been shut. She was sure of it.

Her pulse exploded, her gaze darting back and forth, probing the windows, the perimeter, searching for movement.

Nothing.

He was inside the house.

The jacket that once belonged to Caroline Milton sat on the seat beside her. She grabbed it and slowly stepped out, her boots crunching the baked dirt. Her palms slicked with sweat, her stomach a wasteland of nauseating energy.

Despite the covered windows, she felt eyes on her as she tramped across the trackless sand to the door. The hair on her arms rose at the unnerving feeling of being watched. Whispers of dust spun up beneath her feet. And the hush... It was deafening, thrashing in her ears.

If she screamed, no one would hear. If he fired a gun, no one would come. If he buried her body out here, no one would know where to look.

Any outsider would think she was batshit crazy for walking in alone, unarmed, and without a phone. Maybe she *was* crazy. But she trusted her instinct. Her training and in-depth understanding of Tommy's personality had guided her here. Her wits and intuition would keep her alive.

DOMINATE

"Tommy," she called out a few feet from the door. "I'm alone."

Silence greeted her.

He'd often mentioned how the unfathomable quiet served as a protective barrier around his home. When something penetrated the stillness, he heard it. No one could sneak onto his property.

No doubt he'd detected her approach long before she'd driven into view. She'd anticipated that. Just like she knew the left floorboard would groan when she entered the house. She knew a small kitchen sat off to one side, opening to the sitting room where his mother lost her fight to cancer.

Two bedrooms in the back shared the bathroom between them, and a problematic hole above the shower let in geckos and scorpions. He'd patched it dozens of times, and the creatures still found a way in.

She knew every nook and cranny of his childhood home, thanks to his detailed descriptions over the years. So many dreams had been conjured within these walls. So many hopes crushed. But not forgotten. He chased their shadows through the rooms, the ghosts of those he loved, which was why he hadn't set it afire like the Milton's home.

"I'm not armed." She held up her hands and stepped over the threshold into darkness. "This is Caroline's jacket. Since you don't have any of her possessions, I thought you'd want this. I'm just going to set it down."

A track of clean wood gleamed along the otherwise dusty floor, tracing a path from the threshold to somewhere beyond the shadows. A trail recently made by footsteps. She toed the dust layer around it, noting the thickness. No one had moved outside that track for months. Probably years.

Placing the jacket on the clean path, she straightened and returned her hands to the air. "I'm standing directly in the sunlight. No weapons. No phone. You can see for yourself."

No response.

Her heart slammed against her ribs, her breaths quickening with the rush of her words.

"My name is Rylee. Originally from El Paso. I moved from there ten years ago because…uh… Well, I'll get to that. I know you have a gun trained on me. I don't blame you since you don't know me or trust me. But believe me when I say I'm more afraid than you are right now. I mean, I can't see you, but you can see me. That puts me at a disadvantage. So I'm just going to keep my hands up and slowly step inside. You said this floorboard creaks so…" She put her boot on it, listening to it protest beneath her slight weight. "Don't shoot."

With the windows covered and the door wide open, a single beam of sunlight stabbed through the darkness, illuminating dust particles like sparkles of glitter.

They made their way into her lungs, and she coughed, cringing as the hacking sound echoed through the house. Dusty boards, dusty drapes, dusty furniture. In the middle of the desert, there was no escape from the powdered sand that covered every surface and filled every crack. She coughed again, stirring up a maelstrom of dirt into the torpid air.

"I know you're here, Tommy." She squinted at the impenetrable shadows, her scalp crawling with dread. "Please, talk to me."

A rustling sound swished on her left, and she spun toward it, gulping. "Tommy?"

Another soft noise whispered behind her. She whirled again, and the door slammed shut, dousing her in pitch blackness.

Sharp, icy fear shot through her, stiffening her joints and freezing her lungs. She tried to speak, but her voice abandoned her. She needed to move to a window and rip off the drapes, but her legs wouldn't work.

Why hadn't she thought to bring the flashlight from the truck?

Another dry cough erupted from her chest, and the wheezing unleashed her voice.

"I'm just going to start talking and try to explain, okay?" She cleared her throat, trembling with unease. "I married the love of my life twenty-three years ago. We had a beautiful life, a promising future, yadda, yadda, lots of superfluous words." She hugged her waist, fighting down old anger as her senses strained in the dark. "Ten years ago, I walked in on him banging another woman. Maybe it's not the same loss you experienced with Caroline, but I loved him. Every breath in my body was his. You know what it feels like to lose your entire world. But I'm not as strong as you. I wasn't. I died that day and had every intention of killing myself for good. I told you how I acquired Caroline's jacket. I never should've logged into the account you created for her. But there I was, standing on the edge of the Pecos River Bridge, when you sent the first email. I wasn't going to read it. I was just going to delete the account and jump. I was going to die, Tommy. I had no reason to live. Until I saw the subject line of your message. *I need you*. Do you remember it?"

Her question hung in the dry air, her eyes wide and unblinking. The memory still hurt. The sticky, hateful slime in her stomach never faded. But she'd managed to keep breathing, keep functioning, even if she was dysfunctional as fuck.

She held still, listening for the sounds of his breaths, footsteps, anything to give away his location.

Seconds of tingling silence passed. He hadn't shot her in the head yet, so that was *something*.

DOMINATE

"You must think I'm a nutjob." She wiped at the sweat gathering on her brow. "Anyone would think that if I told them about you. I haven't. No one has seen your emails. But here's the thing, Tommy. I'm not suicidal anymore. I want to walk out of here unharmed. So I made copies of your messages. They won't be discovered *unless* I go missing. If I don't return home when I'm expected, the authorities will find those copies and know that I drove here to meet with Tomas Owen Dine. I don't want that to happen. I'm not here to hurt you. I have nothing to gain from that. I just want to talk." She caught her breath. "Turn on the lights."

Please, don't kill me. Please, don't kill me.

He didn't make a sound. Nothing.

The longer he kept her in the dark, the more fearful and furious she became.

"I know you're pissed." She forced bravado into her tone. "Fine. Yell at me. Let me hear it. Act like a fucking adult and confront me."

He still had some anonymity because she didn't know what he looked like. But this wasn't about him hiding his face. He was fucking with her.

"I know what you're doing with the silent treatment. The bullshit intimidation tactics are beneath you. It's a dick move and a waste of time. Don't forget, whether you like it or not, I know you better than anyone."

"Are you familiar with the rule of threes?" His deep, gruff voice came from behind her.

With a gasp, she pivoted, reaching out and grabbing only air. "You're talking about the rules for survival?"

Where the hell was he? She stumbled through the dark, arms out, and bumped into the back of the couch.

The bastard was playing with her. Not unexpected. If he terrorized her enough, he could break her down to her most basic instinct. Survival. A human could only endure so much before they surrendered.

But she'd come here prepared to endure a lot.

Where were the windows? Or the light switch? The sheer absence of sight and sound disorientated her. She needed to keep him talking.

"Tell me about the rule of threes." She moved on shaky legs, hopefully in the direction of the door.

"It takes three seconds to make a life-or-death decision." His breath licked across her nape. "Three."

"You won't hurt me." She shivered, uncertain.

"Two."

"I'm not your enemy." She reached for the door, seeking light. Or momentary escape.

"One."

Her fingers caught the knob just as his hands clamped over her mouth and nose.

She bucked, fighting on instinct. She grabbed at his fingers and twisted, thrashing her body and going nowhere against the powerful strength of his.

Jesus fuck, he was huge and brawny and utterly immovable. She'd always pictured him as a gangly, pimple-faced, seventeen-year-old boy. But the beast who was restraining her and cutting off her oxygen was nothing short of terrifying.

Her frantic struggling bumped her back against a hard-muscled frame. A frame that towered over her by a foot. He stood like a concrete pillar behind her, no part of him jostling or shifting as she jerked and kicked and wore herself out.

"You can survive three minutes without air." The cadence of his timbre glided over her like velvet.

Three minutes? No fucking way. Maybe if she was unconscious. Even then, the asphyxiation could cause brain damage.

Her lungs burned, and her chest raged with fiery panic. Had it even been a minute?

She renewed her efforts to escape, flailing for air and trying to bite his hand.

"Two weeks ago, I watched my friend do this to a girl hanging on a meat hook." He adjusted his grip, pinching her nose while smothering her mouth. "She was innocent. Unlike you."

Tears leaked from her eyes and gathered at his fingers. She surpassed discomfort and denial and plummeted headlong into frenzied desperation. She was going to die, right here in the dark, in the arms of a man who never showed her his face. With each second that passed, she was certain it was her last.

"You can survive three hours in the extreme heat of a harsh environment." His stony voice penetrated her agony, torturing her dying heart. "Three days without water. Three weeks without food. Three months without hope." His lips brushed her ear. "Welcome to my world, Rylee from El Paso."

Her lungs gave out, and shadows crept in on all sides, raiding all conscious thought until nothing remained.

No bright light. No life flash. No euphoria.

Just an endless absence of being.

THREE

"Did you kill her?"

"Who fucking cares?" Tomas snarled into the phone and nudged the woman's limp body with his boot.

Calling Cole Hartman was the last thing he wanted to do, but he needed information. Who did she work for? What were her connections? Who would miss her? Why had she really come here?

The woman had an agenda, and she'd been diligent about not giving it away.

He needed Cole to do the investigative work, but when his friend answered the phone, the first thing Tomas asked was, *Are Luke and Vera alive?*

Last time he'd seen or heard from Luke was in the limo before the cartel had escorted Tomas off the property.

Not only had Luke and Vera survived, but apparently, she'd strapped herself with weapons, including a grenade, and taken down the whole fucking La Rocha family. Christ almighty, Tomas adored her. She was beautiful, ferocious, and the perfect match for Luke. Hearing that they were both safe in Colombia almost lifted his murderous mood.

Almost.

He grimaced at the brunette laid out on the floor. Killing her was the cleanest way to handle this, but first, he needed to know who she was.

When he'd received her email a week ago, he intended to hunt her down *before* she showed up here. But that plan was fucked to hell when the cartel forced him out of the limo at gunpoint. He'd found himself stranded in California without money, transportation, or an untraceable phone.

By the time he stole a car, stole another one when he ran out of gas, dumped the last car, and hiked the rest of the way to the house, he'd run out of time. With only a day to spare, he'd spent those hours preparing for the woman's arrival.

Electricity to the house was kept on to power the security cameras and satellite. The latter allowed him to contact Cole. But the moment he hiked out of range of the house, the outside world would be inaccessible.

That was ideal for what he had planned.

He couldn't kill her right away, and considering the seemingly harmless, but insidious manner in which she'd been spying on him for ten goddamn years, he knew it would take some effort to crack her.

So when she'd stopped breathing against his hand, he'd resuscitated her.

"Did you receive the photo I sent of her?" He swept his gaze over the unconscious body, ignoring all the sinful dips and curves and focusing on the fragile bones that would shatter beneath his fists.

"Yeah, I got it," Cole said. "She looks dead. Tell me she's not."

He crouched beside her and touched the pulse point on her throat. "She's not. For now."

"Listen up. If she has copies of your emails, you need her alive and compliant. Don't fuck this up. The lives of your entire team are on the line."

Of course, he fucking knew that. He'd made a mistake sending those emails. A horrendous, mortifying mistake that started when he was seventeen. He hadn't known any better then. But he couldn't use that excuse ten years later.

He *would* fix this.

"She's not carrying ID?" Cole asked.

"Nothing. I searched her pockets, her truck, and all the gear inside it. No phone. She even removed the license plates."

"She's smart."

"She doesn't look so smart now." He glared at her sulky lips which, just moments ago, had been sucking for air against his hand like a dying fish.

"Any tattoos, scars, or birthmarks?"

"None that I can see."

"You haven't stripped her yet?"

"I'm not a pervert."

"Right." Cole's disbelieving tone grated. "How long ago did you knock her out? She shouldn't still be unconscious."

"I gave her a sedative."

DOMINATE

Cole didn't need to ask where the tranquilizer came from. When Tomas and his roommates sold their house in Austin, Texas and moved to the Restrepo headquarters in Colombia, he'd transferred their weapons, electronics, burner phones, and medical supplies here, along with nonperishables, bottled water, and petty cash. It had been Cole's idea. A precautionary measure to ensure the team had a safe house in Texas.

Tomas had enough equipment in this house to restrain and torture the woman for months.

"Okay, so next steps..." Cole exhaled into the phone. "I don't condone the kidnapping of innocent—"

"She trespassed on my property, willingly walked into my house, and she's far from innocent."

"She's guilty of invading your privacy. She hasn't killed anyone."

"That we know of. She has a cheating ex-husband." He updated Cole on everything she'd said when she walked in. "I don't know why she disclosed the details of the affair."

"I'll find out. Just stay put and keep her restrained."

"Where are you?"

"Almost there."

"What the fuck? No, turn back. You don't need to be here." Goddammit, he should've known Cole would show up. "I don't need a babysitter or anyone to clean up my mess. I just need information, and you can dig that up at the headquarters."

"I've been working with Luke and Tate for the past week trying to do just that. We scoured the IP addresses of all the activity on the email account. There's no forwarded mail. No suspicious logins. She knows how to erase her tracks."

"She's in law enforcement."

"Her email implied that, but it's not confirmed. I'll stop in El Paso to do some digging before heading your way. Might take me a few days. In the meantime—"

"I'll call you when she starts spilling secrets." Tomas hung up, seething with frustration.

He couldn't stop Cole from coming to the house. But it didn't matter. His plan to break down Rylee piece by piece would begin out there. He turned toward the open door, sweating in the heat that blasted in from outside.

Four hours until sunset.

He spent the next few minutes unloading her truck. On his way back inside, he tore off his sweat-drenched shirt and checked her breathing.

The cuff on her wrist attached to a chain that restrained her to a post. But she wouldn't be waking any time soon.

He sat back on his heels and let himself fully look at her for the first time.

Long brown hair framed a pixie face. A tiny turned-up nose, cupid lips, and symmetrical features rounded out her delicate bone structure. Flawless porcelain skin and a toned physique gave her the appearance of a woman in her twenties. But she married twenty-three years ago? If that were true, Tomas would've been four at the time.

That would put her in her forties now. Hard to believe.

Maybe she had laugh lines when she smiled or crow's feet when she squinted. But with the muscles relaxed in her face, there were no wrinkles or sunspots. No indication that she was older than him.

Her tits sat high. Her waist tucked in, and her jeans molded to slender hips and legs, leaving little to the imagination. The woman was built. Easily fuckable. Insanely gorgeous.

That only made him hate her more.

Shifting away, he turned his attention to the denim jacket that lay near the door. He remembered it well—the soft texture beneath his hands, the scent of vanilla on the collar, and the small front pocket, where he watched Caroline slip the scrap of paper he'd given her the day she died.

If he hadn't written down the account information, he wouldn't be in this mess. Hell, he should've never written down any of his secrets.

Not just his secrets. He'd spewed an unedited, unfiltered stream of consciousness in those emails. He'd detailed his fears, his regrets, every internal battle, every ridiculous notion in his head, every terrible thing that happened to him, and his desires… Fucking hell, she knew his darkest cravings, his filthy fantasies, his obsession with fucking and dominating and his inability to emotionally connect to sex.

He'd confessed every shameful thought to his girl. Because she was dead. He never imagined anyone reading it. Why would they want to?

What a dumb fucking asshole.

Except the writing had helped him. It had given him a sense of control over a life that had spiraled wildly and dangerously into chaos.

He lifted the jacket to his nose and inhaled deeply. Caroline's vanilla scent was long gone. In its place lingered the aroma of an unfamiliar woman. Undertones of lavender drowned in years of deceit.

He hated her with a blinding passion.

Fury burned anew as he stored the jacket safely in his old bedroom.

Then he loaded the woman into the truck and drove her into the desert.

FOUR

Rylee woke with a hangover.

In the middle of the godforsaken desert.

The sun's unblinking eye glared down at her, scorching her from the inside out. Nausea, headache, crushing heat… She rolled to her stomach and retched precious fluid, groaning miserably.

Fresh pain seeped into her palms, where she'd planted them on the ground.

"Ow, ow, fuck!" She pushed to her knees and shook out her blazing hands.

The sand was the sky's co-conspirator, cooking her as viciously as the sun. And there were miles of it in every direction.

He hadn't just dumped her in this desolate wasteland alone.

He'd shackled her.

A thick leather cuff clamped around her wrist, secured with a tiny padlock. The ring connected to a chain that snaked through the sand and circled the base of an old telephone pole.

From one horizon to the other, that pole was the only sign of human civilization.

Deep cracks forked through the parched earth beneath her, burnt into a hard crust, no more hospitable than a sunbaked rock. If Tommy had driven her here in her truck, the tires had made no impression on the ground.

She felt sick. Aside from her churning stomach, dusty throat, pounding headache, achy muscles, and feverish flu-like symptoms, she was frying in this heat, and that worried her more than anything.

How far would he take this?

She remembered dying. Suffocating beneath his hand. Had he killed her and revived her?

Would he kill her again?

Consumed with panic, she stumbled to her feet and jerked uselessly on the chain. The desert stretched out around her, tufted with shrubs and punctuated with small boulders and tall columns of cacti.

Black vultures circled overhead, eying her like carrion. Reptiles sought shelter in the shadows of the rocks where the sand wouldn't roast them. There was no shade close enough nor large enough to protect her. No water. No breeze. Not a cloud in the sky to filter the harsh rays.

Each searing breath sank into her lungs, drowning her chest in lava.

"You fucking prick! Where are you?" Her scream echoed across the barren terrain. "This isn't how an adult faces his problems. You're a goddamn coward!"

She didn't believe that. A coward would've left her for dead. While he seemed to be doing precisely that, he wouldn't have gone through this trouble after asphyxiating her. What was his plan?

The rule of threes.

She cast her mind back to their ominous conversation, recalling the first and only words he'd spoken to her.

Three seconds to make a life-or-death decision.
Three minutes without air.
Three hours in extreme heat.
Three days without water.
Three weeks without food.
Three months without hope.

Dread swelled, as thick and hot as the air.

He'd already enacted the first two. And now…

"Three hours in extreme heat." She gripped her lurching stomach and fought back tears. "Three fucking hours of this? Are you kidding me?"

She couldn't even think about the remaining rules. First, she had to survive the relentless sun.

How long had she been out here?

Pressing a finger against her forearm, she watched the indentation flash from white to pink. Her skin didn't appear to be burnt. Yet.

She'd arrived at his house with maybe four or five hours left of daylight. Would he leave her out here until dusk? Or all night? Shackled and unprotected?

Predators came out after dark. If she didn't perish from sun-poisoning, she'd make an easy meal for a coyote or snake.

DOMINATE

Tommy had done some stomach-turning shit over the years. He'd killed people. Evil people. But he wasn't cruel enough to let her die like this.

The sun perched too high in the sky, but maybe it was an illusion. Maybe dusk was only an hour away. She could make it until then. She had no choice.

Sitting with her back to the pole, she lowered her head to her bent knees and adjusted her hair to cover her face, neck, and bare arms. Her jeans and boots should protect the rest of her.

The danger lurked in the unrelenting heat. What was the lethal temperature to the human body? How long could she survive out here?

Tommy seemed to think the limit was three hours. But she wasn't a hardened, outdoorsy girl. She camped infrequently and always in campgrounds with shade and running water.

God, she needed water. Her throat felt so raw and sandy it hurt to swallow.

She hated him for this. It was unnecessarily cruel and inhumane. But her clinical mind tried to analyze his behavior from an unbiased angle.

He'd witnessed and experienced the worst of human depravity. The torture he'd endured and inflicted on others had desensitized him. She remembered a story about how his team had injected a man with Krokodil, a flesh-eating cocktail that rotted the skin off the bones while he was still alive.

In Tommy's world, brutality and death were as common as nightfall.

He'd been separated from gentle affection and normalcy for so long he'd lost sight of what normal looked like. He could camouflage himself in society, but he would have to undergo a great deal of therapy and self-help to create a lasting positive change. Especially if he ever wanted to engage in a healthy romantic relationship.

She didn't judge him for his psychological shortfalls. She had her own litany of issues. But she would never do something so ruthless as chaining a person in the desert, even if her issues were the reason she was in this predicament in the first place.

Time passed in a blistering haze. She held still within the dark curtain of her hair, sweating in the oven of her clothes. With each second, the withered shag of the earth blurred into a weird, dehumanized hue. Neither taupe nor gray nor sandy brown, the land was the color of death, reflecting back at her.

She tried to keep her spirits up, giving herself pep talks and tracking the descent of the sun. But her nemesis barely moved, its everlasting rays blasting down on her, diminishing her morale.

Salty sweat rolled off her brow and stung her eyes, her clothes unbearably hot and sticky. Gritty sand worked its way into her hair and mouth and coated her tongue with stiff fur. She avoided licking her lips, knowing it would only chap them further.

God, she ached for crystal, cold water. The thought tormented her until she became mad with the craving.

Unbidden, she wet her lips and tasted... *Strange*. She did it again, flooding her mouth with a chemical flavor.

Wiping at the perspiration around her eyes, she held up her hand and stared at a milky residue. Was her facial lotion melting? It should've rubbed off hours ago.

She raised an arm to her mouth and licked. Same chemical taste.

Her heart hammered as she ran her hands over her face and neck. She hadn't noticed it before, but there was definitely a thick layer of cream on her skin.

He'd lathered her with sunscreen.

Oh, Tommy, you miserable, thoughtful, misguided man.

He'd probably done it as an afterthought, telling himself he didn't want to deal with a blistered body. Misguided reasoning, to be sure.

But she remembered the outpouring of devotion and selflessness in the words of the teenage boy before his abduction. He loved a girl with all his heart. He loved his mother and respected the life she'd given him. Following their unimaginable deaths, he'd remained steadfast, never veering into substance abuse or self-destruction. That kind of inner strength didn't just go away. It was innate, sewn into the fabric of his being.

It gave her hope.

A gentle breeze stirred up the wispy sand and brushed across her skin like drafts from a fire. There was no escape from the hellacious temperature. It sat heavily on her chest, making every breath an exhausting effort.

Gradually, the heat chased her into a fitful slumber. Each time she woke, she felt disoriented and confused. In and out of sleep, she fumbled between reality and hallucination until everything smeared together, plunging her into a nebulous hinterland.

At some point, the fog lifted, as did the torrential heat. She rubbed her eyes, drowsy and weak, squinting in the dark.

Twilight had arrived in the desert. The huge, pale moon rose over the edge of the desolate landscape, its beams falling on the murky outline of a vehicle.

Her truck.

It parked several yards away, pointed in the opposite direction.

DOMINATE

Her heart pounded, and her skin shivered, for perched on the open tailgate was the silhouette of a man.

A cowboy hat angled low on his brow, casting his face in shadow. But it didn't hide the bristling tension surrounding him nor the rage in his unmitigated stare, burning as hot as the Texan sun.

Tommy hadn't left her for dead, but she might wish for that before he was done with her.

FIVE

Rylee lay on her side, her hair stuck to her face and stiff with sand. As she slowly rose to sit, her head swam with fuzz. Dehydration. But her arm was free. Tommy had removed the cuff.

He lifted a water bottle to his lips and drank deeply, watching her, taunting her.

She followed the movement of his throat with longing, swishing her tongue in her mouth, trying to gather moisture where there was none.

"I need water," she croaked, her voice covered in dust.

The plastic crinkled in his hand, and he tossed the empty bottle in the truck bed behind him.

"You think I can survive out here for three days without water?" Her anger fired on all cylinders as she attempted to stand. "Is this my punishment for reading your emails?" Her legs gave out, sending her back to the prickly earth. "Fucking harsh, don't you think?"

He stretched out along the tailgate, crossed his cowboy boots at the ankles, and reclined against the side of the truck bed.

Hard to make out his form in the blackness of night, but there was something about his presence that intrigued and allured. Maybe it was his brooding silence. Or the cocksure tilt of his hat. Or the dark, intimidating confidence that radiated from his posture.

Whatever it was, she had no business admiring him with female appreciation. She wasn't here for that. Besides, the motherfucker had just put her through ungodly hell, and he wasn't finished.

DOMINATE

"You're going to regret this someday." She ran her hands over her hair and clothes, attempting to put herself back together. "I know you're ruthless, but you've never harmed an innocent woman. I'm no one, Tommy. I'm sure as hell not your enemy."

"Tell me your full name and date of birth." His gravelly voice rumbled from the shadow of his hat as he produced another bottle of water and set it beside him.

So this was his plan. Take away the basic requirements for survival and dangle them piece by piece as a trade for information.

"What did you do while I roasted in the desert for the past three hours?" she asked. "Did you contact Cole to initiate an investigation on me?"

As expected, he gave no answer.

All they had to go on was her first name and the city where she grew up. There were a lot of Rylees in El Paso. It would take time to identify her and those she cared about.

She had an ex-husband who never remarried and a neighbor with benefits. That was the extent of her liabilities.

But the moment he learned her occupation, address, and boring background, the mystery would be over. He would send her home with a threat to kill her loved ones if she ever leaked information about him. Then he would disappear forever.

That outcome was inevitable, but before that happened, she had a desperate, reckless need to help him.

She cared about him. Deeply. It was a one-sided sentiment, a motivation he couldn't possibly understand because he didn't know her the way she knew him.

He wasn't happy. Not today, not last week, not one second in the past ten years. His friends, the family of ex-captives who had his back, didn't know the extent of his suffering. He concealed it from them because he didn't want to be a burden. He didn't even know how to open up to someone. For a decade, he carried around a terrible weight in his soul, confiding in no one. Except a dead girl.

That in and of itself troubled her.

After his abduction, he lived with his vigilante team. But over the years, his roommates found partners, some of them married, and the dynamics of their tight-knit clan changed. They were moving on.

Unless something changed since his last email, he and Luke were the only bachelors left.

"What happened with the cartel?" She squinted at his shadow, unable to see his eyes in the dark.

Silence.

Exasperated, she glanced around and spotted a black smudge on the ground several feet away. She crawled toward it, marveling at how quickly the sand had already cooled.

"I assume the cartel bought your undercover story? Either that or you escaped." She focused on the dark object and quickened her movements when she realized it was her backpack. "Where's Luke?"

She pulled the pack onto her lap and dug through the contents while watching him out of the corner of her eye. His silhouette didn't twitch. No sound. No attempt to take away her belongings.

It occurred to her that his undercover operation might've gone terribly wrong. They went in to find Tula's sister. Tula, who had fallen in love with Martin and Ricky during a mission in a Mexican prison.

What if Luke hadn't made it out of the cartel headquarters? What if he'd been forced to kill Vera, Tula's sister?

"You said your friend killed an innocent girl on a meat hook." She shivered, her voice wavering. "Tommy? Is Luke okay? And Vera? Please, you have to tell me."

"Why the fuck do you care?"

Her pulse skipped at the sound of his voice. "I'm invested. For ten years—"

"You've been collecting intel on my team. Tell me what you're doing with that information."

"Nothing."

"Bullshit."

"You needed someone to hear you. So I listened. Through every word, no matter how uncomfortable or horrifying, I silently supported you, rooted for you and your friends. I'm still doing that. It's the *only* reason I'm here."

"You're a liar."

"I speak the truth. You're just not ready to hear it."

She took an inventory of the supplies in her pack. Some of her belongings were here. The first-aid kit. Sunscreen. Extra clothes. But he'd removed the rest, the things she needed most, such as water, food, weapons, maps, and the compass.

But he'd left the small lantern and its solar-powered charger. She grabbed it, turned it on, and wobbled to her feet.

Thirst was her loudest ache. It screamed from her stomach and clouded her head. Fatigue and fear followed closely behind, making every step to the truck feel like a mile.

The lantern's dim light helped her navigate the uneven terrain. She didn't have a plan beyond the imperative to be in that vehicle when it left.

Halfway there, a startling, ear-splitting bang ricocheted through her skull. Gravel sprayed beside her boots, and she screamed, staggering backward and falling on her butt.

For a moment, she thought he'd shot her. But the sudden pain in her chest was just her heart ramming against her ribs.

"Have you lost your mind?" she roared, swinging the lantern toward him. "If you don't want me to approach, use your fucking words, not a—"

The light snagged on a long, scaly body beside her. Four feet in length, a diamondback rattlesnake lay unmoving, bleeding from the head.

"Oh, my God." She scrambled to her feet, tripping over a deep crack to get away from it. "Fucking shit. Fuck, fuck, fuck."

Her breathing rampaged as full-body tremors robbed her balance. That venomous thing had been right next to her! And he'd shot it with impossible accuracy.

He'd saved her life.

Maybe she should thank him.

Should she thank him for chaining her in the desert, too?

Fuck that.

"Where's my shotgun?" She thrust the lantern out before her.

"Afraid of snakes?"

"Well, I'm not fucking friends with them."

"Who are you friends with?"

"Just you, as crazy as that sounds." She staggered the remaining few paces to the tailgate.

"You're a stranger. That's a long way from *friend*."

"Give me my shotgun."

"So you can shoot me?"

"So I can defend myself against things like that." She pointed at the dead snake.

"No." He hadn't shifted from his sprawled position, the hat still dipping over his eyes. But a handgun now rested on his lap.

He didn't move the gun or the water out of her reach. But she wasn't stupid. If she went for either, he would stop her, and he wouldn't be gentle about it.

Instead, she focused on the view.

The lantern's glow picked out the contoured muscles of his legs and accentuated his trim waist, *V*-shaped torso, and broad shoulders. Sun-bronzed skin sheathed his biceps and forearms, emphasizing the flex of sinewy strength.

He wore snug jeans, a faded t-shirt, and the rugged hat and boots. The shirt rode up, and the denim rode low, drawing her gaze to the thin strip of brown hair that disappeared beneath his fly.

She swallowed hard and moved the light higher, capturing the arrogant cut of his jaw, the bold line of his nose, and the cruel taunt of chiseled lips.

As fate would have it, he was astoundingly, inconceivably gorgeous. Even with his face etched in godlike fury, he was the most beautiful man she'd ever seen. But she wasn't besotted into thinking that was all he was.

This virile, handsome devil was a dangerous vigilante and killer. He was also a sexual deviant, a kinky freak with an insatiable appetite, who'd lured hundreds of unsuspecting women into his bed.

He'd written about his explorations, and she'd devoured the tantalizing words with flushed cheeks and quivering breaths. She'd also noticed a disturbing progression of depravity over the years, his cravings growing darker, bolder, more painful, veering into dubious territory.

She wasn't a guileless victim. But she was curious enough to slowly reach out and lift the brim of his cowboy hat.

Their stares caught and held, transfixed as the atmosphere shuddered between them. Crackling energy. Red-hot voltage. She felt it everywhere, curling fingers of warmth into parts of her he would never physically touch. He would never try because what she saw in the depths of his gaze was enough to know that he despised her with every jagged shard of his soul.

She'd always been told she had silver eyes. They just looked colorless and gray to her. But his eyes were like that of a tiger, shimmering in hues of molten metallic gold.

They dipped, as though he couldn't help himself, to chase the rise and fall of her breasts. When they returned, she was once again imprisoned in the magnetic beauty of his face.

From the clean, soapy scent wafting off him and the spotless appearance of his clothes, she assumed he hadn't spent the past few hours in the desert heat like she had. A small part of her had hoped he'd been watching her from afar, growing sick with guilt over what he'd done to her.

But the formidable man who reclined on her tailgate didn't care about her wellbeing. Instead, he glared at her like a stranger he wanted to murder.

"Tell me who you are, and this ends now." The dangerous, silky tone of his words cut through the dense night air.

"You hate lies and insincerity because it goes against everything you believe." She licked her chapped lips and rested a hip against the tailgate near his legs. "I'm known for my ability to keep secrets. It's a fault, really. Foolish, most times. Because I'll keep the truth to myself just to protect someone else's feelings."

"I don't need anyone to protect my fucking feelings."

"I'm not." She held his impatient gaze. "I'm telling you who I am."

"That's—"

"You have an incredible heart and are always willing to help your friends and even people you don't know, like all those innocent, enslaved girls. My heart, on the other hand, is subtle. I don't show it or share it with anyone. Not anymore."

Grabbing the gun and the water, he sat up, swung his powerfully muscled legs off the tailgate, and stood. Scowling down at her, he looked alarmingly tall, horrifyingly lethal, and unapologetically mean.

He was going to leave.

Without her.

She dropped the lantern and ran. Around the truck and to the driver's door, she yanked it open and threw herself behind the steering wheel. The keys, her gun, water, food… She frantically searched the cab for something, anything that could save her.

Until a fist caught her hair and wrenched her out of the truck.

He tossed the water onto the seat and shoved the gun under her chin. "If you move, I'll shoot and deal with the fallout of your copied emails. That option is shaking out to be a whole lot easier than playing your games."

"This isn't a game." Her chin lifted above the press of the barrel. "I've known you for ten years, dammit. You're important to me."

He snarled and shoved her away with enough force to send her stumbling onto her back. Sharp rocks broke her fall, and she cried out in pain and frustration.

By the time she hobbled to her feet, he was already in the truck with the engine running.

"Don't leave me." She ran to the window and flattened a palm against the glass while yanking on the locked door. "Please, Tommy. I'm not tough or outdoorsy or equipped for this. I don't know how to survive out here."

He gripped the wheel and stared straight ahead, his jaw carved in stone.

"I won't make it through the night. I need water and…" She lurched toward the back of the truck, keeping her hands on the metal side as if that could stop him wrenching away her lifeline.

A quick scan of the truck bed confirmed her supply of water had been removed. Flooded with fear, she pushed up to climb in.

He hit the gas. The tires spun up sand, and the vehicle bolted forward. She tried to hang on, but her fingers lost purchase, her palms sliding off the edge as he sped away.

"Tommy! Don't leave!" She chased him, pumping her legs, heaving for air, and running as fast as she was physically able.

Until she twisted her ankle on a rock.

"Fuck!" A sob rose up, but she pushed through the agony, her eyes bleeding hot tears. "Tommy, wait! Don't leave me. Please, don't leave me."

She sprinted as the sound of the engine faded. She kept moving, limping, long after the taillights vanished over the hill. Then she fell.

Alone.

No water.

No food.

In the desert.

Three days.

She was fucked.

Rolling to her back, she lay in the sand and cried. The moon watched, pitiless, as she mourned her situation and every miserable second leading up to it.

He could've listened to her. Interrogated her. Tried to get to know her beyond a name and date of birth.

Instead, he chose to let her die.

He'd made his decision.

It hurt. Fucking hell, it hurt deep in her soul. But she'd put herself here. She'd known the risks.

She'd expected too much from him. The man who poured his heart into his emails kept those feelings close. He didn't open up to his closest friends. Why did she think he'd open up to a stranger?

He hadn't given her enough time. Or maybe she'd said the wrong things. Either way, she'd let herself get hurt.

Again.

There was no romantic attachment this time. No broken heart. But she'd allowed pieces of herself to get involved with a man she'd never met.

Even when she closed herself off, she became attached. She was impulsive. Careless with her life. Stuck in a vicious cycle. *Attachment, pain, death, repeat.*

It didn't have to end in death.

Ten years ago, she'd walked off that bridge when it seemed impossible.

Could she walk out of this desert in three days? Without water? Without a map? With no sense of direction?

Impossible.

But if she traveled at night and found shade during the day, maybe?

It wasn't an impossible decision. She could lie here and die. Or she could try.

DOMINATE

Rising to her feet, she hobbled back to the telephone pole. The pain in her ankle dulled by the time she gathered the lantern and the rest of her measly supplies.

The truck had headed west. There lay more desert. A black, undulating sea of sand at night. Vast and lonely, with its excruciating heat looming on the horizon.

She started walking.

SIX

Away to the west, the sun sank toward the unreachable edge of the desert. Dusk was approaching for the third time since Rylee had arrived.

Listless, she lay on her stomach at the rear of a narrow cave, her cheek pressing against the cool limestone bedrock. She might as well have been shackled. Exhaustion, heat, and extreme thirst had held her in the same position since dawn.

If she hadn't found this dark hole last night, she would already be dead.

By her estimation, it had been fifty-three hours since she had food or water.

Fifty-one hours in the desert.

Two full days and nights.

It occurred to her that she'd never truly been thirsty until now. It was an agony like she'd never known. Her skull squeezed around a banging, inconsolable migraine. She couldn't produce saliva or tears. Her throat was so raw it felt as though the lining had been flayed and stretched out in the sun to dry.

In normal conditions, she could've lasted much longer without drinking. But the boiling heat had cut her survival rate in half.

It tormented her until all she could focus on was finding something cool to relieve her suffering. She'd spent the first night and the next day wandering the desert scrublands, searching for a puddle, discarded bottle, underground cave, anything that might contain a drop of liquid.

No luck.

DOMINATE

She'd heard of survivalists drinking their urine. By the time she'd reached that level of desperation, she had nothing left in her body to excrete.

To escape the heat, she'd holed up in the cave all day and thought of nothing but the taste of water. Sparkling, flavored, natural spring, ice jangling, with little rivulets of condensation running down the sides. She'd give anything for a cool sip. Even a splash of hot, stagnant water would be a godsend.

Now that the sun was setting, the urge to venture out of the cave and find liquid dominated her mind. She didn't know how far she'd already walked or how close she'd come to civilization. Everything looked the same, from the towering buttes and dry ravines to the pattern of stars overhead. For all she knew, she'd been roaming in circles.

As she lay there, ordering her boneless limbs to move, a noise sounded in the distance. Her heart took off at a gallop, and her head shot up, pounding with the boom of her pulse.

She tried to listen past the cacophony of her aches. Then she heard it. The undeniable purr of an engine, growing louder, closer.

Digging her elbows into the dirt, she crawled through the narrow space and dragged her pack behind her. When she reached the mouth of the cave, she squinted into the fading light.

There, on the hazy horizon, two headlights bobbed along the bumpy terrain.

She didn't have three seconds to make a life-or-death decision. Frantic to be seen, she grabbed the lantern from where it'd charged in the sun, flicked it on, and thrust it into the air.

Her arm shook with the effort, her body too weak to run.

"Help!" She crawled, stumbled a few steps on her feet, tripped, and crawled again. "Help me! Here! Please, help!"

Her voice had no strength, coughing and hacking with disuse. But the motorist seemed to see her, making a beeline in her direction. She didn't care if it was Tommy or Hannibal Fucking Lecter. If she didn't get water soon, she was dead anyway.

The vehicle slowed, stopping some fifty feet away. As the dust settled around the tires, she made out the silver paint and the silhouette of a cowboy hat inside.

Tommy had stolen her truck again.

Rage warred with desperation. If he'd come to help her, she'd let him without hesitation. But her amicability was long gone. She had a thing about grudges, as in when she held onto one, she held onto it forever.

He'd hurt her irreparably, thereby destroying any concern she'd felt toward him. She no longer wished to help him. She wanted to forget the last ten years and just go home.

Dropping the lantern, she centered all her energy on dragging her legs beneath her to stand. It required more strength than she had, but she did it. Eyes on the truck, she swayed, floundered, and slowly staggered forward.

The passenger-side door opened, and she realized he wasn't alone.

A man stepped out.

No, he was shoved.

His hands waved around as he yelled, trying to right his balance.

What was he saying? Who was he? Why was he shirtless? She couldn't see his face at this distance, but he sounded pissed off.

She quickened her tottering steps, picking over rocks and slanted earth. It was all she could do to remain upright.

"Tommy." She tried to raise her voice. "Tommy!"

Goddammit, she needed help. It was too far to walk. She'd never make it.

The man shouted something and charged toward the truck.

A shot fired, and she faltered.

More shots followed, each pelleting the sand around the man's feet. He reeled backward, dancing around the bullets and screaming.

Tommy shot at him twice more, deliberately missing. Then he yanked the door shut and spun the truck around, facing in the direction he'd come.

"No! Wait!" She shrieked at the top of her lungs, pushing her legs faster, trying to close the distance. "Don't you fucking leave me! Please! I'm begging you!"

He drove off, taking his time around the ruts in the ground, knowing she'd never catch up.

Bursts of dizzying light blotted her vision, smeared with tears and the unshakable pain behind her eyes. Her knees gave out, hitting the ground with crushing agony. She collapsed, catching herself on elbows and fists.

He was gone.

And he'd left her with a stranger whose life meant as little to him as hers.

The man charged toward her, his hands balled at his sides and his unrecognizable face twisted in a snarl.

"How do you know that crazy motherfucker?" He stopped beside her, kicking up dust in her eyes.

"Do you have water?" She coughed, her throat so sore it felt as though it were bleeding. "Anything to drink?"

"Yeah, I'm carrying a jug in my back pocket." He spat a wad of saliva next to his leather loafers. "No, I don't fucking have water. He stripped me down and took everything, including my goddamn shirt."

"No food? Nothing?"

He huffed and gripped the back of his neck, looking around.

They were both dead.

Her stomach clamped around a gnawing knot, and she rolled to her back, staring up at him through a blur of pain.

Blood trickled from the tight black curls that covered his head. More rivers of red ran from gashes around his eyes, mouth, and bare chest. Suit pants clung to his legs, smudged with dust and ripped at the knee.

"How do *you* know him?" She pushed herself to a sitting position, woozy and unsteady.

"I don't."

"Then why did he beat you up and leave you in the desert?"

His eyes crinkled, squinting as he studied her. "Something doesn't add up."

She couldn't guess what he was thinking, but Tommy didn't throw punches without reason. This man must've threatened him, trespassed on his property, or endangered his friends. Whoever the man was, Tommy considered him an enemy, just like her.

He was average size and build, if not a little stocky and soft around the middle. A few years younger than her. Maybe late-thirties. His eyes sat a bit too far apart, but most women would probably find his looks adequate.

She found him completely unfamiliar. "You seem to know me, but I don't know you."

"Where are we?" He spun around, scanning the desert in all directions. "Which way is out?"

"You tell me. You just rode in from somewhere."

"He tied my hands and blindfolded me. He removed that shit right before he kicked me out of the truck." His tongue darted out, licking the blood on his lip. "How did you locate the tracker?"

"What?"

"The tracking device on your truck. Did you know it was there? Or did he find it?"

"Why is there a tracker on my truck?" Her heart rate hit a breakneck speed, thudding in her throat. "Who put it there?"

What had she gotten herself into? Tommy didn't even know she existed a week ago. How would he have been able to find her and arrange to have her tracked?

He wouldn't. But he'd know how to spot that sort of device if he was looking for it.

"*You* put it there." Suddenly wary, she crab-walked backward and scrambled to her feet. "Why? Who the fuck are you?"

"You have no idea, do you?" He clicked his tongue. "Fucking clueless."

"Start talking." She shoved back her shoulders, and the world spun. She braced her legs, and they buckled out from under her, sending her back to the ground with her cheek in the sand. "Fuck!"

He stepped toward her.

"Don't come near me!" She shoved out a hand as if she had the strength to fight him off.

"You've been out here for two days." He crossed his arms over his chest. "Might as well tell me who that man is. Seems he wants you dead more than I do."

He knew how long she'd been here?

Because he'd been tracking her.

"Why do you want me dead?" A chill swept through her bones.

"Didn't say I did." He pivoted and strode toward the cave.

"What are you doing?"

"Getting the hell out of this desert." He snatched her pack and slung it over his shoulder. "Fuck this shit. No job is worth dying for."

"Job?" Her words slurred, her brain chugging on sputtering fumes. "Someone paid you to put a tracker on my truck?"

"Sweetheart, I've been monitoring you for six months." He prowled back to her, pausing just out of reach. "It's been a pleasure watching your sexy ass through my binoculars. Hell, even hours from death, you look good enough to eat."

Dread sank in with the implication of his words. If he wanted to attack her, she wouldn't be able to stop him. She couldn't even lift her head from the dirt.

"What's your name?" Every sound she made caused her pain, every thought an excruciating effort.

"Paul."

"I assume you know my name."

"I know everything about you, Rylee Catherine Sutton."

Not everything. He didn't know how she was connected to Tommy.

"Who paid you to watch me?"

"Someone who is obsessed with every detail of your life—what you eat, where you go, who you talk to, and most of all, who you're banging."

The words bounced around in her head, jumbling into nonsensical mush. She couldn't think past the declining state of her body.

"Who hired you?" she asked again.

"Who are your enemies?"

DOMINATE

Tommy. His friends. Maybe one of them had discovered her six months ago and was working behind Tommy's back to learn who she was. It was the only answer that fit.

"Give me a name," she said.

"My contracts are anonymous, and even if I knew, I wouldn't tell you."

She pressed a finger against her pounding temple. There was one aspirin left in the first-aid kit. She wouldn't be able to swallow it, but if it sat in the back of her throat, maybe it would melt.

"Give me my pack." She held out a trembling hand.

"Can't do that." He glanced at the vast wasteland behind him and turned back, grimacing. "I'd carry you, but it'll slow me down. You're as good as dead anyway."

She dropped her hand, unable to fight or stand or do anything but watch him amble away.

Whatever information he had on her would be useless after she was dead. He was a mystery that would go unsolved, because as she lay there, staring at his retreating form, she suspected he wouldn't make it out of the desert alive.

SEVEN

Rylee woke on her stomach with her face in the prickly sand. The nighttime air spread goosebumps across her arms. But the sky was warming, paling into shades of pink and gray.

She'd made it through another night.

And she wasn't alone.

Hot breath brushed along her spine. Hands gripped the hem of her shirt, lifting the cotton up her torso.

With a gasp, she jerked and tried to roll. But a heavy body came down on her back, pinning her in the dirt.

"Stop." She wheezed, clawing at loose rocks and tufts of plant growth, her voice hoarse, barely a whisper. "Get off me."

"I've been walking around all night," a masculine voice rasped at her ear, "trying to find my way out." A hand wedged beneath her hips and yanked open the fly of her jeans. "Trying not to think about your sweet cunt."

"Paul…" Fear raged through her veins, but her body refused to respond. It couldn't. It had used the last of its energy just keeping her heart beating. "Don't do this."

"For six months, I've wanted nothing more than to do this." He ground his erection against her backside. "If I'm going to die out here, I'm going to satisfy this fucking infatuation once and for all."

"No! You can't!" Despite her terror, she remained calm enough to scan the dirt beneath her face, her fingers digging through the sand, searching for a small rock.

"I can."

"I'm filthy."

"Damn straight, you're filthy. I've watched you fuck your neighbor on the back porch, in your car, and on every surface in your house. Seeing a woman take it in the ass does something to a man. Christ, you don't even know how fucking hot you are."

He'd invaded her privacy. If she had it in her, she might've laughed.

Wasn't Karma a vindictive bitch?

Maybe she deserved to be spied on, but she didn't deserve to spend the last minutes of her life being raped.

He lifted his hips and yanked her jeans and underwear to her knees. Her heart stopped, and her fingers latched onto a skinny stone with a jagged edge. She fisted it and rolled to her back.

With his gaze locked on the exposed apex of her legs, he didn't see her hand moving until it was too late.

She stabbed the rock into his eye.

Direct hit. But not enough strength. Instead of blood, she got his seething, roaring rage.

"Stupid bitch!" He clapped a hand over his eye and smacked the rock from her grip. "You're going to pay for that."

Teeth bared, he rose up and wrenched her jeans past her knees.

She kicked her legs and slapped at his face, but the struggle was clumsy and ineffective. She couldn't stop him from opening his pants and crawling between her thighs.

He gripped her throat and flashed a manic smile. "Your cunt is mine."

His face blurred, fading with the deprivation of air. Darkness closed in, and a loud ringing sounded in her ears.

Then a boom.

Paul's head exploded, spraying the sky with blood, bits of bone, and brain matter.

He toppled to the side, and the pressure released from her throat.

Stunned, she gulped for oxygen, gripped her neck, and snapped her gaze toward the gray horizon, searching for the threat.

Someone had shot him. Killed him. Was it Tommy? Or the person who'd hired Paul?

She whimpered, heaving frenzied breaths, and fumbled to pull up her jeans.

The rev of an engine approached.

Splattered in blood and scared out of her mind, she moved. Muscle memory took over, her limbs bending and dragging her body across the sand.

The cave. She could hide in the narrow hole.

Tires crunched behind her, shoving her panic into the red zone. Her vision began to fade, but she could still hear.

Footsteps.

A slow gait.

Chasing her.

"Please." She cried, crawling on her stomach, desperate to get away. "Please, don't."

She didn't know when she'd stopped moving, but her arms wouldn't work anymore. She continued to fight, mentally reaching for the cave, willing herself to become invisible.

Hands gripped her back and legs, and she flinched, crying harder. Arms lifted her, and she glimpsed a whiskered jaw. A flash of light brown hair.

Her eyes shut, her face pressed against a warm neck. "Tommy?"

He was walking, the sand grinding noisily beneath his steps. But his breaths were louder, sawing in and out next to her ear.

"Hate you." Her limbs weighed a thousand pounds. Everything hurt.

He laid her on a soft bench seat, and she blinked, trying to adjust her foggy vision.

A dashboard. Air vents. Condensation. Beads of it clinging to the plastic. She was in her truck.

Reaching out, she tried to collect those precious drops. But her movements were uncoordinated, the effort too great.

He bent over her, his body heat invading, too close, too much.

Until a trickle of water ran over her lips. The incredible taste startled her. She choked, lapped at it greedily, and tried to grab the source.

He yanked the bottle away and tossed it into the back of the truck.

"Please. Need more." She was fading. Dying.

He slammed the door shut.

EIGHT

The woman passed out. Just as well. Tomas was in no mood to listen to her crying.

The risks he'd taken with her life had been necessary. Not everyone would see it that way, but when it came to his friends, he would accept their anger and disappointment over needlessly putting their lives in harm's way.

Rylee Sutton was a threat. Well, she *had been* a threat. Now he didn't know what she was.

Most people wouldn't last a day out here. The fact that she'd survived without his interference was shocking. He'd watched her like a hawk and skipped sleep, waiting for her to give up or do something stupid like fall into a nest of rattlesnakes.

With the windows rolled down, he navigated her truck across the uneven terrain, holding her head on his lap to prevent it from bouncing.

Sand and blood stiffened her hair, her clothes saturated in grime. Her complexion was too pale for this climate, ephemeral beyond any hope of tanning. Yet the smooth alabaster glow complimented her dark lashes, wing-tipped brows, and long hair. Wild ribbons of brown hung past her breasts, the color as rich and variegated as spalted sweetgum.

Her nose was too delicate, her bones too slender, and her cheeks too silky to have been exposed to the harsh sun. And her mouth… Those lips were far too pouty for his liking. They made a man want to taste and bruise and test how far they stretched around a hungry cock.

Underneath the gore and desert grit, she was outrageously beautiful. A goddamn knockout.

And when she was at her weakest, he'd left her alone with a rapist.

"Fuck!" He slammed a hand against the steering wheel, boiling with anger.

At himself.

At the bastard who'd touched her.

At the fucking shitstorm that had blown into his life.

For the next thirty miles, he forced his eyes on the unpaved wasteland, trying to ignore the guilt and resentment that rode him.

When his childhood home finally came into view, he approached slowly, surveying the property for intruders. Everything appeared in order. Except...

Motherfucker.

A motorcycle sat around the side of the house. Not the sporty, rubber-burning kind that Luke rode. No, this beast was throaty and heavy, made for long hauls on desolate roads. He only knew one guy who was arrogant enough to take an iconic Harley off-road in the desert.

As he parked the truck, the front door opened. Cole Hartman stepped out and leaned against the door frame, tattooed arms folded across his chest and eyes stony in the twilight.

Every time Tomas saw him, the man had more ink on his skin and hair on his face. He looked hard around the edges, fearsome even, like a one-percenter in an outlaw motorcycle club.

"I turned on the air-conditioning in the house." Cole stalked toward him. "I don't know how you can stand this fucking heat."

"I told you not to come." He rolled up the windows and stepped out.

Cole tilted his head, and when he caught a glimpse of the unconscious cargo, his nostrils stiffened. The cords in his neck protruded, and his face turned red above the beard. "What the fuck did you do?"

"Tested her." He strode around to the other side and dragged her out.

"Tested her how exactly? She looks more dead now than she did in the photo you sent."

"Here's an idea. Instead of standing around like a smacked ass, make yourself useful." He cradled her against his chest and shoved past Cole. "Grab a couple of bags of sodium chloride from the bunker."

"She's covered in blood."

"Hadn't noticed." He carried her into the house, and the sudden cold air shot a chill through him. Pausing at the control box on the wall, he raised the temperature. "Don't fuck with the thermostat."

"You've gone off the fucking rails, Tomas."

"The IV drip, Cole. I need it yesterday."

DOMINATE

The bunker beneath the house maintained a mild temperature year-round. It was where they kept all the medical supplies and anything that might perish in the heat.

Cole grunted and treaded toward the interior door that led underground. Tomas headed to his old bedroom.

The bed was narrow like the room, but he had everything he needed to bring her back to life. Settling her on the mattress, he gave her limp body a quick perusal, probing for injuries he might've missed.

Minor scratches and bruises marred her fair skin. No deep gashes or burns. She'd used the sunscreen and kept to the shade when she could.

Blood streaked her face and arms, her shirt soaked and clinging to her firm little tits.

She needed a bath. But fluids first.

Using the supplies he'd already laid out, he cleaned her arm, washed his hands, and prepped the IV tubing and equipment.

When the sound of heavy boots entered the room, Tomas kept his gaze on his task. "What did you find on Paul Kissinger?"

"Nothing yet." Cole handed over two bags of sodium chloride. "He returned to her house yesterday morning, snooping around. Then he left Eldorado and dropped out of signal range. Did he show up here?"

"He tried to rape her."

"What? When?"

"An hour ago." Tomas bent over her arm, hunting for a vein for the IV drip. Hard to do when her little vessels were deprived of fluid. "Goddammit."

"The vein collapsed." Cole crouched beside him, taking up too much room in the small space. "Slow down and try another one."

Neither of them had gone to school to study medicine. They'd learned basic shit in the field, jumping in whenever the cartel's medical staff needed help.

Knowing how to stitch a wound and insert a peripheral IV proved invaluable in their job. Tomas and Kate had taken the most interest in it. Kate wanted to be a doctor and help people. But not him. He just wanted to mend his wounds without depending on others to do it.

He finally accessed a vein, and once the drip started delivering fluid, he sat on the bed and blew out a breath. The intravenous route was the fastest way to rehydrate her body. She would recover quickly. *Physically.*

In other ways, she might never fully heal.

He knew the feeling.

"That's not her blood." Cole leaned over her, picking at the sticky gunk on her throat. "Tell me what happened."

"I found Paul Kissinger lurking on my property. You were right. He put the tracker on her truck."

"What did you do to him?"

"Tied him up. Smacked him around."

"And he confessed? Just like that?"

"No. He told *her*."

Cole's brows knitted, his gaze shifting from Rylee to the doorway. "Where is he?"

"In the desert."

"Idiot. I have a million methods to make a man talk."

"So do I." Tomas grabbed the container of soap and water and gently ran a wet cloth over her face. "Before he showed up, I bugged her pack and dumped her in the desert, too."

"What part of *stay put and keep her restrained* did you not understand?"

"I *did* restrain her. The scrubland is inescapable to anyone who doesn't know its secrets. I was monitoring her. Watching and listening."

"How did you watch me?" Her eyes snapped open, bloodshot and glinting silver. "Were you there?"

He should've given her a sedative. How long had she been eavesdropping?

"Spying again?" He made a tsking sound. "That's a terrible habit of yours."

She kicked her leg, trying to knock him from the bed. A pathetic attempt, given the weakness in her body. She glanced at the cloth in his hand, the IV in her arm, and the blood on her shirt.

"You were there? The whole time?" Her gaze made an uneasy pass over Cole and returned to Tomas. "You watched me suffer for days and did nothing?"

"I stepped in when I needed to."

"When *you* needed." She coughed a dry, raw sound. "Well, now you can step out, let me change clothes, and I'll be on my way and gone from your life."

She tried to sit and failed.

"My backpack." She scanned the room. None of her belongings were in here.

Her attention landed on Cole, tracing his tattoos and lingering on his beard. Tomas waited for her to voice the man's name and spout every incriminating thing she'd read about him in the emails.

Instead, she pressed her lips together and directed a disgusted glare at Tomas.

He glared back, daring her to open her deceitful mouth. He'd written enough about Cole that she could easily identify him. He'd also outlined his assumptions about Cole's background, his shady military training, his ability to slip in and out of any fortress, computer system, or security infrastructure. No one was that good unless they were hiding some scary shit.

The most concerning thing about Cole was his motivation. He wasn't like the rest of them. He'd never spent a night in Van's attic, never had his freedom ripped away, never experienced the kind of loss and hopelessness that made a man long for death. Not that Tomas knew, anyway.

That was the problem. None of them *knew* Cole Hartman. Yet here he was, mired in their lives, and fighting alongside them. For what? Van and Matias stopped paying him a dozen jobs ago. Now he was what? Contracting for them pro bono?

Whenever he was asked about his past life and current endeavors outside of the team, he just smiled or gave vague non-answers. The bastard was as closed-off as Tomas. Perhaps more so.

Tomas didn't trust him. But he'd contacted him anyway, because he was the best at digging up secrets. If Rylee was hiding skeletons, Cole would find them along with every dirty person connected to her.

Eyes locked, she watched Tomas as he watched her. He hated that she knew all of his secrets. His skeletons, regrets, desires, every thought in his head. She also knew that Cole's presence in Texas meant they'd already learned some things about her.

"You were in the desert with me?" Her gaze lost focus, her momentary spurt of awareness dwindling by the second. "I never heard the truck."

He'd parked it out of hearing range and hiked in close enough to watch her through the scope of his rifle. Only once, he'd left her unattended to return to the house and call Cole. That was when he found Paul Kissinger on his property.

"Fine. Don't answer me." She weakly flexed her hand. "That man...Paul. He must be connected to you and your friends somehow. But you don't believe that, so you put him in the desert to spy on our conversation."

Cole leaned against the jamb of the doorway and squinted at Tomas. "What did you learn?"

She was fucking her neighbor. On the back porch, in her car, on every surface in her house.

Seeing a woman take it in the ass does something to a man.

His stomach hardened against the stirring images. "Paul monitored her for six months. She didn't know him."

"*Didn't?*" A muscle flexed in Cole's jaw, twitching his beard. "You killed him?"

"Like I said, he attacked her."

Pulling the trigger hadn't been planned. It just happened. They'd needed the son of a bitch alive to get answers. Oddly, the only regret he had about his impulsiveness was the looming task of driving back and dealing with the body.

"We could've pulled information from him." Cole gripped his nape, his expression etched in frustration. "Now we don't know who he was working for, why he was following her, or how it's connected to us."

"She'll tell me." Tomas met her eyes.

"*She* doesn't know anything." Her jaw set. She didn't look away, fidget, or show any signs of dishonesty.

Maybe she was good at lying.

"Did you find anything on the ex-husband?" Tomas asked Cole without breaking eye contact with her.

"He's clean. Except one thing. She has a restraining order against him."

"*Ex*-husband." Her eyelids hooded over silver pools of fatigue and anger.

There was no surprise in her expression. She'd anticipated them investigating the people in her life once they learned who she was. That was why she'd shown up without identification.

"Tell me about Mason Sutton," Tomas said.

"He's a jealous nuisance. Way too jealous to hire another man to watch me. Where are the keys to my truck?" She touched the catheter in her arm, likely debating the best way to yank it out.

"You're not leaving." He caught her probing hand, stopping her.

"You're not keeping me here for three weeks without food."

"What is she talking about?" Cole straightened.

"Give us a minute." His head throbbed, magnified by exhaustion.

"No." She twisted her wrist out of his grip. "You had your minute. You had two days, you heartless cunt."

He'd prepared an intravenous sedative, just in case. If he restrained her to the bed, she would struggle and risk dislodging the IV.

Mostly, he just needed her to sleep so he could close his eyes for the first time in two days. He was operating on three-percent battery life and rapidly draining.

He reached toward the dangling IV bags and began the flow of the sedation drug, titrating the dose to give her just enough to relax her back into dreamland.

"What are you doing?" Her eyes widened, glazed and unfocused, trying to follow his movements.

"Who are your enemies?"

"The only enemies I've made are in this room. What did you do to the IV? What are you giving me?"

"I know who you are, Rylee Sutton."

She glanced at Cole and back to him. "You should've talked to me instead of starving me in the desert. It would've saved you the trouble of calling in your friend. So what have you learned? That I'm a stupid woman, who waltzed in here alone thinking I could do some good and instead, ended up getting myself hurt? Go, Rylee. Another failure." She exhaled a tired breath. "Look, Tommy, I've learned my lesson, okay? Believe me when I say I'm done. I don't want any part of this or *you*. I just want to go home."

"It's too late for that." He leaned over her, bracing an elbow on his knee. "You wanted me. Now you're stuck with me."

NINE

Tomas had reached a level of worn-out that hurt. Every muscle wanted to surrender to gravity. What he needed was sleep. Any horizontal surface would do.

But there was a corpse rotting in the desert. An unfinished conversation with Cole. An IV drip that required monitoring. An unwashed, blood-splattered woman in his bed. And too many unanswered questions.

"I'll ask again." He put his face in hers. "Who are your enemies?"

Her teeth ground together. "I already told you—"

"We know you're a criminal psychologist, Rylee." Cole gripped the upper frame of the doorway, leaning into the small bedroom. "You aid in apprehending scoundrels and testify against them in court. I'd say you make more enemies than we do."

"Since you know my occupation, you also know that I contract for small-town law enforcement." More teeth grinding. "I deal with petty thieves and potheads. Tracking devices are a part of *your* world, not mine."

"You must be bored out of your mind." Tomas scrutinized her bleary eyes, willing the sedative to kick in faster. "So you show up here with your fancy, underutilized degree, hoping to dissect a real criminal mind."

Her mouth stopped grinding, her jaw falling slack. Her head lolled to the side, losing strength. Then she snapped it back, her tone deadened. "You're the reason I chose that field of study."

"Excuse me?"

"I went to school for criminal justice, but as I got to know you…" Her words slurred, fighting the sedation. "Your emails…changed my major." A long, lethargic blink. "I don't…feel…right. You…drugged…"

Next thing from her mouth was an angry, muttering exhale. Her lashes drooped over her cheekbones, and the tension visibly left her body. She was out.

Finally.

He turned off the drip of the narcotic and swapped the sodium chloride with a new bag.

"She's taken a lot of interest in you." Cole approached the bed.

"That's her problem."

"She's making it *your* problem. Seems she's in the habit of getting mixed up with the wrong men. Nine months ago, she filed a protective order against Mason Sutton. Three months later, Paul Kissinger started watching her."

"You think Mason and Paul are connected?"

"Maybe."

"We need eyes and ears on Mason. Find out what he knows about us."

"I'm on it. He's an orthopedic surgeon. Runs a booming practice. On the surface, he seems too busy to get involved with a troublesome ex-wife. What would be his motivation?"

"Jealousy. Obsession. He never remarried and has more than enough money to hire people to monitor the object of his obsession. Especially since she lives five hours away from him." He let the weight of his head hang, fighting exhaustion. "She's sexually involved with one of her neighbors."

"Evan Phillips?"

"Who?"

"The single guy who lives next door to her. Divorced. Forty-something. Good-looking. Works construction. He's collecting her mail and looking after her house while she's on sabbatical. I'll dig deeper, see what I can find on him." Cole narrowed his eyes. "You look like shit. When was the last time you slept?"

"I need to deal with the stiff in the desert." Sleep closed in, heavy and persistent. He slumped onto his side in the narrow space next to Rylee. "In a minute."

"The stiff can wait." Cole rubbed his whiskers and stared at Rylee's unconscious form. "Go grab a few hours of sleep in the other bedroom. I'll clean her up."

"You're *not* touching her." Christ, that came out sharper than he'd intended. He softened his voice. "This is my mess. I got it."

"Yeah, I see that. Suit yourself." With a grunt, Cole left the room and shut off the light. "Stubborn fuck."

Within seconds, Tomas passed out.

He slept hard and deep, but not long. An hour maybe?

When he woke in the dark, he registered Rylee's body pressed against the front of his. With his arm around her tiny waist and her head tucked beneath his chin, he didn't move.

Had she rolled into him? Or had he subconsciously grabbed her to keep her from escaping?

His eyes slowly adjusted to the dimness, bringing the room into focus. A new bag hung from the IV pole. Cole must've slipped in and swapped out her fluids. Her boots were off her feet. Cole must've done that, too.

She still wore her grimy clothes and reeked of sweat and desert dirt. Or maybe the odor was coming from him.

He removed the phone from his pocket and stared at the locked screen, stunned. He'd slept three hours? *Jesus.*

Without waking her, he untangled himself from her soft, small body. Then he checked her vitals and headed to the bathroom.

After a quick shower, he set out bottles of water and apple juice on the nightstand, checked her breathing, and left her sleeping to go deal with his other unwanted visitor.

Cole perched on the couch in the front room, eyes glued to a laptop.

"Feeling better, princess?" The man idly flipped a black coin-sized disk back and forth between his fingers, his gaze never leaving the computer screen. "You two looked so cozy in there I didn't want to disturb you."

Tomas didn't acknowledge the dig as he lowered into the armchair. "Any updates?"

"The guy she's banging, Evan Phillips, walked through her house an hour ago. In and out in ten minutes. No other movement."

"You think he knows something?"

"I think we can't rule out pillow talk. If they're fucking on the regular, she's telling him things, sharing secrets, like how she's been reading the incriminating ramblings of a dumbass vigilante for ten years."

Pounding heat flared beneath his skin, his system flooding with the ire he'd been holding back for days.

"You have something to say to me, fucking say it." He shot from the chair and stood over Cole, hands clenching. "Better yet, use your fists. You're the one who taught me how to fight. We both know you can kick my ass. If you're going to do it, fucking do it already!"

DOMINATE

Cole slowly shifted his gaze from the computer screen, moved it over Tomas' rigid stance, and stopped on his eyes.

The air thinned, and the tension in Cole's lethal glare grew taut. Then he blinked.

"Nah." He returned to the laptop. "You're beating yourself up enough for the both of us."

Irritation twitched through Tomas' muscles. He spun away and paced the room, noticing the lack of dust on the surfaces. Cole had kept himself busy for the past few hours.

Everything that once filled these rooms had been replaced with new furnishings. Nothing remained from his childhood. No photos. No keepsakes. He'd moved it all to the Milton house and burned it.

His mother's home and the land it sat on was the only tether he allowed himself to keep.

"I was seventeen when I sent the first email." Tomas paused at the kitchen table and rubbed his brow. "It started out harmless. Just the words of a boy who missed his dead girlfriend."

After his mother died, he'd spent two weeks alone in this house. That time in his life left a black hole in his memory, the grief more than he could bear. The only thing he could recall was his urgency to leave, to go somewhere, to be anywhere but here. So he'd left.

"Two weeks after my mother was put in the ground, I drove east. Ended up in Austin." He laughed hollowly. "A small-town kid in a big city. I'd never seen anything like it. So many tall buildings, flashing lights, loud noises, and the people... Christ, they were everywhere, packed together on the streets in every size, color, and creed. I was so fucking out of my element. It's no wonder I didn't last a week."

"That's when Van captured you?"

"I was easy prey. A young, naive boy with a decent physique and no sense of danger, wandering the streets, utterly lost." *Lost in life.* "I walked right up to Van's car and asked for directions. Next thing I knew, I was chained in his attic."

"No one blames you for continuing the emails after your captivity. If writing to her was therapeutic..."

"She was the only one I could talk to. A dead girl. I know that's fucked up. I knew it then, too. But it kept me sane." He released a slow breath and turned to face Cole. "I fucked up when I started writing about you and the team. As much as I covered my tracks and meticulously monitored the account, it was still reckless. Fucking careless. And I'm paying for it now."

"Maybe it's not as bad as it seems." Cole typed something on his laptop. "I hacked into the neighbor's home network. Look at this."

He joined Cole on the couch as the image of a shockingly gorgeous woman filled the screen.

His heart stopped, and his breath fell on a gobsmacked groan. "Holy fuck."

"Yeah. There's more." Cole flipped from one photo to the next, each candid snapshot of Rylee Sutton more intoxicating than the last. "She's not on social media. These photos are from Evan Phillips' personal computer. *All* of them. We're talking hundreds of pictures *just* of her."

Completely enraptured, Tomas couldn't look away from the screen, his gaze greedily feasting on her flawless features, the glossy shine of her brown hair, those sexy full lips, gleaming silver eyes, the healthy glow of her porcelain skin, and the curves of her exquisitely toned body in a glittery dress, a tiny swimsuit, obscenely short shorts—

Cole snapped the lid of the laptop closed, breaking the trance.

"Christ." Tomas cleared his throat, trying not to imagine her naked and failing miserably.

"That battered woman in your bedroom is undeniably attractive. But when she's healthy?" Cole made a whistling sound. "She's the kind of beautiful that makes a man do crazy, desperate shit."

No shit. The last time Tomas had such a gripping, ravenous reaction to a woman was…never.

And he wasn't the only one. Paul Kissinger should've used the last of his energy to find water and survive the desert. Instead, he'd circled back and forced himself on her. A stupid fucking move but at the same time, sickeningly understandable for a guy who'd been ogling her through his binoculars for six months.

"Maybe," Cole said, "we're dealing with something as simple as an infatuated lover. Could be the ex-husband or the neighbor or some random hookup who's feeling extra possessive of a beautiful woman."

That didn't sit well with him. He'd rather Rylee be a person to blame, not a victim. "Does the neighbor have pictures of other women?"

"No."

"Did you come across compromising photos of Rylee?"

"None. No sex tapes or anything that implies that Evan is creeping on her without her permission."

"He has a private photo collection of her." An uneasy sensation coiled in his stomach. "I don't like it."

"I agree. It looks suspicious." Cole turned to him, his gaze probing. "Maybe he loves her. Or maybe he just appreciates her beauty. I mean, if you were fucking a woman who looks like that, wouldn't you keep photos of her?"

No question, he would keep them. And stare at them. Hell, he was never going to fuck his hand again without a visual of her in his head.

"Collecting photos is one thing." He pinched the bridge of his nose, thinking. "But we're dealing with someone who hired a man to watch her. Someone who is obsessed with every detail of her life. *What she eats, where she goes, who she talks to, and most of all, who she's banging.* Those were Paul's exact words."

"Sounds like a domestic issue. I should be able to determine who hired Paul within the next few days. Once we know that, we'll know if it's connected to us." Cole drummed his fingers on his knee. "Best case, she has a creepy admirer and hasn't told anyone about your emails."

"Then we clean up and go home."

"Yep."

He wanted to spank the ever-loving shit out of her and leave a permanent reminder on her ass. But a few threatening words against her loved ones would be sufficient in keeping her quiet when he vanished from her life.

"The worst-case scenario..." Cole rolled that small plastic disk between his fingers again. "She's planning to do something with the evidence she has against us, and she's not working alone."

"She didn't know Paul Kissinger."

"No, but she's somehow connected to whoever hired him. Think about it. We send our people on missions all the time with tracking devices. We bug their cars, their clothes, their bodies." Cole's lips twitched. "I heard Camila once wore a GPS chip in her tooth."

"Yeah." He grinned. "She's fucking crazy."

He missed her. He missed his whole damn team and longed to return to them.

If Rylee was working with someone, it made sense that they wanted to track her whereabouts and jump in when needed. That would explain Paul. She disappeared in the desert, and he showed up to find out what happened.

The device on her truck was the only one Tomas found. He'd scoured her belongings but... "I didn't check her body for chips."

"I have a reliable detector." Cole nodded at his bag on the table. "She's clean."

"And you verified her occupation."

"Yes, but it could be a front. Especially if a three-letter agency is involved." The disk in Cole's hand stopped moving. He looked up and tossed it to Tomas.

He caught it and turned the plastic coin-shaped object this way and that, baffled. "What is this?"

"A high-tech GSM bug. I pulled it from her house and disabled it. There are dozens more there."

"Shit." He inspected it more closely. "I've never seen anything like this."

"Brand new technology. Insanely long battery life. High-speed transmissions. You can't even buy that on the black market. It's impossible to obtain unless you're tied in with NSA or black ops."

A chill trickled down his spine. "You think she could be involved with a government agency?"

"An agency or an agency rogue." A dark look clouded Cole's expression, and he ran a hand down his face. "She could be working for someone. Running from someone. Or she has a lusty-minded stalker with access to cutting-edge espionage tech."

"Fuck." Tomas dropped the bug on the coffee table and slumped back on the couch. "So in summary, she knows everything about us. We know very little about her, and at this point, anything is plausible."

"Pretty much."

TEN

Tomas scraped a hand over his head, impatient to be back in Colombia with his friends and eager to leave the desert memories behind. Ghosts lived in these walls, in the dust, in the arid sand.

He didn't want to be here.

Cole pushed off the couch and ambled to the kitchen. A moment later, he returned with two Bud Lights.

"Thanks." Tomas accepted the cold beer and reluctantly said, "Thanks for coming."

"Yep."

Cole would scour Rylee's life from end to end until he flushed out the truth. In the meantime, Tomas needed to bury a body and babysit the meddling woman.

She wasn't going to be cooperative. By the time she woke, she should have enough strength to bathe herself. And fight him tooth and nail. After the hell he put her through, escape would be her priority.

Her health, however, wouldn't be one-hundred-percent. She hadn't eaten in three days. He could starve her for up to three weeks. That had been his plan—keep her weak and hungry, wear her down, and offer her food in exchange for information.

He'd put the rule of threes in play to fuck with her head and prove his ruthlessness. No air for three minutes. No water for three days. She knew what came next.

He drained the beer. "I'm going to starve her."

"What?"

"You heard me." Resting his elbows on his knees, he met Cole's eyes.

He didn't need to explain himself to anyone, but there was no reason to be a dick. So he told Cole why he'd put her in the desert and what he planned to do with her next.

"Jesus." Cole blew out a breath. "What if she knows nothing, and her only crime is reading your emails?"

"If you tell me you never tortured an innocent suspect during your *unofficial* government career, I'll eat my shoe."

"I can't tell you that. But I will say this. It fucks with you, Tomas. Doesn't matter what cause you're fighting for. When you hurt someone who doesn't deserve to be hurt, that shit leaves scars. Nightmare-inducing scars that keep you awake at night. The guilt festers and changes the makeup of your character."

"Which government agency did that to you?"

"Can't say."

"Are you still working for them?"

"I work for myself."

"What happened?" He directed his eyes at the tattooed silhouette on Cole's arm.

From wrist to elbow, black ink filled in the figure of a woman on a dance pole. Last year, she was the only tattoo on that arm. Now a tapestry of drawings crowded in around her as if he were slowly working his way toward fading her out.

There was so much chaos in the illustrations it was hard to guess if each piece had been a spontaneous addition or somehow part of a premeditated vision. Spider webs, fire, chains, plants, various depictions of the sun, and random unknown symbols—all of it overlapped and blended together, sleeving both arms and one entire pec.

He returned his attention to the inked dancer. "Is she the one you hurt?"

"One of many." Cole stared at his beer. "The only one who mattered."

"How long ago?"

"Years. A lifetime ago."

He'd never seen Cole with a woman. Couldn't even imagine it. At the headquarters in Colombia where they lived, there was no shortage of willing pussy. The cartel loved their girls. But not Cole. Whenever one of the ladies approached him, she was met with a sneer of disgust.

"When was the last time you got laid?"

"None of your goddamn business." Cole stood and strode back to the kitchen, grabbing two more beers.

"That's a bullshit answer. For the past year, I've spent damn near every day with you, a lot of that time on the mats, letting you pound in my face and pick apart my weaknesses. I trusted you with my training. I trust you with this job. But beyond that? I don't know, Cole. Because I don't fucking know you."

Cole handed him another Bud Light, sat in the chair across from him, and took a long draw from his bottle. Then he stared at him. Drank again. More staring.

At last, he leaned back and closed his eyes. "I fell in love many years ago."

"With a stripper?"

"A belly dancer. She floated up to me on the street like a damn angel emerging from a mist. Her smile… Fuck, it was so blinding it stopped me on my motorcycle and leveled my entire world." His leg bounced. Then stilled. "I asked her to marry me. Then I chose my job over her."

"The secret agent job?"

"Don't call it that." He cracked his eyes open, glaring through the slits. "I was sent out in the field for a while. Mistakes were made, and I was forced to fake my death to protect her. By the time I cleaned up the mess, quit the job, and returned home to her, she'd fallen in love with my best friend."

"Ouch."

"She's happy. That's all I ever wanted."

"I don't believe that. I've seen the wedding ring you wear on the chain under your shirt. A woman's ring. She's inked on your arm, and unless you're hiding a health problem, your dick still works. You're still a man. But I'm guessing you haven't had sex with anyone since her."

"There isn't a woman out there who comes close to the one I had."

"Trust me, Cole. You have to let go and move on. If you're afraid of falling in love again—"

"I will always love *her*. End of." Cole steadily met his eyes. No defensive anger. No emotion at all. "My refusal to bed random women has nothing to do with fear and everything to do with self-control."

"I get it. I fucking *lived* it." He softened his voice, recalling his own pain and the celibacy that accompanied it. "Caroline was only fourteen when she died. As innocent as it sounds, I saved myself for her. Then Van happened. A fucking traumatizing way to lose your virginity. He and Liv forced me to perform sexual acts, but I didn't willingly touch a woman for the first time until much later. Those were some dark years."

"What changed?"

"I was so goddamn lonely that I went out one night and got laid. Just like that. I don't even remember her face. Doesn't matter. It was the intimacy that I needed. It pushed me out of the dark." He met Cole's eyes. "You're making a regrettable mistake if you condemn yourself to loneliness for the rest of your life."

Cole's gaze slid toward the back bedroom and locked on something out of view.

Tomas couldn't see around the corner, but he knew she was there. His neck stiffened. "Eavesdropping again, Rylee?"

"Leave Cole alone." She shuffled into the room, looking ragged and filthy and breathtakingly gorgeous. "He's not like you."

Cole winged up an eyebrow.

Tomas tensed as she looked at the front door, scoped out the kitchen, and returned to the door. She reeked of desperation. To find food. To run for her life. Neither was an option until she spilled her secrets.

"Go take a shower." He guzzled down the second beer.

"I want to hear what the psychologist has to say about our conversation." Cole nodded at her. "Go ahead, Rylee."

"I didn't hear all of it." She rubbed her arm where she'd removed the IV and stole another glance at the kitchen. "I'm hungry."

Cole wasn't on board with Tomas' plan, but he didn't twitch a muscle to interfere. At least, not yet. He simply observed her, waiting.

When no one spoke, she stepped farther into the room, positioning herself closer to the front door.

Would she run? Tomas counted on it. What he hadn't expected was her blatant disregard of his presence. Surely, she felt him glaring at her, daring her to look at him.

After a moment of deliberation, she lowered her head.

"Everyone handles a broken heart differently." Her shoulders twitched, her eyes shifty and tired. "Some people only love once, and if they lose that love, they never look for it again. They find other things in life that stir their passions. Like their work. Their hobbies. Or throwing themselves behind an important cause." She peered at Cole through her lashes. "You don't waste your time with hookups because you don't do casual relationships. You had the real thing, and there's no replacement. You're a one and done kind of guy. But a word of warning, Cole. Fate might not be done with you."

"I fucked fate to hell, darlin'." Cole traced a finger along his bottom lip, his voice taking on a menacing edge. "Believe me. That train crashed and burned."

"Okay, but if you're wrong, if love comes for you again, it's going to blindside you and knock you on your ass. You'll deny it. You'll fight it with every breath in your body. But having already experienced it once, you know it's a fight you can't win. So maybe, if and when it happens, give yourself a break. Don't fight so hard."

"Is that your professional opinion? Or personal experience?"

"Professional." Her brows furrowed. "Or personal. Both, I guess." She lifted her gaze, struggling in the effort to drag it across the room, pushing it toward Tomas, and finally, *finally*, she met his eyes. "You told him my husband cheated on me?"

He stared right back, giving her nothing, even as his blood flew through his veins. It wasn't her words that affected him. It was everything she didn't say.

Censure blazed in her glare, fury so hot he felt it flare against his chest. She abhorred him, scorned him, and found him severely lacking. Perhaps that was what struck him the most. Her burning disappointment.

As if she'd come here expecting to find something dramatically different. She must've read something into his emails that wasn't there. Maybe she thought if a man was stupid enough to write the details of his criminal life to a dead girl, he was stupid enough to fall in line with her agenda.

Well, she could shove her disappointment up her ass, because he wasn't that guy.

"Some people have more aggressive ways of dealing with a broken heart." She addressed Cole, but her eyes were all for Tomas. "Like standing on the edge of a bridge and welcoming death. Or writing emails and pouring out their regrets. Or hate-fucking every willing body they come in contact with."

Hate-fucking? That was what she thought he did? Or was she projecting her own issues? That would explain a lot.

"Are you having hate-sex with your neighbor?" He leaned forward, his posture rigid.

"God no."

"How many have come before Evan Phillips?"

"Not nearly as many as you parade in and out of your bed."

"Give me a number."

"Rot in hell."

"You know mine. In fact, you know every detail of my sexual history. I want yours."

"I'm not giving you shit." She backed toward the door, clumsy and nervous. She wouldn't get far.

"You want to eat? Give me the names of your lovers. Timelines. Descriptions. You're going to tell me who you're fucking, everyone you're connected with, and what they know about my friends and me."

"This again?" She took another backward step. "You already know about Mason and Evan. You know my occupation and where I live. Whoever that Paul guy was, I don't know him. He's connected to *you*."

"Then why was the tracker on *your* truck? Why was he watching *you* for six months?"

"I guess you should've asked him instead of dumping him in the desert with me. I told you everything I know about that, and I hope you figure it out. But I can't help you."

She reached for the door, but he was already moving.

"Don't do this!" She fumbled with the handle, breathing heavily and whimpering in her struggle to escape.

He pressed a hand on the door above her head, forcing it shut. "Get in the shower. You stink."

"No! I'm leaving!"

"Have it your way." With little effort, he flung her small body over his shoulder and carried her toward the bathroom.

Her little fists bounced off his back, the rest of her bucking ineffectively as he crossed the short distance. As his gaze intersected Cole's, they shared a look, but he didn't know what it meant.

Disapproval? Indifference? Definitely not encouragement. It didn't matter so long as the man didn't interfere.

In the bathroom, he turned on the shower and dropped her beneath the cold spray, clothes and all.

She yelped and clawed at the shower curtain.

He caught it before she tore it down and shoved her back into the tub. "Do that again, and you'll be showering with no privacy."

"Fuck you." She spluttered in the downpour of water, slipped on her socked feet, and scrambled up again, pressing her back against the shower wall.

Wet cotton and denim clung to her stunning figure. Strings of dark hair stuck to her face, and her silver eyes glinted with ferocity, sharp as honed steel and enthralling beyond reason.

Rylee Sutton was devastatingly sexy when she was mad.

"The soap is behind you." He leaned against the vanity, his jeans too painfully tight to contain his reaction to her. "Use it."

With a feral smile, she snatched the bar of soap and hurled it at him.

ELEVEN

The soap bounced off Tommy's chest and fell to the floor with a dull, anti-climatic *plonk*.

Rylee stared at it, her heart pounding in her throat. "That would've hit harder if I weren't starving to death."

"Then I should feed you." His tone scraped, stinging her nerves. "Just to ensure that the next thing you throw leaves a mark."

"Why are you such a jerk?" She shivered even as the spraying water started to heat and form a cloud of steam between them.

He blocked the exit with his sheer size, wearing a hateful scowl, dark jeans, and a black muscle-hugging shirt. Mist collected on the fabric in a blurry shine, making him look otherworldly, like an angry, avenging warlord.

If he expected her to take a shower while he watched, he could fuck right off.

"Move." She stepped over the bathtub ledge only to be shoved back in.

Indignation warred with fatigue, and the latter won out as she staggered and fell on her butt.

"Goddammit!" She staggered back to her feet and swayed. "Let me out!"

The hollows and slashes of his sculpted cheeks, the twisted sneer of his mouth, all of it carved a cruel expression in his unbearably handsome face. But his looks were overshadowed by the dispassion in his steady, golden eyes. Didn't matter what she said. He had a plan for her, and it wouldn't be merciful.

His gaze took a tour along her soaked clothes as he drifted closer, so close she detected fumes of beer on his breath. The piney, masculine aroma agitated her hunger and stirred other things she refused to acknowledge.

She met his eyes. "I'm not stripping in front of you, motherfucker."

His lip curled, and he leaned back. "You're old enough to be my mother, and that's a hard pass." He tossed the soap into the tub and yanked the shower curtain closed between them. "You have five minutes to undress and clean off the blood."

His nastiness penetrated, leaving a toxic, coiling pain in the deepest chambers of her heart.

"If I don't?" she asked.

"I'll do it myself, and neither of us will enjoy it."

So he'd rather insult her than see her naked. Fine. That was preferable. She could handle spiteful words, even if they hurt.

It was time she stopped thinking of him as the boy she'd connected with ten years ago. That kid was gone, and this man was beyond saving.

She only needed to save herself.

Lightheaded and famished, she shook from head to toe, her fingers uncooperative and trembling as she pulled off the soggy clothes and washed her hair.

If he remained on the other side of the curtain, she couldn't hear him. No amount of curiosity would compel her to steal a peek. Besides, he wouldn't go far.

Even if he thought she was old enough to be his mother.

Over the past few years, she found that maturity in women warded off shallow, insecure assholes—the same way aposematism warned off predators. If he was repelled by her age, it was working.

But his jab still burned her up. She was only forty-one. Fourteen years older than him. Maybe it was biologically possible to birth a child at that age, but she didn't know any fourteen-year-old mothers.

Why was she still thinking about this? Fuck him.

She needed the keys to her truck and an escape plan.

She needed food.

Finishing the shower in a rush, she shut off the water and grabbed the curtain. Then she slowly peered around the edge.

The bathroom was empty, the door cracked. No sound drifted in, but she knew he was out there, waiting with animosity in his eyes.

When she drove here three days ago, she saw this playing out so differently. If that rapist piece of shit, Paul, hadn't shown up, maybe Tommy would've despised her less and listened more.

Or maybe he'd just sounded nicer in email, and she didn't really know him at all.

A towel sat on the vanity, along with a clean pair of her pajama pants and an unfamiliar t-shirt. She hurried through drying, dressing, and using the toilet, left her ruined clothes in the bathtub, and stepped into the narrow hall.

Glancing toward the bedroom, she noticed the bed had already been stripped and replaced with clean bedding. Meticulous as ever, he would undoubtedly have all traces of Paul's blood gone from his property by nightfall.

How strange to be inside this house after hearing about it for ten years. It was exactly as he'd described—dark, cramped, cozy. And *quiet*.

The scent of food invaded her nose. She'd guzzled water and apple juice when she woke, but the gnawing emptiness in her stomach screamed for substance.

Her pulse quickened as she entered the front room.

Tommy sprawled on the couch, a sun-browned hand hanging casually over the armrest. Steam rose from a bowl that sat on the table before him, the aroma of delicious spices pervading the air.

Chili. Out of a box, a can, wherever it came from, she didn't care. Saliva pooled in her mouth, and her belly churned with ravenous need.

"Where's Cole?" She tugged on the oversize shirt, fighting the impulse to attack the food.

"Out." His gaze followed the action then lifted to hers, hard as polished gold. "Sit."

The front door beckoned, but the chili promised instant relief.

She crossed the room and sat across from him, her eyes on the bowl.

He straightened, leaning toward the table, and grabbed the spoon.

"Let's start with your bed partners." Scooping a huge helping of beans and meat, he held it between them and wet his lips. "How many men have you fucked since you started reading my emails?"

For a bite of that food, she could give him an estimate. A staggering number, to be honest, especially for a woman who thought she'd married her one and only. She wasn't ashamed of her sexual history or her voracious libido, but none of it concerned Tommy. If she told him about her past hookups, it would turn them into suspects and put them in his crosshairs.

"I've had one lover in the past year." She didn't want to look desperate, but her gaze kept drifting to the spoon, pulling like a magnet. "Evan isn't a criminal. He knows nothing about you. There isn't a chance in hell he's involved in this."

"Who came before him?"

She shook her head rapidly, frenzied in her hunger. "Tommy, please. I'm starving."

He veered the scoop toward his mouth and wrapped his mean lips around the entire bite, humming as he chewed.

There were a million words in the English language, but not one could adequately express how badly she wanted to stab him with that goddamn spoon.

She could try to take the bowl from him, but she was operating at a fraction of his strength and speed. If she behaved, maybe she wouldn't have to fight him at all. Maybe he intended to share with her.

He shoveled a second helping of chili and hovered it before her. "Give me names."

"Douchebag. Fuckface. Jackass. Mouth breather."

The spoon slid between his lips, another bite stolen.

She saw red. "You want to know why Paul followed me here? Look at your own history, the people you've murdered, the women you've fucked, and the ruthless company you keep. *That's* where you'll find your answer."

"I'm looking at all connections, but the most glaring one is you. The more you cooperate, the quicker this ends." He ate another spoonful, twisting pain through her stomach.

"Who I've slept with has no bearing on this."

"You have no family or friends. It seems the only people who come into your life are the ones who come between your legs."

"That's not true." A hot ember flared at the base of her throat.

"Then tell me, Rylee." He spooned more chili, eating it cruelly in front of her and talking with his mouth full. "Among your acquaintances, who hasn't been in your pants?"

"God, you're such a prick."

He continued eating, watching her with callous indifference as the bowl slowly emptied before her eyes. She could almost taste the hearty beans as they disappeared in his mouth.

"My colleagues." A prickly burn swarmed the edges of her eyes. "I don't sleep with them, and they're my friends."

"Colleagues," he echoed in an acidic tone and wiped the back of his hand across his lips. "Define your relationship with them."

"What do you mean?"

"Have any of them been to your house? Or called you on the phone just to shoot the shit? Or invited you to hang out or grab a beer after work?"

"No." *Not once.* "I don't make friends like that easily. I'm shy. Reserved."

"A shy woman doesn't show up at a known criminal's house by herself. But you're not alone, are you? Whoever you're working with sent Paul to check on you, and when he doesn't return, they'll send someone else."

"Jesus, you're all over the place with your theories. Which is it? Am I being tracked by an enemy, a lover, or some cohort who is helping me plot your demise?"

"You tell me."

"None of the above. I'm so damn shy and guarded it took me ten years to work up the nerve to talk to you. Luring you here to meet you in person is so far out of my comfort zone. I told no one about you or where I was going. I just...I thought you were in danger with the cartel, and I panicked when you said goodbye in your last email. I don't have friends like you do. I'm not good at letting people in."

"You don't have friends because you're a lying, deceitful—"

"I'm afraid of being hurt again." The confession blurted on a rush of anger.

He stared at her like she was the village idiot. Maybe she was. She'd made a terrible mistake coming here. Too late to take it back. But she was educated. Trained to listen to criminals and understand their motivations, views, thoughts, and actions.

If he didn't view her as a person, he would continue to hurt her. She needed to remind him she was human.

"I pretend I don't need anyone." She swallowed, her vision blurring with tears. "I keep everyone at a distance. But deep down, I still dream of finding a life partner, someone who loves me enough to be loyal. *Faithful.*"

"Is that why you're fucking Evan? You want him to love you?"

"No." She wiped at her wet cheeks and looked away. "He's charming and nice and…"

Too perfect. Too doting. Too much like Mason. That scared the crap out of her.

"Women love him," she said. "I'm not his only lover. I mean, we don't have that kind of relationship. We're just neighbors."

"With benefits." His judgmental tone added insult to his narrowed glare.

"You're not in a position to look at me like that. You fuck whomever you want and make those women hurt. *Your* words. Don't you dare shame me for having a sex life."

With a grunt, he turned his attention back to the chili and ate another spoonful.

There was only one bite left.

She balled her hands so tightly her nails dug into her palms. "You're not going to let me eat?"

"Give me the names of your sexual partners, and I'll feed you."

"I don't know their names."

"You don't know who you're fucking? How did you meet them?"

Her hunger outweighed her pride, making it easy to answer. "Dating sites and hookup apps. Their usernames were probably not their real names, and I don't remember any of them anyway."

"Where's your phone?"

He already knew her identity. There was nothing in that duffel bag worth hiding.

"Buried in the ruins of the Milton house," she said. "Southwest corner."

He shoved the bowl toward her.

She fell upon it like a rabid dog, sucking the last bite off the spoon until it gleamed. Heavenly flavors exploded on her tongue as she dropped the utensil and dragged her fingers along the bottom of the empty bowl, frantically scraping out every drop.

"Where are you?" He stood with his phone to his ear. "Okay. Swing by Caroline's house on your way back."

As he recapped the conversation about her duffel bag, she cleaned every speck of chili from the bowl with her fingers and tongue. It didn't come close to putting a dent in her hunger.

He ended the call and turned toward her. "Are the dating apps still on your phone?"

"Yes, but I swear, Tommy, I never told anyone about you. Don't hurt those guys. They were just one-night stands."

"Let's go." He gripped her arm and wrenched her from the chair.

"Go where?" She tried and failed to escape his grip as he dragged her toward the bedroom. "Wait! I'm still hungry."

"Not hungry enough."

"What do you mean?" She dug in her feet and stumbled with the force of his forward motion. "I answered your questions."

As he hauled her away from the kitchen, it became horribly apparent that one bite of chili was all he would give her.

Eating was imperative. But more than that, she felt the overpowering instinct to run.

She went wild, thrashing, punching, biting, kicking, and somehow, she broke free. Her thoughts spun into chaotic indecision, but her body took the reins, bolting through the house and toward the front door.

Blood pounded in her ears, her pulse spastic and breaths bursting.

DOMINATE

Running into the desert would be suicide. She needed her keys and scoured every surface as she flew past the front room. *Nothing.* But she didn't slow.

Outside, she slammed into a wall of hot air, the sky pitch black and her truck nowhere in sight.

Oh fuck, oh fuck, oh fuck.

She darted around the side of the house, searching for anything that might help her escape this miserable wasteland. Where was her fucking truck?

If she sprinted in the direction of the Milton house, could she find her way in the dark? Did she have the strength to travel two miles on foot? Then what? She'd dig up her phone, but it didn't have a signal. And she needed the map in her truck to find the closest town.

Fuck!

"You'll die out there." His chilling voice fell against her back, terrifyingly close.

She spun, backing away from his towering silhouette. "Where's my truck?"

Only a few feet separated them, and he stayed with her, prowling forward as she reeled backward.

Twilight threw the hollows of his cheekbones into shadow and accentuated the handsome planes of his face. He was a vigilante criminal, a lawless punisher, with righteous murder pumping through his veins.

His dangerous lifestyle was echoed in the strength of his hands, the cruelty from his lips, and the sheer power of his body as he trapped her like the sun in the barren desert. Inescapable heat, nowhere to run, and she was starving, the looming threat of another day here as brutal and unforgiving as the man himself.

"Let me go, Tommy." Her heart hammered, and she retreated another step, trembling. "I know you think I'm a loose end, and you're meticulously good at your job, always finishing every task set upon you, even the ones that are bothersome and undesirable. But I'm not a job. You're starving an innocent woman and holding her captive. That violates everything you and your friends are doing. If there's someone truly after me, you should be protecting me not hurting me."

He stepped forward, slow and menacing.

Revenge was his life, in his blood, and he intended to punish her in payment for a wrong that had been done. He was beyond listening.

She turned and ran.

TWELVE

Rocky sand bit into Rylee's bare feet as she sprinted through the dark. In normal circumstances, she would've been terrified of stepping on a scorpion. But there was a deadlier threat on her heels, breathing down her neck, closing in—

His fist caught her throat, his other twisting in her hair. The punishing grip wrenched her off her feet, dragging her knees and scraping her hands along the ground as he hauled her back into the house by her hair.

No amount of fighting or screaming slowed him down. By the time he wrestled her into the bedroom, she was out of strength, out of breath, and he hadn't broken a sweat.

He tossed her onto the bed like a rag doll and followed her down, straddling her legs and pinning her arms above her head.

"You fucking psycho!" She wheezed, trying to catch her breath. "This is wrong. This isn't you. Please, Tommy. Stop this madness!"

The sound of metal clanked above her. She twisted her neck and glimpsed handcuffs in his grasp.

"No!" She renewed her fight, but it was a wasted effort. "Get away from me!"

Within seconds, he shackled her arms to the wrought iron headboard. His thigh pushed between hers. His hand covered her mouth. Then he gave her his weight. All of it.

DOMINATE

Fucking God, he was muscle-heavy. Hard. Dense. Utterly immovable. His heat, his strength, every inch of him pressed her into the mattress, making her whimper against his palm. And his eyes. Damn those eyes. They were so shockingly, brilliantly gold. Gorgeous. Mesmerizing. *Vicious.*

He radiated rebellious, bad-boy intimidation coupled with a virility so potent it made every warmblooded woman's head turn and mouth water.

This was the closest she'd ever physically been to him, and while she loathed him for hurting her, it wasn't enough to dampen her reaction to his masculinity.

A sharp, carnal tug pulled inside her, dirty and wanton. There was a wicked wildness about him that called to her filthiest desires. After accusing him of hate-fucking women, she couldn't stop herself from imagining him doing that to her. Didn't mean she wanted it. No way in hell. But the naked possibility of such a thought messed with her head.

His hand moved from her mouth to wedge beneath her nape, tightening at the base of her skull and yanking her toward his sinful lips. Not to kiss her. He just held her mouth against his, breathing, seducing, making her squirm between want and repulsion.

He'd written in detail about his captivity in Van's attic. Eight weeks of brutal sexual instruction. Van had whipped him and taken his virginity. Liv had taught him how to kiss and suck a cock, but she never fucked him. He didn't have intercourse with a woman for the first time until years later.

The intimate position made it impossible not to think about everything he'd endured. Everything he'd *learned.* He was trained in sexual pleasure and knew how to use it to lure and torture. He was tormenting her with it now, arousing her, confusing her. Just to be a dick.

"I know what you're doing." She jerked her face away.

He gripped her jaw and yanked it back.

She drank in the youthful texture of his skin, his symmetrical, rough-hewn features, the flavor of his breath, the faintness of beer, spicy meat, and all man. The delectable, warm scent of him enveloped her like a fantasy.

While she reeled from his overbearing proximity, she wasn't the only one affected. Electricity writhed between them, twisting the dynamic of their tumultuous relationship and weaving layers of toxic complexity.

They had no business staring at each other like this. There was too much animosity and resentment in the air. But neither of them looked away, their breaths melding into shimmers of hot, poisonous attraction. It punched through her, almost causing the last of her senses to desert her. Christ, she was shaking.

He responded to it by sliding his touch along her jaw, studying her with his fingertips, feathering them along her cheekbones, her nose, her lips. Then his touch grew heavier, harder, pressing against her skin until his entire hand was squeezing her face.

Anger. His reaction to her was pissing him off. Or maybe this was what he'd meant in his emails. When he was intimate with women, he always hurt them.

"Tommy." She shook her head, gasping and trying to break his cruel grip. "You're hurting me."

He was all biceps, abs, and rock-hard thighs, bearing down on her like a brick wall. He must have felt her shifting beneath him because he removed his hand from her face. Then he stared at her mouth, watching her gulp for air under his heavy body.

Lifting slightly, he transferred some of his weight onto his elbow and leg. It was such a small thing, a tiny glimpse of thoughtfulness.

He wanted to make her pay, but that wasn't how his mother raised him to treat a woman. Nor was it the first time he'd shown a trace of compassion.

"I know you put sunscreen on me before leaving me in the desert." She peered into his eyes from inches away. "Why?"

"Your skin is flawless. I've never seen anything like it." His gaze traveled along her throat, the neckline of the shirt, and returned to her eyes. "It would be a shame to ruin something so beautiful."

That was the nicest thing he'd said to her, but she needed a lot more than a compliment from him.

"Keep starving me, and there won't be any flesh left on my bones."

"Starvation is a very slow, agonizing death."

"Three weeks."

"This will end before then."

"How will it end? I know you've killed horrible men, but do you have it in you to kill me?"

"I guess we'll find out."

She drew in his threat on a sharp inhale. "This is why I filed a protective order against my ex-husband."

He glanced at her arms. "Because he handcuffed you?"

"No. He forced his way into my house. Then he forced himself on me."

The heat, the intimacy, and the weight of his body vanished, leaving nothing but cold vulnerability in its wake.

She should've been relieved to gain the space. But she was still restrained to the bed and knew that when he left the room, she would be stuck here with nothing to distract her from the hunger pangs.

"He raped you?" He stood beside the bed, his expression unreadable.

"No. He got aggressive and handsy and wouldn't leave. It scared me enough to call the cops and file a restraining order."

"This happened last year. Yet you divorced him a decade ago."

"He never wanted the divorce and has been trying to get me back ever since. He's a relentless pest, but that's *all* he is. He shows up at my house, at my work, calls and texts and sends gifts. But it's all harmless. He's not a threat."

"Until he forced himself on you. Why are you defending him?"

"I'm not. It's just…I know him. He wouldn't hire someone to watch me."

"What about Evan Phillips?"

"No way. He doesn't have the money to throw around on shit like that. Besides, we're together all the time. He lives right next door. There's no reason for him to hire someone to watch me."

"You'd be surprised what a desperate man would do. He has hundreds of photos of you on his personal computer."

"What?" A chill zinged along her scalp. She didn't know what bothered her more—his announcement or the fact that he had access to Evan's computer. "Hundreds?"

"Yes."

"Wow, okay. I mean, I know he takes pictures of me with his phone sometimes. I didn't know he saved them. But he's with a lot of women and probably has photos of them, too."

"Nope. Just you."

That's fucked up.

But was it really? Evan repeatedly pressed her to take their relationship further. Maybe he liked her more than she thought?

"Just because he has photos of me," she said. "That doesn't mean he hired Paul to watch me."

He stared at her for an eternity, his face unfairly gorgeous. And blank. She would give anything to read his mind.

Growing antsy, she twisted her wrists in the handcuffs and pulled. He'd secured them correctly, ensuring she couldn't escape and while keeping them loose enough not to cause discomfort. She could flip over but would have to sleep with her hands above her head.

Turning away, he grabbed a bottled water from the stash on the small desk and sat beside her hip.

"This is your childhood room," she said. "You were in here when you started emailing Caroline."

His jaw hardened as he lifted her head and helped her drink.

She knew he'd burned all the furniture and everything else that had once been in this house.

"I cried for you that day." She drank another long gulp, draining the rest of the water. "The day you burnt your belongings. I know it was hard for you. But it was also cathartic."

His neck stiffened, and he tossed the empty bottle in the direction of the desk.

"I want to know…" He leaned over her, his eyes ablaze with accusation. "How far did you let your ex-husband go before you told him *no*."

"What?"

"You loved him enough to nearly kill yourself when he cheated." He lowered his head, hovering his lips a hairbreadth away from hers. "When he put his mouth on you, did you open for him? Did you draw him in?"

Her mouth opened now on a shocked gasp. "No, I—"

His tongue swept in, lashing and licking at the stunned flesh of hers. She didn't kiss him back, for this wasn't a kiss at all. It was anger and violence. He grabbed her face and mauled her with his mouth, biting, sucking, and decimating her defenses.

Before she thought to bite him back, it ended. He stared down at her, his breaths fast and hot against her face, his lips swollen and glistening.

"Why did you do that?" she asked, furious.

"To test your reaction."

She ground her teeth. "What did you learn?"

He touched a finger to her mouth and trailed it down her chin, her neck, her breastbone. His eyes followed the movement, his intention clear a half-second before he pinched her nipple through the shirt.

"Stop!" She wasn't wearing a bra and had no protection against the assault. "Don't touch me!"

"Is that what you told him?" He squeezed harder, shooting pain through her breast and stinging her eyes with tears.

"Yes!"

"You told him *yes*?"

"No!" She kicked her legs, aiming a knee toward his back. But she couldn't reach him. She didn't have the strength. "I told him *no*. A million times *no*."

"But he couldn't keep his hands off your hot little responsive body." He cupped her breast in a ruthless vise, adding ungodly pressure as his thumb rolled over the pebbled peak. "Your nipples were hard before I even touched them. My God, you're hungry."

"You sound like a rapist."

DOMINATE

He clicked his tongue. "Are you wet?"

"Are you hard?"

He twisted, slid a leg over the top of hers and pressed the hardest, *largest* erection she'd ever felt against her hip.

Her pulse quickened. Her body shuddered, and her mouth went desert-dry.

That couldn't be real. No goddamn way.

His cock jerked against her, and swear to God, it felt like a baseball bat was stretching the threads of his jeans from groin to knee.

Instinct bellowed at her to retreat, but she refused to wither beneath him.

"I know you get off on hurting women, but I'm a *hard pass*, remember?" She lifted her pelvis and pushed into the threat, challenging his execution. "Go fuck someone your own age."

"I don't want to fuck you, Rylee. I'm only interested in hurting you."

He flipped her to her stomach and shoved the hem of the shirt up her back.

"What are you doing?" She jerked on the restraints and bucked beneath his ruthless hands.

He yanked down her pajama pants and exposed her bare backside.

Her breath left her.

His palm came down with a shocking, fiery *smack*. She gulped, stunned, and opened her mouth on a silent scream.

Another strike. And another. He wailed on her ass with all the fury of a punishing god. She could only lie there and take it like a shameful child. But she wasn't ashamed. She was burning, panting, sinking into his blistering attention in the most sickening way.

It wasn't just the bite of his hot palm or the delicious chill that followed each blow. It was the crescendo of his breaths, the guttural growls from his throat, and the blustering pulse in her ears, in her pussy— all of it echoing in an erotic symphony and growing faster, faster, until there was no pause between the primal beats.

Then he was on her. His hands, his teeth, tearing into her welted flesh, sinking into burning muscle, piercing skin, slapping, biting, and groaning with sexual savagery.

He spread her cheeks and took his mouth to her anus, teasing and tormenting the ring of nerves. His tongue prodded and lapped up and down her crack, delving deep. So deep. Oh, God, he knew what he was doing. If this was him when he lost his temper, she couldn't fathom what he could do to a woman when he was in full control.

It felt too good. Too atrociously depraved and shocking. She'd wanted this level of rough, raw lust for as long as she could remember, to burn beneath the intensity of male heat, to explore the dark, uncharted corners of her imagination, but she'd never found a man who could take her there.

So instead of fighting, she lifted her ass and writhed against him to heighten the sensation.

"You fucking slut." He spanked her again, harder, meaner. "I don't hear you saying *no*. You tease men with this perfect, round ass. You fuck them and forget them and wonder why you have a stalker."

The heat of his mouth replaced his hand, his tongue stabbing between her buttocks, and lower, lower, reaching for her pussy.

Nonsensical sounds bubbled in her throat as she jerked like a mindless thing, trembling, gasping. The throbbing between her legs came at intervals until those intervals blurred into one blinding pulse. It overtook her.

She was going to come.

He tore his mouth away and climbed off the bed.

Her stomach seized and plummeted.

Without warning, he plunged two fingers between her legs, gliding the tips along her soaked slit. She squeezed her thighs together, but he got what he wanted, proving it as he brought his wet hand to her face and smeared her arousal across her lips.

If she felt shame, it was diluted by an inglorious blast of rage. Rage at herself for falling into his trap.

His other hand caught her hair and wrenched her head back at a painful angle. Then he kissed her fully, brutally, with such appalling intensity and hostility that it shriveled her insides.

Shoving her away, he strode toward the door.

True to his word, he didn't fuck her.

He'd hurt her.

"Tommy." She seethed with contempt and panic. "Let me go!"

He shut off the light and left her quivering in the dark by calculated intent.

THIRTEEN

Rylee lay in the dark, listening to male voices drift in from the front room. Cole had returned, and no one had come to check on her. Hunger only scratched the surface of her misery.

The welts on her backside throbbed. The restraints on her arms prevented her from pulling up her pajama pants and cleaning away the damp reminder of her arousal. Tommy had deliberately left her in this position, knowing she would squirm in discomfort and despise herself as much as she despised him.

What sane woman craved the touch of a cruel man? She couldn't even claim Stockholm syndrome because she'd known him for ten years, had willingly put herself in this situation, and felt absolutely no positive feelings toward him.

Except for this sick, sexual attraction.

She needed to get far, far away from him before she lost her damn mind.

He and Cole spoke in low murmurs, too muted for her ears. They were probably going through her duffel bag and dissecting all the messages, apps, and private activity on her phone.

Hopefully, their intrusive investigation would prove she wasn't connected to Paul Kissinger.

How had she not known she was being followed for six months? As frightening as that was, if the person who'd hired Paul wanted to kill her, she would already be dead.

Ironically, this had all began on the one night she'd actually wished for death. Tommy had inadvertently saved her life on that bridge, and now, a decade later, he was intent on destroying it.

Too bad she didn't have the training to negotiate her way out of this. But criminal psychologists were not effective as negotiators.

First off, if she attempted to counsel him, no matter how subtle her technique, he would know what she was doing and rage against the implication that he was crazy.

Secondly, therapy was *not* the same as negotiation. Therapeutic intervention took months or years to achieve positive growth and relief from suffering. She was no longer interested in helping him grow past his trauma. Her only goal now was escaping as quickly as possible.

Thirdly, he wasn't mentally ill. He didn't have bipolar disorder or schizophrenia. He was a sane man, a ruthless vigilante, who knew no bounds and harbored a blatant disregard for laws and authority.

Hours must've passed, and at some point, she fell asleep.

When she woke, Tommy was in bed with her.

Morning light filtered into the bedroom through the open doorway, illuminating the hard, sinewy arm that rested on her hip like an iron bar.

Her pants had been put back in place, and even more surprising, her hands were free.

She lay on her side, turned into him for some reason. All she could see was a flat nipple and taut, tanned skin stretched over the ridges of a chiseled chest.

Her pulse accelerated, her joints frozen. Had he slept here all night? Was he sleeping now?

His hand moved, fingers ghosting along her back. She stiffened.

Swallowing past the resentment in her throat, she tilted back her head and locked onto alert, golden eyes.

"Why did you sleep in here?" she asked, suspicious.

"The other bed was taken."

"So was this one."

"While I despise the sight of you, I'd rather sleep beside you than the sweaty, bearded bastard in the other room." He lowered his hand to her backside and squeezed the abused muscle. "How's your ass feel this morning?"

"Fine." She resisted the impulse to jerk away and give him the satisfaction of a reaction.

"Liar." He gave her a light smack on the butt and rose from the bed. "Go take a shower."

He strode out of the room, wearing workout shorts that hung so low on his hips she could see two deep dimples near the crease of his firm butt.

No one should look that sexy after just waking up. Especially not the motherfucker who was responsible for the stitching pain in her stomach.

How many days had it been since she'd eaten? Four? It felt like forty, and her strength was paying for it. Any escape attempt right now would be laughable. Hence the reason he'd removed the handcuffs.

The room spun as she wobbled toward the bathroom. The only reason she wanted another shower was to wash off the remnants of last night's arousal. She couldn't let that happen again.

Today, she would find a way to leave.

Fresh clothes—taken from her truck—waited for her on the vanity. No undergarments, but there was a tube of ointment. She glanced at the label, realizing it was meant for her welts.

Was that what Tommy did for all the women he fucked? Blistered their asses then tossed them a tube of aftercare?

Her blood boiled, and she snatched the ointment, hurling it across the bathroom.

She made it through a quick shower without passing out, all the while imagining driving her fist into his handsome face repeatedly. As she dried herself off, she caught her reflection in the mirror.

Four days of stress and starvation had already taken its toll. Her cheekbones sharpened under the dark circles bruising her eyes. Her shoulders and ribs were more pronounced, pressing starkly through the pallor of her skin. She looked gaunt. Almost cadaverous. She felt sick.

Reluctantly, she located the ointment and smeared it on her welted backside. That done, she dressed in jeans and a white tank-top, cleaned her teeth, and left her hair dripping down her back.

Then she opened the door to the overwhelming fragrance of pork grease and coffee. The aroma buckled her knees. Staggering, she followed the scented trail into the kitchen.

Tommy sat at the table, a mug in his hand and his eyes drilling into hers. Shirtless and sprawled with his legs spread, he took up too much room, too much air. He knew it, too, with his brown hair all tousled from sleep and his lips twitching with arrogance.

He knew exactly how women looked at him, including the one he starved.

She tore her gaze away and found Cole standing at the stove, frying eggs and bacon. A basket of colorful fruit sat on the counter, along with cheese, bakery sweets, and milk. He must've gone to the store while he was out yesterday.

Salivating and dizzy with hunger, she couldn't endure this. It was cruel enough to starve her. But to torment her with a goddamn breakfast buffet right under her nose was beyond brutal. It was coldblooded and diabolically evil.

Tommy stood, put his empty plate and mug in the dishwasher, and strode past her without a glance or a word. A second later, the bathroom door shut, and the shower turned on.

"Sit." Cole pointed a spatula at the table and turned back to the stove.

If she didn't sit, she would collapse. So she obeyed.

He joined her, holding a heaping plate of food.

Her eyes watered, overflowing with despair. "Would you kill me if I fought you for a bite?"

"No need." He slid the plate toward her and wrapped her trembling hand around a fork. "Hurry up. You only have about five minutes."

Shocked elation jolted through her, but she didn't hesitate. Eggs, bacon, pineapple, glazed donuts—she shoveled it all in, groaning, whimpering, and casting off her manners in lieu of stuffing her face. "He doesn't know you're feeding me?"

"No, and if you tell him, this will be the last time I interfere on your behalf."

Focused on devouring every bite, she didn't come up for air until she'd licked the plate clean.

Cole held out a glass of water, regarding her too closely.

She drank deeply, washing down barely chewed food. "I'm not complaining, but what are you playing at? Good cop, bad cop?"

"If you think I'm the good one, you're terrible at your job."

The bathroom door opened.

Cole reached out and swiped a thumb across her lips, clearing away crumbs. Then he moved the empty plate, setting it in front of him.

Her blood-sugar levels were already rising, surging energy through her system and chasing away the trembling effects of hunger. She was far from feeling like her normal self, but the meal had quickly taken the edge off.

She met Cole's eyes, and maybe he saw the gratitude in hers. But she wouldn't thank him. He was an accomplice in her suffering, and she owed him nothing.

With a smirk, he reclined in the chair and ran a finger along his beard.

DOMINATE

He wanted her to think he wasn't a good guy. He could mostly pull it off with that unnerving smirk on his rugged face and the sheer number of tattoos that competed for space on his strapping arms. And maybe his heart was a little jaded and a lot broken. But those bloody, beating scraps still had the capacity for compassion.

As Tommy walked from the bathroom to the bedroom and back to the hall, she pinched the neckline of her tank-top and scrubbed the inside of the material over the surface of her teeth, trying to remove any evidence of that satisfying meal.

Cole arched an eyebrow.

She tipped up hers in return. She'd meant what she told Tommy that first night in the desert. Keeping secrets was a weakness of hers. She did it too well and often lied to protect someone's feelings.

Tommy emerged, wearing a cowboy hat, black t-shirt, faded denim, and dusty boots. His gaze went to her, the empty plate in front of Cole, and made a pass through the kitchen, taking in every detail.

"We're going for a ride." He prowled toward her, reaching into his back pocket.

She stood. "Where—?"

He slapped a handcuff on her wrist and looked at Cole. "I'll be out of signal range for a few hours."

"Where are you taking me?" She kept her movements slow and her stance weak, feigning starvation, even as every muscle in her body burned to fight the restraints.

"I'm heading out, too." Cole pushed from the table, ignoring her as efficiently as Tommy. "I'll be back tonight."

"Don't go after Evan or Mason." Panic shook her voice. "I swear to you, Cole, they're not involved."

"Come on." Tommy pulled her along by the handcuffs, hauling her out the door and into the morning heat.

She shaded her eyes with her free hand, faltering at the sight of a 1980's doorless, topless Jeep Wrangler.

"Where's my truck?" She turned, searching the property, and spotted a black Harley-Davidson motorcycle. "Please, tell me you didn't get rid of my truck. It took me years to pay that off!"

He lifted her, dropped her in the Jeep's passenger seat, and made quick work of shackling both of her hands to the handle on the dash.

As he walked around the front, she took an inventory of the cargo. A shovel, pickax, large plastic containers filled with water, other containers with unknown contents. Her attention returned to the shovel.

"You're going to bury Paul Kissinger?" Her heart shivered.

He climbed in, buckled her seat belt, did his own, and started the engine. Then he shoved the Jeep into gear and took off.

Speeding over ruts and prickly shrubs, he worked the clutch and the gear shift and... *Fucking fuck fuck fuck!*

Even if she managed to escape the cuffs and knock him out, she wouldn't be able to drive out of the desert. Because she didn't know how to drive a goddamn manual transmission.

She dropped her head back on the seat and groaned.

Endless miles stretched in every direction—an expanse of searing, white-hot hopelessness. Gusts of dusty air blasted in through the open top, whipping her hair around her face and stinging her eyes. If she died and went to Hell, it would probably just be more of this.

"I have a newfound aversion to the desert," she said aloud.

"Tell me about it."

The fact that he responded at all surprised her, but it was his words that drew her gaze.

"What?" He glanced at her from beneath the brim of his hat. "I hate this fucking place and never planned on returning."

That was her fault. She'd given him no choice.

"I'm sorry." And she was. "I demanded you to come here because you were in over your head in that undercover job. What happened with Luke? Did he make it out?"

His hand clenched on the steering wheel, his mouth a slash of grim silence. The silence continued for the remainder of the drive through the desert.

He didn't use a map or GPS to find his way. He knew this land better than anyone.

An hour later, he slowed the Jeep, approaching a butte on the horizon. It looked like all the others in this region, but the flock of vultures circling overhead told her that this butte had a narrow cave at the base. And a dead body.

When the corpse of Paul Kissinger came into view, she wanted to close her eyes and hold her breath. She wanted to turn back.

Tommy parked the Jeep far enough away not to smell the rot. Large black birds of prey darted and swarmed in her periphery. She couldn't look. If she did, she would lose her breakfast.

He shut off the engine and unlocked her handcuffs.

She rubbed her wrists, her senses on high-alert. If she ran, he would catch her. If she stole the Jeep keys, she wouldn't know how to operate the clutch. She was free of the restraints, but not free at all.

"Luke is safe." He turned his neck, blinding her with the golden depths of his eyes. "I talked to him last night." The corner of his mouth bounced. "He fell in love with her."

"With the target? Vera?"

"Yeah." He unbuckled his seat belt and stared out at the desert through the windshield. "If I hadn't left the cartel compound when I did, things would've gone differently. Probably worse. Maybe my departure saved lives. Maybe Luke, Vera, and I would've survived either way." He turned his harsh glare on her. "But you had no business interfering. I don't give a fuck if you're telling the truth about your motivation or lying through your teeth. You're a stranger to me. You had no right reading my emails and making demands."

She swallowed down her objections and considered his words. "You're right. I shouldn't have invaded your privacy. I've made a lot of mistakes when it comes to you. But the punishment you're doling doesn't fit the crime."

"That is yet to be determined." He reached toward the back and tossed a bottle of sunscreen on her lap. "Lather up. We're going to be out here a while."

FOURTEEN

The miasma of death overpowered the desert air, making every inhale a poisonous, stomach-turning affliction. Rylee bent at the waist and gagged, her insides burning in misery.

Tommy stood in a shallow grave, seemingly unaffected by the stench as he swung the pickax over and over. He'd been digging forever, making excruciatingly slow progress in the hard, dry earth.

Since tampering with evidence and hiding a human body were crimes, she refused to help. But it was also a crime to fail to report a death and to fail to report the disposal of the body. Neither of which she intended to do.

She would take the secret of Paul's murder to her own grave. Not because she forgave Tommy for his heinous treatment of her, but because she was indebted to him for this murder. The only reason he killed this man was to stop him from raping her.

The desert sizzled with dry heat as far as she could see. She wasn't even tempted to run. Paul hadn't been able to escape this place, and the grisly aftermath of his failure lay in a pile of vulture scraps. It would be a long while before anyone stumbled upon his grave, if ever.

Even if law enforcement was tipped off to search the area, it would be a race against time and the elements, as the scorching temperatures ensured the remains would quickly decompose. The evidence of homicide would soon dry up with the corpse.

Gruesome thoughts. But comforting. She was so certain the crime scene would never be discovered that Tommy probably didn't even need to bury the body. But he was scrupulous in every job he undertook. He wouldn't leave here until every trace of foul play was gone.

DOMINATE

The sounds of scraping and hammering rent the air. He threw the pickax with brutal strength, breaking up rocks and chipping away at the sandy soil.

Muscles and stamina. He had an abundance of both, flexing through each swing, his lips set in a severe line, his physique as rigid and uncompromising as stone.

She would have to be stupid or blind not to notice his honed, sun-splashed body, his shirtless chest glistening with sweat, and his face overheated and red as Lucifer's was by nature.

The handsome devil paused, tossed off the cowboy hat, and raked damp hair away from his forehead. It was cropped on the sides and back and darker at the roots. The longer strands on top were straight and sun-bleached to a lighter shade of brown. If left untouched by his combing fingers, his rebellious bangs hung to his eyebrows.

It was a youthful hairstyle, one he could pull off without a receding hairline like many men her age had. A reminder that too many years separated them.

He resumed digging, angling away and slamming the ax into the ground. Her gaze followed the action, her lips parted in admiration.

His jeans hung low, molding to his contoured backside and exposing the carved indentations at his hips. His boots bore a thick layer of dust, and all those twitching back muscles streaked with dirt and sweat.

Lethally gorgeous.

Impossible to look away.

He was violence and sex and salvation. Salvation for trafficked women, not for her.

For her, he was corruption.

Damnation.

Death wasn't off the table.

That was the real reason she refused to help him dig. If she stepped into that grave, he might not let her leave it.

But as the day grew hotter and the stench of rot grew riper, she just wanted to get this over with.

With a sigh, she grabbed the shovel and forced her feet toward his sculpted back.

He stilled at the sound of her approach and glanced over his shoulder, his eyes as hot and golden as the blistering sun.

"I'll help." She shrugged. "But it better not be *my* grave I'm digging."

He cocked his tousled head, and a mischievous grin touched his lips.

An honest-to-God smile.

She couldn't have imagined such a thing on his stern face, but now that she witnessed it, she didn't want it to fade. It matched the glint in his eyes and made him look boyish, less threatening, and unreasonably, heartbreakingly stunning.

She was thunderstruck.

He turned back to his task, breaking the spell.

For the next two hours, they dug in silence, taking water breaks in the shade every fifteen minutes.

When he finally deemed the grave deep enough, she crawled out and stood by while he pulled on work gloves and dragged the half-eaten body into the hole.

She gagged and fought surging nausea as they covered the remains with sand and rock. The stench was eye-watering, the sight of squirming maggots and mangled flesh forever branded in her mind.

When the last scoop of dirt dropped on the grave, she charged toward the Jeep, breathing through her mouth and swallowing down bile.

Please, don't puke. Please, don't puke.

She chugged a bottle of water, sweating, shaking, desperate to leave this place and never return.

Footsteps approached from behind. He tossed his dirty gloves and grabbed a water, guzzling it in one long drink.

Dropping her brow against the side of the Jeep, she gagged again. It was all she could do to keep her stomach from emptying precious nutrients.

He moved in behind her and spoke at her ear. "A cock in the ass stops the gag reflex."

Her heart sputtered. "Are you offering?"

"It's a helpful tip."

"So you're offering just the tip?"

"For you, I'll bury it to the root." His breath heated her nape, his body heavy and damp against her back.

Her skin tingled in response, in memory, and she hated herself for it. "Get off me."

"I read the messages on your hookup apps and know for a fact that anal isn't just a notion in your lexicon of filthy thoughts. It's a must-have for your one-night stands."

If he was trying to insult her, he needed a different approach.

"That simply isn't true." She twisted to face him, smirking. "I enjoy all sorts of sex. I'm open-minded that way."

"If I knew that women your age were kinky, I would've bagged a horny old lady years ago."

That hit the mark.

DOMINATE

The outrage this man inspired in her was fast and sticky, climbing through her limbs and burning her hand. She swung, slamming her palm across his face.

He didn't flinch or raise his hand. His chilling calmness was threatening all on its own. "You wouldn't have the strength to do that if Cole hadn't fed you."

Denial tangled in her throat and surged onto her tongue. "He didn't."

He strode toward the back of the Jeep, lifted a huge container of water, and poured it over his head. His wet, powerful physique defied the downpour, standing proud and mighty like an impregnable fortress.

Bronzed by the sun, his chiseled chest provided deep grooves for the rivulets of water to travel. It streamed down his well-thewed arms and darkened the denim at his hips. More trickled over the blunt angles of his face and along the thick column of his neck, racing between the hollows of his bulging chest muscles.

He lowered the container, and a fat, glistening drop clung to the ridge of his brick-hard pec. Finally losing its slippery hold, it cascaded down his flat abdomen and into the thin line of hair that led an enticing path beneath the waistband of his jeans.

"I smelled the bacon on your breath." He stepped forward, his eyes ablaze with malice.

She backed up. "I stole a piece off Cole's plate when he wasn't looking."

In a blur, he dumped the rest of the water on her head. As she sputtered beneath the deluge, he gripped her tank-top and ripped the straps, the neckline, and the material straight down the front.

It fell to the ground in tatters, leaving her braless breasts exposed. She didn't bother covering herself in some pretense of being a shy virgin. They both knew she was anything but.

He watched the water run over her bare chest the same way she'd watched him. The appreciative gleam in his hooded eyes hardened her nipples and boiled her blood.

"You insult my age then ogle my tits?" She grabbed the shovel she'd left against the Jeep. "What kind of bastard are you?"

"A hungry one." He licked his lips, his voice smooth, deep, dangerously masculine. "Remove your jeans."

"Like hell I will." She raised the shovel with both hands.

"Make me hurt you, Rylee." He wrapped his mouth around the words, enunciating slowly. "Beg me."

She swung.

He seized the weapon with a vicious jerk, yanked it from her grip, and flung it out of reach. She slapped his face. Or tried. A fist caught her hair, whirling her off balance. She swung at him again, and he snared her wrist.

"You can't keep your greedy eyes off me." He forced her backward and sideways, crushing her between his body and the Jeep, his breaths coming so hard and angry against hers. "Because you like what you see."

"You have nice hair. Healthy bones. But your personality needs work. Far more than I'm willing to invest."

"Liar. You want me so badly it scares you." He leaned his weight against her, letting her feel the hard, impossibly thick, rigid length of him. "You like it rough and crave an aggressive, heartless man who will smack you around and fuck you like you just kicked his dog."

"You make me sick."

"You lied to me about breakfast, and you're lying now." He wrapped a hand around her throat. "But you're going to make it up to me by taking every inch of my cock."

She couldn't help it. She laughed, a loud, coarse, mocking guffaw that was cut off by his mouth as it slammed down over hers. He kissed her so cruelly and with such sublime devastation of heart and body that it only made her more furious, spurring her to kiss him back with equal venom.

He made a guttural sound deep in his chest as he assaulted her mouth, the thrusts of his tongue lashing against hers, punishing, seducing, making her need him and fear him until the past and present twisted together, doubts and certainty tangling so messily that one couldn't be distinguished from the other.

She arched into him, and he gave her his powerful body, fucking her with his tongue, squeezing her breasts, choking her throat, and smothering her with the fury of their toxic need.

His kiss was born of darkness, in the horrors of an attic, where pleasure could be plucked from hell if one were demented enough to reach for it. And reach for it, she did, with her lips, her hands, her entire body rising to him. He grabbed her hips, trapping her against the Jeep, and devoured her mouth as if he were trying to suck the life from her soul.

He captured her breaths, swallowed her whimpers, and plunged her into a madness of lust and helplessness. His body was a weapon of enticement, his tongue the trigger. He held her hostage with his mouth, his dominance, and she only wanted to give more, more, more until nothing remained.

When he let her breathe at last, his grip still firm above her collarbones, she could do no better than stare.

He stared back, panting, seemingly dazed.

Christ, he was irresistible. Sexy as fuck. Gorgeous beyond human nature.

And mean as a snake.

She hated him. But she loved the feel of his assertive hands, the taste of his cruel lips, and the dark, deadly passion in his labored breaths. She wanted him to touch her. Her breasts ached for it. But she was scared.

Scared he was toying with her.

Scared he would reject her.

Terrified he wouldn't.

"You wrote in your emails that you can't have sex without inflicting pain. Yet you fight for a cause that saves women." She touched his hand at her throat, pulling on his immovable fingers. "I don't know what this is, if it's just two angry people lashing out at each other and using sex as an outlet, but I don't want any part of it. I won't willingly let you abuse me. If beating women gets you off—"

"Beating women?" He slammed a fist against the Jeep beside her head, making her jump. "Touch me, Rylee. Right now." His face twisted in rage, contorting the masterful planes of beauty as he roared, "Put your fucking hands on me!"

His thundering voice rang in her ears and shook her from head to toe. She swallowed, confused by the demand, and lowered her hands to his jeans.

He tensed as she touched the swollen outline of him beneath the zipper. Her fingers trembled as she followed the impressive bulge, down, down, down, still going...

Holy mother of God, what she'd felt last night hadn't been her imagination. He was enormous, thick, and so fucking long. Like porn-star long.

"Tommy?" Startled, she removed her touch.

Flattening his palms on the Jeep behind her, his arms supported his assertive lean and caged her in. He scrutinized her face, glaring, invading her space, and stealing her air with blatant intimidation.

"Pull me out." A deep, insistent command. Taunting.

This wasn't foreplay or seduction. He was being mean. But there was something else going on. Something straining beneath the antagonism.

Interest? Desire? He was hard as a rock, so yeah, he wanted to fuck, and she was the only female within a hundred miles. But he would never rape her. She'd miscalculated some things about him, but she was certain he would need a damn good reason to force a woman.

And that was what she'd detected beneath his growly, imperious command.

Uncertainty.

Vulnerability.

Was he anxious about her seeing him in the flesh and casting judgment? There was only one way to find out.

Her heart galloped as she unbuckled his belt and lowered the zipper. His breath hitched as she bent, wrestling the snug denim and briefs down his brawny thighs.

He didn't spring free or jut upward. His erection was too heavy, too inconceivably massive to do anything but hang. God help her, he was hung. In his fully aroused, undeniably hard state, he was easily ten inches.

Disbelief compelled her hands. She touched without hesitation, drawing a gasp from his lips. The skin was warm, circumcised, and oh-so silky beneath her trembling fingers, the engorged muscle beneath like bedrock. The hair at the base was dark brown and neatly trimmed, his huge, full testicles completely shaved.

He was beautifully formed, and at the same time, monstrous. A woman's body wasn't designed to take an invasion of this size. Not without horrible stretching and…

Pain.

He couldn't have sex without hurting women.

Realization sank into her stomach, stabbing her with guilt and dread.

"Now you know." He curled his fingers around hers, holding her grip to his shaft. "You invaded my privacy, read the personal journals of my life, and jumped to assumptions about my conduct with women." His hand tightened, crushing the bones in hers. "Your narrow-minded, judgmental idiocy led you into a sick, twisted fantasy world, where I star as some abusive, raging beast."

"You are abusive! Your treatment of me is deplorable."

"That's what *you* want." He grabbed her throat and slammed his body against hers, pinning her against the Jeep. "You came here in search of a sadist who breaks laws and fucks the shit out of women."

"No!" She shook her head rapidly, her neck locked in the cuff of his bruising hand.

Without releasing her, he toed off his boots and kicked away his jeans. Then he set his mouth against hers and fed her his infuriating demand. "Beg me."

"Never." She grabbed his thick neck, mirroring his choking grip.

"For a psychologist, you have a shitload of issues." He wrenched her closer and bit the skin beneath her ear. "I'm going to fuck all that pent-up anger out of you."

"Eat a dick." Fuming, she aimed a punch at his arrogant face.

DOMINATE

"I have." He knocked her hand aside and hauled her back against the Jeep. "But you already know all about that because you're a creepy, spying little bitch."

"I was there for you!" She exploded, clawing at his cheeks and kicking him in the shins. "I cried for you. I hurt for you. You ungrateful prick!"

"Oh, Rylee." Laughing cruelly, he dodged her strikes and swatted away her fists. "You break my heart."

"You harden mine." She went after his throat again, trying to strangle him. "Men like you remind me why relationships fail."

"What the fuck does that mean?" He restrained her hands between her bare breasts, his eyes burning with aggression. "Men like me?"

"Playboys. Manwhores. The cheaters and manipulators who fuck their way through the female population without giving a damn about their feelings."

"Pot calling the kettle, baby." He flicked the button on her waistband. "You're the queen of fuck-'em and forget-'em."

He had her jeans open and down her legs before she even registered the sound of the zipper.

Her heart seized, and she dropped to a crouch, twisting out of his grip. Her clothes, now bunched around her legs, tangled up her attempt to run. She fell, spitting and shrieking and frantically crawling away.

He dove for her and grabbed her ankle. She kicked him in the face. He caught her other leg and wrangled off her shoes and clothes until she was as naked as him.

She screamed every curse she knew and scrambled over the rocky ground, scraping her hands and knees. He chased, his breaths hot on her bare ass.

The instant she left the shade of the Jeep, the sun-scorched sand fried her skin. She screamed and scrambled back.

And he was on her, flipping her over and dropping his huge, hard body between her legs.

The astounding sensation of all his hot skin against all of hers was more than she could bear. With his strength so close and his monstrous erection stabbing into her belly, she couldn't escape. Couldn't breathe. Couldn't look away from the furious hunger in his eyes.

He wrapped his hand around her hip and held her firmly to him. She grabbed his hair and pulled with all her strength. He choked her. She yanked harder on his hair, jerking his head.

He glared at her. She glared at him.

Neither of them moved.

Deadlocked.

Seething.

Seconds from boiling over.

They just stared at each other, unblinking, exchanging a look of pure hatred.

Then suddenly, it was on.

They collided in a clash of mouths and teeth and grappling hands. Rolling, slapping, kissing, scratching, they ground their bodies together like horny, deranged teenagers. Each time they inched out of the shelter of the shade, he dragged her back into the Jeep's shadow and attacked her again.

His cock rammed against the juncture of her thighs, demanding entry. Her pussy throbbed in invitation, convulsing and opening in a flood of arousal. But no amount of wetness could prepare her for his size.

She didn't want him. She couldn't fucking stand him. But the burning, tightening demands of her body made it damn hard to resist his bold touch, ripped physique, and the fascinating yet terrifying equipment between his legs.

"You're despicable." She brandished elbows, knuckles, and knees, hammering her sharpest bones into any part of him she could hit.

He ducked his head, dodging her strikes, and veered his mouth downward to chase the curves of her body. He licked and sucked every inch of her from breasts to pussy. She kicked at him, bowed into him, and tore at his hair.

"I hate you!" She jerked her hips, rocking against his face. "Oh God, don't stop. Don't fucking stop, you son of a bitch."

He bit her clit, and she screeched, smacking his head and sinking her nails into his flesh.

"Fuck, woman!" Teeth bared, he shot up her body and grabbed her face.

Livid didn't begin to describe the fire in his eyes.

She yanked him close. He dragged her closer and took her lips, kissing her, fingering her, and grinding against her to the echoes of her own traitorous groans.

They reached for his cock at the same time, wriggling and lining up their bodies, wild and clumsy in their urgency. She knew he would stretch her, bruise her, possibly injure her, and she didn't even care.

She counted on it.

With the broad tip of him notched at her entrance, he wrapped a fist around the base of his shaft. A habit? To prevent himself from sinking in all the way?

Clenching his jaw, he held her gaze and pushed past her opening.

DOMINATE

Sensations unfurled, exploding shimmers of pleasure around the stretching invasion. His entire body shook with the effort to control his thrust, and she trembled with him, moaning, squirming, needing more. More burning, more pressure, more *him*.

She slapped him across the head. "Hurt me, goddammit. I want to feel you."

He stopped breathing, eyes wide and frighteningly angry.

Then a nefarious smile lit his face.

He dropped his hand from his cock, removing that barrier, and impaled her to the hilt with absolutely no mercy.

FIFTEEN

Rylee let out an ear-splitting scream of pain, and Tomas choked on a groan, shaking in the exquisite grip of her body. Christ, he was going to come.

From one thrust.

Holy fucking fuck.

He wasn't a sadist, but damn, this woman had begged for it so beautifully. Not just begged. She'd demanded it.

Hurt me, goddammit.

Yeah, he was hurting her, and she was taking it like a champ. Every inch of him. Each time he hit the back of her hot cunt, she wailed, cursed, and clutched his ass, pulling him tighter, harder against her.

She was tougher than he'd thought, and everything was so wet and warm around him, sucking him in, gripping him like a glove. The sweet smell of her skin, the intoxicating way she tasted, her sexy little cries of hunger and rage—these were things he would never forget. Fucking incredible. Hotter than hell.

That only enraged him more.

Why wasn't it like this with other women? He was so accustomed to the gasps of fear, awkwardness of penetration, and pleas for him to slow down and be gentle. He couldn't remember the last time he'd just let loose and plowed into a woman. Or when he'd actually had sex without holding a hand around his cock.

Never.

Rylee was unlike anyone he'd ever been with. Just his goddamn luck.

DOMINATE

Only four days ago, he'd strangled the life out of her and contemplated leaving her for dead. And that was before he knew the infuriating depths of her stubbornness. The best thing to do now was just fuck her until she broke.

He grabbed her by the throat, growing painfully hard at the sight of her huge silver eyes, the gaping O of her swollen lips, and the jiggle of her perky, round tits as she tried to suck in air.

She was beyond gorgeous. Utterly perfect. He fucking despised her.

Driving viciously against the walls of her cunt, he rammed his tongue down her throat in the most aggressive kiss he'd ever taken.

When he finally let her breathe, she growled and ripped at his hair. But it didn't stop her from kissing him back. Their mouths fused, crashing and mauling like they were trying to dislocate each other's faces. It was violent and crude and emotionally unbridled, releasing an unfathomable flood of passion.

He pounded into her, biting her lips and licking the tears that drenched her face. Sand and grit clung to her hair, his hands, their arms and legs.

The heat was unbearable, the sun relentless. But the fever between them overpowered everything, flowing uncontrollably through their locked tongues, breaths, and hips. Nothing was stopping them.

With a surge of strength, she pushed him onto his back and started to ride him, clawing at his chest, trying to claw away his dominance.

Fuck that. He rose to his feet without disconnecting their bodies, continued to grind her on his cock, and crossed the distance to the cave.

He dumped her on the ground in the shade. She landed with a yelp, and he fell upon her, thrusting deep, power-fucking her into the rocky sand, dripping with sweat, and tearing her up like an animal. She choked him. He choked her right back, and within seconds, she was coming in a torrent of incensed screams.

"Fuck you, Tommy!" She sank her nails into his arms, panting and thrashing and gushing all over his cock. "Oh, Jesus, it hurts so good. So fucking good."

Impaled on the full length of him, she came and came, flailing wildly, unabashedly through the longest orgasm in history. Sweet God in hell, she was the most arousing, extraordinarily beautiful thing he'd ever seen. Such a sexy, uninhibited screamer, who liked it rough, got off on pain, and left shameless scratches all over his body. So fucking satisfying.

But he wasn't satisfied.

He didn't want her to enjoy it more than he was.

Pulling out, he flipped her over in the dirt and spanked her. She fought him belligerently while wriggling her ass for more.

"You're such a slut." He grabbed her hips and slammed into her from behind.

"If I'm a slut..." Panting, she pushed back and forced him deeper. "You're a depraved, twisted pervert. Give it to me, you sick fuck. Make me feel it."

His balls tightened. His skin caught fire, and the pressure in his cock exploded. He came violently, dizzyingly, groaning, jerking through the thrusts, unable to slow down as he fucked her like a dog.

He shouldn't have shot his load that quickly. Hell, he shouldn't have fucking come in her at all.

Irritated, he pushed her away, his cock still rigid and throbbing.

She fell onto her back, legs spread, pussy glistening, and eyes glimmering with filthy, forbidden temptation.

He wasn't done. Not even close.

In the next breath, he was inside her again, his tongue in her mouth, his furious thrusts stabbing between her thighs. He'd never been a gentle lover, but he was really going at it with her, slapping her tits, biting her throat, marking her flesh, leaving hickeys and bruises, and God only knew the damage he was inflicting on her cunt.

He wouldn't pretend it was the moral thing to do or that he was justified in any way, but what followed was the angriest, loudest, sweatiest, most passionate sex of his life.

Every time she climaxed, he spiraled with her, falling deeper, further into her corrupt, dishonest, deliciously tight clasp.

His recovery rate was unprecedented. He'd never been able to go multiple rounds without breaks in between. But with Rylee, he never wanted to stop.

He used her mercilessly—on the ground, against the Jeep, and across the front seat with the air-conditioning blowing at full speed. It went on and on, orgasm after orgasm, in every position. Just when he thought he couldn't go another round, she did this seductive lip-biting thing with an evil glint in her eyes, and blood surged to his cock with a vengeance.

They ended up at the entrance of the cave again where the shade from the butte was the coolest. With his back to the rocky cliff, he held her on his lap, hands clenched on her waist, moving her up and down on his sore, ravenous erection.

Scratches and bite marks covered her gorgeous breasts in a tapestry of destruction and passion. Their bodies were soaked in layers of sweat and come, with sand creeping into places they would never get clean.

"Fuuuck!" She threw her head back, moaning. "I love your huge, gorgeous cock. Even if you are a heartless asshole."

DOMINATE

"Shut the fuck up." He dragged her mouth to his, kissing her hungrily, furiously, trying to quench an unquenchable thirst.

It was impossible. This felt too amazing. She felt too perfect. It was as if he'd been waiting his entire life to experience this. To experience Rylee Sutton in all her lusty, untamed glory.

He separated their mouths and stared at her, enraptured. Then he captured her lips again, his hand falling to the small of her back and gently fitting her against him.

His hips were no longer moving, his body no longer racing toward release. He was still hard inside her, but he just wanted to touch her, enjoy the nearness of her beauty, for no other reason than because he could.

He moved his lips to her throat, licking gently, savoring her salty-sweet taste.

"What are you doing?" She touched his jaw, pushing away his mouth.

With a hand framing her angelic face, he leaned in to kiss her.

She pulled back and wriggled on his cock. "Why did you stop?"

"I'm spent."

"Bullshit." She scoffed with disdain. "You dominate women in your sleep."

As conflicted and angry as he was with this crazy woman, he wasn't so far out of his mind to not recognize she had severe intimacy issues.

Her eyes hardened as if she could read his thoughts. Shoving off his lap, she gave him the finger and strode toward the Jeep.

No, she limped, nursing each step. He'd done that. He'd fucked her so brutally she could barely walk.

He smiled, feeling a sick amount of satisfaction in that.

Until she spoke.

"I thought a guy your age could go for days." She flashed a venomous glare over her shoulder. "Evan might be twenty years older than you, but he knows how to fuck me properly. He *loves* my ass."

Yeah, he knew all about Evan's ass-fucking, but it was difficult to hear.

What was this burning pit in his stomach? The sudden difficulty in swallowing. The loss of vision due to a blinding need to gut her neighbor from neck to balls.

Was it jealousy?

That was new.

So was her insult. He'd been with women who cowered and grimaced and sometimes cried in pain, but they never outright criticized his performance.

She was baiting him. He knew it, but he couldn't stop himself from moving. He just…lost it.

He caught her at the Jeep, bent her over the bumper, and fucked her pussy so hard that her head hit against the scorching metal hood.

Everything was so drenched down there he pulled out and slammed right into her ass. No barriers. No mercy. He put his back into it and went to town, giving her every inch of his cock and soaking up her screams.

Fuck yeah, she screamed, calling him every despicable name she could muster. But her verbal abuse only made him hotter. He loved how her tongue slurred over the vowels, her lilting voice and moaning cries rising up and down like notes on a musical scale.

If he thought she'd made him hard before, it was nothing compared to the excruciating grip of her tight little hole. She kept trying to finger herself, but he wouldn't allow it. He slapped her hand away. She hit him back and ended up coming without the stimulation.

She climaxed just from the stretch of his cock in her ass, soaking his balls, his legs. He shoved a hand between her thighs. Holy fuck, she was a squirter.

Another first for him.

His orgasm crashed into him, and he exploded like a goddamn fire hose, filling her with more come than he'd ever shot before and with such ferocity that he collapsed on the ground in a pile of exhaustion and astonishment.

Straightening, she stretched her arms overhead and rolled her neck. Thick globs of milky white slithered down her inner thighs, her perfect ass welted from his hands and coated in sand.

She wasn't embarrassed by any of it as she turned to face him. Her posture radiated pleasure and contentment.

The image of every man's wildest fantasy.

He'd wasted a lot of goddamn years fucking only young women.

Rylee was so far past modesty, bashful awkwardness, and indecisive teetering. Whether she was confident in her skin or mature enough not to give a fuck, she stood before him, gloriously naked, covered in savage bites, and *smiled*.

It was the first time she genuinely smiled at him.

Christ, he felt it.

Everywhere.

"I have a newfound appreciation for the desert. Best sex of my life." She walked away, wobbly on her legs and sexier than ever.

What they just did, it was destructive. But the twisted, fucked-up aspects of it had made it so much more passionate. They hated each other, and he might just kill her before this situation was resolved.

But he agreed with her. She was the best sex he'd ever had.

He joined her at the rear of the Jeep and lifted the second water container, pouring it over her as she washed her body. Then she held it over him while he did the same.

They didn't speak. Didn't smile. But their gazes touched and held, never shying away.

It wasn't awkward or normal or hopeful or angry.

It just...*was*.

When all the sand and body fluids were rinsed away, they pulled on their jeans. Her tank-top was ruined, so she stole his shirt.

He allowed it because seeing her in his clothes satisfied some weird, territorial instinct he refused to analyze. It was too soon.

They packed up the Jeep and drove back to the house in sated silence. He didn't shackle her. She didn't know how to drive a manual transmission—a prediction he'd guessed accurately when he'd put her in the vehicle this morning.

Yesterday, Cole hid her truck in a storage unit and bought this Jeep in a nearby town. They still didn't know who was watching her, if she was working with anyone, or if she was as clueless as she claimed to be.

Someone connected to NSA or black ops had put high-tech bugs in her house. That someone had an unnerving interest in who she was fucking. And now Tomas was on the list.

Was her ex-husband stalking her? Her neighbor? Or someone less obvious? Whether or not it was her intention, she'd led that someone directly to him and Cole.

That made him edgy, especially as he neared his property.

The house came into view, and he slowed, shading his eyes and scrutinizing every inch of the perimeter. Cole was still gone, as expected. Nothing appeared off-kilter.

"You're tense." She twisted in the seat, watching him. "Do you think we're in danger?"

"You led trouble to my front door."

"Yeah, you keep saying that, but I can't figure out how or why anyone would be interested in me."

He was interested in her. Begrudgingly. Insanely. She'd sneaked beneath his skin, and if he wasn't careful, his attraction to her would become irreversible.

Parking the Jeep, he shut off the engine. As he stepped out, the distant purr of a motor reached his ears. He went still, his senses firing.

"What is it?" She followed his gaze to the horizon, shielding her eyes with a hand.

The engine grew closer, louder. Not throaty enough to be Cole's motorcycle.

"Get in the house." Pulse quickening, he lunged toward the glove box, unlocking it and removing a pistol.

She didn't move.

"Now." He slammed a palm against her butt, sending her in motion.

The sounds of her footsteps moved toward the door, and it slammed shut behind her. She better keep her nosy ass inside.

A black truck emerged on the horizon. Newer model. Expensive.

He concealed the gun in his boot and straightened his spine.

As the vehicle advanced, he saw only one occupant. A male driver. Texas tags on the truck. Not a local, though. The man was wearing a white collared shirt and black tie. No one around here owned a suit or drove a fancy truck.

The pistol sat heavily against his calf. If Rylee hadn't taken his shirt, he would've concealed the weapon in his waistband for easier access.

As the vehicle stopped a few yards away, Tomas leaned against the Jeep, arms folded across his clawed-up chest, and waited like a bored, rural redneck with nothing but time on his hands.

A mid-thirties man stepped out and directed his mirrored aviator sunglasses at him. Lean cheeks, clean-shaved jaw, aristocratically straight nose, ink-black hair worn high and tight—all of it lent him the air of official business.

He reeked of law enforcement. Probably a small-town detective, dressing for the job he wanted rather than the dead-end job he was stuck with.

Only one of two reasons would interest him enough to drive all the way out here. Paul Kissinger or Rylee Sutton. Both missing.

Except Rylee took a sabbatical from work and claimed she told no one she was coming here. The jury was still out on whether she was lying.

"Mr. Dine?" The man strode forward, flashing his shiny, self-important badge. "I'm Detective Hodge."

Tomas spat a wad of phlegm in the sand and glared.

"You're the owner of this property?" The detective paused a few feet away and peered at him over his lowered sunglasses. "Are you Tomas Dine?"

"Yep."

"I'm following up on a missing-persons report. Got a call that Rylee Sutton was spotted at your residence."

Spotted by whom? Paul Kissinger? The bastard must've notified someone that the tracker on her truck stopped here. That, or someone else was tracking her truck.

"If she was seen here," he drawled, playing the part of a moronic cowboy, "then she ain't missing, is she?"

Any moment, she was going to burst out the front door and run off her mouth about being beaten and held captive. Then he would have to shoot the detective and bury another body.

But he wasn't a cop killer. There had to be another way.

"I'm looking for Rylee Sutton." Detective Hodge cocked his head. "Age forty-one. Brown hair. Gray eyes. Tiny little thing. Absolutely gorgeous."

"Gorgeous? Is that in the official description, detective?"

"Well, it's the truth." The detective stood taller. "Have you seen her?"

The front door opened, and here she came. His hand twitched, the pistol burning in his boot.

"Dean?" Her footsteps approached. "What are you doing here?"

Oh, great. She fucking knew the guy. Probably worked with him. Another admirer?

He clenched his jaw.

She walked past Tomas, circling far out of his reach as if she weren't limping from the ramming of his cock. That was when he saw her duffel bag clutched tightly in her fist.

So she'd grabbed her shit and intended to leave with this douchebag. *Clever girl.*

Unless Detective Dean Hodge was compromised.

Tomas didn't know if she was in danger, but if she was, *everyone* was a suspect.

Tension flared beneath his skin, but he kept his expression relaxed and voice calm. "Who reported her missing?"

"Missing?" She turned to him, mouth open in shock, and looked back to the detective. "I'm not missing, Dean. Who said I was?"

Now would've been the time for her to blurt the details of her captivity, but she didn't utter a word of it. Even stranger, she'd pulled on a jacket while in the house, hiding the abuse inflicted upon her body.

"Your ex-husband." Dean gave her a once-over, lingering on her mouth. *What the fuck?* "He said you disappeared four days ago."

"Try ten years ago. That's the beauty of divorce." She cocked her hip. "He doesn't get to know where I am or what I'm doing." She narrowed her eyes. "How did you find me?"

"We put out an alert two days ago. Got an anonymous call that you were spotted here."

Suspicion snaked through Tomas' veins. Either Dean was lying or someone was using him to get to Rylee, whether to deliver a message to her, pull her out of here, or something else entirely.

Everything about this felt off.

Her empty expression revealed nothing. Frozen, she stared at Dean's vehicle. What was she thinking? Escape, most likely.

"Rylee? Is everything okay?" Dean stepped toward her and touched her arm. "How do you know this man? Where's your truck?"

She could tell him everything, just lay out all the gory details right now. The detective would try to arrest him, and he would be forced to shoot or flee in the Jeep. He really didn't want to kill an innocent guy. But what if Dean knew more than he was letting on?

"Tomas is just a friend I met in town." She blew out a breath and hauled the duffel bag over her shoulder. "My truck broke down. Mind if I catch a ride?"

SIXTEEN

Rylee's pulse sputtered frantically as she hobbled toward Dean's truck, sore and uncertain. She was making a decision that not only risked her life but that of her colleague.

Nothing was stopping Tommy from drawing that gun in his boot and shooting them both. But if she let this opportunity slip away, if she stayed here another day, he would continue to starve her and poison her mind.

She'd turned into something she didn't recognize today and grudge-fucked him in the desert. But that didn't make the grudge go away. No amount of sex—no matter how huge the cock—could erase the three days she spent in the heat without water.

Or the cruelty in his eyes as he ate that bowl of chili in front of her.

Or the dozens of other vicious acts he'd committed against her since she arrived.

She needed distance from him to think, figure out who was watching her, and talk to her nuisance of an ex-husband. Why in the hell would Mason report her missing?

Something didn't add up.

Dean followed her without comment, probably confused by her boldness in requesting a ride. She'd made a habit of avoiding all her male colleagues, coming across as a guarded, unapproachable bitch. She was there to work, not get laid.

Early on, she'd learned that something as innocent as eye contact often led to a wrong impression, which led to unwanted attention and harassment. So she kept her head down and avoided, avoided, avoided.

Which was why she had no friends.

As she reached the passenger door of his truck, the space between her shoulders itched.

She turned her neck. Their gazes locked. The desert held its breath.

They stared at each other with a familiarity, an intimacy that hadn't been there before. The voltage, the sparks, the unwanted chemistry that had been present from the beginning was there, too. But it hadn't grown into trust. Not even a little.

Someone knew she was here, and Tommy believed she was working with this person. She was under no delusions that sex had changed his opinion. If anything, he thought even less of her now.

She needed to get out of here.

Without looking away, she opened the passenger door.

His eyes narrowed to slits, his knees slowly bending as he reached to pluck the pistol from his boot.

Dean climbed into the truck, oblivious.

Panic spiked, and she subtly shook her head at Tommy, begging him with her eyes.

Don't shoot him. He's an innocent man.

He went still, scowling at her. Even at this distance, she felt his murderous fury. It competed with the desert heat, blistering her skin and watering her eyes.

She forced her legs to move, stepping into the truck, her nerves on tenterhooks, shaking with the rush of her breaths.

He didn't move as she closed the door. Didn't draw his gun as Dean started the truck and drove away.

Angling her neck, she stared at the side mirror, expecting Tommy to chase or shoot. But he was nowhere in sight.

She held her breath until she could no longer see the house, until she was confident they were out of bullet range.

Then she dropped her head back and released a sigh of relief.

That had been too easy.

He'd let her go.

"You just met that guy?" Dean glanced at her and returned to the unpaved terrain.

"Yeah."

"Doesn't seem like it. I mean, the way he was looking at you…"

She didn't owe him an explanation. "Thanks for the ride."

His hand clenched on the steering wheel. "What's wrong with your truck?"

"Don't know." She cut her eyes at him. "Why was there an alert put out on me? Did you not ask around first? My neighbor would've told you where I was."

"Evan Phillips? Yeah, I talked to him. He said you were acting strangely and left. Couldn't tell us your whereabouts. His statement didn't inject a lot of confidence in your safety."

"Ridiculous." She balled her hands on her lap. "I told him I was going to the desert for a much-needed vacation."

"A vacation with a man you just met?" His tone grated with judgment.

"You're crossing the line, Dean."

"All I'm saying is you should be more careful. That guy was putting off some serious hostile vibes, and I don't like the way he was looking at you."

"Like what?" she snapped impatiently. "How was he looking at me?"

"Like he couldn't decide if he wanted to hug you, fuck you, or throttle your neck. He definitely didn't want you to leave."

Perceptive man. He wouldn't be good at his job if he wasn't.

She pulled the collar of the jacket against her bruised throat.

"He was fun for a few nights," she said, at the risk of ruining her reputation. "But I need to get back to my truck."

She couldn't go home since Tommy knew where she lived.

When she'd spotted her duffel bag in his house, she'd only had seconds to go through it. Her ID, credit card, money, everything she needed was in there except her phone. Didn't matter. Since someone was tracking her, she would've left the device behind anyway.

On her way out, she'd ransacked the kitchen, searching for a weapon. A large butcher knife was the best she'd found. That went into the duffel bag, along with some of her spare clothes she found in the laundry room.

"Where's your truck?" Dean asked.

"May I?" She gestured at his phone, where it mounted on the dash, showing a map of their location and directions back to the nearest paved road. "I can't remember the name of the town."

She had no idea where to go. Somewhere with a motel, a cash machine, and food. Lots and lots of food.

At his nod, she zoomed out on the screen and started scrolling east, searching for the best place to lie low for a few days.

"Where's your phone?" He veered the truck around a deep ravine.

"Out of batteries." She paused the screen on a small town that showed a few restaurants, a gas station, and...*bingo*. A motel.

Pulling her attention away, she glanced at her surroundings. Sand, shrubs, more sand—all familiar but not recognizable. She didn't remember driving in this way, but she'd been watching her GPS map the entire time.

It seemed strange that Dean would travel three hours to follow up on an anonymous tip. If she were anyone else, he would've called in local law enforcement to check it out. But he knew her. They'd worked together for a couple of years. Maybe that explained it.

Maybe she shouldn't be trusting him.

"Is it slow at work?" She returned to the map, panning away from the town she'd decided on.

"Always."

"Is that why you're here? Nothing better to do?"

"I was worried, Rylee." He ran a hand over his head, his gaze straight ahead, avoiding hers. "I don't trust these local guys to do a thorough job, so I came to look for you myself."

It was the right answer, but something niggled.

If someone was after Tommy and they were tracking her to get to him, how deep could they go? Deep enough to involve Dean?

She was in the middle of the desert with a man who showed up at Tommy's house after Paul went missing. Dean could be on the same errand as Paul. He could be delivering her as a hostage to one of Tommy's enemy cartels. Or planning to kill her himself as part of some blackmail scheme.

Jesus, Rylee. Stop.

She was fucking paranoid. That was Tommy's fault. After reading about all the shit he and his team had been mixed up in over the past ten years, she'd developed a scary imagination.

Dean wasn't part of some criminal organization, but that didn't mean she could trust him with her whereabouts. If someone was monitoring his conversations, he could inadvertently mention where he dropped her off.

So she quickly scanned the map, searching for a different motel in the surrounding areas. A motel she wouldn't be staying at.

"Here it is." She announced the name of the desert town and set it as the destination on the map, rerouting the directions. "Thank you for coming for me."

"I'm happy to do it." He paused, eyes on the terrain, and dropped his voice. "What happened?"

"What do you mean?"

"I saw his chest. The scratches and… I don't know. Sure looked like bite marks. *Human* bites."

Heat rose to her cheeks. "We're adults. It was consensual."

And hateful and angry and so fucking hot she would never, ever experience anything as amazing or pleasureful again.

"He's a little young for you."

"Excuse me?" Her neck went taut.

"Hey, don't get mad. I'm just making an observation."

"That was an ageist insult, not an observation. If you have any more of those, keep them to yourself."

Awkward tension filled the cab, producing a bitter taste on her tongue.

For the next thirty minutes, they drove in silence. She should've been thinking about what she was going to do without a car and a phone, but her focus kept pulling back to Tommy, to the fervent way he'd kissed her, touched her, and claimed every inch of her body. He hadn't just physically branded her. He'd indelibly seared himself onto her soul.

His cruelty was unforgivable, but the sex was unforgettable. He was no longer in her sight, but she doubted he would ever leave her mind.

"I'm sorry." Dean turned onto the main road, following the directions on the map. "I shouldn't have said what I did."

Sand turned into pavement, but the desolate surroundings remained unchanged.

She stared out the window at the vista of buttes. "How's the Wagner case coming along?"

"We got a lead on the location of a meth lab."

For the remainder of the drive, they talked about work. A neutral subject. Familiar ground.

When he pulled up to the motel, she looked around and panicked. There was nothing around. Not a car or a restaurant or another building in sight.

She didn't intend to stay here. Not where Dean knew her location. She needed to get to the next town over, where she had options and could hide out for a few days.

He turned off the engine. "Are you sure this is where you left your truck?"

"It's the closest motel to the mechanic." She grabbed her bag and opened the door. "Thank you for the ride."

"I'll come in with you."

"No need." She stepped into the wretched heat.

He reached across the seat and caught her elbow, stopping her. "Let me take you to dinner. There's nothing here—"

"No." She wrenched her arm away. "I'll see you in a month, Dean. Drive safe."

She shut the door on his response and strode toward the motel office.

Inside, the scent of tobacco smoke attacked her nose. A young blonde woman sat behind the desk, flicking ash from a cigarette, her gaze glued to her phone.

Rylee turned toward the window and watched Dean pull out of the lot. She didn't move until his truck vanished beyond the horizon.

"Need a room?" the girl asked.

"I need transportation to the next town."

"Can't help you there, babe."

"You can't call me a cab? Or a vehicle for hire?"

"Nothing like that comes out here." The girl snorted without looking up from her phone. "You'll have better luck using your thumb out on that road."

Rylee glanced at the highway, which hadn't seen another car since she'd arrived.

Shit.

Desperate, she grappled for options. "When do you get off work?"

"In six hours."

Double shit.

She couldn't wait that long. She needed food, a shower, a bed, and a million other things to formulate a plan, and she needed to do all of it in a place where no one could find her.

Tommy might've let her go because he didn't want to shoot Dean. But he would come for her now that the detective was out of the way.

The girl lowered her phone and toyed with one of her short blonde ringlets. "I have a one-hour lunch break."

"When?"

"Right now."

Exhilaration coursed through her as she dug through her duffel bag and removed a wad of cash. "I'll pay you two-hundred dollars to drive me to the next town."

"Okay." The girl shrugged a shoulder. "Sure."

Yes! Mind spinning, she turned toward the cash machine in the corner. "Does that work?"

"Last I checked."

Perfect. She would withdraw enough cash to get her by for a few days and destroy her credit card. "Do you have a trash bag?"

"Umm..." The blonde's eyebrows knitted. "Yes?"

"I need that, too."

The duffel bag would stay here, and only the things she needed would go in the plastic bag. Things that couldn't have been bugged.

If Tommy or anyone else was tracking her, she was going to make it as hard as possible.

SEVENTEEN

For the next three days, Rylee holed up in the shittiest motel room in Texas. Restless, overstrung, and nearing her wit's end, she paced the stained carpet and chewed her nails down to nubs.

When she'd paid for the ride here, she had the girl drop her at a corner store a mile down the road. There, Rylee had bought a range of everyday items, including a cheap, prepaid smart phone. After paying in cash, she carried it all on foot to this smelly, dilapidated, out-of-the-way motel.

By the time she'd checked in, her body throbbed everywhere, a reminder of the beating she'd taken in the desert. Her immediate concern had been taking care of her basic needs—shelter, water, food, hygiene, pain-killers, sleep.

So much sleep.

God, she'd needed that rest. After asphyxiation, extreme thirst, starvation, and unthinkable stress over the past week, she slept through most of the first two days. She never wanted to wake up.

But she couldn't hide forever.

The prepaid phone burned in her hand as she paced the room. She hadn't stepped outside once since arriving. Hadn't called Mason or Evan or any of her colleagues. Hadn't logged into her email at home or the systems at work.

The television stations reported no major news. A web search on Paul Kissinger turned up exactly nothing. As if he didn't exist. She didn't know who had hired him or why. She didn't have names, physical descriptions, eye-witness reports, behavioral habits, a motivation… Absolutely nothing to profile.

She had no plan. No solution. Not a single goddamn thing to go on.

Desperate, she'd pulled up an internet browser and typed random search strings.

How do I identify who's stalking me?
What types of devices are used to track cars?
Can bugs be hidden on a person?
If I'm being followed, what should I do?

Every answer led to the obvious course of action. *Call the cops.* Ironic, considering her occupation. She wanted to call her colleagues but didn't know who to trust. Dean had already helped her, so contacting him was the most logical option.

She wasn't ready to do that. Maybe paranoia was getting the best of her, but something about their interaction in his truck made her scalp tingle.

If only she had family or a close girlfriend to call, someone she could ask for help.

She had no one.

She was utterly, completely alone.

What was happening outside her little bubble? Was Mason looking for her? Was Evan still collecting her mail? She knew in her bones that Tommy was out there somewhere, hunting her right now.

She'd worked herself into a corner with nowhere to go. Her cash was dwindling. Her panic was rising. She was running out of time.

The only thing she'd achieved by coming here was healing her body back to full health. But if Tommy found her, *when* he found her, he would hurt her all over again.

It was horrifying that someone had monitored her for six months. But even more frightening was the thought of Tommy crashing through that door.

The fear he instilled in her was crippling, and she fucking loathed him for that.

Stepping to the covered window, she inched the curtain aside, just a sliver, and scrutinized the empty parking lot. The setting sun created shadows across the cracked pavement and arid wasteland surrounding it.

Nothing in sight for miles. No looming danger. The world went on without her.

As if the past week had never happened.

Maybe she was delusional. Overacting. Wasting her time here. Hiding for no reason.

She released the curtain and yanked down the neckline of her shirt. Stroking her thumb over the curve of her breast, she traced one of the dozens of bite marks that covered her body.

DOMINATE

Tommy had positively happened. He was real. His rage, passion, and intensity had been as authentic as hers, and if she didn't do something soon, he would show up here more furious than ever.

Mason still lived in El Paso, a three-hour drive away. She could call him, and if she detected anything suspicious in his voice, she would have time to ditch the phone and put distance between herself and this town. She would steal a damn car if needed.

But was it worth the risk?

Just to ask why he'd reported her missing?

She really needed to know.

Moving to the bed, she sat on the edge and dialed his number from memory.

He answered on the first ring. "Hello?"

"Why did you file a missing-persons report on me?"

"Rylee." The relief in his sigh chafed her nerves. "Thank God. I've been worried sick. Where are you?"

"Answer the question, Mason."

"Tell me where you are. If you're in trouble—"

"I'm on vacation. So imagine my surprise when Dean Hodge showed up, looking for me."

"Why did they send *him*? I hate that sleazy creep. He has a hard-on a mile long for you."

"You know what's creepy? The fact that you know everyone I work with, even though we've been divorced for ten years, *and* I have a restraining order against you."

"The restraining order expired."

"I'll file another one."

"On what grounds? I love you, Rylee. My life is a goddamn meaningless pit without you. How long are you going to make me pay for a mistake I made when I was a kid?"

"You were thirty-one when you cheated on me, and as you already know, my grudges last forever. Why did you call my place of employment and report me missing?"

The sounds of his breaths rasped through the phone for several seconds. "Your neighbor contacted me."

Shock chilled her spine as she lurched to her feet, heart racing. "My neighbor?"

"Evan Phillips. He said you were acting scared and disappeared."

"That's not at all what happened." Her lungs crashed together as she raced to the window, obsessively checking the parking lot. "If he was so concerned about my whereabouts, why didn't he call the police himself? Why would he call you?"

"You'll have to ask him that question."

"It doesn't make sense. He's collecting my mail. I told him I was leaving and where I was going."

"Because you're fucking him."

"What?" Outrage whooshed through her veins and rang in her ears. "Are you watching me, Mason?"

"I keep tabs on you. Always have. I can't let go, Rylee. I refuse to give you up."

She waited for an itch, a tingle of sentiment, and felt nothing.

Should she ask him about Paul Kissinger? If he didn't hire the man, the question would raise flags and needlessly involve him. If he were already involved, he would lie.

Because he was a dishonest, dirtbag cheater.

She had a remarkable gift for attracting the worst of the worst men.

"Tell me why you think I'm sleeping with Evan." Her voice rose several octaves, all patience gone. "Tell me right fucking now!"

"When he called me, I asked him outright, and he confirmed it."

Was Mason lying about that? Was he jealous enough, obsessed enough, to hire a man to watch her fuck her neighbor?

"I hate it." His voice took on a bitter edge. "I hate every second you spend with other men because it's another second you're not with me. I hate that I had the entire world in my arms, in my bed, and I lost it all. I only have myself to blame. I lost you because I'm an idiot. You were the only woman I'd ever been with, and at the time, I thought…"

"You needed to play the field? How was the grass on the other side? Was it greener?"

"No. God, Rylee. No one compares to you. You're stunning beyond words, and every year that you age, you only look younger and more gorgeous. You're hard-working. Intelligent. Compassionate." His tone deepened. "A hellion in bed. But most of all, you were a devoted and faithful wife. You gave me one-hundred percent of your love, and I squandered it like a fool."

She'd never told him about the bridge. They'd never discussed the affair or anything that happened after. This was the longest conversation she'd allowed him to have with her since the divorce.

"Where are you?" he asked.

"I'm wherever you're not, and it's going to remain that way. If I see you again, I'll file another restraining order."

She hung up and tossed the phone.

A tremor started at the base of her skull and worked its way down her spine. Within seconds, she was shaking. Fighting tears. Shivering in a cold sweat.

DOMINATE

"Fuck you, Mason." She swatted at the moisture that leaked from her eyes, her voice soft, deadened. "Fuck you."

Outside, nightfall descended. She sat on the bed until the room went dark. She didn't turn on the lights, didn't want to draw attention to the room from anyone who might drive by.

She couldn't go home.

Maybe Mason had lied about Evan's phone call. Maybe he was telling the truth, and Evan was…what? Stalking her? Trying to control her life? She was a criminal psychologist, for fuck's sake. Her entire job was examining criminal behavior and diagnosing mental health conditions. How could she not detect red flags with the man she'd been sleeping with for the past year?

She just couldn't. It didn't fit Evan's personality.

He has hundreds of photos of you on his personal computer.

Was that a criminal offense? No, but it made him a suspect. If he was capable of involving Paul Kissinger, Dean Hodge, and her ex-husband in some unknown scheme, he was capable of tracking her phone if she called him.

Contacting Evan was out of the question. Not until she had more information.

And she couldn't rule out the most threatening possibility.

Tommy had a nefarious history with a list of enemies that stretched from Canada to South America. Her connection to him was the emails. How someone could discover that she was reading them was beyond her technical understanding. She'd had access to the *Tommysgirl* account for ten years, yet Paul had only been watching her for six months.

All of this buzzed through her mind as she lay in the dark. Every creak and bump made her jump. Even the silence rose the hairs on her arms.

After failing her marriage, she'd given up her reliance on people. She stopped depending on and trusting in all men. Avoiding relationships protected her from repeating the unspeakable pain she'd experienced on the bridge. Being alone had kept her safe for ten years.

But she didn't feel safe right now.

And she'd never felt so alone.

That night, she didn't sleep well. The next day brought more of the same—eating, napping, and chasing her thoughts in circles. Her supplies were running out, and the room was only paid for through one more night.

She would have to check-out tomorrow and call Dean.

Or hitchhike to another country. A far more appealing option.

Hours after dusk on the fourth night, she turned on the shower and set out clean clothes. While the water warmed up, she stepped out of the bathroom and into the dark room. From the nightstand, she grabbed the butcher knife she'd taken from Tommy's house.

Keeping the lights off gave her a false sense of comfort. If someone wanted to find her badly enough, a dark motel room wouldn't deter them. But she refused to cast a moving shadow on the curtains and make herself an easy target.

Showering in a motel room conjured the most terrifying murder scenes put on film. *Psycho*, *Evil Dead*, *Friday the 13th*, *A Nightmare On Elm Street*. She tightened her hand on the knife handle, working herself into a stupid panic.

A demented serial killer wasn't going to sneak in and slash her in the shower.

Steam drifted out of the bathroom, and her feet remained rooted to the floor. She couldn't bring herself to undress.

Come on, Rylee.

With a calming breath, she crept toward the external door, checked the flimsy lock, and reseated the swing bar latch. Both were secured. But she didn't feel secure.

She shifted to the window and peered through the crack between the curtains. Expecting to find the parking lot empty as usual, she jerked at the sight of a car.

Parked next to the office, it sat empty. A middle-aged man stood inside at the front desk, wearing a suit that looked wildly out of place.

Her blood pressure skyrocketed.

He wasn't a local detective. Not in a full suit. He didn't belong here.

She couldn't breathe.

The clerk stood, bending over the desk, and pointed at Rylee's room.

Trembling, reeling into gasping hysterics, she stumbled away from the window.

He was coming for her.

She spun and raced toward the bathroom, operating on impulse. A hot mist fogged the mirror and hung in the air as she yanked the shower curtain closed. Keeping the water running, she backed out of the bathroom and shut the door.

The gap beneath the king-sized bed allowed just enough space for her to fit. She squeezed herself into the hiding spot, her cheek against the carpet, which reeked of maple syrup and cigarette smoke.

DOMINATE

Once every inch of her was out of view, she lay on her stomach, chin to the floor, angled toward the foot of the bed, with her fingers slick and clammy around the hilt of the knife.

No amount of knocking would convince her to come out and open that door. If local law enforcement wanted to talk to her, they could send a guy who looked like a small-town detective during daylight hours.

The wait was petrifying, the silence deafening. Perspiration beaded on her brow as her panic-stricken heart tore through her chest, searching for a way out.

She didn't detect approaching footsteps. Didn't hear a fist against the door. When the hush broke, it detonated in a spray of splintered wood.

The door swung open, pieces of it scattering the floor inches from her face. A bullet had done that. Without the report of gunfire.

His weapon had a suppressor, like something out of a fucking mafia movie.

He was going to kill her.

She slapped a hand over her mouth, smothering the burst of her breaths as she slid the knife across the carpet in front of her.

The intruder strode in, making a beeline for the bathroom. Shiny dress shoes blurred by. Soundless footsteps. Determined. Deadly.

If she slipped out of hiding now, he would shoot her. Not that she could move. Ice encased her joints. Tears leaked from her eyes, her dread so cold and heavy it pressed her into the floor.

He stopped at the bathroom door and quietly opened it. Then he stepped back and fired into the cloud of steam.

Phut. Phut. Phut. Phut. Phut.

She flinched with each muffled shot, shaking violently as bullet casings dropped to the floor.

He paused. She stopped breathing.

Right about now, he was coming to the realization that a body hadn't fallen in the shower. He would have to go in there and investigate, and that would be her only opportunity to escape.

Her muscles clenched, her entire being fraught with fear and braced to run. How many bullets did he have left? Was he carrying extra magazines?

His shoes pivoted, angling toward the bed.

No, no, no. Oh, God. Please, don't walk this way.

He stalked straight toward her, sending her into a hyperventilating fit of terror.

EIGHTEEN

A tear trickled down Rylee's cheek and dangled from her chin with maddening endurance. More fell as the gunman closed in, his shoes following an invisible line to her hiding spot.

Lying on her stomach in a puddle of breathless terror, she readjusted her grip on the knife and poised it just out of view.

He paused at the foot of the bed, and her pulse went berserk. He lowered into a squat, and her adrenaline kicked in, muffling all sound. Then she lunged, slashing the knife, fast and deep, across his ankles.

With a guttural cry, she hacked again, less effective this time as his legs whirled, soaking her hand in hot blood.

The gun fired with a suppressed pop. She didn't slow her attack. Swiping the blade across his shins, she scrambled out from under the bed. The metal frame ripped along her back, but she didn't feel the pain. Right now, all she felt was the driving urgency to eliminate the threat.

She kept the knife in constant motion, lacerating his legs again and again. Raging fear and frustration constricted her chest. How was he still standing?

A dry click sounded from the pistol. Out of bullets.

His body crashed onto hers, heavy and uncoordinated. She'd maimed him, but he wasn't giving up.

"Who are you?" She twisted beneath him and buried the blade in his thigh. "How the fuck do you know me?"

He roared in agony and grabbed for the knife. She yanked it away and stabbed him in the stomach.

DOMINATE

His hand collided with her face, smashing her jaw with a force that sent her flying backward. She didn't have time to control her landing. The impact with the floor snatched the breath from her lungs, and her head bounced off the corner of the wall, shooting stars across her vision.

She blinked rapidly, panting and disoriented. When her eyes came into focus, he was on his knees, crawling toward her with a hand wrapped around the knife in his gut.

"Why won't you fucking die?" she screamed and threw herself at him, pounding her fists in his face. "What do you want? Why are you here?"

He fell onto his back, choking and smiling through a gurgle of blood. "The bridge."

Her heart stopped and restarted. "How do you know about that? What does it have to do with you?"

With a strangled laugh, he grabbed her throat and wrenched her ear against his mouth. "Thur…nnnn…eee."

She tried to jerk away, but he had a death grip on her neck. He'd lost too much blood to be this strong.

Her hands moved without thought, grabbing the knife, sliding it from his belly, and thrusting it back in. Again. Again. The fist on her throat dropped away as she continued to stab him.

Over and over, she aimed for vital organs—stomach, heart, neck, lungs. She was hitting ribs, struggling to spear the blade past bones. But he wasn't moving. Didn't appear to be breathing.

With a jolt, she broke out of her fugue and scooted away, taking the knife and his gun with her.

Numbness spread over her as she sat in the dark, gulping, unmoving in a crippled state of shock and horror.

She needed to do something. Close the door. Wash her hands. Turn off the shower. Check his pulse.

No. Fuck, no. She didn't want to touch him.

Blood soaked his clothes, the floor, her fingers, the knife. So much of it. Everywhere. He couldn't be alive. No way.

Still, she didn't twitch a muscle, too terrified a sound might resurrect him.

He'd come here to kill her. If she hadn't checked the window, he would've succeeded.

Who in the hell would go through the trouble of killing her? Why? He'd mentioned the bridge, but it didn't make sense. Was someone offended that she contemplated suicide ten years ago?

Mason didn't know about that. No one knew about it.

Except Tommy.

No. It wasn't possible. Tommy wouldn't have sent this man. If he wanted her dead, he would've done it himself.

Minutes passed, and the flow of her adrenaline slowed, bringing awareness to her body, to the pain in her face and back and the uncontrollable shaking in her limbs.

She wiped the knife on her pants, cleaning off the blood. More covered her hands. She needed to get moving.

The sound of an approaching car pierced through her daze. Headlights illuminated the open doorway. Doors slammed. Footsteps advanced.

Her stomach tightened, and she whimpered.

More hitmen? A backup team for the man she'd just killed? Goddammit, she couldn't fight off another attack.

Scooting backward in the dark, she slid between the mattress and wall, set the knife under the bed, and aimed the gun with both hands. It was out of bullets, but they wouldn't know that.

Hidden by the bed, she ducked down low, tucking into a ball, and tried to control the torrent of her breaths.

The tread of heavy boots crossed the threshold. Multiple intruders.

Oh, God, I'm dead. I'm dead. So fucking dead.

The overhead lights illuminated, blinding her eyes. Curled up on the floor, she aimed the gun upward, and another gun pointed back.

"Rylee." Tommy stood over her, his face set in stone, eyes bloodshot, and posture vibrating with unleashed fury. "Lower the gun."

Relief, distrust, fear, anger—so many emotions battled inside her. She didn't move.

"He's dead," a deep, masculine voice said. Chillingly deep. "No wallet or ID."

"Rylee, lower the gun," Tommy said in his domineering tone.

"Fuck you."

The owner of the unfamiliar voice stepped into view and snatched her next breath. "You're one woman against a gang of bloodthirsty savages."

Savage was one way to describe him. Short brown hair. Razor-sharp eyes. Powerfully built. The faded scar that divided his cheek didn't detract from his chiseled beauty. His smirk did. A lethal smirk, that curled arrogantly around a toothpick.

Van.

The monster who had captured and raped Tommy nine years ago.

"Don't underestimate her." Tommy gave her the full force of his eyes while addressing Van. "I'd rather take on you and your attic than this hellcat."

What the fuck? He must be joking.

"I can arrange that." Van clapped him on the back and ambled toward the bathroom.

The shower turned off, and he prowled back through the room, joining the din of footsteps and hushed voices that gathered outside the door.

Tommy unchambered the live round in his gun and wedged the weapon into the back of his jeans.

She tightened her grip on the pistol in her hands. "How did you find me?"

"We had a tail on the hitman." He tipped his chin in the direction of the corpse, his expression unreadable. "You butchered him."

"He deserved it."

He went still, no part of him moving except his gaze, which darted over her, probing, flaring darkly. Deadly eyes. Hypnotic. God, the man was beautiful when he was contemplating murder. "Did he hurt you?"

"I've been hurt worse. Most recently, on your watch."

"Yeah, I hurt you. Unjustly. Unforgivably. So shoot me." He lowered to a crouch, leaning into the crack where she huddled, sucking all the oxygen. "Pull the fucking trigger."

The gun rattled. Her breaths shook.

She couldn't do it. Even knowing the gun was empty, she couldn't take the risk. "I hate you."

"I know, and I'm going to fix that."

She blinked, unsure she heard him correctly. "Fix what?"

"I was wrong about some things." He drifted closer, pressing his chest against the barrel of the gun. "You and I, we're going to start over, but right now, I need to get you out of here."

"No. Fuck that. I'm not going anywhere with you."

"You're in danger."

She met his treacherous stare. "You think?"

In a blink, he snatched the gun from her hand, aimed it at the ceiling, and fired a dry click, without a twitch of surprise.

He'd known the whole time it wasn't loaded.

"Let's go." He held out a hand in the narrow space between them.

More footsteps entered the room. More ruthless friends to aid in her mistreatment.

Reaching under the bed, she grabbed the knife and angled it at his throat. "Back up."

His eyes glinted, and he pressed forward, cutting his neck on the blade. "You can do better, Rylee." He dropped his voice to a heated whisper. "Hate me with your body. It's far more satisfying."

She was struck by how much sharper his words were than the weapon in her hand. He bled from a small cut in his throat while she hemorrhaged in endless, agonizing bitterness.

For reasons she didn't understand, someone wanted her dead. Maybe that someone wasn't Tommy, but... "You starved me."

"A decision I regret. Tonight, I have a new priority, and that is protecting you."

"You can't protect me from yourself."

"No." His gaze, warm and richly gold, never wavered from hers. "You'll have to weigh that risk."

His throat didn't bob against the knife. His hand didn't swing to overpower her. He just waited her out while his friends searched the dead body.

She leaned in and tipped up the blade, lifting his chin. "No shackles."

"Not unless you beg."

"Never. What about the last rule in the rules of three?"

Three months without hope.

"We were ten minutes behind the hitman. I knew I would arrive too late." His face took on an expression she'd never seen there before. *Torment.* "The whole way here, I knew I would hold your dead body, look into your lifeless eyes, and never experience hope again." He touched the pads of his fingers to her throbbing jaw, featherlight. "I don't know what you've done to me, but for the first time in ten years, I have hope in my grasp, and I'm going to fight like hell to keep it."

Just words. Nice words. Profound words, if she were honest. But they wouldn't keep her safe. "I will never forgive you."

"I look forward to all the ways you're going to never forgive me. Lower the knife, Rylee."

He could take it himself. He was stronger, faster, expertly trained in disarming opponents. But for some insane reason, he wanted her to make this step.

It didn't mean anything. She was in danger, and he was the only person who could help her.

She tossed the knife.

With a nod, he rose and held out his hand.

"You should clean that cut." She rejected his waiting hand and pushed to her feet. "Someone else's blood was all over that blade."

He stepped back, giving her space to move out of her hiding spot. The room was empty, the corpse covered with a blanket. Everyone waited outside.

"You have two minutes to clean up." He nodded at the bathroom.

She didn't have to look down at her body. Her skin shivered beneath a sheen of cold, wet blood.

"Who's here with you?" She strode into the bathroom, grateful to find the clothes she'd left in here earlier.

"Half the team." He followed her in and gripped the hem of her bloody shirt. "Arms up."

Sensing the tension in his posture, she let him undress her. "You're expecting more hitmen?"

"Yes." He traced a finger along the torn, burning skin that ran the length of her spine. "How did this happen?"

"The bed frame. I saw the gunman talking to the motel clerk. It gave me time to hide." She washed her upper body in the sink, thinking through the ramifications. "The clerk might've called the cops."

"The clerk was dead when we arrived."

She froze in horror.

"Keep washing, Rylee." He crouched behind her and carefully lowered her filthy pants. "You have one minute."

Another dead body. Three in one week. Because of her. Who would be next?

Shoving down a thousand questions, she focused on scrubbing away the blood.

As Tommy helped her step out of her pants, she was viscerally aware of how close his mouth hovered to her bare backside. His breath caressed her flesh, prickling goosebumps, and his hands ghosted down the backs of her thighs, too tender to belong to the man who'd viciously fucked her in the desert.

"What are you doing?" She jerked her hips, trying to dislodge his touch.

With a firm grip on her butt, he gave her a warning squeeze. Then he released her and grabbed a clean towel.

Seconds later, she was wiped down and dressed in clean lounge pants and a t-shirt.

As he soaped up his neck and scrubbed the cut she'd inflicted, his gaze locked on hers in the mirror. There was something different about him. Something softer in the way he looked at her. It put her on edge.

When he clasped her hand to lead her out, she yanked free from his grip.

"Rylee." He reached for her again, eyes hard.

"I'm not going to run."

She walked out ahead of him and slammed into potent, eye-burning fumes of gasoline. The room had been doused in it.

"Where's my ID? Clothes?" She spun in a circle.

"They grabbed it." He caught her shoulders and pointed her toward the door.

With a hard swallow, she stepped around the covered corpse and into the dark parking lot.

Someone had killed the outside lights, but the moon was bloated and bright, illuminating a motorcycle, two SUVs, and two…four…*seven* human-shaped silhouettes.

The desert heat clung to the night air, but the atmosphere exuded a chill that seeped into her bones. All eyes turned to her, and she stumbled back as if she'd been shoved, crashing into Tommy's broad chest.

"You're safe." He curled a hand around her hip and put his mouth at her ear. "You know them."

Cole was easy to spot with his beard, leather jacket, and formidable lean against the motorcycle.

Next in line was a man with sloping shoulders, a stern expression, and red hair. That could only be Luke. Van stood beside him, gnawing on a toothpick.

Her heart thudded as she took in the others.

A Latina woman sat on the curb, cuddled in the arms of a man with dark blond hair and crystal blue eyes. Lucia and Tate? If they hadn't been joined at the hip, she might not have guessed who they were. But Tommy's emails often talked about how the two were never apart. He'd joked that they probably took their daily shits together.

Which brought her gaze to the imposing figure who stood away from the rest. Stubble shadowed a squared jaw and outlined sculpted lips. Dark hair, dark eyes, Hispanic features—all carved into the image of a shockingly attractive man. But his presence bespoke of something other. Something egregious, inhuman, and evil down to the morrow of his soul.

A shiver snaked through her, for she knew, without looking at the self-inflicted scars on his arms, that she was standing in the withering stare of one of the most ruthless crime lords in Venezuela.

In the name of all that's holy, why is he here?

"I thought you…" Damn, her trembling voice. She cleared her throat. "You live on the other side of the world."

"While I'm honored to make the cut into Tomas' diary of angsty feelings, where I live is none of your goddamn concern, little girl." He grinned, and it wasn't a grin at all.

Her mouth went dry, and her pulse careened into hysteria.

"That's enough, Tiago." Tommy shifted her behind him and gripped her hand.

This time, she allowed it, squeezing tight to his fingers as he removed a set of keys from his pocket.

"If you let him intimidate you, he'll never stop," a woman spoke from the shadows of the SUVs. "He gets off on it."

The striking image of the last silhouette emerged from the darkness, striding forward.

Dressed head to toe in black, she wore badass buckled boots, guns on her hips, and straight black hair to her waist. Slender limbs, all long and graceful, gave her the appearance of delicate femininity. But her bearing commanded attention. Her aura controlled the very air. Authority beamed from her glacial eyes.

Liv.

The queen of depravity and dominance.

She'd molded Tommy into the sexual deviant he was today, and Rylee felt an irrational stab of jealousy over that. But she was also wonderstruck, tongue-tied, and instantly enamored.

The scar that hooked across Liv's cheek replicated Van's in its appearance and story. And like Van's, it only added to her allure. The woman looked like Kate Beckinsale of the underworld—all sexy power, intimidation, and seduction.

"We'll talk in the car," Liv said in greeting and plucked the keys from Tommy's hand. "I'm driving."

This was happening.

Surrounded by criminals, Rylee felt the shadows closing in, tingling her nape and smothering her chances of survival. What had she gotten herself into?

Too late to run. She was outnumbered eight to one.

Eight darkly corrupted felons had traveled all the way here because of her. Because she'd invaded their privacy and gotten herself mixed up in something terrible.

She would have to go with them, wherever that might be, and hope to God they weren't plotting her death.

Tommy held onto her numb hand and led her to the SUV.

Behind her, someone struck a match, and the motel erupted in flames.

NINETEEN

In the darkness of the SUV, images of Rylee's injuries worked through Tomas' conscience. Something had struck her jaw with enough force to leave it swollen and red, and a nasty gash marred the length of her spine. Numerous marks cut and bruised her gorgeous flesh. But the other guy looked much worse.

She'd fought for her life and defeated a professional hitman. Admiration didn't begin to express how he felt about her. A heady, complex cocktail of emotions hammered at him, mixing with adrenaline and twisting in his stomach.

He'd lost her four days ago. Almost lost her for good today.

Just like that, he forgave her for invading his privacy. Her life was in danger, and he felt responsible for that. He shouldn't have let her leave with the detective. He should've fucking protected her.

She wasn't the enemy.

Fate was giving him a second chance. A chance to right his wrongs with her and maybe, just maybe, find happiness again. He wouldn't fuck it up. He'd meant what he told her. Tonight, he would begin anew.

A fresh start.

With her.

His mind had gone there so quickly. The instant he thought she was dead was the exact moment he realized she was more than the best sex of his life. More than a throat he wanted to throttle. More than any word he'd ever written in an email.

He survived Caroline's death. But he knew, deep in his fractured soul, he wouldn't survive Rylee's.

DOMINATE

The simmering sensations at the base of his throat, behind his breastbone, and in the pit of his stomach were an accumulation of violence and desire, chemistry and possessiveness, fire and rage. The extreme passion she produced in him was the antithesis of the tender, doting innocence he'd felt with Caroline.

It was difficult to think about, but he couldn't help but wonder if he and Caroline would've been as compatible as adults as they'd been as children. Caroline had been a gentle soul, sweetly passive, always smiling. If she hadn't died, he probably would've still gone to Austin, grieving the loss of his mother, and ended up in Van's attic.

That experience had fundamentally changed him. Ten years later, he didn't want Caroline's kindhearted brand of love. He wanted explosive, no-holds-barred, raging, brutal passion.

He wanted Rylee.

But she wasn't ready to hear any of this.

"Where are we going?" She sat beside him in the backseat of the SUV with her hands balled on her lap.

Liv drove in silence with Luke in the front seat next to her.

"A safe house." Tomas would eventually have to tell her it was thirteen hours away.

"How did you find me?"

"When you left with the detective," he said, "I called in my team. We traced your credit card and identified the cash machine you used. It took us several days to track down the motel employee who helped you."

"She told you where I was?" She heaved a frustrated sound. "I paid her an extra two-hundred to keep her mouth shut." Her shoulders tensed, and her gaze flashed to him in the dark. "Tell me you didn't hurt her."

Rule number one in this business: *Never leave loose ends.*

But Rylee didn't live in his world. She didn't know.

"The motel clerk took her bounty of cash and drove to San Antonio," he said. "A spontaneous vacation to visit a friend. If she hadn't left town so quickly, we would've located you within twenty-four hours."

"What did you do, Tommy?" She shifted to face him, her voice rising. "Answer me."

He had a lot of bad news to give her. Christ, she'd already been through so much. He wanted to spare her this. For just a little while longer.

"She just butchered a man, Tomas." Liv met his eyes in the rearview, her voice melodic yet icy in its command. "Don't coddle the woman. She can handle it."

He knew that. Fuck, he still wore the vicious marks of Rylee's claws and teeth. He knew exactly how she handled things.

With a steeling breath, he turned toward her.

"The hitman located the girl before we did." He reached for her face, her expression falling, collapsing in agony before his eyes.

"No." She jerked away, shaking her head. "No, no, no!"

"She's dead."

Killed slowly. Body parts removed. All left for his team to find.

Her eyes glistened with tears, but she didn't let them fall. "So the hitman learned my location and killed that poor girl." She inhaled deeply. "How did you follow him?"

"Cole and I stayed behind, working it from a different angle." Tomas hadn't been much help, his technical skills no match for Cole's. "It took days, but Cole managed to trace Paul Kissinger's phone to multiple other devices. I still don't know how he did it, but one of the devices he locked onto was traveling from San Antonio back to this area. We knew that was our guy and scrambled to catch up. When the phone stopped moving at your motel, we were still ten minutes out." A hot clamp squeezed his airway. "Ten minutes too late. I'm so sorry, Rylee."

"I got myself into this." She leaned back and looked out the window. "I won't forgive the way you treated me, but I know you didn't send that hitman after me. That is a result of something I've done, evidently. Not your fault."

"What do you mean?" Suspicion thickened his voice. "What are you hiding?"

"Nothing!" Her gaze shot to his, wide and urgent. "I don't know what's going on, but when I was stabbing that man, he mentioned the bridge." She nervously glanced at Liv and Luke in the front seat and whispered, "He was smiling like he knew a dirty secret. But you're the only person I've ever told about that night."

"Start from the beginning. Tell me step by step what happened from the moment you saw the hitman talking to the motel clerk."

She explained how she left the shower running and hid beneath the bed, hoping to distract him long enough to escape. She had the knife and her wits—two things that saved her life. While it was hard to hear the details of her struggle, he was so fucking proud of her.

"I asked him about the bridge. How did he know about it, and what did it have to do with him?" Her brows pulled together, and she chewed her lip. "He was pretty much dead at that point, but he mumbled something about Thur… Need? Like Thursday? Or thirsty? He never finished."

Baffled and agitated, he drummed his fingers on his knee. He'd briefed his team on everything he knew about Rylee Sutton, including her ex-husband, the suicide bridge, and her sexual history, as well as her hate-fuckfest with him.

DOMINATE

That had been a strange conversation. He never shared shit like that with anyone. But his secrecy in writing emails for ten years had started this mess. They deserved to know all the facts, no matter how personal.

The consensus among everyone was that this had nothing to do with Rylee. They were dealing with a team of sophisticated spies and assassins who were likely using her to get to the Freedom Fighters. Probably a loose end from a sex trafficking ring they'd taken out in recent years.

So how would her near-suicide on a bridge a decade ago have anything to do with this?

The emails.

That was the night he'd started writing.

"I called Mason yesterday," she said into the silence.

Luke's gaze snapped toward Liv, and every tendon in Tomas' body went rigid.

He wanted to bend Rylee over his knee and show her luscious ass just how foolish it was to contact anyone right now. But the damage was already done.

Now he needed to understand the repercussions. "Tell me what was said. Every word."

"I used a disposable phone."

"Purchased from a corner store? It can be traced."

Despite the darkness, her face paled. Then she breathed in and walked through the conversation—Mason's confession that he loved her, kept tabs on her, and wanted her back.

"He reported me missing because Evan called him with claims that I was acting scared and disappeared." She rubbed her temples. "That just isn't true. Even weirder, Evan admitted to Mason that we were sleeping together. Why would he do that? To enrage Mason? To bait him?" She dropped her hands, her voice monotone. "I think Evan is behind all this. It doesn't fit his personality, but there are too many things that don't add up."

He exchanged a look with Liv in the rearview. Her gaze crystallized, issuing an order that shriveled his balls.

Yeah, he knew what he had to do and didn't need her controlling the situation from the front seat.

Fuck, this was going to hurt.

"Rylee, listen." He clasped her hand, clenching tight as she tried to pull away. "Evan died at work today. He fell off a six-story building at his construction site."

"What?" She yanked frantically on her hand, her breaths gusting hard and angry. "No. It wasn't on the news. They would've reported it. He wouldn't fall off a fucking building. He's smarter than that."

"His death is being investigated. They'll rule it accidental, but you and I both know it was foul play."

"He's not dead." Her voice shook, her gaze brimmed with anguish and denial. "He's not dead, Tommy. He's not."

He would give anything to order the caravan off the road and chase everyone out of the car so she could wrap her emotions around this in private.

Nothing like breaking down in front of strangers. He hadn't been able to do it when he lost his mom and Caroline. He didn't leak a tear at their funerals. Couldn't open his soul to a therapist, either. He still didn't know if he had it in him to show weakness in front of his closest friends.

He felt her fighting it, battling the sobs in her chest, and pushing it all down. She trembled with the effort.

She needed to let it out. He knew that from experience.

All those years of writing emails, pouring his fears, sadness, and loneliness into the ether, and to think, someone had been listening to him after all. While he'd mourned his dead girlfriend, Rylee had been there for him through every word.

Now the tables had turned. While she grieved her friend, her *lover*, he wasn't jealous. He only felt an overwhelming, protective need to take away her pain.

Gathering her in his arms, he fought her snarls and weak attempts to break free. Once she settled down, he held her on his lap, cradling her, wrapping her up with his body, and kissing the tears on her cheeks.

"I hear you, Rylee." He pressed his lips to her ear, breathing her in. "All of you. We're still here. Our lives matter. Don't shut down on me."

She stared up at him, her eyes swimming in rippling silver waters. A choking sound strangled in her throat. Another smothered sob. Then she circled her arms around his shoulders, buried her face in his neck, and wept silently, softly. Each painful hitch in her breath ripped him open and pulled her in.

From the moment he met her, she'd sworn her intentions were innocent, claiming that all those years ago, she'd hurt with him, cried for him, and changed her major to psychology. For him. She'd taken a sabbatical and driven to his house because she wanted to help him.

And he'd treated her like an enemy. Now that he knew the truth, he had to live with his crimes. But he wouldn't live without her.

Once they escaped the present danger, and they *would* escape it, he was going to smash through her intimacy issues and convince her she needed him as much as he needed her.

"Evan Phillips didn't make that call to her ex-husband." Luke twisted in the front seat and met his eyes.

"No, he didn't." Tomas didn't have proof, but he knew at gut level her neighbor was an innocent casualty.

Either Mason was lying about Evan's phone call, or someone had called Mason, pretending to be Evan.

The reason for Evan's murder wasn't apparent. It could've been retaliation of the jealous ex-husband, or a message sent to Tomas' team, or just a loose end that needed to go away.

For the next hour, he spoke quietly with Liv and Luke, speculating about possible enemies. Rylee didn't try to push off his lap, her soft whimpers sinking into stunned acceptance. He sat with her in her sadness, his arms tight around her, exactly where he belonged.

If he didn't fuck this up, he could have more moments like this. Moments when he held her while she was happy, scared, excited, or just wanted to sleep.

He hoped she would sleep now, but he sensed too much alertness in her muscles. She was listening, always eavesdropping, as he and his friends reminisced about missions gone by and gossiped about family drama.

Liv had deliberately confined Van, Tiago, Tate, and Lucia in the same vehicle for thirteen hours.

"Forced proximity," she said. "They need to work out their shit."

While that was true, he didn't believe Tiago's crimes would be forgiven anytime soon. The crime lord had poisoned Lucia to keep her sick, forced Van and Tate to have sex, and scarred up Tate's back beyond physical and emotional repair.

Some crimes just weren't redeemable.

While Rylee sat lethargically on his lap, he used the opportunity to dig out the first-aid kit and treat the laceration on her back. For once, she didn't fight him. A testament to the despondent state of her mind.

Three hours into the drive, she lifted her head from his shoulder and squinted at the blackness beyond the window. "Where is this safe house?"

"Missouri." He braced for the backlash.

"What?" Her voice pitched with outrage, and she shoved out of his embrace. "I can't leave Texas."

"Too late."

She scrambled toward the far door. To do what? Jump from the moving vehicle?

He caught her throat, wrenched her forcibly back to him by the neck, and took her mouth. She fought him. Hot damn, she always fought. He groaned against her teeth and kissed her deeper, harder, wordlessly ordering her to return the kiss.

With a hand cradling her ass, he pulled her roughly against him and held her nape in a firm lock.

"Let me go." Straddling his lap, she seethed against his mouth and shoved at his chest. "You're kidnapping me!"

"Shut the fuck up and kiss me." His stomach heated, his mind spinning to untangle the knots of her venom.

Battling her rage with more rage wouldn't yield a lasting relationship with this complicated woman. While his cock loved her ferocity, they were more than sex. More than her hatred.

She told herself she was done with commitment and love and all matters of the heart. But that wasn't true.

"You fear intimacy." He restrained her hands against her back and held her close, chest to chest, mouth to mouth. "But you've been in a relationship with me for ten years."

"You didn't even know I existed."

"That changed the moment you walked into my house and upended my world."

He covered her mouth with his, his tongue insistent, pushing past the stubborn line of her lips. He refrained from using aggressive, overpowering strokes and instead delivered a languorous caress, tipping her expectations into bewilderment.

Her mouth opened on a gasp, and she gave way to his adoring licks. He suckled and worshiped, pressing in and releasing her hands to cup her head and palm her tight, round ass.

For a moment, she melted into him, welcoming his tongue moving in her mouth, against hers. She gripped his shirt and angled her head, delving deeper and whimpering. Not sounds of hunger, but distress.

Intimacy was her limit, and a tender kiss came way too close to that. So when her hands balled into fists on his shirt, he was ready for the blowback.

She punched his chest and sank her teeth into his lip. More strikes. Rabid bites. He absorbed it for a few seconds, knowing she needed an outlet for the pain inside her. He also knew she'd have him covered in blood if he didn't defuse her soon.

"Behave." With his hands framing her face, he slowed down the kiss and earned himself a vicious bite on the tongue.

"Fuck you." She went at his mouth, attacking him in a firestorm of feral heat and scorn.

He nibbled when she bit, caressed when she scratched, and hummed when she growled. He dominated her mouth with devotion, overpowering her hostility with sensuality and sliding her temper into a languid embrace of exploration and affection.

Until she shoved him back against the seat. He allowed it, soaking in her fury and grief, her fists pounding upon his chest, her fingernails scoring his flesh. He caressed her everywhere, softly, compassionately, his touch in extreme opposition of hers.

She tore her mouth away, panting. Angry and confused. Then she fused their lips again.

Her kiss was war and retribution. Punishment for everything he'd done to her. But it was also redemption, heaven, and desire. He loved the fiery taste of her, the all-consuming fervor in her breaths, and the curling of her claws in his hair, ripping, pulling, and holding him close.

He loved that she didn't do anything half-ass, especially when it came to him.

"If you put this much energy into hating me," he breathed against her mouth, "I can only imagine the amount of intensity and passion you'll put into loving me."

"Never." Her eyes glinted like steel blades. "I'll never love you."

"Oh, boy," Liv said from the front seat. "I've heard those words before."

"Me, too." Luke sighed and shifted to glance at them over his shoulder. "Rylee Sutton, you just sealed your fate."

TWENTY

An indignant cloud darkened Rylee's expression, and Tomas wanted to kiss it right off her face. She didn't like hearing that her fate was sealed. She'd fought too hard for her independence and was too protective of her heart to believe her efforts had been for naught.

Tomas, on the other hand, held tight to his newfound hope.

She was stuck with the Freedom Fighters, whether she forgave him or not. She knew their identities, their secrets, and once they arrived in Missouri, she would know the location of Cole's safe house.

Even if Tomas let her go, his friends would not.

Loose ends.

None of that mattered. She was his now. If she tried to leave, he would go with her. She just didn't know it yet.

Cole led the caravan on his motorcycle, shooting down the dark highway in the dead of night. Around one in the morning, four hours into the thirteen-hour drive, he pulled off at a vacant rest stop.

"Bathroom break." Tomas nudged Rylee beside him, reluctant to wake her after it had taken her so long to fall asleep.

She rubbed her eyes and followed him out of the car.

Parked behind them, the second SUV rocked wildly on its frame.

What the hell?

The doors flew open, exploding in a whirlwind of swinging arms and heated voices. Lucia's roar was the loudest, her rapid-fire Spanish shuddering the air.

With a snarl, she raced around the vehicle and attacked the smirking driver.

Tiago.

DOMINATE

"Oh, shit." Tomas gripped Rylee's hand, prepared to toss her into the SUV if guns were drawn.

Tiago stood like an impenetrable mountain, chin up, feet braced apart, as he absorbed the force of Lucia's punches.

"They need to knock that shit off." Cole charged toward the commotion.

Liv's hand shot out, stopping him. "There's no one around for miles. Let it play out."

Tate and Van yelled, too, quieter, calmer than the woman who unleashed unholy hell on her nemesis.

"Deep down," Luke said to no one in particular, "Tiago feels regret for what he did to them."

"No, he doesn't." Cole scoffed and walked off.

"Yeah, you're right." Luke started toward the small building of restrooms. "Satan has no feelings."

Rylee tilted her head, eyes locked on the fight. "If everyone hates Tiago, why is he here?"

"He's here for Kate." Liv lit a cigarette, inhaling deeply. "The longer he avoids us, the more he isolates her from her family. Isolation breeds resentment. He might be the devil, but the devil is intelligent."

"Happy wife, happy life," Tomas said.

Rylee cast him a strange look. "So he wants to be part of this family?"

"I don't know if *want* is the right word." He tensed as the fight grew more unruly.

Tiago's patience was dwindling. He caught Lucia's next punch, knocked it away, and cuffed her throat, choking her. Tate went ballistic, jumping into the fray and tackling Tiago to the ground.

"As an outsider," Rylee said, hugging her waist, "it looks like you're your own enemies."

"You're wrong." Tomas turned toward her, putting his face in hers. "Forget everything you learned in school. We're not your case studies. We don't need your therapy." He stabbed a finger at the brawl. "*This* is how we deal with things."

"With your fists?" She stood taller, meeting his glare head-on. "That's going well, I see."

"We work out our issues with communication. Yes, we communicate with fists. And words. And *sex*."

She pressed her lips together, but her eyes argued loudly.

"We don't want to be fixed, Rylee." He straightened, glanced at Liv, and returned to her. "We can't do what we do and be normal or safe or sane. Think about it. We hunt monsters. We break laws. We torture and kill. Hell, we even fall in love with our prisoners. Or *abductors*, depending on the perspective."

Her eyes widened as they darted around, taking in his team. He could see her mind working, recalling the stories of how each of his friends found love. Liv and Josh, Van and Amber, Camila and Matias, Tiago and Kate, Luke and Vera—they all began as captor and captive, evolving from vicious enemies to lifelong mates. Every single one of them.

The Freedom Fighters needed to be coldblooded and crazy to do their jobs. They also needed some of that madness to fall in love, evidently.

"Our story isn't any different." He caught and held her gaze.

"We're not in love, Tommy."

"I'm not opposed to the idea."

She set her jaw. "You're an idiot."

"Call me that again, and I'll kiss the shit out of you."

Her breath stuttered, and she cleared her throat. "I need to pee."

He glanced in the direction of the restrooms just as Luke strolled out. With a chin lift, he signaled Luke to wait. Having already swept the small building, his friend would stand by while Rylee was inside.

"Go ahead," he said to her.

"I wasn't asking." She strode off, stubborn to a fault.

Behind him, the drama with Tiago fizzled from smacking fists to emotional words.

A quick sweep of the perimeter gave him a view of shadows, dark tree lines, and in the distance, an empty highway. Everyone present carried weapons, and no matter what they were doing, they were all on high-alert.

"We'll get through this." Liv touched his forehead, brushing the hair from his eyes. "No matter who we're fighting. There will always be another fight, and we'll always stand together, righting our wrongs."

"And the wrongs of others." He glanced over his shoulder, finding Van, of all people, standing between Tiago and Tate, speaking to them in calming tones. The argument was over. "Van's come a long way."

"So have you."

"What's that supposed to mean?"

"You've always been more closed-off and secretive than the others. I used to worry about your happiness." She smashed her cigarette beneath a boot and offered him a rare smile. "I'm not worried anymore."

Her sharp brown eyes used to give him nightmares. Now they regarded him with an affectionate sort of intensity that told him their decade-long friendship was invaluable to her.

"I've always been your favorite." He grinned.

"Josh might have something to say about that."

"I can't believe the boy scout let you out of the fortress without him."

"He wasn't pleased. But Matias' plane won't hold all of us, and I'm sick of being the one who stays behind."

She'd spent the better part of the past decade raising her daughter. Livana was an adult now. A badass little vigilante in training. Considering who her parents were, he wasn't surprised.

"Everyone wanted to come on this mission." Liv stared at the dark horizon, the scar on her cheek glinting in the moonlight. "To be back in Texas, where it all began? It's nostalgic."

"Most of us grew up here, but honestly, I never had a desire to return."

"Well, we're headed to Missouri now. I didn't even know Cole had a safe house there."

None of them knew. Cole was a goddamn mystery.

He was also a lifesaver. They needed a safe place to regroup, analyze the evidence they'd collected, and determine how to proceed. That could take weeks, and Tomas' shabby little safe house in the desert was too small and no longer safe. When he'd suggested that they camp out in the desert, Cole shot down that idea and offered his house in southern Missouri.

Tomas' attention flitted to Luke, who paced in front of the restrooms. "I'm surprised Luke left Vera in Colombia, given how new their relationship is."

"She was pissed. But he wanted to be here for you."

"Vera stayed behind because she has a gunshot wound?"

"He refused to let her travel. He'll have a lot of groveling to do when he gets home."

Home. In Colombia, Texas, or Timbuctoo, it didn't matter. Home was wherever his fucked-up, overprotective family was. And Rylee.

"She's one of us now." He nodded at the restrooms.

"You think she's a good fit?"

"For the team? Or for me?"

"Both."

"She's mean enough." He chuckled. "Yeah, she fits. She's carrying her weight in issues."

"Oh, good. I was starting to think she might be too normal for this crowd."

"Nah, she's batshit crazy." A warm whoosh filled his chest, lifting it. "She wouldn't be a psychologist if she wasn't."

"Look at you." Her enigmatic brown eyes roamed over his face. She stepped closer and trailed her fingers along his jaw. "You're falling, and my God, it's stunning." She smiled wickedly. "You're so fucked, Tomas."

He cupped her hand to his cheek, cherishing the connection.

Footsteps approached, and they turned.

Rylee breezed past them, followed by Luke. She shot Tomas a withering glare and stormed to the SUV, slamming the door behind her.

"Jealousy. I don't miss that stage of a new relationship." Liv patted his cheek. "Good luck."

She strolled toward Van and the others, where they'd calmly gathered near the other SUV. Tomas headed to the bathroom to take a piss. Then he joined Rylee in the backseat.

"You want me," he said in greeting.

"I want you to fuck off and leave me alone."

"I'm not him."

"Excuse me?"

"You heard me."

"Yeah." She huffed. "You think I'm hypersensitive and overreactive because the man I loved cheated on me. Here's a news flash. You can fuck whoever you want because I. Do. Not. Love. You."

"Love me or hate me. Either way, I'm yours." He grabbed her jaw and forced her eyes to his. "I will *never* fucking cheat on you."

Her swallow jumped against his hand, her eyes round and heartbreaking.

He was pushing too hard, too fast.

"Get some sleep." He released her, giving her space. "We have a long way to go."

TWENTY-ONE

Cole's safe house was a lakefront estate in rustic Missouri. Any doubts Tomas had about finding a place to comfortably and safely accommodate their party of nine were immediately quashed when he stepped inside the sprawling mansion.

It sat on a dead-end road, where the asphalt met acres upon acres of woodland. No other houses. No sounds of traffic or life for miles around. Total isolation.

"Bedrooms are down that hall." Cole paced through the main living area, flicking on lights and tapping codes into a screen on the wall. "Eat. Get some rest, and we'll reconvene tonight."

No one moved. Tomas didn't know what the others were thinking, but Jesus, it was surreal, this glimpse into Cole's private life. Even Rylee, who had only met Cole a week ago, looked shell-shocked by the grandeur of the place.

Fireplaces dominated both ends of the living room. The cathedral ceiling and natural color schemes directed all attention to the wall of picturesque windows between the hearths.

The view of a private cove, illuminated by the late morning sun, was nothing short of mesmerizing.

"You own this? The estate? The land?" Tomas watched Cole move through the open kitchen. "By yourself?"

"Yes."

"Clearly, we paid you too much for your services." Van prowled along the windows, gnawing on a toothpick and taking in the view.

"Seeing how I've been saving your asses for free for the past year, I'd argue you're not paying me enough."

"You're either with us, or you're not." Liv lowered into an overstuffed chair. "It's not a monetary decision."

"Am I with you?" Cole stalked toward her and bent into her space, nose to nose. "Spell it out. What do you want?"

"Secrets don't keep well for long in this family." She was a fraction of Cole's size and managed to look more threatening as she leaned in, forcing him back. "We hide nothing from one another."

"Except Tomas' emails," Cole said.

"Which are no longer a secret." Tomas clenched his jaw.

"Like I said." Liv raised her chin. "Secrets don't keep in our family."

"If you let me in, I'll do the same." Cole straightened and shrugged off his leather jacket. "This property is the entirety of my wealth. An accumulation of the side jobs, the *risks* I've taken over the past twenty years. But it's more than that. This is my retirement. My sanctuary. And now, I'm offering it to you. To the cause."

Tomas glanced at Rylee beside him, the surprised look on her face mirroring his thoughts. For whatever reason, Cole had just made an exorbitant bid to be part of their exclusive team.

He'd been working alongside them for a year, but always as an outsider. He wasn't forced into this by way of Van's attic. Nor was he marrying into the family. Before now, those had been the only avenues into becoming one of their kindred.

But apparently, he wanted this badly enough to invest his entire future in them.

"How is the kitchen already stocked?" Tiago rummaged through the built-in commercial fridge, his nefarious presence as out of place as his question.

"You're worried about my secrets," Cole said to Liv, "when you should be worried about the Venezuelan kingpin who carries razors in his pocket." He turned toward a scowling Tiago. "I have a caretaker, vetted and trusted, who's been looking after this property for fifteen years. He prepared the bedrooms and stocked the kitchen this morning."

Tiago nodded, his expression brooding. Pensive. "You're already in the fold, Hartman. They need you. Most of them care about you. Trust will take time." He grabbed his bag and strode into the hallway, vanishing around the corner.

Silence descended in his wake. Looks were exchanged. Someone blew out a breath.

"That was awkward." Tomas rubbed his nape.

"Fuck him." Lucia crossed her arms. "He's just sore because he has no friends."

"Fix it." Van pointed a toothpick at her.

She made a growly sound. "Why me?"

"Because Tate and I made our peace with him. You're still hanging onto the past."

"Fine." She slung her backpack over her shoulder and turned to follow Tiago. "I'll do it for Kate."

"You'll do it for *you*." Tate swatted her butt. "And not until you're ready. Let's grab a room."

The massive living space slowly emptied as everyone wandered off. Between Colombia, Texas, and Missouri, the team had been traveling nonstop for four days. Two weeks before that, they'd been in California, taking down La Rocha Cartel.

Now that they were safe, the first order of business was food and sleep.

Within minutes, only Tomas and Rylee remained.

"I'm hungry, not tired." She stepped into the kitchen and snatched an apple off the counter.

She'd slept most of the way here and missed the meal they'd grabbed through a roadside drive-through.

"Eat." He collected their bags and ambled toward the hallway. "I'll claim a room."

"Two rooms."

He didn't bother acknowledging that ridiculous request.

A gradual slope of stairs ascended into a long corridor, the flooring tiled in an artistic mosaic of slate stones. He lost count of how many doors he passed, all with keypad entry. Christ, there must've been eight or nine bedrooms in total. Unless something else was hiding behind these locks.

He stopped at the first open door and gaped.

Inside, racks of guns covered one wall. Dozens of firearms of every size, shape, and caliber. File cabinets, desks, and worktables filled the rest of the dimly lit room, the surfaces covered in laptops, camera equipment, and high-tech clothing and gear.

Cole stood at a table, sifting through stacks of burner phones, all plugged into a power strip that ran along the wall.

"Last room on the right is mine." He didn't look away from his task. "The one on the left is still open."

"Thanks." As Tomas turned to leave, his gaze caught on a transparent garment bag that hung from a hook behind the door.

White satin and lace.

A wedding gown.

Damn, it looked eerily spectral and downright sad amid the plethora of guns and spy tech.

"I should burn it," Cole said behind him.

"I don't know, man." He pivoted, meeting the starkness in Cole's brown eyes. "I burned everything, but the ghosts clung."

"Are they still clinging?"

"Yeah." He scratched his jaw, rethinking his answer. "Actually, I've been too distracted to notice."

"Your dick's been distracted."

"More than usual, and more than just my dick. That woman has her claws in every part of me. Now that I think about it, I'm pretty sure she scared the ghosts away." He chuckled and quickly sobered. "Do you think her ex-husband hired hits on her and Evan Phillips?"

"I don't know yet." Cole turned back to the table of burner phones. "Get some rest. Recharge. We have a lot of work to do and need to be clearheaded."

With a nod, Tomas made his way to the last room on the left. An airy, tidy space with a large bed and private bathroom—all decorated in simple, natural hues. Beyond the windows, trees rippled on hillsides that stretched to the horizon.

He could see why Cole chose this place to retire. It was lush and green. Peaceful. Calming. Completely void of sand, desert heat, and hatred.

With Rylee, he would take her hatred over indifference. Her fire was irresistible, addictive, and he wouldn't dare try to control it if it made her happy.

But it didn't. Her anger made her miserable. He accepted the blame for some of that, not all of it. Nine days ago, she walked into his house with a block of ice around her heart and a grudge against men that was ten years in the making.

Enough was enough.

He dropped their bags near the door, brushed his teeth, and found his angry little hellcat sitting alone at the kitchen island. She'd fixed herself a salad with pre-grilled chicken.

Lowering onto the stool beside her, he reached toward her bowl to steal a meaty morsel.

"No!" She jerked it away, hugging the dish protectively to her chest. "Please, don't."

He yanked his hand back, scalded by her reaction. "Jesus, Rylee. I'm not going to take your food away."

She didn't move, her glare distrustful and defensive.

He'd done that. Adding to her fears of intimacy and commitment, he'd instilled a new one.

Starvation.

What kind of monster was he?

"Fuck." He shoved away from the island and paced through the kitchen. "I fucked up. Cole warned me. He told me if I harmed you and learned you were innocent, that I would wear the scars." His chest hurt, and his stomach coiled in a turmoil of guilt. But he wouldn't give up. Pausing a few feet away, he looked her square in the eyes. "You have every right to hate me. I know you're pissed. So yell at me. Let me hear it. Act like a fucking adult and confront me."

Her lips parted. "The day I walked into your house, those were my words."

"I've been listening." He lowered his head and ran a hand through his hair. "I'm not going to apologize. I won't beg for your forgiveness. Instead, I'm going to make you a promise." He lifted only his eyes, pinning her with a stare she couldn't ignore. "I will *not* repeat my mistakes. Let me be clear. My only priorities are to protect you and keep you healthy. I will not cheat on you. I will not starve you. But I will *hurt* you."

"Why?"

"Because when we're in love, we will hurt each other as much as we save each other."

She sat still for so long he thought he'd lost her inside her head.

At last, she released her death grip on the bowl, set it on the counter, and tucked back into her meal.

He returned to the stool beside her, bracketing her rigid body in the *V* of his thighs. "Tell me what you're thinking."

"I should be in Texas, helping Evan's parents bury their son."

"And get yourself killed in the process? I won't allow it."

"Of course, you won't. You're a domineering prick." She chewed slowly, eyes on her salad and voice soft. "I don't belong here. I'm not a vigilante. I have nothing to offer."

"You just took out an assassin. The man who killed an innocent motel clerk. You succeeded where we failed. I'd say you've more than proved your value in this fight."

"I don't want to be here."

"Tell me why."

She finished the last bite of salad and stood, carrying her bowl to the sink. "I didn't choose this."

"None of us *chose* it. You know our histories. This life chose us."

"I work in law enforcement."

"Van's father was the Austin Police Chief."

"I don't carry weapons."

"Amber, Kate, and Josh don't carry weapons." He rose from the stool and prowled around the island to stand behind her. "You carry a shotgun in your truck, and let's not forget the butcher knife you stole from my house."

She stiffened at his nearness. "I was in danger."

"You're still in danger." Lowering his nose to her hair, he breathed in her mouth-watering femininity. "That's why you don't want to be here."

"Because I'm in danger of getting killed by one of your homicidal friends?"

"No, Rylee." He trailed the backs of his fingers down her arms, making her shiver. "Because you're in danger of falling in love."

"Oh, my God." She shot out from beneath the press of his body and scurried around the island. "What is this obsession you suddenly have with *love*? The man who wrote those emails plowed through hundreds of women and couldn't emotionally connect with any of them."

"None of them were you." He stalked after her. "You blindsided me. Knocked me on my ass."

"I can't stand you." She backed away, rubbing her arms, looking for all the world like she wanted to run.

"You can't stand the thought of me getting too close." He closed the distance, backing her into the corner of the kitchen. "Because I *am* getting too close, and when I ram through that armor around your heart, you think you're going to get hurt again."

"You don't know me." Her back bumped into the pantry door, her eyes darting, searching for a way out. "You don't love me."

"You'll deny it. You'll fight it with every breath in your body." He braced a hand on the door above her head and leaned in. "But having already experienced it once, you know it's a fight you can't win."

"Stop throwing my words back at me!" She shoved at his chest, ducked under his arm, and darted toward the hallway.

"Stop running from them like a hypocrite."

"I'm not running." She held up her middle finger without slowing.

She wasn't *literally* running. But that speed-walk of hers wiggled her ass in a spellbinding way. He followed it like a tractor beam, locked onto the diabolical, heart-shaped curves. Fucking hell, she was built. All toned muscle, flawless skin, fiery temper, and *his*.

The tightening heat in his stomach was a primal demand, his body thrumming for a fight and his eyes fixed on his meal.

"Last door on the left." He trailed after her, chasing, hunting his chosen with a determination that couldn't be extinguished.

She reached the bedroom two paces ahead of him. As the door swung closed, he stopped it with the toe of his boot. Then he kicked it open.

"Get out." She tried to re-shut it, pushing him back, her resistance at odds with the raw lust in her eyes.

He wasn't imagining it. Her breathing unfurled at a ravenous speed, noisily heaving from her chest. Her nipples pebbled beneath the tight shirt, her pupils dilated. She licked her lips, stared at his mouth, and shoved him again.

With a hand holding the door open and his boots planted on the threshold, he didn't budge.

Wild brown hair fell in disarray around her shoulders, the upthrust of her tits so round and tempting. Lashes, sprinkled in dark hues of animosity, hooded the molten silver of her eyes.

He leaned in, shaking with excitement and hard as a rock.

She leaned in, too, angry and gorgeous and not above ruthlessness when it came to getting what she wanted.

Right now, she wanted *him*. The dip of her gaze to his straining fly confirmed it.

"When I shove down your pants," he said, "and sink my fingers in your pussy, you're going to drip all over my hand."

"Doesn't mean anything. I love your monstrous cock."

He throbbed behind his zipper, engorged past the point of pain.

Tension mounted. He didn't force his way in. She didn't push him out. They just stared at each other for an endless, unblinking moment.

Then they moved. He grabbed her as she climbed his body. Lips colliding and hands grappling, they locked in a battle they would both win.

The door hadn't even closed before he had her pinned against the wall. She tore his fly. He wrenched down her pants. In a frenzy of shredded fabric, they managed to rip enough clothing out of the way, and he was in her.

Christ almighty, he was all the way in, plunging to the root and submerged into soaking wet heat. Her hips rose to meet his, questing, demanding, and he gave it to her. Nailing her against the wall, he fucked her with the unbridled force of his strength.

It was so incredibly hot, this unhinged frenzy between them, this mutual, maddening urgency to climb closer and closer until they dug out their souls. They couldn't keep their hands and mouths off each other. Ripping at clothes, kicking away shoes, they were naked and tumbling across the floor in a matter of seconds.

She thrashed beneath him, her eyes the color of rainclouds. Perky, flushed tits. A complexion so pristine and fair. Sinful pink lips—one set bruising his mouth while the other swallowed the full length of his hunger.

His hips moved like a piston, chasing his release. The sensations blew his mind, the pleasure out of this world. He was going to come. Really fucking hard and soon.

He broke the kiss and held her gaze, his balls tightening, the pressure nearing detonation. "Tell me you don't need me."

"I don't need you."

He pulled out, rose up, and finished all over her chest and face, grunting and shaking in a surge of liquid ecstasy. With a firm grip, he continued to stroke from base to tip, milking every drop and spraying jets of come across her shivering flesh.

When his nuts went empty, he climbed to his feet, his insides jumping with wild anticipation of her reaction.

She sniffed haughtily, sat up, and reached blindly behind her. Her hand landed in his bag near the door. Without a word, she pulled out his favorite fur-felt cowboy hat and wiped it across her chest, collecting his come on the expensive fabric. She used the underside on her face, cleaning every drop of him from her skin. Then tossed the hat back in his bag.

He stood there in absolute disbelief, staring at her. His hat would forever be traumatized.

Opening her legs, she ran two fingers along her slit and slipped them inside, her wicked eyes fixed on his. "I don't need you."

The fuck she didn't. She needed his cock, his protection, and above all, she needed his love. But rather than forcing any of it on her, he turned on his heel and strode toward the bathroom.

One round with this woman would never be enough. Already, his dick was swelling with blood, pulsing to get back inside her.

Halfway to the bathroom, her footsteps hit the floor, sprinting after him. He didn't have time to turn before she was climbing up his back and biting down on his shoulder hard enough to draw blood. Then she slapped him across the head.

His temper flared, and he spun. She spun with him, sliding to her feet while landing a torrent of punches on his spine and ribs. His seething frustration culminated in World War III when her open palm collided with his ass.

She fucking spanked him.

He froze and felt her go deadly still behind him.

"Rylee."

"Tommy." Her voice shook.

"You better run."

TWENTY-TWO

The mad ravings of Rylee's thoughts withered beneath the impact of Tommy's searing glare.

Oh, shit. She'd done it now. He was going to kill her.

Her heart rate spiked, hammering at her to flee. But with Tommy, she never did the smart thing.

In a bristling surge of fear, she slapped his face, making his cheeks bloom redder, hotter, madder than ever.

His hands balled at his sides, his cock outrageously long and swollen between his powerful legs.

Beautiful.

Dominant.

Terrifying man.

"Go ahead." She stood taller, despite her knocking knees. "Hurt me just like you promised."

His nostrils flared, and he closed his eyes. When they opened again, his anger was leashed, focused.

"Love hurts," he said. "It lashes out when tempers erupt. I might say shit I don't mean, but I will not strike you when I lose control."

Like she just did.

Her face tingled, chilling at the implication.

"You want me to hit you out of anger, so you can push me away." He touched her chin, lifting it. "You want me to cheat on you, so you can blame me when you run." He lowered his hand. "I won't do it, Rylee. I'll grab your throat in the heat of passion because it burns you up. I'll beat your ass because it makes you wetter than sin. But I will never cheat on you, nor will I ever hurt you out of anger."

"You hurt me when you fucked me in the desert."

"Weak argument. We were both raging. *With hunger.*"

Buzzing ignited in her ears. She shook her head, unable to escape the thrashing of her pulse. "I don't trust you."

"You're too scared to try."

"I'm old enough to be your mother. A hard pass."

"*That* was a lie. A bullshit attempt to chip away your confidence. There's no excuse for it. I was in the wrong. You know all my secrets, and I felt cornered, embarrassed by my mistakes. You had the advantage. You still do. You have the power to destroy me."

"I do not!" She drove her fist against his stone-hard chest. "See? You don't even move!" Another punch. "You chained me in the desert." *Punch, slap, punch.* "You strangled me until I passed out, left me with no water, and starved me for days." She pounded her knuckles in a fit of fury, her eyes hot with tears. "I can't forgive you. I won't. What kind of woman falls in love with a sadistic bastard?"

He stopped the barrage of her fists with a bear-hug, lifted her off her feet, and brought her down on her back on the bed.

"A sadistic woman, that's who." He lay atop her, trapping her hands and hovering his face an inch from hers. "And this bastard loves you."

She felt a cracking, rupturing sensation around her heart, and all at once, something burst, letting in air and warmth and terrible possibilities.

"No." She was breaking open, falling apart. "Stop playing with me, Tommy. If you're going to hurt me, just do it. Get it over with!"

He kissed her. Open mouth. Sweep of tongue. Gentle strokes, slipping along the inside of her lower lip. It hurt. Not like a fist. It hurt like hunger pangs. It was a helpless, gnawing, painful need way down deep inside.

Delving deeper, he roamed the caverns of her mouth with a skill that electrified. Her knees turned to water. Her arms went slack between them, and currents of insidious heat flooded her breasts, prickling the peaks.

He kissed her with tenderness, his hands flowing over her body with devotion, drawing pleasure beneath her skin, making her hungry, needy for more. He tasted of warmth and something rich and masculine and *loyal*. He tasted like her fantasies.

Never, *never*, had she been touched or kissed with such sublime adoration. His tongue moved in her mouth with agonizing respect as his fingers traced her breasts with reverence. His cock lay hard and thick against her belly, leaking from the tip but not stabbing. Not taking.

DOMINATE

She could battle his cruelty with fists. She could fight his ruthlessness with hateful words. She could sink her teeth into his stone-cold rage.

But she couldn't attack his affection with violence. She couldn't hit him when he kissed like this. When he kissed her like he well and truly loved her. She wasn't that hard-hearted.

But she wasn't naive, either.

He would grow bored. Whatever this infatuation was, it wouldn't last. He would miss the excitement of the chase.

His mouth trailed down her neck and suckled her breasts. The pressure of his lips, the swirl of his tongue, it was too perfect, too familiar, as though she'd spent her entire life in his arms.

His hand, strong and long-fingered, slid between her legs, tracing the shape of lower lips and rousing sensitive nerve endings. She throbbed, and his mouth nuzzled her quivering belly. Liquid heat flooded her pussy, and he continued to explore, tease, and slowly dismantle her kiss by kiss.

She wasn't stopping this. She couldn't. He was too talented, and she wanted it too much.

"This is just sex." She twisted her fingers in his thick hair.

"This is our bodies following the demands of our hearts."

"I bet that line gets you laid every time."

"My heart"—he sank a finger inside her—"never felt a damn thing during sex. Until you."

"That's a lie. Everyone's heart pounds when they fuck."

"My heart pounds when you walk into the room."

"You're deranged."

"No, merely in love. With you." He nipped her inner thigh. "Hurry up and love me back so we can do this without fighting."

"You can't love me, Tommy. I'm too broken."

"If you're broken, I'm broken. Christ, you look good enough to eat."

With his shoulders wedged between her legs, he stared at her cunt. Then he caressed her, stroking wickedly and stealing back, gentle around her opening and firm thrusts straight through the center.

Her eyes rolled back in her head, her entire body shaking with the need to come.

"You're not thinking through this." She gasped, clenching around his curling fingers. "You love women."

"I love you."

"You love pussy."

"Yours, no question."

"Do you love my pussy enough for it to be the only one you touch for the rest of your life?"

"Yes." He met her eyes. "I'm one-hundred-percent devoted to the stunning artwork between your legs and the beautiful stubbornness between your ears. So much so that I will answer these infuriating questions honestly every time they arise for the rest of our lives."

He buried his face in her cunt, scattering her thoughts on the tide of her gasps. The heat of his breaths was heaven, his lips firm, the voracious strokes of his tongue exceeding her desires and filling her with more.

Blazing light spread beneath her skin, stirring and shimmering and lifting her higher, higher, higher. Just as she reached the brink of climax, he pulled back. His heat, his kiss, all touch was gone.

"Tell me you need me." He stared at her, his mouth glistening, waiting.

Stunned, she stared back. Confusion crashed into realization and simmered into outrage.

He was trying to control her through orgasm denial? Kissing her with an agenda? Toying with her to get what he wanted?

Fuck him. She refused to surrender like a doormat. She also knew she would never win this fight. He had the stamina and willpower of a superhuman machine.

No more games. She was done.

Done with the manipulation and the cheating and the emotional pain.

"I don't need you." She reached between her legs to get herself off.

He watched her hand but didn't smack it away. His body tensed, but he didn't overpower her with his strength. Didn't try to dominate her in his Draconian way. Something flashed across his expression. Disappointment? Frustration? But he didn't leave.

Instead, he lowered his head and placed his mouth against her hand. His tongue joined her fingers. His fists gripped her thighs, holding her open, and before she could process the unexpected turn of events, he pushed her, hard and fast, through an unstoppable climax.

Rippling waves of pleasure poured through her, trembling her limbs, her moan of completion one of barely contained victory.

But she didn't feel victorious.

She felt like shit. Made worse when he pressed a loving kiss between her legs.

His eyes lifted to hers, blinking, raw, stark with vulnerability. "You're not the only one who's afraid of getting hurt again." He pushed off the bed and stood before her naked, open, his hands hanging at his sides. "It scares me how much I need you."

I need you.

DOMINATE

Three words, so simple and ambiguous, reached into her chest and shook her. They sneaked under her guard and gathered up the most broken parts of her.

I need you.

"Ten years ago," she said, voice cracking, "you wrote those words to your girl."

"And my girl heard them. She listened to me. She was there for me. I need my girl to keep doing that. I need you, Rylee."

"I'm not..." She pressed her fingers to her brow and released an anguished breath. "You were livid because I invaded your privacy."

"I'm an idiot."

For a man who'd spent most of last week glaring instead of talking, she couldn't fathom what the fuck had changed.

Except she knew.

He was telling her, showing her, and she just couldn't accept it.

"Someone else could've bought Caroline's jacket and logged into her account," she said. "I could've been anyone. You can't hinge this on the emails. Why do you need *me*?"

"You challenge me at every goddamn turn. You keep me in check, never backing down. You don't cower in the face of fear, not even when you're trapped under a bed and hunted by a hitman. You're crazy as hell, but you have a levelheaded grip on your moral compass. You think your heart is subtle? That you don't show it or share it with anyone? That's not true, Rylee. I watched you cry for your neighbor. You cried for that motel clerk. And you cried for me when I burnt Caroline's house." He dragged a hand down his brow, his nose, his mouth. "As if all that wasn't enough to send me off the rails..." He looked up, his gaze touching, stroking, heating her body. "You're so wildly, immeasurably, astonishingly beautiful it physically hurts."

Heart thundering, she lowered her eyes to the engorged erection hanging between his legs.

A swallow stuck in her throat.

There was no gain without pain. No reward without risk. She would never know how good it could be unless she got out of her own way.

The truth was she *did* need him. She needed his intensity, his honesty, his possessiveness, his passion.

She desperately needed him to need her.

But she was scared. Yes, she was thinking about Mason and the ten years of pain he'd caused her. How could she open herself up and expose her heart to another decade of agony?

And there would be agony. Over the last nine days, Tommy had proved just how vicious he could be.

He steadily watched her, his demeanor cooling by the second, along with his arousal. She held his gaze, locked in a standstill that made no progress.

With a deep breath, he shot her a shivering look and turned toward the bathroom.

She summoned her pride and remained silent as he walked away, leaving her on the bed with her disparaging thoughts. The door shut behind him, and a moment later, the shower turned on.

Tears threatened as her stomach twisted, but through the churning and lurching, she felt something stronger, more profound. *Longing*.

There was no one more capable of love than Tomas Dine. He'd been devoted to Caroline Milton at a level that had made Rylee envious. At the peak of his sexual prime, years after Caroline's death, he'd remained faithful to her. His emails spoke of nothing but love for the girl.

He'd never blamed her for his pain. Never let her loss define him. He grieved without allowing it to control his life.

If he'd married Caroline, he would've never cheated on her because betraying someone he loved wasn't part of his chemical makeup.

Nine days ago, Rylee drove to Tommy's house with a plan. She wanted to help him move on from his ghosts. But he wasn't the one who needed help.

Her chest constricted, and she rubbed her breastbone.

The truth was there, waiting.

I need help.

I need him.

Deep down, she still dreamed of finding a life partner, someone who loved her enough to be loyal. Faithful.

I found him.

Her winding, battling thoughts went on through his absence and carried through her own shower. He let her have the space, and like a coward, she lingered in the bathroom long after she finished. If she avoided him long enough, he would realize she wasn't worth the effort and seek out someone younger and easier to manage.

A voice in the back of her mind hissed, *You stupid cow. He loves you.*

She hid in the bathroom until her hair was air-dried. Until she was confident he was asleep. He'd been running for days without slowing down. He needed the rest.

Nothing would be decided now.

Wrapped in a towel, she opened the door and froze.

He sat on the floor just outside, his back to the wall and head hanging between his bent knees. Waiting for her.

Her lungs caved in as his golden eyes lifted, searching hers for a specific answer to a specific question.

She clutched her throat. "I hold onto grudges forever."

He rose to his full height, wearing briefs and nothing else.

"Then I'll wait." He held out a hand.

"Forever?"

"For as long as it takes."

Her heart keeled and bucked and pounded, the painful beats speaking to her, telling her something important was within reach, and she should grab it before someone stole it away.

Her damn heart bayed for his.

Fingers trembling, she grasped his hand. He led her to the bed, undressed, and wordlessly slid beneath the covers. She dropped the towel and followed him in.

Their bodies came together on instinct, chest to chest, hips to hips, legs entwined. He held her with arms of corded brawn, his muscular torso and soft, thick cock pressed tight to her body.

She had a full belly, a warm bed, and a beautiful man with his hands wrapped around a part of her she'd never imagined a man would touch again.

Her heart.

"Tommy." She touched his strong, whiskered jaw and sank into the golden rays of his eyes. "I'm your girl."

"From the moment you read my first email." He cupped her face and rested his forehead against hers.

"I need you."

She felt his brows pull together, his muscles tightening around her. Then his hand lowered, drifting down her body to slide between her legs.

"No." She gripped his arm and flattened his hand against her chest. "I need all of you, Tommy. I need *us*. I don't know what that looks like tomorrow or ten years from now, or how our worlds fit together, but knowing you, you already have all that worked out."

"You're mine." His strange expression suggested he was trying out the words, tasting them. "*Mine*."

"And you're mine."

He smiled, a brilliant, lustrous, heart-stopping smile, and caressed his palms along her shoulders. His fingers laced through her hair, and his mouth captured hers, kissing her senseless.

His happiness felt elemental against her lips, stirring a fluttery, whirling, delicious warmth in her chest. They made out without hurry or expectation, touching, kissing, grinning, *living*.

She was reborn in his arms, alive and unrestrained, her emotions unfurling in staggering abandon. So many feelings, sensations, the good and bad, the pain and pleasure, the past and present—all of it mounted and spilled out in a shocking flood. She gave a harsh cry, her body convulsing and belly clenching, untying knots as sobs tumbled from her throat, along with wave after wave of relief.

He held her through it, kissing away her tears. Then he lowered himself onto her, his mouth hungry against hers as he worshiped her, caressed her everywhere, and prepared her to take him.

When he finally pushed inside, it was with slow, rocking thrusts, fitting his hard length deeper, deeper. At last, he hilted himself, bottoming out, filling her with unholy pressure and pure satisfaction. She gasped, then groaned, matching the growls rumbling from his throat.

He paused, their breaths rushing, colliding, eyes locked in wonder.

God, he was so gorgeous—chiseled features, squared jaw, a shadow of sexy stubble, and tousled brown hair dangling over his stern brow.

"You should know," she said, "I might act like all is well, but beneath the surface, I'm dreaming about running my own cartel and pistol-whipping every woman who looks in your direction."

His eyes danced, his smile beaming. "I'll provide all the pistols you need."

By now, she should've been immune to the deep timbre of his voice. But the low, throaty vibrations were as intoxicating as the stretch of his cock.

He circled his hips, forcing her to feel every inch, driving shivers of pleasure through her limbs. Her head fell back. She dragged in air, and his mouth fell upon her throat, licking and kissing and showering her in sparks of love.

Desire stirred along her spine, spreading outward like a slow, burning flame. His strokes caught a timeless rhythm, sinking deep, masterfully controlled and wickedly orchestrated.

He fucked her slowly, loved her thoroughly, his stamina and youth carrying her through hours of unadulterated pleasure. He was a mean son of a bitch, a carnal beast, but without a fog of anger driving their hunger, they took their time and savored the explorations of each other's bodies.

She didn't know how long they played or how many orgasms she'd chased into the rafters. But she knew he was spent when a hoarse groan brought him to a languid, sweat-slick halt.

Rolling to his back, he took her with him. With their bodies still joined, she gently rocked, reluctant to relinquish the motions that brought them so much pleasure.

DOMINATE

Eyes closed, with an arm thrown over his brow, he lay limply beneath her, chuckling softly.

"You're insatiable," he murmured and trailed a knuckle along her thigh.

"Get used to it. I hear women only get hungrier with age."

"Can you have a baby?"

"I don't know." Startled, she slid off of him, staring at his closed eyes. "I've never tried. Can you?"

"Never tried."

"Do you want a baby?"

"I want you." He cracked open an eye, lazily watching her. "Children. No children. Whatever happens, happens. We're going to have an amazing life together."

She nodded, wanting that with a healthy amount of fear and excitement.

Tenderly, she ran her palm down the corrugated ridges of his abs, the skin taut and slick over steel. When she reached the trail of soft, wiry hair, he sighed, relaxed.

As relaxed as his cock. It lay along his thigh, wet with their mingled come, and long. Even flaccid, he was at least seven inches. But she could fit that much into her mouth.

Her fingers moved on their own, encircling him, her mind full of wonderment. She'd spent hours exploring every inch of his body, but this part of him still intimidated her. She hadn't dared to take him into her throat.

She moved between his legs, roving her thumb over the velvety knob. The muscle jerked, but didn't harden.

He lowered his arm, staring at her from beneath hooded lids. "Are you going to suck the life out of me?"

"I'm going to try."

He started to swell in her hand, so she hurried, lowering her head and drawing him into her mouth. The tang of their arousal hit her taste buds, the sound of his grunts spurring her faster.

She lapped and sucked, rushing against the clock as he grew harder and longer against her tongue. This wasn't an act she'd ever been particularly fond of. But the tremors in his thighs, the clench of his hands in the bedding, and his groans... Oh, Jesus, his groans were everything.

Eyes shut tight, he rode out the contractions that rippled along his flat abdomen. *Extraordinary.*

He was too gorgeous, too sexy, too fucking huge in her mouth. But too much of this man was the perfect amount. The perfect amount of gagging, choking, thrusting...

With a growl, he flipped her onto her back and fucked her until neither of them could move.

Then they slept. Hearts beating in sync, bodies entangled, blissfully content, they slept until nightfall.

She woke in the dimly lit room, dying of thirst. Tommy didn't stir beside her.

Careful not to disturb him, she slipped from the bed, dressed in the bathroom, and crept into the hall in search of something to drink.

Voices drifted from the living room at the far end. Soft whispers. The team was awake.

She wasn't keen on facing a gang of armed criminals alone. But if she wanted a life with Tommy, they would have to accept her. She would have to trust them.

Steeling her spine, she adjusted her t-shirt and jeans and strode down the hall.

Halfway there, a partially opened door gave her pause. Light glowed from within, the flooring different from the rest of the house. Polished hardwoods.

No furniture was visible through the crack. Was that…a mirrored wall?

She shifted, stealing another angle, and spotted Cole sitting on the floor near the back wall, surrounded by beer bottles.

Curiosity and concern pulled her closer. She opened the door.

A dance room. Holy shit, it was beautiful. Massive. Twelve-foot-tall seamless windows soared to the rafters. Mirrors covered the other walls, and ballet bars wrapped the entire room. There was a lounge area with a leather couch, a built-in stereo system, and a dancing pole in the back corner.

All built for the dancer who was tattooed on his arm.

Her heart sank to her stomach.

Cole glanced at his watch and dropped his head back against the wall, eyes shut. "Forty-five seconds."

"What?"

"There's a rumor going around that Tomas is packing a ten-inch dick."

The random comments gave her whiplash. "It's not a rumor."

He nodded, finished off his beer, and grabbed two more. "Want one?"

"Sure?" Uncertain, she left the door cracked behind her and joined him on the floor.

They drank in silence.

DOMINATE

Out of the corner of her eye, she watched him look around the room, his eyes flickering as if he were tracking an invisible dancer as she swayed through her routine, her feet scuffing and bouncing across the shiny flooring.

Shadows crept over his expression, and he blinked, looking away.

"Do you want to talk about her?"

"Nope." He popped the *P*.

"How long has it been, Cole?"

How long have you been hurting?

"She married my best friend seven years ago." He tipped his beer toward the door, his voice gruff. "Your forty-five seconds has arrived."

She followed his gaze and found Tommy standing on the threshold.

TWENTY-THREE

Tomas couldn't ignore the territorial feeling in his gut as he took in the unexpected room filled with ballet bars, mirrored walls, empty beer bottles, and his girl.

His gorgeous girl. Swigging beer. With the only single man in the house.

Yeah. He was feeling territorial. They'd just made a monumental step in a fragile, new relationship, and she'd sneaked out of their bed to chug beers with this guy.

Drawing in a deep breath, he slowed his roll and leaned a shoulder against the door frame.

Rylee sat on the floor with her legs crossed, her gaze ticking between him and Cole before settling on Cole. "Forty-five seconds...?"

"The time it took Tomas to throw on his clothes and chase after you." Cole rested an arm on his bent knee, a beer bottle dangling from his hand. "I know the drill. I used to be just like him."

"You used to be overbearing, unpleasantly arrogant, heavy-handed, and moody?" A twinkle lit her eyes.

"All of that and worse," Cole said, expressionless.

"He still is." Tomas slipped his fingers into the pockets of his jeans, fighting the urge to drag her back to bed.

They had a lot of work to do—phone tracking, computer hacking, and high-tech spying—that heavily relied on Cole's expertise. The man shouldn't be drinking, but Tomas wasn't here to nag him. The guy was dependable.

"Do you want me to leave?" she asked Cole.

"I don't care what you do." He leaned back against the wall, settling in with a long draw from his beer.

Turning toward Tomas, she shot him a look that said she wasn't budging from this room. And she wasn't asking him to stay.

The instinct to haul her out and spank her ass warred with all logic and reason. He needed to eat. His friends were already gathering in the living room, and he trusted her.

Proving it, he gave her a smile that caught on her face. She smiled back, and he shifted away, heading toward the kitchen.

As he stepped out of the hallway and around the corner, he paused, tensing.

Across the room, Lucia stood near the windows, crying in Tiago's arms.

What the fuck?

He searched the living room and found Tate sitting off to the side, perched on the edge off a chair. Leaning over his lap, he braced his elbows on his knees, head down, and eyes up, watching the bizarre embrace like a hawk.

Tiago didn't look up, didn't say a word. His attention was engrossed in the weeping woman he held. Lucia wasn't a crier, so to see her sniveling softly against the madman's chest, to witness him gently shushing her, stroking a hand over her hair, and hugging her tight, it was fucking weird.

And heartening.

It was a good sign if Tate wasn't interfering. He didn't look pleased, but he wasn't tearing off Tiago's arms, either.

Everyone knew Tiago harbored a deep affection for Lucia. Nothing like what he felt with Kate. But he and Lucia shared a history. An ugly, brutal history of lies and deception. He'd poisoned her for years. She'd smashed his head in with a lead weight, and through it all, he'd kept her alive, protecting her from enemies and allies in his dark underworld.

Lucia leaned back and wiped her cheeks. Tiago released her, clasped his hands behind him, and stared down at her, speaking softly.

Their relationship was a twisty, complicated knot to unravel, but they appeared to be making progress.

Tomas veered toward the kitchen, grabbed a sandwich from the fridge, and spotted the others outside. Leaving Tate to supervise Tiago and Lucia, Tomas stepped out onto the terrace.

The evening autumn air chilled his skin. Not cold, but so very different than the desert.

Liv, Van, and Luke sat around a table, deep in conversation about the mission that Matias and Camila just finished in Mexico. Another sex trafficking ring annihilated.

The thought brought a smile to his face. Fuck, he loved his job.

Lowering into the chair beside Van, he wolfed down the turkey sandwich and admired the exterior view of the massive one-story manor. Veneered in stone, it wrapped around several outdoor living spaces with walkways that led into the woods.

From the largest terrace, a bridge arched over a ravine, providing access to the covered dock on the lake below. A vista of forest and high bluffs surrounded the calm inlet of water. It was majestic and comforting and felt almost as secure as Matias' fortress in the Amazon rainforest.

"Where's Rylee?" Luke asked.

"Talking to Cole. Did you know he has a full-blown dance room down the hall?"

"Not surprised." Liv leaned back in the chair. "The tattoo is telling."

"Are you surprised by his pushy bid to join our team?"

"He's already with us." Liv shrugged.

"He just wants us to recognize that." Van tapped a toothpick on the table.

"Why? What does he get out of it?"

"Purpose. Belonging." Luke stretched out an arm, indicating the sprawling mansion. "This was built as a safe house. He told me that he used to let people in his profession stay here to recharge and regroup. He gave up that job for a girl, lost the girl, and now all he has is the house. A nine-bedroom estate with gear and tech, designed for people like us. He supports our cause, trusts us enough to bring us here. We give him purpose. A place to belong."

"Makes sense." Tomas looked at Van. "You recruited him how long ago?"

"Six years." Van met Liv's eyes. "When I hunted down Traquero."

Traquero, the slave buyer who brutally raped Liv in front of Josh.

When Van had learned about the assault, he lost his fucking mind and dismantled his sex slave operation. Then he hired Cole to find Traquero so Van could kill the monster, which he did. *Gruesomely.*

Cole didn't show up again until a year ago, when Tate hired him to locate Lucia and retrieve her from Tiago's clutches.

"What do you think we're dealing with, Tommy?" Luke scraped a hand through his messy red hair, his gaze focused. "This can't just be about a jealous ex-husband."

"Occam's razor. The simplest explanation is usually the right one, and the simplest explanation is Mason Sutton." The tension at the base of his skull disagreed. "I feel like we're overlooking something. Can't put my finger on it."

DOMINATE

"If Rylee hasn't told anyone about the bridge except you," Luke said, "how did the hitman know about it? What does it have to do with anything?"

"We won't know those answers until we have a motivation. We need the hitman's identity and that of who hired him."

"That's Cole's expertise." Van reclined back, propping a socked foot on his knee. "Depending on who's behind this, it could take weeks to uncover."

"I talked to Matias an hour ago." Luke traced a finger along the edge of the table. "If this gets drawn out, he and Camila will fly in with the rest of the team."

His friends were restless, itching for action and the thrill of a fight. And missing their other halves.

"We need to put our heads together." Tomas scratched his jaw, gathering his thoughts. "Paul Kissinger started watching Rylee six months ago. Three months before that, she filed a protective order again Mason. Paul found me through a tracking device on her truck. A standard device that is widely available. Far different than the tech that was planted in her house."

"Do we know when that tech was planted?" Liv asked.

"Recently. The components are so new that Cole has never seen its kind before."

Her eyes hardened. "Do you think we're dealing with two unrelated threats?"

"The hitman made contact with Paul's phone. We're still waiting on the analysis from the call logs, but we know there's a connection."

"It could be a criminal Rylee testified against," Luke said. "Or a family member of one of those criminals. Someone with a vendetta against her."

"Or it could be any of the hundreds of traffickers we've taken out. We never leave loose ends, but mistakes happen."

"Whoever this is, they're not after your emails. Rylee's house hasn't been ransacked. No one seems to be searching for the copies she made."

"Unless they already have them." His insides tightened.

Her house was compromised. At some point, very soon, he needed to get those email copies and talk to her about selling the property and moving to Colombia.

He went back and forth with his friends for the next hour. The conversation circled, discarding theories and forming new ones. Eventually, Tate rapped on the window, announcing dinner, and they moved the discussion inside.

Tate and Lucia had prepared a spread of Mexican food—enchiladas, tacos, and other fixings Tomas could name.

Cole breezed around the large dining table, setting up numerous laptops, printers, phones, and other electronics.

Behind him, Rylee stood at a giant whiteboard that had been wheeled in on a stand. The marker in her hand flew across the surface, listing evidence and timelines, drawing diagrams, and collating links between people, places, and events.

While the seductive shape of her ass in those jeans tried to steal his attention, it was her mind that held him rapt, gripped in a state of awe. She'd managed to organize the tangle of conversations he'd just exchanged with his friends into an orderly, concise illustration.

As she worked, he made them both plates of food. Cole hadn't stopped messing with his equipment to eat, so Tomas made a plate for him, too.

Setting the heaping dishes on the table, he approached her back and dragged his nose through her soft hair. "You've done this before."

"Well, I've spent a lot of time holed up in cubicles with detectives, but they don't use evidence boards like this. Everything goes into advanced computer programs. It's a more efficient way to connect findings."

She tapped the marker on her chin, staring at her work. Her other hand absently drifted behind her to rest on his hip. It was a simple thing, just a casual touch, but it meant so much more. It was familiarity, comfort, and connection. It was everything.

"Right now, the one currency we have to work with is time," she said. "There isn't a serial killer on the loose or an abducted person held somewhere. No one's breathing down our necks. So I thought the board would be helpful to kick around ideas."

"Is this what you were discussing with Cole?"

"No." She laughed uncomfortably and turned around, her eyes watching Cole head toward the hall for more supplies. "I talked to him about you, me, my failed marriage, and the woman he built that dance room for. Relationship stuff. I did the talking. He indulged me by not kicking me out."

"He was listening." He stroked his thumb across her pillowy lips. "Listening to a beautiful, brilliant psychologist."

"Oh, my God." She laughed again. "I'm a terrible therapist. Therapists *listen*."

"You listened to me."

"And changed my major because I thought I could fix things." She touched his face, his gaze soft with affection. "Some things don't need to be fixed." With a small smile, she turned back to the board. "*This* has always been my dream. Investigation. Profiling. Criminal justice."

"You're in the right place for that. With us. I know it's too soon to make demands—"

She snorted. "You've been making demands since day one."

"Quit your job."

"Done."

"Just like that?"

"I took a sabbatical because I hate that fucking job. The detectives pull me into their sit-downs when they have questions, but I'm never part of the analysis or action. I watch from the sidelines, bored out of my mind. When I drove into the desert, I was searching for so many things. A new life, friendship, happiness, possibilities…" She pressed her lips against his chest. "*You*."

He was a goner. Utterly, completely lost for this woman.

Pulling her close, he wrapped his arms around her and scoured his fumbling brain for something profound to say. "This is nice."

Lame.

"This *is* nice." She hugged his waist and perched her chin on his breastbone, smiling up at him. "I love the growly, aggressive, tough-guy thing you have going on, but it's also nice to just be able to touch you like this, to hold you without expectation or agenda."

Dishes clinked, voices murmured, boots scuffed—the din of family coming together for a meal.

He held her until she pulled away, turning back to her evidence board.

"Eat." He grabbed her shoulders and turned her toward the table.

She sat with a harrumph and ate with a smile in her eyes.

Cole returned a moment later, found his plate, and carried it to the board.

"This is great, Rylee." He took in her detailed lists and diagrams, the fork absently digging into his food. Then he went still. "What is this?"

"What?" Rylee wiped her mouth and joined him at the board.

"These words." Cole pointed the fork at the guesswork she'd made from the hitman's dying gibberish. "What does this mean? The bridge?"

"That's what he said. I don't know." She stood taller, defensive, her expression tightening. "He said he was there because of the bridge. The rest…I don't know. It sounded like Thursday or thirsty or—"

"Thurney." Cole's whisper shuddered the air, and the plate in his hand slowly tipped.

"Yes. That's it. What—?" She grabbed the dish as it tumbled, unable to stop its descent. "Shit!"

Enchiladas and dishware exploded across the floor, but Tomas wasn't interested in the mess. He was interested in Cole's stark, ghost-white expression as the man spun, scanning the room for something.

"What does Thurney mean, Cole?" Tomas stood, his adrenaline spiking.

Cole's shell-shocked eyes landed on a pile of burner phones. He snatched one and turned away as he punched in a number and held it to his ear.

Who the fuck was he calling?

In the next breath, he barked into the phone, "Call me back on a secure line."

He hung up and stared at the device as muscles flexed across his back.

"Cole." Liv broke the silence. "What's going on?"

The phone buzzed, and Cole lifted it to his ear. "Your location?" A pause. "Lock it down. Where is she?" He gripped his hair, his voice plunging into a seething roar. "Fucking get her. Bring her to the safe house!" He pivoted, pacing, listening to whoever was on the other end. Then he slammed to a stop. "No, goddammit. I want her *here*. It's Thurney. Yeah, you heard me. I'll be in touch."

He disconnected, and a sharp, icy hush lanced through the room. Tomas didn't breathe. No one did as Cole stood frozen, staring at nothing.

Then he turned toward the table, slowly, too calmly, and slammed the phone down on the surface, smashing it into pieces. A collective flinch rippled the air.

"Thurney Bridge." Cole raised his eyes, divisive and chilling. "It's where I lost my life."

TWENTY-FOUR

A thousand questions piled up as Tomas put together everything he knew about Cole Hartman. It wasn't much. The man had more secrets than friends.

One question was answered, though. Thurney Bridge, wherever that was, wasn't Rylee's bridge.

As that detail clicked into place, her lips parted, her gorgeous silver eyes round and glassy. She had nothing to do with this. At least, not at the foundation.

Someone had connected her to Cole and put a hit on her.

Why? Who *was* Cole Hartman?

Tomas had learned some things about the man over the past two weeks, but nothing about losing his life on Thurney Bridge. Except he remembered a conversation they'd had in the desert.

I was sent out in the field for a while. Mistakes were made, and I was forced to fake my death to protect her. By the time I cleaned up the mess, quit the job, and returned home to her, she'd fallen in love with my best friend.

Whatever Cole was mixed up in—then and now—put Rylee and the entire team at risk.

"Are we safe?" Tomas met Cole's eyes. "Right now, in your house, are we safe?"

"Yes." Cole straightened and ran his hands down his face. "This is the safest place in the world." He surveyed the room, taking in the disbelieving expressions around the table, and sighed. "The man I just called was my handler. He was also my best friend until he married my fiancée."

"That sounds deliciously nasty." Van didn't smile.

"The point is, while Danni is no longer my..." Cole's hand clenched. "While she's no longer mine, I still protect her. She was a target during my last mission. A mission that ended with me taking a bullet on Thurney Bridge. Now she's in danger again, and there's nowhere I'd rather her be than in this house."

Tomas was surprised to finally hear the name of the mysterious woman who'd leveled Cole's world.

"Is she coming here?" Rylee tilted her pretty head, concern softening her eyes. "Did your best friend agree to bring her?"

"No." One word and Cole's face clouded over.

"Let's go back to the bullet," Tomas said. "Is that when you faked your death?"

"Yeah. I was wearing bullet-resistant clothing. High-tech stuff." Cole tapped his sternum. "The bullet broke skin, fractured ribs, but didn't enter my body. I fell into the river below and swam out of sight. If I hadn't faked my death, the perpetrator would've killed Danni."

"Where's the perpetrator now?" Rylee asked.

"She's in prison. *That* is a fact I can one-hundred-percent guarantee. I monitor her status. She'll never see daylight again."

"You were shot by a woman?" She arched a brow.

"She was my partner," he growled, his eyes dark and murky. "A traitor to the agency."

"Which agency?" Tomas leaned over the table. "No more secrets, Cole."

"Those aren't my secrets. It's classified, and sharing classified information is punishable by law."

Tiago's dark laugh turned all heads toward the corner of the kitchen, which was darkened merely by his presence and the deadly look in his eyes. "You can't scare this group with threats of your law."

"It's not my law."

"Who the fuck cares? The only law we follow is our own. You're one of us. Now tell us what you were involved in."

"Espionage."

"We need more than that," Liv sang in an eerily melodic voice that crashed into a spine-tingling command. "Trust us, Cole."

Cole paced to the windows and laced his fingers behind his neck. The entire room seemed to strain toward him, tense with anticipation.

He made them wait, building the silence into a volatile, rumbling thunderstorm. Fingers drummed. Shoes tapped. Molars sawed. Patience thinned.

At last, Cole turned and faced them, decision made.

DOMINATE

"I retired from a special unit, a clandestine group, that goes by many names." He folded his hands behind him, feet braced apart, voice monotone. "OGA, ISA, Optimized Talent, Gray Fox... Whenever there's a classified spill, the designator changes. But those inside refer to it as the *activity*. I was a deep undercover operative, deployed to foreign nations to collect information. *Crucial* information. The kind that changes the outcome of wars. Or prevents them, as it were." He rolled his neck, cracking it. "I was the eyes and ears in the shadows, and I was fucking good at it. Until Thurney."

Tomas' head pounded as he came to terms with what they were dealing with. The Freedom Fighters had taken down some scary motherfuckers, solidified a trusted relationship with the Restrepo Cartel, and learned the ins and outs of the criminal underground. But top-secret espionage and government corruption? This was way out of their league.

"What happened on Thurney Bridge?" he asked.

"I was embedded deep within the enemy's ranks. But the enemy, as it turned out, was my partner. She was ambitious and power-hungry and turned her back on her country to make some money." He gripped his neck. "Everyone connected to her was apprehended. No stone left unturned. The *activity* was thorough in this."

"Not thorough enough," Van drawled. "Someone knows about Thurney and put a hit on Rylee, who happens to know everything there is to know about us."

"I can't even begin to guess who it is or what they want." Cole's gaze swept over the laptops and gear that littered the long table. "I need to sit down, pore through the findings, and make decisions on how to proceed."

"*We* need to do that." Tomas pointed a finger around the room. "We're not from your world, and we don't know shit about your tech. But we're your team now. Train us. Put us to work."

"All right." Cole nodded, his expression thoughtful, maybe even relieved. A split-second later, he snapped into full-on work mode. "We need to scrape through every detail of my last mission. Identify the actors—enemies, allies, informants, and everyone in between—and run a cross-connection between those actors and Mason Sutton, Paul Kissinger, and Daniel Millstreet."

"Daniel Millstreet?" Rylee asked.

"The cunt you killed in the motel room. I received confirmation on his identity an hour ago." He strode toward the mess of food he'd dropped on the floor.

"I'll get it." Tomas held out his hand, itching for something to do. "You'll tell us how you found his name?"

"I'll *show* you everything."

TWENTY-FIVE

Over the next two weeks, Tomas sat side by side with his team, absorbed in congressional documents, private phone records, and handwritten reports of Cole's undercover missions. Handwritten by Cole. Godawful penmanship. The scrawl was so terrible it made Tomas' eyes cross. It was also really goddamn impressive.

Under U.S. law, Cole couldn't make copies of briefings or anything related to his job. But on the heels of each operation, he'd written everything down by memory, filed it meticulously, and kept the notes in his armory.

Cole hadn't just given them the key to his entire life. He'd literally put details of national security in their hands. In the filthy hands of vigilante criminals.

If that didn't say *trust*, nothing did.

The first week of digging through reports was an eye-opening experience, the entire team engrossed in their newfound knowledge of government inner-workings.

The classified intel didn't interest Tomas, but it opened a portal into Cole's extraordinarily unique skill set. Bottom line, Cole was a master at milking information. He knew how to talk to informants, manipulate dangerous adversaries, and use social engineering to obtain what he needed.

He no longer had access to government systems and confidential records, but he never needed that access. He only had to identify who had the access and massage them into unknowingly leaking the information he was after.

That had been the core of his job in the *activity*. He slipped behind enemy lines, deep undercover, and went to work, befriending and inveigling.

That was how he'd learned the identity of the hitman. He'd convinced someone, a lot of someones, to feed him innocuous pieces of information until he had enough to put it all together.

Fucking mind-blowing.

Tomas pushed back from the table and rubbed his hands down his face. He'd been bent over documents for hours, and the words were blurring. Stiffness knotted his neck, and his body screamed for exercise.

The house was equipped with a weight room, and they all used it daily. But they weren't accustomed to this type of work. They were the feet on the ground, the fingers on the triggers, and muscle on the front lines. They weren't analysts.

Cole sat beside him, flicking that coin-shaped GSM bug between his fingers, eyes on his laptop. He'd been focused on the bug's technical components, reaching out to unknown contacts, subtly asking around about it, and collecting data. He was convinced the tech in that device held all their answers.

Tomas looked around the living space, taking in the bodies sprawled on couches and chairs, holding laptops and reading through reports. In the kitchen, Tiago and Van prepared lunch while arguing the finer points on how to properly chop cilantro.

Definitely not a typical day for this group. But not once in two weeks had anyone suggested going home.

They didn't know who the enemy was, what this entity wanted, or if it had anything to do with them. Maybe his emails were out there somewhere in the hands of someone who intended to exploit them. Maybe his emails didn't factor in at all.

It didn't matter. They were here, sticking together like wet on water.

His gaze fastened on his favorite brunette across the room. She lay face-down on a rug, her fingers clicking on a laptop and legs bent, rocking her delicate feet in the air. It was a girlish thing to do, reminiscent of Caroline lounging lazily on his bed. But that was the only similarity between the two.

The feelings Rylee stirred in him were so much deeper, darker, and deliciously grown-up.

He rose from the chair and prowled toward her. She hummed as he stretched out over her prone body, bracing his hands on either side of her shoulders and lowering into a push-up position.

"Take a break," he said at her ear.

"I could use some fresh air."

Outside, they took the bridge that led from the terrace to the dock below. The tree-lined shores wrapped around calm water that stretched for miles. Several boats bobbed on the horizon, too far to venture near this inlet.

As they made their way to the water's edge, her hand slipped into his, and he felt a pull in his chest, a breath of undiluted happiness.

At the end of the dock, benches faced the water. He lowered onto one and guided her onto his lap, wrapping his arms around her, warming her skin in the chilly air.

He'd fucked her on this very bench yesterday. Over the past two weeks, he'd taken her in every corner of this property, in every position. His need for her was unquenchable, and she had the enthusiasm to match.

Being cooped up together had given them a lot of time to explore. Not just their bodies. He'd never been one to vocalize his feelings, but she had a way of opening him up and riling not only his temper but also his fears, joys, and hardest memories.

She'd demanded to hear every detail of his mission with La Rocha Cartel in California, including an explanation about the girl on the meat hook. He didn't want to revisit that, but after he shared the story, he realized he could tell her anything. Not just in an email, but in person, while looking into her eyes.

It was another first for him.

They talked a lot, argued plenty, and sometimes, they communicated without saying anything at all.

She curled up on his lap, her nose buried in his neck, choosing the view of him over the stunning vista of the lake. She loved him. The words hadn't left her lips, but he felt them. He felt them in the weight of her stare, the caress of her constant touch, and the sigh of her breaths.

She leaned up, her gaze fastening on his. "I'm going to sell my house."

"Okay."

"I'll need a place to live."

"I'm your home."

She nodded, smiled, and her chin quivered.

He kissed her lips. "Scary, huh?"

She nodded again.

Her dirtbag of an ex-husband had put that fear in her.

Deep down, he hoped that Mason Sutton was behind the hit on her so that he would have an excuse to murder the son of a bitch. He might just gut the fucker anyway.

"Which is scarier?" he asked. "Living with me? Or living alone?"

"I don't want to live without you, so I'll take the scary. I'll take whatever comes as long as I'm with you."

"I know you will."

He kissed her, deeper this time. Then he removed her clothes and filled her until every drop of fear deserted her.

The fear would return again, and when it did, he would fight it with her. Fuck it out of her. Break through it piece by piece.

With every word, every touch, every passing hour, they were moving forward. Together.

Two days later, they were sharing an early breakfast alone in the kitchen when Cole darted in from the hall, carrying a laptop.

"I found the last link." He set the device on the table and pointed at the screen, his eyes tired and bloodshot.

"The *last* link?" Tomas knew Cole was making progress with the data they'd collected, but he had no idea how close they were. He squinted at the screen, which displayed some kind of ledger. "What am I looking at?"

"Mason Sutton's bank records."

"We already scoured those."

"This isn't his personal bank account." Rylee leaned over Tomas' shoulder, eyes on the laptop. "These are financial records for his orthopedic practice. I can't believe you got your hands on this."

"Look." Cole moved the mouse, highlighting a ten-thousand-dollar withdrawal listed under miscellaneous. "Six months ago, he wired this money to another account." He switched the screen to Paul Kissinger's bank records. "There. Ten-thousand dollars came into Paul's account on the same day."

"Goddammit!" Rylee straightened, her eyes aglow with fire. "Mason paid that man ten-thousand dollars? To do what? Kill me?"

"No," Cole said. "Mason hired Paul to watch you and report back your activities, specifically who you were fucking. That's all Paul did until the night Tomas left him in the desert."

The night Paul tried to rape Rylee.

A torrent of emotions flooded Tomas' chest, but regret from killing that man wasn't one of them.

"Mason didn't put a hit on me." Rylee released a slow breath and lowered into the chair beside him.

"I'm still going to kill him." Tomas gripped her knee.

"No, you're not." She ground her teeth. "I'm really fucking angry that he hired someone to stalk me for six months, but you're not going to kill him, Tommy. He's not worth the effort." She turned back to Cole. "How is Paul Kissinger connected to the hitman?"

"He's not. Paul was a run-of-the-mill private detective, skirting around the law and doing dirty jobs to make an extra buck. No question, he was a sleazeball, but he had nothing to do with the hitman." Cole looked at Tomas. "Daniel Millstreet worked for someone else, and he arrived in Texas on the same day that I did."

"How do you know?" Tomas asked.

"Data from the phone we found on his body. Someone dispatched him to Texas. For one reason only."

"To kill you?"

"No. To kill everyone close to me, starting with Rylee."

Her eyes widened. "I didn't even know you before all this started."

"They bugged your house the day you drove to the desert. The moment you walked into Tomas' life, they connected you to me." Cole paced in front of the evidence board, motioning at it. "I've been linking all the data you collected, putting the findings together, and the facts are these." He stopped and met their eyes. "Someone from my past, someone related to Thurney Bridge, wants to hurt me or pull information from me. Maybe both. If they wanted to kill me, they would've sent the hitman after me, not Rylee. I've been in hiding for the past seven years, retired from the *activity*, and they've been patient, waiting for me to return to the United States."

"You've been outside the country all this time?" Tomas pressed his fingers to his brow. "No, wait. You were here a year ago when Tate contacted you."

"I came here twice for Tate, staying only hours each time. And I joined the rescue mission last month to retrieve Luke and Vera in California. Again, I was in and out within hours. This visit is the longest I've been stateside in seven years."

"Why?"

"I've always worked abroad, and I'm always working." Cole released a slow breath. "Someone has been waiting a long damn time for me to return, and they know I'm connected to you."

The hairs rose on Tomas' nape. "They've been watching my house."

"Yes. They knew when we turned up there. You, me, Rylee, and Paul Kissinger." Cole resumed pacing. "The hitman called Paul's phone when he showed up at your house, which suggests that Paul was on the hitlist. Good thing, because that's how I was able to track the hitman's location the night he found Rylee."

"Jesus." Tomas leaned back in the chair, his mind spinning.

"I assume they have eyes on Mason Sutton and Detective Hodge, too." At Rylee's gasp, Cole shook his head. "If they were in danger, they would already be dead. Whoever is watching knows you're not close to them."

"Evan..." Her face fell, and she dropped her head in her hands. "Oh, God, they killed him."

Because she was close to him.

Tomas reached for her, pulled her onto his lap, and rested his lips against her brow.

"I was able to trace the tech on this." Cole held up the GSM bug he'd removed from her house. "Bad news. It's only available to the *activity*."

"What are you saying?" Tomas froze, because he knew. He knew exactly what that meant.

"Someone on the inside is behind this." Cole's expression contorted, etched with barely concealed rage. "Someone inside my old group is after me."

"Someone you know?"

"Maybe. They could be retired, still employed, a rogue, who fucking knows? It's a long, classified list." His lips curled into a smile void of humanity and mercy.

"I don't know if I like that look on your face." Tomas tipped up a brow. "I take it you have a plan."

"I'm going hunting."

TWENTY-SIX

Two weeks later, Rylee followed Tomas up the stairs that led to the top floor of her house in Eldorado, Texas. Every room had been swept for bugs and threats, the property deemed safe by Cole and the team. But her spine tingled anyway, her mood sullen and twitchy.

The place writhed with memories of Evan. She hadn't loved him, and in her heart, she'd said goodbye the day she drove away and left him standing on the porch. But he was a good man, an amazing friend, and hadn't deserved to die.

Pushing away those thoughts, she rubbed her chest and focused on her future.

Her future looked delicious as he strode down the hall in front of her, his gait steady and confident, his muscles flexing through the glide of his strides. Corded arms, narrow waist, chiseled ass—he was sexual heat and male potency, dominance and devotion, utterly loyal and all hers.

Turning his neck, he glanced over his shoulder. Eyes of gold, reflecting the color of his heart.

He wasn't always good-natured, but that mighty heart of his made hers beat like nothing ever had before.

"This closet?" He paused at the door at the end of the hall.

"Yep."

He opened the door to shelves of towels and cleaning supplies. "Where is it?"

"If you were a bad guy—"

He gave her a glare that closed her throat.

"Fine." She coughed. "Since you *are* a bad guy, where would you look for a thumb drive?"

DOMINATE

"Not in a linen closet." He glanced at the other doors. "I would search the underwear drawer first."

"Of course, you would. Panty-sniffer." She crossed her arms. "But I already told you it was in the linen closet."

He scanned the bottles of cleaning products and random clutter, his expression quickly transforming into boredom.

"You win." He grabbed her, lifted her off her feet, and kissed her hard on the mouth. "Show me where you hid it."

Wriggling out of his arms, she removed the vacuum from the closet and opened the dirt bin.

"You're kidding?" His brows climbed, widening his eyes. "How have you not accidentally thrown it away?"

"I don't use this vacuum. It's broken." She dug through the powdered dirt in the collector, removed the tiny stick, and blew off the debris. "My working vacuum is downstairs."

She handed him the thumb drive, which contained all the photographed copies of his emails. Nine years' worth. She'd started snapping pictures of his messages after his captivity in Van's attic.

"Have you ever gone back and reread them?" He palmed the thumb drive, regarding her with affection.

"Never needed to. Your words stuck inside me on the first read-through."

His lips tipped up, taking hers with them. They stared at each other. Smiled at each other. Stared some more. These were her favorite moments, the private eye contact they shared. It wasn't a game to see who would look away first. It was a game to see who would *move* first.

This time, they moved as one, coming together with arms, breaths, and open mouths. He backed her against the wall, and she gripped his hair with greedy hands as his tongue chased hers, caressing and rubbing and drowning her in warmth.

The potency of his kiss was enormous, his love even greater. She threw her arms about his neck, mouths locked, holding him close, knowing she would never let him go.

When their lips melted into panting sighs, he touched their brows together. "The team is waiting."

Everyone had left Missouri to return to Texas. They weren't in her house, but they were in the neighborhood, in the shadows, watching and waiting.

Cole had a crazy plan, which involved baiting and hunting his unknown adversary. This stop at her house was just a detour to grab the thumb drive and her personal belongings.

She was going with them, wherever that took her. It was terrifying and thrilling, but for the first time in her life, she'd found her home.

"I forgive you." She slid her nose astride his.

"I forgive you, too." He dropped the thumb drive on the floor between them and crushed it with his boot.

"I need you."

"I need you, too."

"I love you."

A rush of air escaped his lips, and he grinned. "Wow, that's a great feeling." His grin widened. "I love you, too."

They were back to staring and smiling again.

"You," she breathed.

"No, you."

"How much time do we have?"

"Not enough." He checked his watch. "Twenty minutes."

Someone, probably Cole, had decided this was the ideal window of time to enter her house. She needed to pack the few things she wanted to keep. The rest would be donated and the keys turned over to a real estate company.

"Twenty minutes." He kissed her lips and stepped back. "Pack what you want from the bedrooms. I'll do the downstairs."

"You don't know what I want to keep."

"You sure about that?" He winged up a brow.

"I'll check your work."

With a chuckle, he pocketed the broken thumb drive and ambled toward the stairs. She watched him go with a flutter of hummingbirds in her belly.

He stopped on the top step and gave her a strange look.

"What?" she asked.

"I live a crazy, filthy, dangerous life."

"I know."

"Reading about it in emails isn't the same as living it. I make decisions and do things that sane people would never fathom."

"In case you didn't notice, I'm not the sanest person in the world. You're not going to scare me away."

"Prove it."

"Oh, I will." She pushed back her shoulders.

He nodded, smiled, and vanished down the stairs.

Maybe he was a bad guy, but he'd committed acts of bravery and self-sacrifice and made inconceivable progress in his efforts to decimate human sex trafficking. His victories weren't celebrated or recognized in the news. No one knew what he and his team did in the shadows of the underworld.

Many might consider him a ruthless thug. A villain, even. But in her eyes, he was an unsung hero.

DOMINATE

Her hero.

Nightfall darkened her bedroom. She turned on the lights and went to work, sorting through clothes and collecting keepsakes. She didn't own much, hadn't kept anything from her life with Mason.

When her twenty minutes were up, she'd filled five large duffel bags. Grabbing two, she made her way downstairs.

She dropped the bags in the entry, turned the corner into the living room, and slammed to a stop.

Masked men. Armed. Three of them, all aiming rifles at a naked man who was gagged and restrained on her couch.

It takes three seconds to make a life-or-death decision.

She blinked, paralyzed, unable to believe her eyes.

Mason.

His bulging, watery gaze fastened on her, his cries muted behind a wad of cloth. Rope bound his arms and legs, crisscrossed his chest, and tied around the sofa.

Why was he in her house? Why the fuck was he naked?

Where was Tommy?

Her heart sprinted as she jerked her attention to the three gunmen. Black ski masks covered their faces and hair. Black jeans and shirts molded to muscular builds.

Familiar statures.

Safe.

The masked head in the middle turned in her direction, staring through the narrow eye opening. She knew him intimately, from the tips of those boots to the glint in those golden eyes.

She pressed her lips together, angry, worried, and intrigued.

Don't say his name.

Whatever this was, he'd masked himself to remain anonymous. Every word she spoke in front of Mason would need to be chosen carefully.

Looking closer at the other two men, she recognized Van's arrogant posture and Luke's towering height.

Tommy, Van, and Luke. Masked and armed. Terrorizing her ex-husband.

A sheen of sweat glistened on Mason's body. His belly, softer and rounder than she remembered, quivered with the heave of his muffled sobs. His dick shriveled between his legs as if retreating in fear.

The team wouldn't have lured him here. It was too risky. If she had to guess, he'd showed up unannounced to pester her *again* about coming back to him.

He didn't have Paul Kissinger to report her activity. She'd quit her job—a phone call she'd made two weeks ago—and she'd vanished after she'd called him from the motel room last month.

He had no way to track her anymore. But the team was tracking *him*.

They would've known he left El Paso, which was a five-hour drive away. The window of time to pack up her house made sense now. Tommy knew Mason was coming and wanted to make sure they were here when her ex showed up.

For what purpose?

It took her a few seconds to put this much together and another few seconds to force her feet into the living room.

Tommy's eyes followed her, studying her reaction.

She'd told him not to kill Mason, but she'd never put a limit on anything else. Threats? Torture? There were many levels of pain.

Blood whooshed through her veins as she stepped closer.

Mason bucked and thrashed, howling soundlessly behind the gag. From his perspective, they were both in danger. There were armed, masked men in her house, and he couldn't protect her.

Fuck him. He'd given up that right ten years ago. Besides, if she were truly in danger, he was helpless, naked, and shaking in terror. She would have to save *him*.

She paused by the couch and looked at Tommy expectantly.

Your move.

He lowered the rifle. Then he lowered into the chair behind him.

Van and Luke spread out, taking up positions on either side of him, guns trained on Mason.

"You hired Paul Kissinger to monitor this woman." Tommy leaned forward, his mouth moving behind the mask. "Paul got a better offer and handed off the job to us."

Mason's eyes widened, and his thrashing went ballistic.

She remained quiet, uncertain where Tommy was going with this lie.

"I want my payment in advance." Tommy turned his cruel glare on her. "Undress."

Her heart stopped, and her limbs turned to ice.

What was he doing?

I make decisions and do things that sane people would never fathom.

That conversation had been deliberate. He was warning her. Testing her.

Was this a test?

He reclined in the chair and lowered his zipper. The fly opened, exposing the thick, swelling root of his cock.

DOMINATE

Sex was the destination. In front of Mason, Van, and Luke, he expected her to undress and ride his lap.

I live a crazy, filthy, dangerous life.

His team lived openly in their sexuality. They had monogamous partners now, but they hadn't started that way. Tommy had watched Luke fuck Vera in California. Van had fucked half of the guys. They weren't shy about sex. If she was going to live with them, this couldn't be a sticking point.

It wasn't. Not for her.

She looked at Mason, taking in his traumatized misery.

This wasn't a test. It was punishment. Revenge. Tommy had set this up for Mason, the man who destroyed her trust and continued to harass her for the next decade.

She reached down deep and searched for something, a scrap of a feeling inside her that wanted to save Mason.

All she felt was heat. Fire. A burning desire for justice.

An eye for an eye.

"I watched you fuck another woman." She stepped toward him and removed her shirt. "Do you know how that feels to watch someone you love betray you so cruelly?" She unbuttoned her jeans and kicked them off with her shoes. "I'll show you."

She stood before him in a black bra and panties. A matching set. Lacy and sexy. She'd chosen wisely when she dressed this morning. But she hadn't selected her underwear for Mason. She was interested in one reaction, and it was searing a line of fire down the length of her back.

Pivoting, she found his eyes in the mask, and oh, Jesus, they smoldered.

Luke and Van kept their guns and their attentions on Mason as she made her way to Tommy. She circled his chair, savoring the track of his gaze. It stayed with her, turning his head until she stepped out of view behind him.

Bending over his back, she brought her hands around him, caressing his sculpted chest, dragging up the shirt, and exposing all that glorious muscle.

He moaned as she touched him. He slumped down in the chair as she reached lower, slipping her hand into the *V* of his open fly. Soft hair, swollen root, he was so hard, so long and thick. It took some adjusting and a lift of his hips to wrangle him free.

A muffled cry sounded from the couch, drawing her gaze to the tears leaking down Mason's cheeks. He was hurting. The emotional sort of suffering that stabbed deep.

She didn't rejoice in that. Didn't torment him with a smile. She might've been vindictive, but she wasn't inhumane.

Straightening, she walked around the chair, eyes locked on her man. He sprawled with a casual confidence that watered her mouth and soaked her panties.

His cock lay on his thigh, twitching as his golden stare violated every inch of her body.

She climbed onto his lap.

He did the rest, his hands roaming, pulling her close, and tugging aside the crotch of her panties. His mask prevented kissing, but his eye contact sealed their intimacy. He watched her as he guided himself into her body. He didn't look away as she gripped his corded neck and struggled for breath. He held her gaze as he lanced into her and broke into a hungry rhythm.

She was on top, but he controlled everything. The speed, the thrust, the tempo of her pulse. He owned her, dominated her, and brought her screaming and writhing into blissful completion.

With his forehead against hers, he grunted into her cheek, exploding, spilling himself into her with a deep, rumbling growl.

Mason was full-on sobbing behind her.

As she started to lift, Tommy palmed her backside, holding her to him.

"Thank you," he whispered, too low for Mason's ears.

His jealous-possessive nature had needed that bit of revenge. She'd needed it, too. For entirely different reasons.

Mason wouldn't bother her anymore, and he would think twice before cheating on another woman.

"Thank *you*," she whispered back.

She rose from his lap and quickly dressed while Tommy strode toward a weeping Mason, his wet cock hanging out of his zipper.

With a grip on Mason's hair, Tommy shoved him toward his semi-hard dick. "Lick me clean."

She froze, and Mason went wild.

"Nah, I'm just playing." His laughter sobered into cruel authority. "You will never taste heaven again."

Her lungs released a sigh.

She was done here. No more torment.

Luke and Van stepped forward, guns trained as Tommy cut Mason free from the rope.

"You won't talk about this." Tommy tossed Mason's clothes to him. "You hired us after all."

Free of the rope, Mason yanked out the gag and scrambled to pull on his pants. "I didn't—"

"Don't talk. Not a word. If we catch wind of you blabbering about what you witnessed here, we will find you. And we will kill you."

DOMINATE

Half-dressed, Mason gathered the rest of his things and backed toward the door. His tear-soaked eyes jerked from the rifles to her, his expression ugly with accusation.

"Don't send any more men to watch me." She stepped beside Tommy and placed her hand and her cheek against his muscled arm. "I'm keeping this one."

Tommy let Mason go. He stood at the door and watched her ex sprint toward his car and speed away. Van and Luke grabbed her bags and carried them outside.

"You knew Mason was coming." She touched Tommy's tense back.

"We'll be watching him for a while." He turned and searched her face. "You're not running."

"If you're trying to scare me, you'll have to try harder."

He grinned, blinding her with his gorgeous sex appeal. "We're going to war with an unknown enemy from Cole's world. Does that scare you?"

In a few minutes, they would drive to Tommy's property in the desert. There, Cole would activate the GSM bug he'd removed from her house and lure in the threat. The team would be in position. They would be ready.

"Yep." She shivered with excitement and fear.

Fear was good. It affirmed she was alive.

He leaned in and brushed his lips against hers. "It's going to be complicated."

"Then you definitely need me there."

"To dominate it?" He kissed her, lingering, controlling her breaths.

"We'll dominate together."

COMPLICATE
PAM GODWIN

Book 9

PROLOGUE

Southern Missouri
Seven years ago

Something was missing.

Something significant. Troubling.

Cole Hartman lowered his head to his hands, wrestling with the insidious sense of foreboding. Over the last seven months, it emerged without symptoms, invading gradually, subtly, but with detrimental effects.

Dread was eating him alive.

He sat on the floor in the armory of his safe house, his back to the wall, knees bent, and stomach clenched in knots. Down the hall, his beautiful, free-spirited dancer was likely practicing her choreographic sequences of *the biggest production in the history of wedding dances.*

For as long as he'd known Danni, she'd fantasized about her wedding dance.

Not the dress.

The *dance.*

Hers and his. Their first dance as Mr. and Mrs. Hartman.

Over the past few months, she'd been teaching him the steps. Dancing was her thing, not his, but he didn't mind learning. Hell, rubbing up against her hot little body would never be a hardship. He fucking loved her. So goddamn much it hurt.

But something was missing.

Four years ago, he'd left her to complete a one-year, undercover assignment overseas. They'd only been together for ten months at the time. He shouldn't have gone. He didn't know that year would turn into several more.

Without her knowledge, he'd left her under the protection of his best friend, Trace Savoy. In doing so, he'd inadvertently fucked his fate and shoved his entire world into Trace's arms.

After botching the mission, faking his death, losing Danni to his best friend, and finally, *finally* winning her back, he'd crawled out of hell, alive and victorious.

He'd chosen his job over her, and in the end, she chose him over all else.

His decisions had destroyed her life, and in return, she gave him her heart. *Again.*

The shattered pieces of his miserable existence had been put back together. He didn't deserve her, but when he'd returned from the dead, he put every ounce of life into earning her forgiveness.

He'd fought countless battles through his clandestine career, but seven months ago, he won the only war that mattered.

He won back his dancer.

Fair and square.

She let Trace go.

She chose me.

But something was missing.

The depressing lyrics of James Bay's *Let It Go* trickled through the armory. Racks of guns covered one wall, the rest occupied by file cabinets, desks, computers, phones, and high-tech gear. The kind of equipment that didn't exist outside of his classified unit.

In the corner, her wedding gown hung on a hook. It didn't belong in here. Not in a room crammed with weapons, secrets, and deception.

When he'd taken the dress during their separation, he wanted it in a safe place. He longed to see her wear it as she walked down the aisle, toward him, toward their future together.

Nothing stood in their way now. She'd chosen him. Agreed to marry him. Everything was right in the world.

Except it wasn't.

The soft tread of footsteps approached from the hallway and paused on the threshold.

His pulse quickened as it always did when she was near. His entire being pulled toward her as she entered the room. He didn't move, didn't make a sound, his senses alert, tracking her graceful movements as she floated past his shadowed position on the floor near the door.

COMPLICATE

She took in the space, lingering on the wall of firearms. This was her first glimpse behind the armory door. He always kept the room locked. Kept her out. She shouldn't be here. Her spirit was too bright, too gentle amid the guns and dangerous evidence of his business.

As if realizing that, she quickly turned back to the door and paused, startled, her gaze fastened on him. Then she smiled.

The first smile she'd ever given him had been life-altering. She'd stepped in front of his motorcycle at the crack of dawn, wearing almost nothing. Except her smile. It'd been so big and full of life, it softened his insides, turned his brain to butter, and made him weak.

He didn't regret a second of it.

No man with a pulse could regret her. Danni Angelo was a blonde bombshell with a compassionate soul. Beautiful inside and out.

Grey eyes, fair complexion, she glowed with light and stunning sensuality. Her lithe limbs and athletic physique befit her occupation as a professional dancer. But it was her smile that stole the show. And broke hearts. His heart, specifically.

She'd broken him as much as he'd broken her. Crushed. Mended. And soon to be demolished again. He felt it looming — the pain, the devastation, the inevitability of forever's antonym.

Never was coming for him.

Because something was missing.

It was missing in the smile she wore now. Her bowed lips curved like they always had. Her eyes illuminated with angelic beauty. But it wasn't a *Danni* smile. Not the one that had railroaded him the day they met. Definitely not the one that tilted the universe and knocked him off his feet.

It lacked the energy that made his heart rev. It didn't crackle the air and charge his blood. It was low on sunshine, devoid of music, and desperately in need of life.

Her smile cried out for happiness.

There was no contentment in it. No tranquility. No delirium. Had she been without those things all along?

They'd been inseparable for months, staying here at his lakefront estate, reconnecting, dancing, fucking, focusing on their relationship, and planning their future. They were wrapped up together. On top of the world.

But no amount of planning or intimacy could erase the gaping hole in her heart.

The hole that had been left by another man.

He didn't want to notice it. Didn't want to think about it, talk about it, or do anything to make it real. So he'd ignored it. For seven months, he pretended there wasn't something missing.

They were in love and finally back together, all the while pretending she didn't still love Trace.

It was a point of contention that couldn't be resolved with words or time. Ignoring it wouldn't make it go away. He knew that. They both knew.

It wasn't her fault. She hadn't asked for this. He and Trace had wedged her into a miserable love triangle. Then they'd forced her into a decision.

Choose.

So she had.

Her decision ruined Trace, sentencing him to a life without her.

Her decision left a guilt-ridden hole in her heart.

Her decision yielded only one winner, and he couldn't rejoice in that. But if he was strong enough, he could fix it.

She'd lost him once, and yeah, it had wrecked her. But she'd found happiness again. In his absence, she'd fallen in love again.

The same couldn't be said this time around. She was surviving without Trace, but she wasn't *living*.

This had everything to do with who she was, not who she chose. The woman he'd shared space with for the last seven months wasn't the Danni he knew.

She'd lost her luster, her vivacity, her effervescent rhythm. His carefree dancer was miserable.

Because love wasn't a choice.

He dangled his arms over his bent knees and leaned his head back against the wall, watching her, memorizing her delicate features, while slowly, painfully, preparing for a decision that would decimate him on a fundamental level.

"I thought you retired." She glanced at the tables of charging phones and running laptops. "What is this?"

"I *am* retired. I only come in here to check my messages." He gave the devices a thoughtful look. "I get a lot of job offers."

"Job offers?" She closed the distance and lowered to the floor beside him, mirroring his pose. "What kind of jobs?"

"The kind that paid for this house. The dangerous kind that send me out of the country for months. Sometimes years."

He missed the work, the challenge in it. The danger. But he gave it all up for her and would gladly continue to do so…if she was happy.

She tensed. "Are you considering—?"

"I would never consider a job away from you." He gathered her beneath his arm and breathed in the unique Nag Champa scent of her hair.

COMPLICATE

Curling up against his side, she rested her head on his shoulder and hummed. Her fingers stroked his arm. Her silence tried to invoke comfort. All of it felt forced, but not. Tense, but also tender. She was straining for the happiness they'd once shared. And failing to grab hold of it.

Let It Go played again, strumming the air with the glaring truth. The lyrics bemoaned a relationship that was destined to end, no matter how badly two people held on. He'd selected it without thinking, his subconscious sending him a message.

"This song is so sad." She ran a finger along the line of his rigid jaw, unable to coax him to relax. "Why are you listening to it?"

"I know what you're doing," he murmured, his insides sick with unease.

She dropped her hand.

"You're trying so hard to make this work." His voice cracked. "But the heart wants what the heart wants."

She flinched. "No—"

"He's not physically here, but he's here nonetheless, always between us." He met her eyes with a hard stare. "You're settling."

"Damn right, I'm settling." She fisted her hands. "I'm settling into a beautiful life with a man who takes my breath away. I chose *you*, Cole. I'm *with* you."

"Someone told me once that love isn't a choice."

Christ, this hurt. Unlike the bullet that had struck his chest, Danni would leave a lasting, open wound.

"Why do you think I wanted you to wait six months?" He touched her trembling fingers, caressing her engagement band. "I didn't want you to choose. I wanted it to *happen*. I wanted it to rise inside you and become the beat of your heart." He softened his voice, dying inside. "The most decisive actions are the ones with the least consideration."

"What are you saying?"

"The day you forced yourself to decide, I knew. When Trace walked out that door, I saw it in your eyes." He forced resolve into his expression. "You voiced a decision your heart wasn't ready to make."

Her face turned to stone. But beneath the anger, he glimpsed concession. She knew he was right.

"I've watched you fight an inner battle for seven months." He brought her hand to his lips and kissed her knuckles. "You're fighting a war with your heart."

Creases of pain etched around her mouth. "If that's the case, why did I choose you?"

"I was your first. The logical choice. But the heart isn't logical. Sometimes, we don't know what we want until it's gone."

"It doesn't matter." In her usual stubborn fashion, she climbed onto his lap and steeled her voice. "I love you."

"I know you do." He pulled her against him and tucked her head beneath his chin. "But you love him more."

She sank her fingernails into his shoulders, clutching fiercely, holding on, fighting against the inevitable.

For a moment, he fought alongside her. They belonged together. He could work through this, love her hard, harder than any man ever could, and fill the void Trace left behind. There had been a time when he was all she needed.

Until he ruined it.

Agony rose without warning, scraping jagged shards through his throat.

The damage couldn't be undone. He'd left her, let her believe he was dead, and lost her to another man.

Hot prickles stabbed the backs of his eyes. He couldn't swallow. Couldn't breathe.

He'd ruined them.

Dammit, he just wanted her to be happy, and it wasn't fair to either of them to go on pretending. He'd rather be the one with the gutted heart. Instead of fighting for her, he'd rather fight for her wellbeing and take vicarious contentment in that. This wasn't him being a martyr. He simply couldn't find a better way.

He had to let fate play out. Let her go back to Trace. Let her go.

Let it all go.

His vision swarmed with tears. He didn't make a sound, didn't release the air in his lungs, but he couldn't hide his anguish from her.

She leaned back and whimpered at the sight of his tears.

"Don't make that face." A sob escaped her as she frantically dried his cheeks with her hands. "Don't give up on me."

"I lost you, baby. I lost you the morning I got into that cab and left you crying on the porch." He hauled her against him, his embrace constricting and his mouth at her ear. "I'm not giving up. I'm letting you go."

She shattered in his arms, sucking choppy gulps of air. He clung to her, and she clung back, gripping, weeping. He held her through it, crying with her as she came to terms with reality.

Years of friendship, love, and dreams for the future spooled out around them. She would still have those things. Just not with him.

He would never love again. Never find another Danni. He couldn't even fathom it. She was his soul mate.

COMPLICATE

For endless minutes, they sat in the sadness, deep in their own thoughts, until the tears stopped. Too soon, she raised her head and cupped his face, wearing a look of devastating finality. He wiped away her tears as she dried his.

"No more crying tonight." He kissed her lips, softly lingering.

No words were exchanged as he carried her into the bedroom. No second thoughts were voiced as they undressed. No tears fell as he entered her body for the last time.

They'd been here before. Four years ago, he made love to her and left her. But this time, he wasn't leaving for a job. He was leaving for *her*, and he wouldn't be returning. This time, he stared into her eyes, fucked her achingly slow, and wordlessly said good-bye forever.

After, she lay beside him, studying his face, seemingly dazed. She always admired his looks. Her attraction to him had never been in question. Neither had her love.

The woman loved with her entire being. That was the problem. She loved big enough and deep enough to bind her soul to two men.

"I'm grateful I had you to myself for seven months." He pushed a blonde lock behind her ear.

"I'm grateful for every breath, every dance, every memory you gave me."

Sharp, incendiary pain lashed through him, leaching the strength from his body. Fire burned in his chest, searing his breaths and watering his eyes. He couldn't do this. He couldn't let her go.

He wanted to sink into her again and lose himself in her precious warmth. But if he did that, if he stayed the night, he would stay forever. His fragile resolve was splintering. He needed to go.

So he pulled away. Not physically. Not yet. But he pulled his gaze away from her beguiling beauty. He pulled his emotions away from the surface and shoved it all down, growing cold and rigid in the effort.

She seemed to sense his detachment and went still beside him, silent and accepting. There would be no more fighting from her. She knew the score. She would grieve and move on.

Trace was waiting. His best friend would wait for her forever.

As her breathing drifted into the rhythm of sleep, he touched his lips to her forehead one last time.

I love you, Danni Angelo. Be happy.

Without waking her, he slipped the engagement ring from her finger. She didn't need it anymore, but he did. Christ, he needed every memory of her he could carry.

The tightening in his chest was unbearable, his insides hemorrhaging. He pushed through it and pulled away from her sleeping form.

She had Trace, and Cole had enough job offers to keep him distracted for years. He could do this. He had no choice.

In the dark, he slipped out of bed.

Then he slipped out of her life.

ONE

Chihuahuan Desert, West Texas
Present Day

"Ready?" A thrill coursed through Cole as he met Rylee's eyes.

Huge, silver-grey eyes.

Just like Danni's.

Sometimes, it was difficult to hold that stunning stare, for it conjured echoes and aches of the one he let go.

He looked away, directing his attention to the kitchen table, which gleamed in an array of guns, ammo, and other weaponry. Amid the gear lay the high-tech GSM bug he'd pulled from Rylee's house.

The mystery behind who had put it there remained unsolved. After months of investigating, he and his vigilante team didn't have much to go on. But one thing was certain. Someone had bugged her house to fuck with *him*.

Rylee was just collateral. A means to lure him into the open. They wouldn't hesitate to kill her. They'd already tried.

The question was *who*?

Who murdered her next-door neighbor, two innocent motel clerks, and put a hit on her life?

The best clue they had was a word uttered by a dying hitman.

Thurney.

During a mission eleven years ago, Cole had faked his death on Thurney Bridge. Since that detail was classified, it meant he was dealing with someone connected to that assignment. And they wanted him alive. Otherwise, they would've killed him instead of hunting Rylee.

Most likely, they wanted information. Dangerous, top-secret intel from his work in the *activity*. Or maybe this was a revenge plot against him, and they wanted to draw out his death, slowly and excruciatingly.

Time to find out.

Outside, his seven vigilante teammates stood by, waiting for him to set the plan in motion. Most had already moved into position around the perimeter of Tomas' house. The other nine Freedom Fighters, including the Restrepo Cartel's *jefe*, were en route from Colombia to provide backup and reunite with their family.

Family.

The Freedom Fighters were an entangled, dysfunctional mix of blood relations, enemies-turned-lovers, spouses, soul mates, workmates, and above all, loyal friends. They protected and loved one another with a ferocity that made them unstoppable. They killed, waged wars, and sacrificed everything for one another.

And over the past year, he'd become one of them.

It was strange to have a team again after being alone for so long. Even stranger to have a family he could depend on and trust. Criminals or not, he'd grown to care about these people. So much so that he didn't want to put them in harm's way. Didn't want to risk their lives. The thought of losing one of them scared the hell out of him.

That made them liabilities. If his enemies knew what they meant to him, they would use them as leverage.

"I thought I was ready." Rylee tilted her head, studying him. "But I don't like that look on your face. Are we going to die?"

"Everyone dies, darlin'. That's a guarantee."

"Tonight?" Her face paled as she pointed at the high-tech bug. "When you activate that thing and let them know we're here, what are our chances of survival?"

Fifty-percent chance. Sixty, if he was feeling cocky. Which he wasn't. But he wouldn't share those odds with her. This was her first job as a Freedom Fighter, and her fear was palpable, trembling through her willowy limbs.

Nevertheless, she wanted to be part of this. She was committed to the team. More specifically, she was committed to Tomas, one of their longest-standing members.

"You know this is dangerous." He crossed his arms.

COMPLICATE

Standing over the table, she braced her hands on the surface and leaned in. "A plan that isn't dangerous isn't a plan at all. You can't scare me away."

She wasn't wrong. A few months ago, she drove here alone, with a pocketful of audacity and a reckless plan to meet Tomas Dine, fully aware he was a criminal, a murderer, and livid enough with her to shoot her on the spot.

Her chance of survival had been closer to zero then. Yet here she was, alive, in love with the ruthless vigilante, and ready to fight another fight.

Cole should've kissed her when he had the opportunity. Four months ago, here in the kitchen while Tomas was in the shower, he'd thought about doing more than feeding her breakfast.

It wasn't just her enchanting eyes. She was a remarkable woman. Fierce. Smart. Gorgeous.

Where Danni's hair was blonde, Rylee's was dark brown. Same long, straight style. Same slender, athletic build and graceful mannerisms. Like Danni, she exuded raw, natural beauty. No makeup. No maintenance. No nonsense.

His kind of perfect.

It had been seven years since he'd seen or talked to his dancer. Of course, he noticed beautiful women since then. He craved sex, obsessed over it, and fucked his hand on the regular. He still had a pulse, for Christ's sake. But no one had come close to tempting him.

Not even Rylee.

In seven years, he hadn't felt the luscious curves of a female body. Hadn't tasted soft, warm lips or smelled the sweetness of a soaked pussy. He hadn't encountered anyone who compared to the woman he let go.

But he enjoyed Rylee's company. Perhaps because she looked past his coarse exterior and understood him in a way very few people did. She recognized his pain and seemed to admire him for it.

Her education lent her the ability to see through the bullshit. But he guessed it was her own loss, her ex-husband's betrayal, that helped her relate to him so easily.

"You're staring." She narrowed her eyes. Eyes that made him long for a life he would never have.

"You're beautiful," he said.

"Mm-hmm." She pursed her lips, her expression skeptical. "What's going on, Cole?"

"Just an observation."

"Why *that* observation? Why now?"

"Because Tomas isn't here to take a swing at me."

"Fair enough. Thank you for the compliment." Her cheeks rose. "I'm ready to do this. Are you?"

"Yep." A rush of energy buzzed through him as he grabbed the high-tech bug from the table. "Going live in three, two, one..."

He activated the device and gave her a nod.

Nothing indicated the bug was on, but the moment it detected noise, it would begin recording. Sound clips would be sent to an untraceable phone, and whoever monitored that phone would be alerted of the incoming recording within seconds.

Basic spy technology, but so much more. This bug had been customized with high-speed transmissions, long-reach WIFI, and battery life that exceeded months—all built into a chip the size of a coin.

That level of cutting-edge tech wasn't obtainable outside clandestine groups like NSA and black ops. He'd been retired from the *activity* for so long he wasn't up to speed on the latest tech. Hell, he didn't even know how the bug functioned until he'd taken it apart.

What he did know was that this tiny piece of tech was the key that would lead him to the threat.

Or rather, it would lead the threat to *him*.

"Where are you going?" he asked Rylee, following the script he'd rehearsed with her.

"I'm sick of hiding, Cole." She stared at the listening device, answering exactly as he'd coached her. "We've been moving around, running for months, and you still don't know who planted those bugs in my house. Now you expect me to sit here in the damn desert and wait for something to happen? You don't even know if they're listening to us now."

While holed up in Missouri for the past four months, he and his team spent that time investigating and planning. Now they were back in Texas, ready to finish this, and she'd just given the enemy their location. On purpose.

"This house is the safest place for us," he said.

"This house holds too many haunting memories for Tommy. We're leaving."

"Where the hell are you going to go?"

"Out of the country. Doesn't matter." She moved toward the door, deliberately distancing her voice from the listening device. "I came here for Tommy. I didn't sign up for this, whatever *this* is."

"Rylee, wait." He followed her out of the house and shut the door behind him, loud enough to be detected by the bug.

The plan was set.

Outside, Tomas sat in a doorless, topless Jeep Wrangler, his arm draped over the steering wheel and his golden stare locked on Rylee. "How did it go?"

COMPLICATE

"Noticeably contrived." She climbed into the passenger seat and kissed his rigid jaw. "I should've studied acting instead of psychology."

"You did fine." Cole stopped beside the Jeep, sweating in the evening heat. "Doesn't matter if it sounded hokey. They now know where I am, and when they arrive, they'll believe you're gone."

The last part was paramount. Someone tried to kill her once. He couldn't risk her or anyone else getting captured and used as a hostage to control him.

A glance at the Jeep's cargo confirmed Tomas had packed everything they needed to camp in the desert for a few nights. He also had enough artillery to take out an army. Van, Liv, Luke, and Tiago were already in position, far enough away to not be seen, yet close enough to be here at a moment's notice with guns blazing.

Cole turned toward the house and spotted Tate and Lucia sitting in the dark on the flat roof. The instant they heard an approaching car, they would alert the team, aim their rifles, and lie low enough to be undetected from the ground.

If the threat arrived by helicopter, they were all fucked. A view from the sky would mark the positions of his entire team in the desert.

"Get out of here." He tapped the hood and stepped back, watching Tomas drive off.

As the taillights faded into the shadows of sand and desert buttes, he switched on the transmitter in his pocket. "We're live. Do you copy?"

"Loud and clear" came through his earpiece eight times, once for each of his teammates.

They all carried receivers with sensitive microphones and wireless nano earphones that operated over a radio frequency like walkie-talkies. They would sleep in shifts, check in every hour, and wear the earpieces at all times.

"Out." He muted his mic.

Now, they waited.

TWO

Cole returned to the house, keyed up and primed for battle.

He lived for this shit—the tremor of looming danger, the rush of adrenaline, and the thrill in fighting for something meaningful. That was the reason he'd enlisted to become a Navy SEAL all those years ago—a decision that had hurdled him through the ranks and landed him in a unit so covert and off the record that it didn't exist. At least, not to those who didn't have the clearance.

In the kitchen, he holstered a 9mm in the waistband of his jeans. A blade went into his boot. The rifles he set by the door. He left the listening device on the table to record his movements around the house.

It could be days before someone showed up, depending on how far they had to travel. While he was in Missouri for the past few months, he assumed his pursuers had stayed in Texas, waiting for him to reemerge. They wouldn't be far.

He lowered onto the couch and measured his breathing, taking on the cold, competitive mindset that had accompanied him on every mission over the past fifteen years. He was nothing if not a soldier rooted in grit, preparation, and confidence.

Grit rose from a place of deep purpose. Preparation came only through patience and tenacity. And confidence? That had been drilled into him through experience, training, and resilience.

Kill or be killed. Didn't matter what he faced or how badly the odds stacked against him. He believed in his ability to overcome.

In most missions, he knew his enemies inside and out. But not this one. From this point on, anything could happen.

COMPLICATE

A retrieval team would likely be sent for him. A few armed men. Maybe a dozen or more. That was the best-case scenario. If an army of thugs tried to take him by gunfire or physical force, the Freedom Fighters would rush in and wipe them out, save one. One breathing man was all they needed to torture for information.

But if only one man showed up, that would mean his enemy wielded something more powerful than bullets. If he had any fear, it lay in that unknown variable, a potential misstep he hadn't calculated, like an unforeseen hostage.

Everyone he cared about was accounted for. Trace Savoy had Danni locked up in the tower of his St. Louis casino, claiming his security was as impenetrable as Cole's safe house in Missouri. It wasn't. Which was why Cole had demanded they stay at his house. Trace's refusal to do so was infuriating and unfounded. Evidently, the uptight bastard didn't trust Cole around his wife.

Was it a valid concern? Maybe. Cole had no idea what he would do if he saw Danni again. Right now, all he cared about was keeping her safe.

As for the rest of his friends, he'd spoken with Matias an hour ago. The cartel boss affirmed they were safely on his plane and on their way to Texas. When they arrived, they would wait at an undisclosed location until Cole gave them the go-ahead to approach.

He hoped he wouldn't need Matias' assistance, but he wouldn't reject it. *Give help and get help.* It was a crucial motto in his line of work.

An hour rolled by, and radio check-ins were made. Then another hour, another check-in.

With the use of a dedicated frequency and encrypted communication, their conversations transmitted over secure lines. As an added layer of protection, everyone used nicknames.

Just before the third hour, Tate's voice came through the earpiece. "Come in, chief."

Cole lurched from the couch and closed himself into the bathroom, where the bug couldn't hear him. "Go ahead."

"Eyes on incoming movement. A single light approaching from the east. Looks like a headlight."

"A motorcycle?"

"Affirmative."

"On it." His pulse kicked up. "Stand by."

"Copy."

One motorcycle.

That wasn't a goddamn retrieval team. It was something far worse.

Returning to the front room, he peered around the window curtain, his neck tense and senses on high-alert.

A bright light bobbed over the horizon and headed straight toward him.

Only one.

Goddammit. His gaze darted to the rifles by the door. Useless. Whatever the biker was armed with couldn't be defeated with gunfire.

His heart rate escalated as he stepped away from the window. Perspiration formed on his brow as he chambered a round in his pistol and returned it to his waistband.

Bullets wouldn't save them. Not from this.

A tremor rippled through his fingers as he removed the necklace that hung beneath his shirt. He couldn't risk losing Danni's engagement ring.

It went into the pack he kept in the back bedroom, safely stowed. Then he drew in a deep breath and stepped outside.

The mic on his transmitter remained on, his team silent and listening, waiting on his command.

The rumble of a single-cylinder engine vibrated the air as a BMW motorcycle approached, taking its time. The rider wore a black helmet and appeared small in stature, at least half his size. He realized why as the bike rolled up beside him.

Slender hands gripped the handlebars, connected to feminine arms sleeved in more tattoos than he had on his entire body. In the moonlight, vivid colors of ink formed so many artful designs it would take him hours to make out all the images.

The biker shut off the engine and left the headlight on, illuminating the desert behind him. No visible weapons. No immediate threats on the horizon. She appeared to be alone.

Three feet of space separated them. He was close enough to grab her and physically overpower her. Or shoot her point-blank with the 9mm in his hand.

"Right about now, you're calculating your next move." A sultry Russian accent crooned from the helmet as she lowered the kickstand and slid off the motorcycle. "You activated my bug, Cole Hartman, and here I am. But you weren't expecting a woman. This, I know."

You veren't expecting eh voman. Zis, I know.

He certainly wasn't expecting a Russian woman. He didn't have enemies in that part of the world. But he'd worked there. The *activity* operated only outside of the United States, and since all his missions had been overseas, he spoke seven languages with superb fluency. Including hers.

"I'll help you decide your next move." With each syllable, she pulled her tongue to the back of her throat, adding friction to the *H* sounds and hardening the *R*s. "If you shoot me, your friends will die."

COMPLICATE

"Which friends?" he asked in Russian. "I don't have many."

The helmet cocked, paused. She seemed startled that he spoke her language.

She was probably a low-ranking myrmidon, a subordinate who carried out orders unquestioningly. Most likely, she was chosen for this task because she was a woman with an attractive figure, her purpose to lure and disarm. She wouldn't know anything about him beyond what they'd given her to complete the job.

"I'm not talking about your two friends on the roof," she said in Russian. "They can lower their rifles. They won't need them."

His scalp tingled. How did she know Tate and Lucia were there? Aerial thermal imaging? If that was the case, the position of his entire team was compromised.

Unease slithered down his spine, but he didn't spare Tate and Lucia a glance.

Instead, he switched back to English so they could follow the conversation. "You have an infrared drone up there?"

"I have eyes everywhere," she purred.

Maybe she was bluffing, but either way, his team knew what to do.

"Come in, *esé*." Lucia's voice barked through the earpiece. "What's your 20?"

"Same," Van said. "All present and standing by."

"Any drones?"

"Eyes on the sky. No bogies in sight. No hostiles on the ground. All clear. Try not to get yourself killed, *mija*."

"Roger," she said. "Out."

Relief swept through Cole as he turned back to the woman. "Tell me who you work for."

"No."

"Remove the helmet."

"This, I can do." She reached up and started unbuckling the straps.

Dark jeans caressed her toned curves, the waistband rising high to her midriff and exposing a sliver of smooth, pale skin. The denim folded into wide cuffs at her ankles, and Gothic boots sported random buckles that served no practical purpose.

Her cropped corset looked more like a strapless bra, with black and white polka-dots that clashed with the colorful artwork on her arms. The bodice clung to the round swells of her tits, clinching an hourglass figure that needed no clinching.

Her top dipped so low it exposed a red bird inked across her breast, its beak lost in her ample cleavage. A swallow bird. Vintage in its design. With vibrant swirls and elaborate filigree, the chest piece looked so fucking enticing on her perfect rack it demanded his stare, ensnared it, and wouldn't let it go.

Until she removed the helmet.

Piles of thick, bright-ass-red hair tumbled out, bouncing off her shoulders and falling around her inked arms. Eyes of sea-green stared out of a face so feminine, so delicately formed, that her flawless ivory complexion didn't appear natural.

Nothing about her appearance looked real. Or soft.

Heavy black eyeliner winged out from the corners of her large eyes. Her lashes were so dense and long he knew they were fake. Even the white stone piercing on her upper lip was an imitation of Marilyn Monroe's beauty mark.

Cherry red gloss stained her lips. Plump, sinful, smiling lips. The longer he stared, the wider she smiled. She damn well knew the effect she had on men.

Her beauty was bold, arresting, and deliberately, garishly exaggerated. With her makeup painted on in aggressive strokes and her mermaid hair so shockingly red, he suspected she spent more time primping than firing a weapon.

From head to toe, she exuded a rockabilly vibe, blending old-school rock with Goth subculture, like a retro Russian pinup girl with a wartime air. She would look right at home sprawled on a Soviet tank, wearing nothing but garters and that ruby red smile. Seductive and freaky and one-hundred-percent artificial.

What did she look like beneath the hair dye and caked-on cosmetics? He trusted her beauty as much as he trusted *her*.

"While your eyes are bulging from your head," she said in her thick accent, "the clock is ticking. You will come with me now."

Someone had bugged Rylee's house, sent a hitman after her, and killed three innocent people, and this woman was involved.

The plan had been to lure her here. Not get himself captured.

He laughed. "I'm not going anywhere with you."

"You will, Cole Hartman." She removed a large-screen tablet from the pack on her motorcycle and handed it to him. "Turn it on."

His lungs caved in, and alarms rang in his head. He stared at the offered device, unable to move, crippled by memories.

Eleven years ago. Thurney Bridge. He'd faked his death, lost his girl, and destroyed his life — all because of a video on a phone.

He couldn't guess what she would show him on that device, but whatever it was would force him to his knees.

COMPLICATE

No. Fuck no. Not this.

It couldn't be a threat to Danni's life. Not again. Trace swore she was safe.

The woman huffed with impatience and powered on the screen, displaying a paused video. "Push play."

"Rot in hell." He aimed the pistol at her face, inches from her painted lips.

She didn't flinch or bat a fake eyelash. Instead, her mouth curved up. Her tongue poked out, and she slowly, fearlessly, fucking shamelessly licked the end of the barrel. All the way around the tip she went. Then she drew it between her filthy, lush, red lips.

His dick twitched, heating his anger past the boiling point. He yanked the gun away.

"We're out of time, *tigryenok*." She pouted. "Watch the video."

She pressed play, and as much as he wanted to smack the device from her hand, he was still a soldier. A disciplined operative. Logic over emotion, his mind was in control.

The video showed a tarmac and private airplane hangar, the camera hovering from somewhere overhead. Before it zoomed in on the plane and the people boarding it, he knew exactly what he was looking at.

Matias, Camila, Josh, Amber, Kate, Martin, Ricky, Tula, and Vera. The nine Freedom Fighters who were on their way here.

His throat closed, panic spiking.

How had she obtained this footage? Whoever watched his friends hadn't stopped them from boarding. He'd spoken with Matias after they were in the air. They were safe.

Unless another aircraft was following them.

She switched the screen, displaying a new video. "This is a live feed, streaming from an armed drone."

The drone was in motion, high in a pitch-black sky, and locked onto a target. Equipped with night-vision cameras, it provided an undeniable view of another aircraft coasting at a distance ahead of it.

She tapped on the screen, controlling the drone's camera and zooming in until the tail number on the aircraft's cowling was legible.

He recognized the number instantly and knew it was registered to Matias' plane.

An ache swelled in the back of his throat.

Van's wife, Tiago's wife, Liv's husband, Lucia's sister — every person on that aircraft was irreplaceable. They were family.

The team on the ground was listening through the radio, but they didn't see what he saw. They didn't know their loved ones were in danger.

Didn't matter. They were his people, too.

Cold purpose numbed his chest as he slipped a hand into his pocket and discreetly muted the transmitter, preventing his friends from hearing what came next.

"What's the ordnance on the drone?" he asked calmly.

"Air-to-air hellfire. Enough to take down your friend's plane multiple times."

Fire-and-forget missiles.

Fucking fuck!

The drone didn't need to be in line-of-sight of Matias' plane to hit it with those missiles. They were self-guided. But someone, sitting somewhere in a remote terminal, had to control the drone and pull the trigger.

"Where's the operator?" he growled.

"You'll meet him when we arrive."

"What are the orders?"

"The operator will shoot down the plane at precisely twenty-three hundred."

That was two hours away, which might've felt like plenty of time if she hadn't mentioned a ticking clock more than once.

"Call it off." He tightened his grip on the 9mm. "I'll triple what they're paying you."

"I'm not the one holding the trigger."

Which was why they sent her and not the operator.

"You can make demands, offer bribes, or shoot me with that gun." She shrugged. "The operator will not abort."

"Unless?"

"Unless you and I arrive at his location by twenty-three hundred. No exceptions. If we hurry, we'll make it there with five minutes to spare. I'll even let you watch him call off the strike."

His heart hammered, and adrenaline flooded his system. "Who ordered this?"

"No more questions." She clicked her tongue. "Tick-tock."

If he could get a message to Matias, maybe his pilot could evade the danger. But it was too risky. Matias' luxury aircraft was designed for one purpose only. To transport people. It didn't have the speed or artillery to engage an armed drone.

"I know what you're thinking." She stowed the tablet in the pack on her bike, her accent grating. "If your friends deviate from their course or try to escape the drone, it will fire."

His jaw clenched, his options dwindling with the countdown of the clock.

He would kill for his friends.

But would he hand himself over and endure torture for them?

COMPLICATE

Would he die for them?

THREE

Eleven years ago, the *activity* deployed Cole overseas to complete a job. His last job. Upon his return, he intended to retire, marry his dancer, and live a normal, innocuous life in the suburbs.

The assignment was standard undercover work. He was sent to infiltrate the Romanian mafia, root out a leak of classified information, and return home. He expected to finish within a year.

But when he discovered the source of the leak was Marie Merivale, his trusted partner and ex-lover, his entire world imploded.

She'd taken a bribe from the mafia, betrayed Cole and her country for money, and because she knew he would figure it out, she made damn sure she was ready for him.

When he caught her in France on Thurney Bridge, they stood in a face-off, guns aimed. Until she held up her phone and showed him a live video of an assassin in Danni's house.

There was no leverage more powerful than a threat to Danni's life.

He had a split-second to make a decision. Let Marie kill him and save Danni. Or kill Marie and guarantee Danni's death.

Lucky for him, Marie didn't know about the high-tech, bullet-resistant clothing he wore under his jacket.

He let her shoot him.

The bullet hit his chest, fractured his ribs, and sent him crashing into the river below. When he didn't surface, Marie believed he was dead. Everyone believed it. His unit, his employer, Trace, Danni...

Danni grieved his death for three years while he remained hidden, covertly hunting Marie.

COMPLICATE

The fucking bitch was a trained operative, same as him, and always a step ahead. But he had the element of surprise. She thought he was dead.

Maybe he should've killed her when he caught her, but she wasn't a threat now. It'd taken him three years, but she was finally in prison, serving a life sentence without parole.

All of this flashed through his mind with a horrifying sense of *déjà vu* as he stared at the Russian woman. She'd shown him a video, threatened his friends, and now, in a race against the clock, he had a decision to make.

But this time, it wasn't as simple as kill or be killed. Bullet-resistant clothing and a fake death wouldn't get him out of this.

If he shot the woman, his friends would die. If he died, his friends would die. If he pretended to die, his friends would die.

The only way to save them was to go with her.

But if he did that, he faced gruesome, prolonged torture. They would methodically rip him apart until they extracted what they wanted from his mind.

Unless this was about revenge. In that case, torture would serve no purpose beyond their sick enjoyment. Electrocution, starvation, dismemberment—the ways a man could die were limited only by the imagination.

"It's a two-hour ride." She leaned a hip against the motorcycle and tapped her fingers on the seat. "We're officially late."

There was only one thing he could do in the face of such grim inevitability. He had to trick his brain into fighting for a sense of control and dignity.

Straightening his spine, he pulled in a slow, deep breath.

He wouldn't die for his friends.

He would go with the woman and find a way to survive for them.

"I'm driving." Everything inside him hardened as he regarded the motorcycle, its tires and suspension, and the spare helmet on the back. "I'll get us there in time."

"Leave your weapons and communication equipment."

He ejected the round from his pistol and tossed it. The knife from his boot went next.

With razor-sharp focus, he felt nothing as he switched on the transmitter. "Come in, *ese*."

"Go ahead," Van said.

His entire team was tuned in, listening. Dammit, there was no easy way to say this and no time to mince his words. "Our aircraft has a drone on its tail. Armed with hellfire, it will shoot down our plane at twenty-three hundred unless I arrive at the designated place and time with this Russian cunt."

He glared at her.

She glared back.

The radio went silent. He had to give it to his friends. He'd just delivered the worst news imaginable, and not one of them lost their shit. Not outwardly. They kept it locked down tight. Because they were survivors.

They would survive this, along with every person on that plane.

"I'm going with her," he said. "Listen carefully. This is important. Contact the pilot and tell him not to deviate from his course. I repeat. Do not change course. Do not engage the drone. Or it will strike. Follow these orders, and our aircraft will land safely."

"Copy." Fury leaked through Van's voice. "Do you know who these fuckers are?"

"Negative."

"How do we find you?"

"You don't."

"We will, goddammit. We'll be there with an army."

"When the plane lands, I need you to disappear. All of you. Go somewhere I don't know about."

"They're going to fucking torture you."

"I need you alive, *esé*. Do exactly what I said. Out." He turned off the transmitter and dropped it in the sand. The earpiece followed.

His pulse throbbed in his temples as he shifted toward the house. He couldn't see Tate or Lucia on the roof, but they could see him. They'd heard him on the radio, and they could hear him now as he said, "Stand down."

They weren't stupid enough to interfere, but he wasn't taking chances.

"Now, I will search you for weapons." The Russian's silky accent whispered against his nape, close enough to raise the hairs there. "It'll be better for you if you arrive unarmed."

"Better how? Less torture?"

"Shh." She smoothed her hands down his stiff back and palmed his ass, searching, teasing. She continued down his legs to his boots. "You're well-built. Strong. Virile." She worked her way back up, circling to his front. "Don't let it give you a false sense of power. Physical strength won't save you."

COMPLICATE

She stood before him, her intelligent green eyes fixed on his. Then her hand lowered, gliding between his legs and probing his cock through the jeans.

His body reacted, heating his skin and scratching his voice. "Your name?"

"Lydia."

"That your real name?"

"Yes." She closed her fingers around the outline of his semi-hard dick. "Impressive."

"Don't let it give you a false sense of power. It's simple biology. You're not special."

The corner of her flirty lips kicked up, her eyes glimmering with a look that made his skin shiver and heat.

"You don't know where we're going." She stepped back and tossed him the spare helmet. "Without me, you won't reach the destination and save your friends. Remember that before you throw me off the bike."

That was the only reason he hadn't smashed in her face.

Helmet on, he straddled the motorcycle and fired up the engine. The impulse to give Tate and Lucia a parting glance pulled at him, but he didn't give into it. He focused forward, on the bleak horizon, and steeled himself for the worst.

She slid on behind him, her thighs hugging his hips and hands clasped low on his abdomen. "Head east."

He opened the throttle and shot off into the dark. The uneven terrain hindered his speed. Once he hit pavement, he would have to make up precious time.

The roar of the engine made conversation impossible. Just as well. The ride would give him time to go over things in his head.

For the next twenty minutes, he analyzed everything Lydia had said, looking for clues and hidden meanings. She never mentioned Danni or Trace, and she wouldn't know the *activity* even existed. But whoever she worked for was connected to Thurney Bridge.

He recalled the few interactions he'd had with Russian constituents over his career and couldn't trace any of it back to his last assignment. Lydia's nationality most likely had nothing to do with him. Unless her counterparts were Russian, too. He would find that out soon enough.

The off-road tires sailed across the sand, the desert a graveyard of shadows and scattered holes. Silhouettes of cacti rose up like headstones, the wind warm and invasive. Like her hands.

As his shirt billowed up his torso, her fingers followed, exploring the ridges of his abs. He forced indifference into his posture, neither leaning in nor shoving her away. He refused to give her the satisfaction of a response.

She pressed closer, her hot body flush to his back, as her hand slid between his legs, finding him soft. But not for long.

His lungs expanded with dusty air, his cock thickening. She didn't rub him or open his fly. She simply rested her fingers there, curled around his growing bulge.

It was torture. He wanted her to stroke him, to pull him out and give him a fleeting moment of pleasure before his world became nothing but pain.

But he had far more control than that. In seven years, he hadn't acted on his carnal impulses. Didn't stop his mind from placing her lips around him. He let the fantasy distract him for a few minutes, sinking into images of his cock buried in her throat, her cunt, and deep in her ass.

He had a penchant for anal—the strangling tightness, the forbidden nature of it, and the punishing fear it evoked. Just thinking about it made him hard as a rock.

Lydia squeezed his length, acknowledging his body's reaction. Good for her. If she had any intentions of using sex to manipulate him, she had the wrong guy.

Getting off wasn't high on his personal agenda. His only priority was protecting the people he cared about, and to do that, he needed to arrive at the destination without crashing.

So he shut down the fantasy, shut out the feel of her hand, and concentrated on navigating the sandy land.

She steered him through the darkness, pointing this way and that. No one could find their way out of this desert without a map or GPS. Except Tomas. But she didn't falter in her directions.

Given the high-tech bugs in Rylee's house and the armed drone tracking Matias' aircraft, he assumed Lydia's helmet was equipped with the necessary communication equipment to guide her back to civilization.

At last, he reached the main road, the pavement giving him license to open the gas and fly. She tightened her arms around his waist, hugging his back with her entire body as he bent into the wind.

If a cop clocked him for speeding, he would just have to ride faster and outrace the patrolman. He wasn't stopping for anyone or anything.

His pulse revved with the roar of the engine, the bike vibrating between his legs. For the next hour or so, he didn't pass another motorist. Vacant fueling stations and diners blurred by. No cop cars in sight.

COMPLICATE

The dark nothingness pushed his thoughts into dangerous introspection. He had one goal—arrive before twenty-three hundred. Beyond that, he was terrified of what was going to happen.

Torture was barbaric and uncivilized, but it was effective. Whatever these people wanted, he most likely wouldn't be able to surrender it.

They were going to make him hurt.

Would it be more than he could bear? Probably. Would he survive it? Maybe not. But he'd been trained for this. Trained to put labels on his thoughts and compartmentalize his feelings, all in an effort to gain a sense of control in a situation where he had no control over the process or the pain.

Lydia directed him off the main highway. From there, he took narrow back roads through a desolate wasteland. The few buildings he passed were closed-up and crumbling. The skeletal remains of a ghost town.

He wasn't familiar with this part of Texas. While it seemed they'd been traveling southward most of the journey, there had been a number of turns, and he didn't know how much time had passed.

As the clock ticked toward twenty-three hundred, did he have thirty minutes left? Five? None?

The uncertainty pushed him faster, his pulse racing with urgency.

She touched his forearm and motioned to veer right just as a turnoff came into view. It was an entrance to something, the property encircled by a tall, unkempt chain-link fence. The enclosure served more as a boundary marker than a security measure.

Moving closer, he spotted a large industrial building in the distance. No lights or signs of life. *Weird.*

He sped through an unmanned gate and passed several empty parking lots. The property appeared to be vacant. Until he circled the side.

At least a dozen vehicles sat along an old loading dock. She indicated for him to park there, and the moment he turned off the engine, he yanked off the helmet.

"What time is it?" He twisted, hauling her off the motorcycle with him, hurrying her along. "Call off the strike."

She reached around him and grabbed the key from the ignition, pocketing it.

His palms slicked with sweat as she removed her helmet. His mouth dried as she shook out her hair, taking her sweet-ass time. His blood pressure climbed as she pulled the tablet from her pack.

"Look at that." She smiled at the screen, her accent thickening. "Two minutes to spare."

"We're here. Call it off."

Her incisive gaze traveled down his body. "Remove your clothes."

FOUR

Lydia held the smile on her face, but inside she felt cold. Merciless. There was no room for anything else. Cole Hartman was a doorway, and she would cut her way through him to reach the other side.

His nostrils flared, and his neck corded, muscles and veins straining against his skin. He planted his boots wide apart, seething, damn near shaking with fury and fear.

Yes, fear. He was a battle-honed tough guy, but he had a weakness. An aircraft full of weaknesses. In his line of work, he knew better than to get attached to people. That was his own fucking fault.

"We had a deal." He stepped into her space, his rock-hard chest in her face.

Christ, he smelled good. Wild and earthy, like the dusty wind on a dark road. Dangerous and sexy, like the brawn flexing beneath his shirt.

He was gorgeous beyond all sense of the word. With that chiseled body and those fathomless brown eyes, he could crush a perfectly good heart.

Good thing she didn't have one.

She glanced at the clock on the tablet. "One minute."

His lips curled back, baring straight white teeth in the moonlight. And dimples. A pair of them bracketed his enraged scowl, forming deep divots in his beard. Cute. Like a furious grizzly bear.

With a snarl, he reached over his head and grabbed the back of his shirt, yanking it off in that way men did. Tattoos covered his sinewy arms and sculpted chest. Almost as many as she had. But where her ink glowed with color, his were black, the images impossible to make out in the dark.

He held her gaze as he toed off his boots and unbuttoned his jeans. He didn't look away as he shoved down his pants and kicked them off.

"Call off the drone." He regarded her with an unflinching glare, fully nude and chillingly stoic.

As much as she wanted to look down, she didn't check out his body. She refused to break eye contact. Not even as the door opened and armed men spilled outside.

"Your friends are safe." She watched his expression relax a half-second before it hardened again. "Show Mr. Hartman the live video."

Someone appeared at her side. Without glancing, she knew it was Mike. No one looked at her like he did, the heat of his gaze flickering over her, searching for injuries.

He already knew she was unharmed. The technology in her helmet had allowed them to communicate while she was away. But he wasn't rational when it came to her safety.

He was insanely overprotective.

Holding a laptop, he pivoted the screen toward Cole. It showed the Colombian cartel jet coasting at a distance ahead of the drone. A moment later, the drone veered off, changing course, the strike aborted.

Cole stood motionless, except his eyes. They tracked the screen, his expression showing no hint of relief.

It had taken months of digging and a Hail Mary plan to locate the cartel's private aircraft. They had multiple hangars in South America, all of which were monitored for activity by her team. She'd hoped Cole's most powerful ally, Matias Restrepo, would make the journey to Texas, but she hadn't known when or who would be with him.

She'd lucked out when the whole damn crew boarded that plane.

Without a word, she grabbed Cole's clothes and strode toward the building. Her fifteen-man team moved in around him, heavily armed and highly trained. They were hardened soldiers, their backgrounds diverse, spanning from criminal to retired military. But they were all here for the same reason. A paycheck.

Could they be bribed to switch sides? Not easily. But everyone had a price. If Cole made the right offer, maybe he could gain an ally among her crew.

For that reason, no one would be allowed near him unless she or Mike were present.

She entered through the loading dock, confident that Cole wouldn't give them any problems. If he tried to escape, they would shoot to wound, not to kill. He was worthless to her dead.

He was also too smart to run. Without clothes or transportation, he wouldn't get far in the desert.

COMPLICATE

Past the loading ramps, she turned into a spartan corridor. Dust coated the concrete walls and floors. Overhead, stark fluorescent lights illuminated layers of sand that had crept in from outside and gritty powder left over from the raw materials that had once been hauled in and out of this building.

Years ago, a manufacturing company used this warehouse to split and carve granite blocks into monuments, mausoleums, crypts, and headstones.

She'd needed a secure, out-of-the-way place to do this job, and this was what she got. A building where tombs had been made. *Fitting*.

At the end of the corridor, she passed the factory floor. All that remained were piles of discarded granite and limestone, broken machinery, and dust. Powdery residue clung to everything, each step stirring it into the air and making her sneeze.

She turned away, taking another hallway toward their makeshift quarters.

Over the past four months, they'd converted the storage rooms into private sleeping spaces, hauling in mattresses and other comforts when they weren't hunting and planning and preparing for the right moment to take Cole Hartman.

Getting him here was the easy part. A long, arduous road lay ahead, and by God, she was ready. She'd waited eleven years for this, and she was so close to the end. So fucking close she could taste it.

In her room, she changed into lounge pants and a soft t-shirt. A wobbly old table sat in the corner, covered in cosmetics and beauty supplies. She slumped into the chair and began the mindless task of removing false eyelashes and cleansing away makeup.

That done, she grabbed a bag of Twizzlers and flopped onto her back on the mattress. Pulling out a long red rope of candy, she chewed on the end, lost in thought.

It was after midnight when the door to her room opened. Mike stepped in, carrying a microwaved burrito on a paper plate.

She shoved the half-eaten bag of candy beneath her. Too late.

He pounced, snatching the Twizzlers and dropping the plate on the bed beside her.

"I'm not eating that." She shoved away the food.

He pushed it back. "You need protein, not empty calories." He tossed the candy on the table.

"There's nothing more unhealthy than a frozen burrito."

"Say that again." He crawled onto the mattress, grinning.

Oh, man. She was a sucker for his crooked Bruce Willis smile. He looked like a younger version of the actor—all cocky and handsome with that indestructible, blue-collar edge that women loved. He also brought a level of warmth and humor that no one saw but her.

Mike was her rock, and every day at his side was a good day to die hard.

"Say what again?" She blinked, playing dumb.

"You know what." He grabbed the burrito and shoved it against her mouth.

"Burrito," she muttered around the dried-out shell.

"I love the way you say those *Rs* in that accent." He tipped his head, biting down on his grin. "Like they're stuck in your throat, and you have to hack them out."

"Shut up."

"Eat." He pressed the burrito to her hand.

She pouted but didn't have many options. The only food around here was either frozen or in a can.

While she gave in and ate, he stripped down to his briefs and stretched out on the mattress beside her. There were other rooms and other beds, but he never left her alone at night. As the only woman among a team of single, testosterone-fueled men, she was grateful he had her back.

Neither she nor Mike selected the men assigned with them. Before this job, they didn't know any of these people. She could count on them to obey orders and earn their wages, but she didn't trust them.

She didn't trust anyone but Mike.

With her dinner eaten and the lights off, she collapsed against him, tucked under a muscled arm with her cheek on his chest. His hand found hers, twining their fingers together.

As much as she didn't want to think about Cole, the instant she closed her eyes, all she saw were his. Huge brown eyes. Disarmingly intelligent.

"How did our prisoner react to his room?" she asked.

"As you would expect."

"He didn't react."

"Nope. No last-ditch attempts to escape. No struggle. Not a twitch behind that beard."

Her chest constricted. "He's smart."

"He's trained. But we've gone up against harder men than him."

"Maybe."

"It's not too late to cut our losses and get *F* out of *H*."

"Are you serious?" She popped up, glaring at him in the dark. "What the hell, Mike?"

COMPLICATE

"Calm down. I was just tossing it out there." He gripped a lock of her hair and pulled. "Come here."

She went, returning her head to his chest. "We have to finish this."

"I know."

"No matter what."

His silence rang through the room, his objections deafening. She wriggled closer, resting her brow against his whiskered cheek. His jaw felt like steel, his entire body rigid with tension.

They'd argued about her role in this job, and he wasn't over it.

"I can do this." She ran a hand over his neatly trimmed crew cut, trying to soothe him.

"What if you can't? What if he's as unflappable on the inside as he is on the surface?"

"Everyone has a breaking point. I'll find his."

FIVE

How many days had Cole been in here? Had it been a week? Longer? He hugged his knees to his chest, his body naked and filthy, every inch covered in itchy dust.

No use trying to find a comfortable position on the hard floor. The cell was designed for misery.

Dirty.

Empty.

Pitch-black.

He only saw daylight twice a day when someone opened the door to toss in food and switch out the buckets. A bucket for drinking and a bucket for shitting. Christ, he hoped they didn't mix up the two.

While lying on the cold concrete and living off a repulsive diet of frozen hot dogs, he was forced to listen to the same aggressive, head-pounding, thrash metal song over and over and over. It was a three-minute meth binge on repeat, delivered at a blistering velocity that tried to rip off his fucking face.

He used to love hardcore music, but after a few days of guttural vocals and distorted riffs, the genre was ruined for him. He didn't recognize the song. Not at first. Now he knew every raging word and shredded guitar chord. He hated it. He wanted to stab his goddamn ears with an ice pick.

It was truly painful, digging under his skin and dry-humping at his last nerve.

But that was the point.

Psychological torture.

COMPLICATE

The only time they shut it off was when they opened the door. He tried not to anticipate those moments, but there was nothing else to do but wait.

And wait.

And wait.

At last, the song fell silent.

He didn't move, didn't lift his head from his bent knees. He could still hear the rampant adrenaline of music, the pounding discord permanently embedded in his eardrums.

Footsteps entered his cell, and three frozen hot dogs landed on the floor beside him, rolling in the dust.

He snatched them up and didn't hesitate to shove the processed meat into his mouth, dirt and all. Eating these things cold made his stomach turn, but he preferred that over lukewarm meat. The ice coating assured him they hadn't been sitting out. They should be safe from contamination and food poisoning.

Swallowing the last bite, he hungered for more. But it was always the same. Three hot dogs per visit. Two visits a day.

As an unarmed man swapped out the buckets, Cole stole a peek at the old factory floor beyond.

Piles of stones, discarded materials, and abandoned machinery lay beneath a coating of dust. Amid the waste material, he identified broken headstones.

It was a clue. But without any knowledge of headstone companies in Texas, it didn't help him determine his location.

Not that he could escape.

A group of men stood just outside the door to his cell. Never less than six in total and always armed. None of them spoke Russian.

He would have to physically overpower them before they fired a weapon.

Impossible.

Any attempt to run would only get him injured, and up until now, they hadn't inflicted so much as a bruise. So he remained motionless during their visits, biding his time.

With the buckets refreshed, the guard stepped out. But today, the door didn't close.

The others moved out of view, their footsteps retreating but not going far. Then a tread of clicking steps approached. A slow, confident gait. Click-clack. Click-clack.

He hadn't heard this one since he'd been thrown in this room, but he knew who it was before she appeared in the doorway.

Cheetah-print pants molded to her sexy figure, and her low-cut white shirt had a skull-and-bones pirate flag across the front.

Her fire-engine red hair was pulled into two high pigtails, leaving wisps of long bangs around her face. Same heavy makeup as the night he'd met her, her fuckable lips shiny with wet gloss.

Leaning a shoulder against the door frame, she raised a rope of red licorice to her mouth and nibbled on the end.

He rested his head back against the wall, watching her with lazy detachment.

"Are you hungry?" She bit off a length of the candy, holding it between her white teeth before slurping it into her mouth. "You look like you could use some sugar."

He would kill for a taste of anything but hot dogs, but he wasn't playing her games.

"You haven't spoken since you arrived." She tapped the licorice against her mouth.

At some point, she would tell him why he was here and what they wanted. Until then, silence was the only control he had over her.

She took a visible breath, straining the fabric of the shirt across her tits. Full, beautifully shaped tits that would more than fill his hands.

Her eyes, dark green in the distance. Her lips, a deadly trap around the candy. Her body, toned with muscle and curved to perfection. Yeah, if he were another man in a different situation, he would fuck the shit out of her.

But he wasn't. He didn't pursue women or harbor sexual fantasies about his enemies.

"You can get out of here." She strolled toward him and crouched at his side, smothering his senses in her soft feminine scent. "You can have all the candy you want, the food you crave, a comfortable bed, and a woman to warm it." She tilted her head, regarding him intently. "Multiple women, if that's your thing."

His lip curled. He couldn't help it. He didn't want anyone in his bed but Danni. His appetite for sex was constant, but wanting and doing were two different things. Celibacy was a choice. His self-punishment. God knew he deserved worse after the torment he'd put Danni through.

"Do you want a shower?" She reached out and touched his forehead, gently brushing his greasy hair from his eyes. "You want a toothbrush and clean clothes?" Her fingers drifted to his beard, softly stroking. "You can live like a free man. Or you can die like a prisoner on death row."

If revenge was her endgame, she wouldn't be dangling rewards in front of him.

She wanted something from him.

He waited for it, his heart thundering in his chest. What would she demand in exchange for the bullshit she offered?

COMPLICATE

She glanced down, taking in his nude form. With his knees to his chest and his feet tucked against him, she couldn't see much.

Not that he cared. She could stare all she wanted. She could tease him, touch him, bludgeon him, and cut off his limbs. As long as he had breath in his body, he would not cower to her or her band of merry men.

"I have plans for you, Cole Hartman." She put her face in his, her lips so close he could almost taste the sticky candy on them. "But we have time, and I'm a very patient woman."

She rose and strode toward the door, her spine straight, almost regal, with her pigtails spiraling down her back in tangled glory.

At the threshold, she paused, glancing back. "Think about what I said. We'll talk again in a week or two."

A week or *two*? His molars slammed together, every muscle in his body stiffening to lunge and drag her back. But that was what she wanted. She was baiting him.

He reined in his fear and fought down his anger, blanking his face and maintaining his silence. He gave the bitch nothing, and she gave nothing back.

Except a closed door and inky darkness.

Then the music restarted, striking his ears with a vengeance.

SIX

Days passed. A week. Maybe more. The perpetual isolation wore on Cole, his entire world reduced to hot dogs and the same soul-sucking song on repeat.

He kept his mind and body busy with exercise. Push-ups, sit-ups, lunges, running in place—his options were limited in the confined space. He was losing weight at a rapid pace, and his energy and strength suffered for it.

There were moments when he was convinced that electrocution or dismemberment would've been better. Every minute in the darkness lasted an eternity, every visit from the guards a plaguing disappointment.

He'd never felt so trapped. Restless. Hungry. Unraveling at the seams. They'd kicked open the gates of hell and unleashed a level of torture that left him hopeless and walking the edge of insanity.

Okay, maybe that was the lyrics of the song in his ears, but he felt it. He was fucking living it.

Nevertheless, each time the door opened, he kept his shit together. He didn't beg or reveal a trace of emotion. When the guards taunted him, he met their eyes and showed no response.

It required more self-restraint than he thought he was capable. One of these times, he was going to detonate. He could feel himself slipping, losing his hold on his brittle control.

He wanted to kill them all.

The music shut off again, and the door opened to the man he'd met the first night, the one who'd operated the drone. Fuck, that felt like forever ago.

COMPLICATE

Did his team disappear like he'd ordered? Or were they still in Texas, searching for him?

Locating people was *his* skill set, not theirs. He was the best at extracting information and siphoning minute details. It took time and patience, but he would eventually elicit what he needed from these assholes and use it to escape. But if they got their hands on his friends, they could manipulate him in ways he didn't want to imagine.

"We haven't officially met," the man said. "My name is Mike."

The fact that he looked like Bruce Willis wasn't comforting. Hopefully, Mike would be easier to take down than the action heroes Bruce often portrayed.

"Get dressed." He tossed a pair of jeans into the cell. "I have a job for you."

Relief warred with distrust, coursing through him with numbing adrenaline. He wanted to ask how long he'd been here, but it wasn't an important question. So he saved the words and woodenly shoved his unwashed legs into the jeans.

"Follow me." Mike ambled toward the factory floor, ignoring the armed guards who stood near the only exit.

Cole followed him out while zipping up his fly. The jeans belonged to him but no longer fit. Even with the button fastened, they sagged, hanging loosely below his hipbones. He'd lost too much weight.

It could be worse. He hadn't lost blood or limbs or his sanity.

Not yet.

He stood in a massive, rectangular warehouse the length of a football field with concrete floors and brick walls. The rafters soared several stories above, and windows lined the upper half, far too high to reach. Grime coated the glass, obscuring the view of the sky. But sunlight filtered through the smudges, bright and hot, burning his eyes.

Up ahead, Mike waited with his arms relaxed at his sides and a lopsided smile tipping his mouth. That smile couldn't be trusted, no matter how friendly it appeared.

Cole pulled up his jeans enough to not trip over the dragging cuffs. Then he made his way toward Mike.

Footsteps sounded behind him. Two guards on his trail.

He could disarm one of them and use the weapon to kill them both. Mike didn't appear to be carrying a gun, so Cole could take him out, too. But what about the three men at the exit? And the other ten beyond the door? Since arriving, he'd counted sixteen altogether, including Lydia. If he started a gunfight, he wouldn't make it out alive.

"We're not going far," Mike said over his shoulder, walking ahead.

Pallets of discarded stones and cracked blocks of granite cluttered the length of the warehouse. Steel siding sealed up the doors at the far end. No way out. So where the hell were they going?

His nerves frayed, his shoulders twitching with the impulse to turn back.

Then he saw her.

Past a wall of crates, she stood with her back to him.

His gaze caught on the shimmering beauty of red hair, the nip of a tiny waist, and the flashing tease of creamy white legs beneath her dress.

A fucking dress. In a headstone factory. In the middle of the desert.

It cinched at her waist and flared out around her knees. Black fabric with red cherries. Red heels with little red bows. Impractical as fuck. Eye-catching beyond reason.

He couldn't stop staring.

She turned, angling her face into the glow of the windows. Pale shimmers of light accentuated the delicate curves of her profile and illuminated the stunning spirals and brilliant red tones of her hair. Her bangs looped into some sort of pompadour at the front, with the side parts rolling under and down. Strangely vintage. Fashionably retro. Her entire look screamed 1950s.

He'd never seen anything so shockingly exquisite, so uniquely beautiful. Flawless skin, luscious lips, and voluptuous curves. A statuesque woman with the appearance of a goddess, the heart of demoness, and a fashion style all her own.

She touched her chin to her shoulder and gave a slow blink, her unnaturally long lashes fanning over porcelain cheeks. Then her sea-green eyes latched onto his.

Their stares locked for a full second. Long enough to forget where he was or how he got here. A million things needed to be said, but words didn't exist in the space of their eye contact. Only sensations. Buzzing along the skin. Static in the air. Fire over ice in a heart that couldn't melt.

In that unexpected moment between them, he was a normal man, standing before a woman, with a rush of warmth in his chest. She felt it, too, her lips parting, her gaze losing focus. The world blurred, disorientating, and at the same time, perfectly balanced.

She straightened, turning away, and he released a soundless breath, thunderstruck.

And infuriated.

What the fuck just happened? Did they drug the hot dogs? Or was this a side-effect of prolonged isolation?

He was losing his fucking mind.

COMPLICATE

Nothing about that woman was real. From her dazzling hair color to her cherry red smile, she wore a false face and a glamorous facade.

Mike prowled over to her and slid a hand around her waist with intimate familiarity. She shifted toward him, and their foreheads came together, touching affectionately. He spoke quietly against her mouth and stroked her hair, her arm, her lower back.

The man's entire manner seemed to transform in her presence, his expression softening, shoulders relaxing, his posture leaning as if sucked in by her orbit.

The pathetic fool loved her.

Hard to tell if she reciprocated the sentiment. She didn't reject his touch. She also didn't look at him in the same way. Not in the breathless, gobsmacked way she'd just looked at Cole.

Mike said a few words near her ear and stepped away, his demeanor hardening, turning cold as he focused on Cole.

"I mentioned a job." He clasped his hands behind him, his head down and eyes up. "We want you to work for us."

Like hell he would.

If it was a reasonable job, they wouldn't have threatened his friends, forced him here against his will, and locked him in isolation. No, they knew he would never agree to this.

Assuming they knew his range of skills, they probably wanted to recruit him for a heist or infiltration mission to steal something of value—a person, a treasure, or priceless information. Whatever it was, the job would be dangerous, undesirable, and in no way worth his time or risk.

Not that they intended to give him a choice.

He met Mike's eyes, exuding the cagey, reticent persona he'd maintained over the past couple of weeks. They had no idea what was going on in his head, if he was slowly going crazy or completely unaffected by the situation.

A silent man who didn't stand up for himself was often perceived as ignorant and malleable. He needed them to underestimate him and would continue to play that role until they let their guards down.

"Now, I know you're thinking you could never work for us. But I have something you won't be able to resist." Mike moved toward the wall of crates and slid a box into view with his boot. "You want to eat like a king?"

From the box, he removed a can of chicken, a bag of potato chips, and a bottle of beer.

Cole's mouth watered at the sight of the beer. Fucking Christ, what he wouldn't give for a taste of hops on his tongue.

"Yeah, yeah, I know." Mike chuckled. "It's not really a royal feast, but it's better than the alternative, yeah?"

Better than hot dogs? Damn straight.

"The task is simple." Mike tapped his toe against a pallet of broken granite. "Move these pieces to the pallet over there."

He motioned at the empty platform forty yards away.

The rock pile spanned six-feet high by six-feet wide, and each chunk was wider than his chest. Brutally heavy, no question. His back and feet would bear the brunt of it.

Why did they want debris moved from one platform to another? To test his strength? To torture him psychologically? Maybe they were just bored?

"I want my boots."

"Holy shit, he can talk." Mike pointed at him and arched a brow at Lydia. "After sixteen days of silence, I was starting to wonder."

Sixteen fucking days. He'd guessed it had been that long, but hearing it didn't make it easier to stomach. If they owned this building, which was highly likely, this could go on for months.

Unless the thing they wanted from him had a time limit.

"I know it's lonely in that cell, and you're wondering what the point of all this is." Mike patted him on the shoulder. "Well, we're working up to that. Little steps. Right now, those steps go from this pallet to that pallet. Without your boots. Do a good job and you'll get the food in that box."

He needed the carbohydrates. He desperately wanted the beer. But more than that, it was imperative that he spend as much time as possible outside of that cell. Not only for his mental wellbeing but to observe his captors and do what he did best—listen and learn, make small talk and befriend, all the while subtly extracting information.

So without hesitation, he shouldered past Mike and heaved the first hunk of granite from the pile. His muscles strained beneath the eighty-pound weight.

Sixteen days ago, he would've carried it with no trouble. Today, he felt it in his arms, his back, and his feet as he hauled the load across the warehouse.

Mike stepped away, joining the two guards in conversation. They were too far away for Cole to eavesdrop but close enough to shoot him if he decided to slam a rock into Lydia's head.

She perched on a crate beside the full pallet, watching him drop off his burden and walk back. He took his time. No reason to hurry. The longer it took him to move the pile, the longer he was out of the head-banging cell.

Except that bottle of beer was waiting. An effective incentive.

"Your jeans are falling." She crossed one leg over the other and propped an elbow on her knee.

COMPLICATE

He paused before her, fully aware that his waistband hung obscenely low, exposing the patch of hair above the root of his cock. Her eyes went there, lingering, before lifting to his.

"Such a shame." She sniffed. "You had a beautiful physique when I met you." Her gaze darted toward Mike and the guards and returned to him, her accent lowering. "Do what you're told, and you'll gain back those muscles."

He glanced down at his torso, trying to see what she saw. Was he skinnier? Yeah. But he still had definition. He was still physically stronger than her and could overpower her tiny body if he got her alone.

Hell, if he got her alone, he would wrench that dress over her head and drive his fist between her legs. He would tear up her cunt and fuck her ass until both holes were permanently stretched open, gaping and waiting to receive his cock again.

He didn't have to like her to imagine her wet pussy slurping around his thrusts. In fact, his hatred for her made the fantasy all the more filthy.

"You know what I want?" He lowered his voice, deliberately rumbling the words.

Her eyes dilated, her breaths quickening. "What?"

"*Palimi* with sour cream and caviar."

She flinched, her brows knitting together.

"Russian pancakes." He cocked his head. "Don't you know what that is?"

"Of course, I know. My grandma made them for me." She narrowed her eyes. "You only moved one stone. Are you tired already?"

"Tired of eating processed shit." He leaned down, exhaling in her face. "I want a toothbrush and toothpaste, and right now, I imagine you want me to have those things."

"Finish the job, and I'll think about it." She didn't shift away, but the scrunch of her nose confessed the state of his breath.

Good.

While his whole body needed a thorough cleaning, the fur on his teeth bothered him the most.

He stepped back and dragged another rock off the pile. As he towed it across the warehouse, he felt her gaze on his ass, knowing the top half of his crack hung above the sagging jeans.

Didn't matter how badly he reeked or how much muscle he'd lost. She liked looking at him as much as he liked looking at her. His was an unwanted attraction. Maybe hers was, too.

Or maybe she put on that dress and made up her hair because she wanted him to notice her.

Was she after information in his head? Or was this a ploy to use him and his skill set to acquire something for them?

They had no idea who they were dealing with.

If she intended to seduce him into cooperating, she should start by washing that shit off her face. But even then, she didn't have a chance in hell.

He hoped she planned to use sex to get to him so that it could backfire on her with deadly consequences.

SEVEN

Lydia couldn't ignore the thudding in her ears or the heat swimming in her belly. It produced a terrible glow inside her, giving rise to a complicated question.

What if?

Two simple words, known to spark monumental theories and discoveries. They could also lead to disastrous mistakes.

She wasn't the only one asking the question. It took two to engage in eye contact, and when she and Cole stared at each other, both of them sizzling in the charged air, she saw her reaction on his face. She saw her shock, her curiosity, her *what if?*

Under no circumstances was she expecting his gaze to grab her and twist her up like it did. She wasn't expecting the sheer intensity in his eyes as they imprisoned hers, seeing her as something other than an enemy.

Deep down, beneath the scars of loss and the vitriol that had led her here, she was a woman like any other, with longings and vulnerabilities and dreams that had nothing to do with violence and death.

She'd done well enough to bury that softer side over the past eleven years, and in one goddamn look, Cole Hartman brought it to life.

She blamed the dimples.

And his mysterious confidence.

Not to mention his alluring sex appeal, the rugged build of his powerful body, the sculpted flex of his ass, and the untamed beard that should smell disgusting in its unwashed state but instead only added to his masculine potency.

Damn him for being so devilishly, unfairly handsome.

And damn him for putting these foolish musings in her head.

Watching him heave stone after stone wasn't helping her concentration. She shouldn't be affected. This was a job. If she started warming to him, years of training and sacrifice would be forfeited.

She couldn't afford to lose all the progress she'd made just because the job happened to be a sexy son of a bitch.

She. Could. Not. Fail.

No more what-ifs. No spontaneous explorations of possibilities. Any deviation from the plan was bad for her and this operation. Because one thing was certain. Cole was precisely the type of man who would use her and leave her for dead when he finished.

As he trudged between the pallets, his teeth clenched with exertion. He'd lost muscle mass, but he'd started out with so much. Far more than the average man.

He still had a decent amount of brawn flexing through his frame. And a golden complexion. Pillowy lips. A chiseled face. His expression, when at rest, wore a natural smile. Flirtatious without even trying. Dangerous to the core. He was a gorgeous, tattooed beast.

If she had a type, it was Cole Hartman. She imagined he was every woman's type. Including the one he let go.

Danni Savoy.

The pretty dancer was inked on his forearm amid a collage of unrelated designs and symbols. She glimpsed a motorcycle, an inverted cross, several suns, a leaf, chains, a spider web, and dozens of other illustrations too small to make out at this distance.

The artwork sleeved both arms and half of his chest. And though she hadn't stolen a glimpse of him naked, Mike had mentioned there was a large black snake coiled around his thigh.

This wasn't a guy who put fortuitous ink on his skin. Every piece told a story, a secret, and she wanted to learn them all. Starting with the dancer.

She knew very little about Danni aside from his relationship with her. They'd dated for ten months. Got engaged. Then he took a job that separated them for three years. That job was the reason he lost her to his best friend.

It was also the reason he was here.

Danni was his greatest weakness. She was also untouchable. Married to an obscenely wealthy casino owner, she was surrounded by a team of bodyguards at all times and hadn't left the security of the casino since Lydia's team started watching her.

Cole must've alerted her husband of possible danger. Not that it mattered. Lydia had what she needed to coax Cole into compliance.

COMPLICATE

If he thought his time in that cell had been unbearable, he had no idea what she was saving him from. She was the only thing standing in the way of his unspeakable suffering.

But if she failed to hold up her end of the bargain, he was a dead man.

Keeping him in the dark—literally and figuratively—was for his own good. And hers. She needed him alive.

Strangely, though, he wasn't demanding answers about why he was here and what they wanted. Wasn't he wondering why she used isolation and thrash metal over common methods of torture? Maybe his silence was some sort of tactic.

Hard to tell what he was thinking. Right now, he appeared fully engrossed in his task. A task that had been designed to test his cooperation. He was smart enough to realize that. But there were so many things he didn't know.

Halfway through the pallet, he took a break, standing beside her and breathing heavily. As he licked his lips, she couldn't look away from that diabolical mouth.

His gaze raked down her body and lingered on her legs. Then it made a return trip, stroking her like fire. A fire she intended to play with.

He met her eyes. "Why are you dressed like that?"

"To keep you guessing." She handed him a bottle of water.

"Here's my guess." He drained the bottle in one long gulp and tossed it aside. "You're an attention whore."

"Do you think I'm a whore because I have your attention? Or do I have your attention because you think I'm a whore?"

"I think you're trying too hard. You'd get a lot further with me if you spoke clearly, dropped the act, and washed that shit off your face."

Ouch. He didn't like her makeup? Or her accent?

"Oh, Cole." She rose to her feet, the heels putting her at eye-level with his lips. "I want you to accept me for who I pretend to be."

"You're a fucking freak," he said in a deep, resonant voice. No judgment. All heat. "That much is real."

"Yes, and you like it. You like it so much you want to ride it. See where it takes you. But here's a spoiler." She pressed closer, letting her chest brush against his. "It's a ride you won't ever get off."

"Is that what happened to Mike? He hopped on the ride and lost his balls?"

She glanced over his shoulder and found Mike's hard eyes tracking her like a hawk. His scowl conveyed his displeasure, but he wouldn't intervene unless she was in trouble.

"Mike is my partner."

"Do all your partners love you?"

Nope. Just one.

She rested a palm on the warm, hard ridge of his pec. "I have that effect on people."

"Not on me, darlin'." He bent in, his breath hot against her mouth. "If you want to turn me into a boy toy, if that's your big plan, you need a new one."

Slowly, he edged closer, deleting the space between their lips. His hand slid beneath her hair and around her nape. Warm fingers. Calloused and strong. His beard tickled her chin. Scratchy. Musky. All man. The heat of his mouth blanketed hers. Taunting. Not quite touching.

Her throat went dry, and uncertainty dipped in her gut as she waited, dreading, anticipating. It was the longest second of her life.

But he didn't kiss her. Instead, he scraped his teeth against her upper lip, biting at the flesh above. Then he surprised her again by stepping back, his gaze strangely vacant.

Her skin tingled where his teeth had been. She reached up to touch beneath her nose and... "The fuck?"

The piercing was gone. He'd bitten the jewelry right out of her lip.

He angled toward the pallet and spat the tiny stone stud into the rock debris.

"How?" She trailed her tongue along the inside of her lip, seeking the tiny hole. "There was a back on it."

"Not anymore." He gave her a smile that he'd borrowed from Satan himself. A beautiful smile. Cruel. And far too smug for her liking.

She wanted to smack it off his face. So she did. With an open palm, she slapped him hard, sending an echoing *whack* through the warehouse.

It only made his smirk widen, lighting up his eyes. He didn't even flinch.

"Mighty arrogant," she said, "for a guy who's looking at another two weeks in isolation."

"You won't put me in there that long again." He turned away, grabbed a rock from the pile, and trucked it toward the other pallet.

"Why is that?"

"You'll miss me." He chucked the stone, landing it perfectly onto the platform and saving himself a few steps.

Miss him? She didn't even know him. That was the problem.

She knew he was allied with the Colombian cartel, was in love with a married woman who lived in St. Louis, had a team of criminals whose identities couldn't be traced. And he had information. Extremely valuable information that she needed.

Unfortunately, this wasn't a job she could just aim a gun at and demand compliance. It required discretion, delicate handling, and perfect timing.

COMPLICATE

She met Mike's narrowed gaze across the warehouse. He looked angry. And concerned. He didn't think she could pull this off, but she didn't have a choice.

Cole lumbered back and forth between the pallets, hauling rocks, working muscles, silent and watchful. His eyes were always watching, studying everything and everyone around him.

As he neared the bottom of the pile, he bent to snatch a large chunk of granite. A sharp hiss sounded beneath his breath, and he jerked back, empty-handed.

The piece he'd attempted to lift had a wicked sharp edge, and now, it was stained in blood.

For a moment, he just stood there, his brown eyes fixated on his hand. Beads of crimson welled from a deep gash on his palm and trickled down his fingers, dripping from the tips.

Momentary shock held her immobile, her pulse propelling through her veins. He didn't move, either, probably stunned by the pain.

The gush of blood didn't slow. Rivers of it collected in a growing puddle on the floor between them.

"Put pressure on it." She glanced around for something to stanch the flow.

There was nothing soft or clean in the vicinity. It was a stone factory, for fuck's sake. All hard surfaces and layers of dust.

"Shall I use my filthy hand to put pressure on it?" He cocked his head, chillingly calm. "Or some other part of my unwashed body?"

There was a first-aid kit somewhere in the private quarters. She shrugged.

"You didn't throw me in that room for sixteen days to let an infection take me." His gaze lowered, scrutinizing the material of her dress.

She stepped back, gripping the skirt. "I'm not destroying my clothes to bandage your hand."

"Give me your underwear."

Her head jerked back, her mind running at top speed. But once she got over the shock of his command, she saw it as an opportunity to negotiate.

"There's a rumor going around." She toyed with a lock of her hair. "They say you won't touch a woman."

His jaw twitched, his expression otherwise blank.

"Is it because of her?" She directed her eyes to the dancer tattooed on his arm. "I know you still love Danni. But it's been seven years. You let her go and yet, you're still faithful to her?"

That prompted a reaction. His nostrils pulsed. His shoulders tightened, his whole body fighting to rein in his temper.

"That's right, Cole. I know her name. I know what she means to you, and I know she lives in the penthouse of The Regal Arch Casino and Hotel in St. Louis."

He squeezed his hands into fists, wringing a torrent of blood onto the floor.

"I'll give you my panties if you give me something in return." She winged up a brow.

His eyes fired menacingly, his mouth a slash of unholy objection.

"Calm down." She softened her accent. "This is easy. Just tell me the last time you had sex."

He drew in a long breath through his nose, released it, and said nothing.

"Be reasonable," she said. "You're so close to eating a decent meal. Just give me an honest answer. Then you can wrap up that hand and finish the last few stones."

He straightened his spine and took a step forward. She held her ground, gazes locked.

His heat enveloped her, his scent ripe with sweat and dark masculinity as he put his mouth near her cheek.

"Seven years." His head tipped, his eyes sharp, confident, and oh-so-close. "The panties. Now."

EIGHT

Seven years.

Holy.

Fuck.

Her heart galloped at his proximity, the authority in his voice, and the implication of his words.

Seven years ago, Cole ended his relationship with the woman he loved. Yet he'd remained faithful to her all this time?

Whatever the reason, his answer filled Lydia's chest with giddy warmth. Too much. Damn her, but she respected his self-restraint at a depth that had nothing to do with the job.

There was something so very appealing and admirable about a man who didn't fuck everything in a skirt. And let's be clear. He absolutely could. With a crook of his finger, he could have any woman— single, married, or cloistered in a convent—on her back and moaning beneath him. The man was virile. Sexually charged. A deadly ladykiller.

And celibate.

How rare was that? It told her that sex meant something to him. It also confessed an inhuman degree of self-control. She couldn't abstain like that. She'd never even tried.

Christ, what would it be like with him? Seven years of pent-up intensity? The hunger and urgency? The explosiveness? She couldn't fathom it.

She would soon find out. Except it wouldn't be real. The only relationship she could entertain with him was a false one, steeped in lies and coercion.

Even so, she never backed out of a promise.

Without breaking eye contact, she reached beneath the dress and dragged down her panties. He didn't give her space, not an inch, as she carefully worked the silk past her hips without flashing the room.

In the bent position, her gaze went straight to his fly. It was right there, clinging precariously to the bulge beneath and exposing a trim patch of hair. Amid the short brown curls lay the base of his cock, thick and angled down, trapped by the sagging waistband. Even in his flaccid state, the root was substantial, promising the rest of him would be more than satisfying.

She wanted it. The dirtiness. The wrongness of it. She wanted *him*.

But this wasn't about her.

"I'm waiting." He yanked up his jeans, covering himself and breaking the spell.

She swallowed and let the underwear drop to her ankles. Then she straightened and met his eyes.

If he wanted the panties, he would have to get them himself.

He didn't waver.

Lowering to a crouch, he touched his uninjured hand to the back of her heel. She lifted it just enough to allow the garment to slip free. He moved to her other leg, repeating the action. Only this time, his hand lingered.

She stared straight ahead, trying not to react, even as every molecule in her body homed in on his touch.

Four fingertips, like four low-burning flames, ghosted up her ankle. The pressure was so subtle she wondered if she imagined it. But the goosebumps... Dear lord, she was shivering, burning up, unable to rein in her breathing.

The pads of his fingers traveled up her calf and teased the back of her knee. Her legs liquefied, her thighs aching to part, causing her heels to totter ever-so-slightly. He noticed and closed his hand around her leg, steadying her.

Her cheeks caught fire, her palms hot and clammy. She lifted her foot, stepping out of the panties and away from his torturous touch.

Slowly, he rose to his feet, all six feet and then some soaring over her. Her heart beat uncontrollably. Her lungs panted, her entire body flushed and overheated. And he looked aloof. Unfazed. Disinterested.

Cold as ice.

His indifference didn't thaw as he lowered his attention to the red silk in his hand. With a clinical efficiency, he wrapped the material around his injury, staring directly at her as he used his teeth to tie it off.

She didn't move. She couldn't. The man was fucking potent.

Then, as if nothing had happened, he returned to the pallet and resumed his task.

COMPLICATE

Really, nothing had happened. Nothing had changed.

Except the entire atmosphere had changed. It felt heavy and loud, buzzing along her skin and choking her lungs. Fucking hell, she needed to get out of here and breathe in some fresh air.

But the masochist in her waited.

She waited until he finished. Then she waited as he sat on the floor and tucked into his hard-earned meal. She couldn't detach her gaze from his strong throat as he drank deep swigs of beer. The pleasure on his face was glorious, breathtaking, and inconceivably mesmerizing.

He didn't speak while he ate, but his eyes stayed with her, watching her while he chewed, contemplating her while he finished off the beer with relish.

The muffled conversation between Mike and the guards drifted from across the warehouse. They'd remained within eyeshot, but she barely noticed them.

When Cole swallowed the last bite, he set the empty containers aside and stared at the red silk around his hand. Moments passed before he met her eyes and asked the question she'd been waiting to hear.

"Why am I here?"

"You have something I need." At his silence, she sighed. "Eleven years ago, information of political value fell into the hands of a bad actor."

His stare was steady, unflinching. "Was it stolen from the U.S. government?"

"Something like that."

"Digital property?"

"Yes."

"Who stole it?"

"Marie Merivale." She pursed her lips. "You caught her and put her in prison for life, but the digital property is still missing. I need you to tell me who bought it from her."

He made a low whistling sound and leaned back against the crate behind him. "Who do you think I am?"

Retired military? Undercover operative? Secret agent? The sexiest James Bond in real-life and fantasy? Who the fuck knew?

All she had to go on were rumors. His name was whispered in the shadows of the underground criminal world from Bucharest to Bogota. Too much talk from the women about his sex life — or lack thereof. Not enough talk from the men about his business dealings — no one really knew. But the gossip about his alliance with the Restrepo Cartel had proved true.

As far as she could discern, he once worked for a U.S. agency. But now, he reported to no one and operated outside the boundaries of the law.

"It doesn't matter who you are, Cole. I'm only interested in what you know. I need the name of the entity who bought that stolen property."

"And I need a toothbrush."

"I told you I would think about it."

"Who do you work for?" He drew up a knee and dangled his injured hand over it, regarding her with lazy detachment. "You're not secret intelligence. Definitely not U.S. government."

She smiled. "Does the accent give it away?"

"No, your lack of knowledge does."

She tried not to be offended, but he hit the mark. She'd been trained by a battle-hardened spy, but she didn't work for the NSA or any other agency. She wasn't in the know about domestic or foreign affairs.

She was completely out of her league.

"Why would stolen intel from eleven years ago have any relevance today?" he asked.

That got her attention. If he'd known anything about the information she sought, he wouldn't have asked that question.

"How do you not know?" She searched his eyes, her mind spinning. "You took down the defector who sold the intel, but you didn't know what that intel was?"

He just stared at her.

Well, this was unexpected, but it changed nothing. If anything, it gave her more leverage. He didn't care about the missing property. His only stake in this was his survival.

"How do you know about Thurney Bridge?" he asked.

What? She searched her memory and came up blank. She had no idea what he was talking about.

Hiding her confusion, she tucked away his question to investigate later. "Tell me who bought the stolen intel."

"I don't know."

His tone held conviction, his gaze unblinking. She almost believed him. Almost.

A lot of money, time, and risk had been put into Cole Hartman's capture because he was the only one close to Marie Merivale. He might not have known what she was selling, but he knew every person involved, including the buyer.

Lydia's team had made numerous attempts to interrogate Marie. Fruitless attempts. Federal prison was the safest, most inaccessible place for her to be. Any threats to her life were impossible. She had no family or friends to use against her. She was a dead end.

COMPLICATE

"If Marie wasn't in a high-security prison," she said, "we would've taken her instead of you. Think about that, Cole. If you would've just let her go and returned to your fiancée, you wouldn't be in this dilemma. And maybe your girl wouldn't have fucked your best friend."

His jaw set, and a vein bulged in his forehead.

Shit. She didn't mean to piss him off. That wasn't her goal.

"I shouldn't have said that. For what it's worth." She lowered onto the crate beside him and fidgeted with the hem of her dress. "No matter how perfect you think she was for you, there's always someone better."

He barked a humorless laugh. "You don't believe in love? Or fate?"

"In our line of work, there is only war, and that, *tigryenok*, is always fueled by hate."

"There's a quote—I think it's G.K. Chesterton—that goes something like, *A soldier fights not because he hates what's in front of him, but because he loves what's behind him.*" He lowered his voice, his cadence thoughtful as he rubbed his forehead. "We all have something valuable behind us, compelling us to fight. You already know mine. My friends, the people you threatened, they're my family."

That was the most personal thing he'd ever revealed, and she was so taken with the unguarded nature of his words that she didn't move, didn't dare interrupt.

"I'll be honest," he said, "when you showed me the video of the drone, it scared the shit out of me. Those people are irreplaceable. Not because they're perfect. They're not. But because they're *mine*. Mine to protect. Mine to fight for."

"Like Danni?"

"Yes, including Danni. So here I am, protecting them, fighting for them, not out of hate, but out of love. Because that's what people do." He dropped his head and raised his eyes, peering at her through his thick lashes. "Don't kid yourself, Lydia. There's more to this, to *you*, than hate. What are you fighting for? What do you love?"

An unwanted flutter thrummed in her belly. Everything he said gripped her deeply, his questions stroking hidden nerves. And those bottomless brown eyes... Jesus, they seemed to understand her. She wanted him to see more, to hear and feel her reasons.

She opened her mouth to answer him. And snapped it shut.

It was a trap. A damn good one. If she weren't so jaded, she would've fallen for it.

"I know what you're doing." She sat taller, meeting him stare for stare.

"Enlighten me."

"Maybe you're used to charming the pants off women before they even stop to wonder why, but…" Her breath caught, her eyes narrowing on the panties wrapped around his hand.

The panties, she realized with dawning horror, that she'd handed over without questioning the real reason he wanted them.

"You were saying?" His thumb roved over the silk on his palm, his expression stony.

Heat bloomed across her skin, her anger rising and something else, something stirring low in her belly. She hated him for this. For tricking her, and at the same time, turning her on.

She could be a petty bitch about it and take back the damn underwear. But no, that wasn't her. Instead, she shook it off and gave credit where credit was due.

"I don't know how you did it." She rose to her feet and smiled down at him. "I don't know how you talked me out of my underwear, but well done."

"You wanted me to have them."

Did she? God, maybe she did. "I won't fall for it next time."

"I look forward to it." He leaned his head back against the crate and closed his eyes. "Until next time, Lydia."

She stood there, bewildered and captivated.

Did he just dismiss her?

He was fucking playing her. She didn't know how exactly, but she felt it in her gut.

She didn't know his skill set, his training, or his background, but if the last few hours taught her anything, it was that she faced an opponent who wouldn't be easily defeated.

Without another glance, she strode toward Mike, who waited with an expectant look.

"Return him to his cell." She dipped her voice to a whisper. "Don't trust a word he says. Search him for weapons and watch your back." She scanned the warehouse. "I'm going to double the number of guards on him."

"What happened?"

Cole was too confident, too smart, and sneaky as fuck. She wouldn't be surprised if he'd stolen away a sharp rock or piece of glass when she wasn't looking. But it was his mouth that worried her the most. He knew how to manipulate people.

"Just following my gut." She squeezed Mike's hand. "We'll talk later."

She left the factory floor and strode down the corridor, her mind replaying every word and interaction she'd just shared with Cole. Had she unknowingly revealed something important? What if she'd said too much?

COMPLICATE

Lost in her thoughts, she turned the corner and collided with a hard body.

"Shit!" She looked up, coming face to face with Alec.

"In a hurry?" His smirk made her skin crawl.

"It's been a day." She side-stepped him only to be blocked again. "Move."

"Not so fast." He held out a phone. "You have a call."

The screen showed an unknown caller, but it could only be one person. Vincent Barrington. If he'd been waiting on the other end for any length of time, he wasn't going to be pleasant. Not that he knew the meaning of the word.

Drawing in a deep breath, she snatched the phone from Alec's hand and glared at him until he finally shifted to the side. She exited the building through a side door and took a short sidewalk that led to nothing but desert sand and a postcard-view of the sunset.

"*Privet i trakhat' tebya,*" she said sweetly into the phone.

"Speak English, or I'll replace you with someone who will." Vincent had a high-pitched vocal range with the twang of small-town Georgia. When he was angry, it could shatter glass. Like now. She held the phone away from her ear as he screamed, "When I call, do not keep me waiting!"

She made him wait two full seconds before responding in a monotone. "I was working."

"I don't give a fuck. I want an update."

He'd given her until the end of the year to complete the job. She still had two months. Plenty of time. But he had control issues, a severe lack of patience, and far more at stake in this operation than she did.

"As expected," she said, "he's not talking yet. But he will."

"*But he vill,*" he echoed, mocking her accent. "I want to know *when.*"

"When he realizes it's his only option." Slipping off her heels, she stepped into the warm desert sand. "He asked me how I knew about Thurney Bridge. What is he talking about?"

"I find it concerning that you're interrogating me instead of him."

"I find it concerning," she spat, her voice rising, "that you hired me for a job without giving me all the details to complete it."

"Careful, little girl. You're walking on very thin ice."

She pulled in a calming breath and moved on. "He doesn't know what's on the stolen hard drive."

"Of course, he doesn't. His only job was to uncover who sold the information, just like your only job is to uncover who bought it. Anything else is on a need-to-know, and neither of you needs...to...know."

He drawled out the last part in a condescending tone as if she were stupid for even mentioning it. Little did he know, when she finished this job, he would be the bigger fool.

"Anything else?" She paused, listening, and realized he'd already disconnected. "Good talk, Vincent. You heartless cunt."

He hadn't called to get an update from her. He received those from Alec.

The door opened behind her, followed by the tread of footsteps. A lighter flicked. A cloud of cigarette smoke billowed over her shoulder. She knew it was Alec before he spoke.

"Vincent's getting impatient."

"Vincent was born impatient." She turned to face him, holding the phone in one hand and the heels in the other while wearing a smile that veiled her distrust.

"Step out of the way, and I'll get Cole Hartman to sing."

"What do you know about him?"

He puffed on the cigarette, watching her through the smoke. "Give me an hour with him, and I'll know everything."

"Have you ever tortured a man? How about one who was trained to endure months of unspeakable pain?"

The idiot shrugged.

"The only thing you know is how to run your mouth about shit you don't know." She tossed the phone at him. "Until you have something useful to offer, shut the fuck up."

She strode toward the door, knowing full well he wouldn't let her have the last word.

Sure enough, his footfalls followed. Her muscles tightened, and she adjusted her grip on her heels, holding one in each hand.

As she reached the door, his palm slammed against it above her head, preventing her from opening it. Out of the corner of her eye, his cigarette skipped into the desert.

Over the past few months, her position on this team had been challenged repeatedly. Some of the men didn't like taking orders from a woman. A few thought because they were bigger than her or because she dressed the way she did that it was an invitation to take whatever they wanted.

They all tried. And failed.

She'd been waiting for Alec to make a move. Of course, just like the others, he chose to jump her when she was alone.

Fucking pussy.

"I have something useful to offer." He pressed his weight against her back and ground his hips. "Lift that dress, and I'll show you."

COMPLICATE

"Oh, yeah?" She turned her face toward him, resting her chin on her shoulder.

As if caught by an invisible string, his lips crept toward hers, closer, closer, close enough.

She bent her knees and dropped just enough to twist around and hook the heel of her shoe into the corner of his mouth. He yelped, ensnared, as she used the three-inch spike to wrench his head toward the ground.

His hands grappled to dislodge the shoe. But she had control of his head, and where the head went, the body followed. The technique forced him into a large step, opening up an easy takedown. Wobbly balance, a slight turn in his spine, and just like that, his mobility was fucked.

In the next breath, she had him in the sand, his mouth fish-hooked by one heel, and the other pressed into the inner corner of his bulging eye.

"I'm a twitch away," she said in a bored tone, "from slamming this into your tiny brain. Give me a reason, Alec."

His throat jogged with a hard swallow, his mouth gaping like a dying fish on a hook.

"Your job is to follow orders. My orders and Vincent's." She batted her eyelashes. "That's not so hard, is it?"

He tried to shake his head.

"Just so we're clear." She put her face in his, adding slight pressure on the spike against his eye. "Don't ever touch me again."

A sound of agreement coughed from the back of his mouth.

Good enough.

She rose to her feet and brushed off her dress. Without sparing him a glance, she entered the building, confident he wouldn't follow.

He didn't.

NINE

The next day, Cole received the usual ration of hot dogs, two fresh buckets, and some things he didn't expect. With a menacing scowl, the guard tossed in a toothbrush, toothpaste, and a box of medical supplies. None of it would help him escape, but it revealed a great deal about his captors.

One in particular.

Sitting naked in the dark with thrash metal music banging against his skull, he brushed his teeth, blindly patched up his hand, and thought about Lydia.

She wasn't who she pretended to be. She'd said as much during their conversation, but it was what she didn't say that gave her away.

During the few hours he'd spent with her yesterday, he'd put together a rudimentary profile on her. But he needed more time, a few more interactions to formulate a comprehensive outline of her identity, her mental and moral qualities, and most importantly, her motivation.

Once he understood her stakes, he could manipulate her from that angle.

She appeared to be the one in charge here, but this job was only one piece of a bigger operation. An operation that was controlled and funded by someone else. He'd figured out that much when he asked her about Thurney Bridge. She didn't have a clue what he was talking about.

That meant someone else had hired the hitman who attacked Rylee. Someone else was responsible for killing Rylee's neighbor and two motel clerks. Lydia hadn't been involved.

COMPLICATE

He shouldn't have felt so relieved, but dammit, he couldn't ignore the lightness in his chest. The hope. Irrational fucking hope that Lydia was more than just a criminal for hire, that maybe she had a forgivable reason for threatening his friends with a hellfire missile.

Dangerous thoughts.

He couldn't get attached. His only priority was survival, and if it came down to it, he would choose his life over hers.

He would choose Danni's life over everyone and everything.

They knew where she lived. But he couldn't dwell on that. He trusted Trace to protect her. There was no one on the planet who would keep her safer than her husband.

Resting his head against the wall, he drummed his fingers on the box of supplies. Lydia had given into his demand for a toothbrush, and the guards weren't happy about it. She hadn't stabbed needles under his fingernails or waterboarded him to death, and the guards didn't appear to be happy about that, either.

Other than her obvious relationship with Mike, she wasn't in sync with the rest of her team. They wanted to torture him for the information while she seemed to have a different agenda.

When she looked at him, he didn't see his demise shining in her eyes. Quite the opposite. The flush in her cheeks, the quiver in her legs, the blatant sexual attraction that radiated from her pores—she wanted him.

But it could all be part of the act.

Sexpionage was a common practice among intelligence services all over the world, especially in Russia. It was a filthy tactic to elicit information, executed by trained ravens and swallows who had little left of their humanity.

Lydia had a red swallow inked on her chest. Was it a clue? It seemed too obvious, but if she was a hired swallow, she had only one objective here—to compromise him sexually. She certainly dressed the part, and it would explain why she hadn't tortured him. Her beauty alone would bring a weaker man to his knees.

But beneath the evocative cleavage and overdone makeup, he detected something softer, something akin to…kindness. An unfeeling sex spy wouldn't give her target a toothbrush and medical supplies. Unless that was part of her act? A ploy to seduce him into trusting her?

He pressed his fingers to his brow, his head pounding with the music and the weariness of his thoughts.

What a goddamn mindfuck.

The kicker was he could give them what they wanted right now. He could bang on the door and tell them who bought the stolen hard drive from Marie Merivale. But the moment he gave it up, he was a dead man.

They had no intention of letting him walk out of here. The only thing keeping him alive was the information in his head.

He had to escape.

So he remained silent, biding his time, waiting for an opportunity to make his move.

That opportunity lay with Lydia.

If she intended to fuck him into compliance, he would be the one doing the fucking.

He would fuck her until she sobbed his name, surrendered to his will, and begged him for more.

TEN

Over the next two weeks, the guards dragged Cole out of the dark, tossed the same pair of unwashed jeans at him, and forced him to move the rock pile from one pallet to the other. Back and forth, every day, he hauled granite, strained muscles, and slowly lost his mind.

A meal waited for him at the end of each godforsaken chore — canned tuna, microwaved burritos, a hodgepodge of processed crap. Anything was better than hot dogs, and he needed the calories.

Each day, he gained weight and rebuilt his strength, but the tedious labor wore on him, putting him on edge and stoking his temper.

The guards fed on that, pushing him when he walked, taunting him when he stumbled, and growing meaner by the hour. Their numbers had doubled, at least ten of them present at all times, while Lydia's appearances dwindled to nothing.

In the beginning, she showed up while he ate, dressed in her tantalizing rockabilly fashion and flanked by half a dozen armed men. It was always the same. The same demand in the same detached tone. "Tell me who bought the stolen intel."

He maintained his silence, which seemed to infuriate her to the point that she stopped coming. He hadn't seen her in days.

By the end of two weeks, he had enough.

His patience waned as the guards shoved him toward the waiting pallet of rock. His blood boiled as a boot connected with his spine, hurrying him along. He staggered, righted his balance, barely remaining vertical. His teeth clenched.

If he attacked, it would give them an excuse to retaliate. The motherfuckers wanted a fight, their hunger for blood burning in their eyes. They baited him endlessly for it.

He could take down any one of them without breaking a sweat. But not ten of them at once. He was outnumbered, and they were armed. Challenging them would be a fool's quest.

Mike stood off to the side, arms crossed over his chest, watching. Always present, he never participated in the harassment. He never stopped them, either.

Where the fuck was Lydia? Was she watching from a hidden corner of the warehouse, delighting in his misery? He thought he would have more time with her, to analyze and manipulate her. That plan went to hell when she stopped showing up.

He was running out of options, out of patience. Inch by inch, he lost his self-control. He felt harried, wired, crackling like a lit fuse, burning down to detonation. It was only a matter of time.

Dragging in a deep breath, he resumed walking. Something had to change. He couldn't, *wouldn't,* spend another goddamn day hauling rocks.

He was done.

Just like that, a switch flipped inside him. His feet stopped moving, planted shoulder-width apart, his arms hanging at his sides. He didn't tense, but he braced for it, ready, waiting with fire seething in his veins.

"Move." Someone shoved his back.

He didn't budge.

When the next shove came, he ducked, spun, and slammed his knuckles into the face behind him, willfully initiating an explosive chain reaction of violence and fury.

He hammered his fists, connecting with flesh, but no amount of skill or training could defeat their numbers. Within seconds, his back hit the concrete, his ribs taking the brunt of the blows as men fell upon him, weapons aimed, and mouths grinning through the blood.

They didn't want to shoot him. They wanted to beat him to a pulp.

Manic energy surged through him, clouding his vision. Octane pumped his heart. Blood and sweat slicked his face. His knuckles throbbed, and his eyes burned from the impact of raining fists. Still, he kept punching, fighting, and roaring through the bone-crunching agony of their strikes.

Until the report of gunfire shuddered the air. A single shot, fired from across the warehouse. Everyone froze.

His pulse thundered, and his lungs crashed together. Then, one by one, the weight of ten men lifted off his body.

COMPLICATE

He lay on his back, staring at the rafters through blood-soaked eyelashes. Everything hurt, and he relished it—the madness of the pain, the rush of adrenaline, and the utter freedom in unleashing his temper. He savored it almost as much as the sound of her clicking heels heading toward him.

Fucking finally.

"Tie him up." She handed off her rifle to a guard while motioning at the rest of them. "Put him on that pallet."

Christ, she was a vision. He wiped the blood from his eyes to steal a better look, and holy fuck, he couldn't stop looking.

Black combat boots, a tiny skirt checked in white and black, fishnet stockings to her thighs, silk-ribbon garters over skin like fine china, tits spilling from a black corset, and that hair. God, that hair. It hung in rippling waves of fire, as bright as the red swallow tattooed on her chest.

Pressure tightened between his legs, swelling against his zipper. She glared, and he grinned, no doubt resembling a feral, blood-spattered animal.

"I'm gone for five days, and all hell breaks loose." She held her spine ramrod straight, her little hands clenching in fists at her sides. "Goddamn children. The whole lot of you!"

The men, smeared in their own share of blood, shot death looks in her direction. Some of them pressed their lips tight as if biting back scathing retorts. If she wasn't careful, she might have an insurrection among them.

But for now, they followed her orders without argument. Hands fell upon him, hauling him up and dragging him across the factory floor.

They dumped his ass on a stack of wood pallets. Another stack leaned on its side between the wall and his back. Rope bound the platforms together, forming a makeshift L-shaped chair, perfect for restraining a crazed man.

He gave them hell, struggling and spitting as they tied his arms, neck, and waist to the pallets at his back. But much like the fight he'd just lost, one against many proved to be a wasted effort.

Thirty yards away, Lydia stood close to Mike, their heads bowed together, talking, touching, paying no attention to his useless thrashing.

When the guards finished trussing him to the platform, her voice snapped through the room. "Everyone out."

She didn't spare the room a glance, her gaze still fixed on Mike as she returned to their conversation.

The factory floor echoed with the tread of retreating footfalls. Mike vanished with the guards, and when the door slammed shut, only Lydia remained.

A thrill ran through him. At last, he would have some time with her, and he needed to make every second count.

She turned to him, her gaze as vibrant as the colorful ink on her arms. An abundance of cleavage decorated her corset, the view goddamn distracting as she pulled in a long breath and slowly released it.

Fucking hell, she was killing him. More painful than a fist, more lethal than a bullet, more formidable than an army of men, she brandished beauty like a mythical weapon, gaining the advantage by merely standing before him, looking like *that*.

Soft auburn brows arched above eyes that sparkled with the luster of polished emeralds. Supple red lips gracefully curved downward, unreasonably sensual. Deadly. Like cherries soaked in poison.

He knew she wasn't real. The hair, the garters, the heat in her gaze—all of it was a honey trap to lure him under her spell. He knew this, and yet, he wanted to risk it. He wanted to risk his whole goddamn existence for a taste.

His body burned for her, restrained as it was beneath the rope, his zipper, and the plight of his circumstances. He would be lying to himself if he thought he could fight the intensity swarming through his system.

There was sexual attraction. Then there was *this*. He had nothing to compare it to. Not his relationship with Danni. Not the countless women who had come before her. He'd never felt this hungry, this captivated, this fucking petrified of his own lust.

Maybe regular sexual activity over the past seven years would've diluted the voraciousness of his appetite. Maybe if he hadn't been sitting naked in a dark cell for the past month with nothing to do but fantasize about his redheaded captor, maybe then he wouldn't...

Fuck.

That was it. That was her plan.

Spending time with her would've worked to his advantage. He would've identified her weaknesses, her flaws, and seen her for who she really was. But spending a month alone? With only random glimpses of her to fuel his hungry imagination? That worked to *her* advantage.

Absence makes the heart grow fonder.

Or, in his case, absence made his lust burn hotter. She'd managed to keep her distance while staying ever-present in his mind. She wore a shroud of mystery that he couldn't peel away, leaving him to obsess over the only thing she let him see.

Her extraordinary beauty.

Once she finally let him in, there would be nothing left of his resolve.

It was fucking brilliant.

COMPLICATE

He tracked her with his whole body as she strode past him, seemingly ignoring his presence. Pretending. It was what she did best.

A few feet away, she grabbed a rubber hose and twisted a spigot on the wall, turning on the flow of water.

Twitchy, he yanked at the restraints. With his hands bound on either side of his head and more rope tethered around his neck and waist, he couldn't move his upper half. Physically defenseless.

She pulled the hose toward him, grabbed an empty bucket, and tossed a bottle of body wash onto the pallet beside him.

Given the collection of soap, shampoo, and towels along the wall, this was where the team showered. They'd been living here for at least a month, probably longer, and a stone factory wouldn't be equipped with a room for bathing.

"Are you going to bathe me?" He arranged his face into a smile despite the unease simmering inside him.

He hadn't felt the touch of a woman in seven years, and he knew, he fucking *knew* this woman's touch would be his undoing. But he tamped it down, didn't give her a hint of the turmoil rolling in his gut.

She stood before him and squeezed the handle on the hose, shooting a blast of frigid water at his chest. His breath caught, and his muscles tensed. But once the shock wore off, he threw back his head and hooted with maniacal laughter.

After a month without a shower, it felt fucking refreshing. Cold water saturated his filthy beard and crusty jeans, seeping into the creases of his body and rinsing away layers of sand and dirt.

Nothing restrained his legs. So he stretched them out, spreading them wide and soaking up the spray, all the while whooping with unrestrained laughter.

Until she aimed the spray at his face.

He coughed, choking on water. Then he laughed harder.

She shut off the hose. "You're deranged."

"Turn it back on."

"Tell me who bought the stolen intel."

"If I tell you, will you let me go?"

"I won't return you to the cell."

"Ah." He chuckled. "Is my grave already dug?"

Her dainty nostrils stiffened with a sharp inhale. "I won't kill you."

"No, you're too soft to kill an innocent man. You'll make one of your goons do it."

Without breaking eye contact, she fired a burst of water at his groin. The denim added some protection, but fuck, the jet hit hard. And cold. His balls receded up inside him, his laughter effectively cut off.

She shifted the hose away and filled the bucket.

He relaxed, watching her. "Where did you go for five days?"

"Out."

"Out of town?"

"Out of state."

"Why?"

"Why? Yeah, let's start there." She heaved the full bucket onto the pallet beside him, set her hands on his thighs, and leaned into his personal space, surrounding him with the cherry scent of her hair. "Why did you provoke the guards? What the fuck were you thinking?"

"Your concern is touching." He tilted his head. "Does this mean we're friends?"

"What?" She jerked back, eyebrows pinching.

"I'll be honest." He tugged on the rope. "This doesn't feel very friendly. Unless you're into this sort of thing. Which I am. But only when I'm the one playing with the rope."

"Mm-hmm." She narrowed her eyes, her accent laced with sarcasm. "We both know how many times you've played over the past seven years." Holding her hand up between them, she made her fingers and thumb form the shape of a zero.

"You want to be the one." He wet his lips, his mouth inches from hers. "The one I break my celibacy with."

"No," she said too quickly. "You're...just..." She made a sound of frustration. "You're smarter than this, Cole. Smart enough to know the guards were baiting you."

"Smart enough to know *you* are baiting me."

"Sometimes, I wonder..." Her gaze dipped to his lips and returned to his eyes. "Who's baiting who?"

ELEVEN

Intelligent sea-green eyes stared out of the face of a Gothic angel. Enraptured, Cole stared back, knowing eye contact with this cursed creature was treacherous. Lydia didn't just look at him. She looked *into* him as if she knew his darkest desires.

But that was impossible. While he couldn't resist his attraction to her, he made damn sure he didn't show it. He'd been trained to disguise emotion, a skill that had served him well throughout his career.

Without averting her gaze, she reached for the bottle of soap beside him and squirted a cold glob on his chest. She edged closer, pushing into the *V* of his legs, and boldly perched on his knee.

With her featherlight weight on his lap came the smooth touch of her hands on his flesh, fingers splayed, just the right balance of caution and assertion as she spread the gel to his shoulders and throat.

He sank into the warmth of her caress, fixated on her unreadable expression. What sort of woman was she? Heartless? Tender? Promiscuous? Complicated? He didn't know enough about her to make a judgment. But goddamn, she knew how to touch a man.

Her fingers swept across every inch of his upper body, rubbing gently, working in the lather, unselfish with the soap. With the bucket, she rinsed away the grime, leaving no part of his exposed skin unwashed.

When she reached his hair, her fingernails dug in, scraping his scalp and combing him clean.

He fucking groaned.

It felt surreal, like a day at the damn spa. Not that he would know. He'd never been to a spa, never been pampered or massaged into a pleasure-drunk coma.

He didn't trust the feelings it evoked. She had an agenda. A nasty one. But he let himself, just for a moment, indulge in the sublime ecstasy of her hands on his body.

She spent a lot of time on his facial hair, scrubbing and soaping with rapt concentration. Christ, how he must've reeked. The hair had grown too long, venturing into lumberjack territory. He preferred a quarter-inch military beard.

With his head tipped back, he stared down the length of his nose. "Have you found any creatures crawling in it?"

"No." Her luscious lips crooked up at the corner, amusement glowing in her delicate features. "I'm trying to imagine what you look like without it."

"I've shaved it off many times over the years. I'm sure you've seen photos."

Images of him didn't exist on the Internet or dark web. He made sure of that. But he pretended otherwise as a way to fish for clues and subtly nudge her into giving something away.

"No photos." Her hands moved on to the upper part of his face, cleaning around the contusions he'd incurred during the fight. "I didn't know what you looked like until the night I met you in the desert."

Shock jolted through him, but he maintained a bored expression. "You met me that night because I allowed it. Because I deliberately activated your bug."

She pressed closer, lathering soap around his eyes and cheeks. "Your breath smells good. Minty. You've been using the gifts I sent."

If she wanted a *thank you*, she could eat a dick.

Biting her lip, she stared at his mouth. "I planted those bugs in Rylee Sutton's house, knowing you would take them and eventually lure me to your location. You met me that night in the desert because *I* allowed it."

"They're not just bugs. You planted customized tech, designed for the NSA."

"Now we're getting somewhere." She slid a hand into his hair and pulled, yanking his head back. "The only way you would recognize that tech is if you worked for them."

Or if he worked for something deeper, darker, and more clandestine. But he wasn't about to tell her that. "What does Rylee Sutton have to do with this?"

"A few months ago, you showed up in Texas, stalking her." She released his hair and leaned to the side, her attention on his hand.

COMPLICATE

With his arms fastened to the pallet on either side of his head, he opened his fingers and let her look at his palm. The gash from the rock had healed cleanly over the past two weeks, thanks to the supplies she'd provided.

She gently washed the area around the wound and moved to his other hand. "After vanishing off the map for seven years, here you were, riding into the desert on your motorcycle. You went straight to El Paso, then Eldorado, monitoring Rylee's old and current residences. She was your only focus, seemingly the only reason you came out of hiding. So naturally, she became a target for your pursuers."

"I wasn't in hiding, and I didn't realize I had admirers."

"Pursuers."

"Same thing. I see the way you look at me."

"I see the way you look when I mention your pretty dancer."

He didn't blink. Not a twitch.

Danni had never been involved in his affairs. He'd always kept her in the dark, completely separated from his career. Now, she lived a safe, happy life, doing what she loved. Dancing. She married the man she loved. A powerful businessman and billionaire, who had the resources and unparalleled desire to protect her.

Her photos were out there, her personal information available to anyone who wanted to investigate her. That didn't matter since she was no longer connected to Cole.

It wouldn't have mattered if an eleven-year-old assignment hadn't come back to haunt him.

"You're still in love with Danni," she said, her accent straining. "But you came to Texas to stalk Rylee. Who is she to you?"

"Since *you* were stalking *me*, you should know this."

"I think, initially, she was a threat to your friends. While you were digging into her background, she was off in the desert with Tomas, getting stabbed with a hot dog."

"Stabbed with a hot dog," he deadpanned.

"His hot dog. It's a fitting analogy, given your diet over the past month."

"You're a twisted bitch." His nonchalant tone made her smile.

"I'm right about Rylee. Whatever her connection was to you and your friends, it was personal. You wouldn't have returned to the states, otherwise."

She wasn't wrong, but he kept his face unexpressive.

"You haven't been in the country for seven years." She raised a brow.

Not true. He'd visited on three different occasions. Day trips, in and out. Evidently, they weren't watching him closely enough.

Her thumb trailed along his bottom lip, her eyes locked on the movement. "Where have you been all this time?"

"Enjoying retirement."

"You might've retired from a legitimate career, but I know you're working with the Colombian cartel. You've made a name for yourself, Cole Hartman. How does it feel to be notorious in the criminal underworld?"

That was the intel she had on him? The gossip of crime lords and traffickers? He'd put most of those rumors out there himself. All smoke and mirrors to embellish the truth, incite fear, and mislead enemies away from what he was actually doing.

She had no idea he was part of a vigilante group or that his earlier career was in an organization that no one knew existed. That meant she didn't have connections in the intelligence sectors. So how did she have access to those high-tech bugs?

"Who do you work for?" He nipped at her finger on his lip.

She yanked her hand back. "Tell me who bought—"

"No. I'm not going to tell you what you want to know, and you're not going to let me go. We're at an impasse, Lydia." He flexed his thigh beneath her pert ass. "How long have I been here?"

"Thirty-one days."

"How much time do you have left to complete the assignment?"

"Enough."

"There's always a deadline." He made a tsking sound. "Something has to give."

"You." Her lashes lowered, fanning over porcelain cheekbones before lifting to expose the force of her magnetic glare. "*You* have to give."

"When I don't, you'll take. Am I right?" He glanced at his restraints, his vulnerable position. "How much are you willing to take? How far down this dark hole are you willing to go?"

How evil are you, Lydia?

"All the way." She slid off his lap and opened the button on his jeans. Then the zipper. Her eyes found his, and she yanked on the wet denim.

His stomach coiled. His skin grew hot, and his pulse took off at a sprint.

Enduring the soapy caress of her hands below his waist would be the absolute best and worst thing that could happen. It needed to happen. They needed to get personal and intimate and fucking filthy together, so he could break her open and fuck the stubbornness out of her.

At the same time, he had to remember that she was using the same strategy on him. She intended to ply him with her body, and all the while, he would let her believe she was the one in control.

COMPLICATE

Remaining aloof, he gave her no reaction as she wrestled with the heavy wet fabric. Her tits rose with shallow inhalations, the gorgeous swells testing the confines of her corset, testing *him*.

He didn't move or lift his weight to help, but that didn't stop her tenacious hands. Keeping a firm hold on his waistband, she wrenched the jeans down his legs and off, exposing the hardening evidence of his arousal.

Yeah, his fucking cock was excited.

Seven years of built-up excitement.

Physically, he was ready and raring to go.

Emotionally, he would never be up for it. He missed his girl. He just…

Christ, he deeply, unendurably missed her.

He shoved down all thoughts of Danni, concealing them behind a mask of indifference. But he couldn't hide the erection. It jutted upward like a damn flagpole, begging for soft hands, a hot mouth, and a wet-ass pussy.

She didn't spare him a glance and instead directed her attention to his largest and oldest tattoo. The black snake wrapped around his thigh from knee to hip, its head angled toward his foot with shimmering scales inked in meticulous detail.

"What's the story on this?" She traced a finger along the curve of the serpent's spine, making him harder, hotter.

"I'll tell you about the snake if you tell me about the swallow."

Her hand went to her chest and dropped just as quickly, her expression empty.

He was convinced now, more than ever, that she wasn't a trained sex spy. While she excelled at putting on an act, she hadn't mastered the unresponsive austerity of a swallow. She reacted emotionally on impulse. It was subtle, but he caught the little twitches and nuances before she blanked her face.

Maybe she was pretending to be a swallow? But for what reason? The same reason she left him in the dark to fantasize about her for a month?

Because she was fucking with him. Or trying to.

He relaxed against the pallet, curious to see what she would do next.

She washed him. Starting at his feet, she worked her way up his legs. When he halfheartedly tried to kick her, she gripped his knee to hold him down and slid her fingers along his inner thigh.

Heat swept through him as her hands roamed where Danni's had gone before. In rigid silence, he watched her clean his cock and learn the shape of him, her fingers traveling the same path Danni's mouth had been so many times, so long ago.

He fought down the noises that tried to crawl from his throat. Noises of objection. And consent. And reprehensible guilt.

His molars clenched tight, his breaths snapping past his teeth in choppy bursts. Pleasure fused with torment, his body warring with his mind. He wanted it. He didn't want it.

He needed to focus before he fucking lost it.

The ends of her hair brushed his skin, tickling his legs as she lathered and laved. There was no seduction in her touch, the scrubbing efficient and impersonal. Coldly detached.

She wasn't trying to tease him. This was a bath, nothing more. Yet, it was everything.

He throbbed, burning for her. He thought he might die if he didn't get inside her. At the same time, he didn't want her. She was the wrong woman. She wasn't his girl.

Christ, he needed to man the fuck up and get over that. Right now.

Logic over emotion, his mind was in control.

He was going to survive. And to do that, he had to do *her*.

TWELVE

It was just sex.

If Cole remained in control, if he kept himself detached, he could use it as a weapon.

Not an easy undertaking with Lydia's warmth bearing down upon him, so achingly close, shocking his system. Her sweet cherry scent drugged his inhales. Her beauty, even smothered in makeup, drew him in like a supernatural spell.

She washed every inch of his rigid cock, his balls, and farther back, into the recesses of his crack, her fingers like tiny knives slicing their way through his dignity.

Then she took away her touch, her intoxicating heat, and stepped back. With the hose in hand, she sprayed him off like an animal, her stance and expression matching the blast of the water. Cold, aggressive, merciless.

Something felt off about her. She was normally closed-off, but this was different. She suddenly looked way too wooden, her gaze too unfocused, as if she'd retreated into her head. Either she was trying to put herself in a zone, or she was having second thoughts about seducing him.

By the time she shut off the water, she'd completely killed his erection.

The hose dangled from her hand, her gaze fixed over his shoulder, staring at nothing.

"Lydia."

She blinked. Her brow creased, and her eyes went to his mouth, then lower, taking a winding trip from his chest to his soft dick. "I don't want to do this."

Yes, she did. But not for the reason in which she'd been hired.

"Just give me a name, a location, *something*." She glared at him, her jaw flexing. "You don't give a fuck about that hard drive. Tell me where it is."

"Tell me what's on it."

"If I do, will you give me—?"

"No."

She pulled in a breath, standing taller, her posture vibrating with indignation. Then she tossed the hose, turned on her heel, and strode toward the door.

She was leaving.

Dread slammed into him, exploding his pulse. He couldn't spend another month in the dark. Goddammit, he couldn't lose this opportunity with her.

"You're scared," he said to her retreating backside.

She stopped, her spine stiff as she cast a scowl over her shoulder. "Excuse me?"

"You scrubbed me clean because you intended to seduce me. Because you have it in your head that if you wrap that hot little cunt around my dick, my brain will fry, and I'll tell you everything I know. The problem with that plan is you *want* me. Not just to milk me for information. You want to milk my cock because you're wet for it. You've been wet for me since the day I tied the soaked crotch of your underwear around my hand."

She slowly pivoted, facing him with flames in her eyes. "I am *not*—"

"It scares you, this reckless infatuation you have with me. It scares you so much you're running."

As expected, she gasped, mouth gaping and features twisted in fury. "You arrogant son of a—"

"Don't worry, sweetheart. I'm going to fuck you. I'll fuck you so completely that shit on your face will smear and drip off. You'll lose the fake eyelashes like the piercing in your lip. I'm going to fuck you until there are holes in your stockings, tangles in your hair, and bite marks marring those creamy tits. I'm going to ravage you, ruin you, and I'll do it all while my hands are still bound in rope."

She sucked in sharply, nostrils flaring, and smoothed her palms down her short skirt.

Oh, yeah, she was pissed and trying so hard to keep it in check.

Hiding his smile, he waited for it, for her wrath, her passion, and the complete erosion of her composure.

She didn't disappoint.

COMPLICATE

"You really think because you're a strong, virile man..." She charged toward him, sauntering in her exquisite rage. "That I must surely be dripping down my legs? And that because I'm a woman, I must be quivering in fear of my sexual desires? That this is about me stifling my urges rather than taking matters into my own hands? *That's* the conclusion you're drawing?"

Blood surged to his cock, his balls tightening with every seething word, every assertive step she made in his direction. He held still, his chin tilted up. But he couldn't school his breathing. His lungs danced, heaving enthusiastically in the hellfire of her unholy glare.

"And that because you're a man..." She climbed onto his naked lap, straddling him with her weight on her knees. "It must be *you* who does the *fucking*?"

That word, rasped on her tongue, made him outrageously, painfully hard. He would have to tread with care if he were to last until the end of this.

"You think I should swallow my perceived fear and beg you to ravage me?" She reached between them, wrapped a hand around his cock, and viciously, angrily stroked him. "Do I look scared to you, Cole? Do I look infatuated with your superior manliness? Hmm?"

She yanked hard on his cock, wrenching a grunt from his throat. Her vicious tugging grew meaner, rougher, aggressively working him into a lather.

He pressed his lips together to trap his groans, unleashing ragged exhales through his nose. His muscles contracted, hardening and heating as he fought the onslaught of pleasure and pain.

Her eyes stayed with him, blazing with censure as she lowered herself, lower, closer, until the wet silk between her legs pushed against the crown of his erection, still held cruelly in her fist.

Trapped in the restraints, he couldn't stop her. Not that he would. With a few taunting words, he'd deliberately goaded her into running back and finishing this.

But the position made him uncomfortable, his need for dominance burning violently through his body. He craved control and fought the compulsion to aim himself and quest about until he impaled her.

He had to let her do this, let her believe she held the reins. If she suspected otherwise, he would be back in that cell at once.

She regarded him as if searching for subterfuge. Of course, she knew it was there. But she would ignore it. She wanted this too badly.

Do it, he commanded with his eyes.

Her fingers drove under the barrier of her underwear, shoving the crotch aside. He couldn't see beneath the skirt, but he felt her spreading the soft flesh of her cunt. While her hand was moving, she lifted a knee, squatting over him in a more dominant position, and met his eyes.

He held his breath. She seemed to be holding hers. Then she pounded down hard, plunging the full length of him into soaking wet paradise.

Scalding hot.

Inconceivably tight.

Blinding rapture.

Holy God in heaven, he was inside her, inside a woman for the first time in seven years. He didn't move, couldn't breathe.

He'd forgotten what it felt like. Over the years, he'd recalled the sensations, the incomparable ecstasy of a pussy sucking and gripping his cock. But his recollections paled by comparison. Nothing in memory had ever felt this goddamn magnificent.

Then she moved, ripping the air from his lungs. Her hips caught a diabolical rhythm, circling, grinding, and flattening him to the pallets. Her hands anchored against his palms, pressing his tethered arms to the wood slats on either side of his head.

He squeezed her clenched fists, and a scalding noise rose from her chest. He couldn't help it. He groaned with her, throwing his head back while watching her from beneath heavy eyelids.

She was the most wickedly erotic creature he had ever encountered, her thick, spiral-curling red hair tangling around a voluptuous rack and clinging to a heart-shaped face dominated by the scornful eyes of a *femme fatale*.

Her cheeks flushed with the exertion of her thrusts, her complexion smooth and pale as cream. She was as petite and light as a flower, but there was nothing fragile about her. She slammed down on his shaft with venom, every ram of her hips meant to punish not reward, her fingers stabbing into his hands, her face streaked with contempt.

She used him like a piston, burying his shaft to the hilt, up and down, push and pull, her pace feral, shimmering with hostility. The heavy globes of her tits bounced with aggression until a nipple popped free, the little pink bead hard enough to cut glass.

Perspiration leaked black rivers from her eyes, her lip gloss faded from the swipes of her tongue. Sunlight poked through the smudges of the overhead windows, slanting across her face and rendering her almost immortal, like a dark Fae princess from another world and era. Ethereal. Deceitful. Tragic.

He'd never seen anything more beautiful.

COMPLICATE

His attraction defied reason. She was everything Danni wasn't. Salty instead of sweet. Calculated instead of free-spirited. Her makeup and tattoos lent her a hard, artificial appearance, not the soft, natural look he preferred. And her heart was cold and closed-off. Not warm. Definitely not attainable.

Or maybe she just wanted him to think that.

Bowing into him, she rode his cock and huffed strangled gasps of air against his mouth. She was so close he wanted to kiss her. Almost as much as he wanted to bite her and make her bleed.

Instead, he lifted into her vigorous need, grunting, ramming his hips, and washing them both with brutal sensations. All else ceased to exist, everything but her body, her breaths, and the intensity of her livid gaze.

Her eyes were like pieces of kryptonite, deep green and luminescent, weakening him by the second. His dick wanted release. His mind wouldn't allow it. He wouldn't give in.

But as they moved together, their tempos syncing and gazes locked, he felt a sliding sensation. Deep in his chest, he felt a tilting, tumbling avalanche that had nothing to do with the earthquaking motion of their bodies.

Before his brain caught up, his mouth was on her, kissing her so thoroughly he damn near exploded inside her.

He didn't pull away. He couldn't. She kissed him back with the same desperation, and the feel of her tongue rubbing and tangling with his was all that mattered.

They melted together, holding each other hostage with their mouths, their thrusts, and harmonious tremors in their bodies. Her hands moved to his face, fingers clamping firmly around his jaw, her lips crashing against his with the force of her passion.

Lost in the throes of frenzied lust, she used him for her pleasure. It was the moment he'd been waiting for, watching her get worked up, feeling his cock sink past her defenses, and knowing her race to completion was no longer about the job and all about the demands of her body.

At that moment, he held the control. He'd mastered her with his hands tied.

Breaking the kiss, he leaned back and admired his handiwork.

She stopped moving, her cheeks flushed, and her snug little pussy clenched spasmodically around his buried cock. She released shallow, rapid-fire breaths and blinked slowly, with great effort, as if struggling to concentrate.

When she realized what she'd done, that she'd lost control of herself, her expression hardened.

Was she angry? Oh, fuck yeah. Ten strangling little expressions of her rage curled around his throat, her blunt nails pressing against his airway in a bid to choke him.

Just as quickly, she regained her composure, released his neck, and shoved his face away.

But she wasn't finished.

Rising on her knees, she pulled off of his cock. He bobbed against her thigh, wanting back in as she reached under her skirt and swept her fingers along the flesh he still hadn't seen.

Her free hand went to his shoulder, holding her upper body steady as she proceeded to rub her cunt. Her knuckles brushed against his unspent cock, teasing him as she chased her release. She shook with the effort, moaning, muscles straining, lashes fluttering, her eyes smoldering with animosity.

A sound of feral relief stole from her throat, and she screamed, groaning, trembling, and coming undone.

Fucking glorious. Hotter than hell. Had he been inside her, he might've shot his load, which was precisely what he didn't want to do. He refused to give her that.

And to think, she intended to deny him.

It's a ride you won't ever get off.

She thought she could torture him with orgasm denial. Little did she know, he had the discipline of a monk.

Climbing to her feet, she swiped her soaked fingers across his mouth. He licked his lips, tasting her, while holding her blistering glare.

Her teeth clenched. "Tell me who bought the hard drive, and I'll relieve that ache between your legs."

"No, thanks. I'll relieve it myself."

"You're going to jerk off in that filthy cell? Where you can't hear yourself think?"

"Yep." He stretched out his legs, delighting in the way her hungry eyes caressed his swollen cock. "I'm a dirty...dirty...dirty man."

"I could shackle you while you're in there."

"You don't want to do that because you like thinking about me touching myself. But when I do, it won't be *you* I'm thinking about. My heart lies elsewhere."

A flicker of hurt crossed her expression, and she looked away, pretending indifference by straightening her clothes and tucking in her tits.

"You, on the other hand, will not get off without me."

Her head shot up at that, eyes wide. "What did you say?"

"Nothing touches that pussy but me. Not Mike. Not your men. Not your fingers. Your body belongs to me."

COMPLICATE

She made a sound of disbelief that morphed into a sneer of disgust. Then she spun away and stormed to the exit without looking back.

Later, she would think back and relive every thrust, every grunt, every intimate second of eye contact, and she would think about his command.

She would attempt to touch herself because she wanted to hate him. But she wouldn't go through with it because she wanted him. And that want would bring her back for more.

He might not survive it, but he would be ready for her.

THIRTEEN

Three days later, Lydia stood over Cole's nude body, fighting an inner battle between duty and decency.

For as long as she could remember, duty had always won out. She'd lied, cheated, stolen, kidnapped, and sold her soul to the devil in the name of duty.

Her purpose was greater than Cole's life, her own, and that of anyone who tried to stop her. She was prepared to do anything and everything to finish this.

Or so she thought.

As she took in the rope that secured his powerful frame to the factory floor, her stomach churned with an unexpected sense of wrongness. What she was doing to him was unacceptable. Indecent. *Unforgivable.*

Was she developing a goddamn conscience after all these years? Or was it worse? Was she developing feelings for her prisoner?

Lima Syndrome, the inverse of Stockholm syndrome. She knew it could happen. She just didn't think it could happen to her.

It needed to stop.

The moment she met Cole, she knew this wouldn't be easy. Mike had known long before, which was why he'd fought so hard against this plan.

Cole belonged on a motorcycle with a rifle on his back, flying down a lone highway on some hell-raising mission. He didn't belong in restraints, stripped of his clothes and his freedom, and forced to endure another rape.

COMPLICATE

Because that was what this was. No matter how hard his dick grew in her hands. He wasn't a willing participant. He was a prisoner, and in the last three days, she'd raped him three times, each time finishing herself off while denying him a completion.

The first time, she convinced herself he was right there with her, fucking her as passionately as she fucked him. She thought, when he was seconds from climax, that he was too injured to come. He'd just fought off the raging blows of ten men, his face swollen and covered in blood. But he hadn't flinched when she'd washed his wounds. It was as if he didn't even feel the pain.

The second day, she orgasmed too quickly. With the memory of his feverish, toe-curling kiss still fresh in her mind, she was on the brink of coming before she even got his cock inside her. When her orgasm hit, she collapsed in a boneless puddle against his chest, gasping and so lost in the pleasure she'd forgotten to deny him a release. And yet, he didn't come. As if he were deliberately holding it back.

By the third day, she started questioning who was controlling whom. Just like the times before, she bathed him, teased him, and made him hard as a rock. Then she sat on his lap and rode him to the cusp of orgasm. He grunted vehement sounds with his teeth clamped tight. His eyes blazed. His sinews flexed, and she pushed him harder, faster, testing the limits of his self-restraint.

Instead of denying him a release, she teased him toward it.

She teased and teased until she wore herself out.

Still, he didn't come.

How in the fresh hell was that possible?

Desperate to beat him at his game, she'd ordered the guards to shackle him during his time in the cell, preventing him from touching himself. His only relief would come with her, and much to her despair, that went both ways.

She slept beside Mike every night without a moment of privacy. It was for the best. She wasn't here to engage in self-pleasure. Except, whenever she closed her eyes, Cole's gorgeous face was waiting. His smirking lips. That bottomless brown gaze, searing into her thoughts.

Too often, she caught herself daydreaming, recreating the delicious sensation of his tongue in her mouth, the scratch of his beard on her cheeks, the sultry sounds of his breaths, and the intensity of his strokes.

Didn't matter how tightly the rope cinched around him, he was incapable of holding still while inside her. He fucked her from the bottom, with his cock, his mouth, and the dominance in his dark glare. Every single time.

And he didn't come.

Today, when the men dragged him from the cell, she had him arranged on the floor, arms stretched above him, his gorgeous physique on full display.

After he'd lost so much weight in the beginning, she started feeding him high-calorie, high-protein meals. Then there was the rock hauling, the workouts in his cell, and the sex—all the thrusting and grunting and flexing. He'd regained his strength and then some.

With his back to the floor and the rise and dips of his musculature so round and defined, there were only a few points of contact where his body touched the concrete.

No man should have that many curves. God help her, she'd traced every sinuous muscle with her own hands and knew how outrageously hard and masculine he was, as if each sinew and tendon had been carved with an artist's chisel and stacked together to form a dangerously arousing masterpiece.

The granite bricks of his ass drew his lower spine into a sexy arch, leaving a shadowed tunnel beneath. The circumference of his biceps exceeded that of her thighs, and his shoulder blades, sculpted like marble wings, supported the weight of his upper body on the floor.

His powerful legs—wide at the calves and thighs—were in remarkable proportion to the pillar of his heavy, thick cock. Striae of muscle flanked his eight-pack abdomen, the terrain of his torso like a rippling sheet of metal, hard and flat enough to bounce quarters.

Zero-percent body fat. Not an inch of softness anywhere. Utter perfection through and through.

She might've felt like a despicable pervert, ogling him the way she did. But his gaze, as sharp as a freshly honed blade, violated her just as rudely.

His eyes especially enjoyed the tops of her breasts as they expanded and contracted with her breath. She wore a dress he'd seen before—the black one with red cherries. Yet he stared at it as if it were the first time, feasting upon every stitch and lingering where hemlines met skin until she felt stripped and just as naked as him.

He liked what he saw, if his engorged cock were anything to go by. He never had trouble getting hard.

Each time she came to him, he didn't fight against the rope or make demands. He didn't gnash his teeth or shout at her.

In fact, he hadn't spoken to her at all today.

He never said a word to the guards. Other than the fistfight three days ago, he tolerated their taunting, shoving, kicking. His endurance of pain and hardship without any display of feeling didn't seem human.

COMPLICATE

How could a man sit in a pitch-black cell, shit in a bucket, and never voice a single protest? How could he listen to the same song on repeat for over a month and never complain? He didn't grumble or whine or express any sign of dissatisfaction.

She'd offered him better accommodations, better food, a warm bed, sex with multiple women, anything in exchange for the location of the hard drive.

Anything but his freedom. She couldn't give him that, and he knew it.

Any other man would've surrendered by now. No one had this much stoicism. Even she was starting to lose her nerve.

So what was his deal? He had the patient self-control of a robot, like an upgraded model of the Terminator.

Except when he looked at her, when it was just the two of them, she saw a human man beneath the steel. A confident, lusty, hotblooded man with so much heat in his eyes she caught fire.

Like now.

He stared at her like he wanted to eat her alive. Like she was the only thing that existed. But she wasn't. He loved the dancer.

Maybe that was how he maintained such ironclad discipline over his orgasms. His heart wasn't in this. Of course, it wasn't. Nothing they did together was consensual.

Even if it was consensual, would it have changed anything? The man had been celibate for seven years because no one was good enough for him. No one but Danni Savoy.

It only made Lydia want him more, and that was fucking dangerous.

She lowered onto the floor beside him and slid her palm beneath the rope across his chest, soaking in the warmth of his skin. He was so well-built, his pectorals smooth and hairless, the crevice between them deep and inviting. She wanted him to touch her, to be free with her body as she was with his. But if she untied him, he would hurt her. Possibly kill her. She'd given him no choice but to hate her.

"Do you want to end this today?" she asked. "All I need is a name."

One brow, higher than the other, twitched with the force of his stare.

With a sigh, she focused her attention on bathing him. But as her fingers and palms delighted in his texture, firm shape, wiry beard, soft hair, all she wanted of his hands was that they would touch her with the same burning passion as his gaze.

When she finished the final rinse, his gravelly voice broke the silence.

"It's just the two of us. Wash off the makeup. Remove the clothes. Let me see you."

She couldn't do that. The persona she wore was a safeguard. It protected her identity.

"No." She looked down at his swelling erection. "How you can be so patient is beyond me. Doesn't it hurt?"

"Watching you stare at it is my favorite part." His hands flexed above his head, straining the rope that bound his sinewy forearms. "Your eyes get this disturbing jolt of light, like you want to tear your teeth into me." His voice dropped, rasping with dark sensuality. "There's something deranged and alluring about watching a woman devour what she wants with rabid intent." His eyes hooded. "Go ahead, Lydia. Wrap those filthy lips around me and eat."

Heat bloomed between her legs, pulsing angrily. "I'll use my teeth."

"I'll be disappointed if you don't."

"And you called *me* a freak."

"Takes one to know one." His cock nodded in agreement.

Happy to oblige, she positioned herself over him, straddling one of his restrained legs. Then she lowered her head.

With the flat part of her tongue, she teased the tip of him. He didn't move. She sucked on the plump head, tasting him in languorous strokes. He didn't breathe.

Her lips stretched around his thickness as she slowly drew him in, deeper, harder, opening her airway, until her mouth reached the soft hair at his base.

She fought her gag reflex, breathing through the fullness in her throat as a series of twitches rippled across his abs. His leg trembled between the clinch of her thighs, and his addictive male scent flooded her senses.

As she made her way back up, she found him watching her, his lids half-mast and lips parted, breathless. Christ, that look on his gorgeous face, the sheer intensity in his eyes, awakened her pulse and spread fire through her circulation.

Without averting her gaze, she sucked him with vigor. The heavy hardness of him pressed down on her tongue, leaking salty beads of arousal from the tip. She lapped it up and felt her own moisture trickling down her thighs.

Since the hem of the dress fell to her knees, she'd gone without panties. Ideal for her position with his leg locked between hers. She rested her pussy against his thigh and let him feel the wetness, rubbing against his hard muscles and soaking his skin.

COMPLICATE

His groan of pleasure was the greatest reward, spurring her to grind harder as she took him deep into her throat. Her fingers gently kneaded and tugged at the soft heavy bag below his shaft. She hummed around his girth, swallowing a gush of pre-cum and savoring his clean, salty flavor.

She'd performed this act countless times with dozens of men in her adult life, none of which had left a lasting impression. But she would never forget this one. Not his taste, nor his velvety texture, nor the molten desire in his sexy brown eyes.

The man was fucking hot, and the more she pushed and pulled and licked, the more he failed to conceal his reactions. Muscles contracted on top of muscles. His feet scraped and dug against the floor. His exhales chased his inhales, his jaw tipping up, straining with the tautness of his body.

She added her teeth, scratching up and down his silky, turgid flesh, and his groaning turned to growls. His erection grew impossibly harder, and his spine bowed with the force of his need.

Her mouth was beginning to take its toll.

She pushed on, devouring him with slobbery, teeth-cutting, vulgar strokes. There was nothing clean or sweet about the way she sucked cock. But this kinky bastard didn't care. He liked it sick and depraved. The dirtier, the better. Same as her.

With a hand clenched around his sac, she squeezed his dense balls while pressing a fingertip against the tight, silken entrance of his rectum.

"Fuck." He gasped, shaking and flexing, his eyes wild as he stared down the length of his body. "What are you doing?"

"You like your ass fingered." She stroked the little clenching knot of flesh.

"Help me out here because I'm getting mixed signals." His chest heaved, and a twitch kicked up the corner of his lips. "Are you trying to deny orgasms? Or force them?"

Damn him and that lopsided smirk.

She flicked her tongue against the head of his cock and licked deep into the tiny slit, earning another trickle of salty fluid. "Depends."

"On?" He struggled to push the word past his choking breaths.

"You."

Beautiful, strapping, rugged, seductive, iron-willed Cole Hartman. She had eleven years of patience and planning riding on his willingness to cooperate.

It was hopeless.

This man wasn't going to help her in exchange for an orgasm. He was stronger than his baser needs. Smarter.

And he didn't want her.

She knew it weeks ago. But she had to try.

So she renewed her efforts, worshiping every inch of his gorgeous cock. She sucked him with everything she had, working her fist along his length, applying just the right balance of tongue and teeth.

His hips snapped upward, desperately trying to ram himself into the back of her throat, and his groans ran away from him. He was an ensnared beast, seething and bucking in the tethers of his restraints, testing the strength of the rope.

"What do you want from me, woman?" he snarled.

A loaded question. One she could only half-answer. "You know what I want."

He halted abruptly but for the flexing of his need in her mouth. His jaw hardened, and the air changed, growing colder, thinner. His gaze fell flat, and his muscles loosened beneath her.

She continued sucking him, but he wasn't feeling it.

Neither was she.

His erection didn't deflate, but the energy between them all but dissipated, the moment gone.

"Hurry along with your games, Lydia," he said in a cruel tone. "I'm growing bored."

Her stomach sank.

He didn't want her. No amount of seduction would change that.

She'd wasted a month trying to force a different outcome. Because she knew that the suffering he'd endured at her hands was a whole lot better than the brutality that would come from Vincent Barrington's men.

But she'd failed. White torture, psychological manipulation, isolation, blow jobs — he was immune to it all.

Disappointment constricted her chest. She needed more from him. Far more than the hard drive's location.

She needed him to help her *retrieve* it. But she couldn't tell him that. Not until she trusted him. Until he trusted her. And that would never happen.

Because he despised her.

He despised the way she looked, the way she spoke, the things she did. Could she blame him? She'd threatened his friends, captured him, and raped him. She was a horrible person.

With her heart in her throat, she sat back on her heels and admitted defeat. She only had one option left, and if that didn't work, Vincent would get rid of her and let the team slice, dice, break, and ultimately kill Cole for the information in his head.

She couldn't allow that. Not while there was still blood in her body.

FOURTEEN

Determination chased away the trembling in Lydia's legs as she strode to the bag she'd left nearby.

The guards were never in the warehouse during her sessions with Cole. But Mike was. Always. He remained close, out of view, armed, and ready to step in if Cole managed to overpower her or escape his restraints.

Knowing Mike listened to her having sex with another man was upsetting. But they shared an unusual bond with a complicated background. They would survive this like they'd survived everything else over the past eleven years. *Together.*

She glanced in the direction of the exit, unable to see his position around the corner. But he was there. She bet her life on it.

From the bag, she removed a laptop, launched a recorded video, and set it on the floor beside Cole's head.

He glared at the rafters, refusing to look at the screen. The same reaction he had the night she showed him the footage of the drone. He wasn't stupid. He knew that whatever she intended to show him would hurt. It would hurt worse than anything he'd endured so far.

She pressed play on the video and stepped back, detaching herself from his impending pain. God, how she'd tried to avoid this. Tried and failed.

Because the way to Cole Hartman wasn't through his stomach or his dick.

It was through his heart.

The video began, streaming sultry music through the warehouse. His entire body turned to stone.

Slowly, his neck twisted, his eyes shifting toward the screen. His expression, starkly blank, gave nothing away. He lifted his head, straining to see around the bulge of his bicep. She couldn't see the video, but she knew it well.

The glittery costume, sensual hip rotations, long golden hair, and room full of admirers were but a backdrop to the main attraction.

Danni Savoy was stunning. With huge gray eyes, flawless skin, and a body that dripped sex, she wasn't just a gorgeous woman. She was a gorgeous belly dancer. Dear God, the woman stood on that stage and danced like no one was watching—shameless and serene, self-possessed and sinfully, enchantingly talented. And everyone was watching.

The video captured ten minutes of her performance, focusing on the gyration of her hips, her pretty face, and most importantly, the vulnerability of her position. She wasn't locked away in hiding. She was dancing in public for all to see.

Lydia didn't have to voice the threat to Cole. The footage spoke for itself.

"This is where you went for five days," he said in an eerily calm tone.

"Yes." She'd driven seventeen hours to St. Louis to locate Cole Hartman's heart. "Your dancer is extraordinary. Painfully beautiful. If I were into women, I would be obsessed with her, too."

"I'm not obsessed with her." His dark gaze snapped to hers, stony and unbreakable. "*She* doesn't belong to me, Lydia. *You* do."

His erection, which had lost some of its life, hardened anew. With his magnificent body laid out like an erotic buffet, rigid and vibrating, he exuded an animal magnetism that made her feel things, *want* things that she couldn't freeze out.

It was impossible not to desire him. Any woman with a pulse would throw herself at his feet. So to hear him say that she belonged to him? It satisfied an ache she didn't even know she had.

It also distracted her from the job.

He continued to stare, watching her with a brooding intensity in his eyes, the video seemingly forgotten. Why wasn't he freaking out and asking about Danni's safety?

Because this was Cole, always in control and one step ahead.

"She might not belong to you." She crossed her arms, her pulse thudding. "But you belong to her."

"My position says otherwise. You have me, Lydia." He eased up on the rope, relaxing his limbs, unabashedly sprawled and fully erect. "Come here, and I'll show you."

It had to be a trap, but she was already moving toward it, kicking off her heels as she went.

COMPLICATE

The music on the video changed, increasing in crescendo. Danni's hips would be kicking and shimmying along with the beat, but he didn't glance at the screen, didn't remove his eyes from Lydia.

As she reached him, she lowered to her knees and slid over his sculpted body, her hands and lips roaming everywhere, trembling and conflicted. But all the doubts in her mind couldn't stop her from crawling up his chest and touching his beard, his rugged face, those chiseled lips.

"Closer." Panting, he lifted his head and offered his mouth. "Give me your lips."

As if yanked by a fist attached to her throat, she fell into him, kissing him with reckless abandon.

He growled, pushing his tongue into her mouth and taking over. Her insides turned molten as she ground down on him, rubbing her pussy against his flexing abs.

Then she broke the kiss, shocked by how wet she'd become. She was leaking all over him and rocking mindlessly, frantically, desperate to be filled.

Rope bound his arms, chest, and legs, but his hips had freedom to move, and holy sweet Jesus, did they move. He bucked beneath her, twisting and angling as if trying to reposition her, as if dead set on taking her this way.

Maybe it was a trick. Or maybe he really did want her. The video started over, blaring its music, but he never looked at it. His gaze never left her mouth.

She grabbed his face and kissed him again. He groaned, thrusting his tongue, bruising her lips, his muscles contracting and writhing beneath her.

Reaching between them, she gripped his cock and stroked him mercilessly. His entire body went rigid, his breathing choppy and urgent, as slippery strings of pre-cum coated her hand. She increased the pressure, ringing him with her thumb and forefinger until he was groaning, thrusting, panting.

"Goddamn, Lydia. Oh, fuck." He grunted, his sinews straining and creaking the rope. "Put me inside. Right now."

Sharp longing spilled through her, shaking, building, and hurtling her toward delirium. But it wasn't enough.

She needed him.

Shifting backward, she clamped her thighs around his waist and brought her tender flesh against the underside of his cock. He was so fucking hard, so insanely turned on he couldn't catch his breath.

What had sparked it? The glimpse of his dancer on the video?

With more force than was necessary, she smacked the laptop shut and shoved it away. Then she gripped his length between her legs and slammed down on him.

"Ah, God. Fuck yeah, that's incredible." His voice scraped, thick with desire. "Now just sit there like a good girl and let me do the fucking."

Excitement and pleasure shimmered in her blood, heating her breasts and racing her pulse. He arched against the restraints, plowing into her, digging his cock deep, deeper, ramming into the back of her cunt.

Blissfully, maddeningly, she moaned. It felt so good it hurt, building too quickly, too viciously. He stabbed into her harder, faster, his hipbones driving into her buttocks and circling, dragging his length at new depths and angles, and shattering every nerve ending inside her.

Her fingers slid from his face to his flat nipple, her nails burying into muscle and pinning her need against his thrusts. Her other hand clung to his broad shoulder as she leaned toward his mouth, seeking.

He caught her lips, kissing her deep, then deeper with each brutal stroke of his cock. Her hands sought, and his body shook with exertion and pleasure. Somewhere in the recesses of her awareness, she knew she shouldn't enjoy this. But his kiss generated a craving in her neglected heart. As arousing as it was terrifying, she couldn't separate her emotions. She could not stop.

She needed more. More of his hunger. More of his kisses. More of his hot, hard maleness sliding and flexing against her.

And he gave it to her, deeper, harder, fucking her mouth as passionately as he fucked between her legs. They were sweat and spit, feral lust and smacking flesh. Together, they were explosive. Unstoppable. Dangerous as hell.

He thrust again and again, the heat so fierce, the sensations so shockingly uninhibited, she burned. Melting from the inside out, she clutched at the rigid muscles of his arms and sank into his strokes.

His aggressive kisses held their mouths together. She opened to him, her lips and thighs, welcoming the invasion, inviting him to take and touch as he wished.

She wanted his hands on her, groping and bruising. She needed his arms around her, wrenching her closer. But he was still restrained. He couldn't touch her, couldn't hold her, and she resented that.

His teeth caught her lips, biting wildly, the kiss breaking and reconnecting with the frenzy of their hunger.

"I have a weakness," he grunted against her mouth.

"Only one?"

"Right now, it's the only one that matters." His hands balled into fists above his head, his eyes locked on hers. "Give me your ass."

COMPLICATE

"You want to fuck my ass?" Her breath fled. "That's your weakness?"

"You have no idea." A shudder ran through him. "You're so goddamn hot, so unbelievably slick and greedy. The tight fist of your cunt..." He snapped his hips, hammering into her. "Fuck, you make me crazy. I can't even imagine what your little asshole would do to me."

A gaping, throbbing sensation ignited between her legs, dripping, swelling, aching to be punished.

"Jesus." He gasped. "I can feel you clenching. You want it. Christ, I knew you wouldn't pass up a dick in your ass."

"You're so fucking kinky." She stretched over him, chest to chest, mouth to mouth, with her hands braced on his restrained arms. "I want *your* dick in my ass."

"Then spread your cheeks, woman. Don't make me wait."

She was far from an inexperienced newcomer to anal. When she was younger, she had a regular lover who preferred her ass over all else.

Relaxation, arousal, and lube were crucial in making it enjoyable, and holy hell, she had all of that working for her right now. She'd never been so turned on, so utterly loose and ready for it. And wet. So goddamn wet her fluids were everywhere, leaking into her crack and running all over his thighs.

She rose on her knees, disconnecting them. He grunted at the abrupt loss of contact, his body stiff and waiting. The folds of her dress kept her covered as she reached behind her and angled his erection between her flexing cheeks.

The head of him sluiced through her slippery crevice until he notched against her back entrance, pushing against the tight outer ring. She breathed in, out, and slowly lowered, pushing down, down, all the way to the root.

So much pressure, the fullness, the overwhelming stimulation... Her body gushed in response, and his echoed her every spasm. He wasn't breathing, his mouth hanging open, his eyes wide and glazed.

Then she lifted, stretching around him and crying out before sinking again.

He choked on a groan and started pumping away, harder, faster. "I'm going to come."

"Wait." Her hand skidded down his abs to his hip, holding him fast, while she fumbled beneath the dress to rub her clit.

He didn't wait. His muscles went taut. His spine arched, and he roared, thrusting feverishly, erratically, and jetting a torrent of hot liquid warmth into her ass.

He came.

At last, he fucking surrendered.

Despite not finding her own release, she couldn't help but savor the victory.

"Wipe that look off your face." His voice cut through her like a whip, shockingly cold and mean. "Get off me."

She flinched, frozen, with him still buried in her rectum.

"Get up!" He punched his hips, dislodging her, his eyes blazing with fury. "Get the fuck away from me."

FIFTEEN

Stunned and teetering, Lydia fell off Cole's lap and landed on the floor beside him.

"What the fuck is wrong with you?" She shoved to her feet, shaking with her fists at her sides.

"Are you fucking kidding me? You've been forcing yourself on me for days, and you have the nerve to ask what's wrong with *me?*"

Footsteps pounded behind her, sounding Mike's approach. When he reached her side, she shivered at anger rolling off him. But neither she nor Cole spared him a glance, their gazes locked.

"Orgasm denial doesn't work on a man who doesn't want to come." Cole laughed cruelly. "He has to be interested."

"You just came—"

"I *literally* fucked you in the ass, Lydia. With my hands tied. Let that sink in for a second."

It sank, and it sank *hard*, caving in her chest and leaving a trail of ice.

After a long, heart-pounding pause, Cole went in for the kill. "The only pleasure I derived from that orgasm was knowing that while you're coming to terms with how fantastically you've been manipulated, you get to feel my payback dribbling from your filthy asshole."

Bile hit her throat. She was going to throw up.

Mike lunged forward with his pistol drawn, his expression murderous.

She swung out an arm and caught him across the chest, halting him. She needed to hear this. No matter how badly it hurt.

With a growl, he snatched Cole's jeans from the floor and tossed them over Cole's soft cock.

Grateful to not have to see that part of him, she moved to the hose and twisted it on. She could, in fact, feel him dripping down her legs. An irritation that would soon be remedied.

Cole and Mike watched as she lifted the hem of the dress and sprayed off the slime between her thighs. She kept herself covered, but it wasn't her finest moment.

Her humiliation was absolute, but she hid it beneath a mien of rancor, which she directed at Cole, shouting with her eyes. *Fuck you.*

The corners of his mouth twisted up, defiling his gorgeous face. So antagonistic, that smirk.

"Danni is surrounded by bodyguards, right?" He glanced at the laptop and returned to her. "You can't touch her. If you could, she would be here with a gun aimed at her head. The casino has top-notch security, so you couldn't even plant bugs. You had to wear a camera on your clothes and sit in the restaurant with all the other patrons just to capture a recording of her."

Her throat closed.

He'd known all along. That explained why the video hadn't upset him.

Everything they just did together had been deliberately contrived. None of it had been real. How hypocritical of her to think otherwise. She'd been coercing him all along.

Except that wasn't entirely true. She was using him and at the same time, saving him. She wanted him to survive. And for a fleeting moment, when they were together, she wanted him simply because she wanted to be with him.

"The video was only good as a scare tactic. A hollow threat," he said, his voice rumbling, crawling beneath her skin. "You're desperate. That tells me you searched for my friends and couldn't find them. Danni was your only option."

Mike stiffened beside her, his finger twitching against the trigger on the pistol. He wouldn't shoot unless he had to. He wasn't that impulsive.

She'd tried to track Cole's friends. But while she was getting him settled in his cell, his friends had fled the states. They were nowhere to be found.

"Why are you telling me this?" She turned off the hose and dried her legs with a towel. "Why not just tell me where the hard drive is?"

"We both know I'm not walking out of here. You're not going to kill me. But there are fifteen men, including your boyfriend here, who are gunning to rip me apart."

COMPLICATE

She ground her teeth, feeling pretty fucking homicidal. "You don't know me or what I'm capable of."

"No, but I've learned a lot over the past month. Enough to know you're too soft to torture me."

"I wasn't too soft to fuck you, was I?"

"You convinced yourself I was into it, but you feel guilt. Puts a new light on the walk of shame."

Her cheeks heated, and a ringing sound blared in her ears. She hated him for this. Hated how easily he dissected her.

"You don't have the stomach for torture, and you're not cold enough to be a Russian swallow." His jaw tightened, twitching his beard. "You're not even Russian."

The blood drained from her face, chilling her skin. Oh God, how did he know?

She didn't dare speak, too afraid she would give away more than she already had.

"During the first week, you had a good handle on the accent." Furrows formed between his brows. "It was stiff, but convincing. Then it started to slip. The more comfortable you were around me, the more your inflection relaxed. Especially when you're aroused. That's when I hear the Midwestern drawl. Chicago, I think."

"She's lived in the states for years." Mike shook his head, refusing to give up her ruse. "Of course, she picked up an American accent."

"That's what I thought until she made a glaring mistake." Cole met her eyes. "The day I told you I wanted *palimi* with sour cream and caviar, you didn't correct me. You played it off like you knew what I was saying. But you don't. *Blini* is a pancake. A Russian staple for breakfast. *Palimi* isn't even a word."

Her lungs collapsed, and her hands slicked with sweat. She'd fucked up, and if Cole saw through her disguise, who else had? If Vincent Barrington was half as smart as Cole, she was dead.

Mike stepped forward, and she recognized the look in his eyes. He was ready to end this with a bullet in Cole's head.

Cole knew too much. He couldn't live, and given the *fuck-it* vibes radiating from him, he'd already accepted his fate.

"Mike." She set a hand on his forearm and dropped the accent. "This isn't finished."

He glanced behind them, confirming they were alone. Then he gave a nod.

"Why Chicago?" she asked Cole.

"Your *th* sounds get lazy. Instead of *zis,* you slip into *dis. Da* hard drive, instead of *za* hard drive. You've used *fer* instead of *for,* among a dozen other little tells." Cole switched to Russian, speaking each word with flawless articulation. "You use Midwestern slang that doesn't make sense to native Russians."

He was right. Goddammit, she knew it happened sometimes and tried to cover it. But nothing slipped past him.

She blew it. The gig was up, and she had no idea what to do.

Pacing, she grasped at strings, desperate to fix this. "Tell me who bought the hard drive, and I'll let you go. Right now. Just give me a name, and you're free."

Mike went still, his gaze cutting to her. This wasn't part of the plan, and he didn't like it. If Cole went free, he would hunt her down. After everything she did to him, she expected nothing less.

"You won't let me go." He twisted his arms in the rope. "Even if you tried, you won't succeed. You're not in charge."

"What are you talking about? I'm leading this—"

"Thurney Bridge."

Her neck went taut. He'd mentioned that before, and she'd looked into it. There was a bridge in France by that name, but she found nothing else. Nothing related to Cole Hartman.

"Five months ago," he said, "a hitman killed Rylee Sutton's neighbor, two motel clerks, and when he attempted to kill Rylee, he mentioned Thurney Bridge."

Vincent Barrington. That corrupt son of a bitch. Putting hits on innocent people? What else was he doing behind her back?

"That wasn't me." Her heart pounded. "I don't know anything about that."

"Your boss was behind it."

"He's not my boss."

"*He.*"

Shit. She'd just given way another detail. For the love of God, she needed to keep her mouth shut.

"Your boss knows the connection between me, Thurney Bridge, Marie Merivale, and the hard drive," he said. "That suggests he has access to classified information."

She pressed her lips together, refusing to confirm or deny.

"So how do you fit in?" He slowly released a breath through his nose. "You posed as a Russian swallow to get hired for this job. Your boss sent you here to capture me and seduce me into talking. Not an uncommon tactic, but complicated. Physical torture would've been simpler."

COMPLICATE

She shared a look with Mike. Trusting Cole was out of the question, but if she disclosed their strategy, there might still be a way to use him.

"I wasn't just hired to seduce you into talking." She met Cole's steady gaze. "I was hired to seduce the person in possession of the hard drive."

"So you can steal it."

"Yes. My employer doesn't give a fuck how I get it, just as long as it's in his hands by the end of the year."

Cole nodded, his expression pensive. "You kept me alive, with all my limbs, because you need me to help you steal it."

"That would make things easier."

"I don't do retrievals of that nature." He relaxed into the floor, his chest glistening with sweat and scratches from her nails. "I'm not a goddamn thief."

"I know. That's why you're in this position."

"What do you know about me?"

"For the past seven years, you've accepted jobs that involved finding missing persons and information. Information such as secret trafficking routes and criminal headquarters, which often puts you deep in the bowels of cartels and organized crime syndicates. But you've never taken a job related to politics or government intelligence. I assume you're bound by loyalty to your country or some sort of legality related to the job you held in the government. How am I doing so far?"

"Not bad. Your boss gave you this intel?"

"Yes."

Vincent knew a lot about Cole, but he'd only given her the bare minimum. Without Vincent, she wouldn't have connected Cole to the hard drive. She wouldn't have even known he existed.

"You deceived your boss about who and what you are." Cole inclined his head, eyes tapered. "He believes he hired a sex spy when in reality, you're here with your own agenda. You don't intend to deliver the hard drive to him. You want it for yourself."

A chill swept down her spine, and her neck twisted impulsively toward the exit, her eyes scanning every shadow and nook in the warehouse. If Vincent or his men knew the truth, it was game over.

Vincent thought she didn't know what was on that hard drive. He believed she and Mike were just here for a paycheck.

"He's going to kill you," Cole said, reading her mind.

"Not if I kill him first. Listen to me." She crouched beside his hip and set a hand on his thigh.

He flinched and bared his teeth, looking for all the world like he wanted to rip her to shreds.

"You hate me. Fine." Her heart in knots, she removed her touch. "But if we work together, we can survive this."

"Burn in hell."

"I'll pay you. Name your price." She was talking out of her ass. She had no money. "I'll pay you whatever you want for your cooperation."

"What was your exit strategy, Lydia? You seduce me and learn the hard drive's location. Then what? How were you going to sneak out of here, with me, without giving your boss the information he wants?"

She lowered her gaze to his body, taking in his strength, his sheer muscle mass.

"I see." Disappointment roughened his voice. "You thought I'd be so blinded by your pussy that I'd lead you out like fucking G.I. Joe, maybe take some bullets for you in the process. And if I survived, I'd be useful in infiltrating the next target."

"You have powerful friends. Once we get out of here—"

"You want my friends to help you? The same friends you targeted with hellfire?"

"The drone wasn't armed."

"Lydia," Mike growled.

"You were bluffing?" Cole barked out a laugh. "Fucking awesome." In the next breath, he sobered, his eyes hard as steel. "Give me the name of the motherfucker who's funding this shit show."

"He's—"

In a blur, Mike pounced, swinging the pistol and whipping it across Cole's head. The smack echoed through the warehouse, leaving Cole knocked out cold.

She gasped. "Why did you do that?"

He turned his furious gaze on her. "You said too much. If you tell him who's involved, he'll go after the hard drive himself."

"That's what we want." She grabbed a towel and a bucket of water and knelt beside Cole's head.

"We want it in the right hands. You know how valuable it is." He raked his fingers through his hair, yanking at the roots. "Jesus, Lydia. You can't trust him. You don't know anything about him."

She bent down and wiped the wet rag along the gash near Cole's temple. A trickle of blood fell from the cut, but it would heal cleanly without stitches. Mike knew how to strike with minimal damage.

"I don't trust him." She applied pressure to the wound and let her fingers trail down his sculpted face.

Mike's expression clouded as he watched her. "You trusted him with your ass."

She sucked in a sharp breath, hurt by the disgust in his tone. "Don't you dare shame me for that."

COMPLICATE

"Lydia." Sighing, he closed his eyes and pinched the bridge of his nose. "I'm not..." He dropped his hand and stared at her with bloodshot eyes. "Look, I get why you did it. Why you let him..." His stance widened, shifting with the weight of his frustration. "Just tell me you're not falling for him."

"What?" She blinked. Then choked out a laugh. "No. God. This is bigger than me, Mike. It's bigger than *us*."

"I know." His eyes narrowed on her hands in Cole's hair.

"Good grief." She tossed the towel in the bucket and stood, staring down at Cole's limp body. "He beat me at my own game. I seduced him. He seduced me. He won. That's all this is. I don't know the extent of his skill set, but I can tell you this. He's a master at reading people. He knew how to strip me down and make me talk before I had a clue what was happening. But he doesn't know everything. We can let him go. Let him live."

"Lydia."

"We're a lot of things, but we're not murderers. If we leave him here, he's dead." Her chest squeezed. "He's never going to talk. He'll let them kill him first."

"This is so fucked." He paced away with his hands clasped behind his neck. "We're not giving up."

"Never." Her pulse quickened, her voice breathless.

"All right. Go back to the room." He squatted beside Cole and reached for the jeans. "I'll dress him and return him to the cell."

"What if he tries to talk to the guards? If he tells them what he knows...?"

He flashed a menacing smile. "I'll gladly knock his ass out again."

SIXTEEN

Lydia dozed off. She hadn't meant to close her eyes, but when she opened them, a rude buzzing crashed through her grogginess.

"Fuck!" She scrambled off the mattress and stumbled through the room, hunting the vibrating sounds of her phone.

Where the hell was Mike? He should've returned by now.

She spotted the buzzing device on the table amid the clutter of cosmetics. Snatching it up, she gasped at the time. Jesus, she'd slept for two hours?

Because…Cole. He'd put her body through the wringer and mangled her emotions. But she couldn't think about that now. The unknown caller wasn't going to be happy about waiting through five rings. Six.

"Yes?" She hacked the greeting from the back of her throat, overly conscious about her fake accent. "You need something?"

"Change of plans." Vincent's high-pitched drawl set her teeth on edge. "I'm moving up the deadline."

"You can't do that." She tightened her hand around the phone, making it creak. "We had a deal."

"It's already done. The team is extracting the information now, and once they have it, they'll pass it along to you. Then you will retrieve the package. Maybe your cunt will be more effective on the next target."

Her blood pressure hit the roof, and she reached out a hand, catching herself on the table, attempting to steady her legs and quash the panic in her voice.

"Whatever," she said with as much boredom as she could summon. "The payment doesn't change."

COMPLICATE

"You'll get your money. Just don't fuck this up."

"I'm very good at my job."

"You keep saying that. Yet you've produced nothing."

"I delivered him here."

"Yeah, all right, I'll give you that." He hardened his tone, which succeeded only in making him sound whiny. "You will stay out of the way until the others get the information you need. Then you will finish this. Understood?"

He expected her to sit here while they butchered and killed Cole.

Yeah, whatever you say, boss.

She swallowed down her rising fury. "Yes."

He disconnected.

She'd never met him in person, and maybe she never would. But as she tossed the phone and dragged on a pair of black jeans, she vowed that, before she surrendered her last breath, she would witness the glorious annihilation of Vincent Barrington.

Quickly, she pulled on a white t-shirt, combat boots, and checked her appearance in the mirror. The false eyelashes barely hung on. Black eyeliner melted down her cheeks and smeared into her blush. Bright red lipstick slanted over her chin as if streaked by a river of drool.

She looked like a redheaded Harley Quinn, freshly fucked, one-hundred-percent psychotic, and ready to party.

Yeah, her makeup was utterly ruined — *thank you, Cole* — but it still did its job. It hid her true face.

On her way out, she grabbed a handgun, slid in a full magazine, and clipped a spare mag on her hip. Then she took off down the hall.

Passing the break room, she counted four guys gathered around the table eating and drinking beer. She slipped by unnoticed and turned the corner, pausing at the bathroom. Two men inside. She intersected two more farther down the corridor.

One of them stopped her. "Where are you going?"

"I need a shower." She gave him a look. "That's not an invite."

He held up his hands and backed away, smirking as his eyes drifted down her body.

"The warehouse is all yours, honey." He turned and paced off in the opposite direction.

Had he just come from there? God, she hoped Cole was still in his cell, and Mike was keeping guard.

As she measured her steps, trying to appear calm, Vincent's words coiled in her belly.

The team is extracting the information now.

That could mean anything, but her mind conjured knives cutting through flesh, extracting bones, organs, and any part of Cole that would bring out the answer.

By the time she burst into the warehouse, she was sweating and out of breath.

Silence surrounded her, thrashing in her ears. No one was here. She spun toward Cole's cell.

The door stood open. He was gone.

Oh fuck, oh fuck, oh fuck. Where the hell was he?

Where was Mike? Was he in trouble? If Vincent's men overheard her conversation with him, if they were hurting him…

Horror glued her boots to the floor. Terror pulled through her gut. A helpless void resonated in her chest.

The loading dock.

It was the only place they could be. Unless Cole and Mike were taken somewhere. Somewhere she would never find them.

She raced out of the warehouse, down the eerily quiet corridor, toward the dock.

What if it was a trap? Were they waiting for her to come running? Had they figured out why she was here?

Her eyes darted behind her, expecting one of the doors to open and hands to shoot out.

Paranoia pushed her harder, and dread dug in its claws. She wrestled with it, fighting it down, burying it deep enough to control her breathing. Then she forced herself to holster the weapon in her waistband. She couldn't burst in with guns blazing. Not without giving herself away.

At the entrance to the loading dock, she pulled in another calming breath and opened the door.

Voices drew her attention to the far side. She flattened her back to the wall, remaining out of view. Then she peered around the corner.

Alec stood beside a massive machine, his attention on the cast-iron bridge that rose overhead, twenty feet in length, with steel pillars supporting each end. She didn't know anything about the tools required for cutting stone into grave markers, but it didn't take a genius to understand how this one worked.

Suspended from the center of its bridge was a circular saw, at least six feet in diameter. Rusty, broken teeth fringed the outer edge. It was large enough to cut blocks of granite into narrow slabs.

Or human bodies into little messy slivers.

She worked her throat against a knot of fear.

The machine didn't function. None of the junk left behind was operational. Unless someone had fixed it? Was there a mechanic on the team?

COMPLICATE

"What's it going to be?" Alec folded his arms across his chest. "Your hands? Or your feet? Or you can keep your extremities and tell us the location of the hard drive."

Her shoulders bunched to her ears, and her heart landed somewhere in the vicinity of her stomach. She silenced her breathing and leaned forward, straining for a better look.

Five men stood around the machine, including Alec. *And Mike.*

A vein of relief swept through her.

Angled slightly away from her position, Mike rested his hands in his pockets, exuding the appearance of cool indifference. But she knew him.

She knew his shoulders held too much stiffness. His neck elongated with the tensing of muscles, and trenches rutted his hair from his fingers repeatedly pushing through it. He was anything but relaxed.

He was also the only man not armed.

Alec and the others must've taken him by surprise, and now he was pretending to go along with this to avoid raising alarms. *This* being the torture of Cole Hartman.

Cole lay on the platform beneath the giant circular saw, his body restrained to the steel structure. He didn't move, didn't make a sound.

"We'll start with your hands, then." Alec flicked a lever on the machine.

An ear-splitting screech cracked the air, springing the rusty saw to life and making her jump.

No, no, no!

She stared in horror as Alec hit another switch and lowered the enormous whirring blade. Cole's arm lay two feet beneath it, trapped in rope. He didn't struggle or twitch a muscle. The fucking asshole was just going to lie there and let that saw take his hand.

Mike's shadowed eyes flicked back and forth, lingering on the men's holstered guns. He was going to attempt something. Something stupid like swiping one of their weapons. Dammit, he was going to get himself shot.

Perspiration formed on her spine.

At the speed in which the blade lowered, she only had seconds.

A huge breath filled her lungs as she drew her weapon. Then she bolted forward, the sound of her approach swallowed by the chest-rattling squeal of the machine.

Alec spotted her first, his brows leaping to his hairline. Twenty-feet away, she fired.

Missed.

Fucking shit! She sprinted forward. He reached for his gun.

Fifteen-feet. She shot again and hit him in the chest. He dropped instantly.

The need to gasp set her lungs on fire, but she couldn't draw air. Adrenaline spiked her blood as she set her sights on the remaining three.

Their guns, already drawn, turned toward her as the spinning blade continued its descent, the toothy edge blurring inches from Cole's arm.

All at once, Mike grabbed one of the men, and a bullet fired, whizzing past her ear as she squeezed the trigger.

Over and over, she shot off rounds, charging forward and blowing through the magazine until the only man left standing was Mike.

Without taking a breath, she fell upon the machine and smacked the lever. Her heart stopped, waiting in agony as the motor ground to a soundless halt, freezing the circular saw.

The blade sat against Cole's sinewy forearm, drawing a bead of blood around the serrated, rust-colored edge. So goddamn close, and he never struggled. Never moved a muscle.

Her pulse pounded as she dragged her eyes over the rest of him. Boots, dirty jeans, powerful legs, shredded abs, tattooed chest and arms, and a scraggly beard that only enhanced his intimidating, masculine appearance.

No visible injuries.

"Other than the cut," she said, quickly flipping the switch to lift the blade, "you're not harmed?"

His silence pulled her gaze to his, and lord have mercy, those molten brown eyes imprisoned her, suffocated her, and refused to let go. He was so beautiful, so utterly unruffled and fearless, just watching her, breathing calmly, *alive*.

As she met his stare head-on, she swore she saw that look again, the one from before when she thought she felt something forging between them. Something real and not of this cold, ugly world.

Tingling sparked through her arms and fingers, and she gulped a breath.

"In less than a minute, we're going to be under fire." Mike scuttered back and forth behind her, collecting weapons. "Time to go."

The moment she'd shot the first bullet, the report had alerted the rest of the team of trouble. Any second, ten men would explode through that door with more firepower than she and Mike could defend.

"Hurry." He slapped a knife onto the platform beside Cole and sprinted across the ramp toward the parked vehicles.

Two motorcycles sat out there somewhere among the cars and trucks, with the keys in the ignitions.

COMPLICATE

"We'll take the bikes," she shouted after Mike and cut one of Cole's arms free.

Then she set the blade in his hand so that he could remove the rest. As he calmly sawed his way through the rope, she replaced the magazine in her gun and stepped back, keeping the weapon trained on him.

Outside, Mike darted from one parked vehicle to the next, slashing all the tires. All but the two bikes they would leave with.

"Have you ever killed a man?" Cole freed his arm and moved to his legs, regarding her from beneath his dark brows.

"N—" Her voice cracked, and she cleared her throat. "No."

"You did good. Most people hesitate the first time." The corner of his mouth quirked up as he glanced at the gash on his arm. "You didn't."

"I made a choice." She held the gun with both hands, her fingers clammy and ribcage wrapped in rubber bands. "Don't make me regret it."

He cut through the final restraint and shoved to his feet, his gaze instantly falling on the dead bodies, scanning their clothes. She knew what he was looking for, but Mike had already taken the weapons.

She might've sabotaged the entire fucking mission to save Cole's life. But that didn't mean she and Mike trusted him with a gun. If he was the revengeful sort, she wasn't safe.

She would never be safe again.

An ache swelled in her chest.

Walk away, Lydia.

He stared at her, expressionless, and she stared back, miserable and heartbroken. There was so much to say. If things had been different, if she were a gentler person with better circumstances...

There was no time.

"Go." She stepped forward, aiming the gun at his handsome face. "You're free. Take the second bike and get out of here."

"Lydia!" Mike yelled from outside as the engine of a motorcycle rumbled to life.

Cole's dark gaze lifted toward the door thirty yards behind her, and his eyebrows pinched. In the next heartbeat, the door crashed open.

"Run!" She raced toward the ramp and found Mike waiting at the far end on the motorcycle.

Shots fired, pelting the ground behind her and whistling past her head. The spare bike sat twenty-some yards in the other direction. But rather than darting for it, Cole remained at her back, breathing down her neck.

"Get out of here!" She pointed at his ride. "That way!"

The volley of bullets multiplied as more men poured onto the loading dock. A couple of them were closing in, gaining on her. She couldn't outrun the spray of lead.

As she started to turn and fire back, a hand gripped her arm.

Everything happened so fast, the chaos of gunfire ricocheting in her ears, disorienting her as Cole yanked her off the ramp.

Her back hit the ground, and he fell atop of her, dodging bullets with laughter in his eyes.

What the fuck? Her heart thundered so violently she thought her ribs were cracking. And he was laughing?

"First gunfight?" He grinned down at her, his shirtless chest smothering her in heat.

Yes. But before she could answer, he plucked the pistol from her grip, extended his arm, and returned fire.

Pinned beneath him, she craned her neck and watched the men scatter. Two of them dropped, hit by Cole's bullets. At least six more took cover.

On the other side of the ramp, Mike sped forward on the motorcycle, firing his gun at the shooters on the loading dock.

Cole used the diversion to wrap his arms around her and roll them across the ground, seeking cover. He found it beneath a nearby box truck, where he yanked her up and dragged her around to the other side, shoving her behind it, shielding her from gunfire.

Buying them time.

A moment.

With her back pressed to the vehicle, he leaned in and flattened a hand on the steel above her head. Her breathing tumbled into asthmatic hysteria while his remained normal, controlled, unnervingly composed.

But his eyes told a different story, the dark depths pulsing with the hungry fires of hell.

This wasn't the man who fucked her ass and knocked her away with a nasty sneer. This devil was far more deadly, possessive, protective, deeply passionate, and complicated. She stared into the soul of a man she could fall in love with.

The longing that gripped her was enormous, the pull toward him more than she could bear.

"Go." She shoved at his chest.

Gunfire boomed just beyond the truck, growing closer. Amid the mayhem, she heard the motorcycle, the engine revving, speeding toward her.

"Leave." She slammed her palms against his shoulders and pushed harder. "You're free!"

He stepped back, swaying with her shove. Then he was on her again, cupping her head with both hands. With the gun in his grip, the length of it lay against her cheek as he held her, forcing her to look at him.

COMPLICATE

"Darius Skutnik." His thumb tenderly stroked across her cheekbone.

"What?"

"The *nașu* of the Romanian mafia. The godfather." He brought their foreheads together and breathed against her lips. "He has the hard drive."

Shock and elation stole through her, weakening her legs and her voice. But she didn't need either as he lifted her up his body and kissed her hard on the mouth. His tongue knifed past her lips. His beard scratched her face, and his fingers dug into the backs of her thighs.

She grabbed his shoulders to pull. No, to push. It was too much. *He* was too much.

He wrenched his mouth away and turned just as Mike rolled up on the motorcycle.

"Let her go." He trained the gun on Cole. "They're coming."

Cole shifted and set her on the seat behind Mike. As he pulled back, her heart tore. Another retreating step, and her trembling hands slid off his shoulders, down his biceps, her fingers curling, hanging on.

He slipped free, and her palm came away wet. Soaked in blood.

"Oh my God." Her eyes darted to the hole in his arm, her bloody hand reaching for him. "You were shot?"

Footsteps stampeded toward the truck.

Cole's gaze stayed with her for another second before he tore it away, spun, and fired the pistol.

"Hold on!" Mike opened the throttle, and the motorcycle lurched forward. She wrapped her arms around him and twisted, watching as Cole shot into the fray and sprinted toward the second bike.

Her hair whipped around her face, obstructing her view as Mike put more and more separation between them and the gunfight. She didn't breathe until she heard the roar of another engine. She didn't straighten her neck until Cole appeared off in the distance, bent low over the bike as he sped through the desert in the opposite direction.

Twilight approached, streaking the horizon in ribbons of orange and violet. Within seconds, the swirling shadows swallowed his form. He was safe.

Gone.

A painful clot amassed deep inside her, and a terrible burn bubbled from her chest, forming a lump in her throat and searing the backs of her eyes. Everything she felt was irrational and wrong, but it was real.

What she felt for him was real and raw and unbearable.

She screwed her eyes shut and rested her cheek against Mike's strong back, her arms holding him tight.

They survived. All three of them. And Cole had given her a name. Now she knew the location of the hard drive.

This wasn't over.

Not the job.

And not this other thing…this unresolved connection.

She knew at gut level she hadn't seen the last of Cole Hartman.

SEVENTEEN

Drenched in sweat and trammeled by exhaustion, Cole stood at the bathroom sink in Tomas' vacant house and patched up the gunshot wound.

It was a clean shot through his bicep, with an entry and exit point. It would hurt like a bitch for a while and fuck with his muscle movement. But it could've been worse.

He could be lying beneath the stonecutter in a hundred sliced-up pieces.

Once he finished treating the injury, he slumped onto the couch and contemplated who to call first.

Maybe because the image of red hair was heavy on his mind, he dialed the only ginger he knew.

Luke answered with a heavy exhale of relief. "Holy shit, you're alive."

"Thanks for the vote of confidence."

"The doubt was real."

"I'm safe, in case you're wondering."

"Where are you?"

"Making a pit stop at the house in the desert."

He couldn't stay here. Lydia knew about this place, which meant the person she'd just betrayed knew about it, too. He just needed to grab some gear. Shit, shower, and shave. Then he would be on his way.

"You've been missing for a goddamn month," Luke growled. "Where have you been?"

Despite the overload of fatigue and unease, Cole managed a smile. It was nice to have people who cared enough to worry about him.

"Calm down." He chuckled. "I made it out with all my parts intact."

"We thought you were dead."

"No, you didn't."

"We had a funeral service and everything. Van cried. Huge crocodile tears. It made everyone uncomfortable."

"Fuck off."

"Seriously, man." Luke's voice sobered. "We've been freaked the fuck out. What happened?"

"I spent a month in a pitch-black cell, eating hot dogs and listening to thrash metal music."

"Are you fucking with me?"

"Wish I was."

"What about the freaky Russian pin-up girl? Did she do that to you?"

"She isn't Russian." His heart drummed at the mention of her, his thoughts a conflicting jumble of anger and desire. "She restrained me, fucked me, and saved my life."

A stretch of silence ensued, followed by Luke's exhale. "I can't tell by your tone if you participated or if it was torture, so I'm just going to come out and ask. Were you raped?"

Coming from Luke, it was an earnest question. He'd been raped by Van, and most recently, by a strap-on worn by a crazy bitch in La Rocha Cartel.

"Dubious," Cole said. "In the end, I fucked her in the ass."

He gave Luke a rundown of the events, walking through the details, and answering one-hundred-and-one questions.

Once Luke was up to speed, Cole asked, "Is everyone back in Colombia?"

"Yeah, we're all here. We stayed in Texas for a few weeks. When we couldn't find you, we assumed you'd been transported out of the state. Or out of the country. We didn't know. So we returned home where we could regroup in a safe place and wait for you to make contact, per your orders."

"You did good."

"Now what? There's a lot you don't know about these people. What are you going to do?"

"I can leave the country and join you guys in Colombia. If they're hunting me, they won't be able to find me there."

"You're talking about hiding." Luke made a huffing sound. "We both know you won't do that. You're going to go after her."

"I'm going to *track* her. Whatever she's involved in is big. Bigger than she can handle. She's in way over her head."

COMPLICATE

"You want to help this woman?"

"No. I don't want anything to do with this shit. But I need to know. *Fuck.*" He scrubbed a hand over his head, on edge and needing sleep. "I need to know who she is and what she's trying to achieve."

He would stay in the shadows and remain unseen. No contact with her. No exceptions. Whoever she betrayed today wasn't going to let her live. That hard drive held something valuable. Valuable enough to orchestrate an elaborate plan that involved a fifteen-man team, a Russian swallow, and the capture of a retired operative from the *activity*.

A shit storm was brewing. He felt it in his bones.

"How can we help?" Luke asked.

"I need to follow her every movement without being seen by her or whoever might be hunting her."

"You need Romero."

"Yep."

Romero was the computer whiz kid who had been instrumental in helping Luke and Vera escape La Rocha Cartel earlier this year. The kid had designed and maintained the proprietary technology that secured the cartel compound, but his range of tech skills went far beyond that.

"I'm heading through the halls to look for him now." Luke's breathing picked up, confirming he was on the move. "He can hack into security systems and run facial recognition software on the camera footage, but he'll need information. Names, aliases, physical descriptions, whatever you have."

"I can give him hair color, eye color, height, weight, a detailed description of every tattoo on her body, what she was wearing when she left the desert, how she dresses, which direction she headed, and so on."

"Okay, cool. I'll call you back in a bit. In the meantime, you need to get out of that house."

"On it."

It took him ten minutes to pack all the clothes, weapons, tech gear, and travel documents he would need for an extended mission. More time was doled to showering and shaving off his beard, as well as all the hair on his head. He grabbed Danni's engagement ring and secured the chain around his neck. Then he devoured a can of chili.

When Luke called back, he put Romero on the phone, and Cole gave the kid every detail he had on Lydia and Mike. It was probably more information than Romero would need. The tattoos alone would make Lydia stand out like a beacon.

"Give me a few hours," Romero said. "Should I contact you at this number?"

"Yeah, it's a secure phone. Thanks, Romero."

"You bet."

Six hours later, Cole was sitting on a bench outside Dallas Fort Worth International Airport when his phone buzzed.

Concealed behind sunglasses and the bill of a baseball hat, he lifted the device to his ear. "What do you have for me?"

"Two hours ago," Romero said, "a woman and man matching your description bought airline tickets at George Bush Intercontinental Airport in Houston. They're traveling under the names Lydia and Micheál Johnson."

His pulse kicked up. "Excellent work, kid."

He'd gone to the airport in Dallas on a hunch that they would fly somewhere. But he didn't need to be in the same airport to follow them to their destination.

"Their flight leaves in three hours," Romero said. "Headed to London. You want the flight info?"

"Nah. I just need to know where they go after they land. Can you track them overseas?"

"Now that I have the names they're using and digital images of their faces, I can track them anywhere."

"They probably travel under multiple aliases."

"I won't lose them," Romero said with excitement in his voice.

"I know you won't." He stood and grabbed his bag. "I'll call you when I land."

"I'll be here."

As he strode into the airport to buy a ticket to London, a voice in the back of his head told him to forget this quest. He had no stakes in it. Nothing to offset the risks he would be taking.

Except the woman.

In seven years, no one had come close to capturing his interest. He was officially, certifiably enthralled, and until he understood why, he wasn't walking away from this.

EIGHTEEN

Rome, Italy
Six months later

Lydia's hand grew hot and sticky in Mike's unbending grip as he led her through the exclusive nightclub. Prolonged exhaustion and stress lived in her bones, the weeks blurring into months until she'd lost track of where she was and how much time she had left.

But she didn't lose track of faces. She memorized every detail of every person she passed, knowing any one of them could be connected to her.

Her shoulder blades twitched, her spine tingling with the feeling of exposure. Not just from the backless dress, but from the constant sensation of being watched.

She and Mike weren't just hunting. They were being hunted.

Her neck tightened with the impulse to look over her shoulder. But she kept her eyes directed at Mike's broad back and reached out her senses, probing the shadows around them.

Her short blonde bob and skintight sequin dress blended in with this crowd. The wig hid her hair, and heavy makeup covered the tattoos on her arms and chest and completely altered the contours of her face.

She looked like a drag queen, and Mike played the role of her gay lover. He'd grown out his brown hair and dyed the shaggy mop black. His fashionable linen suit, yellow bowtie, and lopsided Bruce Willis grin underscored the facade. Who knew he could look so adorable?

Every week brought a different city and a different disguise. Through Romania, Italy, Spain, England, France, and Moldova, they tracked the highest-ranking made members of the Romanian crime family, all the while staying one step ahead of the threat on their heels.

Vincent Barrington's men.

She'd already killed two of his assassins since leaving the states. More would follow. Vincent needed that hard drive. His livelihood depended on it, and his only means to find it was through her, Mike, or Cole.

Since she'd betrayed Vincent and escaped with Mike and Cole, Vincent's objective would be to kill them all—and hope to get the hard drive's location from one of them before they died.

She assumed Cole was faring better than her. He had money, powerful friends, and wasn't out in public, stalking the Romanian mafia. He'd disappeared that day in the desert, and she hadn't seen or heard from him since.

Sometimes, she thought she sensed him. When the hairs on her nape prickled, when a flutter stirred in her belly, when the shadows of an alley or dark corner of a pub seemed darker, more intense, she *felt* him. But she never saw him.

She needed to forget all about those bottomless brown eyes, the sinful slide of his tongue, the guttural sounds of his groans when he fucked. God, she needed to stop torturing herself.

Not that she had the time or resources to look for him. Every second that she wasn't running reconnaissance and surveilling the Romanian mob, she was trying to outrun Vincent's men.

Tonight, she was doing both.

The discotheque sat on the Tiber River with a stunning view of Rome. The mirrored decor was grungy, vintage, the space almost exclusively black. The rafters vibrated with the electronic beats of techno, funk, and dance tracks. But she wasn't here for the music.

She'd heard this was the place to spot a Romanian mercenary or two. To penetrate Darius Skutnik and steal the hard drive, she needed more than her body. The job required stealth, and she had a particular sort of criminal in mind. A technically trained criminal with a passion for cybercrime.

But first, she had to deal with whoever was following her.

Bodies swayed, gyrating and grinding and bumping against her as she followed Mike deeper into the horde. Amid flawlessly dressed ladies and trendy, aftershave-scented men, he stopped walking, pivoted around, and brought her chest and hips flush with his.

"Hi." She smiled and slid her hands up his strong neck.

COMPLICATE

"Hey." His lips crooked up, and his body caught the thumping rhythm.

She rolled with him. Or *tried*. He was a much better dancer, his movements natural and loose as he pulled her tight and placed his mouth at her ear.

"Black shirt, black tie. Crooked nose." He splayed a hand over her tail bone, the other curling around her waist. "At your seven o'clock."

Spinning slowly with the music, he turned them in a full rotation so that she could cast her gaze about the room without appearing obvious. She spotted the man Mike noticed, recognizing him immediately.

He leaned against a high-top table off to the side, pretending to stare at something behind her.

Mike shifted her away, letting the throng of dancers sweep them into the undulating wave of heat and sex.

"He was in Paris last week." She hooked her arms around his neck and rested her cheek against the clean-shaved curve of his jaw as her hips reeled and plunged with his. "In the train station, when we were leaving."

"And in London the week before that."

"He's our guy."

One of Vincent's. They had to kill him. Once they did, it would buy them a few months to infiltrate the Romanian mafia before Vincent deployed more hired guns.

It was a fine line they walked, trying to get close to the mafia without Vincent figuring out *who* they were tracking. If he learned the location of the hard drive, all would be lost.

"The veranda out back is ideal." She stretched on her toes to speak in his ear. "Last I checked, no one was out there."

All the smokers congregated on the huge veranda in front with a full bar.

"I'll go." It was easier for her to do it since she could employ her feminine wiles—give the man a look, flash a little cleavage, lead him into a dark corner, and slide a steel blade between his ribs.

"No, you did the last two. I want this one." He squeezed her hip, his breath against her neck. "I'll have a smoke on the veranda and wait for him. Stay here in the crowd. Keep an eye out. Don't fucking wander off."

They were both armed. She wore a stiletto strapped to her garters on her inner thigh. He had multiple blades concealed beneath his suit, as well as two pistols.

The guns were for emergency. The last thing they needed was a showdown with the *polizia*.

"Do it *quietly*." She narrowed her eyes then danced off into the fray.

The gunman wouldn't engage her in a crowd. Vincent didn't pay his employees enough for them to risk getting arrested. The last two had been run-of-the-mill street thugs, looking for quick money. They'd waited until she was alone, where there were no witnesses, before they attacked.

Sidling up to a group of laughing women, she danced with them while watching the man out of the corner of her eye. His gaze discreetly tracked Mike through the nightclub. He took a sip from his cocktail, watching over the rim of the glass long after Mike vanished beyond the doors of the veranda.

Mike was alone in a poorly lit area. An easy target. Why wasn't the man going after him?

Maybe she and Mike hadn't been marked after all. They'd changed disguises since Paris and London. Was she just being paranoid?

No, it was too coincidental. Of all the nightclubs in all the cities, why would this guy come to this one, if not for her and Mike?

People bounced and whirled around her, blocking and unblocking her view. Her heart rate quickened as she repositioned, trying to keep an eye on the threat while remaining inconspicuous.

In her periphery, he finished his drink and set it on the table. Then he stood.

She held her breath, her hips twitching, barely dancing.

He didn't turn toward the veranda. Without looking in her direction, he prowled directly toward her.

Goddammit!

What was he going to do? Drag her off the dance floor? Shoot her in front of all these people?

Mike wasn't here. She was alone among strangers. Maybe that was the only incentive this guy needed?

The din of clinking bottles, pouring liquor, shouting, chatter, laughter, drunken revelry — it all melded together and swirled around her as she held her position. Running would be the absolute worst thing to do. She needed the cover and protection of the crowd.

He wove around the dancers, never making eye contact with her. But he was undeniably headed for her. Twenty feet away. Fifteen.

She moved deeper into the crowd of writhing, sweaty bodies, shoulder to shoulder, bouncing in sync. Hands and hips, heat and breaths, men and women — strangers rubbed up against her and slid away, only to be replaced by another and another.

A friendly pair of arms came around her from behind, hugging her waist. A solid chest pressed against her back, bringing with it the scent of leather from the jacket he wore. Or maybe it was his skin? He was all around her, the flex of lean masculine muscle grinding intimately, brazenly, with her body.

COMPLICATE

Ten feet away, her pursuer paused, looking everywhere but at her. Then he veered off to the left, fading into the throng.

She relaxed against the stranger's tall frame behind her, letting him guide her into a sensual dance. If she stayed with this guy long enough, maybe her pursuer would go after Mike.

Christ, the guy knew how to move his body. The rock of his pelvis controlled the pace of hers, and his hands wandered with bold, confident strokes down her hips, molding around the fronts of her thighs, and slipping aggressive fingers beneath the short hem of her dress.

Whoa! Down boy.

Rough breaths pushed past her lips, and her insides melted into lava. So erotic, his touch. So dominating. Possessive.

Dangerous.

She gripped his forearms, pushing them away, but they were too strong. Unmoving.

Familiar.

With a gasp, she tried to turn toward him.

He stopped her in the cage of his arms, tugging her in close and dragging his hard, whiskered jaw along her neck. "You're a terrible dancer."

That voice, the gravelly rumble, the dark, silken cadence.

Cole Hartman.

Her entire body went rigid, and her lungs went up in smoke.

"Don't go stiff on me. Relax your hips." His palms ran down the outsides of her thighs, charging her blood with seductive energy. "Your stalker is watching."

Evidently, she had more than one stalker, and this one wanted far more than a quick paycheck.

His mission was personal.

NINETEEN

As months of paranoia hardened into reality, Lydia's heartbeat exploded, ramming against her chest.

She'd wronged Cole unforgivably. Of course, he would come after her. She should've trusted her instinct.

He wanted revenge, but not here. He wouldn't kill her in public. Too messy. Too many witnesses.

Until she figured out his plan, all she could do was play along.

Wiping the shock and fear off her face, she leaned back against his chest and angled her mouth toward his bent head. "How did you find me?"

"I never lost you." He twisted her around, dragging her pussy right up against his muscled thigh.

Stunned by his words, his proximity, and his unrecognizable appearance, she could only stare. "You never had me."

"Oh, I've had you." With his leg between hers and his hands on her waist, he drove their hips together, flexing and thrusting in the delicious rolling movements of sex. "I've had every hole in this body."

She didn't need the reminder. Most nights, she sneaked away from Mike and pleasured herself in the bathroom to the memory. Cole had been an unforgettable experience, no matter how tainted the circumstances. She'd forced herself on him, and he'd fucked her right back. Tit for tat.

He kept her moving with the grind of his body, maintaining the ruse of a flirtatious stranger. God help her, he looked like one.

A tattered *Misfits* t-shirt peeked out from beneath a black motorcycle jacket. Black boots. Dark jeans. Clean, spiked hair. No beard. Just a shadow of stubble. And dimples.

COMPLICATE

Treacherous dimples. Deep, sexy, ensnaring little dips of deception. They made him look boyish, harmless, and so goddamn gorgeous her hands shook with the effort not to touch his sculpted face.

"What have you done to yourself?" She gave into the compulsion and set her fingers on his scratchy cheek, trying to reconcile her memory of him with the image before her.

He leaned forward, bending her and putting a sexy roll into movement before yanking her back up. "You prefer the beard?"

"Can't decide."

The beard shouted male dominance, maturity, and sexual virility. The five o'clock shadow attempted to affect the same rugged masculinity with deliberate untidiness while not actually being unkempt.

He probably smelled different. Cleaner. Less musky. A disheartening thought. She desperately missed his manly scent. But without all the hair, his dimples dramatically popped.

She needed to stop staring at them.

The song changed, and she forced her gaze around the nightclub, searching for the other stalker.

"He's on his way out." Cole pulled her in close and pivoted, putting the front entrance in her line of sight.

Sure enough, the man with the crooked nose headed to the door and slipped outside.

Had Cole been watching Vincent's man watch her? Had he not planned on revealing himself to her? He seemed only to pop in because Vincent's goon was approaching.

How long would Mike wait before he gave up and came back inside? Another ten minutes? Long enough for Cole to get what he came for?

"Are you going to kill me?" She dragged her gaze to his, burning in the heat of his twisting, writhing, gloriously ripped body.

"Can't decide."

"I keep thinking I should've let the stonecutter take your dick."

"I haven't stopped thinking about you, either. Your perfect rack. Your sloppy cunt." He palmed her backside, grinding her body against his thigh. "Your tight little asshole clenching around me. Fucking heaven."

With each word and rocking gyration of his hips, he slid closer, hotter, his hands traveling everywhere, feeling her up and down. If there was a lie in that smoldering look, she didn't sense it. The man was a baffling contradiction.

"You said you weren't interested." She pushed at his chest. "You fucked my ass to manipulate me."

"Is that what I did?" He pulled her back in. "Or what I *said*?"

"You said it. Sure felt like you did it."

Was he fucking with her? Then? Or now?

He touched the blonde tips of her wig, his knuckles brushing against her jaw. "I prefer the red."

Interesting. The wig matched the color of Danni's hair.

"It was fake." She smacked his hand away.

"Was any of it real?"

Her pulse thrummed. "You tell me."

Their gazes locked, and electricity crackled across her skin, resurrecting her fear, for with it rose the flames of reckless longing. Their hips undulated together, and her insides buzzed, sparking with blistering desire.

She never knew sexual tension like this existed. It seethed beneath his touch, growled through his heavy breaths, and dripped down her legs because dammit, she wasn't wearing panties.

Their grinding became so obscenely sexual she knew they were making a scene. But she couldn't shove him away, and he showed no signs of stopping.

Fused at the hips, they connected in rhythm and motion, pushing and pulling, slowing down and speeding up, dancing as one. Not fighting. Not trying to kill each other. They molded together and clung, sinking into the addictive burn. The hunger. The danger.

She shivered, her breaths growing faster with the heavy rush of his. Nothing was sexier or more sinful than grooving up against this man. She wanted to live in his arms and do this for the rest of her life.

But doubt and duty trickled in.

Why was he dancing with her? Touching her? Staring at her like he was into her? Was it another trick?

How many women had he fucked in the past six months? After seven years of celibacy, surely he hadn't gone back to abstaining. He was too sexually charged, too goddamn filthy-minded to go without.

And his dancing? Yeah, he had moves. All the moves. He was by far the best dancer in the discotheque. Maybe in all of Italy. She didn't have to stretch her mind to guess who'd taught him.

So what was he doing with her? With his good looks, sexy confidence, and dirty dancing, he wouldn't be hard up for pussy. He could get it anywhere, anytime.

Even now, every woman in the nightclub was eye-fucking him. The ladies corralled around, shaking their hips, waiting for him to toss away his current distraction and notice them.

COMPLICATE

If he noticed them, he didn't show it. His dark brown eyes never strayed from her. The longer he held her in his gaze, the more adventurous her hands became. Chiseled pecs, solid shoulders, corded neck, pillowy lips—she touched him everywhere, rubbing, caressing, stroking, and burning up.

She was soaked between her legs, made worse by the blatant need hardening his body. He didn't ram his erection against her, but he couldn't hide it. She was intimately familiar with its shape in every stage of hardness. She knew his girth as he stretched every orifice of her body with dominating force.

She knew it and missed it terribly. She missed *him*.

The scent of him warmed her senses with outdoorsy undertones of leather and earth and masculine pheromones. Yeah, even without the beard, he still smelled deliciously lickable and distinctively him.

He rocked against her, changing up the tempo, bringing her hips in for a slow grind. Then he gripped her nape, bringing her mouth in for a heated exchange of breaths, teasing her with a brush of lips, taunting her with the promise of more.

Every action was sensual and calculated, wildly hungry and terrifyingly confident. Damn, but he knew what he was doing.

He scared the shit out of her.

So when his mouth fully captured hers, she tensed and tried to pull away. He grabbed her head, trapped her waist, and deepened the kiss, chasing her tongue and decimating her resistance.

Controlled by desire, they attacked each other in a frenzy, dancing and moaning to their own music, spinning in their private orbit of touching, kissing, biting, licking, and grabbing. Whatever this was, it was impulsive, carnal, dangerous, and *real*. They weren't capable of stopping. It was too potent, too infectious, taking over and twisting them up.

He kissed her until she melted. Until they were panting together and pulling at each other's clothes. She needed more of his touch, his hands on her skin. Her body had never felt more alive, her breasts heavy, and her breaths shallow and fast.

She was so caught up in it she hadn't realized they'd drifted away from the crowd. With her eyes screwed shut and all five senses wrapped up in Cole, she didn't know he'd danced her into a nearby passageway until her back hit the wall.

Her eyes flew open, and the air evacuated her lungs as he pinned her body with the weight of his. There was no one in view, this part of the club currently unused. It was just her and him and the fingers trailing up the outsides of her thighs.

This was it. He'd separated her from the crowd, pulled her away from witnesses. He was going to fuck her or kill her. Probably both.

She deserved it. She'd let him seduce her *again* and was officially too stupid to live.

"What do you want from me?" She lifted her chin.

"The truth."

Don't trust him. It's another manipulation.

She was prepared to fight, but she wouldn't kill him. She couldn't, and that put her at a severe disadvantage. She blanked her expression.

"Who's Mike?" he asked. "Who is he to you?"

"My partner."

"You're fucking him." A shadow passed over his beautiful face.

"Why do you care?"

"Do you love him? Every night, every city, you share a bed with him."

"You creepy pervert." A chill ran down her spine. "You're watching me?"

"Who are *you* watching? I told you where to find the hard drive. He's in Romania, not in a nightclub in Rome. Why are you here?"

"You told me *where*. I'm working on *how*."

"Explain."

"Are you going to help me?"

Please, help me.

"No." His eyes hardened. "Who's trying to kill you?"

"You?"

"Who else? These men who are hunting you...they're connected to the team in Texas. But I can't trace their employer. Who is it? Who hired you to seduce me?" At her silence, he asked, "What's on that hard drive?"

"Help me retrieve it, and I'll tell you."

"Tell me how you're connected to it, and I'll think about it."

"What?" Her breath hitched. "You will? You'll help me?"

"No. Fuck." His jaw flexed, and he swiped a hand down his face. "I can't, Lydia. I spent a year embedded in the Romanian mafia, searching for the traitor who sold that hard drive. Darius Skutnik knows me. He knows my face, my disguises, my loyalties. My cover's blown. Bridges burned. And besides, I don't get involved in political or government affairs. Not anymore."

"Then why are you here? Why are you following me?"

His expression clouded.

COMPLICATE

"Is this about revenge? Do you want an apology?" She cupped his strong jaw, holding his gaze. "I won't give it. I'm not sorry. I'm not sorry for meeting you or fucking you or learning how strong and resilient you are. You scare the bejesus out of me and fascinate me and turn me on like no other. If I were a normal girl with average problems, I would chase you and date you and do all the normal-girl things with you. Because this? You and me? It's *real*." She lowered her hand. "You wanted the truth. That's *my* truth."

She pressed her tongue against the back of her teeth, immediately regretting her verbal ejaculation. She'd said too much, overexposed herself, and couldn't take it back.

How many times would she stumble and fall over this man?

Maybe this was the last time. Maybe he would try to kill her now, and she would finally learn to keep her guard up around him.

"I'm not interested in normal girls." His finger traced circles on her thigh, invoking goosebumps.

In the span of an eternal moment, her life flashed before her eyes. She lived, and she died, but she didn't regret. He'd woken her from a long, cold dead sleep, and she wouldn't change that for anything.

Slowly, his hand dipped between her legs, going straight to the stiletto like he knew it was strapped there. Of course, he knew. She'd rubbed it up and down his leg while they were dancing.

He made no attempt to take it as his fingers crept upward, seeking something softer, warmer, more welcoming.

A tremor crashed through her, and she rose on her toes, trying to slow the climb of his hand. "What do you want from me?"

"This." He kissed her, deeply, possessively, and sank a finger between her legs. "This greedy pussy's been leaking all over my jeans."

She whimpered, her hands clenching on his shoulders, pulling.

"I want your surrender." His chest pressed against hers, his teeth scraping her gaping mouth as if he were trying to crawl inside her. "Give it to me."

She was already careening toward it before he added another finger, and another, dipping inside and plunging to the knuckles. His tongue knifed through her mouth, assaulting, owning, and twining her fear and need together.

As if he had all the time in the world, he played with her ache, teasing her soaked flesh, and mounting her lust until she clung to him, moaning and panting against his hot lips.

He seduced her with his mouth, his smoldering looks, and oh God, his touch. His fingers unfurled ribbons of heat within her, clenching her inner muscles, and dribbling past flesh that had become far too hungry for him. It was stupid and irresponsible and…

"There." She widened her thighs to deepen the thrust of his fingers. "Please, Cole."

"Good girl."

"We both know I'm not, but I love the way you lie."

He slapped his free hand against the wall above her and bowed in, twisting his fingers between her legs. Then his thumb circled her clit and broke the dam.

Her body split apart in waves of orgasmic pleasure. Shimmery stars seized her vision. Trembling bursts of electricity washed up her legs and rendered her senseless, boneless, until noises she didn't recognize tumbled from her mouth.

He continued to stroke. His fingers. His tongue. Hot and aggressive, he pulled her under and submerged her in the sweetest delirium. Her head tipped back. Her eyes fell shut, and her flesh rippled with unadulterated, carnal bliss.

She shook, stunned and overcome, high on ecstasy and thoroughly mortified.

Mortified, because the voice that broke through her haze didn't belong to Cole.

"Don't move, motherfucker." Mike stood behind Cole, aiming a knife at Cole's stomach and a gun beneath his jaw. "How do you want to die?"

"Buried three-knuckles-deep." Cole had the audacity to wriggle the knuckles still buried inside her.

Mike's lips pulled back, baring his teeth, his eyes blazing with fury.

It was one thing for her to get naked with Cole in Texas when seduction had been part of the mission. Mike had been passionately against it but went along with the plan because there'd been no other way.

But this was a whole other thing. She had no explanation for why she was pressed against him in a dark hallway with her dress shoved to her hips. No explanation would assuage Mike. This had nothing to do with the job. Cole wasn't even supposed to be here.

Mike didn't kill unless it was the only option. But given his current signals—flushed neck, bulging veins, wild eyes, grinding teeth, and not one but two weapons drawn—he saw only one option. Cole's lifeless body.

This wasn't a bluff. Mike was going to kill him.

Heedless, Cole removed his hand from between her legs and held up his soaked fingers, stretching them apart to display the thick, milky strings of her come. "She's a gusher."

"Mike." Pulse racing, she clasped the hand that held the blade against Cole's stomach. "Don't do it. He's baiting you."

"I'm going to fucking kill him." He pushed against her grip.

COMPLICATE

"No, you're not." Cole slipped a sticky finger between his lips and groaned with satisfaction. "She won't forgive you if you do. You don't want to lose her." He licked another digit, his eyes shutting briefly. "Goddamn, when a woman tastes this good, I imagine you'll do anything to keep her."

He curled his tongue around the next finger, and the next, slurping with relish.

"Stop antagonizing him." Her hand started to sweat around Mike's grip, battling over control of the knife.

The gun beneath Cole's jaw was less concerning. Mike wouldn't fire it and risk getting them arrested.

"I would've left some for you to taste." Cole flicked a menacing glare over his shoulder at Mike. "But you're dipping into this pussy every night, aren't you? That's why you're itching to gut me. You don't like to share. I get it. I don't share, either."

"Enough." She pushed at Cole's chest, attempting to upset his balance.

He jerked, and they all moved at once. She went for the knife at Cole's stomach. Mike fought her grip, trying not to cut her as Cole swiped the stiletto from between her legs. In a blur of motion, he twisted between her and Mike. His torso tensed, flexing with the snap of his arm as he stabbed the blade toward Mike's shoulder.

She opened her mouth to scream, the sound cutting off as the dagger sank. Blood spurted, not from Mike but from the neck of someone else. A man with black hair.

Her heart stopped. Mike spun away, and Cole stabbed the knife again, cutting through the throat. Blood spilled over his hand. The man dropped to the floor, and she stared down at a face with a crooked nose.

Vincent's man.

Her hands trembled, her pulse thrashing in her ears, sounding out the muffled thump of the music.

Goddammit, she was smarter than this. She didn't get distracted. She didn't let assassins sneak up on her.

"Get out of here." Cole wiped the stiletto on the dead man's pants and handed it to her. "Go!"

The chatter of feminine voices sounded around the corner. People were close. A whole nightclub of people. Anyone could step into view and sound the alarms.

"Come on." She concealed the knife beneath her dress and tugged on Mike's clenching hand. "We need to go."

Cole bent over the body and dragged it into a shadowed corner. She looked up, scanning the ceiling with surging panic.

"There are no cameras." Cole met her eyes, his voice thundering with command. "Get the fuck out of here."

Heart hammering, she held his gaze for a moment longer, and he stared back, forging the connection in fire.

They needed more time, more moments. If only he would agree to help her, if they could find a way to trust each other…

"Let's go." Mike gripped her elbow and led her away.

They walked straight out of the club without stopping or looking back. Outside, the summer night air wrapped around her. She didn't breathe until they reached a less-congested part of the busy street. There, a few blocks from the nightclub, they lingered in the shadows without speaking.

Patrons milled along the stone walkways, flitting in and out of the nearby bars. The alleyways between belched a thousand unbearable stenches caused by calls of nature. She thought she might throw up, not from the rank air but from her unbearable nerves.

Huddled in a dark doorway with Mike's arm around her, she had a direct view of the discotheque's entrance. Her neck grew taut as she waited for the sound of sirens. Her molars clenched painfully as she waited for Cole to step outside.

Ten minutes passed.

Fifteen.

He never emerged, and the *polizia* never came.

"He hid the body and found another exit." Mike clasped her hand and pulled her down the street, getting them out of there. "If he's smart, we'll never see him again."

She didn't want that, did she? Her chest constricted. "He just saved our lives."

"If he hadn't distracted you, you wouldn't have needed saving."

Good point.

Walking alongside him, she twined their fingers together and acknowledged the guilt stabbing her insides. "I'm sorry."

"No, you're not." He glanced at her sidelong, the anger still alive in his eyes. "What did he say to you?"

Lowering her voice, she recapped every word she'd shared with Cole. When she fell quiet, his expression darkened, and he quickened his gait.

She jogged to keep up, wobbling in the heels. "What's wrong?"

"What's wrong?" He stopped abruptly and turned to glare at her. "He followed you across Europe for six months. You haven't just become his mission. You've become his obsession."

TWENTY

London, England
Eight months later

Lydia had become a dangerous obsession.

An obsession that had brought Cole to this tattoo parlor to do something he never fathomed.

Why?

She was an anomaly. A goddamn mystery. He knew so little about her, and that only made him crave and crave and crave. His thirst for knowledge demanded he unravel her.

Who was she? Where had she come from? Why was she always on the move?

Why am I still following her?

It had been fourteen months since she'd saved his life beneath the stonecutter. He'd given her the location of the hard drive, and she wasn't even trying to infiltrate the Romanian mafia.

Instead, she visited strip clubs, nightclubs, fluttering from venue to venue in red-light districts across Europe. *Dancing.* Or attempting to dance. She had terrible coordination.

Still, he loved watching her. Stalking her. He couldn't let go of this infatuation.

She and Mike never used the same last name twice. Their identification documents were forged. They paid for everything in cash, traveled light, and spent little, sleeping on trains and staying in low-rent hostels and dingy hotels.

They must've had a plan, but for the life of him, he couldn't figure it out.

"Almost finished." A twenty-something Englishman wiped a towel along Cole's forearm, admiring the artwork. "You ready to see it?"

He hadn't looked at his arm. Not once in five hours as the tattoo gun stabbed into his skin. He couldn't bear to watch the inked symbol of Danni slowly disappear. He just wanted it gone.

Out with the old obsession, in with the new one.

Breathing deeply, he turned his gaze on the fresh ink.

From wrist to elbow, a deadly snake coiled tightly around his arm, leaving no unmarked skin between the tight spiral of its thick, scaly body.

It was a diamondback rattlesnake, commonly found in the Chihuahuan Desert where he'd met Lydia.

Warmth spread through his chest as he held it up for a closer inspection. Shocking bursts of red poked out from beneath the twisting, winding predator. Red feathers.

He turned his arm, revealing the head of a red swallow peering out of the snake's constricting hold.

His lips twitched with morbid satisfaction. "It's perfect."

"Ace." The tattoo artist grinned. "You got a pet snake, mate?"

"A pet bird."

"Ah." The man's eyes twinkled as if he comprehended the meaning.

He didn't. Cole didn't even understand it.

As the Brit wrapped up his arm, the TV on the wall streamed endless commercials, each one to the tune of a Christmas jingle. It was the first week of December, and the holiday season was choking the life out of the air.

Blinking lights, glittery ribbons, peppermint coffee, swarms of shoppers, singing, and laughing—the spirit of Christmas forced itself on everyone, everywhere. He couldn't escape it. Not even here. Sitting in a dark, grungy tattoo parlor on the outskirts of London, he felt it jabbing under his skin.

He despised this time of year, for it only served to remind him just how goddamn lonely he was.

He'd turned thirty-eight this year. Thirty-eight Christmases, and he'd spent half of those alone. He should've been used to it by now. But he couldn't forget the holidays he'd shared with Trace and one he'd had with Danni. Those were good times. The best.

Maybe that was why he hated Christmas so much.

"Hell of a time to be an American." The tattooist nodded at the TV, which had switched to a world news report about American politics.

COMPLICATE

It was an election year in the states, and though the election had ended a month ago, the country was in an uproar over who had unofficially won. The President-elect wasn't a politician. He was a business magnate, software developer, and philanthropist.

His presence in the White House promised to shake things up. Maybe that was what the country needed, but Cole didn't hold out hope. He knew too much about the collusion and cronyism that existed within the U.S. political system.

"Can you turn that off?" He flicked a hand at the TV.

"Sure."

Christ, he was in a mood. If he were honest, his head hadn't been in a good place for months.

He needed to see her.

No, he needed more than that. He needed to feel Lydia's warmth under his hands, taste her cherry lips on his tongue, and hear her husky voice whispering his name.

He longed to make contact with her, but he couldn't. He wasn't the only one watching her. Whatever she was involved in, people were hunting her. They would've been tracking him, too, but he kept himself hidden.

Until eight months ago.

In a total lapse of sanity, he'd approached her in that nightclub in Rome. He'd done it to protect her. Mike had left her alone with a damn assassin in the building.

Dancing with her had gone too far. He'd needlessly and recklessly indulged. Holy fuck, he'd indulged in every inch of her luscious body.

He couldn't do that again. He couldn't be seen with her. Couldn't get involved.

He told her he wouldn't help her, and he meant it.

When he finished his transaction at the tattoo parlor, he returned to Central London and walked the streets, soaking in the historical ambiance while evading the Christmas shoppers. He was looking for something, searching for a distraction from his thoughts.

Lydia was somewhere in the city. According to Romero, she'd arrived yesterday by train.

He told himself he wouldn't walk by her hotel this time, that he wouldn't watch her from the shadows. But he knew it was a lie. She was the only reason he'd flown in this morning.

Wandering aimlessly with his hands tucked in his pockets, he kept to the side streets, kept his feet moving, tried to keep his thoughts away from the object of his obsession.

Late into the early morning, the foot traffic died down, the tourists all tucked into their temporary beds.

Was Lydia out dancing in some dodgy nightclub? Or was she in bed, too? With Mike?

His stomach buckled, roiling with acid. The undetermined state of her relationship with Mike twisted him up. He tried not to think about it, but his imagination was a bitch.

So was his jealousy.

It awakened toxic memories. Memories of the months he'd shared Danni with Trace. He wouldn't do that again. Not with any woman. No matter how fucking lonely he was.

His breaths quickened, forming angry white clouds in the chilly air as he strolled across Westminster Bridge. He stopped at the center with no one around and stared down at the inky water of the River Thames.

He needed to give up this pointless quest and return to the states. Better yet, he should go to Colombia and spend the holidays with his friends. His family.

For a moment, he tried to imagine it—sitting around some elaborate Christmas tree at the Restrepo headquarters, drinking, opening presents, and celebrating togetherness. He wanted that, longed for it, right up until everyone paired off and went to bed.

Where would that leave him?

Alone and pining for the love he'd lost.

Fucking pathetic.

He laughed aloud, and the ache in his voice caught on the cold breeze, tumbling toward the river. He sounded insane—in his mind and out loud. Even the voice in his head thought he was nuts.

Maybe he was having a breakdown? Or going through some sort of mid-life crisis?

Or maybe this was what it felt like to finally let go? He'd carried the guilt around for twelve fucking years, and tonight, he'd let some of it go.

He erased her from his skin.

His feelings about it were complicated. He felt a torrent of anger and relief, guilt and redemption, grief and hope, and never-ending loneliness. It was difficult to parse through when all of it twisted up around Lydia.

"This isn't about her," he murmured. "Stop being a goddamn pussy and move on. This is long overdue."

He reached beneath the neckline of his jacket and yanked his necklace free, breaking the chain. Danni's engagement ring sat in his palm, glinting in the moonlight. Such a tiny thing, yet so heavy with broken promises and lies and loss.

He'd carried the weight of this thing for too long. Danni was happy, and he could get there, too, if he stopped punishing himself.

COMPLICATE

It was time to let go.

His vision blurred, and his eyes burned with sudden, uncontrollable anguish.

Fuck it.

He blinked away the moisture and flung the ring into the river.

Then he closed his eyes and let the tears fall. Silently, lightly, they gathered at the creases of his mouth, and he wiped them away.

He felt numb. Hollow. But so much lighter.

Removing the phone from his pocket, he dialed the number he'd called countless times over the past fourteen months.

"Hello?" Rylee's groggy voice whispered over the line.

"Did I wake you?" He did the time conversion in his head. "It's only eleven at night there."

"No. Yes. It's fine. Hang on."

Sounds of rustling indicated she was crawling out of bed, probably trying not to wake Tomas.

"Okay," she breathed. "You there?"

"I did it."

"What? What did you do, Cole?"

"I inked over the tattoo and threw the ring into the River Thames."

"Oh."

"Oh?" He exhaled and rubbed his pounding head. "I thought you would...I don't know...have something therapeutic to say."

"I'm processing. Give me a minute."

He hadn't seen her or any of the Freedom Fighters since the night he left with Lydia in the desert. That was fifteen months ago. But he talked to all of them regularly, keeping them updated on where he was and what he knew about Lydia and Mike.

"So," Rylee said, "after twelve years of holding onto the symbols of a life you wanted, you let them go. Good for you. What prompted it?"

"I don't know."

"Yes, you do." She sighed. "You finally realized you don't want that life anymore, that maybe you never did."

"I disagree. I would take back Danni if—"

"*Staaaahp.* Do you actually believe you would be content settling down in the suburbs with a wholesome little wife, an unremarkable job, and the same uneventful, unchallenging routine day in and day out for the rest of your boring existence?"

With Danni? He would've made it work. He would've been happy with her.

And miserable in every other aspect of his life.

"Something opened your eyes," Rylee said. "Something or maybe…*someone* with a flair for tattoos, knives, garters, mystery, and danger."

His groin tightened. "She's a threat."

"That's not why you've been stalking her for fourteen months. Do you remember what I said to you when we met?"

"You said a lot of crazy shit."

"A lot of crazy, *smart* shit. You remember."

Yeah, he remembered.

If love comes for you again, it's going to blindside you and knock you on your ass. You'll deny it. You'll fight it with every breath in your body. But having already experienced it once, you know it's a fight you can't win. So maybe, if and when it happens, give yourself a break. Don't fight so hard.

"That's not what this is." He dragged a hand through his hair and started walking toward his rented apartment. "What she did to me is unforgivable. She can't be trusted. Ever. She's a goddamn risk."

"If she consumes your mind, she's a risk worth taking. Take the risk, Cole. Or lose the chance."

"I already did that with Danni. I took the risk *and* lost the chance."

"That's why second chances were invented. It's never too late to begin again, have a dream, and make her yours."

"She already has someone."

"That didn't stop Trace when he went after Danni, and look how that worked out for him."

"Ouch." His jaw flexed. "Direct hit below the waist, Rylee."

"Did it clear your head?"

"No."

"Come home. If you don't feel anything for this woman, bring your ass back to Colombia, spend the holidays with your family, and put some distance between you and this thing you're wrestling with."

"Not yet." His voice cracked, and he cleared his throat. "I can't."

"I didn't think so. When you're ready, we're here. You know that."

"I know."

"Try not to take too much longer. We miss you."

"I miss you, too," he said quietly, uncomfortably. But he meant it.

"Night, Cole."

"Good-night."

An hour later, he lay on a cold mattress in an unfamiliar apartment and thought about Lydia.

He didn't know her natural hair color. She wore it in every shade and style possible, usually wigs, always eye-catching. But he preferred it red, and that was how he imagined it every night when he wrapped a hand around his cock and beat off.

COMPLICATE

He thought of the thick, silken, blazing red mass of waves tumbling off her shoulders and curling around the pink peaks of her gorgeous tits. He thought of the hair between her legs, imagining it a lighter shade of red and glistening with her arousal as he penetrated her with his tongue, his fingers, and hungry cock. He thought about her rebellious little chin lifting toward him, her lips parting, begging to be kissed as he teased her, worshiped her, and gave her everything she wanted.

Christ, he was hungry. So fucking ravenous for her. He finished too quickly and continued to stroke, milking the final drops, trying to prolong the transient moment of pleasure.

When the sensation passed, and his body grew cold, he lay there in the dark, breathless, empty, and more alone than he'd ever felt in his life.

TWENTY-ONE

Dublin, Ireland
Three weeks later

If the idea of Christmas heaven was bundling up under layers of clothes and slushing through wet snow across cobbled streets in an epically festive pub crawl, then Dublin was the place.

Cole didn't mind the cold, and frankly, nothing warmed the blood like a hot Irish whiskey in a cozy Irish inn. So in the dark hours of Christmas Eve, he sat in the quiet corner of a small pub off the beaten path and treated himself to a few of those hot toddies.

Outside, the wind beat against the windows in an icy serenade, forming frozen lace on the glass, delicate and jewel-like. Fire crackled in a nearby hearth, and periodically, the door opened with the draft of snow and incoming Dubliners.

Woolen hats pulled over reddened ears. Scarves wrapped around rosy cheeks. They arrived in pairs, small groups, but never solo as they stamped their boots on the entry mat and made a beeline to the bar.

For this small island of emigrants, Christmas was a time for family and friends. Many returned home to Ireland to spend the season with their loved ones. Others reconnected like the older couple across the room.

With their hands clasped together at shoulder height, they slowly danced in front of the hearth fire, smiling, swaying, locked in eye contact, and lost in their own private world.

Love.

It was the greatest gift they could give each other.

COMPLICATE

Physical closeness. Emotional warmth. Partners for life. They shared a lasting, soulful kind of love that lifted every part of who and what Cole was.

In that moment, in his dark, solitary corner of the world, all he wished for was another beating heart, one less empty chair, and one more pair of gloves resting on the table beside his.

He'd learned how to fly solo, how to sleep alone, and how to solve his problems unassisted. Over the past twelve years, he'd become a lone wolf, and it had made him a successful, unstoppable force in his job.

But what it left was a form of loneliness that he couldn't mend by himself.

What it left was a sad man who sat alone in a pub on Christmas.

Throwing back his whiskey, he dropped some money on the table and returned to the streets.

The toothy bite of winter wind nipped at his face. Ice crackled underfoot. Carolers crooned in the distance, and shop window displays flickered beneath strings of rainbow-colored lights.

Grafton Street at Christmas was a wonderland, and for anyone who believed, they could pluck the magic right out of the air.

But he wasn't a believer in the spirit of anything. Not in a world where he walked alone.

His teeth chattered as the cold seeped into his gloves, numbing his fingers until they ceased to bend. Burrowing deeper into his leather jacket, he pulled his beanie low on his head and stuffed his hands in his pockets. Then he walked.

He tried to walk off the chill and the direction of his thoughts, all the while keeping constant vigilance on his surroundings, always on the lookout for threats.

Miles later, he took a cab to Dublin 22 and walked some more.

His breath rose in white puffs and faded into the dark, frozen sky. Naked winter trees lined streets that slept peacefully beneath no boots, save his.

The houses around him were home to those in full swing of togetherness, their merriment shining from decorated windows. But out here, he felt only the beat of his heart. A lonely beat, but strong, and growing stronger on the cusp of a decision.

Treading slowly, he kept to the shadows, out of sight, his senses on alert. As if the snow had stopped time and covered all the distractions, he couldn't see anything but what was right in front of him.

He wasn't lost. He knew exactly where he was and what he was doing as he stared up at a three-story, mid-terraced house made of fieldstones and ancient wood.

With neighbors attached on either side, the old, dilapidated property belonged to Micheál and Shannon O'Sullivan.

Micheál O'Sullivan. *Mike.*

Shannon O'Sullivan. *Lydia's real name?*

Were they married? This seemed to be their permanent home. They'd been holed up in there for two weeks, the longest they'd stayed in any one place since leaving Texas.

He shouldn't be here.

The wind whipped sleet into his eyelashes and chafed the exposed skin above his beard. But the freezing chill brought a crispness to his thoughts.

Once he walked up to that door, he was involved in this. Connected to her. Committed.

There were a lot of risks.

She could shoot him. Her husband could shoot him. Those who hunted her could shoot him.

They could try.

Under a black sky of wintry snow, he backed away.

Around the property and along the surrounding streets, he slipped through the shadows and swept the perimeter. There was no one outside. No late-night wanderers. No Santa. No reindeer. No hitmen. No present danger.

Dark windows veneered the O'Sullivan house on both sides, suggesting they were asleep or not home. The thought of catching them in bed together sucked the life from his soul, but he wasn't stopping.

He'd gone as far as he could on this path alone. His next step forward would be with her, and he was prepared to fight.

When he was buried inside her in Texas, she was with him. When he kissed her in Rome, she was with him. Every time he had her body, she gave him her passion, her beautiful desire. And Mike had tolerated it.

Fuck Micheál O'Sullivan, and fuck their relationship.

Keeping to the darkest areas of the walkway, Cole ghosted to the door with a single-minded focus.

The porch creaked beneath his boots, and he paused. A chill crawled over his scalp. Breathless, he glanced back, searching the perimeter for movement. All held still.

As he reached for the handle to check the lock, the wind wiggled the door, cracking it open. It hadn't been latched. What the fuck?

Alarms fired in his head, tensing his muscles. Quickly, he removed his bulky gloves and drew the handgun from the back of his waistband. Holding it up and out, he expelled a soundless breath and pushed open the door.

COMPLICATE

Dark, deafening silence enveloped him. He slipped out of the doorway and pressed his back to the adjacent wall, staying hidden. The narrow entryway accommodated only a stairwell that rose into more pitch-black darkness. No other doors on this level. No other rooms. Nowhere to go but up.

He kept the gun trained as he stepped toward the bottom stair, steadily, quietly. Until the shadows moved in his periphery.

The darkness beside the staircase dispersed, and Mike prowled forward, blocking the path to the stairs. He wore a heavy coat, no doubt concealing a myriad of weaponry.

"What do you want, Cole?" Mike asked in a heavy, distinctive brogue.

He felt his eyebrows shoot up. "You're Irish?"

"Born and raised in this house, you thick knacker scumbag." Mike folded his arms across his chest, his expression etched in hostility. "Why are you trespassing on my property?"

Blood thrashed in his ears, his fingers aching with tension. "Where's Lydia?"

"Leave."

"Move. Don't make me shoot you."

"You won't." Mike smiled cruelly, repeating Cole's words from Rome. "She won't forgive you if you do."

"Who is she to you, Micheál O'Sullivan? Is her real name Shannon? Your wife?"

"Shannon was my mam. God rest her soul." Mike's mouth tilted down. "And no, Lydia and I haven't tied the knot."

Relief thrummed through him, but it still didn't explain their relationship.

He glanced at the top of the stairs, probing the thick blackness. Was she up there, standing just beyond the reach of his sight? He was seconds from knocking Mike out and scaling those steps.

"Who is she to *you*?" Mike cocked his head, his body rigid and unmoving.

"She's a risk," he said honestly. "A risk I want to take."

"Of course, you want to take her." Mike laughed, his accent thickening. "You're a manky stalker. Following her around for months and months. You have a problem, pal. An obsession."

"Yeah, I have an obsession, one that takes dedication, discipline, and sacrifice." His voice vibrated with a growl. "I'm not walking away from this. Nor will I leave it up to chance or fate. Not this time. I'm taking this risk because, without her, there can only be a lonely goddamn existence."

Mike blinked, his expression cast in shadows. After a long, fraught silence, he opened his mouth, but Lydia's voice cut him off.

"I love you, Micheál," she said from the dark landing above. "More than anything in the world. So I say this with the utmost respect and adoration." Her tone turned to steel. "Get lost."

Cole's breathing quickened, and he wrestled to control it. A swell of heat spread inside him, blooming into a fire so intense it made his pulse spark and flutter.

Cautiously, Mike stepped forward until his chest pushed against the barrel of the gun, which brought a playful smile to his face.

"If you hurt my sister, I'll remove your bollocks with a bloody spoon." Mike clapped him on the shoulder and strolled toward the door. "Merry Christmas, fecker."

Sister.

Not lovers.

The door shut, and he closed his eyes, just for a moment, savoring the pure and utter joy in that revelation.

Siblings.

"Lock the door," she said.

His skin heated with buzzing energy as he stowed the gun in the pocket of his jacket and engaged the outrageous number of locks, bolts, chains, and bars on the house's only entry point. "Mike won't be able to open—"

"He'll be gone all night."

"Where?" He stepped toward the stairs, straining his eyes, trying to see her at the top.

"Wherever there's pussy. He hasn't left my side in…I don't even know. It's been a long time."

"He trusts me with you?" He climbed a step.

"He trusts you'll be here all night and that you'll shoot anything that tries to come through that door." Her voice grew breathy, and she coughed, hardening it. "Did you mean it? What you said? Or are you just here for sex? I know you're not going to kill me. You would've done that by now."

"I meant it." He felt his way up the railing, ascending into the dark. "Where're the lights?"

"No electricity on this level. Old wiring." She shifted, creaking the floor just a few steps away. "You never lost me."

"No." He measured his footfalls, his entire body strumming, attuned to her voice. "I followed you out of the desert and across the Atlantic. I've been following you ever since."

"Four-hundred-and-forty-one days of dedication. Why?"

COMPLICATE

"Because you were mine, Lydia." Hot anticipation coiled inside him as he reached through the dark and caught her nape. Then he hauled her gasping mouth to his. "You're still mine."

Their lips collided, tongues seeking and connecting. She flung her arms around his neck, and he lifted her, stumbling blindly until her back hit a wall.

The kiss caught fire, desperate and starving, building into a tameless, unholy fever. The aggressive savagery with which she met the strokes of his tongue only made him harder. Jesus Christ, he was so fucking hard for her.

His hands threaded through her hair. Long, silky, heavy waves of hair down her back. He found her delicate neck, her slim shoulders, and continued downward, searching for skin beneath her clothes.

She wore a baggy t-shirt. Nothing on her legs. By the time his fingers reached her pussy and sank deep into her heat, he was ready to explode.

Goosebumps prickled her thighs, and she shivered in the chilly air. He needed to move her to a warm bed, where he could take his time looking at her. He'd never seen her without clothes, and dammit, he needed to *see* her.

With his hands cupping her firm, bare backside, he turned and carried her up the next set of stairs. Her legs circled his waist. His palm pressed against her lower back, and he curled his middle finger deep into her asshole. A placeholder, to let her know he was coming for it.

Her gasp tore their kiss. He bit at her lips, her neck, nipping at her shoulders and marking her flesh with his teeth.

"I own you." His mouth covered hers, claiming her with rough, unbridled hunger.

"I own you." She molded his urgency to her own with a fierce passion.

"You don't have an Irish accent."

"I'm not Irish." She frantically kissed his face, panting. "Mike and I have different mothers."

"You're going to tell me everything."

"Yes."

"I want it all, Lydia. All of *you*."

"Take it."

TWENTY-TWO

A possessive hum resonated in Cole's chest. A wanting wrenched his gut. He ran a shaking thumb across Lydia's lips, unable to stop himself from touching her. Then he kissed her, claiming her with the sweeping, stroking blade of his tongue.

Mouths locked, hands grappling, they bounced off the wall, bumped into the railing, stumbled over the last stair.

The third level greeted him with more darkness. But a sliver of moonlight poked through the curtains, giving shape to furniture and obstacles as he carried her through the space. A modest room with an open kitchen and a couch.

Without breaking the kiss, he headed toward the door that led to the only bedroom. Except he didn't make it past the next wall. He crashed against it, deliberately falling against her, trapping her tight little body beneath his mindlessly grinding, humping, trying to assuage his blistering need.

He tore off his jacket, dropping it. She lowered her legs and fumbled with his zipper, opening it. His shirt and hat went next. Then his boots, his jeans, until he wore nothing but ink.

She bit her lip, breathing heavily and eyes slitted, trying to see him in the dark.

"Need light." He gripped her waist and looked around.

"Bedroom."

With spiking urgency, he hoisted her legs around his hips and attacked her mouth. She weighed nothing, her body twisting as she wrestled off her shirt.

COMPLICATE

Her sexy moans and whimpers drove him crazy, vocalizing unspoken wants. He quickened his gait, each step increasing the friction and persistence between them. Her hot mouth fell upon his neck, his shoulder, showering him in a frenzy of kisses as her hands clawed and pulled, scratching his back and tangling in his hair.

"You grew back your beard." She kissed the scruff from one cheek to the other and cupped his face. "You're so handsome, Cole Hartman."

"Lydia." Groaning, he bumped into the bedroom door and slapped a hand along the wall, hunting for a light switch.

"The table."

He knocked over a slew of shit in his path and wiped out everything on the nightstand in his quest to find the bulb. "How do I turn the damn thing on?"

She laughed against his mouth. Then she threw back her head and laughed harder, the musical sound alive with relief and breathy with need.

He tossed her onto the bed and focused on the lamp. There. He caught the chain and yanked.

A dim glow illuminated the small, spartan room. Curtains blacked out the single window. No adjoining bathroom. No pictures on the walls. No knickknacks. Just a bed and the most beautiful woman he'd ever seen sprawled atop it.

Red hair. *Natural* red on her head and between her legs. Porcelain complexion, almost flawless, save for the freckles that speckled her brow and nose. Without the makeup and the wigs and evocative clothing, she looked outrageously innocent and young.

"How old are you?" He feathered his fingers up her calf, shaking with the force of his desire.

She shivered. "Twenty-seven."

"I'm eleven years older than you."

"Afraid you can't keep up with me?" She stared up at him, panting, her sea-green eyes dazed and hooded, and her lips… Sweet hell, those full, fuckable lips pouted as she opened her legs, taunting him. "Let's go, old man."

"Shut the fuck up and let me look." He sat back on his heels and soaked in the sensual lines of her body.

She arched into a sensuous stretch that mounted the pounding in his blood. She was perfect. So painfully, insanely gorgeous.

"You're stunning. Jesus. You're always beautiful, but this face…" He trailed a knuckle along her graceful jawline. "Your real face shines in breathtaking contrast to the one you paint on."

"Cole." She reached out a hand and scissored her legs back and forth, restless, needy.

He caught her fingers, entwining them with his. Until her eyes widened.

"Oh, my God." With a gasp, she sat up, her attention locked on his new tattoo. "You removed her?"

"I didn't belong to her." He met her riveting gaze. "I belong to someone else."

He twisted his arm, showing her the red swallow caught in the serpent's deadly clutch.

Her hand fell to the bird on her chest, and little ruts formed between her brows. "I don't know what to say."

"Do you hate it?"

She shook her head, slowly at first, then faster, harder, her eyes tearing up. "I love it."

His chest lifted, soaring. "Lie back."

As she relaxed into the bed, he followed her down, sliding over her and dwarfing her tiny frame. She hooked her legs around him, and their lips came together.

And their bodies.

For the first time, he felt her skin flush with his, the soft warmth of her nudity rubbing and quivering beneath him.

With a shaky hand, he reached between them, cupping her, watching her eyes. Long, auburn eyelashes fluttered closed. Warm, supple, soaked flesh welcomed his caresses. He traced his fingertips around her opening, evoking short rapid inhalations on her cherry red lips.

Passionate woman.

So easily aroused.

"Cole, please." She lifted her hips, wriggling, demanding.

He swatted her thigh, chastising her for her impatience. But his own was just as bodacious.

Shifting down her body, he pushed the bedding away, freed her legs, and opened her wide. She shuddered, whimpered, and reached for her clit. Such a shameless, wanton creature.

He knocked her touch away. "My hands are no longer tied, Lydia. I command. You obey."

"Even with your hands restrained, you were always the one in command."

The throbbing stiffness of his cock demanded he do dirty, dirty things. From the moment he'd met her, he fantasized about eating her, front to back, inside and out.

"How many cocks have been here after me?" He speared his thumbs into her pussy and spread apart her needy flesh.

COMPLICATE

"I've never been one to abstain. I gave away my virginity at a young age and…" She stroked a hand through his hair, blushing. "I just really love sex. But since I met you, I've found something I love more." She shrugged. "I'm in love with love."

He grinned. "That's a pretty drastic leap from *There is only war, and that is always fueled by hate.*"

"I've taken a lot of leaps recently." She slid her fingers down his face. "I'm on birth control, and I haven't been with anyone since you."

The tension in his shoulders loosened. "You're the only woman I've touched in eight years."

"Why?"

"I was waiting for something extraordinary." He glided his thumbs up and down in opposing directions, working her tight little pussy into a sticky, squelching suction of need. "I was waiting for you."

Her breaths punched out in disbelieving rasps as her fingers threaded through his hair. "You're making me really, really fucking hot, Cole. If you don't put something inside me, I'm legit going to die."

Gazes locked, he flashed her a grin. Then he buried his face between her legs.

She cried out. Spasms rippled against his tongue, drenching her with more heat and saturating his beard. Her heavenly taste flooded his mouth, and he groaned, needing more.

He draped her legs over his shoulders and dragged her pussy hard against his face, really getting in there, tucking into his sweet meal. His beard scraped against her thighs, turning her skin red, and the strokes he inflicted between her legs teased out more of her desperate sounds, painting them in a picture of devotion and greed.

She writhed and thrashed beneath him, her hair splayed across the pillow in luminous waves, trapping the lamplight in metallic shades of red. The texture was softer, fuller, more luminous than he ever imagined it could be.

His starved mouth inched up to her other hair—the short red curls on her mound. He pressed his nose in the patch and inhaled deeply, basking in her pheromones and the sinfully ripe scent of her musk.

"You're smelling my pussy." She half-laughed, half-moaned. "God, you're so filthy."

"Just getting started."

Moving his tongue away from his first conquest, he licked his way backward, along the sexy slit of her body until he reached the next opening.

With his hands locked behind her knees, he pushed her thighs to her chest, angling her tightest channel heavenward. Then he shoved his tongue inside.

She made a scandalized sound and clenched the tight ring of muscle, trying to keep him out as her hands swatted and pushed. "What are you doing?"

"Your ass and my dick are going to spend a lot of time together. I'm talking about regular visits. At least once a day."

"Oh my fuck, you weren't kidding? Anal is your weakness?"

"It's my weakness at a premature-ejaculation level." He gripped himself, collecting the thick, abundant pre-cum from his tip. Then he held up his wet hand. "I'm leaking all over just thinking about it."

She burst out laughing. "You traumatized my brother doing that."

"Oh shit. In Rome."

"Yes, in Rome. Mike and I have been forced into some awkward situations together, but that was the first time my come was shoved in his face."

"I'm not sorry." He stabbed his tongue again, rimming her, violating her, and making her scream.

Once he had her thoroughly loosened up and drenched in both holes, he gripped her hips and dragged her toward his lap, tight against his cock.

The four times they'd had sex, he'd been restrained by rope, unable to move the way he needed with her on top. Not a comfortable position for a man of his nature. So this was going to feel fucking fantastic, having her under him, pinned beneath the drive of his need.

"It was real." She trembled, gripping his arms. "In Texas, when we fucked, every second of it was real. I never faked my desire for you."

"It was real for me, too. That last time, when I took your ass, my cruelty was unforgivable. The things I said afterward were lies. I'm—"

"Don't apologize." She pressed a finger to his mouth. "We're not doing that. We're not going to regret the actions that brought us together, okay?"

"No regrets." Poised between her thighs, hard and thick and pulsing with eagerness, he lined himself up and met her eyes.

In that look, he felt as though he were already inside her, and she was inside him, their connection sparking, twisting, soldering into something brighter, denser, and more profound.

Then he pushed, sinking inside her body, stroking his tongue into her wet mouth, and burying his cock to the hilt.

Jolts of overwhelming sensations coursed back and forth and everywhere. They held themselves motionless, her lips parted around a soundless cry as he attempted to master his breathing and not bust a nut.

Her lissome beauty was intoxicating. Impossible to look away. Not to mention the pleasure that gathered where they were joined. The strangling grip of her pussy brought a flush of sweat across his brow.

COMPLICATE

He flexed within her. He couldn't help it, and the pulsing sent her chest into motion, rising and falling and thrusting her gorgeous tits upward.

With the dip of his head, he took the taut nipples into his mouth, sucking and biting until she groaned and yanked his hair.

"I'm dying a mini-death here." She pulled his mouth toward hers. "Fuck me already."

He obliged, bruising her lips, attacking with teeth, and shutting her up with the swift, invasive thrusts of his body. He held her gaze as he fucked her. He never looked away as he stretched her and filled her so full and deep she had no time to brace herself when the first orgasm hit. He watched as she exploded around him, and his pleasure rose in dark, swirling torrents, pushing him to join her. But he fought it off, unwilling to surrender so quickly.

Before she caught her breath, he flipped her over and plowed into her from behind.

Over the next couple of hours, he took his time with her, exploring her body, worshiping her curves, and pumping his seed in all of her holes.

He found his ultimate release in her ass, his cock buried to the root and his eyes jammed shut against the violent, jetting spurts of his climax. Seconds later, she joined him from below, moaning through yet another orgasm. He lost count of how many she'd had.

On hands and knees, she collapsed beneath him. He rolled to his back, his cock throbbing and sore. Deliciously used.

She panted beside him, her hair plastered to her flushed, sweaty face and her eyes aglow with dazed satisfaction. A huff of laughter broke through her gasps for breath. She swallowed, heaving and short-winded, and laughed again.

Happiness looked good on her. Dazzling and magical. She was absolutely extraordinary and so vibrantly, naturally gorgeous. Her beauty was true to life.

"What the ever-loving hell, Cole?" A beaming smile lifted her cheeks as she crawled toward him, climbing up his chest and sliding a lazy kiss across his mouth. "You've been holding back on me."

"Ready for round two?"

"Oh, no, no, no. You just blew through ten rounds. Pretty sure you broke my vagina."

"Let me see." He shoved a hand between her legs.

With a yelp, she stumbled back and off the bed. "I'm going to feed you, you beast." She turned and sashayed toward the door. "Then we're going to talk."

TWENTY-THREE

Contentment sifted through Lydia as she sat at the kitchen table, watching Cole dig into his second bowl of mutton stew. He hummed as he chewed, his eyes hooded with pleasure.

She savored the moment, knowing it wouldn't last. A somber conversation loomed ahead. And the job. She had to finish the job by the twentieth of January. Less than a month. If she didn't, it would be out of her reach.

"I can't believe you're here." She propped her elbow on the table and rested her chin on her hand. "I've never cared much for Christmas presents, but you just gave me a dozen unforgettable ones. I'll never walk the same again."

"I hate this time of year." His eyes twinkled as he stared at her over his spoon. "At least, I *did*. You might've changed my mind."

He slid the bite of stew between his chiseled lips, licking the utensil.

The temperature of her body rose several degrees.

Was he trying to be sexy? Or was it an involuntary reflex, like the salivation happening in her mouth?

Seriously, though. Why was he so beautiful?

His facial hair was thick but not long. Nothing like the beard he wore in Texas. Neatly trimmed, soft, and tidy, the length lay somewhere between stubble and a full-on beard. The scruff took those boyish dimples and made them so manly. She loved it. She really did.

COMPLICATE

Two small pink scars glowed amid the tattoos on his arm. One in front and one in back, they marked the pathway of the bullet he'd taken in Texas. If he hadn't stayed at her side that day, that bullet might've gone through her.

He wore his jeans with the button unfastened. Nothing underneath. No shirt. A lot of ink. Tousled, just-been-fucked hair. Lethal from head to toe. Sexy as fuck.

The man looked like he'd been playing football his entire life. A linebacker with a solid eight-pack and enough aggression to push back an army. Beneath all that brawn and those adorable dimples was a guy she could have a beer with, or tear up a dance floor with, or run into a gunfight with, or share a dozen orgasms with. He was the most dangerous person she knew, and maybe, just maybe he was the safest.

"Thank you." She smiled softly.

"For the orgasms?"

"For spending Christmas with me."

"I should be thanking *you*. Earlier tonight, I was sitting in a pub alone, feeling woefully sorry for myself." He slurped down another spoonful of stew. "This is our first Christmas together. The first of *forever*."

"Whoa. Forever is a long—"

"*Forever*." The sharpness in his tone cut through her. "I get all of you, Lydia. Every holiday. Every non-holiday. Every damn thing for the rest of your life."

She straightened, stunned, disturbed, and strangely aroused.

"Having second thoughts? It's too late for that." He pointed the spoon at her. "You opened that door, knowing what you were letting in. You welcomed me into your bed, knowing what kind of lover I was. A celibate one, in fact, until I met you. Because I *don't* do casual sex. I'm a partner for life. A dedicated, faithful, protective, possessive, jealous, obsessive partner. Welcome to my world." He flashed her a wolfish smile, all teeth and somewhat scary, and returned to his bowl. "This is deadly. Seriously, the best stew I've ever eaten. What's in it?"

Whirling, she opened her mouth and tried to untie her tongue. His deranged declaration tangled her up and strung her out. But after several hard swallows and a calming breath, she knew he was right. She knew exactly who and what she was letting into her life when she told Mike to unlock the door.

"Mutton chops," she said. "Potatoes, onions, water, and magic. It's Shannon O'Sullivan's recipe. She always made her homemade stew when it snowed. It warmed us down to our toes, like we were somehow imbibing some of her hardiness, her glow. I think it's because she made it with love. That was her magic ingredient." Her chest warmed with the memory. "I have a lot to tell you, Cole. I don't know where to start."

"Mike is your brother. Let's start there."

"We met twelve years ago. I was fifteen. He was sixteen." Her shoulders loosened, her love for Mike all-consuming. "My mother was a Russian swallow. I don't remember her. I was two-years-old when she died. I was born in Russia, but my dad raised me in Chicago. He was American."

His gaze dipped to the tattoo on her chest, the symbol of her mother. "You really are Russian."

"My bloodline, yes. But I never lived there. I'm American."

"And Mike?"

"He was raised in this house by his mother, Shannon. He didn't know our dad, never met him. Mike and I didn't know about each other until Dad died."

"How did you find out?"

"My dad named Mike's mother as my legal guardian should something happen to him. I was fifteen when a lawyer showed up at my door and told me that my dad was gone, I had a brother, and this woman I didn't know would be my guardian. I was uprooted from Chicago and sent to Dublin, and man, oh man, I was angry. I was an angry, grieving, rebellious teenager with a penchant for stealing. And suddenly, I was Shannon O'Sullivan's problem. You know what she did?"

"She beat your ass?"

"No." She laughed. "She loved me. That's what she did. She loved me with every breath in her body. And so did her son. A brother I never knew I had. They took me into their humble home, made sure I had everything I needed, and they gave me love."

"Where the hell did you all sleep?" He glanced around at the cramped space, the small kitchen, the couch, the single bedroom.

"Shannon and I slept in the bedroom. And this was Mike's room." She pointed at the couch. "After Shannon died, I demanded he sleep beside me. When we travel, he sleeps beside me. We have a unique relationship because we didn't grow up together. We're best friends. Siblings, too. But it's our friendship that binds us." She pulled in a guilt-ridden breath. "I know you thought we were fucking, and I let you believe it. It's a ruse he and I employ to ward off unwanted attention."

"Male attention."

"Yes."

"He's protective of you."

"That's an understatement. When I met him, he was the biggest troublemaker in Dublin 22. The leader of the troublemakers. I was a thief when I arrived here, and he made me a better thief. I went from picking pockets to luring powerful businessmen back to their hotel rooms and scraping their phones while they were in the shower."

COMPLICATE

"Scraping digital information?" His eyes darkened. "Information that, I assume, you sold on the black market?"

"Yep. I saved up a shitload of money from those jobs."

"Did you fuck these men before you robbed them?"

"Sometimes. Look, Mike and I got mixed up in some dirty shit. We needed money. A lot of it. We've been planning our revenge for our father's death for years. So we ran criminal schemes and robbed people to fund it. It was the only way we could afford to do this for as long as we have."

"Why didn't Mike meet your dad?"

"Dad was protecting him and Shannon. He kept their existence a secret. Something he couldn't do with me because I didn't have a mother."

"Who was he?"

"Richard Pictam."

"That's your real name? Lydia Pictam?"

"Yeah." She looked down at the table and picked at a deep scratch in the wood. "I loved him so much I idolized him. He was my entire world. My protector. He had this rugged rebelliousness about him, an air of danger, but he made me feel safe. Untouchable. Like I could do anything because he would always have my back. My own personal action hero." She sucked in her cheeks. "I wanted to be just like him. So I ran the streets, got into trouble, picked fights, and acquired some bad habits. But he's the one who taught me how to defend myself. Combat training, weaponry, tactical skills—he taught me everything I needed to know to protect myself." She looked up and met Cole's eyes. "He was an NSA agent, part of the Special Collection Service."

"Ah." He sat back and wiped his mouth with the back of his hand. "An intelligence spy."

"Yeah. He worked jointly with the CIA abroad to penetrate foreign communications networks."

"That explains how you got access to those customized bugs. But how the hell did he hook up with a Russian sex spy?"

"No idea. He never talked about my mother. I don't even know how she died." She shrugged. "Shannon O'Sullivan held his heart, and he protected her and Mike until the day he was killed."

"How did he die?"

"That's a critical question." A dull pain pressed behind her breastbone. "With a dangerous answer."

"Come here." He pushed back his chair and gripped her hand, pulling.

She went into his arms, her heart so swollen with years of grief and anger she didn't know how her ribcage continued to contain it. He slid an arm behind her legs, and in one swift motion, he hoisted her up and onto his lap.

And just like that, her chest felt instantly lighter.

"I used to have a pet snake." He rested his mouth against her head. "My foster family gave it to me."

"Foster?"

"I'm one of those unlucky few who spent eighteen years in foster care. But I always considered myself lucky. I lived with nice families. Good people."

"But none of them were permanent."

"No." He rubbed his hand up and down her arm. "I said I would tell you about the snake tattoo, if you told me about the swallow. You told me about the swallow."

"And now you have two snake tattoos."

"I used to have more on my arms. I had them removed after I faked my death on Thurney Bridge."

"What?" She jerked back.

"A story for another time." His fingers found her hair, absently playing with the tangled strands. "The pet snake I had in high school gave me a dangerous reputation, especially with the girls. It got me laid. A lot."

"Bullshit."

"I swear." He laughed. "What I learned was that snakes represented danger, and having a dangerous reputation earned respect and elicited fear. No one fucked with me. It gave me the confidence to take what I want."

He held out his arm, punctuating his point with the tattoo of the serpent taking what it wanted. *Her.*

She traced a finger over the ink. "I don't know if I should be honored or scared."

"You're safe with me." He cupped her face and pulled her in for a deep kiss. "Always. I protect what's mine."

"I do, too." She kissed him in turn, tongues entwining, deep and languorous. Then she leaned back and combed her fingers through his unruly brown hair. "Twelve years ago, my dad was involved in an operation with a CIA informant in Russia. I don't know the details, only that it pertained to Russia's interference campaign in U.S. elections. My dad was sent to Russia to meet with someone, to do something. I don't know. It's all classified. But he never came home. He was murdered in a hotel room, and the murder was recorded on a hard drive."

His entire body tensed beneath her. She twisted on his lap and studied his expression, watching as he absorbed and processed her words.

COMPLICATE

"My dad's colleague and loyal friend in the NSA was there," she said. "He was the tech guy, monitoring from another room. He turned in the hard drive, but it was stolen and sold by Marie Merivale."

"To the Romanian mafia." He narrowed his eyes. "How did you get this intel? It's classified."

"My dad's NSA friend has done a few things for me over the years. He told me about the hard drive, gave me those customized bugs, and erased my identity and Mike's so that we wouldn't be connected to our dad."

"That's why I couldn't find anything about you. Neither of you exists."

"I don't know the identity of my dad's friend and have no way to contact him. He wishes to remain anonymous and separated from all this. I imagine he's protecting his own family and his career. I get it, and I'm grateful. Without him, I would've never learned the truth about how my dad died."

"Who murdered him?"

"Vincent Barrington."

"What?' He stopped breathing, and his hand clamped down on her leg. "I don't think I heard you correctly."

"Yes, you did."

"Vincent Barrington, the United States President-elect. *That* Vincent Barrington?"

"Yeah."

TWENTY-FOUR

With a thudding heart, Lydia stiffened on Cole's lap, watching his expression morph from shock to confusion to steely resolve.

This was it. She'd given him the single most important secret of her life. He could choose to help her. Or he could fuck her eight ways to Sunday, steal the hard drive, and sell it to Vincent himself.

"Why?" he asked on a heavy exhale.

"Why did Vincent do it? Why was he in that Russian hotel room twelve years ago? Why did he kill my dad? I don't have those answers, but I can confirm that he wants that hard drive as badly as I do."

"It was Vincent who hired you to capture and torture me in Texas?"

"Yes. Fifteen months ago, he hadn't announced his intent to run for U.S. President, but I knew it was coming. Mike and I spent a fucking decade investigating him, watching his every move. All that effort, and we could never get close enough to kill him. He has so much wealth and power. Mike was on his payroll for years as part of his security team, and even then, he couldn't get near the man."

"How did *you* get on his payroll?"

"Through Mike. He suggested using a Russian swallow and offered up my contact information."

"You're the daughter of an NSA agent who was murdered by Vincent Barrington. You should be in protective custody, not *working for him!*" A vein bulged in his forehead, his entire body rigid. "What if he learned your identity? Jesus fuck, Lydia. Do you know how fucking dangerous it was to put yourself on his radar?"

COMPLICATE

"Yes, Cole." She pushed off his lap and paced through the kitchen, clenching her fists. "That's why I wore all that makeup and dyed my hair and learned Russian. I concealed my identity. Doesn't matter anyway, because he's already sent eight people after me since my stint in Texas, and more will come. He wants me dead."

"Fuck." He leaned over his lap, elbows braced on his knees, and shoved a hand through his hair. *"Fuck!"*

"It's a lot to take in. The President-elect put a hit on your friend, Rylee, and her neighbor. And God knows who else? But he couldn't kill you, because he needed you to surrender the location of that hard drive. If the video goes public…"

"He won't just be impeached. He'll be arrested."

"Instead of living in the White House, he would spend the rest of his life in a 6x9 cell."

"We need that hard drive."

"Now more than ever." Uncertainty buzzed through her, clashing with hope. "Does that mean you'll help me?"

"I'm committed one-hundred-percent. To this. To *you.*"

"Okay." She released a ragged breath and reached for the kitchen cabinet. From within, she removed a package of Twizzlers. "He's not the President yet. We still have time to expose him before he becomes the most powerful person in the world. This is no longer about revenge for my dad. It's about keeping an extremely dangerous, corrupt man from taking control of the most important position in our country. He won that election with Russia's interference campaign. Imagine what he'll do once he takes office. He'll rip our country apart."

He slowly nodded as if coming to terms with the stakes and the gravity of the situation. "You must have a plan, but I can't for the life of me figure it out. What have you been doing for the past fourteen months? Besides driving me completely insane?"

"You're the one stalking me, Cole Hartman." She bit a rope of licorice out of the package, smiling as she chewed it down. "I couldn't infiltrate the Romanian mafia. I'm not a super-secret spy or government operative or whatever you were. I'm just a girl."

"With a really great rack."

She glanced down at her chest, which was exposed in the wide-open gap of her silk robe. She spread the material wider and cocked her head. "Is it great enough to seduce a high-ranking member of the mafia?"

"Not without getting your ass blistered." His gaze turned to stone, his voice gravelly. "Remember that part about me being jealous and possessive? You don't want to see what happens if you try to seduce anyone but me."

She arched a brow. "Moving on. What does the mafia want with that hard drive?"

"Profit. They sat on it, waiting for its worth to reach its highest potential."

"Which is now. It incriminates the President-elect. So they'll sell it to the highest bidder?"

"Yes, and the highest bidder would be Vincent Barrington."

"Yet they haven't sold it to him." She rubbed her nape, frustrated. She'd turned this round and round in her head so many times. "Vincent doesn't even know they have it."

"Good point." He drummed his fingers on his knee. "So they must intend to use it as blackmail. To control him once he's in office."

"They'll have a huge goddamn bargaining chip if that's the case. Do you know what the Romanian mafia is known for?"

"ATM-skimmings and cybercrime."

"Yep." She gnawed on her candy, her mind spinning. "That brings me to my plan. Do you want to hear it?"

"I'm on pins and needles," he deadpanned.

"PaulVer."

"What?"

"PaulVer Rize. You haven't heard of him?"

"No, should I?"

"I'm disappointed, Cole. He's only the most notorious hacker in the world. He stole more than 200 million payment card accounts from major retailers in the U.S. He created back doors in several corporate networks and pocketed an estimated 300 million dollars from one company alone." Her pulse accelerated, and her hands fluttered through the air as she talked. She could feel herself getting excited. "He's on fire."

"You want him to hack into the mafia and steal the video file?"

"Yes. They would've made copies as a safeguard and stored them on a server somewhere. I just need PaulVer to hack in, snatch the file, and blast it all over the Internet."

"Wow." He leaned back and clasped his fingers behind his neck, his expression thoughtful. Then his lips curled into a smile. "That's fucking brilliant."

"Thank you." She released a slow breath. "Only problem is no one knows who he is. PaulVer is his hacker name."

"I'll start digging around, see what I can find on him."

"Already did that. For fourteen months, Mike and I have chased him and his hacker friends all over Europe. You know where he spends his time?"

"In strip clubs."

COMPLICATE

"And nightclubs and anywhere there are dancing girls. No one knows what he looks like, and those who do would never say. There are a lot of rumors about him, but the one that is consistent in every club in every city he visits is that he's drawn to talented female dancers. When he sees one that impresses him, he gives her a painted Easter egg."

He stared at her, incredulous.

"What?" She widened her eyes. "I'm not making this up."

"It's ridiculous."

"I thought so, too. At first. Until I saw one of these Easter eggs with my own eyes. Then I saw more. Mike and I have literally been on an Easter egg hunt for the past year. After bouncing between strip clubs to dance clubs all over Europe, we know which clubs are his favorite and the type of girl he approaches. He targets the most beautiful, most talented dancer in the club, comes up behind her, and slips a painted egg in her hand. By the time she examines the strange object and turns around, he's gone. No one has ever seen him."

"Have you ever witnessed it happening?"

"No. I'm always watching for it. But I never spot an occurrence until after a girl makes a fuss over the egg in her hand and waves it around. Of course, these women have no idea the meaning or that it has anything to do with a notorious hacker. It's not like they're dancing in these clubs to win a painted egg. They just shrug it off. Most of them just leave the egg on a table."

"So that's your plan? Try to catch him handing off an egg and confront him? Then what? Make him an offer to hack the mafia for you?"

"Yes. I've also been trying to draw him to me. With enough glamour and the right dance moves, I was hoping he would put an egg in *my* hand."

He laughed. The mean son of a bitch actually threw his head back and laughed.

"Fuck you." She crossed her arms over her chest and flung him her most venomous glare.

His amusement cut off, and in its place rose a brooding, stony-faced, intimidating man. He stood and prowled toward her, getting right up in her face. "You are undeniably the most gorgeous woman in all of those clubs. But you can't dance."

"Yes, I can." She slammed her fists on her hips and met him stare for stare, noses touching.

"Let me clarify. You can't dance as well as the dancers I've seen in those clubs." He kissed her lips. "But you can learn."

Her chest hitched. "You like my plan."

"I fucking love your plan. It offers the least amount of risk with the greatest chance of success. If this hacker is as good as you say, he can snatch that video file and transmit it all over the world in one night from the safety of his computer."

"I just need to learn how to dance. You think you can teach me?"

"No. But I know someone who can."

"Danni Savoy." Her stomach clenched beneath a fist of insecurities.

"You good with that?" He narrowed his eyes.

"Will she agree to it?"

"I can convince her."

Why? Did he see this as an opportunity to rekindle old flames?

"Whatever you're thinking, stop." He cupped her face and drew her mouth to his. "She's a solution to a problem. That's all. How badly do you want this hard drive?"

"You know the answer to that."

"Yeah. You wanted it badly enough to capture an innocent man, lock him in the dark for thirty days, and torture him with the worst thrash metal song ever created."

She cringed. "I said I regretted nothing, but I really do regret that. I'm sorry."

"I survived. And I'll take hot dogs and terrible music over that stonecutter any day."

She wrapped her arms around his strong shoulders and rested her forehead against his. "So you'll call Danni?"

"I'll call Trace and have them meet us in Missouri. I have a safe house there."

"We only have until Inauguration Day. Less than a month."

"Danni will have you dancing like a pro in less than a week. Then you'll get your Easter egg."

Her heart melted, falling, crashing, and breaking open for this man. "Take me to bed."

His eyes made hungry promises as he lifted her. "I'm going to take you on this table first."

TWENTY-FIVE

Hours later, Cole lay in bed, staring into the sleepy, sea-green eyes of Lydia Pictam. Such an exquisite creature. Arresting. Rebellious. Fearless. *Mine.*

He ghosted his fingers along the outer curve of her breast, savoring the soft noises each caress drew from her cherry lips. Every touch reinforced their connection. A connection forged so deeply inside him his bones thrummed with it.

After he took her on the kitchen table, he fucked her again in the shower. Still, he couldn't stop touching her, looking at her. She was a dream. An erotic Christmas angel.

And a remarkably good listener.

He'd spent the last couple of hours talking her ear off. He told her everything, holding nothing back. Thurney Bridge, his fake death, Danni and Trace, his career in the *activity*, and his current endeavors with his vigilante family.

His activities and relationships with the Freedom Fighters fascinated her the most. Her questions were hungry, her attention enraptured. She wanted to meet them, get to know them, and she would.

After their shower, he'd made several phone calls.

The first was to Matias, requesting transportation on the private jet back to the states. He wouldn't risk putting Lydia on a commercial flight. Not with Vincent Barrington gunning for her. Matias gladly agreed to pick them up the day after Christmas and fly them to Missouri.

He called Romero next, inquiring about PaulVer. No surprise that the kid knew of and admired the notorious hacker. Romero validated PaulVer's expertise, saying that if anyone could break into the Romanian mafia, it was the Romanian hacker known as PaulVer Rize.

The final phone call was to Trace, the conversation terse and to the point as always. He checked in with Trace several times a year, but he never asked for anything. So his request had taken his friend by surprise.

"I need a favor."
"Are you in danger?"
"No more than usual. I need you and Danni to go to the lakehouse."
"Are we in danger?"
"No. But this is important. I'll explain everything when I arrive in two days."
"I'm not agreeing to this."
"Yes, you are. This is connected to Thurney Bridge, but bigger. I haven't asked anything of you in eight years. I'm asking for a week of your time. Danni's time, actually. I need her to teach someone how to dance."
"Who?"
"A woman."
"Is she your woman?"
"In every way."
"Well, fuck. Now you have my attention."
"Don't be a dick. Just be there."
"We'll be there."

"It's officially Christmas morning." Lydia twisted her fingers in his hair, playing with the messy spikes. "Merry Christmas."

"You need to sleep. We have a lot of planning to do today."

"I'm all hyped up on adrenaline."

"And candy."

"And sex."

He gripped her waist and tucked her in close. "I can fuck you into a coma."

She groaned against his chest. "Definitely need a rain check on that."

His thoughts flitted to the plan with the hacker, sparking a question he was meaning to ask. "Any theories on why he uses Easter eggs as his calling card?"

COMPLICATE

"Easter is a big holiday in Romania, and they love their hand-painted eggs. They empty the eggs and paint the shells, creating these fragile little artistic masterpieces. It could also have something to do with the Easter eggs used in computing and video games. You know, the hidden messages and secret responses that programmers love to sneak in? It's like this guy wants to leave a mysterious trail, hoping someone will take the time to find him."

"We'll find him. The question is, will he help us? I assume he's motivated by money? How did you plan on paying him?"

"Is it that obvious that I'm broke?"

"I've been watching you for a long time. I assumed your money was running out."

"Oh, it ran out. That's why we came back to Ireland. We decided to sell this house and use the money to keep going until we finish."

"Don't sell it. I'm funding this venture going forward."

"I can't ask you to do that."

"You didn't, and I'm doing it." He ran his hand through her hair, thinking through the logistics. "How much does a hacker like PaulVer charge for one of these heists?"

"PaulVer doesn't charge anything. He's already filthy rich. If the job interests him, he'll do it pro bono. And trust me, the job will interest him. There's nothing these black-hat hackers love more than sticking it to the man, especially if the man is a greedy, corrupt, self-serving politician."

They talked a little longer about the hacker. Then they drifted into stories about their tattoos, explaining how each one came about and the meaning behind them.

As she fell asleep in his arms, he felt untroubled, clearheaded, and happier than he ever remembered being. She rejuvenated his soul, elevated his spirit, and gave him a new reason to fight. It might be cold and dark in this tiny room, but there was beauty in it, inspiration, and a promising future.

She was all those things, and he was so damn glad he'd taken the risk.

TWENTY-SIX

Cole woke Christmas morning with a hard-on. Nothing unusual about that. What had changed, however, was the soft, warm body rubbing up against it.

Lydia stretched with a lazy, drawn-out hum in her throat. Her colorfully inked arms reached overhead, her sweet ass shimmying and shaking as she extended her body to its full length.

She did all this in the cage of his arms. Then, in one fluid motion, she turned so that she was astride him, wearing nothing but a beaming smile.

"Good morning." He smiled back, spellbound by her beauty.

"Nothing says *good morning* like morning wood." She rocked her hips, teasing her pussy along his rigid length.

Her hair, wildly tangled and gloriously red, tumbled down her chest, inviting him to twine it around his fingers and pull her down for a kiss.

With a nudge of her jaw, she flicked her tongue along the seam of his lips, urging him to play.

He pinched her nipple hard and chased the gasp inside her mouth. Then he chased her hot little tongue. They kissed slowly, languidly, in a greeting of sighs with no expectation beyond the pleasure of closeness.

Leaning up, she took her lower lip between her teeth and dipped her chin to her chest. "Other than my brother, who doesn't count, I've never woken beside a man." She snapped her head up, eyes wide. Then she scrambled out of bed in a sudden burst of energy. "Where is he?"

"Who? Mike?"

COMPLICATE

"Yeah. He should've called." She yanked the curtain aside, spilling light into the room, and searched the worn carpet. "Where's my phone?"

He followed her out of bed and dragged on his jeans, the quickening of his pulse feeding off hers.

"Here." He spotted it on the floor beside the nightstand, where he must've knocked it off last night.

He tossed it to her, waiting as she unlocked the screen.

"No missed calls. Dammit, Mike." She dialed and held the phone to her ear while sliding on her silk robe. "Voicemail." Her brows knitted together as she left a message. "Come home. You're worrying me." She disconnected and dropped her arms to her sides. "He should've returned by now."

"You said he was getting laid." He yanked on his shirt, keeping his voice calm despite the shiver in his veins.

"I know, but it's Christmas." She turned and faced the window, her hair falling in rampant waves of red down her back.

Gray, watery light washed the sky, illuminating thin patches of ice on the house behind hers.

"I'll go look for him." He pulled on his boots and strode out of the bedroom. "Do you know where he went?"

"No, but he wouldn't have gone far." She followed him into the kitchen. "Somewhere on foot. He doesn't have a car or money for transportation."

He found his jacket and beanie on the floor and pulled them on. The gun sat securely in the coat pocket. He left it there, not wanting to alarm her.

"It's not a good idea for you to walk out of this house in the daylight." She stepped toward the window that faced the street and eased back the curtain. "If Vincent's men are watching..." She gasped, squinting at something outside. "What...is...? Oh, my God, that's blood."

As she tore away from the window and darted for the stairs, he slipped by her and yanked back the curtain. The third-story view showed the pathway to the street. Snow blanketed the trees, the front yard, the pavement, and...

He stopped breathing. That was blood. A dark red trail of it from the street to the front door of her house. Footprints surrounded crimson splatter. Stumbling, falling impressions from shoes.

"Lydia!" He took off down the stairs, hitting the second level to the sounds of sliding locks. "Don't open that door!"

She opened the door.

Then she stumbled, clapped her hands over her mouth, and released a shrilling, keening wail. "Nooooo! Not my brother! Oh, God, please, no! Not him!"

The sounds coming from her made his blood run cold. His muscles went taut, and his pulse skyrocketed as he bolted down the remaining flight of stairs.

Drawing his gun, he watched in horror as she fell to her knees on the porch, making herself a wide-open target for whoever was out there.

Lydia! Inside! Now!" He leaped over the final steps, weapon raised, and hooked an arm around her chest, dragging her back inside.

As she kicked and screamed and tried to claw away from him, he took in the grim scene.

Mike lay face down on the porch, half on, half off the short stoop, with an arm outstretched, reaching toward the door. The dusting of snow on his lifeless body suggested he'd been there a while.

Gunshot wounds were visible on his calf, lower back, and right shoulder. He'd been shot from behind, but it couldn't have happened nearby. They would've heard the report of gunfire.

That meant Mike had run here with those injuries. Given the trail of blood that led down the street and around the corner, it was a miracle he'd made it home.

The shooter was out there somewhere, probably waiting nearby. In Mike's attempt to reach Lydia, he might've inadvertently led the threat right to her door.

She wailed in Cole's arms, her legs buckling and her hands grappling, trying to get to Mike. It fucking hurt—the sounds of her agony, the sight of her brother, the goddamn fucking needlessness of it. His chest burned. His throat closed, and his training took over.

She had a vicious amount of strength as he muscled her backward, fighting to keep her out of view of the doorway. With her back to the wall, he flattened an immovable hand against her chest. His other imprisoned her chin, forcing her shattered gaze to his.

"I need you to push it down," he said sternly. "Push it way, way down where you don't feel it. It'll be there later, but right now, I need you to bury it, Lydia. Bury it and focus. I need you alive and with me."

She stared at him out of glazed eyes, not seeing him. Not seeing anything but hopelessness.

"He's my rock." Her face collapsed. "My world. He's all I have left." A sob ripped from her throat, followed by an avalanche of mewling convulsive gasps.

Any minute, someone would drive by and see the body on the porch. The saving grace was the overnight snow. It would discourage people from wandering out this morning. And it was Christmas. Most were tucked around their decorated trees, opening presents and listening to holiday music.

COMPLICATE

"Look at me." He tightened his grip on her jaw until her eyes cleared and locked on his. "You have three minutes to go upstairs and pack what you need. I know you can do this. You can do it because you're strong as fuck, and you want to live."

She shook her head, knocking more tears loose. "Every day at his side was a good day to die hard."

"You know what?" He put his face in hers. "Today is a good day to *live* hard because that's the only way we're going to avenge his death."

That got her attention.

She gripped his wrists and worked her throat, swallowing down the sobs. More tried to rise, overwhelming her breaths. She whimpered, choking, and her gaze started drifting away, toward the door. He was losing her.

"Breathe with me, Lydia. In and out. In and out. Just like this." He inhaled, exhaled, slowly, loudly, forcing her to follow along. "Good girl. Keep breathing. In. Out. Focus on my breaths. There you go."

He held still, watching her power through the anguish until her legs regained strength, firmly holding her up. Her shoulders squared. Her jaw stiffened, and her breathing evened out.

"Christ, you're so fucking strong." He grasped her nape and brought their foreheads together. "You've got this. Three minutes. Go."

He stepped back, and she walked stiffly up the stairs, moving quickly, up and around the corner.

Returning to the doorway, he stayed out of view and scanned the perimeter. No movement. Then he stepped outside and quickly rummaged through Mike's clothes while keeping an eye on the street.

Both of Mike's guns were holstered, suggesting he'd been caught unaware and didn't have time to fire off a shot.

Cole collected the weapons, a wallet, phone, and... He pried open Mike's frozen hand and lifted a small wrapped present.

A Christmas present with a tiny red bow.

"Goddammit, Mike." He pocketed the gift in his jacket, his chest aching. "This is going to fucking hurt her. She's going to mourn you for the rest of her life."

But she wouldn't do it alone. Cole would be with her in whatever capacity she needed.

Once he'd gathered everything he thought she would want to keep, he piled it in the entryway and surveyed the snow-covered surroundings.

His blood heated with the sprint of his pulse, every instinct inside him demanding swift action. They needed to go before someone called the gardai. They needed to disappear, but Lydia didn't have a car, and cabs didn't travel through here.

They would have to flee on foot.

With Mike's murderer on the loose.

He twisted at the sound of her footsteps on the stairs. As he shifted to turn back to the front, a resounding boom cracked the air. The gunshot discharged from the street and splintered the doorframe an inch away from his head.

His lungs emptied. He aimed the pistol and dropped low to the ground, his senses reaching for Lydia.

"Stay down." He thrust a hand behind him, stalling her descent on the stairs. "Lock the door behind me. Do not open it until I return. Understand?"

"Cole—"

"Lock the door!" Adrenalized and laser-focused, he slipped onto the porch, ducking low and shutting the door behind him.

At the sounds of engaging locks, he melted into the shadows of the hedgerow lining the property.

Surrounded by parked cars, icy trees, wheelie bins, and terraced houses, he probed the spaces between, frozen in wait for some sign of movement.

Then he saw it. Across the street between two houses, a man dressed in black stood out in stark contrast against the wintry backdrop. The dark clothing would've aided him last night, but in the daylight, it only helped Cole.

He bolted toward the shooter, weaving in and out of cover while refraining from squeezing the trigger until he had a clear shot.

Then he fired. Missed the target. The man spun around the corner of the house while blindly shooting back, forcing Cole to wait behind a car for breathless seconds until the thug stopped spraying lead.

A moment of silence. Then Cole gave chase.

The gunfight moved through the quiet neighborhood. Bullets pelleted cars and shattered house windows. He didn't aim at homes, conscious of civilian casualties. But his adversary didn't give a fuck. The bastard ran down the street, heedlessly swinging the gun behind him and shooting everything in a vicious sweep.

Somewhere in the distance, Christmas music played. A car horn honked. Stomping footsteps rang out—the shooter's, Cole's, and others in the periphery, stampeding in the opposite direction.

He chased the man for blocks, jumping fences, crossing icy yards, dodging passing cars, and racing down busy avenues. Meanwhile, Dublin 22 stirred to life. And several streets away, the blare of sirens erupted.

The gardai were coming.

Given the fast approach of the sirens, he had thirty seconds tops.

COMPLICATE

Up ahead, the shooter ran into a wide intersection. Cole trailed him, twenty feet behind. The man abruptly stopped at the center and pivoted, weapon raised.

Cole halted in the street with no nearby cars or trees to take cover. With no choice but to engage in this standoff, he trained his pistol with both hands and met the man's eyes.

Timing was everything.

"I don't want to shoot..." He squeezed the trigger mid-sentence.

His gun clicked dry. Empty.

Oh, fucking fuck.

The shooter tipped his head, and a cold-blooded smirk twisted his lips. He held his gun out one-handed and took a cocky step forward, aimed to kill.

Cole knew his next breath would be his last, and as he drew it into his lungs, the squeal of tires sounded. A motor revved, and a speeding car flew into the intersection and slammed into the gunman. The impact hit him like a freight train, bending him in half. The wrong way.

The body buckled beneath the car, succumbing to the brutal spin of tires and bouncing the vehicle like a speed bump.

His mouth dried, his muscles locked in shock. It took a full second to snap out of his stupor and focus on the snow-covered car.

It skidded to a stop. The tires spun in reverse, and it raced backward, running over the body a second time. Hope swelled in his chest.

Ice coated the windows, blocking his view of the driver. But as the door swung open, he already knew, his feet racing forward, his heart rate exploding.

Lydia poked her head out.

"Cole!" Her neck twisted toward the sound of approaching sirens. "Hurry!"

He slid past the open door, crashing in behind the steering wheel and shoving her into the passenger seat. Then he hit the gas, bouncing over the body and speeding down the street.

She stared at the side mirror, watching the flash of chasing lights, her voice numb. "Are you shot?"

"No."

He wanted to scold her for disobeying him and leaving the house, but under the circumstances, he wouldn't dare. She'd lost her brother and saved Cole's life. Her courage took his breath away, leaving him gobsmacked and awe-struck.

"Where did you get the car?" He pushed the small sedan to its mechanical limits as he squealed around bends and tore through intersections, weaving, dodging traffic, and trying to outrun the gardai behind them.

"I stole it. Where are we going?"

Her voice was wooden, her posture stiff. He couldn't fathom how she was doing. She kept it buried, just like he'd demanded.

"Looks like I lost the gardai." He gripped the wheel, his eyes on the rearview and his neck aching with tension. "We'll dump the car, go to my rented apartment, and stay the night there. Tomorrow, we fly to the states."

Without Mike.

He didn't make promises that everything would be okay. All he could do was hope that when revenge came, it would bring her some sort of closure, something more justified and bearable than leaving her brother lying dead in the snow.

Until then, he would hold her through the pain.

TWENTY-SEVEN

Cole didn't know how to do this, if he was doing it right or making it worse. He wasn't a grief counselor. He'd never tried to console someone through the loss of a loved one.

Watching Lydia suffer and being helpless to fix it was the hardest thing he'd ever done.

She'd held herself together until they reached the apartment. Once they were safely inside, he removed their clothes and carried her into the shower.

That was where she lost it. The anguish pouring out of her tore the flesh around his heart. She cried so hard she vomited. She cried until she hyperventilated. Her pain was all-consuming, strangling her from the inside out.

It made him realize with gut-wrenching misery that when he'd faked his death, Danni had gone through something similar. She'd told him later that her grieving process had been so ugly that she'd drowned herself in grain alcohol for months. He thought he'd understood what she was saying. But he hadn't.

He understood now. Every harrowing tear, each body-wracking sob, the immeasurable, yawning despair that rendered the soul forever scarred—he felt it all with Lydia as he held her in his arms.

Tucked beneath layers of blankets in the bed, he entwined his body around her and cradled her through the night. Eventually, her choking sobs waned, giving way to exhaustion and listlessness.

She didn't speak beyond one-word responses, but he refused to rush her. She needed to go through this at her own pace. When she was ready to talk about it, he would listen.

Right now, his job was to take care of her.

He forced fluids and tried to make her eat. He kept a constant vigilance on the perimeter, overly cautious and paranoid about being followed. Everywhere he traveled, he chose lodging with the best security. This apartment was no exception. But it was no longer just his life he was protecting.

He was responsible for her safety, physical wellbeing, and emotional health.

Hefting the thick mass of her hair in his hand, he laid it against her shoulder, smoothing it, caressing it where it fell in soft waves of satin against her throat and chest.

From roots to tips, he gently finger-combed the strands. Over and over, with each rhythmic stroke, her eyelids grew heavier, the furrows in her forehead flattening out. The hitches in her breaths came with longer stretches in between until they vanished altogether. She was finally falling asleep.

"It's really hard not to love you, Cole."

The feeble sound of her voice startled him, but it was her words that gave him pause. He didn't have to ask why she would try *not* to love him. He knew from experience that love was a risk, its longevity never guaranteed. At any moment, it could be taken away.

Her father, Shannon, Mike—everyone she'd ever loved had been taken from her. Maybe it was safer to avoid all forms of love.

But after eight years of being alone, he knew it was far better to experience all the ups and downs with a partner, to fight together, and spark joy in each other. Loneliness was never a better option.

"Do it anyway," he said.

Her fingers twitched against his chest, her voice a thready whisper. "Did you just order me to love you?"

"Yes."

"I'll think about it."

"Take your time. I'll wait."

Danni had said that love wasn't a choice, and she was right. Love was a chance.

A chance worth taking.

She whimpered and cleared her throat. "It hurts, Cole."

"Tell me what to do." He pulled her tighter to his chest.

"This." She melted against him, accepting his embrace. "Don't let go."

"Never."

Not this time.

She fought the pull of sleep, but at last, her body won out and dragged her under.

COMPLICATE

Reluctantly, carefully, he slipped out of bed, stepped into the bathroom, and called Rylee. She listened as he updated her on everything that had happened since the moment he decided to walk into Lydia's house.

When he finished, she blew a breath into the phone. "God, Cole. My heart is so happy and sad at the same time. I'm glad she has you right now."

"I don't know what I'm doing."

"She needs you to watch over her and hold her hand while she grieves. Just keep doing that." Her voice softened. "I look forward to finally meeting her."

"This is almost over."

"Matias selected the team for the heist you're planning with the hacker. They're on their way to you now. He's bringing the best. Obviously, I'm not with them."

"You'll be on the next mission."

"I know. Get back to your girl, and I'll see you in a few weeks."

"Night, Rylee."

"Night, Cole."

He made two more calls, touching base with Matias and Romero. If the gardai or Vincent Barrington's men showed up here looking for him or Lydia, Romero would know. The kid was linked into the apartment's security system, as well as multiple security cameras throughout the surrounding blocks.

With that comforting news, Cole returned to Lydia and grabbed some much-needed sleep.

The next morning, he was all business. From the moment they woke, stepped out of the apartment, caught a cab, boarded Matias' private plane, and lifted off the tarmac, every thought in his head and measure he took focused on the safety of Lydia and the team.

It wasn't until they were high in the air that he released a sigh of relief.

Lydia sat beside him in the front of the jet, staring out the small window as they ascended through the clouds. She hadn't spoken much since she woke, and her limbs barely moved. Almost as if she were in a state of catatonia.

"Lydia." He rested a hand on her denim-clad thigh.

She turned to him, the skin around her eyes red and puffy despite not having shed a single tear today. "Don't ask me if I'm okay."

"I won't."

"But you want to know how I'm doing."

"For sure."

"It changes by the second. I feel strong one moment and utterly paralyzed the next." She rubbed her breastbone, wearing the weight of her heart in the shadows on her beautiful face. "I don't want to cry, and I don't want to pretend I'm fine. So I'm balancing on this plateau in emotional limbo."

"It's okay to cry," he murmured.

"There's a time and place." She gripped his hand and squeezed. "I want to do that with you, when it's just us. Which is weird because I'm not a crier. I was a ball of rage when my dad died, and I was a pillar of strength for Mike when Shannon died. But now, God, this is so much harder. It feels too heavy to carry. But I know I can. I will. Because of you." She unbuckled her seat belt and twisted to face him fully, resting a hand on his whiskers. "You've seen me at my worst. As if all the things I did to you in Texas weren't bad enough. Now you've seen me cry for ten hours straight."

"If that's your worst—"

"I puked all over your feet in the shower."

"I was there."

"Exactly," she said quietly. "You were there. You're still here."

"I'm committed, Lydia."

She said nothing and drew her gaze away, her smooth cheeks and pert freckled nose illuminated by the window light. Then she leaned toward him and rested her mouth against his shoulder, her hands curving around his ribs.

He encircled her slight body with one arm and pulled her onto his lap. "I want you to meet my friends."

"They should want to kill me, not help me."

"I told them your drone was a bluff. You already know who they are and what we do. They appreciate a good deception tactic." He stroked along the length of her tumbled hair. "You're exactly the kind of person they want fighting alongside them, not against them."

"I want to meet them."

He stood, taking her with him, and led her to the rear of the cabin.

Matias had assembled a six-person team for this operation. Seven, if he counted Romero, who remained in Colombia surrounded by his equipment. Matias had an elaborate computer lab built for the kid, complete with his own geek squad.

He reached the cabin's lounge area, and six pairs of eyes greeted him, spreading a feeling of weightlessness in his chest. He'd been gone fifteen months, and he fucking missed these assholes.

As he opened his mouth to start the introductions, Lydia beat him to it.

COMPLICATE

"Matias." She stretched out a hand toward the black-haired Colombian. "Thank you for the ride."

Matias unfolded his hulking frame from the couch and rose to his full height. "It's a pleasure, Lydia." They shook hands, and Matias motioned at the others. "This is my wife, Camila, and her sister, Lucia. The token white guy is Tate."

"I fucking hate this guy," Tate said to Lydia. "If I weren't in love with his sister-in-law, I would've snuffed him already."

Lydia's eyes widened, her lips parting in shock.

Cole smiled at the interaction. He didn't know how much she'd retained from the other night when he walked her through the backgrounds and relationships of all his friends. But she knew their roles and connections to one another. No doubt she'd heard some terrifying rumors about Matias. His brutal, mafia-style code of respect made him the most feared cartel capo in Colombia. But when he wasn't striking terror into the hearts of his enemies, he was annoyingly charming.

"Ignore them." Kate climbed out of the adjacent seat and gripped Lydia's hand, holding on for a long moment. "I'm Kate, the resident doctor-in-training. I'm just here to patch up any injuries."

"Nice to meet you."

"Same. I'll be honest. We've all been so curious about you. Cole's not the most forthcoming guy, so to see him with you..." She cupped a hand around her mouth and stage-whispered, "*with a woman*, well, it's a little tantalizing."

Laughter rumbled through the cabin.

Lydia found his gaze, and he thought if she weren't hurting so badly, she might've smiled.

"This is my husband, Tiago." Kate flicked a finger behind her. "Don't mind his death-glare. I promise his body-count has gone way down in the past two years. He's almost rehabilitated."

A smile slid across the lounging male's face as he yanked her onto his lap and sank his teeth into her neck, making her yelp.

Tiago Badell, the once-notorious Venezuelan crime lord, had to put forth a lot of effort to integrate into their tight-knit family. His past with Lucia and Kate wasn't pretty, and his demeanor radiated an air of cruelty that hadn't diminished with time. But they trusted him. He wouldn't be here if they didn't.

"Here. Sit." Camila gave up her seat and moved to Matias' lap. "Hang out with us. Tell us about your brother."

Lydia stiffened, and he touched her back, trailing a knuckle down her spine.

"You're not ready. I get that," Camila said softly. "I'm sorry we didn't get to meet him."

"You don't have to talk at all." Lucia pursed her lips. "Or you can tell us some of Cole's dirty secrets in your Russian accent. We've known him for years but not the way you know him." She winked.

"We're done here." Cole started to pull Lydia toward the front.

She pulled back and stepped toward the empty seat beside Camila. "Just a warning, I'm not the best company right now. But I'd like to hang out and get to know you guys."

That was a good sign. Any sign of life was promising. He knew she faced a tough road ahead, and there would be days when the grief overwhelmed her. But he liked seeing her among his friends. He loved it, actually. The interaction would soothe her and drive home the fact that she wasn't alone. She also needed to establish trust with them since they were all headed into an operation together.

In one week, they would fly back to Europe and visit the clubs where she'd seen the most Easter eggs. With any luck, her new dancing skills would lure the hacker into the open. Then this would all be over.

The nine-hour flight from Dublin to Missouri passed quickly, thanks to the nonstop conversation. He had a lot of catching up to do with his friends.

Lydia listened to their stories without comment, her intelligent eyes taking everything in. She wasn't standoffish. She was fighting an inner battle, drowning beneath the gravity of the past twenty-four hours.

He watched her closely and caressed her constantly. Every touch she returned in kind, affirming her strength. She wasn't shutting down. She was fighting through this.

It was after dark when they arrived at the lakehouse. He didn't recognize the black Rolls-Royce Wraith in the driveway, but he knew it belonged to Trace Savoy. The man had a passion for expensive luxury cars.

As he stepped out of the rented SUV and unloaded their bags, Lydia stopped him with a hand on his arm.

Footsteps moved around them as the others collected their things and headed toward the front door.

"It's been eight years." She searched his eyes.

Eight years since he'd seen Danni.

"I know." He brushed a red lock of hair from her face.

"Aren't you the least bit freaked out?"

"A year ago, I might've been apprehensive. But today? With you? Not at all. I'm not excited about introducing my friends to Trace. Too many strong personalities in one room is a recipe for trouble. But they'll behave."

She nodded and stepped into him, hugging his waist and resting her forehead on his chest. "Thank you for doing this."

COMPLICATE

"I want this." His blood heated. "Maybe not as badly as you do, but I want revenge for the same reasons. For everything you've lost and for the safety of our country."

"Good." She straightened and twined her fingers with his. "Let's go teach me how to dance."

When they entered the house, Trace met them at the door. Alone.

A glance over Trace's shoulder revealed a vacant living room and kitchen. No Danni.

Goddammit. If she didn't come—

"She wasn't feeling well." Trace read his thoughts and nodded at the hallway. "She's taking a nap."

Tension released from his shoulders as he took in Trace's crisp black suit, six-foot-four frame, and brooding scowl. Always scowling. Predictably broody.

To those who didn't know Trace, he exuded a severe, imposing, pretentious demeanor that reeked of money. His inheritance had made him obscenely wealthy, and he owned The Regal Arch Casino and Hotel, which had grown into a booming enterprise. But he hadn't always been a cutthroat businessman.

He met Trace in the *activity*. They were operatives in the field together, inseparable for years while running dangerous missions. Spending time with someone like that, doing what they did, built a level of trust that couldn't be imitated. They knew each other's weaknesses, fears, dirty habits, every secret. They were brothers in arms. Best friends.

When Trace took a promotion to be his handler—essentially his boss—it had been a great fit. They already had a relationship built on trust. For the next few years, Trace guided him through every operation, and he trusted Trace not to get him killed.

Their work relationship ended when Trace's parents died. He retired and donned a tailored suit. But they remained best friends.

Until Danni.

All those memories came rushing back as he met and held Trace's stark blue gaze. He waited for the blistering resentment to surge with it. The betrayal. The toxic jealousy. But none of it inflamed. Because it no longer existed.

As he stood face-to-face with Danni's husband, he only felt resolution, contentment, and gratitude.

"Thank you for coming." He stepped forward.

There was no awkward shuffling of shaking hands or halfhearted side-hugs. They went straight in for the hard, constricting embrace of old friends, with arms wrapping around each other and fists pounding on backs.

Trace had maintained his lean muscle, evident in the flexing strength of his squeeze. Eight years hadn't physically aged him. If anything, the years made him even more disgustingly handsome and distinguished.

When they separated, Cole turned to the quiet, stunning redhead at his side. "This is Lydia."

Her eyes shone with alertness and curiosity as she shook Trace's hand. "Don't be alarmed, but I know everything about you."

"Everything?" Trace arched a stern brow at Cole.

"All of it." He nodded. "She knows our history, our careers, and every detail of our tangled relationship with Danni. Full disclosure."

Trace looked back at Lydia, his expression softening with something akin to wonderment. "She's the real deal then."

"It doesn't get more real than this." Cole clasped her hand.

She didn't smile, didn't speak. But her fingers squeezed his, clenching and releasing in silent agreement.

He introduced Trace to the team. They knew everything there was to know about one another. They'd just never met in person.

"I'll show you guys around." Tate led the others toward the hallway.

Kate, Matias, and Camila had never been here. Everyone else was well acquainted with the property.

With nine bedrooms and ten bathrooms, it had been designed to serve as his safe house and accommodate large teams of operatives. Plenty of space for this group to spread out and make themselves at home.

"These walls hold a lot of memories." Trace stared after the team, watching them disperse. "Not all of those memories are good."

Eight years ago, he and Trace had brought Danni here and forced her into a decision. They'd shared her in this house. Fought over her. Cried over her. This was where she'd said goodbye to Trace after telling him she'd chosen Cole.

Cole could never live in this house. It wasn't his home. It only served as a safe place to regroup and make plans. That was why he'd offered it to the Freedom Fighters. This property was as much theirs as it was his.

"Why am I here?" Trace clasped his hands behind his back and tipped his head down, his sharp eyes flicking between Cole and Lydia. "I want the whole story."

"You'll get it, but we should wait for Danni."

"I'm here." Her voice drifted from the hallway, followed by the light tread of her footsteps.

COMPLICATE

His hand went to Lydia's thick red mane, stroking the silky length. He did it without thought, a subconscious gesture of possessiveness, as if he needed to prove that he wasn't available. Which was ridiculous. He didn't need to prove anything to anyone, least of all, Danni.

She emerged from the corridor, her blonde hair falling around her shoulders. The flowy skirt of her Bohemian-style dress rippled around her ankles as she approached, her gray eyes instantly locking on his.

Beautiful, as expected, she glowed with sunshine. Her cheeks rose with a smile, her face bright and shimmering with happiness.

She went straight to him and hugged his waist, and that was when he noticed the change.

"Whoa." He gripped her shoulders and held her away, his attention dropping to the small round bump beneath the dress. "You're pregnant?"

"And miserable." Her smile widened. "Terrible nausea."

If misery gave out a steady light, flushed the skin with warmth and radiance, and stretched the mouth into a permanent smile, then yeah, she was absolutely miserable.

He'd never seen her this happy. It flowed through her expression and bearing and emitted outward in infectious sparkling waves.

That was all he ever wanted for her, and he felt deep pleasure knowing he'd made the right decision eight years ago in this very house when he let her go.

"I imagine there's more to your misery than the nausea." His gaze flicked to Trace. "You're going to be a father." He tsked, shaking his head. "That should be illegal. The poor kid."

Trace's lips twitched, struggling to maintain his scowl.

"Danni, this is my girl." He turned, staring into vast green eyes, where the reflection of trust and acceptance floated atop a fathomless sea of strength. "Lydia, this is Danni, your dance instructor."

TWENTY-EIGHT

"Hi." Lydia pushed the syllable past a tight throat.

She wasn't nervous or apprehensive or even jealous. Cole gave her no reason to be any of those things. When he looked at Danni, there was no longing in his deep brown eyes. No passion or possessiveness. He gazed upon the pretty blonde with kindness and warmth. Like brotherly love.

Like the way Mike had looked at Lydia.

The painful tightness in her throat ebbed and swelled with the vacillation of her emotions. Mike was gone, and while she coped with that insufferable reality, she wasn't in the mood for pleasantries with Cole's ex-girlfriend.

The obligatory exchanges—*Nice to meet you* and *How was your trip?*—where they traded hollow stares, waited for a turn to talk, and skated around the fact that they'd both had sex with Cole—all of it required more energy than she could muster.

But she was here for this. One-hundred-percent. Trace and Danni were sacrificing a week of their time to help her. The least she could do was slap on a friendly face and participate.

"Let's skip the awkwardness." Danni crooked a finger at her and walked through the brightly lit living room toward the open kitchen. "You look like you could use a beer."

"A beer would be great."

COMPLICATE

The four of them gathered around the kitchen island. Open shelving on rustic wood walls displayed dishes and cookware. The floor-to-ceiling windows on the back of the lakehouse offered a panoramic view of the raw wilderness. The natural rock and wrought-iron terrace off the kitchen connected to a bridge that led to the private dock below.

Inside, the motif was clean, spacious, and monochromatic, as if designed to pull visitors toward the exterior views of the lake and woodland.

It felt safe here. Isolated. Quiet.

"It's weird." She lowered onto a stool at the island, speaking to no one in particular. "For the first time in years, I don't feel like I have to look over my shoulder."

"Do I get to hear what you two are involved in?" Danni set opened bottles of Bud Light in front of Lydia and Cole and poured a scotch for Trace. "Or is this another classified spy mission?"

Cole met Lydia's eyes, his expression grave, silently warning her that he was about to rip off the Band-aid and talk about Mike.

She nodded and steeled herself.

He pulled up a seat beside her, sitting comfortably close with his legs spread around her stool. Then he shared her story with Trace and Danni.

Her father's death, Mike's death, Vincent Barrington's corruption, the years of dogged determination she and Mike had invested, essential details of her personal life, the operation in Texas, her ugly truths — it was all exposed and so hard to hear.

But as she listened to the narration of her whole existence from Cole's point of view, she didn't cry. She didn't even feel vulnerable. She was riveted. The way he viewed her life was astonishing.

He saw her hopes and struggles as something beautiful and painful and strong and poignant and incredibly human. He didn't perceive her as a thief or a rapist or a horrible villain. She couldn't mistake the raw compassion in his voice. He ached for her. He felt her. He related to her on every level.

That was when she realized that the things she carried around weren't so different from what he carried around.

It was profoundly overwhelming and powerful.

As the night wore on, the others popped in and out of the kitchen, grabbing food and hanging out for a while. Tiago and Kate walked down to the dock. The rest of them eventually went to bed.

After midnight, they moved the conversation to the living room, where Cole lit fires in the hearths that sat on either end of the wall of windows.

Trace lounged on the brown leather couch, looking for all the world like a Viking king in a stuffy suit. Tall and muscled, intimidating scowl, blonde hair, strong features, and a stern brow that, even in its resting state, gave him a brooding mien.

With Danni curled up against his side, he'd shed the jacket, the collar of his starched shirt gaping open. They couldn't have looked more relaxed.

Cole sprawled in the armchair across them as they discussed Trace's casino business and Danni's leave of absence from belly dancing. She was four months pregnant, her baby bump barely noticeable beneath the dress. But she touched it often, wearing a whimsical smile.

Lydia watched Cole through the night, expecting him to steal looks in Danni's direction. But every time she looked at him, he was looking back, watching her as if she were the only person in the room.

Obsessive stalker.

Beautiful, complicated man.

His presence in her life felt surreal. The whole evening was pleasantly bizarre. For whatever reason, the four of them fell in lockstep with one another as if they'd been hanging out every weekend for decades, as if eight years hadn't separated Cole from his friends. Instead of stiff pleasantries, they spoke openly and honestly, hiding nothing.

"When Cole told me he was going to ask for your help…" She stood beside Cole's chair, running her fingers through his hair. "I was fully prepared to make jokes about the tension between the three of you. But there's no tension. No awkwardness. You're all just…old friends."

"We went through some tough months together," Danni said. "But it worked out."

"It worked out for *me*. From where I'm standing, you made a mistake choosing the uptight, scowly suit over the sexy, rebellious stalker. But hey, your loss is my win."

Trace scowled. Hard. Scary.

Danni burst into laughter.

Cole caught Lydia's waist and pulled her down on his lap. "Are you trying to cause trouble?"

"Just testing the waters."

"You're doing great," he murmured against her ear. Then he looked at Danni. "Your wedding gown is hanging in the armory. Take it with you when you leave. Donate it. Make diapers out of it. You won't hurt my feelings. It's yours."

Danni didn't seem surprised that Cole still had the gown. Lydia wasn't, either. For a battle-hardened vigilante, Cole was remarkably sentimental.

COMPLICATE

"There's a girl who volunteers at the homeless shelter with me." Danni smiled. "She just got engaged and doesn't have much money. I'll give it to her."

"Your engagement ring is in the River Thames."

Danni nodded, her expression thoughtful. "You've been alone for a long time, Cole." She shifted her gaze, locking onto Lydia. "I was afraid I wouldn't like you. He needs a strong woman, and I didn't think anyone would ever measure up. I'm not sure that *I* measured up. But here you are, exceeding my expectations. I know you're hurting. I *feel* it. I can't even fathom the sheer force you're exerting to keep the tears at bay." She stood, slowly approaching, and leaned down to touch Lydia's chin. "It's an honor to be here, to meet a woman who matches Cole in strength and backbone. It's an absolute privilege to help you avenge the deaths of your brother and father. You already have the beauty to catch the eye of this hacker guy, and by the end of this week, you'll have the moves. Your dancing will be so hot you'll have every man in the club coming for you." She winked at Cole and stepped back. "I hope you're prepared for that."

Cole made a growling sound in his throat.

All Lydia could do was mutter a raspy, "Thank you."

Danni exceeded her expectations, too. It was no wonder why it had taken Cole so long to let her go.

"I'm glad you asked us to come." Trace pushed off the couch and grasped Danni's hand. "We missed you, Cole."

"Same." Cole caressed his fingers along Lydia's shoulder as he asked Trace, "Are you headed to bed?"

"Yeah. The girls have a long week ahead of them." Trace rubbed his jaw. "I want to spar with you. It's been a while."

"Sure, I'm happy to kick your ass. Just like old times."

"The way I remember it, you can't even kick your own ass."

"I'll remind you how it is when you're screaming like a little bitch, and I have to ball gag you."

"The conversation has suddenly taken an uncomfortable turn," Lydia mumbled.

"See you in the morning." Trace chuckled.

It was the first smile she'd seen on his face. Didn't make him look any less rigid.

Shortly after Danni and Trace went to bed, Cole grabbed their bags and led her down the long corridor of bedrooms.

"I'll show you around the property tomorrow." He stopped at a doorway midway down the hall. "This is where you'll be spending most of the week."

He flipped on a light, illuminating the dance room. He'd told her about it in Dublin, saying he'd designed it for Danni but now had no practical use for it.

"We need a sparring room." He shut off the lights and tugged her onward. "After we destroy Vincent Barrington, I'm going to repurpose it."

"Makes sense."

He guided her into the last room and shut the door. Full-length windows covered two perpendicular walls. A massive king-sized bed took up one corner, and an ornately carved wood-burning hearth sat in the other. From the rich wood flooring to the opulent crown molding, he'd invested a lot of money in this place.

As they showered and got ready for bed, she realized how much she didn't feel like herself, her limbs heavy with fatigue and sadness. But every shared look and interaction with Cole felt easy and comfortable. Seamlessly in sync. They'd earned that. After the trials of the past year, they deserved harmony with each other.

"I have something to give you." He removed a small box from his bag and guided her into bed, following her in.

"What is it?"

"I've debated when to give this to you, thinking I should wait until after the mission. But here's the thing. You're so fucking strong you don't need kid-glove treatment. You're not fragile or broken. If you can't handle something, I'll know and tread with care. So I'm going to give this to you. Then I'm going to fuck you." His voice grew husky. "Because that's what you need. It's what we both need."

Her breaths shredded, and her nipples went taut beneath her thin t-shirt.

He noticed, his dark gaze zeroing in as he lifted his hand. Through the cotton, the blunt nail of his thumb dragged over the tight peak.

Heat fluttered her veins. "Let's just skip to the last part."

"No." He took his touch away, grabbed whatever he'd set behind him, and placed it on her lap.

"What is this?" She lifted the small wrapped present.

"Mike was holding it when he died."

The room grew cold, and her heart thudded in her throat. "I don't want to open it."

"Then don't."

"I have to. I have to confront this head-on, or it will take over my life. If the grief wins, Vincent wins."

"You need to grieve, Lydia. It frees up the painful energy."

"I *am* grieving." She yanked at the red bow on the gift, her vision blurring. "I just don't have to drown in it. I'm channeling it into my revenge. *That's* how I'll free the pain."

COMPLICATE

She wouldn't fail. She couldn't.

"Mike was such a sentimental gift-giver." She ripped off the glittery paper on the small box. "This is going to break my heart."

"It's not going to break *you*."

With an aching chest, she opened the package and removed a lightweight ball of newspaper. Her hands trembled as she carefully tore away the wrapping and revealed the gift inside.

A hand-painted egg.

"Oh, Mike." Heaviness invaded her limbs as she soaked in the gorgeous, familiar brush strokes. "He made this."

"He painted it?"

"Yeah." Her eyes burned. "He was so artistic. He designed a lot of my tattoos, including the swallow on my chest."

She rolled the hollow, fragile egg in her palm, examining the detailed illustration of the same red swallow sitting on the limb of a cranberry tree.

Searing pain rose through her throat. Her gasping prompted him to inch closer and wrap his warm strength around her.

"The bird…" Her voice broke. "The bird represents my mother, and the cranberries… That's Shannon. Or maybe it's him and me, too. The three of us used to dance around the house, singing songs by *The Cranberries*. Our favorite was 'Ode To My Family.' Shannon loved the band, and though Mike would never admit it, he loved it, too. He always sang the loudest."

A tear trickled down her cheek, and more followed.

Cole positioned her with her back against his chest, holding her and wiping the wetness from her face.

"I really hope he didn't spend his last night on Earth emptying this damn egg and painting it." Her heart hurt unbearably. "He was supposed to get laid." She choked on a sob. "He wasn't supposed to die."

She let herself cry for a moment before swallowing it down and repackaging the gift. "He knew how much I wanted PaulVer to give me an Easter egg. After a year of trying and failing, I was so frustrated with myself."

"So he gave you an egg himself."

"Yeah." She set the package on the nightstand and twisted around, straddling his lap. "I'm okay. The pain feels really heavy, and everything around me has slowed way down, like I'm trying to move through thick mud. But you keep me centered, focused. Thank you."

"Don't thank me. I'm here for you."

"I keep picturing his body lying there in the snow. He's just lying there alone, cold, abandoned. I don't have any religious or life-after-death beliefs, but I can't bear the thought of him shoved into a refrigerator drawer, anonymous, forgotten."

"His body was moved to a funeral home and will remain there until you decide—"

"How do you know?"

"Last night at the apartment, after you fell asleep, I called Romero. He took care of it."

"How?"

"Digital records. He hacked into the Coroner's Office and changed the orders for the body's final destination."

"Oh my God, Cole." She stared at him, overcome with indebtedness and adoration and…more. So much more.

Deep inside, beneath the sorrow, something was building, thickening, and growing unstoppable.

"Thank you." She framed his gorgeous face with her hands and kissed him. Her pain, devotion, desire—she poured it all into the warm union of lips and tongues.

He groaned, breaking the kiss, and they stared at each other. They stared as if they were both expecting some form of emotional breakdown from her. When none was forthcoming, he curved his hands around her hips and hauled her impossibly closer.

"I want you to be happy." He kissed her slowly. "And naked."

His tongue stroked. Her breaths shortened, and his fingers traveled everywhere. Caressing turned into grabbing. Soft nipping into passionate biting. Heartbeats accelerated, pounding harder, growing louder.

She met him lick for lick. His cock hardened, swelling against her leg as his hands roamed, worshiping, tearing at her shirt. She twisted to tug the garment over her head, exposed and bare.

He looked at her, panting. She looked back, wanting.

She needed his body pressed against her. His warmth. His protection. His talented fingers deep inside her. His beautiful dick. His possessiveness. The taste of his kiss. The heat of his mouth. She needed him.

"I'm addicted to you," she breathed.

"I don't want to be an addiction. I want to be the love of your life."

Then he was on her, his mouth attacking her breasts and his hand between her legs, shocking her with three assertive fingers delving into her wetness. There was no warning, no warm-up. The intrusion bowed her back and reverberated to the soles of her feet.

COMPLICATE

He bit her nipples and fucked her with his hand. She bit his lips and pulled his hair, trembling, moaning, burning for him alone.

"I love seeing how much you want me." He raised his soaked fingers in her periphery.

She kissed him harder, momentarily shutting him up.

With a firm grip on her waist, he pulled her tight against his erection, withdrawing only to yank her back again in a slow, teasing grind. She whimpered, needing him, wanting him to fuck her, her fingers gripping the striated lines of his muscled back, her breasts aching fiercely.

"I'm going to put you on your back with your knees against your shoulders, and you're going to take it." He rocked beneath her, hips circling, grinding her on his lap. "I'm going to be so deep inside you you'll feel me from your cunt to your throat."

She couldn't wait.

Rolling her to her back, he looked into her eyes and sank into her body, inch by inch, stroking, panting, working himself in. He groaned loudly, and she nearly choked on her own rapture.

With her body folded in half at the waist and her knees on her shoulders, he fucked into her ruthlessly, tirelessly, his eyes fevered and breaths heavy. The pressure on her muscles created a tightness in her pelvis, increasing the sensations with each delicious thrust he delivered.

His tendons and sinews contracted and stretched as he dug into her, deeper, harder, lunging, spearing, putting his magnificent body to work. The position gave her hands access to his ass, and God help her, she couldn't stop groping him, her palms molding to the rock-hard shape, basking in the movement of those round sculpted muscles.

He was a high-performing, wild animal with endless endurance. She dissolved beneath his potency, her legs losing strength in the restraints of his hands.

Once he thoroughly pounded the deepest parts of her, he eased up and gave her a break from the stretch. Adjusting her here and there, he straddled one of her legs and hooked the other over his shoulder, scissoring her in a side-straddle.

Her arms lay boneless above her head, putting the upthrust of her chest into his ravenous reach. His hands kneaded her breasts, his fingers punishing the nipples, and his intense gaze never leaving hers as he gave her the most sublime pleasure with the thick, long strokes of his dick.

He had full control of her body in this position, and he took it, impaling her in fluid, possessing thrusts. Her breaths came faster, his caresses rough and greedy. His hips snapped in a fury.

He rode her with a single-minded focus, parting that jaw, staring into her eyes, and chasing her urgent sounds with growly, winded grunts. Then he drove her into a back-arching, body-shaking, screaming orgasm so powerful that she damn near blacked out.

As she fell apart beneath him, he threw his head back and braced himself on outstretched arms, stiffening, shuddering in the throes of his release.

His roaring, volcanic pleasure was such a glorious sight to witness. She could spend the rest of her life doing nothing else but watching him come.

His dark bedroom eyes looked dazed, lust-drunk, and terrifyingly, thrillingly in love as he stared at her and bucked, jerked, and thrust his way through ejaculation. His lips parted. His neck corded, and his gaze clung. He seemed helpless to hold the smallest part of himself back as he spent himself in an endless climax within her.

She was melting. Slipping. Falling like a feather on the wind. As long as she was in his arms, she never wanted to touch the ground.

TWENTY-NINE

"Touch the ground." Danni rudely snapped her fingers, setting Lydia's teeth on edge. "When you shimmy down, go *all* the way down. Fingertips to the floor. None of this halfway bullshit. And loosen those hips! Start again from the top."

After five days of dance instruction, Lydia wanted to wring the woman's neck. The sweet little blonde from the first night had vanished the moment she donned a leotard. Danni Savoy was a goddamn Dance Nazi.

Every time Lydia tripped, forgot a step, or copped an attitude, she was met with Danni's withering glare. If her spine bent incorrectly, it earned her a stinging pinch from Danni's hand. If she did a butt-wiggle instead of a figure-eight-sway, she got a scolding swat on the ass.

Her feet ached in the heels. Her muscles protested every brutal, repetitive movement, and her heart fought it all, because more than anything, it just wanted to heal.

The days and nights swirled into a fugue of sweating and swaying and tapping and sliding. She was naturally uncoordinated, stiff through the hips, and not always receptive to Danni's criticism.

But she was making progress. Huge progress.

Watching herself in the mirror, she focused on transforming her feelings into movements. Music had the power to connect the soul with the senses, and for the past five days, Danni had been teaching her how to achieve that.

"Let your body loose. Like this." Danni gripped her hips from behind, moving her, demonstrating for the thousandth time how to catch the rhythm. "A stiff frame can't move. Surrender your joints, your muscles, your breaths. Allow the music to control your movements all the way to the floor. See?"

Despite Danni's pregnancy, she had no trouble sweating it out on the dance floor for twelve hours every day. Lydia studied Danni's reflection in the mirror, mimicking the descending, rippling silhouette of Danni's cute body as they undulated together, down, down, down to the ground and back up.

Techno music thumped from the speakers. Just one of the many dance genres she'd learned how to groove to. Different nightclubs offered different kinds of music, and she needed to adapt to each style as the music changed.

And so it went. Hour after hour, day after day, Lydia practiced no less than fifty dance moves and transition techniques.

At her request, Cole stayed away during the lessons. He was too distracting, his gaze too invasive and penetrating. She couldn't work with him stalking the perimeter of the room, consuming her senses, demanding her attention.

But they always reconnected at night amid tangled sheets. With each possessive thrust, it was no longer enough just to hear him roaring her name as they finished together.

She wanted more.

Lovers had come and gone throughout her life. She remembered none of them, never pursued anything more than a five-second fling.

Cole wasn't a lover. He was an unprecedented, decadent experience. His perseverance, dedication, and loyalty was unlike any man she'd ever been with. And let's be honest. There was no one as insanely, unreasonably gorgeous as Cole Hartman.

Whether they were sharing conversation, food, or body fluids, she didn't want it to end. She often caught herself thinking about her life after this mission, and she always circled back to one undeniable truth. She wanted a future with Cole.

Mike would've wanted that for her. On Christmas Eve, he let Cole into their home, into their life, because he *knew*.

Cole belonged to her. He was the one. If she didn't believe Cole's words, she only had to look into his unyielding brown eyes. She would have to cut off his legs if she ever tried to run from him. Until his last breath, he would chase her to the ends of the earth.

He wouldn't need to, for he already caught her, heart and soul.

COMPLICATE

"Wow. Look at you." Danni danced around her, smiling and snapping her fingers to the music. "You got your groove, girl. Damn, you're on fire!"

She observed her form in the mirror, letting the repetitive electronic beat lift and drop her hips as she slid through the box step.

With each booty shake, she felt less restrained. More confident. With the subtle kicks of her pelvis, her movements glided like oil, more relaxed, freer, sexier. If her feet still ached in the heels, she didn't notice. She only felt the tune, the percussion, and the *music*.

She was so lost in the zone she didn't notice Danni had drifted away until the song ended.

"You're almost ready." Danni leaned a shoulder against the wall of windows, her attention fixed on something outside.

"What's left? I swear I've learned every dance move in existence."

"You've mastered all the techniques and steps you'll need." Danni touched her throat, her cheeks flushing as her gaze remained glued on the window. "What's left is the fun part. I'll teach you how to flirt and...fuck."

"Sorry?" She wiped the perspiration from her forehead and treaded toward the window. "Are you *blushing*? What are you looking at out...? Oh, shit."

Outside, dormant grass stretched from the rear terrace to the surrounding tree line. At the center of the lawn, Cole and Trace rolled across the ground, grappling, sparring, shirtless and sweaty. So goddamn sexy.

Her mouth watered. Her skin caught fire. Her stupid knees went weak.

"Oh, shit," she repeated, entranced by the display of muscle and ferocious power.

They weren't alone. Cole's friends stood on the sidelines, bent forward, shouting, laughing, and cheering on the sparring match. Tiago, Matias, and Tate were shirtless, their workout pants clinging to their muscled physiques.

Lucia and Camila wore exercise clothes, too, with their black hair pulled into ponytails. The sisters looked so similar it was hard to tell them apart.

Kate sat off to the side with a textbook on her lap, cramming for an upcoming exam.

"Trace missed his sparring partner." Danni touched the glass, her expression somber. "I ruined a beautiful friendship."

"*You* didn't ruin anything. Their relationship took a beating and evolved through the hardship. They're still friends. I mean, they still call each other when they're in trouble."

"You're right." Danni nodded. Then she grinned, her eyes glowing with sudden mischief. "Let's take a break."

They shared a smile and slipped off their heels. Then they raced out of the dance room, through the house, grabbing coats and sneakers before heading outside into the chill of January.

The overcast sky draped the yard in a wintry gray. The shirtless guys seemed unaffected by the cold, their grunts and shouts bursting in clouds of steam. Those who stood on the sideline looked just as tousled and sweaty as Cole and Trace. They must've been taking turns sparring.

As she and Danni joined the group, the atmosphere buzzed with energy. Over the past five days, she'd spent more time with Danni than anyone else. But during meals and evening lulls, she got to know the entire group.

Hearing their histories firsthand had given her a whole new respect for this vigilante family. Their experiences in Van Quiso's attic hadn't destroyed them. It made them stronger, closer, and those unbreakable bonds had formed a team of survivors willing to take the law into their own hands to decimate the most depraved criminals in the world.

They were the personification of justice.

She never had a plan beyond Vincent Barrington's arrest and incarceration. Never let herself imagine what she would do next.

Until now.

The sounds of seething breaths charged the air. A few feet away, Cole held the dominant position over Trace, where they lay on the grass, chest to chest, wrestling for a chokehold.

With Cole on top, he had the advantage, throwing his body weight behind the forearm that pressed against Trace's throat.

Then he looked up, his molten brown eyes homing in on her, softening, heating, then widening as a fist skidded across his jaw and slammed his head backward.

Oops. She winced.

Trace laughed in triumph. Cole scrambled back, flinging a sloppy kick to ward off Trace. They staggered to their feet and circled each other, catching their breaths. Then, with their glares narrowed in determination, they dove back together in a blur of limbs.

"I've never seen that guy get distracted." Tate stood beside her, his crystal blue eyes twinkling with amusement. "It's nice to see him with a distraction. Especially one that puts a goofy smile on his face."

"I hope he doesn't get distracted next week. Did you guys iron out the itinerary?"

COMPLICATE

"Yep. We narrowed down your list of nightclubs, using Romero's facial recognition software to identify patterns. There are a handful of clubs between Italy and Romania that are frequented by the same group of men. According to Romero, this group was present on the nights that you spotted Easter eggs."

"Is PaulVer one of these people?"

"We don't think so. We've investigated all of them. They're nobodies. Wealthy, bored nobodies who like to party. No I/T training or apparent computer skills. They're probably just his friends, people who know his schedule and show up to party with him. I doubt they even know he's a hacker. Most of these hackers are in the closet, hiding behind their keyboards, committing federal crimes, and telling no one."

"So these friends...if you know their identities, Romero should be able to track where they are, right? We'll know which city and nightclub they're at?"

"Exactly. Assuming PaulVer goes where they go, it'll be like shooting fish in a barrel. We'll show up where they are. All you have to do is lure PaulVer out of the shadows. Once he puts an egg in your hand, we'll have him."

"Yeah, and while I'm doing that, I'll be luring Vincent's men, too."

"That's why we're here. Cole called us in to protect you while you're dancing." Tate bumped his shoulder against hers, winking. "We're really good at killing bad guys."

"I know, and I'm grateful." She turned toward him. "I mean it, Tate. I don't know how I'm going to repay you."

"We would do this job even if you hadn't lost your family. Vincent Barrington *cannot* become President. Period. And when we take him down, there will be more evil fucks to pursue. This is what we do, and you're part of it now." He smiled, flashing his teeth. "Welcome to the family."

Blood hummed in her veins, circulating a depth of joy that she didn't think she'd feel again without Mike.

A pained grunt drew her attention back to the sparring match. Trace doubled over, and Cole went in for the attack. With both hands, he grasped Trace's head and brought a kneecap to Trace's nose, followed by a kick to the solar plexus. Trace stumbled backward, but there was no blood. No apparent bruising. They were sparring, holding back their punches, not trying to kill each other.

Trace regained his footing, but it was too late. Cole took him to the ground and twisted him into an arm lock, forcing Trace to tap out.

In a blink, Cole was on his feet again, prowling toward her with an impish glint in his eyes. When he reached her, she stepped back, evading the aggressive grab of his hand.

"You want me? Come and get me." She retreated faster, dodging another swipe. "Is that all you got?"

He growled, throwing himself at her. She feigned right, compelling him to move with her, then changed direction at the last minute and broke free.

She took off at a sprint, delighting in the sound of his chasing footsteps.

River-rock streams and mulched footpaths trailed off into the woods. Other paths led to the terrace and exterior doors of the house. She followed the cobblestone sidewalk that curved around the wing of the estate.

The chilly breeze nipped at her cheeks, but the coat kept her warm. She glanced back, and her pulse ignited. Holy shit, he was right there in arm's reach, shirtless, his expression so intensely hungry her heart tripped...right along with her feet.

She staggered, and his arm swung out, grabbing for her hair. With a yelp, she bolted forward, the strands slipping from his fingers. She picked up her pace, leaping over rocks, laughing, and trembling with desire.

Halfway around the side of the estate, he caught her by the neck and hauled her back, crushing her mouth against his. The kiss split open in a sweep of tongues and searing heat. Her back hit the side of the house, and he moved in, syncing their hips and grinding with the rhythm of their rushing breaths.

He tore her coat open, popping the buttons. Then he shoved her tank top and bra to her neck and pressed his bare chest against hers, burning her skin.

"Cole." She gripped his thick arms, trying to keep up with the impetuous passion of his kiss.

His aggressive lips worked her into a fever, his tongue lashing and twining with hers. God, she loved his sinful mouth, but it was his dimpled smile that stole her heart. He leaned back, giving her a glorious, up-close view of those delicious divots. Then he dove back in, his lips hot on her neck, and his hands running everywhere.

With his body bearing down against hers, they rubbed together, rocking, sliding, and panting. His sculpted physique bunched and flexed against her as the sound of his fervent breaths spun her up and turned her inside out. Every gasp and sizzling exhale confessed how badly he wanted her.

Holy fuck, he wanted her. He was so hard, so damn long and swollen beneath the thin cotton of his workout pants. He was going to take her right here, outside in the cold, where any of his friends could walk by. He didn't give a fuck, and neither did she.

COMPLICATE

He yanked her leggings to her ankles and pulled one side completely off, along with her shoe. It freed up her legs, which he lifted and spread, pinning her against the siding with one knee shoved to her shoulder. He held it there as he wrestled down his joggers and freed his cock.

His eyes met hers for the span of a moment, and in that precious space between them, she felt the promise of a future, a beautiful destiny, their hearts fused, their bodies entangled, and their souls forged as one.

As he pushed inside her, he watched her like a man in love, his eyes drunk on happiness, and his dimpled mouth parted in wonder.

Utterly possessed, she captured that mouth and sank into the flames.

He fucked her against the house. Then he fixed her clothes, carried her inside, and made love to her in his bed. Neither of them said the words, but she felt it in every touch, every kiss, every whispered breath.

"Only two days left." She lay in his arms after, stroking the stubble on his chiseled jaw.

"I want to dance with you."

That wouldn't be possible at the nightclubs in Europe. She would have to dance alone to draw in the hacker. The team would take up posts around the perimeter, watching for threats and keeping her safe.

"I have a confession." She made a face. "I hate dancing."

"Okay."

"Okay? I don't think you understand. I'm doing this for my dad. For Mike. When it's over, I'll be happy to never step onto a dance floor again."

"What about slow dancing?"

"With you?" Her chest fluttered. "Yeah, I'd be down for that."

"Good." He brushed their lips together. "I still want a fast, hip-grinding dance with you. Just one."

"Okay." She would happily give him anything he wanted.

As it turned out, he got his wish on their last night in Missouri.

After dinner, Danni asked everyone to gather in the dance room. The entire gang stood around—Cole, Trace, the six Freedom Fighters—watching Danni circle Lydia at the center.

"You mastered the technical part of club dancing." Danni paused behind her, sliding soft, sensual fingers down her inked arms. "There's another aspect of this that isn't dancing at all. It's basically flirting. Grinding provocatively. Fucking with your clothes on."

Across the room, Cole stiffened, his eyes narrowing.

"Calm down." Danni pointed a finger at him and returned to Lydia. "You can do this with the women on the dance floor. Take everything I taught you and make it sexual. Touch them in ways you both like. It's about turning each other on. But there *will* be men, and they're going to flock to you with their tongues hanging out." Danni shifted back to Cole. "Most of the people who frequent nightclubs aren't there to dance. They're there to participate in a clothes-on, fluid-free orgy. Loud music. Simple, mindless beats. Lots of sweaty people who can't hear one another talk. It's a non-verbal, dry-humping fuckfest without the penetration. If you want to succeed in this mission, you will swallow your caveman ego and deal with it."

Lydia burst into laughter. She couldn't help it. Cole looked so miserable.

His nostrils flared. His face turned red, and his jaw clenched to the point of breaking. But after a few seconds, he gave a nod.

"We're going to practice." Danni dimmed the lights and moved to the stereo as she addressed the room. "Doesn't matter if you can dance or not. You're here for the orgy. Lydia needs to test her skills with random bodies rubbing up against her. Let's see some dirty dancing."

Danni started the music—a rapid iteration of electronic beats. It took several seconds for Lydia to loosen up enough to move. When she did, she kept her movements subtle and tight, remaining right where she was, waiting to see what the others would do.

Trace moved first, heading straight to his wife and wrapping his body around her back. They rolled as one, dipping and sliding like they'd danced together a million times. No doubt they had.

Cole stayed at the edge of the room, his hands at his sides, swaying to the music with his eyes locked on Lydia, stoking a fire in her belly.

Someone came up behind her. Small hands rested on her hips. She turned, finding Kate's pretty face smiling back, her body rocking with confidence.

Within seconds, she was surrounded. Tiago, Matias, and Tate favored the two-step side-to-side motion. Simple. Relaxed. Not a hint of awkwardness or discomfort. The women were bolder in their movements. None of them were dancers, but their assertiveness and self-possession more than made up for any lack of technical skill.

This group didn't have a shy bone between them, and sweet Lord, they were sexual.

Through the next few songs, each of them danced with her in turn, rolling their bodies with smooth, deliberate, erotic suggestion, hips to hips, pressing in tight, and grinding with the motion of sex.

COMPLICATE

Cole didn't lose his shit. He stood at a distance, never looking away. Perhaps he was testing himself, watching her writhe with his friends. Or maybe he was teasing her, making her wait until she was so sexed-up she would explode if he touched her.

As the group slowly paired off to dance with their mates, he approached. She trembled.

He circled her, placing a hand on her waist as he moved out of sight, keeping his touch on her at all times. When he came back around, he edged closer, aligning their bodies chest to chest and rolling his hip. One hand cupped her jaw. The other hung loosely at his side and slightly behind him, making it impossible *not* to grope his ripped physique.

She ran her palms down his torso, tracing the indentations and ridges of muscle through the shirt, and teasing the button of his fly.

"You're beautiful," he mouthed.

"So are you." She smiled, feeling warm and gooey and so undeserving.

She wasn't worthy of this incredible man, but she'd laid her claim and wasn't letting go.

Grabbing his face with both hands, she rose on her toes and captured his lips. He kissed her back and pulled her closer, controlling the movement of her muscles, setting the pace, and letting her feel him.

His body was made for this, hips thrusting, mouth moving against hers, and hands palming her ass. He danced like he fucked, commanding, leading, and she followed without question. She loved his touch on her skin. She adored his breath on her neck. She craved the hard heat of him, and he gave her what she craved, total permission to feel.

To feel with her hands.

To feel with her heart.

To bask in the beauty of their bond.

They danced through several songs, kissing and grinding until her legs burned and her mouth went numb. Slowly, the room emptied, each couple quietly drifting into the hall.

Danni and Trace swayed in their own world, their bodies entwined and mouths locked in passion. Then Trace lifted her, cradling her in his arms, and carried her out of the room.

Cole moved behind Lydia, rocking and molding his hands to her curves and dips. His lips caressed her neck seductively, lovingly, luring her into his hungry orbit.

"I want to strip you down and lick your body from top to bottom," he said at her ear.

Then he led her to the bedroom and did exactly that.

The next morning, they said goodbye to Danni and Trace. It wasn't weird or strained, and it didn't feel final. The couple might not be part of Cole's vigilante world, but she knew she would see them again and often. She would make sure of it.

Her chest filled with nervous excitement as the rest of them packed up and headed to the private airport where Matias' plane waited. As she boarded the plane and flew toward her destination with her hand tucked tightly in Cole's, she recognized that she wouldn't be here without him.

Without him, she would still be in Ireland, financially broke and emotionally destitute. Or dead.

When she started this mission twelve years ago, she had one purpose.

Revenge.

When Cole started this mission fourteen months ago, he had a different purpose.

Rescue.

He'd claimed her in Texas, and at that moment, he'd become her champion. He'd fought against it. She'd fought it, too. But in the end, he laid down life and limb to do what heroes did.

He rescued his girl.

THIRTY

Brașov, Romania
Two weeks later

The nightclub was rainbow lights and primal beats, throbbing like a heartbeat over a loudspeaker. Lydia didn't need the music to rev her blood. She was hyped up on adrenaline and nerves.

Tiago led her through thick swirls of dry-ice smoke and sweaty hordes of writhing bodies. This was their sixth nightclub in two weeks, and she was beginning to think their intel was wrong.

There had been no Easter egg sightings. It had nothing to do with whether she could dance. PaulVer simply wasn't at the venues they visited.

Inauguration Day was in five days.

Five days until Vincent Barrington became the President of the United States, the most powerful man in the world, and utterly untouchable.

She tightened her grip on Tiago's arm as he muscled his way through the throng. The entire team wore disguises—wigs, hats, fake tattoos, and flashy club attire. Her ink lay completely hidden beneath layers of makeup, her wig a vibrant shade of blue.

For the tenth time, she yanked down the hem of her silver body-con dress, but within two steps, it worked its way back up her thighs. The glittery material barely covered her ass and breasts. Cole's expression had darkened when he saw it, but he didn't dare say a word.

The dress did what it was designed to do. It drew attention.

She felt the gaze of every man she passed, despite the danger wafting off her intimidating escort. Tiago wore all black, save for the long, brown fur coat and matching fedora on his head. With his shirt unbuttoned to his belt and his six-pack on display beneath the fur coat, he looked like a goddamn pimp.

She didn't glance around the club for Cole. He would be close. Always within eyeshot. Since they were both targets for Vincent's men, it was safer if they weren't spotted together, even with the disguises.

When Tiago dropped her off at the dance floor, Camila and Lucia were already there, dancing together. She didn't make eye contact as she sashayed past them.

The acoustics in the rafters thundered with the music and the pound of countless feet. Beams of lights crisscrossed over the crowd in an array of blues, acid greens, hot pinks, and gold. The booming rhythm fused with the bouncing bodies, and she joined them, rolling her hips, tossing her head, and miming sex with every person—man or woman— who approached her.

There was no talking, no need to fake an accent. This was all about tactical flirting, eye-fucking, heavy petting, groping, panting, and humping with clothes on. In the carnal beat of the music, in the heart of the nightclub, a hundred people bumped and writhed in a public gang bang.

While everyone danced to that lustful vibe, she danced for Cole. She knew he watched her. He saw every woman who touched her, every man who humped her, every flirty, grabby dancer who tried to reach under her dress. She kept the unwanted molesting at bay, refusing to give anyone what belonged to Cole.

The dancing lasted hours. Perspiration glistened on her brow. Her breaths labored, and her muscles burned with exhaustion. As the night wore down and the crowd began to thin, she knew it had been another wasted effort.

Disappointment crashed through her, but she kept moving, dipping her hips with someone at her back, dipping with her. Masculine hands molded to her hips. A warm mouth nuzzled her neck. Then she felt it—the sudden chill as he stepped back, the brush of fingers against her wrist, and the round egg-shaped object touching her palm.

Her heart rate exploded, her elation bursting in shimmery waves. She couldn't contain it, her cheeks rising with the stretch of her laughing smile as she thrust her free hand in the air and extended her index and pinkie fingers in the sign of the devil horns.

To anyone watching, she was just waving her arm to the music. But to the team, her hand sign just alerted them that the man at her back was the target.

COMPLICATE

She spun around, but the man had already turned away, his head down and shoulders hunched around his ears. She glimpsed dark hair and an average-build as he quickly slipped through the jumping crowd.

Cole had demanded she not engage or chase the target for fear he would panic and run off. Her job was to lure him in and mark him. The team would do the rest.

Without any pockets, she reluctantly dropped the egg and glanced around the dance floor, noting the absence of Camila and Lucia. They were already on the move, trailing the hacker. As she turned toward the exit, she came face to face with Cole.

Electricity sparkled across her skin, heating her up. She wanted to scream, *We have him!* But she pressed her lips together and kept herself in check.

Within the shadows of his baseball cap, his beautiful features showed no reaction, no shared excitement. This was his *work face*, the one he wore in fight mode, when he was hyper-focused, detached from emotion, his mindset cold and competitive. She'd seen this expression often during his captivity in Texas.

He pulled her closer and rocked his hips with purpose as he led her off the dance floor. Then he gave her a discreet nudge toward the exit. She walked ahead of him, knowing the rest of the team was focused on the target. They would stay with the hacker until he left the building. Then they would engage.

Since her role was finished, Cole's only priority was getting her out of the venue and somewhere safe. Once they had PaulVer in their possession, Cole would take her to him so she could help plead their case.

Outside, she quickly crossed the busy street, keeping close to the shadows of buildings, parked cars, anything that provided cover. After being hunted for over a year, stealth and concealment had become second nature to her.

Any stranger walking along the sidewalks could be a hitman.

At the end of the block, she hid in a recess of the building and glanced back. Cole was nowhere in sight, but he was there, somewhere. He would never let her out of his sight.

Their rented vehicles waited just around the corner. She headed there, rounding the bend, and stopped.

A man stood in the empty side street between the medievalesque buildings made of stone and arched windows. He faced the opposite direction, but she recognized his build, his dark jacket, and short black hair.

Twenty feet before him, Camila strutted forward, wearing red leather pants and stiletto heels. The drape of her off-the-shoulder shirt was deliberately baggy, hiding the weapons beneath it.

"PaulVer," she purred, laying on the seductive ruse. "You speak English?"

He stiffened, his shoulders curling forward and hands flexing at his sides. A small satchel hung against his hip with the strap crossing his upper body.

"I don't know that name." His English was succinct, despite the heavy inflection of a Romanian accent.

Lydia's muscles trembled as she flattened herself against the corner of the building, remaining hidden.

Matias and Lucia leaned against their rented SUV, which was parked at a distance behind Camila, well in view of PaulVer. Kate would be inside the vehicle. Tate and Tiago stood in the shadows at the edges of the side street, mere feet from PaulVer's position. Their unmoving forms would be difficult to detect by an unsuspecting eye.

Behind her, people strolled along the main road, coming and going between the bars and nightclubs.

After a moment of searching, she spotted Cole crouched beside the building across the street. He held a gun at his side, his gaze flicking between her and PaulVer.

"I have a proposition for you, handsome." Camila slowly placed one heeled shoe before the other, sashaying her hips as she approached.

"You have the wrong person." He pivoted, revealing a shockingly youthful face before he ducked his head and strode in Lydia's direction, not seeing her.

Jesus, the guy couldn't have been older than eighteen.

As he hurried away from Camila, nervous tension tightened in Lydia's gut. Fourteen months of searching and hoping, and her answer was walking straight toward her. She knew the team wouldn't let him get away, but it took everything inside her not to jump out and grab him. She would do it in a heartbeat if she weren't being hunted by Vincent's goons.

Tate swept out onto the street, walking casually behind PaulVer. Then Tiago emerged, joining the slow, heart-pounding chase.

PaulVer marked them and tucked his hands in the pockets of his skinny jeans, picking up his pace, gaze on his sneakers, and reeking of fear as he inadvertently strode directly into Lydia's path.

He must've decided to head back to the nightclub. In about three seconds, he would turn the corner and see her. She would have to engage him, try to push him back onto the side street and out of view without making a scene.

Something stirred behind her, lifting the hairs on her nape. She didn't have time to consider who or what before someone crashed into her back. A split-second later, gunshots rang out.

COMPLICATE

The impact of two-hundred pounds slamming into her knocked the wind from her lungs and sent her pummeling toward the ground.

More gunfire erupted, booming through the side street.

The next few seconds slowed to a crawl.

As she hit the ground beneath the weight of her attacker, PaulVer froze. His shoulder kicked back as if punched by an invisible fist. He staggered. His eyes bulged, locked on her. He reached for his chest, then his arm, and pulled his hand away, smeared in blood.

He was shot.

Oh, God, he was shot.

No, no, no!

A guttural sound barreled from her throat, and her stomach rolled in violent waves. Trapped in the cage of unbending steel arms, she could only watch in horror as PaulVer crumpled to the ground a few feet away. *Lifeless.*

She twisted her neck, her lungs screaming for oxygen, and found Cole stretched out atop her like a shield of flesh-and-bone armor. He'd saved her life *again*, but with that realization spiked a blood-chilling fear for his life. While she lay safely beneath him, his entire body was exposed to the bullets whizzing past her head.

All around her, the team returned gunfire. The deadly exchange of lead lasted a long, agonizing minute. Then the street fell quiet.

"All clear," Matias shouted.

"Cole?" She whimpered, panicking. "Cole, are you-?"

"Not hit." He dropped a kiss on her temple and rolled off her back.

Three dead bodies scattered the sidewalk behind her. Vincent's men.

She stumbled to her feet, frantically scanning the side street before her. The team had taken cover during the gunfight. Were any of them hit?

The wrath of a million bees swarmed her bloodstream as Cole shouted, "Report in!"

One by one, each person on the team responded with "Not hit."

As she exhaled some of her tension, the blare of sirens broke out in the distance.

"Move out!" Cole crouched beside PaulVer's body and tossed the kid over his shoulder.

She raced ahead, leading him to the SUV with Tiago and Kate.

"Is he alive?" Kate asked from the backseat.

"He's breathing." Cole fell into the seat beside Kate and dumped the kid between them.

Lydia jumped in the front passenger seat next to Tiago, and before she got the door closed, Tiago hit the gas, shooting forward.

The other four teammates sped down the street in the second SUV. Tiago followed closely behind, skidding around turns and running through stop signs.

"Is he alive?" Blood thrashed in her ears as she twisted to face the backseat.

"Yes." Kate bent over the kid's body, eyes narrowed on his shoulder while Cole held a small flashlight on the wound. "It's a graze. Not deep enough to need stitches." She laughed, coughed against the back of her hand, and laughed again. "He passed out from a scratch."

Cole's face broke out in a grin, and within seconds, everyone in the vehicle was laughing, including Tiago as he tore through the streets, outrunning the Romanian Police.

"Search his pockets," Lydia said. "See if there's an ID."

Cole rummaged through PaulVer's clothing in the dark. "No, ID. But this was in his satchel." Cole held up a slim laptop.

His eyes, chocolaty and warm, latched onto hers. They stared at each other, letting the moment sink in.

"You did it," he whispered, setting aside the laptop.

"We did it."

Now they just needed PaulVer to do the rest.

Cole inched forward and gripped her neck, bringing their mouths together. He kissed her softly, adoringly, humming his happiness. She returned the kiss, sharing in his joy, her soul swelling and reaching for his.

"It's almost over." He smiled against her mouth.

"Doesn't feel real."

The trailing sound of sirens faded. Then disappeared completely. They'd lost the police, but Tiago didn't slow. He flew down the sleepy Romanian streets, keeping pace with their friends in the other SUV.

"He's waking," Kate whispered, taping up the bandage.

Cole leaned back, letting Lydia bend toward the backseat.

"Hey, there," she said softly. "Remember me?"

A heavy rasp pushed past PaulVer's teeth, his thick black eyebrows twitching as he dragged open his eyes.

His dark brown gaze struggled to focus, his eyelashes blinking rapidly, until finally, he centered his sight on her.

"You're my angel," he said dazedly. "My beautiful, perfect angel. Do you like the egg?"

"I love it. Thank you for giving it to me. I've been trying to earn one of your gifts for over a year."

"You..." He was sprawled in the backseat between Cole and Kate, seemingly unaware of where he was. He hadn't taken his eyes off Lydia. "You knew about the Easter eggs?"

COMPLICATE

"I know it's your calling card, and each night you go out, you give one to your favorite dancer. It's very mysterious. You like that, don't you? You like leaving a trail of mysterious eggs that no one will ever figure out."

His boyish smile appeared out of place with the sexual heat simmering in his foggy gaze. The kid was certainly unconventional and strange. But eccentricity was often associated with intellectual giftedness. As the most notorious hacker in the world, he was undoubtedly a genius.

"How did you find…?" His face paled, eyes widening as he shot up and gripped his bandaged arm. "Oh my God! I got shot!"

"The bullet grazed you. You're fine."

He didn't seem to hear her as he wildly looked around the car, taking in the other passengers.

"Who are you?" He pulled his feet up onto the seat, gasping and scrambling to get away with nowhere to go.

Cole gently held him in place as she reached out a hand, touching the kid's knee, trying to soothe him.

"We didn't shoot you, PaulVer. We're a vigilante team." She met his terrified gaze. "The shooters were assassins hired by Vincent Barrington. The President-elect is trying to kill me and anyone involved in exposing his crimes."

He stilled, his expression awash with disbelief. Then his breathing sped up, his voice rising in volume and urgency. "Let me out. Stop the car. Let me out of the fucking car!"

Everyone in the civilized world knew who Vincent Barrington was. She couldn't expect him to believe her fantastical claim, and at this point, there was no calming him down.

Matias drove the other SUV, leading them to the rendezvous point. In the meantime, she just needed to tell PaulVer her story and hope he wasn't too scared out of his mind to listen.

"Twelve years ago, Vincent Barrington killed my father in a Russian hotel room. My father was NSA, and the murder was recorded. That recording is in the hands of the Romanian mafia. I need you to get that video file."

He shook his head rapidly, but the pace of his breaths lost momentum. He was listening, despite his fear. He was listening because he was too smart not to pay attention.

She started over from the beginning, filling in details about her dad, her ruse as a swallow in Vincent's employment, Mike's death, her fourteen-month hunt for his Easter eggs, and his ability to bring justice for all of it.

"You're vigilantes." He swallowed, eying Cole with suspicion. "Like…you kill people?"

"We killed the fuckers who shot you." Tiago jerked the wheel, deliberately causing PaulVer to tumble into Cole.

She exchanged a look with Cole, attempting to borrow some of his composed patience.

"We're part of a vigilante team that eliminates evil people." She reached up and pulled off her blue wig, letting him see her natural red hair, her identity. "Human sex traffickers, pedophiles, and greedy, corrupt politicians." She sighed. "Look, I'm only asking if you can hack into the Romanian mafia's network and steal the recording, watch the video, and decide for yourself."

"You won't kill me?"

"Do you traffic women and sell children to predators?"

"No!" He made a horrified face.

"Do you murder innocent people?"

"No. I've never killed anyone. I steal from monopolized corporations and give the money to people who need it." He rolled his lips. "And I like pretty dancers. But I don't...I would never hurt a woman. I just like to give them my painted eggs."

Her chest swelled with hope, but she felt the tension in the car. Everyone was on edge, holding their breaths. There was so much at stake, hinging on an eccentric, fearful teenage boy.

He lowered his feet to the floorboard and leaned toward her, bracing his elbows on his knees.

"I found a back door last year." He raised his dark eyes to her, his accent thickening. "I'm already inside the mafia's network."

Her pulse took off, dancing through her veins. She was so strung out, so anxious and overjoyed she thought she might puke.

"Help us." She lifted a trembling hand to his hairless jaw and let him see the tears welling in her eyes. "Please."

"What will you do with the video?"

"Twelve years ago, it was turned into the NSA. I don't know who saw the footage, but they did nothing. They covered it up and let it fall into the hands of the mafia. I'm reluctant to trust anyone in the government, especially now that Vincent Barrington is five days from becoming our President." She drew a breath. "I was hoping you could disperse it, broadcast it all over the Internet, make it impossible to cover up. Americans need to know who they voted into office."

He leaned back and stared out the window, watching buildings and street signs blur by. "Turn left here and head north. There's a Starbucks up the road. They have a strong WIFI signal."

As Tiago veered left and followed PaulVer's directions, Cole called Matias and told him where to go.

COMPLICATE

"Thank you." Her ribs expanded with the unstoppable release of years of pent-up emotion.

A tear escaped, running down her cheek, and Cole moved in, gripping the back of her head and kissing away the salty river.

"I'm sorry." She laughed uncomfortably. "It's a long time coming, and I'm emotional."

"A moment I don't want to miss." He touched his forehead to hers.

Tiago pulled into the vacant parking lot of Starbucks and parked behind the building. Matias pulled in beside him.

There, PaulVer sat in the SUV with his laptop and dug through the mafia's network files. She'd given him her father's name and every keyword she could conjure, which he loaded into his software program to scan the mafia's metadata.

Then they waited on pins and needles.

Most of them stood outside the vehicles behind the building. Out of view of the street, they watched and listened for the Romanian police.

The sirens never came.

Three hours later, PaulVer stepped out of the SUV and handed her the laptop. "I think this is it."

She stared down at the paused video, her stomach twisting in knots. "Did you watch it?"

"Yes." He frowned, his face appearing older somehow. "It's bloody. Definitely Vincent Barrington committing murder."

"You don't have to watch it." Cole cupped her jaw, pulling her gaze to his. "Once you see it, you'll carry the image with you for the rest of your life."

"My imagination can't be much better." She pressed play and clutched Cole's strong hand.

On the screen, her dad walked through a hotel room and opened the door. Vincent stepped in as her dad shook his head, speaking rapidly.

"There's no sound?" Her voice shook.

"No," PaulVer said.

Her dad looked calm, albeit a little surprised and annoyed to see Vincent. When the door shut behind Vincent, it happened fast. Vincent pulled a knife from behind him and slashed it across her dad's throat. A clean cut, deep and fast.

He hadn't seen it coming, which meant he trusted the man.

If she had to guess, her dad had set up the video recording because he was expecting a visitor. Possibly the Russian informant he was supposed to meet. When Vincent showed up, he probably didn't want him there because he was expecting someone else.

He wasn't expecting to die. Richard Pictam had taught her everything she knew about combat fighting, weaponry, and self-defense. No one could get the drop on him. Unless he trusted them.

Regardless, the video quality was perfect, the identities on the footage irrefutable.

"That's him." Tears quivered through her voice. "Give it to the world."

Cole wrapped his arms around her from behind, holding her tight as PaulVer switched screens on the laptop and hit a button on one of his software programs.

"It's sending now." He bounced a little on his toes. "It's hitting social media platforms, major news networks, and government agencies all over the world. Inboxes everywhere are receiving the file. It's done."

"Thank you." She pulled away from Cole and flung her arms around PaulVer's neck. "Thank you so damn much."

When she pulled away, the kid blushed and stared at his feet.

She turned back to Cole, and he was right there, waiting, smiling with two gorgeous, irresistible dimples.

"It's over," she whispered.

"It's only just begun." He caught her nape and hauled her in, taking her mouth with pure and vulnerable passion.

In his kiss was heartbreak and risk and choice and chance and a million dreams all condensed into a moment.

A moment hard-won.

In his kiss, she won love.

THIRTY-ONE

Dublin, Ireland
Two weeks later

Lydia visited the house in Dublin 22 one more time. She thought she needed the closure, but now she didn't know. Her heart was a mess.

"I don't know why I'm here." She paced through the small kitchen, looking around for anything she might want to keep.

"Do you want to go through his clothes?" Cole sat at the table, watching her steadily.

She and Mike didn't own anything. No pictures. No clothes worth keeping. Nothing of value. Instead of collecting material objects, she'd collected tattoos. Her memories of him were inked on her body. She had the egg Mike painted, and she kept the image of his lopsided smile safely in her mind. That was all she needed.

There hadn't been a funeral service. No big send-off. After she had him cremated, she and Cole flew to London, stood on the Westminster Bridge in the moonlight, and poured Mike's ashes in the River Thames.

She let her brother go.

"I'm still trying to come to terms with it all."

"There's no hurry, Lydia. Take your time, and I'll be right here with you, every step of the way."

He hadn't left her side since the night they released the video. PaulVer had done exactly what he'd said. The video went viral, and within twenty-four hours, Vincent Barrington was arrested for murder.

She and Cole had been glued to the news stations for the past two weeks, watching the drama unfold as Vincent was handcuffed and hauled away. The trial would make history. Those in the NSA who covered up his crimes would be named and charged, too.

Vincent Barrington would never see daylight again.

Cole had asked her if she wanted more justice than that. He said he couldn't make promises, but he would find a way to have Vincent murdered in prison.

She didn't want that. Death would be too easy. For a man who had lived so extravagantly off the rewards of his corruption, a concrete cell and penal labor would be the worst kind of hell.

Let him rot behind bars.

She treaded to the window and pulled back the curtain, gazing out at the dead lawn and the quiet street beyond. The snow had long melted, taking the trail of blood with it.

"There's nothing left here but haunting memories," she murmured.

"Then you need a reminder of the good ones."

The chair squeaked as Cole stood, drawing her attention. He tapped on the screen of his phone and set it on the table. A moment later, a feminine Irish voice sang from the speaker.

Doo doo doo do, doo doo doo do.

Her sinuses flooded with searing, sticky emotion. Her vision blurred. Gasps rose and fell from her chest. By the time the first tear fell, he was in her arms, holding her, rocking slowly as he sang along with "Ode To My Family" by *The Cranberries*.

He kissed her softly as she sobbed out the agonies of her heart. He danced with her in the living room where Mike had slept without complaint. He swayed with her in the kitchen where Shannon had made her magical stew. Then he made love to her in the bed where he'd given himself to her completely and irrevocably on Christmas Eve.

He stared into her eyes as he entered her body as if it were the first time. No regrets passed between them as he stroked inside her, taking his pleasure and giving it back with the devotion of his lips.

He would never leave her. Never let her go. She felt that promise as he looked into her eyes, fucked her achingly slow, and said, "I love you."

"I love you, Cole. Thank you for taking the risk with me."

"You were worth the risk, Lydia. You made me whole again."

He made her whole, too.

She'd lost her family, and though they could never be replaced, he'd given her a new one.

COMPLICATE

They shared a complicated history, but love was their magic ingredient. With a kiss, it annihilated twelve years of revenge and eight years of loneliness. If that wasn't magic, she didn't know what was.

THIRTY-TWO

Cayman Islands
Two years later

Today was the day. Nervousness might have been a natural response in Cole's position, but he lived for this shit—the tremor of looming danger, the rush of adrenaline, and the thrill in fighting for something meaningful.

It didn't get more meaningful than this.

White-crested waves rolled in from the sun-bleached horizon, lapping at his sandaled feet. He strolled along the beach, hands resting in the pockets of his swim shorts as his eyes moved from sand to sunbathers, from cobblestone pathways to crowded beach-side bars.

The panorama captured the essence of a laid-back paradise along with the elegance of a luxury resort. But he wasn't here to work on his tan.

The warm midday sunshine injected frissons of energy beneath his skin. He was here to keep his eyes open and senses honed, for today, he would see a year-long dream finally come to fruition.

The blue skies were clear as far as he could see. Even the weather smiled on his plans.

Up ahead, a good-looking guy ran down the beach and leaped in a burst of strength, catching a football midair. His cheerleaders jumped from their loungers and clapped their hands, whistling.

As he turned to launch the ball back to the group, he met Cole's eyes.

Joshua.

COMPLICATE

He hadn't always been a gun-toting vigilante. Before Liv, he had a promising future as a professional football player.

His green eyes glinted with his smile. There was no resentment there. No misgivings.

With a nod to Cole, he sent a message.

Nothing was amiss. Everything and everyone was in place.

Cole continued on, strolling toward the group. Liv, Amber, and Van watched as Livana raced toward the spiraling football that Joshua passed back. She missed the catch, laughing at her fumble while her gaze made a furtive sweep of the perimeter.

As the only child of Van and Liv, she had big shoes to fill. But Cole had spent a lot of time training her over the years. She was sharp, fearless, and deadly with a gun.

He ambled past the group, smiling a friendly greeting.

Van sat beside Amber on the lounger, leaning in to tease the string on her bikini top. But like his daughter, his eyes were razor-sharp, probing the surroundings until they landed on Cole.

A toothpick rolled at the corner of Van's smirk, cocky and chilling. Scary as fuck.

But Cole trusted him with his life. He trusted all of them.

While Joshua entertained them with his athletic dexterity, they played their parts as clueless vacationers, lounging and soaking up the sun.

No one knew they were killers. Every single one of them. They were a highly-trained, fiercely passionate team of vigilantes, and they were here to take down a multi-national criminal enterprise that catered to pedophiles.

There were one-hundred-and-twenty child predators mingling at the resort, all gathered for an annual convention. On the surface, it was a fun-in-the-sun holiday for business. But what happened after dark behind locked doors was so sick, sadistic, and inhumane that it called for justice without lawyers and trials.

It called for the Freedom Fighters.

When the team received the signal, they would dig their firearms out of the sand and take justice into their own hands.

Cole veered off the beach and headed into the resort, swapping warm oceanic air for air-conditioned breezeways.

He passed through one of the many indoor bars and spotted Luke, Tomas, and Vera at one of the card tables, playing poker with their targets. Handbags sat at their feet, concealing their weapons.

A hand brushed his arm, and he turned his neck, coming face to face with Rylee's huge silver eyes.

"Hey, handsome." Her cheeks rose with a smile. "Enjoying your stay?"

"Tremendously. You?"

"Everything's perfect." She winked and sauntered off to rejoin the group at the card table.

He crossed through the spa next. Tula, Martin, and Ricky sat in massage chairs, receiving pedicures. Evidently, men did this sort of thing, if he could call their targets *men*.

Old, fat fucks lounged in the other chairs, talking among themselves as women scrubbed and rubbed their feet. They had no idea they were about to die in those seats after spending their final moments on earth getting their toenails clipped.

Fuck them.

They would never touch another child again.

Ricky looked up, grabbing his gaze and giving him a chin lift. *All clear.*

Cole continued his perimeter sweep through the halls, his attention flicking to the shadows, to the opened and locked doors, and other possible escape routes. He and the team had scoured the property from end to end and every dark corner in between. This operation was a year in the making, and he didn't want any surprises.

There were three pool areas with vast spaces for their targets to congregate. He found Matias and Camila sitting at the edge of the first pool.

Camila looked stunning in her red bikini. Her husband, on the other hand, stood out like a douchebag with his floppy sunhat and white sunscreen slathered on his nose.

Fucking ridiculous. But necessary. As the capo of the Restrepo Cartel, he couldn't risk being recognized.

"Nice hat," Cole said in passing, biting down on his smile. "Can I ask where you got it?"

"Yeah, you can pick one up for yourself at..." Matias gave him the finger. "Fuck off."

"Behave." Camila elbowed her husband and glanced at Cole, whispering under her breath, "We're ready."

She rested a hand on the bag beside her, her eye glimmering with excitement.

With a nod, he followed the paved pathway to the next pool. Tate and Lucia stood at a high-top table, drinking colorful cocktails while surveying the area.

Lucia gave him a thumbs-up, and his heart rate accelerated, his blood thrumming for a fight.

COMPLICATE

He located Tiago and Kate in the final pool, their positions in place and expressions calm.

Everyone was in their assigned zones, locked on their targets.

There were targets they couldn't account for, the ones who were in their rooms or lingering in areas of the resort that required a key. That was where he came in.

And his favorite thief.

He picked up his pace, making a beeline to the outdoor bar at the center of the property. As he turned the corner, the first thing he saw was her fire-engine-red hair.

The thick waves tumbled down her back in lavish, unbridled glory. She sat on a stool at the bar, her spine straight and legs crossed like a lady. But that was where her decorum ended.

She wore an ultra-sexy rockabilly swimsuit, black with a cherry-themed print. The sweetheart neckline and figure-hugging shape drew the eye to her voluptuous tits, where they swelled up and out to here as she leaned toward the man beside her, whispering shamelessly in his ear.

A rush of heat tightened between Cole's legs as he prowled closer, his gaze raking her body, soaking in every dip that he knew so well.

Her beauty was just as bold and arresting as the first night he met her. Only now, he knew that gorgeous face wasn't just makeup and eyelashes. Beneath the cosmetics, she radiated. Her fair complexion, her natural red hair, and those sexy little freckles that dotted her nose—all of that only added to her badass perfection.

He was so fucking in love with this woman he made her his wife last year.

She was his forever. His happiness. And right now, she was instrumental in finishing this job.

Stalking around the perimeter of the bar, he listened to her conversation with the man at her side. Her Russian accent had improved over the years, and she laid it on thick, drawing her target under her spell.

She ordered him another drink, never once making eye contact with Cole. They were so attuned to each other, she knew he was there without lifting her fake eyelashes in his direction.

Watching her employ her seductive powers on her targets shouldn't turn him on as much as it did. But there was something really fucking satisfying about seeing every man in this bar openly gawk at her and knowing that no one could touch her. She was his. Period.

He waited for the moment she would make her move. Her target was the only man at the resort who held the codes to the property's top-notch security system.

Her target owned the resort and ran his multi-national child trafficking organization within these walls. He was paranoid by nature, and never removed his fingers from his phone on the bar.

Until she slid a rope of cherry licorice from her purse. She looked away, feigning innocence as she sucked it between her lips, conjuring the image of a blowjob.

Her target homed in, leaned in, his attention on her mouth, forgetting himself, and at last, forgetting his phone.

She held his gaze, licking on her candy as her free hand swapped his phone with a lookalike from her purse.

Just like that, she fucking did it. She had the codes.

His pulse raced as he slipped away from the bar, watching as she started coughing, hacking, pretending she was choking on the Twizzlers.

With a wobbly exit, she grabbed her purse and pounded on her chest. "I'm okay. I'm okay. So sorry. I'm just going to use the ladies room."

The lookalike phone she left behind was locked and uncharged. It would distract the owner for a while as he tried to power it on. By the time he realized she'd stolen his codes, it would be too late.

Cole stepped out of view, following her at a distance as she made her way toward the beach. Her gorgeous ass swayed in the swimsuit, her gait graceful and confident.

His stomach tightened as he pursued her, waiting for the hand-off. A few feet ahead, PaulVer stepped out of the shadows of a pool house. She dropped the phone in his hand and continued walking, slapping her flip-flops along the pavers.

The night PaulVer had unleashed the shit storm surrounding Vincent Barrington, Matias had offered him a position on the team. The kid hadn't hesitated, and he'd been invaluable ever since. Especially in operations like this one.

Now that he had the owner's phone, he would scrape the codes to break into the security system. In about three minutes, the faces and identities of his team would be wiped from the security footage, like they were never here. The entire system would be hacked, and every door in the resort would be unlocked for their attack.

Cole's chest expanded with the rampant, pounding beat of his heart. He quickened his strides, chasing Lydia to the beach. Their weapons waited there, buried in the sand near Van and Liv.

They had a few minutes before PaulVer gave them the *go*. So Cole stole one.

He stole a moment with his wife, grabbing her from behind and wrenching a beautiful laugh from her throat.

COMPLICATE

She spun toward him, smiling, showering him in sparks of brilliant chaos. It took courage to walk this dangerous life with him, and she was built for it, born for it. His perfect mate.

"What are you doing?" She leaned up, running her nose along his whiskered jaw. "We have bad guys to kill."

"So bloodthirsty," he growled. "Kiss me, woman."

She tilted her smile heavenward, offering up her glossy cherry lips.

The instant he kissed her, he breathed all the more deeply. Together, they shone brighter. A serenity of souls, fighting in a dark world and reaping their forever.

"I'm in love with you," he said.

"I'm in love with love, and you, Cole Hartman, are all of that."

"Ready?"

"Forever or bust."

"Forever it is." He kissed her again and laced their hands together. "Let's go."

OTHER BOOKS

LOVE TRIANGLE ROMANCE
TANGLED LIES TRILOGY
One is a Promise
Two is a Lie
Three is a War

DARK COWBOY ROMANCE
TRAILS OF SIN
Knotted #1
Buckled #2
Booted #3

DARK PARANORMAL ROMANCE
TRILOGY OF EVE
Heart of Eve (novella)
Dead of Eve #1
Blood of Eve #2
Dawn of Eve #3

DARK HISTORICAL PIRATE
King of Libertines (novella)
Sea of Ruin

STUDENT-TEACHER / PRIEST
Lessons In Sin

STUDENT-TEACHER ROMANCE
Dark Notes

ROCK-STAR DARK ROMANCE
Beneath the Burn

ROMANTIC SUSPENSE
Dirty Ties

EROTIC ROMANCE
Incentive

ABOUT

New York Times and USA Today Bestselling author, Pam Godwin, lives in the Midwest with her husband, their two children, and a foulmouthed parrot. When she ran away, she traveled fourteen countries across five continents, attended three universities, and married the vocalist of her favorite rock band.

Java, tobacco, and dark romance novels are her favorite indulgences, and might be considered more unhealthy than her aversion to sleeping, eating meat, and dolls with blinking eyes.

EMAIL: pamgodwinauthor@gmail.com

Made in the USA
Monee, IL
19 November 2023

46915034R00371